A SUBTLE AGENCY
OMNIBUS
THE METAFRAME WAR:
PART ONE

Graeme Rodaughan

Cover art by Huw Jones

For Linda, for her unfailing love and support that always leaves me in awe.

I would like to thank a number of people who have assisted with my progress as an author, including Alex, Tim, Lisa, Lena, Marie, Eldon, Michael, Christopher, Perry, Nick, Andrew, Laura, Daniel, Ginger, Jody, and the regular crew of Beta and ARC readers at the Castle Dracula (now Castle Terror) group and my many friends and followers on Goodreads. You have all contributed more than you know to my craft and your support and encouragement are invaluable for this journey.

Books by Graeme Rodaughan

The Metaframe War Series

A Subtle Agency
A Traitor's War
The Dragon's Den
The Day Guard
The Crane War
The Key of Ahknaton
The Metaframe Adept

Omnibus Volumes

A Subtle Agency Omnibus (includes A Subtle Agency, A
Traitor's War, and The Dragon's Den)

Dramatis Personae

The Ancients

Ahknaton, Ruler of the Southern Realm, High Priest of the Temple of Thoth. Master Architect. Ramp Master.
Hakron, Second prince of the Southern Realm. Master Scribe. Ramp Master. Ahknaton's brother
Mekra, Princess, Ahknaton's wife.

The Vampire Dominion

Cornelius Crane, King of the Vampire Dominion
Chloe Armitage, General, The Americas, ex Order of Thoth and Crane's chief enforcer
Haras Mosule, General, Middle East, ex Red Empire warrior of the 3rd rank
Dieter Franz, General, Western Europe
Clayton Maze, General, Africa
Shen Zhen, General, East Asia
Marcus Drake, Chloe's aide de camp
Jean Philippe Allemande, Metaframe Sorcerer
Rawlings, Centurion, praetorian

The Order of Thoth

Ramin Kain, Head of the Order of Thoth
Samuel Luther, Ramin's chief of staff and aide de camp
Deon Lamar, Order Traveler (Spy Catcher)

The Exiles

Arthur Slayne, (Exiled) Master Strategist, Force Leader, Weapons Grandmaster, Speed Talent.
Anna Slayne, (Exiled) Operative
William Slayne, (Exiled) Operative, Arthur's son
Anton Slayne, Anna and William's son

Gang Wu, (Inactive) Weapons Grandmaster, Chef and Proprietor of the Noodle House restaurant
Li Wu, Gang's daughter, Weapons Master

The Mirovar Force Team

Francis Mirovar, Force Leader, Weapons Master
Juliette Mirovar, Loremaster, Netmaster, Combat Surgeon
Yvette Mirovar, Operative
Jay Creeley, Operative, Weapons Master
Peter Lamb, Operative, Armorer, Strength Talent
Chiara Romano, Operative, 2nd Combat Surgeon

The Walker Force Team (UK)

Richard Walker, Force Leader
Joan Lewis, Loremaster, Netmaster
Mary Turner, Operative, Netmaster,
David Wilkinson, Operative, Weapons Master
Karen Chapman, Operative
David Khan, Operative, Weapons Master
James Cox, Order novice
Michael (Mikey) Wilson, Operative
Francine (Frannie) Parker, Operative

The Red Empire

Shabbah al Ahmar, aka 'The Red Ghost,' aka Dalien Morte. Head of the Red Empire
Al Ghurab, aka 'The Raven,' Operative inserted into the Order of Thoth
Al Eunza, aka 'The Goat,' Operative
Al Far, aka 'The Rat,' Operative
Thueban Kabir, aka 'The Great Serpent,' aka 'Taipan,' Weapons Grandmaster, warrior of the 3rd rank
Nasr al Dam, aka 'The Blood Eagle,' Fist team leader, warrior of the 2nd rank
Tamsah al Ramil, aka 'The Sand Crocodile,' Fist team leader, warrior of the 2nd rank

Shadowstone

James Haley, Head of Operations, United States
Louise Wesson, Team Lead, Green-4 spectrum team
Sean Higgins, Operative, information technology specialist
Gary Johnson, Operative
Harvey West, Squad Leader, Indigo-6 spectrum team
Gordon Heathmont, Director Shadowstone United Kingdom.
Frank Quiver, Major, Command Officer Squadron F
Victoria Hansen, Flight Officer, Blackwidow pilot, Squadron F

Other Players

Luke Walker, Sergeant Detective, Boston Police Department
Sarah Murphy, Head, Crime Scene Response Unit

Sam, Homeless Shelter Attendant
Barry, Homeless man

Mr. Wang, Head of the Tiger Clan
Sleazy, Tiger Clan gangster
Fats, Tiger Clan gangster
Ferret, Tiger Clan gangster

Dillon Browne, Gang Leader
Caleb Moore, Dillon's enforcer
Aaliyah Williams, Dillon's girlfriend
Gabriel Williams, Aaliyah's younger brother
Ethan Jones, Gangster,

John Tilson, Captain, US Special Forces
Smith, Sargent, US Special Forces, Tilson's 2IC.

Justin Blake, Force Leader (South West) Weapons Master, Strength talent. Former student of Gang Wu

Gracie Williams, Flight Lieutenant, RAF
Tom (Tommie) Wilkes, RAF Regiment, soldier

Glossary

The Vampire Dominion: Established in the 1850s by Cornelius Crane. The Vampire Dominion has built an organized community of vampires that work together to maintain the primacy of vampires, and the secrecy of their existence.

The Order of Thoth: Established in 3023 BC by Hakron the Scribe with the twin purpose of protecting the Key of Ahknaton and eliminating vampires from the world.

The Red Empire: Established in the third century BC, by a faction of the Order of Thoth. The Red Empire view themselves as the true inheritors of Hakron's vampire hunting legacy.

Shadowstone: The Shadowstone organization was established in the second half of the 19th century by Cornelius Crane as a means to co-opt the military and intelligence elements of nation states to the purposes of the Vampire Dominion.

Praetorians: The praetorians predate the existence of the Vampire Dominion. They are an elite vampire force established and ruled by Cornelius Crane.

The Metaframe: Also known as The Divine Engine of Thoth, is an interface to the fundamental rules of the universe that when properly invoked allows reality to be changed.

The Key of Ahknaton: A device that enables safe access of the Metaframe

Prologue – A Subtle Agency

"Imagine if you could change the rules of the game, what rules would you choose?" – Unknown

* * *

Southern Egypt, The temple of Thoth, 3023 BC

Thunder boomed and echoed across a sky howling with madness.

Lightning bolts sheeted between bubbling masses of black thunderheads, and crimson sunlight slashed across the rock and sand before the temple of Thoth.

Hakron shivered with more than the sudden cold and drew his cloak more tightly around his lean frame. He glowered at the roiling clouds all but obscuring the setting sun and thought furiously to himself, *This storm is not born of nature.* He took a step back beneath the cover of the stone pillars and the vaulting roof of the temple of Thoth.

An attendant, shaking with fear, moved from the shadows within to stand beside him. He flung a dusky hand out, pointed into the distance and whispered with an aged hoarse voice, "Our Master comes."

Hakron glanced down to his side, noting the dull sheen of perspiration on the man's shaven scalp. He placed a comforting hand on the man's shoulder and said with firm calmness, "This devilish storm has undone us all. Now harden your resolve, the Great Thoth will see us through any calamity."

The man looked up at Hakron and blinked silently. The great horn of the temple of Thoth resounded across the valley. Its sharp note breached the thunder as it welcomed the high priest of Thoth and first prince of the southern realm, Ahknaton, to the seat of his power.

Hakron watched from above, as his older brother pulled his chariot to a sudden halt before the temple entrance. Attendants rushed forward to take hold of the frightened horses that drew the chariot.

Ahknaton swept down from the back of the chariot, his jaw clenched and his face pale with fury. He carried the limp form of his beloved wife, Mekra, within the cradle of his powerful arms.

Mekra's beautiful hair fell like a raven's wing. Her left arm hung limply; her hand clenched into a rigid claw. The swollen mark of a scorpion's sting stood in bold defilement on the back of her wrist. Grief tore at Hakron as Mekra had claimed the hearts of both men, and he braced himself against a pillar to avoid falling to the flagstones.

1

Ahknaton strode grimly up the broad stone steps of the temple's entrance, carrying the body of his young wife into the temple. He drew close to Hakron and their gazes met over Mekra's limp form.

The depths of his brother's anguish washed over Hakron and he recoiled as if slapped. The agonized fury within his brother was a palpable force, as trenchant and bitter as the storm assaulting the heavens above the temple.

Ahknaton looked into the temple and swept past him.

Hakron turned and rushed after him, keeping pace with Ahknaton's long strides as they went deeper into the temple.

Ahknaton moved past the main altar toward an archway near the back of the temple. The temple guards and priests quickly stepped aside to allow him to pass. The attendants had already lit oil lamps and pitch-soaked torches for the evening. Ahknaton gently shifted his wife to his left shoulder and took hold of a burning torch as he approached the archway.

Hakron moved to stand before him.

Ahknaton stared at him, snorting dismissively. "Hakron, you will not bar my way."

Hakron looked at his brother with glistening eyes. "I feel your pain brother. I am not here to stop you but to offer counsel."

Ahknaton paused, his head leaning against the still form of Mekra on his broad shoulder. In the pale light of the oil lamps, she looked like she was merely sleeping as fresh tears rolled down Ahknaton's cheeks.

Hakron had never seen his brother weep before. He was mad with grief. An unbelievable realization flashed through him. He stepped forward, and grabbed his brother's shoulders, and declared incredulously, "You intend to use the Divine Engine of Thoth."

Ahknaton's face hardened and he snapped, "Of course."

Hakron froze, momentarily dumbfounded with disbelief. Ahknaton shrugged off his grip. Pushing past him, he rushed through the archway and into the antechamber that led to the hidden depths beneath the temple.

Snatching a lit torch, Hakron hurried into the antechamber after his brother. He ran down a long sloping hallway leading to the first landing. He then switched back to descend again in the opposite direction. The powerful figure of his brother ran in front of him. His pace undiminished by the burden of carrying Mekra over his shoulder. Hakron strove to catch up with him. He drew upon the techniques that Ahknaton had taught him to accelerate both mind and body but even running faster than any man could expect to run, he was unable to close the distance between them.

Hakron reached the second landing, and followed his brother down a spiral staircase, and into the Halls of the Gods. The halls were a dangerous and deadly maze of shifting walls and counterweighted traps. Caustic pits, acid sprays, razor sharp nets and crushing blocks of stone waited for the unwary. Ahknaton had designed the traps to bar the passage of anyone without the secret knowledge of how to navigate their murderous paths.

Ahknaton shouted over his free shoulder, "Only a fool would hope to stop me, but you can witness divinity in action. Someone should record what happens tonight, and you have a gift for words my brother – so follow me if you dare."

Hakron had helped his brother build the temple and the levels beneath it. He darted forward, navigating his way past the traps.

Exiting the maze, he descended along another sloping hallway toward the chamber of the third landing. Embedded into the landing's floor was a secret door that only Ahknaton knew how to unlock. There was a deep rumble of moving stones and shifting counterweights. Upon reaching the chamber, he discovered a circular hole in the floor.

He rushed to the edge. Beneath him, the retreating sphere of Ahknaton's torchlight disappeared down another spiral staircase. Hakron followed his brother, taking the stairs two or three at a time until he reached the bottom. He passed through a vaulted archway and entered the Chamber of Worlds.

Lifting his torch high, Hakron illuminated massive walls of polished stone. He found himself staring into the empty space of an inverted pyramid. Beneath him, the lower levels crowded into the darkness at the limit of his torchlight. Halfway down the levels of the inverted pyramid, Ahknaton raced toward the bottom.

Chasing after his brother, he ran, leaping from level to level until he reached the bottom. He went through an archway and down another descending, curved hallway.

Hakron emerged from the hall into Ahknaton's Tomb Chamber. The intended location for Ahknaton's final resting place. It was bare, except for a raised plinth on which a sarcophagus could rest. Beyond the plinth, was an opening, the height, and width of a tall man. It was another secret door – left open for him. Through it, the glow of Ahknaton's flaming torchlight diminished into the distance. He dashed forward, fearing there was no time left to stop his brother summoning the Divine Engine of Thoth.

Hakron sprinted down the narrow hallway and into the chamber of the Engine.

Ahknaton had placed his torch into a wall sconce. Mekra lay as if asleep in the center of the room with Ahknaton's cloak wrapped into a pillow for her head. On the far side of the chamber, Ahknaton stood tall. He withdrew a polished, black, obsidian stone, the size of a pebble, from a pouch at his belt. He held it aloft in triumph.

Hakron stared at the stone – Ahknaton's key. It seemed a god had captured the starry sky and locked it within the stone. Its surface wet, and glistening, writhing like a living thing within Ahknaton's grasp.

"Stay back!" Ahknaton shouted.

Hakron warned fiercely, "You cannot be sure what will happen if you try to change the Engine."

"There is no doubt the power can be used to save Mekra," Ahknaton declared with a desperate passion. "It is her only chance."

"Her soul is already facing the judgment of the Gods," Hakron urged. "It will be a violation of divine law for her to come back now."

Ahknaton promised, "I will remake the law – even divine law must bow before Thoth's Divine Engine."

"My brother," Hakron pleaded. "Thoth's engine is too complex for any mortal to understand. If you change it, you could unmake the world and all within it!"

Ahknaton pointed to the body of his beloved. "Do you imagine that I care about the risk – you fool – I have lost everything in this world."

Clenching the key, Ahknaton's face filled with concentration and the world trembled in response.

Hakron's heartbeat thumped in his ears. The air stilled within the chamber. The shadows beyond the two torches thickened, deepening into darkness beyond memory. The circles of torchlight sharpened; faint motes of dust lying marooned in their light.

The walls faded, becoming blurred and insubstantial. The Divine Engine of Thoth emerged into view. A swirling mass of luminous spheres, each a brilliant point of subtle color moving in a steady flow around an invisible axis. The Engine's bright light eclipsed the shadows of the flickering torchlight.

The chamber snapped into razor sharp clarity. The presence of the Engine, rendering every sense to a high pitch of acuity. Time slowed and Hakron's mind raced. Power flooded his limbs and his thoughts clarified. The orbits of the spheres revealed a unified order. A perfect balance between movement and stasis, between order and chaos, and between good and evil.

Ahknaton thrust the key at the swirling lights and a dark glow encompassed his fist. With a voice filled with desperate longing and powered by a will beyond measure, he demanded, "She must live again!"

The Divine Engine of Thoth responded with a clap of thunder that shook the stones of the chamber. A single sphere reversed its orbit, changing from golden yellow to a deep blood red. For a moment, the world paused in dreadful stillness; then the Engine vanished in a rush of air.

Hakron staggered backward. A tidal wave of force rippled out in an instant from the center of the Engine. A wave that reformed the reality of the everyday world eliminating what was no longer possible and enabling what must now occur.

Hakron regained his balance. The chamber was once more lit by the pale glow of the flickering torchlight. His skin crawled over his back and arms. He involuntarily took a step backward, coming to a halt against the cold stone wall of the chamber. Something had just moved in the room, something that should not have moved at all.

Mekra stirred. The hairs on the back of Hakron's neck rose in a primal response. He stared, unable to look away as she sat up, her gorgeous brown eyes glittering like jewels, blinking with surprise in the soft glow of the torchlight. Her skin glowed once again with the abundant health that had so recently deserted her.

Ahknaton sighed. The key dropped from his hand to clatter on the stone floor.

Mekra's eyes locked avidly on her husband's face. Smiling with delight, she invited huskily, "Ahknaton – my love – come to me."

Needing no urging, he scooped her up into his arms, twirling her around the chamber. She melted into his muscular arms, her lips finding his throat and nuzzling into the firm groove she found there.

Stepping quietly away from the scene, Hakron edged nearer to the entrance of the chamber. Caught between rank terror and urgent curiosity, he lifted his torch high so that he could clearly witness a miracle of the gods.

Ahknaton whispered, "We will be together now, forever in victory over death itself."

Hakron frowned. Mekra began to stiffen, her hands clenching hard onto Ahknaton's shoulders. He winced with sudden pain, startled by her strength. The shift in her mood was palpable, filling the chamber with a fell charge of dark power.

Mekra, her face frozen with horror, called out, "What have you done?"

"I have saved you," Ahknaton cried, a sliver of doubt creeping into his voice.

"No!" Mekra screamed. "You have doomed us both!"

Mekra's grip tightened on Ahknaton's massive shoulders. He crumpled to his knees, groaning with agony. A bone suddenly snapped like a dry twig and Ahknaton cursed through gritted teeth.

Hakron edged into the chamber entrance, transfixed by what was happening before his eyes.

Mekra's face twisted with a horrific need. She reared her head back, sharp fangs sprouting in her gaping mouth.

Ahknaton, his heroic physique useless against her supernatural strength, flopped like a rag doll in her hands.

Mekra blurred forward, sinking her fangs into his neck. Blood splashed before she fixed her mouth over the wound. She sucked eagerly at the red tide flooding down her throat.

Watching from the chamber entrance, Hakron's gaze darted from the lust and horror alternating on Mekra's face, to the uncomprehending shock rising like a dark sun over Ahknaton's face.

In moments, Mekra drained the life from her beloved husband. She staggered back as he slumped to the floor.

Mekra cried out with outraged grief and horrified despair. Her scream tore at the walls, slicing like a razor within Hakron's head. She fled from the chamber, slamming him into the wall as she blurred past him with inhuman speed, uncaring of his fate in her anguish.

Hakron awoke and looked around. The torches still burned, Ahknaton's body still lay lifelessly on the cold stones of the floor, but of the Divine Engine of Thoth, or of Mekra, there was no sign.

Retrieving the key of Ahknaton from where it lay on the cold stone floor, Hakron left the chamber.

Surfacing into the Temple, Hakron counted eleven men, all dead. Cast aside by a newborn demon as she emerged from the depths below. He clenched the key of Ahknaton tightly, terrified that he would lose it. He walked to the entrance of the temple, the storm was gone and the night sky was clear. A river of stars arched across the night sky a celestial echo of the Divine Engine of Thoth.

The Engine knew Ahknaton was coming, the storm was a warning.

A sudden gust of cold wind swept up from the desert sands, the fine grit catching on the lines of tears on his face, which he hurriedly wiped away with his forearm.

No time for tears. No time for grief.

He stood tall, scanning the night sky and the desert. He stared into the darkness, listening intently, but there was no sign of Mekra. His heart churned; a ship tossed on an unsteady sea. He breathed, slower and slower, and grief gave way to resolve.

What my brother has done, I will devote my life to undo.

He called out to the night, "Something must be done, and something will be done. This I swear by the almighty Thoth."

The silence heard him and drank in his words.

Hakron, the second prince of the southern realm and master scribe of the temple of Thoth, left that night, never to return.

Chapter One

"Power that is secret will endure." – Cornelius Crane, King of the Vampires

* * *

Boston, April 28th, 20:25

The white limousine purred down the darkened street.

General Chloe Armitage rested on the back seat, watching the houses as she passed by, her extraordinary senses drinking in the world around her. The faint glow of warmth from the recent footprints of a man walking his dog. The rhythmic sound of the heartbeats of the people in their homes. The smell of garden beds, freshly turned soil and a recently buried cat that had begun to bloat with corruption. A sea of information on which her mind could plumb the depths of, or soar far above.

Chloe tapped her knee with an impatient finger. Her companion, Marcus Drake, sat beside her, he looked at her quizzically for a moment. She lifted her hand, dismissed him and looked away. She was thankful he didn't speak; she didn't want or need his concern. His personal devotion was useful and surprising given the century-long curse that bound him to her will. Even after so much time he still loved her.

She found his loyalty a mystery, especially given how her own circumstances mirrored his. She'd long and intimate knowledge of a binding curse.

The faint glow from the car console reflected her face in the window beside her. She glanced at her dark brown hair, straight and fine, cut into a professional Bob. Her hair neatly framed her exquisite face. She contemplated her flawless complexion for a brief moment. Her gaze flicked up to her vivid blue eyes. She pouted her full lips and noted the perfection of her red lipstick. She'd need all her weapons tonight.

She smiled briefly in careful anticipation of the night ahead and focused her mind using skills taught to her as a child. Accelerating her perceptions, her thoughts raced ahead as the world receded into a slow dream.

Chloe's mission objective was clear, to retrieve the ancient Egyptian Papyrus of Hakron the Scribe from the Slayne family, and deliver it to her master, Cornelius Crane, lord of this world. Tonight, represented the culmination of nearly two centuries of planning and searching to find the Papyrus by Crane and his five generals.

However, one thing troubled her, why was there no mention of the boy?

Crane's informant within the Order of Thoth had betrayed the location of the Slaynes and yet the parameters of the operation only included the parents, Anna and William Slayne. Her own research had revealed the existence of Anna and William's son, Anton Slayne.

Chloe was the last of Crane's generals recruited via transformation into a vampire and magically cursed to never harm him. She'd risen to prominence amongst the five by delivering the Key of Ahknaton into Crane's hand; taken from a secret vault beneath St Peter's Basilica. Delivery of the Papyrus would cement her primacy as first amongst the generals.

Crane had offered her any reward she may care to name, but she'd declined the offer, as there was only one thing she really wanted and it was beyond his ability to give – her true liberty.

When I have provided you the Interpretive Codex, and you have all three of the artifacts of the Metaframe, what then my lord? What price will you pay for my continued service? You have bound me with magic so that I can never harm you, but for all your genius, knowledge, and wisdom, you fail to see that the binding may have a loophole – and you know nothing about this boy who is so dangerously like his grandfather.

The limousine slowed down and began to turn. Moments later, the luxurious car pulled to a halt. The street ended in a quiet suburban court and she looked out at a pleasant, unremarkable, middle-class home. Relaxing her focus, she decelerated her mind and the world snapped back into motion. She smiled with anticipation, after tonight, this peaceful street would never be the same again.

Marcus stepped out of the car, dressed in a finely tailored pinstripe suit that fitted his tall, powerful frame perfectly. He moved quickly to open the car door for Chloe. She stepped from the car with feline grace, her body equally at home in a national ballet troupe or on an Haute Couture fashion catwalk. Smoothing her elegant black pants suit, she walked purposefully to the front door. Marcus fetched a long black case from the trunk of the car and followed a step behind her.

The limousine driver drove the big car away, parking about fifty yards down the street.

Chloe stood before the door and rang the doorbell.

* * *

'Because the peace of God is with them whose mind and soul are in harmony, who are free from desire and wrath, who know their own soul.'

The doorbell rang.

Anton Smith put down the Sanskrit copy of the Bhagavad Gita he was reading and looked at the clock – it was 8:30 pm. He considered ignoring the doorbell, he had spring semester exams starting in a week, and it was simpler to pretend no one was home than go downstairs and answer the door. He'd completed studying for his first-year subjects, mathematics, ancient languages, and archaeology. He knew the material well and was confident of doing well for someone on an ice hockey scholarship.

He was honest enough to admit that he was killing time with the Gita. The book belonged to his mother who had taught him the Sanskrit language before he was ten and he'd caught her infectious passion for Indo-European Mythology. Anton expected his parents to come home in another one to two hours from their faculty dinner at Boston University. Then he could borrow the car and hang out with his friends. It was Saturday night, he'd turned eighteen two days before on the twenty sixth of April, and it was time to celebrate.

Picking up a mini-soft basketball, he lounged back in his desk chair. He casually looped the ball toward a small hoop on the other side of his bedroom. It sailed through the air and went straight through the middle of the ring. He glanced back at his computer screen. The Hockey East League website covered the display. The previous season had finished a couple of weeks ago. Boston University had lost by a single goal in the Championship game.

Anton stared at the screen, nonplussed by the result. *We won every game all season – but not the one that mattered – how did that happen?*

The doorbell rang again.

Rubbing his face with both hands he stood up and remarked to himself, "This guy is persistent, I'm going to have to get rid of him."

He walked downstairs in his socks. He wore a simple gray, long sleeved BU Hockey T-shirt, and jeans that hid the rugged athleticism of his six feet one-inch frame. Anton jumped the last couple of stairs and arrived at the front door just as the doorbell rang for the third time.

He opened the door. Before him stood the most beautiful woman he'd ever seen in his life.

She was tall, only a couple of inches shorter than himself. A brunette with vivid blue eyes and a flawless skin like cream. She wore a professional black business pants suit with a short jacket, and a translucent scarlet silk chiffon shirt that displayed the round curves of her breasts within a stylish black bra. Just standing still, she was a seductive mix of poise, elegance, and class, with a face that commanded attention.

Anton stared at her, rendered speechless for a long moment.

She smiled at him, revealing perfect teeth framed by full, sensuous lips, and declared with a polished English accent, "Mr. Slayne, please let me introduce myself, I am Chloe Armitage."

Slayne? ... What?

Anton decided he must have misheard her and replied, "Hi, I'm Anton." He immediately mentally kicked himself for not thinking of something suaver to say. Fortunately, she didn't seem to notice his sudden lack of cool.

Chloe swept her right hand back toward the large man who stood a couple of steps behind her. He was big, blond, hard and looked like high-class security. "This is my associate, Mr. Drake. We work for an organization with a long-term interest in your family," she paused briefly, a slight smile curling her generous lips as if quietly amused by something she knew that Anton didn't, and said, "and I believe we have information you will find quite fascinating."

Anton caught up on what the vision before him had said; they had the wrong man. Disappointment flooded through him and he apologized, "I'm sorry, my name isn't Slayne. It's Anton Smith. There must be a mistake."

Arching an eyebrow, Chloe inquired again, "Mr. Slayne, Anton, if I may?"

Anton nodded and shrugged, perplexed by her insistence on getting his name wrong, but willing to go along with whatever was happening. The last thing he wanted her to do was leave.

"Anton, we have much to explain," she waved her left hand elegantly toward the empty hall behind him. "Perhaps you could invite us inside and we can clarify any questions you may have."

Anton considered her proposal for all of half a second. After all, it wasn't every evening that a statuesque super-model landed on your doorstep and asked to come in. He smiled broadly and said, "Sure, please come in."

Anton directed them past him to the lounge room, just off the main hall. He closed the front door and followed them into the room. They were standing there waiting for him. They hadn't assumed they could just sit down. His new guests' politeness struck him. Their manners were old school – very old school.

"Please sit down and make yourself comfortable," Anton said. "Can I get you anything to drink?"

Marcus shook his head. He sat down in a large single chair, and placed his long black case next to it, leaned back and studied Anton speculatively.

Chloe took a seat on a long lounge opposite a coffee table.

Her blue eyes locked on his and she requested with a charming smile, "A glass of water will be fine."

Anton fetched the water. It was clear study was over for tonight. One thing puzzled him enormously. She seemed certain his family name was Slayne. Intrigued, he wanted to understand what was going on. At the very least he definitely wanted to get to know Ms. Chloe Armitage better. After all, what on earth did he have to lose by spending time with an exquisitely beautiful young woman?

Returning to the lounge room, Anton placed the glass of water on the coffee table in front of his guest.

Chloe inclined her head slightly in a silent thank you but ignored the glass as Anton sat down in a chair opposite her. She leaned forward and declared, "Anton, as I said earlier, the organization I work for is very interested in your family."

Anton studied her for a moment. She was certainly serious about something. It was time to find out what. He began with a direct approach and asked, "Okay, who do you work for and what is your interest in us?"

Chloe glanced at Marcus and requested, "A card if you please."

Marcus opened the case, and extracted a business card which he silently handed to Anton.

"Thanks," Anton said, taking the card. He began to wonder if Mr. Drake would ever speak. He turned the card over with his fingers and glanced at it. Gold letters on a black background covered the card and read, 'R.I.S.C, Risk, Investigation, Security, Consultants. Chloe Armitage. Director, North American Operations.'

Anton turned the card over a couple of times as if there might be something more to see. The business card didn't shed any light on who these people really were. It didn't even have contact details or an address. He put the card down on the coffee table and raised a quizzical eyebrow.

Chloe arched an eyebrow and said, "We deal with information, we connect the right people with the right information."

Spooks? Anton thought, a sliver of unease crawling through his gut, and he asked, "What do you want with my family?"

"Anton," Chloe inquired. "Are you sure you know who your family are?"

Anton was momentarily nonplussed. *What sort of question is that?* "Of course, I do," he reacted indignantly. "I'm an only child living with my parents who are full professors of Archaeology, Ancient languages, and Indo-European Mythology at Boston University. We have lived here in Boston all my life. I have no cousins because my parents were only children and all my grandparents are dead." He shrugged, and spread his hands wide. "Accidents and sudden illnesses seem to follow my family, okay?"

Chloe momentarily bit her bottom lip, looking straight into Anton's eyes, she declared earnestly, "I can prove two things. One, your family name is Slayne, and two, your paternal grandfather Arthur Slayne is alive and well. Anton – people close to you have been keeping secrets – don't you think that now you're eighteen you're old enough to know what those secrets are?"

Anton took a step back mentally. What on earth was going on here? None of it made any sense and how on Earth did she know his age? "C'mon this is crazy," he said. "You can't be serious – this has to be a joke, right? Has someone put you up to this?"

Chloe leaned back, crossing one long leg over the other. She steepled her fingers in front of her chest and declared, "Anton, I'm deadly serious."

"Huh?" Anton grunted. He didn't want to believe it. She was either telling the truth or she was an extremely convincing liar.

"Okay Anton," Chloe said. "I can see you're feeling uncomfortable, and that's not why we're here." She uncrossed her legs, and leaned forward, reaching part way across the coffee table. "I propose we show you the evidence we have, and you can make up your own mind. I promise you this, if you are not convinced, we will walk out your front door, and you will never see us again." She looked straight into his eyes and smiled warmly. "Now, what could be fairer than that?"

Anton paused; something wasn't adding up. This was all too strange. An alarm began ringing quietly at the back of his mind, a small red flashing light that whispered one thing: *danger!*

"Five minutes," Chloe promised. She swept a hand in the direction of the front door. "If you're not satisfied, we're telling the truth, we're out of here."

Anton hesitated, his home suddenly unfamiliar, alien, close with ancient secrets, and yet she sat bare feet from him, vibrant, alive, filled with an uncanny allure and seemingly the most real thing present in this moment.

He realized with a shock he was holding his breath and let it out with a sigh. He drew in his next breath; her subtle perfume filled his nostrils. He'd never smelled its like before. It was indescribable and almost robbed him of the ability to think.

"So, what is it going to be Anton?" She murmured, barely more than a whisper. "Take a risk and find out the truth, or play it safe and continue wondering what this meeting was all about for the rest of your life?"

She'd made her point in such a reasonable way that rejecting her offer seemed stingy and cowardly. The alarm at the back of his mind fell away to silence. Anton found himself agreeing with her, and said, "Okay, show me what you've got."

Chloe flicked a glance at Marcus. He reached into his case and withdrew a dozen high quality color photographs which he handed silently to Chloe. She arranged them neatly, one at a time on the coffee table and remarked, "Anton, have you noticed how few photos your parents have of their marriage?"

Anton frowned, it was true, his parents only had a handful of photos.

"It's because they were not allowed to keep photos like this one," she declared, putting a photo that was clearly of his parents on the table. "Of William and Anna Slayne with your grandfather, on their wedding day."

Anton reflexively began to deny what he was seeing, *No, William and Anna Smith,* but remained silent, his mind grappling with questions, *or is it Slayne?*

Next to his father was a fit, middle-aged man with a full head of wavy dark brown hair, strongly defined features, high cheekbones, strong chin, a sensual mouth and piercing blue eyes who was the spitting image of both William and Anton. He was a little shorter than his father, more Anton's height and build.

Chloe tapped the photo with her finger and said as if instructing a student, "The Slayne genes are strong in the male line. The three of you could easily pass for brothers."

Anton lifted the picture and examined it carefully, it looked genuine.

"Here are more photos from your parents' wedding," Chloe indicated with an elegant sweep of her hand over the coffee table.

The photos were crystal clear. His parents seemed completely at ease with the older man, hugging and smiling with him, the man that Chloe had identified as his grandfather, Arthur Slayne. He had to admit as he picked up photo after photo, it all looked real.

Anton picked up the last photograph. A profound sense of familiarity struck him. He'd met this man before. A very old memory rose up from his early childhood. The man had lifted Anton effortlessly and placed him onto his shoulders for a ride. He found himself tearing up and put the photo down.

His heart told him the truth; it was all real. Blinking furiously, he wiped a tear away with a trembling hand and took a deep breath.

Chloe gestured toward the glass of water on the coffee table. "Would you like a drink? I'm not that thirsty."

"Thanks," Anton replied, picked up the glass of water and drank half of it down.

"There are also these recent photos," Chloe said, laying out a series of shots taken quickly in a burst with a modern digital camera. There was a date-time stamp in the bottom corner of each photo.

The string of photos revealed a vibrant street scene from two months earlier. A festival filled with floats, sparkling costumes and crowds of people in a parade. In each photograph, there was a man who looked much like the man with his parents on their wedding day. Although now he wore a dark-brown fedora hat. His hair was longer and it had some visible gray in it. He wore a shirt cropped at the shoulders and open down the front. He looked lean and physically powerful as if he could run a marathon and then go fifteen rounds in a ring with a champion prize fighter. He had a long, slim, gently curved, black case in his left hand and he was staring fiercely at something across the street that was out of shot.

Anton wondered if the case contained a sword. "It's the same guy," Anton declared, rubbing his hands through his thick wavy hair. "So, where was he?"

"Rio. At the carnival in February this year, and clearly very much alive."

"Okay, my grandfather is still alive. So, why don't I know that?"

"Anton, you and your family have been hidden with a lie for all of your life – for at least nineteen years."

"You're kidding me," Anton said, shaking his head with disbelief. "Why on Earth? … Why?"

Chloe watched Anton closely and stated matter-of-factly, "Because your grandfather is a murderer."

Anton stared at her, his eyes wide, his mind frozen.

"Well, that's the official story," Chloe said, arching an eyebrow and making herself look delightful. "I personally think he is innocent and was framed for a crime committed by another – but I lack definitive proof."

Anton shook his head. The alarm at the back of his mind began ringing again. A weird sense the real world was on the verge of melting away joined it. Something terrible was coming but he couldn't put his finger on what it could possibly be. He frowned and asked, "Why do you think he is innocent?"

"I have excellent professional reasons to study your grandfather. I probably know him better than anyone else in the world, and I can guarantee it's not in his nature to murder anyone. He would consider it dishonorable." Chloe smiled slightly and stated firmly, "And one thing Arthur Slayne has always been is a man of honor." She paused for a long moment and looked into the distance as if immersed in an old memory.

The look of ancient remembrance on her youthful face sent an uncanny shiver up Anton's spine.

"He is amongst the two or three best swordsmen alive," she remarked softly as if her mind was somewhere far away. "And I have a great respect for him – even admiration."

"So, it was a sword he was carrying in a black case in Rio?"

"Indeed, it was," Chloe agreed, returning her attention to Anton and smiling. "He is, in a vernacular that you might easily understand." She air quoted with her fingers. "A bad-ass!" She smirked, seemingly amused by what she'd just said.

That was awkward. 'Vernacular that you might easily understand.' She looks like she is about my age, but who speaks like that at eighteen or nineteen?

Anton didn't find it funny. A sliver of fear ran up his spine, jagging its way into the base of his brain. He glanced across at the brooding presence of Mr. Drake who had remained steadfastly silent since his arrival. Would the man ever speak? Could he speak? Anton decided to forge ahead and asked, "Okay, my grandfather is alive, and my family and I are in hiding – so why are you here? It's not such a great secret if you know about it."

With growing animation, Chloe said enthusiastically, "Indeed Anton, you're very astute. I shouldn't know about it, but I do. But you need not worry, I'm on your side. The people who oppose your grandfather, who framed him for murder, and caused him to put you and your family into hiding – well, I despise them with a passion."

Chloe stood up, emphasizing her words by chopping her right hand into her left. She stared at him, her eyes fierce, cold and hard, and declared in tight, sharp tones, "They're cowards. They have no honor. I promise you; I will not rest until I see justice done."

She paused for a moment, her eyes softening. She leaned across the coffee table, her subtle perfume wafting over Anton again.

She smelled lovely and Anton began to relax. How could anything dangerous smell and look so good?

Gripping Anton's hand with warm urgency, she gazed into his eyes. She was mesmerizing, Anton wanted to lean in and kiss her generous lips. She was so inviting, and yet, at the same time there was the barest hint that somewhere beneath the surface of her warm smile were cold depths beyond imagination.

Chloe gently pulled him closer. There was a fathomless power just beneath her gentle touch. She leaned next to his ear and whispered, "Anton, justice must be done, and I am sure you will do great things in its name for you are a true son of justice."

Chloe let him go, sitting back on the couch, she looked up at the clock on the wall.

"Anton, when do you expect your parents back from their faculty dinner?"

Anton murmured without thinking, "A little after nine, maybe later."

Chloe turned to Marcus and declared in fateful tones, "It's time."

A sudden dread curled into cold life in Anton's guts. He'd never mentioned that his parents were at a faculty dinner.

Marcus flipped open his case, taking out a soft white cloth and a vial. He crushed the vial in his bare hand, the liquid contents spilling onto the cloth.

Staring at Anton, Marcus grinned crookedly and asked with a deep voice, "We can do this the easy way or the hard way, which will it be?"

Anton's mind raced. *There's no time to get help. Who is the bigger threat? Drake or Chloe? He looks strong, but is he fast? I know that I'm fast. Front door, back door – which is closer to a clear path? Go to the front door. Once I am out on the street, he won't catch me. Who is she? Looks my age, dresses like a CEO for a fashion label and sounds like she's a hundred – weird.*

15

Chloe looked at him calmly, and urged, "Relax Anton, I can hear your heart racing from here. Look, I like you – I really want you to survive this, but unfortunately for your parents." She gently shook her head. "Not so much."

Leaping backward over the chair, Anton sprinted toward the front door. The move put the lounge chair between himself and Marcus. The coffee table blocked Chloe. He got three steps before hands like steel traps landed on his shoulders. It was like running into an iron bar. His feet kept going, spinning up into the air and Marcus slammed him onto the floor.

The breath went out of his lungs in a huge whoosh. He started to gasp. Marcus jammed the drugged cloth over his face and he reflexively inhaled the sickly-sweet substance on it. A moment later, Anton's world went dark.

* * *

William 'Smith' turned the Chevy Suburban into his local court. The car's big headlights illuminated the garage door which opened automatically before him.

His wife Anna sat beside him. Placing her hand on his right knee, she lightly drew it along the hard muscle underneath his suit trousers. It sent an immediate electric tingle straight into his groin.

He glanced sideways; her face was glowing with a fascinating sense of mischief.

She smiled coyly and suggested, "Nightcap?"

"Absolutely," he replied with a grin.

"Champagne?"

"We have two bottles chilling in the fridge."

"More than enough."

William pulled the car to a halt. The garage lights had come on automatically, gleaming off the new car's polished white paint.

Anna and William lingered. They shared a single long passionate kiss, then broke away, exiting the car and racing each other to the door leading into the house. Anna got there first, William hugging her from behind as she opened the door. William wrapped his right arm around Anna's waist and lifted her easily with one hand, carrying her across the threshold and into the house.

Anna pinched him. "Discipline," she whispered urgently. "You know that you're not allowed to show how strong you really are."

William gently put his wife down and sighed. "There is no one here to see, and besides – you're petite enough not to arouse suspicion."

Anna looked up at William, her blue eyes flashing. She punched his shoulder, hissed and said, "Anton is here." She grabbed the edges of his jacket, pulling him closer, till their faces were an inch apart, and whispered, "He's not ready for the truth."

It was an old argument, and for a long time, he'd simply gone along with Anna's will on the matter, but as his son had blossomed into a young man, he'd become convinced they should tell Anton the truth about his family, and his heritage as a Slayne.

William stroked Anna's blond hair and whispered, "He's mature enough, I think that you underestimate him. He needs to know. What would he do if something happened to us?"

"We're well hidden; only our friends at the Noodle House and your father know who we really are. Our strategy has worked for nineteen years, and it will continue to work for a while longer – we can wait until after he graduates."

"Love ..." William frowned slightly. "We're holding him back. He's a freshman who could cope with some of the work that my postgraduates do. How many eighteen-year-olds can read and write Latin, Ancient Greek and Sanskrit, cope with advanced calculus, and are widely read across half a dozen disciplines."

William knew that Anna loved Anton just as much as he did, and he wondered if they would ever agree on this point.

"My gorgeous man," Anna declared, leaning closer, and kissing him passionately. After a timeless moment, she pulled away. "We're exiled. If the Order find us, they will kill us to keep their secrets. If the Dominion find us, they will kill us because of who and what we are. We have to be careful and protect him."

Anna kissed William again, vibrantly, strongly, completely. William, his lips tingling, returned the kiss with every fiber of his being.

Exiled or not, to have Anna as his wife was a living miracle. William hugged her close. They turned together, walking down the hall toward the kitchen. The formal lounge opened up beside them and they saw him at the same time.

Anton tied to a chair, his head slumped forward, unconscious or worse.

William felt time slow down to a crawl as the secret training provided by his father kicked in. His senses exploded in acuity as every detail of the scene became razor sharp. Anna stilled beside him; her heart accelerated as she went through the same process. He heard a scuffling sound from the lounge, someone was already moving – fast.

There was one ... no, two opponents and not yet seen.

The wall next to him exploded toward him like a slow-motion movie. He moved, impossibly fast for a human. Turning, positioning for whatever was coming through the wall. There was a puff of plaster dust, followed be a spray of wooden splinters as the frame in the wall gave way. He was big, blond, and came through the wall like it comprised tissue paper instead of

17

a hardwood frame. He snarled at William, and launched his attack with fists like steel mallets.

Vampires!

William blocked the first strikes, the 'Ramp' as the training provided by his father came to full fruition. He pivoted out of the way of the rush, but the vampire turned as well, matching his speed. William launched a flurry of counter attacks which the vampire rapidly blocked, their hands and feet snapping through the air like cracking whips. The vampire matched his close-quarter skills, then he closed with William, attempting a grapple. William caught him on the side of a jaw with a punch that would have killed an ox. It felt like hitting concrete, the vampire's head snapping back, blood and bone spraying high across the wall as he broke the big vampire's jaw.

Undeterred the vampire kept on coming, locking William up in hands like stone. He tried to break the hold and twist away, but instead, the vampire threw him hard, face down on the floor. A moment later, the vampire was on top of his back, dragging both his arms backward. He felt the ligaments in his shoulders and elbows begin to give way as pain arced through his body like lightning.

Choking back a scream of agony, he raised his head up as far as he could to see his wife pinned to the wall by a tall brunette with her left hand on Anna's throat. His wife's feet dangled six inches off the floor. The vampire's right hand held stiff like a knife, poised an inch away from Anna's left eye.

"Stop!" she commanded. "Or else she dies."

William's heart sank – he recognized who it was.

Chloe Armitage, and ... this must be Marcus Drake on my back.

Drake's heavy knee pushed hard into the middle of his back as he dragged back on William's arms. His joints creaked and the bones of his shoulders ground against each other. William was six feet three inches and two hundred and seventy pounds of dense muscle and bone. He could bench press over four hundred pounds without the benefit of the Ramp. With the Ramp, he could recruit every muscle fiber in a given contraction. One hundred percent recruitment of muscle fibers as opposed to the normal human response of twenty percent. The Ramp made him five times stronger than normal and the associated physiological shifts of the Ramp reinforced ligaments and bones to handle the loads. But even with those capabilities, he didn't have half the strength necessary to break Drake's hold.

William let go.

Drake immediately bundled him into a chair and tied him up with chains and padlocks. He strained against them with all of his tremendous strength, but they did not give way.

"Sized to hold vampires – you can't break them," Drake declared with a smirk.

William looked across the room, the three of them were each confined to a chair at the points of a triangle about ten feet on a side. The vampires had moved the other furniture back against the walls and cleared the middle of the lounge room. Armitage and Drake stood in the center of the triangle and faced him.

Drake massaged his jaw; a trickle of blood streaked his chin.

Armitage gave him a neatly folded handkerchief, and directed primly. "Don't make a mess."

Drake wiped his jaw, spat into the cloth. He grimaced gap-toothed and remarked ruefully, "He hits hard."

"I don't want to hear about it – it will heal." Armitage declared, focusing her attention on William.

William stared back at her. It was clear the Vampire Dominion had discovered his family. The fact they were still alive meant his family was not the victim of a casual hunt. He wished the vampires were simply hunting, as death would most likely have been quick. No, this was far worse. The vampires were here for a purpose other than feeding, and he truly dreaded the possible paths this could go.

They were in a helpless position. He could only hope this pair of vampires would make a mistake. An error he could exploit to allow them all to escape, or at the very least save the lives of his wife and son.

William considered the situation and determined that he was most likely a dead man, but if by dying, he could save the lives of his wife and son, he would do so without hesitation.

* * *

Chloe studied William, smiled warmly and said, "Before we start, let's wake Anton. It's best to make sure he doesn't miss anything."

After all, she mused, *much of what will happen tonight is for his benefit.* She moved over to the coffee table which rested hard up against a wall. Marcus's open case sat on it. She retrieved a vial from it, unstopped it and waved it under Anton's nose. "Awake Anton," she called out. "Awake!"

The effect was immediate and dramatic. Anton convulsed as if given an electric shock. He was bound to the chair with plastic ties at his hands and ankles. He collapsed back, as limp as a rag doll.

Anton raised his head, and shook it as if clearing it, and swore irritably, "What the hell." He glanced around the room, taking in the scene. His face paled and his eyes widened with shock. "Mom, Dad, what's going on?"

"Stay calm Son, we'll get through this together," William declared grimly.

"Be strong, Anton," Anna cried out. Tears welling up in her eyes.

Chloe wanted to slap them, she really wanted them to know precisely how helpless they were. She wanted to tell them the truth and make them understand the reality of what was going on. As necessary as deception was to her strategy, she took no joy from lying – it left her feeling tainted. She hungered for a time when she would be able to live a life of absolute honesty, a life of truth without the need for subterfuge. And what a glorious world that would be.

She stood in the middle of the room, waiting for the Slaynes to calm down, to become still. *Necessity makes liars of us all,* she admitted silently to herself. She sighed, and everyone in the room looked at her.

"Well, if you don't want to be here – let us go," William said.

Chloe's eyes widened and she blurred forward. "Don't presume to know what I'm feeling." She slapped William hard across the face. His head rocked back as if struck by a baseball bat. She'd hit him with artful perfection, maximizing pain without knocking him out – she needed him to be conscious.

"Right, let us begin the preliminaries," she declared, fetching a smartphone from the case. Flicking on the camera function, she took three photos of Anton, front, left and right, as if taking mug shots. She winked at him and said in soft tones, "I'll need these later."

She put the phone back in the case and extracted four pieces of polished metal. In moments, she snapped, twisted and screwed the pieces together to form an elegant, gleaming saber.

"Not my favorite sword," she said while flourishing the shining blade. "The weapon of an assassin from the court of King Louis the fourteenth of France, but it is easily hidden and will serve for tonight."

Chloe returned to face William and promised with perfect certainty, "You will give me what I ask for." Turning, she addressed the room. "Or you will discover a fate far worse than you could possibly imagine for your family and yourself."

Anton, Anna, William, and even Marcus stroking his healing jaw, stared at her as the room fell into silence.

* * *

Dread gripped Anton's chest with ice cold fingers. How could this happen? Who were these people? What did she want?

He pulled at his bindings, but there was no getting free. The plastic was already starting to cut into the skin at his wrists. He looked at his parents, they were bound with steel chains and solid padlocks. *Why the difference? Sure, Dad is strong; he can out lift me – but chains are overkill – aren't they?*

Armitage interrupted his silent torrent of questions. "William Slayne, exiled member of the Order of Thoth and sworn enemy of the Vampire Dominion. I, Chloe Armitage, First General and right hand of King Cornelius Crane, hereby put you to the question," she announced. "Answer me truthfully and you will be granted quick death as befits your mortality – lie to me – and I will deliver you to a life of eternal punishment."

Flourishing her saber, she ran the blade over her palm and blood splashed onto the carpet. "This I swear before vampiric witnesses on the sacred blood of Mekra, mother of us all."

The blood drained from his father's face, and his mother gasped in shock. What were the Vampire Dominion and the Order of Thoth? Who was King Cornelius Crane and what did he want with Anton's family? The world had gone mad!

Armitage advanced on his father – her hand had already stopped bleeding. She leaned in on William, her face inches from his own, and asked directly, "You have the Papyrus of Hakron the Scribe – do you not?"

William shook his head. "I don't have it."

"I will bury you in a silver coffin," she promised. "I will convert you before we seal the lid. You will live for thousands of years confined in the dark, paralyzed by silver and unable to move. Tormented by thirst, you will be unable to die … are you sure you don't have the Papyrus?" Armitage stood straight and waved her hand around the room. "Are you sure it is not here … hidden somewhere in this house?"

William paused for a moment, shaking his head. "My father destroyed it, to ensure it could never come into the possession of the likes of you."

Armitage laughed derisively. "Arthur Slayne, the great archeologist, the great champion of the Order of Thoth, destroys one of the only three artifacts in the world that together give access to the Metaframe. Access he could use to destroy the Vampire Dominion. The greatest warrior of the Order of Thoth turns down the most powerful weapon, just to keep it out of our hands." She arched an eyebrow. "Please forgive me if I find that hard to believe."

What is the Metaframe? Anton asked himself silently.

Tilting her head slightly, Armitage stared hard at his father and said, "You have courage William, I will grant you that, but you are also foolish. I take my oaths seriously; you have sealed your fate. But what of the fate of your wife and son? What of Anna and Anton? What will become of them?"

William's jaw worked, but he said nothing, while his muscles bunched and strained against his chains.

Armitage stepped behind where Anna sat, placing the edge of the saber against the side of her neck, just below her ear. "I could slice bits off her as you watched. I wonder, would that be enough to motivate you?"

Marcus took up a position behind William, taking hold of his head with both hands, forcing him to face his wife.

Armitage stepped aside, her hand blurring, thrusting the saber through Anna's right shoulder. She twisted the blade. Anna's agonized scream drowned out the snapping of her bones.

"Leave her alone!" Anton shouted, overwhelmed with a need to protect his mother. "If you need to torture someone – torture me!"

Armitage turned to him, leaving the saber embedded in Anna's shoulder. "If necessary, your turn will come, but that will depend upon your father, and on which force is stronger? His resolve to protect the Papyrus or his love for his family."

Turning back to William, she paused for a long moment. "Do you want to try again? Now please remember carefully, for I am tiring of this game – where is the Papyrus?"

"Okay," William whispered, then half-shouted, "OKAY!" William stared at Anna with wide eyes as she gasped in pain. He uttered the words without looking away from his beloved wife, "There is a wall safe. The Papyrus is in it. It is behind the painting above the fireplace."

Armitage caught Drake's gaze and then flicked her head toward the picture. Drake let go of William and took the painting down. Behind it was a wall safe with a combination lock.

William muttered in a voice heavy with defeat, "The numbers are sixteen left, twenty-three right, seven left and thirty-four right."

Drake dialed the numbers. His head cocking slightly at the end, responding to a sound beyond Anton's ability to hear. He grinned, and pulled open the safe door. He recoiled, lifting his left hand like a shield, hissed and jumped backward about a dozen feet as if scalded. "Silver!"

Armitage looked back at Anna and withdrew her bloody saber.

Anna screamed again, her hands trembling with shock, blood spreading in a wet stain on her shoulder.

Armitage advanced on the safe, pushing the door back with the gore-soaked point of the blade, and looking inside the safe.

"Indeed," she said with a wry grin. "You have some silver sitting on top of a Papyrus." She used the point of her saber to push several silver coins and small bars out of the way. She fished out the Papyrus with her blade and caught it as it dropped free from the safe.

"I'm sorry Anna – I'll have to put this back," Armitage remarked with mock regret. "It's stopping you from bleeding to death, and it wouldn't do to have you die by accident." She jammed the saber directly back into the wound, perfectly matching the original cut. This time, Anna didn't scream. Gritting her teeth, she kept her silence.

His mother's agony swept through Anton like a physical blow. He was helpless; tied to a chair as vampires tortured his parents. It was worse than a nightmare, at least with a nightmare, it was possible to wake up. If anyone had told him this could happen, he would have called them crazy – and yet it was happening – the world had gone mad.

Armitage carefully opened the Papyrus. It was a scroll about six feet long and a foot wide, covered with intricate hieroglyphics. It looked faded, fragile and ancient. She scanned the Papyrus quickly. Pausing about halfway through, she frowned and rolled the Papyrus back up, and slapped it down carelessly beside the case. She walked back to the center of the room, steepled her fingers beneath her lips as if pondering what to do next. She turned toward Anna and commanded flatly, "Marcus, break her leg."

Drake's fist blurred faster than Anton's eye could follow. His mother shrieked as her right thigh bone shattered beneath Drake's hammer blow.

Anton swore, "What the fucking hell – we gave you what you wanted!"

His face flushed with blood, William shouted in frustration, "How dare you! I will make you pay!"

Armitage waited while Anna's screams reduced to quiet sobs. She turned toward William and arched an eyebrow. "I gave you the opportunity to be honest, to tell the truth, and what did I receive in return – lies and empty threats. You disappoint me, William Slayne. I thought you'd be a better man than this."

William snarled. "Let me free and give me a sword, and we'll see if you remain disappointed."

Armitage tilted her head slightly, putting her finger on her chin, her eyes filled with a fell light. "... Tempting – but I think not. A vampire's blood oath forbids mercy and death by my sword would be merciful."

William snapped, "I have no fear of dying."

"Of course not, you're a Slayne, but you no longer have the option of dying – do you?" Chloe promised, with quiet emphasis. "The time will come when you'll want nothing else but to die."

William stared at her in silence, his jaw clenched and his eyes gleaming like hard stones.

Anton implored her, "You have what you came for – what more do you want?"

Armitage picked up the Papyrus from the coffee table and threw it into Anton's lap. "You can have that if you want – it's a fake." She sighed. "Hakron the Scribe encrypted the real Papyrus. By reputation, it reads like utter gibberish written by a madman. An order is apparent in this," she shook her head once, "rubbish. A lesser mind than Hakron's wrote it. It's a worthless fake designed to deceive the unwary."

"Do you have to talk so damn much?" William said with a growl. "Just kill us already, your talk is worse than the torture."

Anton and Anna stared at William. Anton wondered what on Earth his father was doing. Did he have a strategy? Anton hoped so with all his heart.

"Oh, William," Armitage declared, shaking her head. "There are things far worse than simple death, as you already know."

Horror swirled into a great, dark cloud within Anton as Armitage walked back to where Anna sat chained to her chair. His mother reflexively recoiled as Armitage approached, but she was unable to avoid her captor pulling her head back, and biting deep into her throat in a classic vampire attack. Armitage wrapped her mouth around the wound and within a handful of seconds his mother's skin paled, while veins darkened on her throat as her blood rushed into the vampire's maw.

Anton's mother gasped in shock, while his father groaned in despair.

"Oh my God," Anton whispered. He wouldn't have believed it if he hadn't seen it with his own eyes; vampires were horribly real. He was at a loss to imagine what could happen next. Witnessing his own mother drained of her blood by a creature that in any sane world would not even exist. Surely, it couldn't get any worse than that.

Armitage stepped away from Anna. She licked a stray drop of blood from her finger, sighed with obvious pleasure and remarked as if speaking to the room, "There must be something about the Ramp. The blood of the Order is exquisite."

"You will rot in hell if I ever get my hands on you," William promised, his voice shaking with helpless fury.

"Oh William, I'm sure you will be there long before me." Armitage walked over to Drake's case, and retrieved a large hypodermic syringe from it. She went back to stand next to Anna. She faced William, hitched up her left sleeve, and promised with absolute certainty, "You have insisted on lying to me. I'm sure you will regret that choice." She plunged the syringe into the vein in the crook of her left elbow. She drew back on the plunger, and filled the syringe with her blood.

Anton looked on in uncomprehending horror while his father shouted, "NO!"

Armitage plunged the filled syringe directly into Anna's heart – just to the left of the sternum as if she was a paramedic delivering a vital dose of adrenalin to a heart attack victim.

The effect was immediate. Anna's eyes bulged, and she writhed in agony while William cried out in despair. Anna's limbs twitched and vibrated. Inbetween low moans, she cried out, "No ... Please God ... NO!"

Armitage stepped to the side, studying William intently. He wrenched his eyes from his wife and stared back at their tormentor, his face twisted with hate, fury and despair.

Armitage commanded in stern tones, "Tell me where the real Papyrus is."

William shook his head, whispering hoarsely, "No – I can't do that."

Armitage's eyes softened and she promised, "I will give her a clean death."

William shook his head in silence.

"Marcus, prepare to free her," Armitage directed, "but keep her on a leash."

Armitage turned back to William and inquired with a knowing look, "Who do you think she will feed on when the bloodlust of a virgin vampire overwhelms her? I assure you; the choice will not be rational. Will it be you, or will it be Anton? I trust her maternal instincts will protect Anton, which means that she will feed on you."

"You're a fiend!" William declared furiously.

"You are wrong William," Armitage corrected him, as if instructing a dull and tiresome student. "I am simply doing what is necessary. You could have avoided all of this upset and trouble – just tell me where the real Papyrus is."

"Dad tell her," Anton pleaded in desperate tones. "Before it's too late."

His father stared at Anton with eyes filled with disappointment and shook his head slowly.

A shocking realization swept through Anton; it really was too late. He felt sick to his stomach. If by dying, he could end this horror, he would willingly die. His stomach churned, he'd never seen his father disappointed in him before now, it was shocking beyond belief. The world had gone insane. If the floor opened up and demons erupted from a fiery hell to drag him down – it would seem normal compared to what was happening right now.

Armitage approached William, and stood beside him. She caressed his cheek, and he twisted his head away from her hand. She leaned down, whispering in his ear but just loud enough for Anton to hear her words, "Now William, please listen closely. Marcus and I will stand ready. When your wife begins feeding on you, we will watch carefully, and Marcus will drag her off before she drains you completely. Now Marcus is very strong, even for a vampire. It's one of the reasons that I like to keep him around, so don't assume that he can't do what I need him to. Then I will inject you with my blood and in about five minutes you will be a newly converted vampire with an overwhelming and uncontrollable need to feed on the nearest human being – and who would that be?"

She left the question hanging between them and straightened up. The transformation of Anton's mother completed. Armitage glanced at the gleaming blade piercing Anna's shoulder and asked her henchman, "The saber?"

Drake pulled the weapon from Anna's shoulder, and handed it back to his mistress.

Anna winced and then smiled. "William, my love. The pain is gone. I can feel my thigh, it's healing. I feel strong." She moaned as if aroused, tossing back her long blond hair, she wet her lips with her tongue and declared huskily, "William, I need you."

Anton watched in horror as his mother's attention focused on his father. It was like watching a starving snake looking at a juicy fat rat.

Armitage stood behind his father, resting her a hand on his shoulder. She said softly into his left ear, "After I convert you and you finish feeding on your son. I will convert him as well and stake him out in the backyard to await sunrise. You and your wife I will imprison in silver at opposite ends of this world. Where is the real Papyrus of Hakron the Scribe? Tell me now, and I will kill your wife cleanly and spare your son's life. I have given a sacred oath and I will honor my word."

William looked down, his face twisting with anguish. "It is behind the picture that you took down, hidden in the frame."

Anna thrashed against her bonds, her eyes flashing with a terrible lust, she screamed, "Free me! I must feed!"

Armitage ignored her, shredding the frame and extracting another Papyrus. She checked it carefully for about two minutes while Anna ranted and raved in her chair. She briefly closed her eyes, breathing deeply, she wiped away a tear with a trembling hand.

Anton's mother's face snapped around toward Armitage.

Armitage stepped aside, smiled briefly and with an air of quiet inevitability, she declared, "I am true to my word." Her saber blurred through a flashing arc and Anna's head slipped from her shoulders to the floor.

Anton screamed with horror while William wept with despair.

"Marcus, clear this room and take William Slayne to the car."

In moments, Drake rendered William unconscious with the same drug he'd used on Anton. He cleared the coffee table of the photos, and the business card, gathering it all together into his black case. He then carried William's limp body from the house.

Armitage approached Anton, still tied to his chair, tears streaming down his face. She flicked the saber and his mother's blood disappeared from the blade. She poked him lightly in the chest, enough to break the skin, getting his attention with a little physical pain. "You are the one that invited us in." she said in cold, cutting tones. "You – in your ignorance and helplessness –

became the bait that made your parents vulnerable. It is entirely your fault that they are dead or imprisoned forever." She smiled at him without warmth and said, "On the bright side – you get to live."

Armitage tapped him again on the sternum with the point of her saber. "One other lesson before I go." She leaned in close, her face inches from his own. Her eyes locked on Anton's as she instructed with a soft caressing voice, "Your parents have told you that they loved you and wanted to keep you safe, but I ask you this – who spent years lying to you and who told you the truth?" Stepping back, Armitage slashed his bindings.

Anton reached out, trying to catch her, but by the time the plastic ties had hit the floor – she'd already vanished from the house. He stared wide-eyed around the room in silence. The house lay still like a felled corpse. His mother slumped lifeless in her chair, her head at her feet. His father had disappeared and was destined for a supernatural punishment.

Anton dropped to his knees before his mother's corpse, and howled like an animal caught in a trap. Overwhelmed with emotion, devastated beyond words, he was drowning in grief and utterly alone.

* * *

Anton staggered up to his room.

This is insane, this is insane, this is insane. The words kept circling like trolls around his mind. He couldn't think. Images flashed randomly through him, constantly replaying the horror. The saber slicing into his mother's shoulder. Armitage draining her blood and licking her finger afterward. His mother's transformation into a blood lusting monster, followed by the lethal brutality of her beheading.

It's my fault. Armitage's words threaded through his mind like cold dark needles. He couldn't breathe, he was dizzy and lightheaded. *I'm hyperventilating.* He sat on his bed, put his head in his hands and started breathing through his nose. *Slowly, in, out, hold my breath, in, out, hold my breath.*

A thin veneer of sanity returned. He couldn't stay. This house was no longer a home, but where could he go? His mind raced, switching between options before trenchant memory dragged it back to scenes of recent horrors.

He whispered in desperation, "How can I unsee what I have seen?"

Canvassing many options in a frenzied rush, he quickly packed a backpack with a few essentials.

He stopped, standing like a statue in the middle of his bedroom. He couldn't call the police. How would the conversation go? He whispered derisively to himself, "Hello officer, vampires beheaded my mother and abducted my father," he snorted, then smacked his face, his hand sliding down to cover his mouth, his eyes wide and staring into empty space. A patina of the surreal covered his world. The authorities would be useless. He concluded in a hoarse whisper, "The cops will think that I did it, or Dad did it."

How could he live with this? What about his friends? They'd be expecting him tonight. Anton picked up his smartphone and it shook in his hands before dropping back to the desk. Vampires had murdered his mother and abducted his father. There was nothing stopping them coming back for him. The last thing he wanted to do was get any of his friends involved. He was dangerous to be around. He'd have to be a no show for tonight. Anton resolved to disappear. His friends could not know where he was. It would keep them safe, and might keep himself safe too. He checked his wallet; he had a little over sixty dollars on him. He had another thousand in his savings account. He grabbed his passport. He didn't know if it would be useful or not, but better to take it and not need it, than leave it behind and discover it was essential. He left his phone on his desk, anyone who might call it – he didn't want to answer.

Anton gave the room a long, last look. He could forget about exams; he was never going to graduate. The ice hockey scholarship was in the bin. He felt a sharp pang of deep disappointment as he realized his budding professional sports career was over. The feeling lasted all of a second before an ocean of guilt washed it away. "Damn it. How could I be so selfish?"

He rubbed both hands through his thick dark hair, before dragging them down his face. His mother was dead and vampires had abducted his father. There was no time for self-pity.

"Damn it all to hell. Weapons? What can I use against these damn vampires?"

A dozen movies and TV shows flicked through his mind. He put aside the idea of finding Armitage or Drake in their coffins and staking them through the heart. They didn't look like they spent any time in a coffin. Guns, you would have to be very fast to shoot someone who could move in a blur.

Then he remembered their aversion to silver. They didn't like silver – they avoided it with a passion.

Anton put on his runners, a cap and a dark jacket with a hood. He stuffed some spare clothes into his backpack and put his sunglasses on top of them. He went downstairs and into the lounge room.

His mother's corpse still sat in her chair. He'd been unable to touch her before. It was too macabre, and his emotions lay like strips of raw meat in his soul. Armitage had told him, it was all his fault, he'd been bait, and his parents had been unable to defend themselves because of him. His breathing became fast and shallow. He stood, staring at his mother, the safe and the silver momentarily forgotten. Fresh tears welled up in his eyes.

"Fuck it!" Anton snarled. "Why am I still alive?"

Armitage had whispering into his ear, '*I am sure you will do great things.* She'd wanted him to live. She had a purpose that involved him.

Anton shook his head as his rage overflowed the walls of his soul, and he screamed in inarticulate defiance. He panted for a long moment, his soul on fire, and vowed to his mother's corpse, "There is no way I'm ever going to help that bitch!"

He went to the safe, there was the silver and nothing else. Taking the coins and small bars, he added them to his backpack. As he left the room, he deliberately avoided looking at his mother's corpse for the last time. He wanted to remember her as she was when she was alive. A vibrant, inquisitive woman with a kind heart, and not as she was now – a real life horror show.

Anton went to the kitchen, added a pair of water bottles, some hard cheese, nuts and dried fruit. Anything he could easily carry that would last more than a few days.

He left the house through the back door, made his way over the fence and into the nearby forest preserve and garden cemetery. Then he ran; as he left his home behind, he had an uncanny feeling of hidden watchers tracking his every step, that the woods were full of eyes.

His skin crawled, he stopped, turning to stare into the shadows behind him – but there was no one there. Listening carefully, he could only hear the silence of the surrounding gardens. There wasn't even the whisper of a breeze. The trees stood still, silent sentinels over the nearby gravestones, and the only intrusions were the faint noises of the city beyond. He turned again, running hard for two minutes, putting another eight hundred yards between himself and his home.

He had to get away from here. He had to disappear. He pulled to a sudden stop. *What about my father?* Witnessing his mother's torture and murder had overwhelmed him. He'd momentarily forgotten about his father. Anton was the only person who had any knowledge of what had occurred, he was the only one who could save his father or avenge his mother.

Responsibility fell like a dead weight upon his shoulders. Rage, grief, guilt, terror, and despair, warred within his soul. His stomach knotted. He collapsed to his knees, overtaken by convulsive vomiting. He pushed himself back from the mess, sitting back against a nearby tree. Breathing in the smell of the vomit made him feel nauseous again, and he gave way to the compulsion. He sat back again, wiping his mouth with his hand. He took a swig from one of his water bottles, swishing it around his mouth before spitting it out. He took a long pull on the bottle and the water soothed his throat.

Questions lay siege to his soul. Armitage had done everything possible to make him hate her. Did she want him to try and kill her? Why would she want him to do that? Surely her purpose can't be her own suicide. There must be something else going on.

Anton's emotions churned. His thoughts were leaves flying carelessly within a firestorm. His father had said to Armitage, '*I will make you pay.*' His words struck through the chaos within, fanning Anton's rage.

Ghosts of the recent past flew through his soul, whispering, '*It's your fault, be afraid, there is no hope, don't care, be numb.* But he did care, he couldn't give up. He couldn't let it go. He couldn't let any of it go.

A chaotic sea threatened to engulf him, reaching desperately, he found sanctuary from the chaos on an icy rock of fury. Dragging himself out of the clinging wasteland of madness he stood tall upon the glacial ice. It burned with pale fire while lightning played behind his eyes. Anton lifted his gaze. His eyes hardened as he promised with dreadful conviction, "I will make you pay."

He continued in quiet tones of ferocious intent, "I know who you are Chloe Armitage. I will find out what you are and how to kill you, and when we meet again – then you will pay for what you have done."

Slinging his backpack over his shoulder, he strode off. After ten minutes, he reached the edge of the garden cemetery, and stepped onto a sidewalk. He paused for a moment, considering his father's fate with a heart in which anguish and cold fury stood opposed in a frightful detente.

I may not be able to save you dad, but if I find you, I promise you that I will release you.

* * *

Chloe lifted her Shadowstone smartphone to her ear.

It was already dialing the call. The system relied on quantum encryption technologies that rendered the call both untraceable, and indecipherable to anyone but the intended recipient.

A familiar voice answered after the second ring, "James Haley speaking, what can I do for you, Ma'am?"

"James, I need a cleanup crew at this residence," Chloe requested, sending through the GPS coordinates of the Smith family home in Boston. "Deal with this personally. There is no room for error."

"Yes Ma'am, I will organize a team immediately and ensure the site is completely sanitized."

"I have an additional assignment for you and your team. One of the terrorists escaped, I'm sending photos of him now."

Chloe forwarded the photos of Anton taken in the lounge room earlier that night. The photos were close ups of Anton's face and didn't reveal his restraints.

"His name is Anton Smith," she directed. "I want him found and tracked, but under no circumstances are you to approach, contact, or engage with him in any way. Report immediately back to me once you have established a sustained trace on his location."

"I will have a Panopticon search running in less than a minute after this call ends," James replied.

Chloe could almost hear him nodding his head as he promised, "We will find him, Ma'am."

"Be sure that you do."

"Yes, Ma'am."

Chloe hung up.

James Haley, head of the United States arm of the Shadowstone organization, would follow her orders to the letter. Chloe had worked with him for years, trusting him as much as she trusted anyone – which is to say not much – but she understood him and knew he could be relied upon to get things done. He was an able and effective operator, previously with the CIA, Shadowstone had recruited him with the promise of being, 'where the real action is', in the 'blackest of black ops,' in a 'genuine transnational global organization working for world peace and the greater good.' The situation with Anton Slayne was delicate, she needed staff capable of subtlety. James was capable of being subtle and playing an effective role.

She'd contemplated the idea of bringing James fully into the Vampire Dominion, but that would require the approval of Cornelius Crane. An approval Crane was unlikely to grant. Crane was rigorous in keeping total vampire numbers below his *'magic'* limit of one thousand. He had never provided a reason for why he limited vampire numbers to less than a thousand, and Chloe had lost interest in trying to find out why. She deemed it a quirk of her boss.

Chloe turned to the Papyrus. It sat next to her on the back seat of the limousine. She lifted it up, unrolled it and read it again. She replayed in her mind the act of reading it for the first time in the Slayne lounge room. Nothing had changed, every detail of the Papyrus was identical with her memory.

An eidetic memory is as rare amongst humans as amongst vampires. It was one of the skills that had attracted the Order of Thoth to induct her before her eighteenth birthday. It was an ability she'd kept secret from Crane.

She put the Papyrus down. Leaning back, she closed her eyes, savoring its content. She remembered the position of individual fibers, of slight variations in pigment where Hakron had needed to renew an ink pot. She easily recalled every detail, every image, delighting in what she saw. She could hand the prize of the Papyrus of Hakron the Scribe to her master, while retaining a perfect copy for herself.

Chloe's eyes shone with pleasure and she smiled broadly. The limousine pulled to a halt within a hangar owned by R.I.S.C at Boston's Logan Airport. Marcus transferred the bound and gagged, but now awake William Slayne to a sleek, black helicopter.

The nightfalcon was an advanced evolution of the blackhawk helicopter, the new design commissioned and funded by the Vampire Dominion. Crane had assigned this particular helicopter to her personal use. The pilot was a vampire, a member of her personal staff. The helicopter began to spool up with a low whine as great doors in the roof of the hangar started clanking open. Chloe boarded her nightfalcon, taking a seat in the main cabin.

She addressed the pilot, "To the citadel."

"Yes, General Armitage," the pilot replied.

Marcus joined her in the cabin, closing the door as the helicopter took off. It rapidly cleared the hangar and sped off toward New York City.

* * *

A terrorist had escaped.

James Haley worked his smartphone, inserting the three photos he'd just received from General Armitage into the Panopticon system. He swapped to his computer terminal. Logging into the Panopticon, he punched up the search program. He selected the photos and set the search program running with a high priority flag.

The Panopticon responded with a three-dimensional plot of the world. A web of red markers spread across the screen. Each tiny red flag indicated where searches completed with a negative result. The markers operated at a very fine resolution; it was like watching a set of red waves spreading out from nodes located in all the world's major cities. Boston showed an orange rash where the Panopticon found hits on the target in records older than an hour. There were no yellow or green markers. Not a single camera linked to the Panopticon had registered Anton Smith within the last hour or last minute respectively.

James ran his cursor over several options, clicking as he went. The system responded by expanding the Boston view until the perimeter of hits in the last week filled the screen while simultaneously cross-referencing hits to establish a target profile. In seconds, James had a name, a student number, a social security number, a smartphone number, email accounts, bank accounts, Facebook and other social media accounts. The system even began estimating the target's characteristics, habits, predilections, and personality type based on usage of all other systems.

James rapidly scanned the profile, musing to himself, *Well, Anton Smith, you're a little young to be playing in the big league. I wonder what you did to attract all this attention.*

He looked around his office, a set of hi-definition, multi-screen monitors dominated the walls. One of them showed current satellite tracks. James smiled to himself and thought out loud, "That's convenient."

He opened a new program, vectoring a camera on a military satellite currently passing over the northeast corner of the United States. He fed in the GPS coordinates of the Smith residence and the satellite camera zoomed in on Anton Smith's home.

He flicked on a filter to get an infra-red view. There was nothing alive inside the house. James stared intently at the screen for about five seconds, and then his fingers rapidly flowed over the keyboard before he paused for a moment waiting for a response. The satellite camera swapped in a new filter and the telephone network rang the smartphone number on Anton Smith's profile. In the center of his monitor, a small red star came into existence and started flashing over a room at the top of the house. He flicked the camera back to its standard operations, and leaned back in his chair.

The phone was home; the boy was not. Who would leave home without their phone? Someone was in a hurry. It mattered less what he was running from, than where he was running to.

James had been with Shadowstone for eight years. He'd seen a lot of things in that time, not all of which made sense. His initial induction had emphasized the need to maintain stability in the world, and to combat those forces that would bring chaos and death. A true fight between good and evil where devoted service to the greater good licensed any and all actions.

He'd always pursued a life that would make a difference, first with the US Army Green Berets, and then with the CIA. At thirty years of age, the man who had previously held his current role had tapped him on the shoulder. He'd pursued the opportunity and within three months General Armitage had interviewed and accepted him into the ranks of Shadowstone. In the last eight years, he'd worked to keep the world hanging together, to ensure stability and order, to keep governments operational and the little guy safe. He'd done everything he could for the greater good.

However, there were many operations like this current one, sanitation ops, the cleansing of all evidence of the operation of a group of operatives reporting directly to General Armitage. There was an echelon of agents that operated at a layer above where he was, who were definitely outside his chain of command, and who participated in all the real missions.

General Armitage had told him the enemy had special training and combat techniques and only her elite agents and special forces could effectively combat them. James shook his head. He believed that he belonged on the front line with the special forces on combat operations.

Instead of combat operations, Operational Security, OPSEC, was his primary purpose. Information suppression and the keeping of secrets. The Order of Thoth and the Red Empire opposed Shadowstone. Terrorist organizations that made Al Qaeda and ISIS seem like amateurs. Revolutionary organizations that would bathe the world in blood to achieve their objectives of the overthrow of the current world order. They were a clear and present danger, but he'd never met a single operative from either group – and that wasn't what he'd signed up for.

James was a man of action, but instead of confronting the enemy he found himself riding herd on a stunningly effective surveillance system and a set of cleanup crews. But now a terrorist had escaped, it was an opportunity to prove what he could really do. He put aside his wool gathering and focused on the task at hand.

He did not need to look up who was available to assign to this operation. The closest spectrum team was Green-4, sixteen highly skilled operatives organized into four-man squads led by Louise Wesson. He rang her smartphone, all the Shadowstone operatives carried smartphones equipped with completely secure quantum encryption.

Louise Wesson answered immediately, "Yes, Sir. What are your orders?"

"We have another clean up op. This time it's Boston. I'm sending site and target profiles through to your phone. If you encounter the target, do not engage; instead, standoff, track only and await further orders. Is that clear?"

"Yes, perfectly Sir. I will get the team in motion. We're at Fort Dix at the moment, it will take us a minimum of four and a half hours to get the sanitation vans and my available staff to Boston … that gives us an ETA of 03:00 hours."

"Get moving, I will meet you on site," James directed.

"Already moving, Sir."

"Outstanding."

James hung up the call. He fetched his jacket from a coat rack next to the door of his office. He went to the nearest elevator and descended to the building's parking garage; he would need his car's specialized set of equipment.

It was going to be a long night.

* * *

Chloe Armitage's nightfalcon descended smoothly through the open hangar doors on the roof of a massive Manhattan skyscraper.

Top end military grade weapon systems had tracked the helicopter for the last five miles as it approached the building. Sophisticated sensor arrays that no city officials were aware of identified her helicopter as a friend, allowing her craft to safely pass disengaged missile and rail gun systems. The building, at number 350 on Fifth Avenue, had 108 floors above ground level. The hangar and building defense systems took up floors 107 and 108 as a combined space.

The operations of the Vampire Dominion occupied all the floors above the hundredth floor and included the personal quarters of Cornelius Crane, King of the Vampires.

This was his citadel.

As the helicopter landed, Chloe turned to Marcus and ordered him, "Take Slayne to our containment facility on Rikers Island, get him set up and wait for me to arrive."

Marcus nodded and replied, "Yes, Chloe."

Chloe exited the nightfalcon and walked briskly to the elevator. She carried the Papyrus in a tubular case tucked under her left arm.

Crane's praetorians guarded the building. They were elite vampire warriors dressed in modern matte black combat armor, carrying long curved swords, and M249 light machine guns. A pair of them saluted her, stepping aside as she reached the elevator doors.

Chloe ignored them; deference was a one-way street in the Vampire Dominion. Inside the elevator, she leaned forward, staring into a biometric eye scanner, a small green light came on above it. She pressed the button for the operations center on the 103rd floor. Moments later, she strode into the tactical heart of her operational domain. Forty stations and screens surrounded her, a dozen vampires at work in the room, a skeleton staff for the current low threat environment.

The cold war detente was in full swing. She remembered when vampires working in shifts crowded the room. The beating heart of the Vampire Dominion's war against the Ramp masters of the Red Empire and the Order of Thoth. Those were the days; when a swift blade and tactical brilliance made all the difference. The quietude of the modern world left her with a gnawing dissatisfaction. A desire for a return of more challenging times.

The vampires in the ops center stood up, saluting her as she came out of the elevator. She walked briskly past them, indifferent to their actions, and they returned to their duties. She strode to the end of the room where a single set of stairs gave access to the floor above — to Crane's personal quarters.

She shared access to the 104th floor with the other four generals and Crane's personal secretary. All of them captured by the curse of the Haitian voodoo priest, Jean Philippe Allemande, which had eliminated their ability to harm Crane.

As she took her first step on the stairs, another biometric scanner took in her body shape and style of movement. At the first landing of the stairs, a GAU-17/A minigun tracked the center of her body mass. The gun sported six barrels and fired 7.62mm depleted uranium rounds. It could deliver four thousand rounds of pure hell per minute. The system recognized her and the deadly weapon swung out of the way.

She'd walked up these stairs more times than she cared to remember. Each time, she found herself musing about the nasty accident that would occur if the system ever made a mistake. She enjoyed the details of technology, but she considered it a weakness to rely on it too much. She stepped past the wicked looking barrels of the minigun without a second glance at the formidable weapon.

At the top of the second flight of stairs, she approached a forbidding door of polished steel. Only someone on the other side of the door could open it. She waited a moment and a nearly invisible seam opened vertically in the reflective surface. The two sides, thick enough to stop a shaped explosive charge, silently pulled back into the walls. Cornelius Crane, king of the vampires, had just granted her access to his personal quarters.

Chloe stepped into the inner sanctum of Crane's citadel. The whole floor was an extended suite done exclusively in the high style of the 18th-century French aristocracy. She walked calmly along a broad entry hall. The walls had shallow nooks holding exquisite pieces of art. Crane favored the European Renaissance masters. The halls and rooms displayed a collection of Da Vinci, Michelangelo, Donatello, Raphael, Botticelli, Titian, Hieronymus Bosch, and woodcuts by Albrecht Durer — all authentic, and many famous.

The fakes and copies littered the walls of the museums of the world — the originals were here. Crane was a collector; and art was one of his many passions. Chloe noted as she walked past the art that he'd collected her too, and for a time, she'd been his passion.

She entered into his library. He'd been collecting books since the 11th century. Shelves and volumes lined the walls from floor to ceiling. Additional works rested in climate-controlled cases to preserve them. The great minds of the last five thousand years filled the room. More than a dozen languages were required to read what was written here, and Crane had mastered all of them.

After Crane had personally converted her into a vampire, Chloe had spent her early decades as his lover, confidant, and protégé. She'd spent many years in this library when it was still in London during the 19th century.

Walking through the main room of the library, she glanced down at an elegant French 17th-century table. Resting on the table was an original copy from the first print run of 'Dell'arte Della Guerra,' also known as 'On the Art of War' by Niccolo Machiavelli.

She'd read that very volume, written in the original Italian within the first year of her relationship with Crane. Her mind grasped the open page at a glance. She almost stopped walking as one of Machiavelli's quotes from the page came to her mind. 'No enterprise is more likely to succeed than one concealed from the enemy until it is ripe for execution.'

How apropos, she thought, *but why does he have this very page open for me to see as I pass by – does he suspect me?*

She halted in front of Crane. He sat behind a polished wooden desk, dressed simply, in fine robes and slippers. He glanced at the tube she was carrying and said with an avid grin, "Chloe, I see you have brought me a gift. Let me see it."

Chloe took the Papyrus from the case, unrolling it across the breadth of his desk.

Crane laughed. Standing up to his full six feet six-inch height. His long arms reached out, pinning the scroll at each end. He leaned over the Papyrus, peering intently at it. "It's magnificent, both intricate and unknowable without the Codex. Hakron was a genius, the equal of his brother."

"Two of the three are now together, Cornelius," Chloe remarked, using Crane's first name which he allowed when they were alone together.

"Yes. I have been searching for nearly a millennium, and now we have two artifacts in less than forty years. If I believed in it, I would say the hand of fate was at work. But no, these are the fruits of persistence, hard work, and to a great degree – your own skills." Crane rolled the Papyrus up again. Placing it within a golden tube, he rested it on his desk. He looked deeply into Chloe's eyes and requested, "You must name a reward."

Chloe's mouth tightened and she replied, "You know what I want, and it cannot be given."

"Well, yes … such a quaint notion … Liberty. But of course, – you must choose something else."

Chloe tilted her head slightly, smiling innocently. "I am sure that one night I will think of something worthy of my service."

Crane stared at her; his brown eyes filled with hidden thoughts, and declared, "I am sure that one night you will."

Chloe stood quietly in silence, forcing him to continue.

"Turning to other matters," Crane declared with a brief frown. "You had your personal helicopter transport a human to Rikers Island. It looks like you have more work to do tonight."

"Yes, I do. He is the son of Arthur Slayne."

Crane raised an eyebrow in surprise. "I expected you to kill them both."

"I made a sacred blood oath during the interrogation – he violated it. I am merely completing the punishment."

"So be it, such operational matters are your prerogative."

Chloe nodded.

"Is there anything else to report?"

"Nothing of any import."

"You have done excellent work tonight. Please get some rest. You're dismissed."

"Thank you, Sir," Chloe replied deferentially. She inclined her head in a short bow. Taking three steps back, she turned and walked away. She exited Crane's chambers through the polished steel doors, a slight smile curling the edge of her mouth.

He has no idea of the existence of Anton Slayne. I will have to ensure he never finds out the truth – until it is too late.

* * *

Cornelius Crane watched Chloe leave his library. He waited until he heard her exit the floor, then he remotely closed the main door behind her.

With the Papyrus tube in hand, he turned around, gazing at the art piece hanging directly behind his desk. It was the triptych, Garden of Earthly Delights, by Hieronymus Bosch. Cornelius had been the unknown patron who had commissioned both this work in 1491 and a deliberately imperfect copy completed in 1493. The copy now resided in the Museo del Prado in Madrid and had done so since 1939. The interwoven fantastical images spoke to his soul; it was his favorite masterpiece.

Together, the three panels of the triptych stood over seven feet high and thirteen feet wide. He approached the middle panel. The largest of the three, it depicted scenes of lost innocence. He touched an almost imperceptible stud on the bottom of the panel, it swung free, revealing a hidden doorway.

It was a narrow space, crouching, Crane stepped up into the doorway, disappearing into the darkness beyond. He moved into a secret room and soft lights came on automatically. It was a mini-library, filled with rare and obscure books. All manner of parchments, scraps of papyrus and wood carvings lay on shelves along the side walls. Cornelius kept all the knowledge and lore of the Metaframe here. What had been known over five thousand years before by Hakron and Ahknaton as the Divine Engine of Thoth.

Cornelius had come to understand that the Metaframe underpinned the physical reality of the world. While extremely difficult to access, once reached, anyone could change the rules of the universe as easily as a programmer might change lines of computer code. The shocking implications of that power had driven him to dedicate himself to ensuring that no one would ever access the Metaframe again.

He approached the bare rear wall. In front of it stood three short marble pillars, each about five feet high and a foot across. On the middle pillar rested a polished black obsidian stone. Its surface glistened wetly in the pale light, seeming to capture the night sky in miniature.

It was the Key of Ahknaton, retrieved in 1978 from a secret vault under St Peter's Basilica in the Vatican City. In 1625, Michelangelo had placed the key in a hidden chamber guarded by an ingenious maze filled with deadly traps. Himself a senior member of the Order of Thoth, he had made the safe keeping of the key his life's work.

Arthur Slayne had interrupted the mission to recover the key. They had fought within Michelangelo's secret vault, the three of them, Slayne, Chloe and himself. Cornelius shook his head with the troubling memory. He'd never seen anyone fight as well as Slayne had that night.

Slayne's masterful skills and extraordinary speed had saved his life. Anyone else would have died in a moment, but his survival that night had sparked an interest – an interest that led to the events of this night.

It was a pity Arthur Slayne was not one of his generals. What a treasure he would have made.

Cornelius placed the golden tube containing the Papyrus of Hakron the Scribe on top of the left pillar. It had never left the hands of a member of the Slayne family line for over five thousand years and now it was here.

Now it was safe.

He turned to contemplate the bare, third pillar on the right. The Interpretive Codex remained beyond his reach. Chloe Armitage was his best asset and she would be pivotal to bringing it here.

Cornelius turned around, staring out into the brightly lit main library without seeing anything in particular – his mind obsessed with his most useful operative. But what then? Her capability and ambition were dangerous. In the long years ahead, she may find a way to breach Allemande's curse. With the three in his possession, it would be safer for everyone if she was no longer with him.

"When the time comes, she must go," Cornelius promised to himself in the stillness of his secret library.

* * *

Chloe Armitage had used her pass to swipe her way into the bio-hazard waste section of the Rikers Island Waste Treatment Plant.

Originally commissioned in the late 1920s by the city of New York. The waste treatment plant had almost never happened. Cornelius Crane operating in the background had shaped the decision making, forestalling an alternative plan to convert Rikers Island into a prison.

It was now an ongoing commercial concern, operated by front companies owned by Shadowstone, and therefore owned by the Vampire Dominion. Even detailed inspection by city officials would not show all of what really went on at the facility. By day, the main plant processed all manner of waste, including medical waste from New York City and surrounding district hospitals. By night, vampires exclusively staffed the smaller bio-hazard waste section. It processed the remains of vampire feasts held at Crane's citadel and other locations in New England sanctioned by Crane where vampires could feed in secret. Similar facilities operated across the United States and the rest of the world; disposing of the evidence of vampire hunger.

When Crane shifted his operations from London to New York City in the early 1920s, he'd built the towering citadel on Fifth Avenue over the New York subway. He'd cut a secret railway line out to Rikers Island and funded the establishment of the waste treatment facility. He'd made it widely known amongst vampires exactly what the bio-hazard waste section was for. Chloe had punished vampires for breaking the rules and dumping bodies where humans might find them. Chloe and the praetorians routinely culled indiscreet vampires from the ranks. The vampires who survived the purges were all obedient and religiously tidy about their feeding habits.

The existence of the Vampire Dominion was a very well-kept secret.

Chloe made her way into the depths of the bio-hazard waste facility, to a door the human staff who worked there could not pass through. She tapped her pass on the sensor. The door clicked and she pushed it open. The next section was known only to the upper echelon of the Vampire Dominion, Crane, the generals, and their immediate staff. It was a facility for containing vampires, a vampire prison. Crane rarely used it, as non-compliance by a vampire to the edicts of King Crane was typically a fast form of suicide. The primary exceptions were the generals. Crane had handpicked them, and he'd gone to the trouble of having them cursed to improve their usefulness to him. With Jean Philippe Allemande dead, they were not replaceable. When they made mistakes, instead of killing them, he would punish them with imprisonment in silver.

The most recent example had been a stint by Dieter Franz. The general in charge of continental Europe, who had made a terrible error of judgment in 1945. Chloe had hauled him back to the US in disgrace, before interring him in a silver coffin for thirty years. The internment had temporarily cost Franz his sanity. It had taken him several years to recover his mind and become useful once again.

Chloe opened the final door, entering the last room at the very bottom of the facility. In the room was 'The Machine,' and Marcus stood next to it. William Slayne lay tightly strapped into the device and unable to move. She was pleased to see Marcus had used duct tape to silence him.

She was thankful for his thoughtful consideration. She'd never liked the tiresome sound of screaming and if at all possible, she preferred to avoid it. Most of the time in combat with Chloe, people didn't scream – they didn't get the chance to. The incident with Anna Slayne earlier in the night had been distasteful, but necessary to the success of the mission, and Chloe excelled at dealing with necessities. "Marcus, you have done well," she said warmly, reaching up and kissing him on the cheek.

Marcus beamed and reported, "We're ready."

"Excellent."

"Do you wish to feed?" Marcus asked with a deferential tone in his voice.

Chloe shook her head. "No, thank you. I am replete. Please, be my guest – he is all yours. You deserve it. It has been a long and trying night."

She looked around, there was a table prepared with syringes and other medical paraphernalia. Marcus had been thorough in his work. She picked up a fresh syringe and filled it with her blood. There was a sudden movement on the edge of her vision as Marcus sank his fangs into William Slayne's throat. She watched him feed, noting his self-discipline when he stopped short of draining his victim dry.

"Good work, Marcus," she said with warm enthusiasm.

Marcus stepped back and she inserted the syringe needle into William's heart. Depressing the plunger, she pushed a full load of her blood directly into his left ventricle. Bound into immobility and silence. William's eyes bulged and his skin developed a clammy sheen.

A clock ticked noisily in the background. Chloe stepped back, waiting patiently. After five minutes, the transformation was almost complete. She indicated with a flick of her eyes at Marcus what she wanted done.

Marcus ripped off the duct tape.

"Wait! Hey!" William yelled.

It was all he was able to say as Chloe punched a green button on a console next to the machine. The metal arm that William lay strapped to, arced forward 180 degrees and slammed him into a coffin made from pure silver. The restraints around him automatically released with puffs of high-pressure air, retracting in a matter of milliseconds.

Before William could react, the coffin lid slammed shut and a dozen heavy bolts snapped into position. A set of whirring robotic arms automatically screwed the bolts into place. A giant mechanical claw attached to a pulley and a motorized runner system on the ceiling reached down, hooked up the coffin, and slotted it neatly into a waiting vertical holding chamber in the floor. Finally, a lid slid shut over the chamber leaving no trace of the coffin beneath.

To all intents and purposes, William Slayne had vanished from the face of the Earth.

Chloe took Marcus's hand and looked up into his eyes. She said huskily, "You have done very well tonight, time for some recreation back at my penthouse."

Marcus smiled broadly.

She stroked his chest, staring hungrily into his eyes. "Now where did you park the helicopter?"

Chapter Two

"The most useful deceptions are those the target will actively resist questioning." – General Chloe Armitage

"Take a potent lie, wrap it in the truth and hammer it home with trauma." – General Chloe Armitage

– Quotes from an Instructional Video, Target Capture and Conditioning, Shadowstone Covert PSYOPS Manual – Appendix B

* * *

Boston, April 28th, 23:40

Anton scanned the departure board at South Station, the main hub for ground transport out of Boston.

It showed a Greyhound bus leaving for Montreal in ten minutes, with the following Montreal bus leaving on Saturday morning at 07:00. The five-mile hike from the forest preserve behind his house to the station had allowed him to begin to calm down and collect his scattered thoughts. He ached with sadness, broken only by flashes of livid fury. Despite his best efforts, his swirling thoughts still flew like lost birds over the chaotic ocean of his feelings.

There were so many unknowns. Where did Chloe Armitage live? Who was King Cornelius Crane? Was there an army of vampires? How do you kill a vampire? How would he find out what he needed to know? It wasn't information that you could get at the local library. How would he survive without the vampires finding him again? And where on Earth was his father? And, if he found him – could he save him? He had no answers and was on the run. Anton had considered going north to Montreal, getting away from Boston to find somewhere out of the way to regroup and gather resources. Montreal seemed as good a place as any to start with. As he stood in front of the departure board, the clock ticked away the opportunity to board the 23:50 bus.

How did the vampires keep it all secret? Why wasn't their existence general knowledge? He backed away from the departure board. With his peaked cap pulled down low and his hood up, he found a seat in the waiting room. He sat down, bowed his head and became just another nondescript passenger waiting for a late-night bus out of Boston.

Chloe Armitage had spoken of the Vampire Dominion. The vampires had organized themselves. They must have someone keeping their secrets during daylight. He whispered beneath his breath, "I'll need to find the secret keepers."

She'd also said his father was a member of the Order of Thoth as if they were the bad guys. What was the Order of Thoth and how did they fit into all this? She'd said the Order had exiled him, but why? Was it something to do with his grandfather? If his grandfather was such a *bad ass'* warrior, why wasn't he around to protect his family? Why did his mother have to die? Anton's fists clenched to white knuckle intensity as rage flared through his soul. Hot tears squeezed out of his eyes and he wiped them away furiously with the back of his hand. He looked around, but no one had noticed his distress.

Armitage had also left him alive so that he can do something for her. He vowed silently that she would burn in hell before he would help her with anything. He leaned back, his backpack beside him. He pulled the peak of his cap low over his eyes as if he was resting. He spent most of the next hour going over in his mind what he knew, what he didn't know, what were the opportunities for action, and what were the priorities. As the time passed, his emotions subsided and he formed a plan of action.

The vampires would have to deal with the evidence, they would have to keep it secret. If he acted quickly, he could find out who the secret keepers were, and that would be a good start. With the Montreal option abandoned, Anton approached the ticket window. He spoke with the teller, and confirmed there were available seats on the express bus to New York. It was due to leave in fifteen minutes time at 01:00.

Armitage had taken photos of him. They would be looking for him. He needed a false trail. He needed some breadcrumbs for them to follow. There was a nearby ATM, he went to it, withdrawing nine hundred and eighty dollars from his savings account, it was most of what he had. He went back to the ticket counter, using EFTPOS to buy a one-way ticket on the next bus to New York City. Two transactions, leaving two breadcrumbs.

He walked casually to the toilet block. Stripping off his cap and jacket, he stuffed them into his backpack. Two minutes later, as he left the toilet block a random bit of graffiti caught his eye, it read, 'Vampires Rule!'

"No kidding," he remarked to himself. It was time to poke the sleeping bear. With three minutes to go before the bus was due to leave, Anton went to a public payphone and dialed 911. In hushed tones, he identified himself as Anton Smith, quickly relating the basic details of the evening to the 911 operator. He told her that two assailants had murdered his mother and abducted his father. He described them as a strikingly good-looking brunette and a tall, powerfully built, blond man. Both dressed in business attire and under thirty years of age. He named them as Chloe Armitage and Marcus Drake. Anton hung up the phone, and jogged to gate one, where the bus to New York City was boarding the final passengers.

Before boarding the bus, Anton slowed to a walk and glanced up for a long moment at the camera dome in the ceiling at the gate.

Taking a seat at the back of the bus, he put on his cap and jacket, pulling his hood up and over his head. *She took photos of me; she expects to find me again. Breadcrumb number three – let them see me getting on this bus to New York. In three minutes, time – I'll be off this bus, and underneath their radar.*

* * *

James Haley was on the I-91 heading north toward East Hartford on the way to Boston, when his Shadowstone smartphone pinged with an automated message from the Panopticon.

He had a hit on the target. He commanded his smartphone, "Heads up." The smartphone, networked with the car to display a ghostly image onto the windscreen. There was enough resolution in the translucent image that James could easily read it, without it obscuring his vision of the road ahead. The image detailed a debit card transaction for a withdrawal of nine hundred and eighty dollars in the name of Anton Smith. Smith was running.

"Well, that was easy," James remarked to himself. The smartphone pinged again, the details of a bus ticket to New York flashing up onto the windscreen. James pursed his lips; shaking his head, he pulled the car over to the emergency stopping lane. He picked up his smartphone, dialing back to the New York City Shadowstone office, where the staff duty officer manning the desk answered the call.

James ordered the duty officer, "I need an immediate Panopticon tracker on the 01:00 express bus from Boston to New York City. I need four operatives at the Port Authority Terminal before 05:20 this morning at gates sixty to sixty-five to confirm sighting on a target. Photos are on their way. Do not engage the target, tail and track only. Is that clear?"

"Yes, Sir," the duty officer replied. "It will take about five minutes to establish a Panopticon tracker on the bus. I will immediately assign a team to the PA Terminal."

"Do it."

"Yes, Sir."

James hung up the call. As his car accelerated, merging back into the traffic, a third Panopticon ping hit his smartphone and an image of Anton Smith getting onto the bus flashed up onto his windscreen.

Anton Smith was making all the newbie mistakes. James shook his head with disappointment. *This won't take long to clean up, what a waste of my time.*

* * *

Luke Walker, Sergeant Detective with the Boston Police Department, pushed back the safe door with a pen and peered inside.

He stared into the empty space within the safe. Was it a robbery gone wrong? He considered theft a possible motive. Turning from the safe, he surveyed the crime scene. The other two members of his squad, detectives John Kelly and Sean O'Reilly, worked the crime scene, taking photographs. The Crime Scene Response Unit led by Sarah Murphy examined the body, in situ, and as yet untouched. The junior members of the CSRU were busy setting up filtered floodlights to search for body fluids, fingerprints and other evidence the perpetrator may have left at the scene.

The woman's head lying on the floor next to her feet drew his gaze like a moth to a flame. Luke shook his head with dismay and sighed. It was a particularly grim crime scene.

He'd been with the police department for nineteen years, joining a week after his eighteenth birthday. He'd been with the Homicide Unit for the last ten years, six as a Sergeant Detective leading his own squad. He'd seen knife attacks before, but this was the first beheading, and he'd a sincere wish that it be his last.

Luke carefully threaded his way through the furniture toward where Detective Kelly was teasing something from the edge of a huge hole in the wall. Kelly held it up with a pair of tweezers, it was a torn piece of dark, pinstriped fabric. He reported, "It was caught on a wood splinter in the middle of the wall." Kelly frowned and put the fragment into an evidence bag.

The vaguely human shaped hole stretched a yard across, and rose from floor to ceiling. The plaster dust and wood fragments in the hallway, and the direction the wood had broken in, clearly indicated that whatever went through the wall had come from the lounge room. Luke had an image in his mind of a large man smashing through the wall, it would neatly fit the shape of the hole. He snorted – it was like something out of a damn cartoon.

However, given the thickness of the wooden members, it was doubtful that anything human would have survived the impact. He stroked the broken edge of a beam with a gloved finger, the wood was hard and strong, with no sign of rot or weakness. He shook his head, nonplussed by the evidence. What the hell had really happened here?

Luke looked into the hallway where O'Reilly had just completed taking photographs of footprints in the plaster dust. There were two sets, about size thirteen or fourteen, similar to his own. He tilted his head, his mind integrating what he saw in the patterns in the pale powder.

There had been a fight in the hallway. Two big men duking it out like the old west. Instinctively looking up, he saw it, blood splatter high up on the wall. Someone had taken a hard hit.

"Kelly, get a blood swab and bag this. O'Reilly, get this on camera," he directed, drawing his detectives' attention to the top of the wall. Kelly began swabbing blood and bone fragments, putting them into a vial. Luke turned his attention back to the corpse in the chair.

Sarah Murphy, the head of the CSRU attending the crime scene was kneeling beside the body. She was collecting clumps of blond hair from the carpet with a brush and bagging it in labeled evidence bags.

"Anything?" Luke asked as he came over, standing opposite his colleague, the corpse between them.

"It's interesting," Sarah remarked. "It looks like she was beheaded with a single blow with a very sharp instrument."

Luke was relieved. An image of a Jihadi sawing at Anna Smith's neck with a knife faded away.

"However, there are some really odd things," Sarah said, frowning. "Her hair is all over the floor, clearly sliced off at the same time as her head, indicating the killer cut her head off here. However, there is hardly any blood splatter. Her blood should be everywhere," she lifted her hands and spread them wide, "where is it?"

Luke stroked his chin. Did the perp stage the crime scene? He asked, "Could she have been killed somewhere else, and the body placed here?"

"It's possible. In that case, I may find foreign material from the original site mixed in with the hair, but the hair looks clean – there is almost no blood on it or any other matter."

Luke looked at the hair in the bags and on the floor, so neatly cut – it seemed a problem and he remarked, "Wouldn't her hair just get pushed out of the way by a blade?"

Sarah nodded. "Normally I would say yes, however with a razor-sharp blade, moving very fast, the hair doesn't have time to get out of the way."

"What sort of weapon?"

"Probably a big knife or a sword, but we haven't found the murder weapon yet. It is possible the perp took the blade from the crime scene." Sarah used a stainless-steel probe to indicate the still intact top of a vertebra at the rear of the wound. "And given that the cut appears to have neatly separated the C4 and C5 vertebrae, an expert wielded the weapon. The chances of inflicting this wound by accident would be astronomical."

"So, you're telling me the victim was sitting in this chair when the perp, an expert swordsman, cut her head off with a single blow, and there is almost no blood here. I'm leaning toward the idea the perp drained her blood somewhere else, then staged the body here."

"Perhaps something like that," Sarah replied, nodded slowly. "Her blood must be somewhere. Once we get her back to the forensics lab, we'll learn more about what happened to her."

Luke pointed to a large blood stain on the victim's right shoulder and an obvious cut in her dress there. "What's that – another wound?"

"Yes," Sarah answered. "Looks like it went straight through the shoulder joint, cracking open the bones and severing the Thoracoacromial Artery. The pain would have been extreme – like having your arm ripped off – and given the blood around the cut, it happened before she died."

"Torture?"

"Motives are for you to answer?"

"I respect your professional opinion on this."

"… Yes, both cuts are surgical in their precision – whomever did this knew exactly what they were doing – and they did it fast, a single strike each time."

"Any idea on time of death?"

"I would estimate four to six hours ago. I can be more exact once we get her to the lab."

Luke looked at his watch. "An EMT team will be here in about fifteen minutes to transport the body, it's already been cleared with the Medical Examiner's office."

"Good, we will be ready by then."

Luke nodded and turned away. A family photo on the mantelpiece above the fireplace caught his eye. They were a good-looking family; happy, proud parents, at their son's graduation from High School. There was no mistaking the body in the lounge room belonged to Anna Smith. He took the photo out of the frame, and flipped it over. There was a message written on the back. 'Anton's Graduation.' With last year's date below it. A proud and happy family – they looked perfectly normal and well adjusted – so what had happened to them?

Luke frowned and whispered to himself, "Too normal by half." He bagged the photo and walked to the front door of the house, collecting his two detectives as he went. "Kelly, O'Reilly, start taking statements from the neighbors, see if anyone knows anything. Hopefully, someone heard or saw something useful."

He stood on the front porch of the house as his detectives moved beyond the police line and started identifying neighbors. He lifted the photo, staring at it intently through the plastic sleeve. He committed it to memory. He'd received a brief over the radio as he drove to the crime scene. The boy had called 911 from a payphone at South Station just before 01:00. A couple of hours after the death of his mother. That'd give him plenty of time to concoct a cover story. His father was missing; the boy was on the run – who had a motive to murder Anna Smith?

Anton Smith had reported a pair of assailants. Luke had checked the names. There was any number of Chloe Armitages, and Marcus Drakes in the world, but none known for being criminals on the Boston Police Department databases. Luke knew he had to find Anton Smith. He was either the perpetrator or the primary witness. He was running – but who was he running from? The police or the real murderers.

He felt a tap on his shoulder and turned around.

"You need to see this," Sarah insisted in hushed tones. Trembling momentarily, she turned away and walked back into the house.

Luke pocketed the Smith family photo, and followed her back into the lounge room. The other two CSRU staff were still at the crime scene, standing back from the body, staring at the head on the floor. They were both young; the woman looked like she was about to cry and the man had his hand over his mouth, as if he wanted to say something, but was frightened to say it.

Sarah squatted down, using her probe to lift a sheath of hair away from Anna's cheek. "Look here, at the top of her throat – puncture marks."

Luke frowned, and crouched down on one knee to examine Anna Smith's head. There was a strange combination of puncture wounds; partially healed with faded scar tissue on her throat. "A dog bite?" he asked. "Looks like it's a week old at least."

"I don't know, but I doubt it – it's too controlled – there is only the one bite that we can see. A dog attack would leave bite wounds all over her body. But look at this," Sarah said, inserting one end of her forensic probe into the largest of the puncture wounds. The probe descended in about half an inch. "The bite would have severed the carotid artery – it should have killed her – but you can see the wound has partially healed and the artery itself has closed over. It's bizarre."

Luke felt a shiver go up his spine and he rubbed his chin with his hand. "That's impossible."

"Not only that – I double checked the shoulder wound, and the Thoracoacromial Artery had also closed over and the entry and exit wounds were partially healed."

The young CSRU tech spoke in a harsh whisper, his hands on his head, "It was a vampire."

"Shut up!" Luke growled. "This is the real world, not a damn TV show. There will be a rational explanation for this." He glowered around the room. Someone had staged the crime scene to mess with their heads. What sort of monster was Anton Smith?

Luke stepped away from the body, he suddenly needed fresh air. He went back out on the porch. He dialed the duty desk at the district office. The officer on duty picked up the call and Luke commanded him, "Initiate an arrest warrant for Anton Smith. I want him found, he is our prime suspect for the murder of his mother and the disappearance of his father."

The duty officer responded and Luke closed the call. He frowned, shaking his head. A son murdering his mother, it was a vile disgusting crime. He vowed to himself to close this case. Finding justice for the dead drove him, and he would not stop until Anton Smith had paid for murdering his mother and disappearing his father.

* * *

James Haley slowed the car to a crawl as he approached the entrance of the court where the Smith family home resided.

The red and blue strobe lights of a pair of Boston Police Department cars lit up the court entrance. A big white Crime Scene Response Unit van stood on the far side of the police cars. A navy blue, Ford Explorer SUV, typical of the type used by the Boston Police Department was beyond the CSRU van. 'Do Not Cross' police tape lay strung along the sidewalk and around the front yard of the Smith residence. All around the court, neighbors, and other onlookers huddled in small groups. Several people held their smartphones up to video the event or take photographs. Four uniformed officers kept everyone clear of operations as a pair of detectives took initial statements from neighbors.

Interviewing of potential witnesses had already begun. James growled in disgust and said, "What a circus! This is so FUBAR! Who tipped them off?"

A tall, thick-set bald man with an air of command about him, was on the front porch staring at something in an evidence bag. Was it a photo? One of the CSRU staff tapped the photo-holding detective on the shoulder and he turned and followed her back into the house.

James assessed the situation. The Investigator-In-Charge and the head on site of the CSRU were clearly troubled by something. He whispered to himself, "What did they just find? I need to shut this down and fast."

He switched off his car's engine. Flipped open his laptop and logged in. The laptop networked back to the Panopticon with high-speed encrypted satellite links. He lifted his smartphone, zooming in with the phone's camera on the police vehicles, associated staff, and onlookers. The phone began networking directly with the Panopticon.

"Okay, who am I dealing with here?" he asked himself. Two minutes later he had summarized files on all the police staff currently on site, and who they reported to.

James read the first line from the Panopticon response out loud, "Sergeant Detective Luke Walker is the Investigator-In-Charge with responsibility for the disposition of the crime scene and the evidence. He is responsive to the District Attorney or the Medical Examiner." He fell silent, tapping the side of the laptop as he read deeper into the files, scanning and reading pages at a glance. He quickly concluded, "I need to be a delegate of the DA."

James put his laptop aside. Opening his car's glove box, he withdrew a small black box from within it. He released the biometric lock on the box with his thumbprint. Inside the box was a set of fake IDs. Each ID matched his biometrics, backed up with fully defined sets of data across more than a dozen government and private systems. With them he could easily impersonate a range of different roles and authorities. These *ghosts* even drew salaries from their host organizations – one of the side benefits of working with Shadowstone – superb renumeration.

James flicked through them, picking out the most appropriate one for dealing with this situation. James, aka Jim, Alexander, an FBI agent from the Manhattan Joint Terrorism Task Force Annex. The JTTF Annex was a Shadowstone front organization seamlessly integrated with the real FBI.

Now all he needed was the paperwork. He ran another program on his laptop. A minute later he had a filled form, signed by the Suffolk County District Attorney assigning Jim Alexander as his delegate for the Smith case. He hit Ctrl-P on his laptop, a printer built into the car's console under the glove box whirred into life, pushing out a high definition, full color copy of the signed delegation form.

James carefully and neatly folded the form and put it aside. A Boston Emergency Medical Services Ambulance passed his car, entered the court and parked in the driveway of the Smith residence. He shook his head as two EM technicians got out of the Ambulance.

Where the hell was the Green-4 spectrum team? He looked at his watch, it was pushing 03:00, Louise Wesson should be here any minute. He dialed her smartphone.

"Sir?" she answered.

"Where are you?" James demanded.

"Two minutes away from your location. We're in Jamaica Plain now."

"OK. Slow down just as you reach the court. I'm parked here and I will lead us in. Once in, wait for further orders."

"Yes, Sir. Will do."

James hung up and started his engine. In moments, he could see two black Chevrolet Express vans in his car's mirrors. He rolled forward into the street, swerving into formation in front of them. As a group, they drove into the court, and parked opposite the Smith residence. James slotted the DA delegation form into an inside pocket of his jacket, got out of his car and walked to the edge of the police line.

One of BPD uniforms approached him, and stated, "Sir, this is an active crime scene, and you're not allowed access."

James flashed his FBI credentials. "I'm with the FBI JTTF out of the Manhattan Annex. Who is the investigator in charge on site?"

The officer hesitated for a moment, and then produced a list on a clipboard and requested, "I will need your details."

"No problem," James replied, adding the name Jim Alexander, and his FBI ID details to the proffered list.

The officer waved James through and instructed as he passed by. "You're looking for Sergeant Detective Luke Walker, you can't miss him, he's the big, bald guy in a suit."

"Thanks, Officer Jones," James said, with a brief smile as he walked past the officer. Be polite. Get the names right. Do it by the book. Be firm, but don't be a total bastard. Works every time.

James walked up the porch steps to the open front door. He reached the landing as Walker emerged, followed by a grim looking EM tech.

Walker looked James up and down and declared brusquely, "Who are you, and what are you doing on my crime scene?"

James handed Walker the DA delegation form and stated, "I'm Special Agent Jim Alexander with the FBI JTTF out of the Manhattan Annex."

Walker opened the form and read it. Shaking his head and scowling as he quickly got to the end of it. "Well doesn't that just take the cake."

The EM tech looked at Walker, and then James, and then back at Walker and asked, "Should I get the body bag?"

James addressed him and directed, "No, go get your buddy and sit in your ambulance. One of my staff will debrief you and then you can go."

Walker asked indignantly, "How the hell is this a terrorism case?"

James ignored Walker's question, signaling Louise with a wave of his hand to come over. He turned back to the cop. "Look, it's nothing personal. There are bigger forces at play in this case. You're a good cop, I can see that. You've done everything by the book and I bet you're already putting a case together."

He clapped a big hand on Walker's shoulder. The two men stood eye to eye and he said, "We're brothers in arms, fighting the same fight. I'm already briefed on this case. You've got a runner, the son, Anton Smith ... he's the prime suspect, isn't he?"

Walker growled with annoyance, but replied, "I've initiated an arrest warrant. We're already closing in on him."

James would have to rescind the warrant. He made a mental note to sort that out later. "I'm sure you are," James declared confidently. "It's time to call your team together. My staff will debrief everyone and collect all bagged evidence. In fifteen minutes, the handover will be complete."

"You can't hand over a crime scene in fifteen minutes!" Walker stated, aghast.

"My team is highly professional. We'll get it done." James glanced out at the court, Wesson and another eight plainclothes Shadowstone operatives were standing in a loose group back from the police line. They were not signing themselves in as per standing orders. They did not have multiple prepared identities. They were waiting for him to clear the path for them.

"Look, Sergeant Detective Walker, I need you to remove your team from this site ASAP. It is imperative that all evidence is immediately handed over to my team."

Walker shook his head, looked disgusted and mouthed, "Shit!" under his breath, but turned and yelled into the house, "Close it down everyone, the FBI is here and they have 'juris-my-dict—'" he halted for a second, then said, "jurisdiction over this case."

He turned back to face James, and they locked gazes for a moment until the detective looked away.

In five minutes, the Boston authorities evacuated the house. The Shadowstone operatives debriefed the BPD staff, while collecting evidence bags, taking additional notes and recording everything on video.

James went back to his car. He retrieved a pack of cigarettes and a lighter. He lit up, taking a long pull on his cigarette as he watched Wesson lead the debriefs. He mused silently as he smoked, *It isn't what they know, it's what they can prove that matters. There's often something strange in these cleanup cases.*

He took another pull on the cigarette. It had been a long night, and he enjoyed a few minutes of peace and relaxation as he wondered, *What would it be this time?*

He finished a second cigarette as he waited for the last of the BPD staff to leave the site. He watched as his operators moved in, clearing the onlookers back to their homes. *Nothing to see here, move along, go back to your homes, the danger has passed, you're all safe.* It was the same consistent message used every time. The Green-4 team operatives repositioned the vans and started pulling out their specialized equipment. He butted out the cigarette, putting it carefully into the car's ashtray. He'd never leave evidence of his presence behind. *We're ghosts in what we do.*

James pushed off from the car. He walked through his team, clapping people on their shoulders, and checking equipment on backpacks. He addressed his team, "Okay guys, let's be careful, let's be thorough. Make it a good job, a clean job, and get it done."

Convinced they were fully prepared, he led them into the house.

It was time to sanitize the scene.

* * *

Louise Wesson, Shadowstone operative, recently recruited from a very specialized cell within the Operations Directorate of the CIA took personal responsibility for managing the removal of Anna Smith's body.

Around her was a hive of well-organized activity as Green-4 operatives first sprayed a clear, odorless mist and then followed with flashes of intense ultraviolet light. The treatments evaporated any biological evidence remaining in the house. When they finished the job, there would be no trace the Smith family had ever lived there.

Louise was thankful for the forensic gloves that she wore as she picked up Anna Smith's head and put it in a body bag with the rest of her remains. She started zipping the bag closed when she saw something that made her pause. She whispered, "What the hell."

She reached into the bag, pushing back the hair from Anna's cheek. The floodlights positioned by her team allowed no mistake. Bite marks? She pushed her gloved little finger into the largest hole, it went in nearly to the first joint. The hole was right on the carotid artery and too deep to survive – and yet the artery was still intact? What the hell, was someone playing games?

Louise's lip curled into a derisive smile. She zipped the bag closed with a sudden movement and stood up. She commanded her team, "Okay boys, move this trash out and complete the sweeps."

She stepped back as two of her operatives picked up the body bag and took it outside to one of the waiting vans. She looked back around the lounge room with fresh eyes. If this family had been her target, there would be three bodies here, not one. This was not a professional hit. Who would bite someone's throat out and then chop their head off? And where was all the blood?

Louise shook her head, continuing with the task at hand, she had a device that looked a lot like a smartphone and which behaved like a powerful torch. She walked through each room, scanning all the surfaces with the light from the compact unit. At the end of the sweep, she'd not found any biological traces of the Smith family. She tapped her earpiece and reported calmly, "All clear, Sir."

Haley's voice called back through the comms channel, "Let's wrap this up, there is still more work to do tonight."

Louise walked out of the house, dropping her gear off in the nearest van. She approached the driver of the other van which had Anna Smith's body in it and said to him, "Get this corpse and the other trash to Rikers Island for disposal."

"Yes, Ma'am," the operative replied.

Haley stood by his car, waving her over.

She strode over, joining him beside the car.

"We have a local office. We need to check in on our target," Haley directed.

"Yes, Sir."

They got into the car, and Haley drove them away from the court. She'd been working with Haley as one of his direct subordinates for six months. She usually made correct assessments of people in the first five minutes. She'd found Haley to be very hard to read, and that intrigued her. The only other person she'd met that was more impenetrable was the woman who had interviewed her for her current role – General Chloe Armitage. *Now that was one stone cold killer,* she'd mused to herself after meeting Armitage for the first time.

She'd found a shell just below Armitage's surface that surrounded secrets she would never discover, and that annoyed her. She enjoyed knowing how other people ticked, what their buttons were, what they would respond too, especially under stress. It was her skill, knowing people, and being able to anticipate what they would do. Louise typically asked questions and got back more information than the person answering the question ever suspect they gave away.

Haley drove the car into the center of the city of Boston, descending into an underground parking garage.

"That didn't look like a terrorist incident," Louise said, glancing across at her boss. "It also didn't appear to be the actions of a mad man. It just looked – different."

Haley snorted. "Every newbie always asks a variant of that question." Parking the car, he turned to Louise and stared directly into her brown eyes. "There's some odd shit from time to time, but our job is clear, protect the security of the anti-terror operations. So just do your job, you will live a lot longer that way."

Louise usually felt fear as a form of excitement, but there was something in the way that Haley had just spoken, a supreme confidence in consequences, that sent a genuine shiver of dread up her spine. She shutdown the desire to frown, it was not her way to wear dangerous emotions like fear on her face. She followed him silently out of the garage and into the offices of a front company owned by Shadowstone. Haley flicked a pass over a reader and the door swung aside. As she passed through the doorway, Louise read a set of gold lettering on the door. R.I.S.C, Risk, Investigation, Security, Consultants.

I've been working for Shadowstone for six months. I have more questions now than when I started. Questions were part of the process, but sooner rather than later – she needed answers.

* * *

Anton arched his back, stretching cramped muscles, he repositioned for a better view of his home.

There had been a brief but intense discussion in front of his house between the Boston Police Department detective and the suit who had shown up waving a badge. Anton hid under bushes in a neighbor's front yard. Unfortunately, too far down the street to hear precisely what the two men said. The suit had won and the Boston police, CSRU staff, and the ambulance had all left. Two black unmarked vans and the suit's own dark gray sedan remained in the court. He counted nine other people in the suit's team, eight men, and one woman, and they all deferred to the suit.

He studied the suit closely; he wanted to make sure he never forgot this man. He was tall, about six feet four inches, powerful looking, more a wrestler's rather than a boxer's body. He had short, dark brown hair, a little gray starting to show at the temples, and a pronounced receding hairline. He had strong features, big nose, big jaw, and big hands. He looked tough, hard, and dangerous.

Anton added the suit to an internal list of objectives. He was another one he would need to deal with. One day the suit would get what he deserved. Anton vowed to himself that he would never give up until he'd achieved justice for his mother's murder and his father's abduction.

Men with backpacks of equipment, sprayers and wand like lights had worked in the house for about half an hour after the Boston police had left. Anton had never seen anything like it. There had been a series of flashes of intense blue light, like a welding arc through the windows of his home. As to what was actually happening inside his home – it remained a mystery. He surmised that it must have something to do with keeping the vampires' secrets.

He added that to his rapidly growing mental 'to do,' list. Find out who was keeping the existence of vampires secret from the world and how they were doing it? They'd just killed his mother, abducted his father and destroyed his life. He figured he had nothing better to do than bring the whole fucking mess down. The only real question was how?

Anton's eyes hardened and he watched the unfolding actions closely. He had to learn everything he could if he was to have any chance against his enemies. Two operatives carried his mother out in a body bag, unceremoniously throwing her into the back of one of the vans. Anton clapped a hand over his mouth. His eyes widened, his face paled and his fists clenched tight enough for his fingernails to gouge his palms. Rage was a fiery torrent running like a wild animal through his soul. For a long moment, he was beyond words, biting down on his left fist to avoid getting up and running over to try and kill the men. Anton shut his eyes, burying his face into the ground.

He screamed silently, *I've got to get this together, it's no good just running out there, they will kill me or worse in seconds. That's not what my Mom and Dad would want. They would want me to be smarter than that — where are they taking her?*

Anton lifted his head a couple of inches. The sole woman was talking to the driver of the nearest van. Anton turned his head, straining to hear what she said. The distance muffled her words, but he could just make out, 'Rikers Island' and 'disposal.' What was at Rikers Island? That's where they were taking his mother for disposal.

The men completed packing their gear into the waiting vans. Within another minute, everyone had left. The woman leaving with the suit in charge in his dark gray sedan. Anton turned, dragging himself through the bushes. He crouched, scuttling to the backyard of the house. He clambered over the back fence. In moments, he was through another backyard, down a driveway, and onto another street.

The neighborhood street was strikingly normal, it almost seemed like a different world to the nightmare he'd left behind. He'd confirmed his suspicions. There was an organization working for the vampires and keeping their secrets. There was an around the clock threat, humans during the day and vampires at night. Anton pulled his cap down close above his eyes. Pulling the hood of his jacket tightly over his head, he slung his backpack over his shoulders. He needed to find somewhere he could sleep, somewhere he could be anonymous.

Anton started walking to the city for the second time that night. He walked without looking back. There was nothing left where his family had died except awful memories of horror committed by an exquisitely beautiful young woman.

A woman who was nothing less than a monster.

* * *

James Haley finished off his fourth cup of coffee.

The clock read 05:21, he stood with his feet apart, and his arms folded across his chest. He faced a wall of computer screens displaying a current track on the 01:00 express bus from Boston to New York City as it pulled into the New York Port Authority Terminal. He had four fully briefed operatives covering gates sixty to sixty-five at the terminal.

Shadowstone had applied the Panopticon tracker on the bus shortly after it left South Station in Boston and the bus had been in continuous motion ever since. The Panopticon tracker consisted of every available camera on the Bus's pathway and hacked cameras within the bus itself. They recorded Anton Smith getting on the bus, the bus had been in continuous motion since they had initiated the tracker, he should still be on it when it arrived in New York.

His men would visually confirm his arrival. They would then tail him, maintaining around the clock contact with the target until new orders were issued. Every available camera in the terminal that could sight the bus from Boston swiveled automatically on their mounts to bear on the target vehicle. No one was getting off the bus without being surveilled from multiple angles.

A large screen displayed a top-down satellite view of the terminal with blue markers on the locations of his operatives and a red outline around the bus. The Panopticon integrated and cross-referenced all the data feeds. It ran a threat board on another large screen, where predictive algorithms scrolled a prioritized list of proposed risks and potential issues that may need James' attention. The threat board was green, his operatives stood in position, and the bus pulled to a stop.

Louise Wesson carefully scanned the screens displaying video feeds from within the bus, and said, "I don't think he's on the bus."

"What the hell?" James growled incredulously. Turning to face her, he snapped, "Well, we will soon find out."

It took less than three minutes for the bus to empty. People milled about as the driver unloaded the luggage compartment on the side of the vehicle. Above the head of each person on the screen was a Panopticon red dot – not a match with the target. James clenched his hands into fists. "Damn it, he got off somehow." He looked at the data on the Panopticon tracker on the 01:00 bus out of Boston. It started at 01:04:54. There was nearly a five-minute window to get off the bus without the Panopticon seeing him.

"He expected to be tracked, he is smarter than you think," Wesson said calmly.

James rubbed his chin. "Not only that, the bus must have stopped out of sight of any road monitoring camera. There is no record of the bus stopping." The boy was not such a pup after all. He snorted. "It won't make any difference. We'll—"

"Sir, the target is not here," an operative at the terminal interrupted, his voice relayed by encrypted satellite link.

"Roger that, Johnson. Pull the team back to Fort Dix," James replied, then addressed Wesson, "As I was saying, we'll blanket the Boston area and pick him up again."

"What if he has simply used another method to get to New York, or anywhere else? He may have stolen a car or hitchhiked."

James returned to his terminal, initiating another Panopticon search. The main screen on the wall began to fill with a sea of red, with a cluster of orange hits in Boston. He stated, "The evidence shows that he is still in Boston."

"The evidence shows that he knows that someone is looking for him and he is actively protecting himself," Wesson said as she flipped close a printed file on Anton Smith and stood up from her desk. "Sir, did you read his file in full. Sure, he's young, he's just turned eighteen, but he has an IQ above a hundred and fifty. I think we need to be careful that we do not underestimate him. He could be on the way to anywhere within a thousand miles of Boston by now. He took out over nine hundred dollars from his account. He could have hiked over to the airport and hired a light airplane. No need for a security check, he could be in the air by now."

"The airports are heavily surveilled. The Panopticon would have flagged him by now."

Wesson stared at him in silence for a moment. James sighed, his lips pressed into a thin line and he acknowledged her silent point, "Of course, unless he's covered his face extensively, we only have photos of his face."

Wesson said, "Yes, my read on this is that he wanted anyone looking for him to think that he has left for New York City. In reality, he most likely has gone to ground. He will be frightened and alone, he will want to stay in familiar territory. He will stay in Boston."

"Well, we will soon find out if you're right," James remarked as he set the search on the Panopticon to continuous mode. Every camera that the system could reach in the world would be looking for Anton Smith twenty-four-hours per day, seven days a week. "The Panopticon sweeps will find him soon enough."

Wesson arched a quizzical eyebrow. "Do you want to put money on that?"

James stared at her, his eyes narrowing menacingly. "Do you want a career change?"

For a second their eyes met, and then Wesson looked away.

James stared at her for a long moment. *Know your place girl.*

* * *

It was almost midnight.

Anton leaned against a brick wall across the street from the Lighthouse Center Homeless Shelter. It was a typical red brick Victorian era building nestled in the South End neighborhood of Boston. He was exhausted, he'd been awake for more than forty hours. He'd discarded the idea of using a youth hostel or a hotel. Those places had cameras, demanded ID, and would cost a lot more than a shelter.

He needed to get his finances sorted before he ran out of cash. He had to conserve what he had. He didn't know when or how he was going to get more. How does anyone make a living underneath the vampire radar?

He pushed himself off the wall, and crossed the street to the shelter entrance. He went up a short flight of steps, pushed open the door, and entered the shelter's reception area. There was an old guy behind the counter wearing a Boston Celtics cap and an odd assortment of clothes that looked like he'd picked them randomly out of the shelter's laundry. The old guy looked at him with rheumy eyes and barked, "We're all full up!"

Anton yawned fit to break his jaw and put a hand on the counter to steady himself and stated, "Hey buddy, I would be happy with a piece of floor."

The old guy squinted at him. "Fuhgeddaboutit – it's against the rules!"

Anton's heart sank. He couldn't even get a piece of floor in a homeless shelter. He had a sudden vision of himself waking up under a three-day-old newspaper on a park bench. Is this what he'd come too?

"You can't stay here – you're gotta go somewhere else!" The old guy half-shouted, shooing Anton toward the front door.

Anton shook his head in defeat. He stepped back from the counter and turned to go. He was halfway out the door when someone grabbed his arm and pulled him to a halt. He looked over his right shoulder. A young woman, dressed in jeans, a pale green sweater, and white sneakers stood beside him.

She smiled and ordered him in a no-nonsense tone, "Hold on a second there, big guy." She pulled him back from the doorway. "I was out for a quick break and Barry was manning the desk. He is a bit of a fixture around here and he can be a bit overzealous sometimes."

"He's a hockey player – he doesn't belong here," Barry declared trenchantly.

"Look, I'm Sam," she said, extending her hand.

Anton took it, she had a firm grip and a friendly smile.

"Grab a seat right there," Sam instructed, guiding him to a chair.

Anton sat down gratefully. Every minute was a struggle to stay awake. He could fall asleep in this chair if people would only leave him alone.

"Would you like a hot drink? Chocolate?" Sam asked.

"Yeah sure,' he agreed.

"Me too," Barry called out eagerly. "Don't forget me."

Sam smiled. "Barry, no one who has met you would ever forget you." She turned back to Anton, her long brown hair swishing over her shoulders, and insisted, "Now just wait here."

She strode down the hallway, ducking into a nearby room. Two minutes later she emerged with three mugs of hot chocolate. The three of them spent the next five minutes sipping their hot chocolate while Barry related, ball by ball, the last game between the Boston Celtics and the Los Angeles Lakers for the 1984 championship.

"That's an amazing memory you've got there Barry," Anton said over the last of his chocolate.

"Yeah, he's one of a kind," Sam agreed, patting Barry on the shoulder. "Okay then, I best get you booked in stranger." She opened a ledger behind the counter.

Anton frowned.

"What's your name, I can't keep referring to you as the 'Big Guy,' now, can I?"

"Ant … Anthony,' Anton replied.

"Okay, I can roll with that." She paused, smiling softly at him. "The handsome Mr. Anthony with no last name."

Anton looked Sam directly in the eyes, lifting his eyebrows in silent supplication. She shrugged her shoulders and said, "I'm not going to turn anyone away when we still have a cot available."

She signed him in as Anthony X.

"Come this way soldier," Sam directed, leading Anton down the hall, and up a flight of stairs. The next floor held four separate dormitories, each with four beds, and a communal bathroom at the end of the hallway. She showed him the fire escape and then his bed, it was the bottom bunk of a double. The other three bunks held warm bodies; the top two guys lay quietly, but the man on the other lower bunk snored loudly.

"Sorry for the symphony," she commiserated gently, shrugging her shoulders.

"I'm beyond caring, thanks – this is great."

Sam patted Anton on the shoulder and said, "Well, you have a good night." She sauntered off down the hall, her hips rolling in her jeans.

Anton just managed to hear her say "So buff," to herself as she got to the stairs. He got himself onto his bunk. Swapping his backpack for his pillow, he managed to pull his shoes off, before rolling back into the bed.

Sam, thirty hours ago I would have been interested.

He crashed into a dreamless exhausted sleep.

* * *

Cornelius Crane relaxed on a lounge in his library, opposite him sat two of his five generals in separate chairs, Chloe Armitage, and Haras Mosule.

Chloe wore a crimson dress, with a small black hat and black shoes. She sat simply with her hands in her lap and her long legs neatly crossed. Haras wore his customary black pants and boots, white shirt and short black jacket. His long wavy hair fell loosely across his shoulders and he regarded his companions with intelligent brown eyes.

Cornelius addressed his generals, "It is rare that I have my two best generals in the same room at the same time." He leaned forward, pouring three drinks from a decanter on a low table between them. "This is Yamazaki Single Malt Sherry Cask 2013 whiskey – surprisingly, it is both Japanese and excellent."

Haras smiled and suggested, "Perhaps we should have Shen Zhen here, it's from his region." He reached forward taking the glass. He sniffed it, closing his eyes before sipping it. "Delicious."

Cornelius had long thought it remarkable that alcohol and nicotine had an impact on vampire physiology, and yet most drugs were simply ineffective. He had projects running in a network of secret labs to explore the boundaries of the vampire condition. When needed, it was a simple matter to create new test subjects. He was fascinated by the exploration of the possible. Science was a wonderful thing; his many secret and not-so-secret laboratories and research facilities guaranteed the Vampire Dominion remained at the forefront of all human knowledge.

Chloe and Cornelius both took a glass each and sipped the whiskey. The alcohol provided zero nutrition, only human blood could sustain a vampire, but the flavors of alcohol and tobacco remained enjoyable. When someone had been alive for nearly a thousand years, simple pleasures mattered. Cornelius put the empty glass back on the table and declared, "I have a mission for you both."

Chloe and Haras glanced at each other and then fixed their attention upon him. Cornelius's eyes narrowed slightly, even as the ghost of a smirk curled the edges of his lips. He knew they would hate having to work together, but the competition between them would motivate them to produce their best efforts. It was time to bring Haras up to speed on current events. Cornelius declared with a note of triumph, "We now have the Papyrus of Hakron the Scribe."

"What?" Haras asked incredulously.

Chloe smiled slightly at Haras from the other side of the lounge.

"Indeed," Cornelius declared, raising an eyebrow. "We now have two of the three Metaframe artifacts. It is time to claim the third."

Haras rubbed his chin and said, "Easier said than done. The Red Empire guard their prize well, and we have no knowledge of where their citadel is."

"That's where the two of you come in. The Red Empire's activities against us consistently track back to the Middle East. I'm sending both of you by shadowstar drone to a Shadowstone facility outside of Jerusalem. That will be your base of operations. You will have two of my praetorian guards with you and substantial local and international Shadowstone resources."

Chloe's eyes widened and she declared, "We have ongoing critical operations against elements of the Order of Thoth in North America, disturbing those operations buys risk for us all."

"This is the priority," Cornelius stated firmly, chopping his right hand through a flat arc. "That's the end of it."

"Of course, Sir. We will discharge our duty," Chloe replied, her voice betraying the faintest trace of sarcasm.

Cornelius tilted his head slightly, and declared, his voice laced with an undercurrent of threat, "I'm sure you will do your duty with the enthusiasm it deserves." He'd assigned two of his best praetorians to the mission. He'd specifically instructed them to keep an eye on his generals, just in case either of them decided to run any side missions of their own. Increasingly, Cornelius felt that Chloe held something back. It wasn't anything specific that he could point to or put his finger on. Just a vague sense of her pursuing her own purposes, even when they clashed with his own.

Cornelius paused for a moment, and then addressed his generals, "Let us be clear. I am sending you to Jerusalem to find the head of the Red Empire, to take the Interpretive Codex from him and return it here. That is the only mission. Is that clear?"

"Yes, Sir," Haras agreed.

"Yes, Sir," Chloe said a moment later.

Cornelius refilled the glasses. "Then let us drink." He stood up and raised his glass. "To the Vampire Dominion!"

Haras and Chloe rose and said in unison, "To the Vampire Dominion!"

All three vampires downed their drinks.

Haras placed his empty glass on the low table and frowned. "Sir. If we leave now, we will get to Jerusalem three hours after sunrise."

"Have you both recently fed?" Cornelius asked, and both his generals nodded. "Then fly now, you can wait in the drone at the Shadowstone site outside Jerusalem. That way you don't waste half of tomorrow night on travel."

His generals variously nodded, or assented, paid their respects, and left the library. They would ascend to the hangar deck where a helicopter would fly them out to the airfield at Fort Dix. In less than three hours a hypersonic shadowstar drone would transport them to Jerusalem.

Cornelius sat back down on the lounge and rubbed his chin. The mission would reveal much about Armitage's loyalty. He mused, *Success or failure in this mission? In either event I will learn more about her usefulness — or lack thereof.*

He harrumphed and narrowed his gaze. Either result was acceptable.

* * *

Anton started to wake up, his head resting on a pillow with a faint odor of laundry detergent.

He winced. Sunlight was coming through the window, striking him in the face. He rolled over onto his side to get away from it – then bolted hard upright, cracking his head on the bottom of the bunk above him.

"Ahhh," Anton yowled, looking frantically around the room. He shouted in desperation, "Where's my backpack?"

His memory of the previous evening came rushing back. He'd swapped the pillow for his backpack – to keep its contents safe. He didn't have far to look, finding his backpack under the end of his bunk. He snatched it close, it came easily, it was way too light. He looked inside and groaned in misery. "Some bastard has cleaned me out." His spare clothes, wallet, cash, food, and silver were all missing. He threw the empty backpack against the wall. He looked up to the ceiling, slumping back down onto his bunk. He leaned forward, putting his head in his hands and moaned, "No, no, no."

For a long moment, he felt the energy drain from his body, and the empty dorm closed in around him. A claustrophobic pressure exploded from the base of his spine. He dry retched, a sickly bile filling his mouth. Filled with disgust, he spat it out onto a used bath towel lying on the bunk opposite.

Suddenly revolted, as only God knew what was on that stray towel. He threw it back onto the opposite bunk, wiping his damp hands on his jeans. He sat back, the light in the room dimming as a cloud shielded the window from the sun.

Anton shivered, his hands trembling. His breath condensed in misty plumes as the temperature of the room plummeted. The shadows darkened in the room. A sense of something uncanny and weird filled him, like the world was about to spin completely out of control. A tightness filled his guts, then exploded into a dreadful foreboding as an overwhelming sense of presence filled the room.

There was something horrible hovering invisibly near him. What was it? The light outside the room evaporated as if the sun had vanished. The windows darkened to the solid black of interstellar space. The single naked globe dangling from the ceiling provided the only illumination. The window blew in with an icy blast of air, showering the room with fragments of glass, wood, and stone. A flash of darkness jagged like black lightning across the room in front of him.

He recoiled backward; his head twisting left to follow the black lightning. His eyes widened; this couldn't be happening. Chloe Armitage stood at the entrance of the room. He couldn't move, he could barely breathe. She wore a diaphanous black gown, off the shoulder and split high on the thigh. She carried a golden goblet before her in her left hand and her right hand rested casually on her hip. Her dark hair was long and pulled back through a delicate golden crown. His heart thumped in his chest, but he remained frozen, caught like a fly in a spider's web. He blinked, and she was in front of him. Her face barely inches from his own, he could feel her breathing slowly against his face. Her magnificent blue eyes stared into his and he screamed silently in helpless terror.

She smiled in a way that didn't reach her vivid eyes, her fangs descending over her bottom lip. She lifted the goblet to his lips and whispered into his ear, "Drink Anton, for this is my blood."

She tilted the goblet, and the warm, bitter contents filled his mouth. He witnessed helplessly as he swallowed and drank the blood. She tilted the goblet to near vertical, Anton arching his head back to avoid spilling any of the precious fluids. The bitter metallic tang had fled, replaced by a sensual, flesh infusing succulence. A liquid fire rose within him, fanning a flame of urgent desire.

The empty goblet fell loosely from her hand. She reached forward with a finger, stroking his chest from the notch of his throat to the top of his jeans. His shirt fell away neatly cut in two by the edge of her fingernail. She reversed the stroke, her fingers now spread wide, pushing up over the hard muscles of his stomach and across his chest in an avid, possessive sweep. Her touch crackled with energy, leaving his skin screaming for more. With both hands she pushed him back onto the bunk. The contents of the goblet singing through his veins. She reached down, ripping away the front of his jeans with her bare hands before sitting astride him.

An overwhelming desire galvanized him. His hands came free of the force that had trapped them but he didn't push her away, he pulled her closer, thrusting his hips and entering her. He arched forward and she went with him – two equals in union.

She wrapped herself around him, drawing him in as close as possible, and murmured into his ear, "Eat Anton, for this is my body."

A drumbeat thudded through his soul, lightning flashed and crackled, and then she was gone.

Anton's heart raced. He dragged in breath after breath as he picked himself up from the floor. The window stood intact, there was no broken glass, splintered wood or shattered stone. The sunlight was streaming through the window, and he could see dust motes floating lazily in the room.

What was that? A vision? Was it madness?

He felt a terrible need for a shower.

Will I ever be clean again?

Twenty minutes later he was striding away from the Lighthouse Center Homeless Shelter as fast as he could without actually running. Around him, the fine folk of Boston sat down to breakfast in stylish cafes, drinking soy lattes and discussing topics that had nothing to do with pursuit by a monstrous vampire.

* * *

Chloe Armitage completed strapping herself into a self-contained life pod within the hypersonic shadowstar drone.

Beside her, in his own pod, Haras Mosule did the same. Behind them sat Crane's two praetorians, Peter Dench, and Washington Jones. If the drone suffered a catastrophic failure, the life pods would become escape capsules.

The voice of their pilot, operating out of a Shadowstone command center at Fort Dix called through their headsets, "The drone will launch in five minutes. Flight time to Jerusalem will be eighty-six minutes. Our target altitude is eighty-two thousand feet, with a cruising speed of four thousand two hundred miles per hour. ETA in Jerusalem is 09:05 local time, Sunday the 30th of April."

Ninety-one minutes flight time, then nearly fourteen hours waiting in the drone for sunset. The drone's liquid hydrogen fueled, Scimitar engines, spooled up. The drone began to taxi out of the hangar. A twenty-four-inch, high-definition monitor linked to cameras in the skin of the aircraft rested in front of her face. In the windowless drone, she could easily see the progress of the flight.

Chloe turned her mind to the mission at hand. She switched the monitor to network mode and opened her Shadowstone email account. She'd sent James Haley an email requesting daily status reports on the progress of tracking Anton Smith. She looked at her inbox, there was nothing urgent or important, she never received email from the other generals. She knew that Crane was well versed in modern technology but rarely used it himself. The other generals were a mixed bag ranging from Clayton Maze and Haras Mosule, both of whom were skilled users, but seemed to view technology as a necessary evil; to Dieter Franz and Shen Zhen, who both avoided the trappings of the 20th century, let alone the 21st.

She sometimes wondered why Crane had picked these people to be his generals. He'd never explained why. The only other person who might know, was the Haitian voodoo priest Jean Philippe Allemande. He'd provided the curses that bound the generals to never harm Crane. He'd been dead for more than a hundred years. For his services, Crane had rewarded Allemande with vampirism in the 1850s. He'd remained in his native Haiti and lived the life of a ghoul lord for over forty years before Chloe had purged him from the vampire community. She'd extracted a final curse before she'd executed him, a binding curse on a young US Naval Lieutenant, named Marcus Drake.

She switched the monitor off. She needed to plan. Assisted by the quiet solitude of the life pod, she closed her eyes and relaxed. The objective was clear, she needed to meet 'Shabbah al Ahmar', the aptly named Red Ghost, the head of the Red Empire. Crane was sure he was in possession of the Interpretive Codex, the second document written by Hakron the Scribe, and essential to correctly interpret the insane gibberish of the Papyrus. The two documents together enabled mastery of the Key of Ahknaton and, therefore, access to the powers of the Metaframe. She did not need to retrieve the Codex for herself, she only needed to read it, her eidetic memory would provide her with a perfect copy.

Chloe was the only person alive who knew the power of her memory. It was one of three special abilities she kept as closely guarded secrets. If Crane knew about her secret powers, he would not hesitate to slaughter her on the spot to remove the risk she would one day usurp his throne. She considered her plans carefully, *I will need to mislead Haras Mosule, and Crane's henchmen if I am to again meet secretly with the Red Ghost. Perhaps it is time to take Haras off the chessboard. He is too clever to leave as a loyal servant of Crane.* Her eyes closed and she smiled grimly, *Perhaps a little private purging of the ranks, it had happened before, why not again?*

She opened her eyes, staring at the dull gray of the monitor, her mind spinning far away. *Or something subtler? Could I turn him to my purpose? Yes, especially if I kept him unaware of the ultimate goal.*

The drone took off, the powerful acceleration pushing Chloe back into her seat. Her lips curled into a smile as she explored the implications and contingencies of her plans, there would be plenty of time to determine the specifics of what she needed to do.

* * *

Anton had spent the last three nights sleeping rough on the streets.

He still had fifty dollars left in his savings account. He'd avoided using his debit card again. He expected the human secret keepers for the vampires would be watching for just that sort of move. As much as he needed the cash, he didn't want to do anything that would allow the vampires to find him again. He maintained a low profile, cap on, hood up. He kept an eye out for cameras and avoided public spaces. He was losing weight, and growing increasingly desperate to the point of near panic. It was almost midnight, the mid-week trade in Chinatown had finished for the night. Anton hissed, "Sssssssss," and pushed a skinny cat off the top of a garbage can.

A moment later, he was fishing around in the can outside the back door of a Chinese restaurant – it was slim pickings. The food must be good. There was almost nothing thrown out in the trash. Anton barked a single disappointed laugh. He'd reached the point where he could feel upset by not finding something to eat in a garbage bin.

He looked up at a low wattage bulb attracting insects over the back door. Beneath it hung a simple wooden sign with neatly painted black letters that read, 'The Noodle House. Prop, Mr. G Wu.' A sudden realization hit home. "Mom and Dad's favorite restaurant, we used to come here all the time when I was growing up," Anton murmured to himself. He flicked a wary glance left and right. He backed away and whispered, "I shouldn't have come here, what am I doing – looking for the familiar? Anyone looking for me could do the same."

There was a faint click. The back door of the restaurant opened and a man wearing a chef's cap stood silhouetted in the doorway, his face draped in shadow. He pointed at the open garbage can and called out, "Hey, you shouldn't," he did a double take, "what? Anton? Anton Slayne?" he took a step forward, reaching out with his right hand.

The Chinese chef knew his real name; Anton barely controlled the panic surging through him. "Damn it," Anton swore, stumbling backward.

The man strode forward into the shadows of the alleyway and asked in urgent tones, "Anton, what are you doing here? What's happened?"

Anton turned, running back up the alleyway. He put on the speed that had won medals at state level four-hundred-meter track events. He covered about ten feet before the chef went past him like he was standing still.

Anton slid to a stop.

The man stood in front of him and stated calmly, "I am a friend of your family. You do not have to fear me."

If he was a vampire, Anton was done for. He was going to die in some stupid alleyway.

"Let me introduce myself, I am Gang Wu," he said, waving his hand toward the restaurant. "And this is the Noodle House. Let's go back inside and get something nice to eat." He glanced past Anton at the open garbage bin. "You must be really hungry."

What were the options? Friend or foe? If he was a vampire, then why bother with all this talk. Wouldn't a vampire have tried to kill him by now? Anton's stomach rumbled. He took a deep breath. "Okay." He followed Gang into the back of the restaurant.

"Li … Li," Gang called out as they arrived in the kitchen. "Bring some towels, we have a guest, and make some nice hot tea."

Gang guided Anton to a stool and instructed him. "Sit here, there's no need to hunt in the garbage. I have excellent dumplings. The best in Chinatown."

The delicious smells of the kitchen convinced Anton. His stomach cramped with hunger, and he stated, "I'm starving."

Gang started cooking and said, "This won't take long, shrimp dumpling, pork dumpling, sautéed Shanghai greens. Li! Where is the Tea?"

"Father!?" called a voice with more than a hint of exasperation. A young woman came through the archway from the restaurant, she was carrying an armload of white hand towels. Rolling her eyes at her father, she dropped the towels onto a spare bench. She looked at Anton with large brown eyes, frowned, and said something in rapid Chinese.

"Li!" Gang objected, waving his kitchen knife. "He is not a stray dog; he is Anton Slayne."

Li sniffed once, then twice, and remarked acidly, "Really? I thought a Slayne would be cleaner and not so scruffy looking."

"He'll scrub up okay. Now, please, some tea for us all," Gang requested, spooning half a dozen dumplings onto a plate. He handed them to Anton, and gave him a fork. "I don't know if you can use chopsticks. Try these shrimp dumplings, they're delicious."

Anton blew on the steaming dumplings. Their rich fresh aroma filled his nostrils and his mouth watered. He was sure he'd never been this hungry in his life. He lifted the first one to his mouth. "Ummmm," he hummed, his eyes closed. Then he looked at Gang, and grinned with heart-felt pleasure. "Oh, they're so good!" He then started into the rest of the plate, and in a minute, they were all gone.

Li placed a teapot and three cups with saucers on a nearby bench and stated matter-of-factly, "The tea will be ready soon."

"Now for the pork dumplings," Gang declared and gave Anton the second plate. He followed the pork dumplings with a third plate of sautéed Shanghai greens. He then sat back, waiting for Anton to finish eating.

Anton ate the pork dumplings and started to weep, tears rolling down his cheeks. "This is … just … so good of you." He sobbed, overwhelmed with nameless wracking emotions.

"Hey, hey," Gang said, taking the plate away and putting his hand on Anton's shoulder. "Long, deep breaths young man, slow it down."

Putting his head in his hands, Anton cried, rocking slowly back and forth as horrors held back for days came forth in a rush.

Gang waited for Anton to regain some composure. In quiet tones, he inquired, "What's happened, Anton? Now I am frightened. Has something happened to Anna and William?"

"Vampires killed Mom on Friday night. They took Dad away and said they would bury him in silver," Anton stated in a rush. It was the first time he'd told anyone what had really happened. He rubbed his face with both hands, they came away wet. His chest heaved in another sob, then he quietened and started to breathe more normally.

Gang stood up; his face pale with shock. Li put her hands over her mouth, her eyes wide with horror.

"You must stay here," Gang declared decisively. "This is terrible news. Someone must have betrayed their secret."

Anton looked Gang in the eyes and asked, "How do you know so much?"

"I was a student of your grandfather. Back then, there was much trouble in the Order ... murders and lies. Your parents and your grandfather had to go into hiding."

"I don't know what the Order is. Chloe Armitage – the one who killed my mother and took my father away spoke of the Order of Thoth."

Gang paused for a long moment, and then queried softly, "This vampire, can you describe her, and did she have a henchman?"

"She's quite tall for a woman. She's young, maybe nineteen or twenty at most, with dark hair cut short in a Bob. Beautiful blue eyes, sounds posh, looks like a supermodel, and yes, she had a man with her, tall, solid, blond, named Marcus Drake."

Gang pursed his lips, giving a soft whistle. "Anton, you're still with us – which is a miracle." He stroked his chin. "Li, maybe something stronger tonight, pass over the shot glasses." He reached beneath the bench and retrieved an ancient bottle. "Sake, family reserve."

He poured out a stiff drink for each of them. Stoppering the bottle, he put it back beneath the bench. They sipped their sake, and it burned with a smooth fire down Anton's throat.

"I will contact your grandfather," Gang declared. "I must tell him what has happened. As for the Order, it is enough for tonight that you know we have been fighting vampires for the last five thousand years. You are with friends now."

Anton put his hand out and Gang took it, clasping his arm. Anton said, "Thanks, Gang," he looked over at Li, "and Li. I can't thank you enough."

Li arched a quizzical eyebrow and smiled. Gang shook his head slightly and said sagely, "There is only one reason why you didn't die with your mother. It serves the vampire's purpose that you live."

"She said things to me," Anton said in a low murmur.

"Beware of what Armitage has told you," Gang warned. "Every word serves her agenda. Now off for a shower. I don't often agree with my daughter – but in this instance, she is absolutely correct. You do resemble a scruffy, stray dog. Li, show him the bathroom and the guest room."

Li indicated an open doorway with a flick of her head and directed, "Follow me."

They left the kitchen and Gang called after them, "Tomorrow, I will teach you how to wash dishes. We're a kitchenhand short, and you can help out while you're here. I have special techniques that I will share with you. You will be the best dishwasher in all of Chinatown."

For the first time in days, Anton smiled. Li led him to the building next to the restaurant. It was the Wu family home. Twenty minutes later, Anton had showered and was falling asleep in a comfortable bed.

Chapter Three

Terrorism link to Friday night murder

By Stephanie Hurd | Mercury Correspondent APRIL 29,

The murder of a woman in Jamaica Plain has been linked to terrorism with the case being handed from the Boston Police Department to the FBI.

Police had been notified of the murder and attended the house where the body of the woman was found in the early hours of Saturday Morning. An arrest warrant for a suspect was issued but was later rescinded after the FBI took over the case.

The FBI from the Manhattan Joint Terrorism Task Force Annex has jurisdiction for this case, said Boston police spokesman, Harold Jacobs in a phone interview Saturday.

The FBI Special Agent in Charge, Jim Alexander, declined to comment on the case, stating that policy dictated that active operations against terrorist cells were not a subject for media discussion.

– Boston Mercury Newspaper article on the Internet.

* * *

Boston, May 5th, 23:00

Anton finished washing the last of the dishes, hanging up his scrapers, brushes and dish washing cloths.

He looked up at the clock, it was eleven pm. Flicking off the kitchen lights, he left the restaurant, and made his way to Li and Gang's home. Entering the ground floor, the sharp crack of wood on wood resounded from the backyard, and he went to investigate what was happening there.

A square wooden deck about ten yards on a side dominated the backyard. A peaked roof, supported by four thick pillars at the corners covered it, providing an all-weather open-air training environment. In the middle of the deck, Li and Gang sparred with pairs of wooden sticks. Anton watched in growing amazement at the remarkable display of skill and control as Li and Gang trained with each other. After three minutes, they paused, stepped back and bowed to each other.

"I see that we have an audience for our Arnis training," Gang said.

"Would you like to join us?" Li asked, looking at Anton with an open challenge in her eyes.

"It's time to begin your training. Vampires hunt you. The Order of Thoth is your natural home," Gang declared.

"How do I begin?" Anton asked, spreading his hands wide.

"You have already started with that question," Gang said. "But before we start with 'how' we must answer 'why.' Why do you want to learn what we have to teach?"

"To defend myself, to avenge my mother's death, to rescue my father," Anton declared with quiet intensity.

"The first part of your answer makes sense, the rest not so much," Gang said. He paused, frowned, and said in serious tones, "Your father is beyond saving. The vampires will have turned him. Burial in silver is a punishment for vampires. As for your mother, do you really want vengeance to be the center of your life?"

"Chloe Armitage needs to be destroyed."

Gang nodded once, then stared hard at Anton and said, "The man who walks in the shadow of vengeance is a different man from the man who walks in the light of justice."

Anton was momentarily nonplussed. What Gang just said sounded like fortune cookie wisdom, and he asked, "... Is there a difference?"

"I see for you there is no difference." Gang hesitated for a brief moment, his eyes tightened for a second, then he said with a wry smile, "But you are also young, inexperienced and foolish."

"Thanks," Anton replied, sarcastically.

A second later he was face down on the woven mats embedded in the floor, his arm twisted up behind his back. Li had dropped him; just as quickly she was gone. Anton rose to his feet, rubbing and rolling his shoulder.

Gang said with a commiserating smile, "Never mind Anton, I was even more arrogant than you are at your age. You will find out that humility is an essential virtue or you will not survive."

Anton took a deep breath and conceded, "Okay. I'm sorry."

Gang leaned toward him. "If you approach Chloe Armitage with anger in your heart, she will gut you like a fish."

"I'm sorry, I just don't see how humility is going to help me fight vampires and defeat her."

"Humility will allow you to master what you need to learn, and to be fully present when the moment comes to use what you have mastered."

Anton frowned and promised, "... Okay, I will try."

Gang snorted. "Try!" he laughed. "We'll see about that."

Anton frowned again and asked, "Are you always going to be laughing at me?"

"Well … yes," Gang replied with a smile. "I'm sure your training will be very amusing."

"Are you serious?"

"Very serious."

"You're kidding me?"

"No – the more serious something is, the more we need to laugh at it."

"… Okay." Anton agreed hesitantly.

Gang sighed. "Now before we proceed, there are things you must know and agree to, or else you must walk away from here and never come back."

Anton nodded slowly. "Okay, sure."

"The Order of Thoth is a harsh mistress, and I mean harsh. I'm not talking about 'Wishy Washy 101' at the local University. There are some hard and fast rules you must understand and agree to. Is that clear?"

Anton nodded again.

"Then let us begin with rule number one. Once you join, there is no going back. The Order is for the rest of your life. Once you commit to the Order, the only way to leave is via the grave. Is that clear? Do you understand and accept this rule?"

Anton was willing to do anything to deal with the vampires and responded without hesitation, "Yes. I understand."

"Rule number two. As a member of the Order, you will keep the Order secret, and you will keep the Order's secrets. Is that clear? Do you understand and accept this rule?"

"Yes, I understand."

"Rule number three. As a member of the Order, you will obey the orders of your superiors without hesitation? Is that clear? Do you understand and accept this rule?"

Total obedience, or he had to walk away with nothing and Armitage would get away with everything she'd done to his family. Whatever was necessary, he'd do it. He declared, "Yes, I understand."

"Do you agree to and accept all three rules?"

"Yes. Absolutely."

"Okay then," Gang directed. "Anton, please take off your shirt."

"Huh?" Anton grunted.

"Rule number three Anton," Gang reminded him, arching an eyebrow and tilting his head.

"Okay, sure," Anton replied. He took off his shirt, dropping it to the floor.

Li stared at Anton for a long appraising moment and slowly smiled.

Gang put a consoling hand on Anton's shoulder, and said with quiet emphasis, "I must warn you, what I'm about to do, I've never done before, but your grandfather taught me how to do it."

What was he going to do? Hit him hard in the face? Some sort of initiation test? Whatever it was, it was sure to be painful, but undoubtedly necessary. Anton put his questions away, braced himself, and declared forthrightly, "I'm ready. Go for it."

Gang shaped the fore and middle fingers of his right hand into a stiff knife. He stared intently at Anton for a brief moment and then his hand blurred over Anton's torso in a tightly controlled sequence, striking him deeply a dozen times in less than a second.

Each strike sent a shockwave through Anton's body. Anton felt silvery light flaring at the base of his spine and racing up his body. The light burned with an intense cold fire fountaining through the top of his skull. His eyes rolled up in his head and he fell to the floor unconscious.

Anton woke up, a living flame ripping through every fiber of his being. A silvery-white fire was consuming him from the inside out. He desperately wanted to scream, but only a high-pitched screech got past his clenched jaws. A white wall of agony swept through his skull, threatening to blow his head apart.

An eternity of trembling and shaking came and went, and then he lay still. Panting for breath; gentle hands rested firmly on his shoulder and hip, and someone rolled him into the recovery position.

Suffering beyond anything he'd ever experienced before overtook his body in waves. Great floods of agony washed through him, all but taking his sanity away. Time disappeared and there was only the dark ocean of anguish in which he was drowning. All light vanished as eternal night descended and overwhelmed his mind.

There was a gap in which nothing existed, not even himself.

A frail spark reignited and the dark gave ground to the light.

Utterly alone and surrounded by darkness; he sobbed once with abject terror, but no one heard.

A rift cracked open between the past and the future – two opposite worlds beckoned with equally seductive powers: oblivion or life. Now was the time to give up, to let go, to receded into the welcoming darkness. However, one need prevailed against the dark, *I care, I can never give up.*

Forced to choose, he drew his next breath and the darkness retreated. The spark grew with the returning of the light. The ocean of pain ebbed away, slowly replaced by intense pins and needles as his body and mind returned to a calmer state.

Oh my God ... oh my God. Anton opened his eyes. He pushed himself up into a sitting position, then doubled forward, wracked by a fit of harsh coughing.

Li put her hand softly on his shoulder and said, "That's your lungs learning to really breathe for the first time."

Anton couldn't speak for a long moment, then regained enough control to gasp through chattering teeth, "What ... was ... that? What did you ... do to me?"

"I just switched you on," Gang replied with a chuckle. He slapped Anton on the shoulder. "That's the first time I've seen that work."

Pushing himself up off the floor, Anton groaned and said ruefully, "Switched me on? I feel like a Mack truck just ran over me ... twice."

Gang shrugged his shoulders, and then nodded once. "But now you can Ramp."

Anton shook his head. His nose had started bleeding and he smeared the blood away with his forearm, and asked, "What's the Ramp?"

Li gave him a hand towel, Anton pressed it to his nose, and turned back toward Gang.

Gang spread his hands wide and addressed Anton, "The Ramp is an epigenetic phenomenon. The outcome of a set of techniques that bind muscles and rewire nerves. There are very real physiological changes that enable us to reach our full potential as a human being. Those changes enable us to match the speed and capabilities of vampires. They allow us to enter combat with vampires and win."

"You could have warned me," Anton said ruefully.

"If I had told you how much it would hurt – would you have chosen differently?"

Anton shook his head. "No."

"Good answer. By the way, not everyone survives the process, most die."

"Most die? I'm not surprised. I thought I was definitely going to die. It was a big risk, was there no other way?"

"There is no way you can stay in the Order as a fighter without the Ramp. I trusted in the fact you are a Slayne. You have over two hundred generations behind you of continuous membership in the Order. If anyone was going to survive the process, it would be you."

Anton flicked his gaze from Gang to Li and back, and asked, "So the both of you have been through that?"

Gang stated with a broad grin, "No, of course not. We both started training at three years of age, and achieved the transformations you just went through over fifteen years of dedicated work."

Anton winced as Gang slapped him on the back and said, "You got off easy, you got the condensed version."

Anton smiled wryly, then grimaced as he stiffly took a step forward.

"You can't train an adult body for the Ramp," Li said. "It's no longer adaptable, what my father did was the only way."

Anton's blood nose stopped dripping. He rubbed his forehead, and picked up his shirt. He staggered, utterly drained and exhausted, then righted himself. The beginnings of a whopper of a headache clawed at his skull, but his soul took flight, as if he'd just won a championship game. He asked, "So, what happens now?"

"All I have done is open the door," Gang instructed. "You still have to walk through it. The development of skill and control is still in front of you. Please believe me when I tell you there is much for you to learn, but for now, drink plenty of water and get some sleep."

"Thanks, sounds like excellent advice," Anton replied, walking gingerly to his room. Everything hurt like hell, there seemed to be no end to the way his body could experience pain.

Gang called after him, "I'll have a big breakfast for you in the morning. You'll need it."

Anton waved at Gang, and made it into the house. He managed to down a couple of tall glasses of water in the bathroom before flopping into his bed and falling immediately asleep.

* * *

Chloe Armitage and Haras Mosule stood on top of a rampart at the Tower of David citadel in Jerusalem.

The evening light show had finished and the revelers had all left. Except for two unfortunate souls whose bodies were in the back of a Shadowstone van Peter Dench was driving to a designated disposal facility. The other praetorian, Washington Jones, stood a dozen yards away on another part of the citadel wall. All four vampires wore barely visible in-ear communication headsets that provided secure communications via encrypted satellite links to any location in the world.

"We're wasting our time," Haras complained loudly, staring out over the old city of Jerusalem. "We have been here nearly a week without a hint of Red Empire activity. We need a new strategy."

Chloe arched an eyebrow.

"First we need good intelligence," Haras said. "We need to find the secret citadel of Shabbah al Ahmar. The Red Empire typically maintain a forward base of operations. They moved the last one in 1850, two days after Crane converted me, and before Crane could launch an attack on it. The Red Ghost of that time had acted quickly when vampires took his chief lieutenant alive. Back then, the forward operations citadel was in Istanbul, the city that I grew up in as a child. It's a distinct possibility the Red Empire have moved back there and now they simply run operatives through Jerusalem to lay a false trail. It's a task for Shadowstone and the

Panopticon to find the Red Empire's men and track them back to their lair. Then we can come in and eliminate the Red Empire's main force."

Chloe tilted her head and said wryly, "You talk of war when our mission is one of stealth."

"You've never shirked a battle before."

Chloe's lips twitched with a slight smile. "Of course not, but open war with the Red Empire is not our mission."

"We don't have enough information to execute our mission as it stands."

"Crane must believe the Red Empire is here. Otherwise, he wouldn't've sent us. We're too valuable for him to waste our time here."

Haras gripped the top of the rampart and stared out at the city. "But we're wasting our time."

"The Red Empire must be here somewhere – we need a new method of searching."

"I will take Jones. If you catch up with Dench, we can split this city into two halves. I will take the west side—"

Chloe seized upon his offer like a trap snapping shut. "And I'll take the east side."

A flash of light lit up the edge of the city, a plume of flame rising into the night sky. They both reacted to the flash at the same time, turning as one to look at what was happening. Jones appeared next to Haras. Another pair of flashes followed hot on the heels of the first. The plume of flame thickened into a tower of smoke six miles away in the direction of the disposal facility.

Chloe activated her ear piece on broadcast and ordered, "Dench, report in ... Dench?"

The only sound on the line was static.

"He's gone, Ma'am," Jones stated in shocked finality.

Jones opened his Shadowstone smartphone, bringing up a Panopticon satellite feed covering the area of the explosion. He held the phone out so that Haras and Chloe could see what was on the screen. The Shadowstone van lay dismembered by the explosions, people cowered in the street, frozen with fear, or running away. A pair of men approached the remains of the van cautiously. Even with a satellite view, they could see the men point toward the center of the remains of the cabin and shake their heads.

The thud and crump of the explosions reached them. The signature squeal of tearing metal discernable to their vampire hearing.

Haras opened his own smartphone, immediately running a program. In seconds, it gave a quick succession of beeps. He grinned hungrily and declared, "We have targets, three of them."

"Same here," Jones reported, showing them his screen with three green dots streaming away from the explosion.

"I will take the one heading northeast," Chloe declared decisively.

"I will take the one heading south," Jones declared.

"I will take the last one," Haras stated.

"Keep your earpieces active. Stay in touch, and try and capture them alive," Chloe declared. "We need information, not kills."

"Good hunting," Haras said to the other vampires before leaping over the edge of the rampart. Landing at the base of the tower, he ran toward the west, disappearing into the night.

Jones followed him down, also vanishing into the darkness.

Chloe paused, long enough to smile with satisfaction. *One pawn sacrificed and one knight distracted.* She leaped over the edge, running off to the northeast, her phone providing her the same Panopticon tracking information guiding the others. In less than ten minutes, she'd covered the distance and converged on her target's location.

He disappeared down a sewer. From the tell-tale heat plume, he was clearly ramped, almost certainly a Red Empire assassin.

"Entering the sewers, I will lose comms in moments," Chloe broadcast to the others.

"Noted," Haras replied.

"Yes, Ma'am – I've found mine," Jones responded.

Chloe dropped through the sewer entrance into the maze of pipes underneath the city. The rip and crack of gunfire, rapidly followed by sword-on-sword combat erupted over her comms link. She ran into the darkness; her vampire senses leaving no doubt she was following her prey. His warm footprints left a visible trail on the cold concrete. She was on a service walkway, above the wet and noxious contents of the sewer. She didn't need the Panopticon system now, she was close enough to her target to follow his footprints, distinctive human body odor and the almost imperceptible noise of his movements. Her comms link gave a little hum in her ear as it lost contact with the satellites. She shut it down and slowed to a walk.

Human hearts were beating within the sewer. There were five of them and they were close. Chloe rounded a bend, where five Red Empire assassins confronted her. One was the sweat-drenched runner she'd pursued. They were all armed with long slim-bladed swords and Uzi 9mm submachine guns. They carried their blades drawn and their Uzis aimed directly at her.

The lead assassin lowered his weapons and asked, "General Armitage?"

"Yes," Chloe replied.

"We are to take you to meet Shabbah al Ahmar."

"As was agreed."

"You will need to disarm, and to wear a hood as the location is secret."

"As was expected," Chloe said. She took off her sword belt and handed it to the leader of the squad.

One of the other assassins approached with a thick black hood and she allowed him to place it over her head. She mused to herself, *A moment of truth; I will get to find out if Shabbah al Ahmar will keep his word.* She declared loudly through the heavy weave of the hood, "Lead on, I will follow you by sound."

The squad of assassins moved away, and Chloe followed as they proceeded to traverse the sewers of Jerusalem to the secret citadel of the Red Empire.

* * *

Hands with the barest hint of a tremble carefully removed Chloe's hood. Someone was trying to hide their terror and just failing to do so.

The hood slipped away. Her hearing had alerted her as to what to expect and there were no surprises. She was in the middle of a large hall without windows. There was a high vaulted ceiling. The walls were of smooth gray stone with the lighting supplied by modern electric fixtures overhead. There was an oppressive sense of mass above her. She was underground.

Surrounding her were twenty-five armed warriors. The hand-picked elite of the Red Empire led by the man standing two yards in front of her, Shabbah al Ahmar.

She smiled at the Red Ghost. She'd met him twice before. The first time on a battlefield, but without closing. The second time by mutual choice in a place of secrecy. He had given her his personal name, Dalien Morte.

His hatred for Cornelius Crane eclipsed all other forces in his life. Chloe did not know the origin of Morte's hatred; it was enough to understand its power. He'd been willing to bargain and had delivered a shared agent in the Order of Thoth operating in her heartland, al Ghurab, the Raven.

In exchange, she would provide high-level operational intelligence from the Vampire Dominion.

Morte glowered at her and demanded, "What brings the right and left hands of the Demon to this land?"

Chloe replied calmly, "Crane believes the Interpretive Codex is in the hands of Shabbah al Ahmar and he wishes to possess it."

"Does he believe that four vampires … no," he snapped his fingers, "three vampires can breach our defenses?"

Chloe arched an eyebrow, tilting her head slightly and said with the merest hint of a smile, "… I'm here."

Like a wolf circling its prey, Morte stalked around her and declared incredulously, "You would dare to challenge us here, alone and unarmed?"

Chloe smiled softly, her eyes glistening with an avid desire. She remained poised and still, without a hint of fear.

Around her, men loosened swords in their scabbards. Safeties clicked open on Uzi submachine guns. The bullets within them reeked of silver. The anticipation in the room rang like a bell. All these men had trained from childhood to do one thing very well – to kill – and especially to kill vampires.

Morte snorted once and answered himself, "Of course not. You play your own game."

Chloe arched an eyebrow. *Which is why I'm talking and you, and your men are not dying on my blade.* "Yes," she conceded. "Shall we begin?"

"What do you have to offer?"

"I will provide you with the exact location of the Key of Ahknaton, and the Papyrus of Hakron the Scribe. All I require in payment is to verify you have the Interpretive Codex."

Morte sneered derisively. "What makes you think that I have the Codex? Crane is delusional."

"Crane's information is good. You have the Codex."

Morte frowned. "You are very certain about such a doubtful claim."

"Unless the Red Empire has lost the Codex, it still has it, as it has been in your family line for five thousand years."

"What you offer is insufficient," Morte declared with a scowl, silently conceding his possession of the Codex.

Chloe smiled warmly. "I also offer my continued good will and future opportunities for mutual benefit ... which is an offer of great value."

Morte stroked his short dark beard for a long moment. "So be it. I need to ensure you have no recording equipment, such as a contact lens with data storage capabilities. I need you closely examined before you can approach the Codex."

"Of course," Chloe agreed.

Morte glanced at one of his men and commanded, "Search her."

A young member of the Red Empire force stepped forward with a device the size of a smartphone. Chloe stood still as he swept the device over her body, running it carefully and slowly in front of her face. The device gave a quick chirp as a green light flashed on the screen.

"She's clear," the young man reported, and rejoined the ranks surrounding her.

Morte touched his earpiece, speaking rapid commands in Arabic. A minute later, the large doors at the end of the hall opened and an old man dressed in a simple gray robe walked into the hall. He carried a long, silver scroll case. Bowing low before Shabbah al Ahmar he handed over the case.

Morte dismissed him with a wave of his hand, and moments later the doors were once again closed and locked.

Chloe continued to look straight ahead. Her stance poised and relaxed as the breathing and heartbeats of unseen guards beyond the doorway whispered in her ears. She assessed her situation, *Another eight outside this room.*

Morte stepped away from her. He opened the case, and extracted the scroll within. He walked away from her and placed it flat on a lectern at the rear of the hall. The scroll was much shorter than the Papyrus of Hakron the Scribe, only a foot square.

Chloe remained still, revealing nothing. With such a short piece of papyrus it must be instructions only. She seethed with anticipation, she was close, so very close to what she sought.

"You must approach without any clothing or equipment of any sort," Morte demanded.

Chloe arched an eyebrow. "… Agreed." She wore loose combat fatigues. She undid her belts and webbing, her hand automatically reaching for her scabbard on her left hip. She smiled wryly as she clutched empty air. Looking to her right, the leader of the squad that had escorted her was holding her sword and belt. She wondered if he comprehended the rare value of the blade, fashioned from meteoric iron by a genius sword smith in late 17th century Japan. Without doubt, she would soon hold it again.

Chloe completed her disrobing, placing her clothes in a neat pile on top of her combat boots in the middle of the room. The room fell into near-perfect silence as the assembled Red Empire assassins witnessed her walk with naked confidence toward the lectern.

Every eye watched her with avid attention. Every sword stood raised in ruthless salute. The doors to the room remained securely locked and offered no escape. Twenty-five heart beats accelerated as she reached the lectern, stood behind it and glanced down at the Codex.

The arcane symbols on the Papyrus coalesced within her mind. A mind fueled by nearly two centuries of access to the wealth of Crane's unique library. A mind gifted with an eidetic memory. *So that is how it works, how remarkable to devise such a code in such an ancient time.*

Chloe looked up from the Codex and briefly scanned the assembly of Red Empire Assassins. For a long moment, her eyes unfocused as she merged the instructions of the Codex and her perfect memory of Hakron's Papyrus into a single image. She realized the truth of the Key of Ahknaton, the Metaframe and the genesis of the vampires.

Intense joy bloomed within her, surging euphoria rushed up her body and fountained through the top of her head. The realization was both shocking and profound. In a rare moment of abandon, she laughed out loud. *Vampires were an accident — who knew?*

81

The men in the room swayed before her, her laughter momentarily unnerving them. Their confident stances shifted to defense as they murmured warnings to each other. Low muttered words reached her, "Capture her. Torture her. Kill her."

Chloe slowly stroked her chin – just once before her hand dropped back to the lectern. Her eyes widened, a ghost of a smile curling her lips, she took a deep breath and sighed softly. She was suddenly intrigued with the possibility of seizing the Codex and fighting her way out of the citadel. The daring nature of the deed excited every fiber of her being. No vampire had ever accomplished such a thing. The theft of the most holy artifact of the Red Empire from the heart of their citadel. She was the premier warrior of her kind, unequaled in skill with the blade. If any vampire was going to complete the feat, it would be her.

She contemplated the twenty-five Red Empire assassins surrounding her. Twenty-five Ramp masters, each a highly skilled and experienced killer versus her unarmed self. Her mind accelerated, racing through options, calculating results versus risks, anticipating action, and counter-action. In a moment, a path of probability opened, revealing a set of actions that made the chance of success substantially better than a coin toss.

Temptation flooded her soul. The assassin standing ten feet to her left would be the first to fall. His sword would become her own. The man standing opposite him would rush to attack her and he would be next to die. Then with a sword in each hand, she would reap the lives of the elite warriors of the Red Empire.

The leader of the escort squad would be the sixteenth man to die. She would leave a blade in his heart and then with her katana, the *Red Dragon,* in her hands, she would kill the remaining nine in ... fourteen seconds.

She would leave Dalien Morte to the last. To give him time to fully understand the depths of his failure in allowing her to enter the heart of his citadel. With the room cleared, she would reclaim her clothes. Then with the Codex in her left hand and the Red Dragon in her right, she would leave the citadel, slaying all who would oppose her departure.

The rush of wonderful joy she felt now would sublimate into divine bliss.

She tapped the sides of the lectern with her fingers and stepped back; rationality curbing her passionate desire. She could not deliver the Codex to Crane. Once he possessed the Codex, it was certain he would soon decide he no longer needed her. With Allemande's curse in place, she was unable to defend herself against him. She would surely perish and her vision of a new world order would die with her.

Chloe took a breath, and addressed the assembly, "You do not trust me. Given that you do not know me, that is understandable, but tonight you will discover that I keep my word. This is the Interpretive Codex, and I will answer Shabbah al Ahmar's questions in full."

Morte ordered the doors opened, the Codex taken away, and the room cleared. Within a minute, Chloe and Morte stood alone.

He stared at her, frowning and stroking his beard, and declared, "Everyone felt it. Your joy at seeing the Codex and your disappointment that you could not take it with you. So powerful were your emotions, these men could not help but react. You are dangerous beyond belief."

"I'm only dangerous to my enemies. My friends, on the other hand—" Chloe left the statement hanging. Arching an eyebrow, she smiled at him and said wryly, "However, I am at a disadvantage, you are clothed and I am not."

"Of course, please dress."

Chloe put her clothes back on and declared, "The answer is simple. Crane keeps The Key and the Papyrus in a secret room within his personal quarters in his citadel. The citadel is at 350 on Fifth Avenue, New York City. His personal chambers are on the 104th floor. The defenses of this building and the surrounding city are formidable and designed to thwart an attack by the Order of Thoth or the Red Empire."

Morte pursed his lips. "That is sufficient." He grinned, his dark brown eyes flashing with triumph. "You may go now."

"Thank you for your … hospitality."

Morte touched his earpiece and gave orders, in moments the original escort squad returned to the chamber. However, this time, the assassin who had led her into the sewers was bound with chains.

He addressed his men. "Give General Armitage back her weapon and this man, and return her to where you found her. Ensure her safety while she is in your care."

Morte faced Chloe. "Al Eunza owes the Red Empire a life debt, his acceptance of this mission of sacrifice will allow his true name to be remembered in honor, instead of shame."

Chloe nodded. "If his name is to be honored, I shall ensure his death is by the sword as befits a servant of the Red Empire."

Morte nodded his head once.

Chloe accepted the black hood and followed her escort away. She reflected on what she'd observed before the hood had darkened her sight, *His heart has still not returned to its normal range after seeing me nude. I will be able to leverage his desire. Now I need to bring Marcus to Jerusalem and lead Haras and Jones on a merry chase for a few weeks to allow this mission to take on the semblance of a real search.*

He thinks himself secure in this hole in the ground, but little does he know that even though I wear this hood – I can remember my steps perfectly.

* * *

For the umpteenth time, Anton punched the air.

Li locked up his arm, ducking underneath his shoulder, she twisted him around, throwing him face down on the mat. He rose to one knee, sweeping with his foot, but Li had already leaped back out of range. Jumping to his feet, he gave ground as Li tested his defenses with a series of kicks that were just fast enough to get past his blocks and evasions. In moments, she finished him with a side kick that propelled him off the training deck.

"Ha!" Li grinned. "I'm amazed, you lasted more than ten seconds that time."

Fantastic, I finally lasted more than ten seconds in a fight with a woman half my size and it has only taken two and a half weeks to get to double digits. Anton picked himself up, getting back onto the training mats.

Li held up her hand and declared, "Enough."

Anton frowned and declared, "I can do more."

"Physically, yes," Li conceded, "but not today. We need to focus on your Ramp control." She walked over to a rack holding Shinai and Bokken training swords made of flexible bamboo and hardwood respectively. She picked one of the bamboo Shinai, flexed it experimentally, and seemingly satisfied with her latest weapon she returned, and stood in front of Anton. She lifted the Shinai and asked, "What is this?"

"A Shinai training sword," Anton replied.

"Those are just words, what is it?"

"It's a Shinai."

"You're not allowed to name it. What is it?"

"A bamboo sword."

"That's just another name, a tag. Do you think the sign out front of the Restaurant 'is' the Noodle House?"

"No, of course not," Anton agreed, becoming exasperated.

"Tell me what it is without words."

"… Huh."

"Tell me what it is with silence."

"…"

"Let it be what it is … don't put words on it," Li instructed.

No words.

For a long moment, Anton felt his internal voice go silent. *That's weird,* he thought as his mental voice came back. "Hey, I just stopped thinking for a few seconds."

Li leaned forward and smiled mischievously. "That's the easy part." She whirled the Shinai through a flat arc, striking Anton on the shoulder with a sizzling crack. "Now do it while I'm hitting you."

Anton leaped backward and swore, "What the hell?"

Li whipped the Shinai forward again, striking him on the other shoulder.

"Hey?" Anton shouted, struggling to avoid the next blow.

Li moved faster than his eye could follow, striking him twice more, left and right beneath the ribs.

Anton tried to blank his mind, but he kept thinking about what Li would do next, trying to anticipate her actions and avoid her hitting him.

Li blurred, using the Shinai to trip Anton, and he landed on his butt. Before he could rise, she pressed the Shinai against his chest, pushing him flat on his back.

"You're very attached to thinking, aren't you Anton?"

"I guess," he conceded from the floor.

Li nodded. "Well, let's go with that. A thinking man's explanation before we proceed, Okay?"

"Sure," Anton agreed. Anything was better than having his ass handed to him by a girl.

Li sat down opposite Anton. "Mastery of the Ramp begins with listening."

"Okay, I thought I was doing that."

"Anyone can listen with their ears, what the Ramp requires is listening with the mind."

"Uh huh?" Anton grunted.

Li paused for a second and then stated, "There are four types of listening, and three transitions between them. The four types are indifferent, ordinary, silent and profound."

"What are the differences between them?"

"Consider a conversation, indifferent occurs when your mind wanders away, and you hear nothing of what the other person is saying. Ordinary is when you hear the other person's words, but you are also thinking about what you want to say, so you are not really paying attention to their words. Silent is when you just hear the other person's words, and your own mental chatter is absent."

"And profound?"

"Profound listening is when you cease to anticipate hearing anything at all."

"You said that there are three transitions."

"Yes. The first transition from indifferent to ordinary is based on orientating yourself in space, you become mindful of your present location. The second transition from ordinary to silent is based on silencing your internal mental voice."

"That seems to be the hard part."

"A lot of people mistake that internal voice as being themselves, but it is just an activity of the mind. You still remain present when it is silent. It's actually simple, once you're used to it. The third transition from silent to profound is based on orientating yourself in time. Arresting your mind within the present moment, no future, no past, just the present. This is the key to mastering access to the Ramp. It is also the hardest part to learn."

"So, I stop thinking and anticipating?" Anton asked.

"Yes," Li answered. "It is the only path to the Ramp."

"How do I know what to do in a fight?"

"A combination of training to automate your reflexes and Ramp mastery. Profound listening is the key to open the door to Ramp mastery, it is not Ramp mastery. A Ramp master's mind accelerates so much the perception of time speeds up. The experience is of the world slowing down. It is the accelerated mind, allied with transformed physical skills that enable us to match a vampire in combat."

Anton remembered the first night he'd met Gang, and how Gang ran past him in the alley as if he'd been standing still.

"Is there a catch?"

"Two of them," Li answered, and started ticking off her fingers. "Firstly, when ramping, your body runs hot and no one can sustain the Ramp for a long time. Secondly, a noisy mind will drop you straight out of the Ramp. Don't get distracted – it will get you killed."

Anton nodded. "Okay."

"It's been said that a Ramp master's actions precede his thoughts," Li said sagely. She leaned forward and looked into Anton's eyes. "Perhaps one day that will be true for you too. Let's try again, this time unarmed."

Li put the Shinai back on the rack. Turning in an instant, she attacked Anton with a flying kick. He ducked away as Li flew over him, whirling around, he found Li already in position, striking him with hand and foot combinations. Li expertly pulled the strikes on contact. Anton found himself becoming quite within his mind as his world shrank to the moment.

He moved aside as Li launched a kick which he caught in a lock, twisting toward her he lowered his shoulder to catch her in a throw.

Reversing his attack, Li swept his feet out from under him and he landed flat on his back with Li on top.

Li's thighs wrapped firmly around Anton's hips. She locked his right wrist, twisting it painfully as she pushed his forearm into his throat cutting off his ability to breathe.

Anton started to smile.

Li's long hair fell like a curtain around their heads. Her large brown eyes widened as her face hovered inches above his own. "Right!" She snapped. Leaping up, she commanded, "Yesterday you said you could do two hundred burpees in a set, so let's see it – or was that the idle boast of someone who thinks too highly of himself."

"Okay," Anton agreed with a grin and started doing the burpees.

Li took the Shinai back off the rack. Positioning it in front of Anton as he was jumping up from the prone position, she instructed, "Jump over this."

She's enjoying this, Anton thought, as he jumped over the Shinai. He focused on the moves. Li kept inserting the Shinai in front of him and he kept jumping over it. As the repetitions continued, she raised the bamboo higher and higher, until she was holding it straight out from her shoulder for each jump.

With each rep Anton glanced at Li's face. She was watching him intently. He found himself sinking into a quiet place where there was only the rhythm of the motion and Li's eyes watching him. He lost track of time. There was just the night, the cool air laced with the perfume from Gang's roses, and Li. Just Li, a poised, coiled presence next to him. He felt like he could do this forever, and wondered if he just might.

"Stop," Li directed, pulling the Shinai away. "That's five hundred, and you're still going like a machine."

"I've always had plenty of endurance."

"That was phenomenal, I think your body is adjusting to the Ramp much faster than I would expect. Time to get a drink and a shower, we'll continue tomorrow."

Anton smiled. "Great, will do."

Stepping off the mats an image of the vampire Armitage beheading his mother came unbidden into his mind. His thoughts darkened, his smile fled, and he vowed to himself, *Your time is coming closer, I will master the Ramp and I will kill you.*

* * *

Gang logged into his laptop and checked the online bookings for the Noodle House.

He was looking for a very specific booking with a pre-order. It would be from, 'Mr. T Masters, a table for two, an order for the duck special, with the new special secret sauce.' Gang had updated his website the day after Anton had arrived, and listed the new dish. It was an agreed signal to Arthur Slayne.

If Gang needed to contact Arthur, he would advertise he had a new secret sauce. If the need was urgent than it would be a special secret sauce. Arthur would set the time and date for the meeting via the booking. The actual meeting would be at a predetermined site – not the Noodle House. Only Gang, Li, and Arthur knew of the arrangement.

It was three weeks later and there was still no booking. What could have kept Arthur from seeing or acting on his message in that time?

"What's happened my old friend," Gang whispered to himself. He was not one to worry unduly about anything, but he had to admit to himself he was concerned by the lack of a response from Arthur.

Gang remembered back six months to when he'd last seen his old force team leader, replaying the conversation in his mind. There had been a large map of South America laid out on Gang's dining room table. There had been trouble in South America – big trouble.

"I will be going to Brazil," Arthur declared. "Crane has a special project in the Amazon." He stabbed the map with a forefinger and traced out a large circle. "Somewhere in this region, there is a mixed team of Shadowstone operatives, molecular biologists, and support staff. In the background, a team of praetorians are providing security."

"What of the Order, are they doing anything?" Gang inquired.

Arthur shook his head. "They're doing nothing. Kain won't lift a finger. I'm sure he's Crane's pet."

"What's Crane's objective? Those scientists worry me."

"Me too, molecular biology suggests genetic manipulation, cellular technologies, and techniques for changing the physiology of a human being or a vampire, but why the Amazon? I need to find out."

"Do you need my assistance? Li could hire some help and run the Noodle House while I'm away."

"Ha," Arthur laughed. "You trust Li with your baby?"

Gang grinned. "Yes, I know. As unlikely as it may seem at times, I really do trust her abilities, she is really very mature for her age."

Arthur took a sip of whiskey from his tumbler and shook his head. "Not this mission my old friend. Stealth all the way, I will be most effective on my own. Thanks for the offer, though. You know I appreciate it."

Gang frowned for a moment. His old friend had always had trouble asking for help. It was a trait that one day might get him killed. "Well then, good hunting," Gang said, offering the traditional toast.

"Good hunting," Arthur replied heartily.

Both men drained their drinks. And then Arthur left Gang's home and vanished into the night.

Gang felt sick to his stomach as he came back to the present. How would he tell him of the turning and imprisonment of his son, and the death of Anna? At least, Anton was alive and well. Gang took a deep breath, let it go slowly, and his distress fled with it. It was time to accept what had happened and focus on the differences he could make. Perhaps tomorrow Arthur would send his message.

He smiled, the boy was whip-smart, driven to learn, and absorbing information and skills like a sponge. He was progressing much faster than

Gang had expected, the Ramp activation he'd put Anton through was playing a large part in that. The ongoing re-routing of the nerve and muscle bindings greatly facilitated the acquisition of physical skills. The transformation of the Ramp enabled the rapid acquisition of any physical ability. Anton was mastering skills in weeks what would normally take years. He was rapidly gaining speed, strength, and a comprehensive fighting ability. What he still lacked was effective control of the Ramp. But that would come with time, Gang was sure of that.

The clock ticked over to 3pm. It was time to attend an afternoon practice session with Anton and Li. Gang picked up a large jar of herbal balm, walked out of his home office and down to the training deck.

It was also time to progress from the flexible bamboo Shinai to the hardwood Bokken. The balm would be useful for the many bruises Anton would soon acquire.

Gang chuckled wickedly for a moment. Anton was the perfect study in the collision between a powerful desire to learn and the trenchant pain necessary to satisfy that desire. He reflected for a moment. Arthur would be proud of his grandson's progress, very proud. And who could ask for more than that.

Gang thought of his daughter, Li. She was the light of his life, and had kept him alive after the tragic accident that had claimed his wife and son. He couldn't be prouder of the young woman she'd become. He'd done everything he could to prepare her for a world ruled by vampires. As powerful as she was, he vowed to himself to work Anton hard. She would need him. A Slayne at her side, with the Slayne fighting heritage in full flower would help keep her safe.

He brushed sudden tears from his eyes and sniffed. What more could a father do?

* * *

Li frowned as another couple left the restaurant without completing their meal.

She'd let them go without asking them to pay. Apologizing profusely as she led them through the front door. Raucous laughter greeted her as she came back into the main room. The boss of the Hu Shizu, the self-styled 'Tiger Clan,' Mr. Wang, completed one of his trademark jokes. The core of his crew sat around a large circular table covered with the remains of the Noodle House's best dishes and finest wines.

Mr. Wang looked around, snapped his fingers loudly and demanded, "Bring the sake!"

Obnoxious creep, Li thought furiously. She walked gracefully forward with two bottles of sake and nine shot glasses on a tray. She placed the tray on a nearby trolley, pouring the sake into the glasses. She quickly distributed the shots around the table. *Here you go,* she thought. *Fats, Stinker, Rats, Slinker, Ferret, Weasel, Greasy, Sleazy and Creepy – I hope you choke on it.*

The gangsters leered at her as she worked. They were all watching her every move. Tracking their avid gazes, she internally shook her head behind her polite, friendly, front of house facade. *What were these guys expecting? A lap dance?*

A rough hand slid over her hip, squeezing her buttock through her red silk dress. The forced smile fled from her face and her eyes narrowed with indignation. She glanced down at the offending hand gliding over the smooth curve of her bottom. She lifted her eyes and stared into the face of the hand's owner, Mr. Wang – the head of organized crime in Chinatown.

Hold it together, step away quietly, and don't rip his head off, Li advised herself and stepped out of reach.

Mr. Wang's hand dropped back into his lap and he said loudly, "You should come and work for me, you could earn a lot more than you make here."

Li whirled and glared at the crime boss for a fraction of a second. *What a pimp! I would rather suck my own eyeballs out with a straw than work for a sleazebag like you.* She raised a fresh smile over her seething anger and replied with a trace of feigned regret, "Mr. Wang, I'm very happy working here with my father."

Mr. Wang stroked his chin, his gaze lingering over every curve of her body. He said avidly, "A beautiful young woman such as yourself could become a star in my best club."

Oh my God, he wants me to be a high-class whore. Li reached deep, managing a simpering titter as if flattered by his assessment of her 'assets.' "Oh Mr. Wang, I wouldn't do anything without my father's permission."

Mr. Wang laughed, and boomed his enthusiasm, "That's it, you're perfect, so innocent, and so honorable. My club's patrons will go wild. I will dress you in gold – you will be a great sensation."

Gritting her teeth behind her smile, Li kept her feelings hidden. Silently reminding herself to maintain her cover, and keep her family's secret. It took more will then she anticipated, but she rose to the occasion. She bowed her head submissively, and took a step backward.

Mr. Wang's chair scraped across the floor, his arm snaking around her waist, dragging her onto his lap.

Li vowed to herself to get a better cover. Next time she would be an ex-navy SEAL. Then nobody would dare mess with her.

"Surely it is time for the young bird to fly the nest," Mr. Wang purred as he looked at her with half-lidded eyes. "I could show you a life far beyond that of a waitress."

"Mr. Wang," Li replied. She shook her head, her eyes wide with feigned innocence. "There is nothing you could offer beyond my life here."

Mr. Wang grinned lustily, pulling her close so that her breasts crushed against his chest. His face closed within inches of her own. She couldn't miss his sallow greasy skin, his stained and yellow teeth, and the pungent reek of stale tobacco smoke enveloping him in a noxious cloud.

"Oh, my dear. If I have nothing you desire, then I'm sure you will continue to enjoy the comforts of your home here in this – 'Noodle House' – for as long as it lasts."

A loud snigger erupted from the other end of the table. She pinpointed the gangster, *Sleazy*, with a sharp glance. The mood around the table shifted in seconds from boorishly enjoyable to coldly threatening.

A familiar presence appeared nearby. She looked up; it was her father.

"Can I help," Gang said calmly.

Anton stood at her father's shoulder radiating cold fury.

Mr. Wang pushed Li off his lap, and she stepped lightly away.

Waving his hand through a wide arc, Mr. Wang asked, "This Noodle House, is it well insured? You never know what could happen … storm, flood – or even a fire." He leaned back in his chair and stroked his chin. "It would be such a shame if this fine little enterprise just went up in smoke."

Gang chuckled. "Ah, Mr. Wang, my insurance is excellent."

Mr. Wang frowned, his mouth drooping sourly. "Your daughter does not want to work for me. Perhaps you could make her see sense."

Gang's eyes twinkled. "Does the lightning obey the wind? She is very strong-willed. She will make up her own mind – she always does."

Mr. Wang smiled at Gang, but his eyes were icy cold. "Mr. Wu, you've been here for years with this little business, so small, I overlooked it." He nodded at Li. "And yet tonight I find your daughter. It's like kicking over a dull gray stone and discovering a diamond."

Li glanced at Anton, his face was flat and still, he stared at Mr. Wang with something dark and terrifying lurking just behind his eyes. *Uh oh. Anton shouldn't be here right now.*

"I'm sorry Mr. Wang, but my daughter will be staying here," Gang declared.

Mr. Wang sneered. "Do you know who I am – how dare you refuse me."

The gangsters around the table leaned back, letting their coats fall away to reveal an array of handguns, knives and short-hafted axes.

Gang took a breath and put a steady hand on Anton's hip. "Mr. Wang, we don't want any trouble."

Li thought furiously. Not how to deal with the lecherous ambitions of the local crime boss, but how to stop Anton exploding. His emotions were still a hot raw mess. She edged behind her father, as if trying to hide, but actually seeking to position herself to tackle Anton.

The last remaining patrons left their seats, exiting through the front door. In moments, only Li, Gang, Anton and the gangsters remained in the main room. The rest of the staff had retreated into the back alley behind the kitchen.

Gang and Mr. Wang stared at each other in silence for a long moment.

"Well, it would be a shame if anyone got hurt through thoughtless action," Mr. Wang said darkly, standing up. "I will give you both a week to think about my offer."

"A week won't make any difference," Gang declared.

"Nor would a lifetime," Li said briskly.

Mr. Wang laughed coldly. "Well, we will see about that." He turned and led his men from the restaurant without looking back.

The last one to leave was the one who had sniggered, Sleazy. Pausing at the door, he caught Li's gaze and made a sexually obscene gesture with his hands, then tapping his chest, he whispered hoarsely, "You and me slut."

As the door began to swing shut, Anton ramped, running through the opening and into the street.

"No!" Li shouted. She ramped hard, following Anton out into the street where she caught up with him. Gang was a step behind her. Anton had just missed the last gangster as he barreled out into the street.

"Hey you!" Anton shouted at Sleazy.

The gang was in front of them and they started to turn around.

Li gripped Anton's arm, snapping, "Drop back down."

Anton stared at her for a moment and then shook his head as if waking from a dream.

Li looked back down the street. One of the gangsters, *Ferret* had drawn a Glock 9mm pistol and it was pointing right at her. Mr. Wang put his hand on the gangster's arm and pushed down. The gangster looked at his boss with 'why not?' written all over his thin face.

Mr. Wang indicated up the street with a nod and a shrug, and ordered in a harsh whisper, "Not here."

Li and Anton turned, looking up the street. About fifty feet away a newly mounted CCTV camera covered the sidewalk in front of the Noodle House.

Li's heart sank as she dragged Anton back inside the restaurant.

"Damn," Anton swore.

As they got back inside, Gang greeted Anton with a shake of the head and stated, "No hood, no good."

"I'm sorry," Anton said. "I don't know what happened."

"What were you thinking?" Li demanded.

"I just lost it. I'm sorry – I wasn't thinking at all."

Gang put his hands on their shoulders. "Use tonight to get ready to leave at a moment's notice. We're not leaving yet, maybe nothing will come of this, but be prepared for a quick departure."

Li and Anton both nodded.

"But before you go, this place is a mess. Please help the staff to clean up, they will be hiding out the back. I will have to make some plans about Mr. Wang."

"Yes, Father."

"Yes, Gang," Anton agreed.

Li looked at Anton, her eyes hardened and she promised to herself, *'I wasn't thinking at all.' The next training session is really going to hurt, and I mean hurt.*

* * *

James was nursing a scotch after a delicious meal of spicy lamb ribs at a New York City restaurant fifteen minutes from his apartment.

He was certain the taller of the two bar girls wanted him to ask her back to his place. They had been flirting with each other for the last fifteen minutes. His smartphone pinged, retrieving it from his coat pocket, he glanced at the screen.

"Damn," he swore under his breath. He put the drink down with a twenty-dollar note, smiled at the pretty girl behind the bar and headed for the door. Saturday night was over. He voice-dialed Louise Wesson as he reached the street, she immediately picked up.

"We have a hit," James informed her.

"Anton Smith?"

"Yes, he's still in Boston. Got a great face shot on CCTV. He was outside a restaurant in Chinatown," James said, striding down the street toward the parking lot.

"Will we tell the General?" Wesson asked.

"No," James replied, shaking his head once. "We will notify her once we have this contact tied up and presented with a red ribbon. We'll need some good men."

"Johnson and Higgins are both available."

"Get them moving," James commanded, "We'll need to establish a stakeout location. Bring a surveillance van. I will meet you at our Boston R.I.S.C office ASAP. We will coordinate further action from there."

"Yes, Sir, I'm on it," Wesson replied enthusiastically.

"Excellent," James said and hung up. He reached his car on the near edge of the parking lot and got in; moments later he was on his way to Boston.

He vowed to himself. *This time, Anton Smith, you will not escape us.*

* * *

Gang checked his online order book. There was still no booking from a Mr. T. Masters for a table for two, for the duck special with the new special secret sauce. He was beginning to fear for his former master, *Arthur, my old friend. Time is running out.* It had been nearly a month since he'd put up the message. What had happened to his former teacher?

Arthur Slayne had planned for the possibility that he may not be able to respond. Gang remembered the plan clearly. If there was no reply for a month, he was to act as he saw fit. Tomorrow was the fourth of June, a month after he'd first sent the message. He would have to make a decision.

It was obvious Anton belonged in the Order. Gang frowned as he thought through the ramifications of the Order becoming aware of Anton Slayne. There was the business surrounding Anton's grandfather. Arthur stood accused of the murder of the previous leader of the Order of Thoth, George Madison.

Despite circumstantial evidence that made him the only suspect, Gang was certain Arthur was innocent. A young Order lawyer named Samuel Luther had pressed the charges against Arthur, but it had been Ramin Kain who had stepped forward to claim the rulership of the Order. Ramin's candidacy had gone unopposed and he'd been confirmed in the role of Head of the Order at an Order Conclave nearly twenty years ago.

Gang had strong suspicions about Ramin Kain, if those suspicions were well-founded, then Anton's emergence would not be welcome. In any event, the family name of Slayne had become tarnished over the last twenty years, Anton would find much hostility in the Order, and few friends. He would need to handle the return of a Slayne to the Order carefully.

The death of Anna Slayne and the capture of William had come as a shock. Circumstances had forced the activation of Anton's Ramp capability. The process was extremely risky, but fortunately, Anton had survived, and his progress since then had been a phenomenon. After a month, he was already three times faster and stronger than he was when he'd arrived. His fighting skills were excellent and he picked up new skills extremely quickly, his learning vastly enhanced by the physiological changes occurring from the Ramp. However, he was still very emotionally fragile after the trauma of losing his parents. The incident earlier in the restaurant had been a clear example of how his emotions could overwhelm good sense.

Gang determined to spend more time with Anton, to talk things through, and assist him to gain a deep mastery of his feelings.

He remembered another student of Arthur Slayne, Francis Mirovar, force leader for the Order with responsibility for the northeast. They had been friends and sparring partners when they were both students, and Gang had followed his progress with interest after the Slaynes had gone into hiding.

He considered that Francis could have been Head of the Order, and wondered why he hadn't opposed Ramin Kain for the Office. Francis Mirovar had remained neutral while many blamed Arthur for the murder of George Madison. Francis had a strong reputation for a strict code of honor and was one of the best leaders within the Order.

Gang also counted Francis Mirovar a close personal friend before the ascension of Ramin Kain.

Francis was the nearest force leader. He would be the best to contact if they needed to find refuge in the Order. He would need to re-establish contact with Francis to ensure they could find refuge in the event of trouble.

Gang's mind turned to the topic of Mr. Wang and the Hu Shizu. He did not fear for his own life, or even Li's life from direct confrontation with the Tiger Clan, it was the immediate threat to the lives of others that concerned him. The sanctity of innocent life was at the foundation of Order belief. Gang needed to protect the people who worked at the Noodle House or lived nearby from becoming collateral damage in any conflict with the gangsters.

Collateral damage was just a euphemistic lie. It was simply another name for murder. All his regular staff would need a night off next Saturday. He would need a skeleton crew of extra 'helpers.'

Gang sighed. Small stupid issues drove the fight with the Tiger Clan. The real risk was that defeating Mr. Wang's gangsters would draw the attention of Shadowstone and the Vampire Dominion in numbers beyond Li's, Anton's and his ability to defeat.

The conflict with the Hu Shizu had progressed too far for a peaceful resolution. He couldn't simply leave with Li and Anton, if Mr. Wang's desire remained thwarted, his rage would reach past his family and the Noodle House, to the families of the innocent people who worked there. Gang determined that whatever the risk, they would have to stay and fight, and end the days of the Tiger Clan for good.

With Arthur out of the picture, perhaps permanently, and with Anton's parents lost, it was imperative they rejoined the Order as active members.

Gang sighed again; his heart heavy with sadness at the prospect of losing an old friend. He'd accepted Arthur's request to stay in Boston and watch out for the Slayne family. He'd moved here with his wife, and son, and soon after, Li had been born. He'd focused on raising his family, running a successful restaurant and exercising his passion for innovating combat techniques with swords.

He'd kept a low profile in the Order, not seeking promotion or embroiling himself in the constant politics that seemed to come in disruptive waves through the upper ranks of the Order.

Then five years ago his wife and son had died in a car accident. Those were dark days; it was only the presence of Li that had given him the strength to continue with life itself. The randomness of the loss had shaken the foundations of his life, and he'd since devoted his life to ensuring that Li had the skills to look after herself against any opponent, as he could not guarantee that he would always be there for her.

When he considered how powerful his daughter had become, hot tears ran down his cheeks. His sadness over the loss of his wife and son giving way to a father's pride born of deep admiration and love for his daughter.

Gang had invested a lot of his life into the Noodle House, and he could feel his home slipping away. There were so many good memories of his wife and family within its walls, but his family's time there was coming to a close, he was certain of it, it was like watching storm clouds roll in and overtake the sun. Everything will be swept away and swept away soon. He mused sadly, *Time to place fresh flowers on Tatsu's and Qiang's graves, it may be a while before Li and I can visit them again.*

With that thought, Gang logged out of his computer and went back to the restaurant to see how the cleaning up was progressing.

* * *

It had been three days since the original Panopticon hit on Anton Smith.

James Haley, Louise Wesson and their team of two Shadowstone operatives had set up a surveillance site opposite the Noodle House. Their stakeout occupied the top floor of a three-story building. The equipment in the surveillance van had been repositioned into a room facing the street with a panoramic view of the front of the Noodle House and the Wu family residence. The building they were in was vacant, Shadowstone had taken out a one-month lease on it via a front company ensuring no one would disturb them.

Sean Higgins, a short, wiry IT guru hired by Shadowstone from the NSA had wired up telescopic microphones and cameras on the roof top to cover both target buildings.

Gary Johnson, an ex-CIA/NSA operative had placed a tiny, camouflaged, remote camera on the back wall of the Wu property. Due to a pervasive screen of roses, the camera did not give direct access to the back side of the Wu residence, but it provided an infra-red feed of activity in the backyard directly to the stakeout's computers.

James had directed the Panopticon to co-opt all nearby CCTV cameras and had positioned them to provide optimum coverage of the restaurant and the residence. He had his laptop open, and the screen showed a Panopticon satellite feed at a fine grain of detail covering a hundred-yard square centered on the Wu family's backyard. Green markers labeled Anton Smith, Li Wu, and Gang Wu littered the screen. He'd been able to capture the necessary photos of Gang and Li Wu over the last twenty-four hours and had added them to the search parameters for Anton Smith on the principle of tracking the known associates of the target.

He'd quickly determined his targets had a training environment behind the house. The training deck lay shielded from surveillance by a roof over the training area and a high brick wall at the back of the property. He'd also verified the roof across the training area provided effective screening from satellite sensors across the electromagnetic spectrum. The training deck was an information black hole.

James glowered around the room at his team and declared, "We should have a damn policy for identifying information black holes that are fully shielded from satellite observation." After eight years of working with Shadowstone, it looked like he'd finally found genuine Order of Thoth terrorists and the shielded training environment looked like a genuine marker.

It was 19:30 on a Tuesday evening. Gang and Li Wu had closed the restaurant for the night. They had just completed thirty minutes of physical exercise with Anton Slayne and were now training with weapons on the training deck.

"Hey, Boss, take a look at this," Johnson said, sharing his desktop display to the main screens on the side wall of the room. Everyone swiveled and watched as human shaped heat blobs moved across the screen. They would suddenly change position, and there would be flaring heat plumes that would expand and die from each of the three forms.

"What is that?" James asked, perplexed.

Wesson stared at the screen and remarked incredulously, "I've never seen anything like it."

General Armitage had informed him once, that the Order of Thoth and the Red Empire had special training and techniques. This must be what she'd been talking about. James glowered at the screens and stated softly, "God only knows."

"Listen to this," Higgins insisted, putting the sound he'd just heard through his headphones through a speaker. It was a metallic clatter, timed with the heat plumes. It sounded like someone had pulled a drawer full of cutlery out of a cupboard and upended it onto the floor, but not as chaotic as that would sound, more musical, like a metallic drum, with an inherent pattern and order.

"Now hear what it sounds like when I slow it down by a factor of three," Higgins said, and the sound resolved into clear metal on metal clashes.

"They're sparring with swords," Wesson remarked, frowning.

"And they're fast ... real fast," James said. "You've got this on record?"

"Yes, Sir," Higgins and Johnson answered in unison.

"Give me five minutes." James went into a separate room and closed the door. He immediately voice dialed General Armitage's smartphone number.

The phone rang twice before she answered, "James, what do you have for me?"

"We have Anton Smith."

"Good work. What is the situation?"

"He is currently staying with a Chinese/American family in Chinatown, Boston. We have a surveillance team in place at a stakeout opposite the Wu family's restaurant and residential home."

"Anything else?"

"I'm sure they're Order of Thoth. They fit the profile you provided perfectly. We have been able to scan their last training session with infrared cameras and telescopic microphones. They move extremely fast, and are highly skilled with edged weapons."

"Excellent work James. I expect a summary report in fifteen minutes, now your orders are to remain at your station and maintain the surveillance. If they move, track them and keep them under continuous watch. It is imperative that you do not engage them, I will come to your site tomorrow night."

"Ma'am, I could get two full combat teams on site in less than three hours. We could take this cell out tonight."

"My orders stand," Chloe confirmed, a frosty edge to her voice. "I expect you to implement them with your usual efficiency. Is that clear?"

James hesitated for a second, he desperately wanted to close this terrorist cell down – permanently, and with disappointment leaking into his voice, he replied, "Yes, Ma'am, understood."

"James, I understand and appreciate your enthusiasm. But you must be patient, your time will come."

"Yes Ma'am, thank you, Ma'am."

The line went dead, and James went back to the main room.

Wesson lifted an eyebrow as he walked in and asked, "Orders, Sir?"

"Stand watch, track them if they leave."

"Yes, Sir," Wesson replied, focusing back on her monitors.

James poured himself a black coffee from a pot on a table, settled into his chair and began preparing the summary report for the General.

The Shadowstone team recorded another two hours of almost continuous training.

"What's this 'Ramp' they keep talking about?" Higgins asked.

"Some sort of Chinese voodoo?" Johnson said.

"Add it to the list of known unknowns. We'll deal with it later," James directed.

The red blobs on the infra-red monitor disappeared from the training deck.

"Looks like they've hit the showers," Johnson remarked.

"Can we get some Chinese?" Higgins asked.

James sighed and agreed, "Why not? Try and find me some steamed dumplings, just a mix, and some soy sauce, I love that."

Higgins quickly left the room and James leaned back in his chair, reflecting on his conversation with General Armitage. *So, my time will come will it, not soon enough, not soon enough by far.*

* * *

I need to get back to New York and Boston, and Crane needs to ask me to come back.

Chloe gently tapped her fingers on a paper pad as she waited for Haras Mosule to complete his report to Cornelius Crane.

"We have no new captures or kills since the last report," Haras declared in a matter-of-fact tone.

Crane frowned from the wall display and declared acerbically, "After more than a month we have three Red Empire casualties, one dead praetorian, and zero useful information — those are not numbers that impress me — are my generals losing their edge?"

"No, Sir," Haras declared. "The Red Empire are very difficult to find. They would rather die than allow capture. We need more resources or a different strategy. If you were to allow us to create new vampires, we could draw them out."

"Vampire creation is out of the question. You will have no control over those you transform. They could easily run amok and reveal the secret of our existence."

Haras nodded.

"At General Armitage's request, I replaced Praetorian Dench with Marcus Drake, a member of her own staff rather than another praetorian. I will now provide another two praetorians and an extra team of Shadowstone operatives. They will come from our Shadowstone force in England. They will all be in Jerusalem by the tenth of June."

"With all due respect Sir, the Shadowstone operatives are not much help. In fact, since we arrived, three operatives have simply disappeared without trace." Haras reported.

"What!" Crane growled. "In future, include the losses of Shadowstone operatives in the main report. Is that clear?"

Haras blinked. "Yes, Sir."

Crane smiled without humor as he stared at each of them in turn. "Now something you must all understand, the six Shadowstone operatives I will send you are all participating in an enhancement program of my own design. They're not yet the match of an Order of Thoth operative or Red Empire assassin, but they're certainly faster and stronger than a normal human. They will provide an essential daylight capability that will assist you to meet your mission objectives."

A program Chloe believed would end in tears. She was certain vampires should never try to enhance humans with capabilities that could one day match their own.

Haras nodded and replied, "Thank you, Sir."

"Now General Armitage, your report."

"Yes, Sir. There is nothing substantive to add to General Mosule's report on the Jerusalem situation. However, just over thirty minutes ago, I received information from a Shadowstone team in Boston. They have an active Order of Thoth cell under direct surveillance; the Wu family."

Crane paused for a long moment.

He knows about them! What does that mean?

"How many Order operatives?" Crane inquired.

How many is he expecting? Has he discovered Anton Slayne? He can independently read the Shadowstone reports – I must tell the truth. "Three Sir."

"Normally this would be within your remit, but with you allocated to your current mission, I am shorthanded for generals."

"We could send Marcus back to deal with the Wu family."

Crane shook his head. "No, Marcus has no rank within the Praetorian organization. They will not obey him and you are both needed in Jerusalem. I think that I will need to deal with this local issue personally."

She couldn't let that happen. He would discover Anton Slayne. "Sir, if I may suggest, there is an extraordinary opportunity here that has not yet been discussed."

Crane raised an eyebrow. "Yes?"

"The Mirovar team. Recent Shadowstone reports indicate they remain active in the northeast and it appears they've recently moved from a safe house in Rhode Island to another location. We could use this Boston cell to draw the Mirovar team out into the open and then crush them all at the same time."

"And how do you propose to do that? To – as you say – draw them out?"

Chloe let Crane's skepticism pass her by. "By causing these Thoth operatives in Boston to run, and to call for help. Then we find the Mirovar team's new safe house and destroy them all. They're the key operational force located in the vicinity of your citadel, and the only group that could potentially launch an attack that could threaten you."

Crane sniffed. "I think you're overestimating their capabilities versus the defensive systems of my citadel. There is also no evidence they even know the location of my citadel."

"Be that as it may, there is still a significant risk to your safety. I could return to the United States and be in Boston before sunrise. The operation to draw out the Mirovar team would take less than a week. Once I have completed the task, I will return here. I will be gone for less than a week."

"One week?"

"One week," Chloe promised.

Crane grinned wolfishly. "So be it. You will return to Boston immediately. Drake will remain in your place until your return. Drake, you're seconded to General Mosule until General Armitage returns."

"Yes, Sir," Drake agreed.

Crane stared directly at Chloe and declared, "General Armitage, I will hold you to your word – I expect the heads of the Mirovar cell on a platter within a week."

"Yes, Sir. Certainly, Sir."

The meeting turned to other operational topics which engaged Marcus Drake, Washington Jones, and Haras Mosule. Chloe gave her respects and left the room. She departed to the adjoining Shadowstone airfield where a hypersonic shadowstar drone was waiting for her. Half an hour later, she was flying at 82,000 feet with the digital windows open, she normally enjoyed the near space view of the Earth curving beneath her, but not on this flight.

That was close. She tapped the end of her armrest with her finger. Now she had to work out how to draw out the Mirovar team in a week. Francis Mirovar was a very slippery fish – just how was she going to do it? It was not often that Chloe felt rushed by shifting circumstances, she did not like it, not one bit. *Why did I make that promise? ... There was no other way. I will have to adapt, and adapt quickly.*

Chloe spent the rest of the flight reconsidering and adapting her plans.

Chapter Four

BODY

SHADOWSTONE INFORMATION REPORT, NOT FINALLY
EVALUATED INTELLIGENCE

COUNTRY: (U) UNITED STATES (USA)

THE GENERAL SITUATION:

A. THE OPERATIONAL TEMPO OF TERRORIST
ORGANIZATIONS WITH A REVOLUTIONARY AGENDA HAS
BEEN STABLE SINCE THE LAST REPORT.

B. THE ORDER OF THOTH IS THE PRIMARY TERRORIST
ORGANIZATION OPERATING WITHIN THE UNITED STATES.
THE RED EMPIRE HAS NO IDENTIFIED OPERATIONS WITHIN
THE UNITED STATES.

C. IN THE FIRST QUARTER OF THIS YEAR, ABANDONED SAFE
HOUSES HAVE BEEN IDENTIFIED AT GRAY MOUNTAIN
COCONINO COUNTY, ARIZONA, AND AT NARRAGANSETT
RHODE ISLAND.

(... REDACTED IMAGES ...)

D. ANALYSIS OF EVENTS INDICATE AT LEAST FOUR
OPERATIONAL ORDER OF THOTH CELLS WITHIN THE
UNITED STATES.

~~TOP SECRET/FGEO~~
RQ
#5390

NNNN
CLASSIFICATION: ~~TOP SECRET~~, SECRET

— Content from a partially declassified preliminary Shadowstone
information report.

* * *

Boston, June 10th, 07:00

Bright sunlight splashed off the iron roofs of the outdoor farmers' market.

Anton pushed a shopping trolley along one of many market aisles. On both sides were arrays of fresh produce; Li selected and purchased items, crossing them off a list as Anton placed them into the trolley.

Gang had given Li and Anton the list earlier that morning and asked them to go to the market for supplies to cover the family's needs for the week. Normally, they would buy all the food in bulk and have it delivered fresh to the Noodle House for the weekend trade, but not today, as the restaurant was not taking bookings for the weekend.

Gang had emphasized the need to ensure there was no one around if the Tiger Clan showed up in force. From the way he'd spoken, he clearly believed there would be a confrontation tonight.

Anton did not feel any concern for what might happen. The sun was shining, the sky was blue, and Li smiled as she handed him a bag of apples. He wore a new gray hooded sleeveless top, his peaked cap and sunglasses. His garments matched the warmth of the day and kept his face away from prying cameras.

It was peaceful and pleasant; he was enjoying being with Li without her constantly hitting him. The training sessions all week had been especially tough, his bare arms revealing bruises, scrapes and a sutured cut where Li had allowed her sword strike to make contact. More bruises lay hidden beneath his clothes.

They had shifted from the hardwood Bokken to metal swords five days earlier. Initially, Anton had been deeply worried he might accidentally hurt Li. By the end of the first day with the katanas, he realized there was no chance he would make contact with her as she was always a step ahead of him.

Anton and Li were nearing the end of the aisle. The list was nearly complete, with the trolley filled with all manner of fresh fruits and vegetables.

Suddenly, Li jumped backward. Something big and hard hit him from behind his left shoulder, throwing him into a display of cabbages. The trolley went flying, tipping over onto its side, spilling everything they had bought onto the concrete floor.

Rebounding back to his feet, Anton stood next to Li. The stall holders were screaming at him in angry Chinese. He ignored them. Six of the gangsters from the previous Saturday night surrounded Li and himself.

Li whispered urgently, "Don't kill anyone, we need to get away from here."

Directly in front of Anton was Sleazy, the one who had insulted Li. The gangster flipped open a pair of butterfly knives, one in each hand, and lunged at Anton. Anton ramped, turning outside the lunge, and trapping Sleazy's right wrist. With a quick twist, he snapped the bones and Sleazy screamed, slashing wildly at Anton with his other hand. Stepping back from the gleaming knife blade, Anton dodged aside as the rest of the gangsters attacked.

Two of the gangsters went after Li, solely armed with wet cloths. The image of Marcus Drake and a drugged cloth rushed through Anton. This was another snatch and grab. They'd doped the cloths.

The Ramp faded and Anton slowed down. Instantly running out of space, blades came toward him from all directions. It was impossible to see and dodge everything slashing toward him.

Spontaneously ramping, Anton trapped a stabbing arm, dragging the gangster forward, and driving the knife he was holding into the lunging arm of one of the other gangsters. Using the first man's body as a pivot, he leaped over him, collecting another gangster in the face with his knee as he went over the top of the ring of men around him.

Now behind the gangster, he kicked out the man's left knee, pushing him hard back into the melee where he toppled over one of the other men dragging them both to the floor. The man with the broken knee began rolling on the ground clutching his shattered joint and groaning with agony, while another gangster dragged a bloody knife from his forearm.

To his left, he heard a guttural scream. Li was standing, poised and taut, a yard in front of the looming form of Fats. Another gangster rolled on the ground a yard behind her, his right elbow bent backward at an extreme and unnatural angle.

Anton didn't have time to watch Li defend herself from Fats. The other three gangsters had regrouped and were charging toward him. Sleazy, his right arm cradled low, lunged with the butterfly knife in his left hand. Anton blocked the lunge with his right hand and drove in hard with his left hand, his fingers extended like a knife penetrated deep into the man's diaphragm. With a great whoosh of air, he folded forward over Anton's hand, before falling away to the side. One of the other two gangsters slashed at Anton as he twisted away, catching his arm, a line of blood appearing on the outside of his bicep.

Anton grimaced, and the grinning gangster who had cut him slashed again, but before his blade could land, Anton punched him straight in the face. His nose imploded, splattering across his cheeks, he fell backward, unconscious before he hit the floor.

The last gangster, his nose already bloody after collecting Anton's knee, lifted a thick bladed chopper. He swung it overhand directly at the top of Anton's head. Ramping again, Anton stepped underneath the strike, trapping his assailant's arm and pushing forward while ducking beneath the gangster's armpit. Twisting and turning, he ended up behind the gangster with the chopper released and now in his own right hand. The man followed the arc of his arm, falling to his knees in front of Anton.

His eyes widened in helpless terror as he stared into Anton's furious face. Anton's arm snapped down, the blade following like a shining stone.

Li's foot flashed in front of him, kicking the chopper from his hand. She dragged him away from the kneeling man. He resisted for a moment, then released the terrified man and went with her.

"Come quickly," Li ordered.

Ignoring their produce on the ground, and a circle of unconscious, moaning, and sobbing gangsters, they vanished into the market crowd.

* * *

The morning sunlight streamed between the tree branches and dappled the grass beneath with patches of golden light.

Anton, Li, and Gang sat at an outdoor wicker table, where Gang had supplied a generous breakfast of Congee, boiled eggs, toast, butter, homemade strawberry jam, a selection of cut fruit, glasses of freshly squeezed orange juice, a pot of strong black tea and a jug of fresh milk.

Gang declared, "Eat first, fill your bellies, drink some tea, and then we will discuss important matters. Starting with what happened at the market an hour ago."

The three of them ate quietly for about five minutes, Gang poured three mugs of steaming tea, and followed with a dash of milk to each mug. Gang sipped his tea and said with a flourish of his right hand, "This tea is excellent. Its flavors are strong, decisive and authentic. Just like the conversation we will now have." He looked at Anton and asked, "Would you like to tell us what happened this morning?"

Taking a deep breath, Anton reflexively felt the fresh dressing over the cut on his arm. Li had sutured it ten minutes ago. He expected Gang would grill him about the brawl in the market, and was sure he deserved it. "I know Li will have spoken with you," he stated contritely. "And that's okay. We got into a brawl with the Tiger Clan, they jumped us with knives. A pair of them also carried wet hand towels which they must've doped with something. They were obviously after Li. Their boss clearly wants her and he doesn't care who he hurts as long as he can have her."

Gang nodded.

Anton paused, wrestling with turbulent emotions stirred up by the recent violence.

Gang waited patiently, sipping his tea. Li sat quietly, her tea untouched and cooling in front of her.

105

Anton looked at Gang, finding no judgment in his eyes, only a compassionate interest in his welfare.

Gang inquired softly, "Li's safety is important, but that wasn't the real issue today was it, Anton?"

Anton sighed and admitted, "I wanted to kill him."

Gang studied him and advised, "Anton, it is good you struggle with the acquisition of power. I would be concerned if you were not facing these issues."

"I really wanted to kill him, and I would have enjoyed it," Anton confessed. "I love the training," he grinned sheepishly at Li, "even though it hurts. I love the Ramp, and what's happening to me, the increase in power across the board. I love it all, and I want it all."

"It's good to be stronger and faster. But you must remember the average human being, even misguided ones like the Tiger Clan, are not the enemy."

Anton nodded.

"The average vampire, and I mean the average vampire is three times stronger than you are now. Some of them, like Marcus Drake, are substantially stronger than that. They're also faster, and Chloe Armitage is twice as fast as you are now. In combat, they will either push past your blade and hit you, or hit you before you can defend yourself."

Gang frowned and inquired, "Did you maintain good personal security this morning? Didn't lose your hood, hat or sunglasses?"

"Yes, Gang. Everything stayed put."

"Good work. We have to keep ourselves secret from Shadowstone and the Vampire Dominion. I must emphasize this point – it is essential we remain hidden. If we're discovered by our enemies, then we are most likely doomed."

Gang paused, sipping his tea, allowing Anton to absorb the point he'd made, then said, "It's important we don't reveal our skills in public. There are—"

"Father, they were trying to kill him," Li interrupted. "And kidnap me."

"Be that as it may, you can't be ramping in full daylight, and probably in front of a CCTV camera."

"We were quite restrained," Li argued. "In fact, anyone watching would simply see a pair of skilled Kung Fu experts defeat a gang of thugs in a Chinatown market – it's a cliché."

"Except there are six gangsters in Tufts Medical or Massachusetts General emergency rooms by now. And what's on the news? How long before a video shows up on YouTube? Shadowstone are explicitly looking for incidents just like this – and they will not see Kung Fu experts – they will see Order of Thoth operatives."

"Shadowstone?" Anton queried.

"Yes. Shadowstone," Gang said in clipped tones. "They're a very-well funded, well organized, para-military international spy organization owned and operated by the vampires, but staffed by humans. They have a mass surveillance system with artificial intelligence features called the Panopticon. They're always watching for us. It's why we must remain well hidden. ... unlike this morning."

Aha! Shadowstone are the secret keepers, snapped through Anton's mind. He was surprised by the core of tension within Gang, he'd never seen him the least bit agitated. There was a lot more going on here than he'd understood. Gang was worried about something and if Gang was worried, then Anton should be worried to. There was something bigger going on and he wanted to make sure Gang knew he would do whatever he could to help. He said, "Gang, the only reason I'm still alive is because Li and you gave me refuge. What do you need from me?"

Gang rubbed his face with both hands, then said, "Anton, this is not your fault. You've been with us for what, five weeks, perhaps a little more than that, and I know I've charged Li with beating you into shape, and she's done a great job. But you're still very early in your training, there is much you still have to learn. I have been remiss, there are things you must know before we go any further."

Anton nodded; he was all ears this morning.

"I have been trying to contact your grandfather since the day after you arrived, but I have not heard from him. Which while accounted for in your grandfather's plans, is unexpected. He may be in serious trouble."

Li rubbed her temple as if she was getting a headache.

"Is there anything we know for sure?" Anton asked.

"No. Just that he hasn't responded. It's possible he is simply in a location where he has no Internet access."

Anton looked intently at Gang, a question burning within him. *What kept my grandfather from protecting his family?* He put the question aside and asked, "Can you tell me about him? I barely remember him."

"Arthur Slayne was a prominent force leader and the obvious succession plan to George Madison, our previous head of the Order of Thoth. He—"

Anton held up his hands and asked, "I'm sorry Gang, ah, what's a force leader?"

"I will try to explain terms as I go, you will have a new vocabulary by the end of the morning. A force leader commands a team of operatives, they have total authority over their teams, and how they operate. The Head of the Order typically comes from the ranks of the force leaders, many of your ancestors have been force leaders, and quite a few have been Head of the Order."

"If a force leader has total authority over operations, what does the Head of the Order do?"

"Set policy, coordinate actions, settle internal disputes and guard the integrity and secrecy of the order. The Head cannot order a force leader to any action, but must rely on persuasion and soft methods of negotiation. The role of Head of the Order is intensely political."

"What about the third rule, operational obedience?"

"Doesn't apply to force leaders and the Head of the Order," Gang frowned. "And that's something I'm sure Ramin Kain wants to change. He'd love direct control of operations."

"Who is he?" Anton asked.

"The man who succeeded George Madison as the Head of the Order, and he's a particularly slimy political animal. You're familiar with the term 'Cui Bono'?"

"Literally 'to whose benefit?'."

Gang nodded. "Ramin Kain was the principal person to benefit from the murder of George Madison and the subsequent conviction in absentia of Arthur Slayne for the crime – by replacing Madison as Head of the Order and removing his main rival."

"What happened?"

"Officially, Arthur Slayne murdered George Madison and Mary Creeley in their sleep. Not that I believed it for a second. Arthur is no murderer; he had no motive and he was on good terms with Madison."

"How was he convicted, what was the evidence?"

"There was no evidence, there were only lies."

Anton pushed his hand back through his hair, perplexed. "How does that happen?"

"There was a coup d'état."

"What the hell? The Order is at war with the Vampire Dominion, and there is a coup d'état? Factions versus factions? You would think that people might just focus on the main game – on killing vampires."

"The Order is very high-minded. Order members either originated or advanced many of the core inventions within human history, such as agriculture, writing, mathematics and science. But there are always people who can hide the darkness within, blend in, and wear a mask in public that hides their own selfish interests. There is a cabal, centered on two men, Samuel Luther, and Ramin Kain. The Kain/Luther cabal is currently in power within the Order."

"So, Samuel Luther and Ramin Kain framed my grandfather for murder?"

"Yes. I believe so, but I can't prove it."

"So, there is no legitimate authority within the Order?"

"Only the appearance of it. Anton, please do not underestimate these men, they're in a powerful position. There are many in the Order who will follow their lead and who will defend their lives because of their own loyalty to the Order itself."

Anton frowned. "So how goes the war against the vampires with this cabal in charge?"

Li snorted. "Quietly."

"Li has it right. Since the rise of Ramin Kain, there have been no vampires of any significance killed by Order operations – especially within the northeast."

"There have been many young vampires killed, freshly turned, less than a year old," Li said.

Gang nodded. "Ramin Kain has established a reputation for finding new vampires. He claims he has a special intuitive capability, a power to 'sniff out young vampires.'"

Li touched Anton's hand and leaned toward him. "We think the new vampires are being deliberately created and then thrown to the Order for killing."

"Cui Bono," Anton said.

"Cui Bono indeed," Gang agreed. "The current regimes in both the Order and the Vampire Dominion benefit – there is a secret detente."

Li said, "Strategically, Crane gets a quiet flank while he directs his efforts at the Red Empire. Kain gets to look like a hero of the Order, and secures his own position against challengers."

"Hang on a moment, who are the Red Empire?"

Li shook her head once, and stated forcefully, "Zealots!"

"Another faction," Gang stated matter-of-factly. "The Red Empire broke away from the Order more than two millennia ago."

Li instructed Anton. "They're much larger than the Order and just as happy to kill Order members as vampires."

Gang said, "The key difference is the Red Empire has no problem killing the innocent in the pursuit of killing vampires."

Anton asked, "There is no unity amongst those who can fight the vampires?"

"None whatsoever," Gang answered.

"No wonder the vampires are so dominant," Anton said. Taking a deep breath, he let it out slowly. "So, while all this has been going on, what has my grandfather been doing?"

"Operating independently and fighting the good fight," Gang declared. "He focuses his efforts directly on Cornelius Crane. Crane has multiple labs and research centers around the world. We don't know what his aims are, but they're surely not good for humanity. Arthur seeks to find out what the vampire king is doing, and thwart his plans."

"What about now?"

"The last I heard; he is operating in Brazil."

"On the night my family was attacked by Armitage and Drake, she showed me photographs of my grandfather in Rio during the Carnival earlier this year."

Gang pursed his lips. "It's concerning that Armitage managed to have recent photographs of Arthur."

"She used them to prove my grandfather is still alive."

Gang stroked his chin, leaning back in his chair. "This throws fresh light on something that has been troubling me. As I said earlier, I have attempted to contact your grandfather and he has not replied. Clearly Armitage also knows he is in Brazil and at least one of her operatives got close enough to take photos. I now fear the vampires may have captured or killed him."

"Dead?"

"With Arthur Slayne, I wouldn't assume he was dead unless I had seen his cold corpse with my own eyes, but yes, we must consider the possibility."

Well, that would explain his absence – if he is dead. Anton mused to himself and then asked, "He was carrying a long slim black case in the Rio photos, was that a sword?"

Gang nodded. "The Black Dragon, his personal weapon. There is a story behind that sword which must wait for another day."

"What would happen if the Order were to catch up with my grandfather?"

"Probably a blood bath," Li said drily.

Gang glanced at his daughter, and then turned back to Anton and said, "The Order convicted him of a capital crime. There is no court of appeal. There is a standing kill order on him from Ramin Kain."

"Is the Order actively looking for him?"

"No force leader that I know of is trying to catch him. If they happen to stumble across him – who knows? He has a powerful reputation, he's not liked, or admired, but his skills are respected and, in some cases, feared."

"Feared?" Anton asked. The thought that people would be afraid of his grandfather seemed odd to him.

"He is extraordinarily capable in combat," Gang stated. "He was my master, and I would fear to fight him. He fought both Crane and Armitage at the same time, back in '78 in a secret vault beneath St Peter's Basilica in the Vatican – and he survived. I know no one else who could have done that."

"That's more than forty years ago, how old is my grandfather?"

"Over seventy."

"He's ripped for his age. He doesn't look seventy, more like a very fit forty to forty-five-year-old man. How does he do it?"

"A side effect of the Ramp, it slows the aging process, not like a vampire of course, but you stay fit and healthy for much longer than normal."

Li arched an eyebrow at Anton and said, "First you have to survive if you are going to get a chance to live that long."

"Speaking of survival, what about the Tiger Clan, you're expecting them tonight aren't you?" Anton asked.

"Yes. They're sure to attack and in numbers. We've wounded their honor. They will learn from this morning's brawl that we're tougher than they thought. However, that will not deter them. They're mean spirited, but not lacking in courage." Gang smiled wickedly. "I have made some inquiries, there is a fellow that owes me a favor, who is no friend of the Hu Shizu. We will have some help, of a sort, later tonight."

"Is there anything I need to do?"

Gang frowned, and ordered, "Pack your backpack. Be ready to travel on a moment's notice, and get some rest."

The tension within Gang that Anton had sensed earlier had returned.

"Tomorrow we must say goodbye to the Noodle House," Gang declared. "It probably will not survive tonight."

"Even with the helpers?"

"Even so," Gang declared. He smiled wanly and sighed. "All things must pass, even this home."

Li put her hand to her mouth, got up silently and walked away.

"This is the only home she has known," Gang said. "It is worse for her."

"Can I help?"

"Give her space. And tonight – be ready for anything."

"Yes, Gang."

Anton helped Gang clear the breakfast dishes and then returned to the garden where he laid down on a patch of sun-dappled grass, reflecting quietly on what Gang had told him. *Perhaps my grandfather is dead, or got a raw deal, but still – where was he that was so important that he couldn't protect his family?*

* * *

General Chloe Armitage sat across from James Haley in a secured room at the surveillance site opposite the Noodle House.

She listened to the recording of the conversation Gang and Li Wu and Anton Slayne had in the backyard over breakfast. She accelerated the playback on the machine to five times faster than normal. The conversation streamed through her headphones and she accelerated her mind to match the machine. In three minutes, she'd memorized everything in the recorded conversation. It was quite the treasure trove. Chloe asked James, "Have these recordings been backed up yet?"

"They're already on the Panopticon storage farm," he replied.

"Set the security level to FGEO – Personal Stamp – CA."

"Once I set security to 'For General's Eyes Only,' I won't be able to retrieve them again."

"Precisely."

James nodded. "Yes, Ma'am."

"Who else knows of this?"

There was a noticeable rise in James' heart rate directly after she asked the question, and he hesitated for a moment before responding, "Only myself, the rest were at breakfast, I didn't mention it."

Chloe smiled, "Excellent."

"Orders, Ma'am?"

That was a good question. What orders should she give him after his exposure to so much secret information? How much should she tell him? He wasn't supposed to know any of this. He was a Shadowstone operative. He was part of an organization built to protect a secret it was never meant to understand. There would always be 'situations' where one or more operatives would find out more than they should know. The praetorians typically culled them from Shadowstone – permanently. On rare occasions, on the back of great merit, the Vampire Dominion would induct them into the ranks of the vampires and disappear them to a far-flung region of the world until those who might recognize them had passed away from natural causes.

The answer was clear. Just enough to lead him to act as she required. Chloe stared at James for a long moment and ordered firmly, "Forget what you have heard today."

James nodded. "Yes, Ma'am. It's obviously nonsense – they believe in vampires."

"Indeed, obvious nonsense," Chloe agreed with a slight smile. "Be prepared to track the Wu family when they depart tomorrow – do not lose contact with them – that is all."

"Yes, Ma'am," James replied. He rose and left the room, closing the door behind him.

Gang Wu suspected that Ramin Kain was in league with the Vampire Dominion. Chloe considered Wu could well be right. However, there was only one vampire who could get away with such an arrangement – Cornelius Crane. Li Wu had made an error in thinking that such an arrangement was about allowing Crane to focus on the Red Empire. No, while that was a useful side effect, the main goal was to allow Crane to focus on the acquisition of the three Metaframe artifacts.

Her mind flashed through the most important question. Was Arthur Slayne, Brazil, and Crane's super soldier program linked? She vowed to find out the facts. Chloe paused, reviewing her immediate plans. She needed to draw the Mirovar team into the open with the Wu family and Anton as bait and take some heads. She needed to get Crane to focus resources back into the northeast and not send her back to Jerusalem. She would need a credible threat to make him do that – something she didn't yet have.

The details of Chloe's new plan had not yet jelled together. She felt a stab of annoyance at the promise she'd made back in Jerusalem. A promise she was running out of time to keep. She sighed once, stood up and walked into the operations room. James and Louise Wesson were observing monitors, the other two, Johnson and Higgins sat at their stations managing their equipment.

Chloe addressed the room, "Report."

"Yes, Ma'am," Wesson replied. "We have something unusual."

"Yes?" Chloe asked.

"Four vans have arrived," she said, "parking further down the street than they needed too. They're all registered with a local pet food company. There were twelve men in them, no women, they've all gone into the Noodle House. There are no other patrons yet, so they either have a single booking or something else is about to happen."

Chloe smiled briefly, making an instant intuitive assessment. Ms. Louise Wesson was smart and useful. She would keep an eye on her progress within Shadowstone. There were always opportunities for people with talent.

"Thank you, continue to observe and monitor the site. No matter what you see tonight, do not take any action without further orders from myself. Is that clear?"

"Yes, Ma'am," James and Louise both answered.

Johnson and Higgins also gave their assent.

Chloe left the operations room, and ascended a set of stairs to the roof. The sky was cloudless, the night cool, a full moon had cleared the horizon in the east. She stretched her arms up, arching her back, luxuriating in the experience of complete power and freedom that nightfall had brought.

The conditions were perfect for hunting. The roof of the building was flat, surrounded by a five-foot high parapet. Chloe leaped up on top of the parapet. Standing tall, her hands on her hips, she extended her senses to their maximum capabilities, and focused her attention on the building opposite. Sensing human heat signatures through the walls, she counted twelve and three. The new arrivals, Li and Gang Wu, and Anton Slayne. Anton covered the rear, the other two stood back from the kill zone before the main entrance. She listened carefully to the quiet murmur of conversations from the men in the Noodle House. *Ms. Wesson is correct. No one has ordered any food, these men are waiting, I can almost smell the anticipation from here. There will be a battle tonight.*

With a predator's patience, she settled in to wait and see what would happen.

* * *

Li held her katana sword within its scabbard at her left hip.

Her mother's ancestor, Kanenaga Yoshindo, had crafted the Green Dragon in Japan during the winter of 1675. A marble sized emerald gracing the end of its handle distinguished it from its four siblings.

The front door of the Noodle House swung open. The men of the Hu Shizu, the Tiger Clan, filed into the restaurant, immediately spreading out across the front wall. They stood, variously grinning or impassive, armed to the teeth with submachine guns, 9mm handguns, knives, short swords, hand axes, and baseball bats embossed with hard strips of gray metal. In their midst swaggered the large form of Mr. Wang. Apparently unarmed, he puffed on a thin cigar wedged between his thick lips.

"Out," Mr. Wang shouted to the men at the tables.

Gang's helpers rushed out the front door and into the street.

Li glanced at her father and thought, *that's convenient, after all, they're not here for the fight.*

Her father grinned, winking at her, then frowned and whispered, "MAC-10s, .45 or 9mm, very high rate of fire and a tendency to pull high."

There would be a lot of bullets coming their way. As the last of the helpers disappeared out the front door, it swung shut behind them. Li and Gang stood side by side at the back of the restaurant. They both let their scabbards fall to the floor, lifting their swords into attack positions above their shoulders – ready for action. The more than three hundred and forty-year-old blades gleamed in the soft light of the restaurant's lanterns, their shape and edges the very measure of perfection.

"You bring a knife to a gun fight?" Mr. Wang declared derisively.

Li promised fiercely, "When your souls enter the afterlife, you will be able to tell those you meet there that your passage was provided by the White and Green Dragons."

Mr. Wang pulled out his cigar and laughed, long and loud.

Li's eyes tightened and her lips pressed into a thin line. The Green Dragon resting in lethal stillness above her left shoulder.

The sound of glass breaking shattered the tense quiet. The gangsters had breached the back door. Anton's party was about to start. Mr. Wang abruptly stopped laughing and shouted, "Cut them down!"

Li and Gang ramped to their maximum ability.

Mr. Wang's men laughed or snarled. Their short, snub-nosed submachine guns erupted in blooms of gray smoke as streams of .45 rounds ripped through the restaurant.

Li and Gang had stood as close to each other as they could before they moved. They'd provided a single target to the Tiger Clan, and every man had aimed his gun at the same location.

Where they no longer were.

Li's mind raced, she could see the rapid puffs of smoke erupting from the barrels of the short submachine guns as each round went off. The spent brass casings were flying everywhere. The gangsters were close enough together that the gun smoke and casings were obscuring the view in front of them.

To her right, her father had already covered half the distance between the kitchen and the first of the gangsters at the far edge of the group. He was moving from table to table, his feet barely touching the surface as he flew through the room. The White Dragon held in both hands, high above his head. The gangsters reflexively started to track the moving targets in front of them, swinging their guns around.

The gangsters stared as Gang and Li moved a yard or so in front of their streams of fire. Panicked fingers pressed hard against triggers as they tried to bring their submachine guns to bear. The MAC-10 carried up to thirty rounds in a magazine. At best, it could fire a thousand rounds per minute. They would run out of ammunition in two seconds.

Li reached the wall next to a gangster, slashing the Green Dragon through his neck as she took three steps along the wall to curve in behind him and put herself in the middle of four other men.

The man's head rolled off his shoulders, his blood fountaining into the air. He slumped forward to the floor, his submachine gun continuing to fire aimlessly, clutched tightly in his dead hand.

Beyond the men surrounding her, she could see her father's sword was already red with blood as he pushed into the far side of the gangsters. At the back of the restaurant, lights flashed as gunfire erupted in the kitchen, and ricochets rang like bells off dangling pots.

The men beside her dragged their guns around as they pivoted toward her. For one of the men, it was impossible to move quickly enough as Li brought the Green Dragon down through a diagonal slash, cutting him from shoulder to hip. His suit splashed red in an instant, he started to fall away a look of shocked amazement frozen on his face.

Before he hit the ground, Li leaped vertically upward as the remaining three men opened fire. The remaining rounds in the guns opposite them cut two of the men to ribbons. The fourth man's gun ran dry, he reached for a 9mm handgun as Li landed and ran him through. He fell backward squealing as Li drew the Green Dragon clear of his gut.

The guns in the restaurant fell silent, their magazines running out of bullets. Through the gray smoke, Li veered to the right to avoid a thrown knife and assessed the situation with a glance. There had been fourteen gangsters to start with. Now reduced by five on her side, and another six on her father's side. Leaving three left, including Mr. Wang.

The knife thrower was nearest. She ran past him toward Mr. Wang, slashing the Green Dragon across his belly, disemboweling him. He had a fresh cast on his right arm, it was the gangster she'd nicknamed Sleazy. *Karma's a bitch.*

Li arrived in front of Mr. Wang. His face twisted with hate and rage, he pulled the pin on a fragmentation grenade and started to push it toward her. Li shouted a warning, "Father!"

She reversed her sword. Striking Mr. Wang hard across the face with her left fist. His knees buckled, the grenade falling at his feet. Li used her forward momentum to swing past the crime lord, landing next to her father. They both leaped behind a thick dining table, overturning it to make a shield.

Behind them, they could hear Mr. Wang groping near his knees for the grenade. He shouted, "Damn—"

The grenade detonated.

As the dust settled from the explosion, silence descended within the Noodle House.

Li checked her father, "Are you okay?"

Gang declared with a broad grin, "Never better – he definitely had that coming."

She looked to the kitchen. *Is Anton, okay?*

* * *

Mr. Wang screamed, "Out."

Anton readied himself as best he could. Gang had given him a katana sword. Anton had made great strides toward mastery of such a weapon but it seemed unwieldy and clumsy given a general lack of space within the kitchen. He put the big blade down, picking up a pair of thick bladed foot long carving knives from a nearby rack. They felt balanced and lethal in his hands. There was more conversation from the restaurant and he resisted the urge to get closer to Li and Gang. What if they needed his help? What if Li needed his help? But no, his job was here, to guard their backs.

Mr. Wang laugh loudly from the front of the restaurant.

The glass in the back door shattered, and someone shouted a harsh command from the front of the restaurant.

The back door burst apart. Six gangsters armed with submachine guns, knives, and baseball bats streamed into the kitchen, while gunfire erupted in the restaurant.

Anton ramped as the gangsters in front of him swung their MAC-10 submachine guns up and fired directly at him. He pivoted away from the guns. Rolling across the kitchen table top as bullets whipped past his head, slamming into the heavy fridge doors at the end of the kitchen. Dangling pots and pans above the table rang out as bullets plowed into them and wild ricochets flew everywhere.

Anton rolled off the table. The gangsters broke into two groups, streaming around the table. Two ran directly toward him, their guns blazing. He ducked, and rolled underneath the table. Crouching into a tight squat, he pushed up and sideways with his shoulder. The heavy metal table rose up, flipping over and smashing two of the gangsters into the floor; leaving Anton exposed to the remaining four gangsters, one of whom was the looming *Fats.*

The gangsters still standing, dragged their guns around to aim directly at him from point blank range. The nearest two held their weapons less than two feet from where he stood. He could see their fingers beginning to squeeze down hard on the triggers.

One dreadful thought raced through his mind. *I'm going to die.*

He spontaneously ramped to a level he'd never experienced before, time slowing to a crawl. Anton felt a singular sense of calm and clarity of purpose. He dropped his knives. Leaning toward the two gangsters, he flipped his hands up, catching their wrists and pushing their gun hands high as he surged between them. The bones in their wrists broke, unable to survive the sudden acceleration. Their submachine guns fired, the bullets streaming wildly into the ceiling as gray gun smoke billowed around his head. His forward momentum carried both men with him, placing the man on his right in between himself, and *Fats* and the last gangster near the back door. The man on his right shuddered as bullets intended for Anton filled his body.

Whirling in a circle, Anton dragged the man on his left into the line of fire. He collapsed, the other gangsters blowing his life away with their submachine guns. He used the dying man as a step ladder to leap high above them all before descending in front of the last two men.

The smaller one dropped his empty MAC-10, lunging with a long-bladed knife in his left hand. Anton trapped his wrist and kept moving forward. The man began to scream as his arm fractured. Anton laughed out loud and pivoted, his right foot lashing into *Fats*, catching him just below the ribcage. The big man folded around his boot, before flying through the back door and into the alleyway.

Anton half turned as he came to a halt. The last gangster's arm lay twisted at an unnatural angle. Anton struck the shrieking man at the base of his skull with an open hand, crushing his spine and sending him into oblivion.

A rush of euphoria exploded through him. *I survived, but what sort of wild Ramp was that?* He looked around, searching for threats. The other two gangsters, hit and half crushed by the table, were out cold and possibly dead. Anton turned, stepped into the back doorway and searched for *Fats*. He lay deathly still a dozen feet away in the middle of the alley. Blood streamed from his mouth and nose, forming a pool around his head.

A blast cracked like a whip inside the Noodle House. "Li!? Gang!?" Anton shouted. He rushed into the main restaurant, the euphoria he'd felt a moment ago, blown away like a leaf on the wind.

They met in the middle of the restaurant. Li silently looked him up and down. Gang grinned at him. Anton, grabbed them by the shoulders and asked urgently, "Are you both okay?"

Li replied, "Sure, and you?"

Anton nodded, "I'm good."

Gang asked, "Is the kitchen clear?"

"I think so but there are two who could still be alive."

"Let's check," Gang directed.

They all moved back to the kitchen and Gang and Li examined the men that Anton had slammed with the table. Gang nodded and stood up. Li rose up next to the other body and declared, "This one is dead."

"Looks like you got all the ones who came through here, well done," Gang said.

"What now?" Anton asked.

"Now our helpers will start their real work."

"To clear the bodies?"

"Yes. Mr. Chan owns several businesses including a large and prosperous pet food company. He has many brothers, cousins, and nephews. Everyone who was here earlier pretending to be a patron is a close family member and entirely trustworthy. They will clear the bodies and clean up the building."

Li smirked. "You would be surprised what ends up in dog food cans."

Strings of firecrackers began exploding in the street. Anton started at the noise and Gang's smartphone began to ring. Gang answered it, and had a short conversation in rapid Chinese. Gang hung up, and said, "Mr. Chan is celebrating the removal of Mr. Wang. His crew will be here in moments. The firecrackers will mask what just happened. Casual onlookers, startled by the gunfire, will run into the street, or look around. They will only see Mr. Chan's firecrackers and it will convince them there were only fireworks." He nodded decisively. "Let's return to our home and calm down."

Anton noticed that his hands were shaking, and agreed, "Yes, let's do that."

Gang slapped Anton on the shoulder as they walked out of the Noodle House and into the Wu family home. "You did well Anton. You did the right thing. All those men wanted to kill us, and you helped save our lives."

Li said, "You watched our back. Thank you."

"Thanks," Anton replied as he walked with them. With every sense heightened and his soul thrilling with victory, he silently wondered, *Was I supposed to enjoy that as much as I did?*

* * *

Chloe had watched with interest as another set of vans arrived near the Noodle House.

Four had parked out the front, and another two had gone to the rear of the restaurant. Twenty men had left the vans. They'd been eager and energized. Their faces filled with intent. Their movements sure and purposeful.

The battle had unfolded before Chloe's supernatural senses. Gang and Li Wu, and Anton Slayne had been easy to identify from the telltale signature heat blooms of the Ramp, and their effectiveness versus the gangsters. Chloe noted to herself, *There is a qualitative difference in Anton's Ramp, he is just like his grandfather, he has the same talent. However, he has no mastery yet. They will now run from here, and draw out Francis Mirovar and his team.*

Chloe opened up her smartphone and ran an app she'd received from Dalien Morte. A cloud-based virtual phone that provided quantum encrypted untraceable secured call and text messaging services. Shadowstone was not alone in its ability to preserve secrets. She sent a text message to a number provided by Morte, it read, 'Request Contact.'

Ten seconds later a text message arrived on Chloe's display. It read, 'They have killed themselves, and are now ghosts.'

Chloe responded with another text. 'The dagger is red with their blood.'

Another text message came back. 'Contact me again in three minutes.'

Chloe waited three minutes and dialed the other phone number. A voice, depersonalized and masked by the communications software answered after the first ring and said, "Yes?"

"Tell your master there is a Shadowstone facility in Jerusalem at these coordinates," Chloe directed, and sent the GPS coordinates as a text message. "The Vampire Dominion have sent two praetorians and six enhanced Shadowstone operatives to Jerusalem. They're a direct threat to your master and they need elimination."

"I will pass this message on. Is there anything else?"

"Only this – who is Francis Mirovar?"

"My Order of Thoth force leader."

The line went dead.

Interesting, Chloe noted, *the Raven is with Francis Mirovar's team.* She then used Shadowstone technology to send a text to Marcus Drake. 'Some friendly advice, on missions, always be ready to fight, and find your own place to sleep.'

Chloe smiled broadly; her long-range plan against Crane was progressing well as Anton continued to develop his capabilities. She walked along the parapet to the side of the building. Her limousine lay parked in a back alley with her driver waiting inside. She leaped over the edge, falling the three floors to the empty alleyway below, landing easily on her feet, she made her way to the car.

Getting into the back of the vehicle, she commanded, "Back to the airport. I need to be in New York City as soon as possible."

"Yes, Ma'am," the driver replied.

Chloe relaxed in the back seat of the car as it pulled smoothly away, reflecting on what she had learned this night. *Soon the Order of Thoth and the Red Empire will distract Crane with rising threats on both sides and allow me to break my promise to him to deliver Francis Mirovar and his team. Anton, what a find he is, if he can match his grandfather, he will be the perfect weapon for my final strategy.*

Life was a never-ending thrilling adventure.

I need to keep working on Anton's motivations. He trembles on the edge of bloodlust – I need to push him over that edge and make him embrace the wild power within.

* * *

James Haley stared at his screen, replaying the video for the third time.

The result was still the same. A set of specialized cameras, telescopic microphones and motion trackers on the roof of the building provided a ghostly, but detailed video stream of the interior of the restaurant. The video showed a hail of submachine gun fire throughout the main room of the restaurant. Gang and Li Wu simply moved from the back of the room to the front of the room, and a handful of seconds later more than a dozen heavily armed thugs were on the floor.

In the back of the restaurant, Anton Slayne had taken on another six gangsters armed to the teeth with the same result; including one big brute of a man thrown through the back door into the rear alleyway as if fired from a circus cannon.

James replayed the video again in slow motion on the main screen. The gangsters moved as if standing in treacle. Gang and Li Wu moved much faster. Every step launching themselves forward, ahead of a storm of bullets that ripped apart the furniture and walls behind them.

Johnson exclaimed incredulously, "That's impossible!"

Higgins demanded with avid fascination, "Whatever they're on, I want some of that."

"Can it," James commanded harshly. "What we just saw doesn't leave this room."

"Huh?" Higgins grunted.

"Scrub the local server disks – do it now before this is swept onto the Panopticon server farm."

"Yes, Sir," Johnson replied.

"On it," Higgins responded.

"I want the disks reformatted, and run scramblers on them – this data must never be recovered."

His team worked at fever pitch to comply. The Panopticon would sweep a copy of all new data on the local server disk drives every ten minutes. To ensure the data disappeared it was necessary the reformat processes had begun across all the local disks to avoid the next sweep picking up the new data.

As the two men worked, Wesson caught his eye. Her face paled, she smiled wanly as if she'd just received a death sentence.

James looked back at his men. *Is this something we were never meant to see? Who can dodge bullets and walk away from a gun fight, and no one knows about it? And how did Gang Wu find out so much about Shadowstone? He knows who we are. What the hell is really going on here? Who is Anton Smith, or should I say Anton Slayne?*

* * *

Louise Wesson watched the replays of the fight in the Noodle House with a growing sense of horror.

She'd counted six men through the back door, and fourteen through the front door. All armed with submachine guns and an assortment of edged or blunt weapons. The front door gangsters had emptied their clips, around four hundred rounds of ammunition. The Wu family should have died, instead, they were still standing, and it was the gangsters who were lying in pools of blood.

From the first bullet to the grenade going off took less than nine seconds. She vowed to tread carefully; it is always possible to know too much. In her previous career, she'd already pulled the trigger on more than a dozen CIA operatives who had understood more than they should have. She assessed the risk. The next twenty-four hours would be critical to her survival.

James Haley ordered the destruction of the recordings of the fight in the Noodle House. It would become a data black hole, significant by its absence. There may be questions, but no one else would be able to assert what had been on those disk drives. She caught his eye, he looked stressed, but still confident and in control. He would most likely be the trigger man, the one to purge the team and clean up the mess.

She studied James, an ironic smile gracing her lips. *Will you be my killer? I guess I will find out soon enough.*

* * *

Anton sat at the dining room table with Gang and Li.

Gang opened a bottle of sake and arranged three glasses in front of them. He poured the shots and lifted his glass, Li and Anton followed his lead.

"Best done quickly," Gang urged, downing the shot and grinning at Anton.

Li followed suit. Anton drank his shot, the liquor was exquisite, a rare and aged reserve.

Gang poured a second round, and again they emptied the glasses. This time, Gang stoppered the bottle and put it aside. For a long moment, they sat there simply looking at each other.

Anton's hands had stopped shaking. The aftershocks of combat smoothed away by the physiological changes of the Ramp and the soothing effect of the sake. "What happens now?" Anton asked, his voice was quiet and reflective. "What will happen to the Noodle House?"

"Mr. Chan will look after it for me, we can trust him. Tonight, we rest and tomorrow we move to an Order safe house. Francis Mirovar will pick us up and escort us to a safe house. He is a force leader of long standing and very senior within the Order. I managed to contact him after breakfast. He has promised that he will come and I trust his word."

"They're coming here?"

"No. We'll meet them near the Boston docks. I have an address, that's all I know for now."

"Do you know where the safe house is?"

"No."

Anton tilted his head quizzically and said sardonically, "We're a bit in the dark, aren't we?"

Gang nodded, sighed and said, "It's because I have been inactive for years. Plus, neither Li nor you are officially in the Order."

"Hang on, what about those promises that I made weeks ago, just before you switched on my Ramp capability? I thought that was enough to be in the Order."

"Well, they're definitely the first steps and very much a real part of being in the Order. However, we have to wait for an Order Conclave to confirm your membership."

"A meeting of the Order; when do they happen?" Anton asked.

"In due course there will be one, and I'm sure that both Li and yourself will be confirmed as full members of the Order."

"What happens if we're not confirmed?"

Gang hesitated.

Li said, "The Order keeps its own secrets."

So, they will kill us, that's comforting to know, Anton thought sarcastically. He stared hard at Gang and inquired, "How do we make sure we're accepted and confirmed?"

Gang said, "You just need at least one force leader to accept you. Operationally the force leaders have tremendous authority. Someone becomes a force leader by common assent based on their capability to fight vampires, keep their team alive and avoid killing the innocent. Acceptance by a force leader is a sure path to confirmation."

"Speaking of Order membership, how is it you can be inactive? I thought that being in the Order was an either/or proposition."

Gang stroked his chin. "Well, it's a funny sort of situation."

Anton arched an eyebrow, and Li tilted her head and declared sardonically, "Is it now?"

Gang blinked at their reactions and laughed. It immediately became infectious and they all laughed together.

Anton felt all his tensions from the conflict evaporate away. He marveled at how Gang had a way that made him feel welcomed. *Yes, but no, it's more than that, I feel that I really belong here – with them – like family.* Anton found himself wiping away tears from his eyes, as the laughter around the table naturally subsided.

Gang mock sniffed. "Well, as usual, I get no respect."

Li got up out of her chair and hugged her father, and declared softly, "I respect you more than anyone else."

Gang's face worked with emotion as Li sat back down. He took a deep breath and instructed, "To put it simply, only a force leader can accept you into the order, and into his team, and only a force leader can throw you out. Anton, can you see where this is going?"

"Arthur Slayne was your force leader."

"He is my force leader until he is dead – conviction or no conviction. I don't have to answer to anyone else unless someone can prove Arthur is dead. The sanctity of the force team within the Order trumps all other rules."

"There are a lot of rules I don't know about."

"You know the most important ones. You have only been with us for a little over a month. You can't learn everything about a five-thousand-year-old organization in that time."

"If my grandfather is still your force leader, then you must have had contact with him. Perhaps a lot of contact with him over the years."

Gang nodded once. "Yes, that is true."

Anton sat back in his chair, shaking his head slowly and said, "I've been completely in the dark for so long." He felt a sudden wave of sadness. Did his parents not trust him with the truth? How would he ever be able to answer that question? He had to know more, and asked, "When my grandfather was convicted, what happened, did you fight?"

"I wanted to, but Arthur insisted I remain out of any conflict. I believe he anticipated this day would come. The rest of the team scattered, and like your grandfather, they're lone wolves fighting against the vampires, I have no idea how many still survive."

Anton paused, digesting what Gang had told him. "So, we will work with Francis Mirovar?"

"Yes. He has promised to shelter us until the next conclave. Have you packed everything that you need? We will leave tomorrow morning after breakfast."

"I think so," Anton replied.

Gang pushed his chair back and stood up. He caught Anton's gaze and said, "Wait here, there is something else you will need." He disappeared into his room for a minute, returning with a long case. He placed it on the table before Anton and opened it. Resting inside on a bed of black velvet was a sword identical to Li's and Gang's, except that it had a deep blue sapphire in the handle. He looked into Anton's eyes and declared, "This is the Blue Dragon. This is what you will need to kill vampires with."

Anton felt his heart jump as he realized the generosity of Gang's gift.

"This is my brother Qiang's sword, it is right that you should have it," Li declared, her eyes glistening with tears.

Gang said, "It is an heirloom of our family, inherited from my wife Tatsu Yoshindo's family line, from the island of Hokkaido in Japan."

Anton felt overwhelmed. "It's beautiful – are you sure you want to give it to me?"

Gang declared emphatically, "Yes. You have earned it tonight by fighting with courage."

Li nodded.

Anton put his hand over his heart and said, "Thank you, I don't know how to repay you."

Gang smiled. "With victory over our foes."

Anton nodded. He picked up the sword and drew it from its scabbard. The blade was majestic, flawless and beautifully balanced. He flourished it; the katana felt like a natural extension of his arm.

"Remarkable," Gang said. "You look just like your grandfather when I first met him."

Anton lowered the sword. "I do?"

"He has the Black Dragon."

Anton returned the sword to its scabbard, placed it back in the case, and asked, "How many of these swords are there?"

"Li's maternal ancestor, Kanenaga Yoshindo, made five swords during the winter of 1675. He forged them from iron drawn from a fallen meteor. The original stone from which the metal came glowed with an uncanny light. The blades are stronger and sharper than any other swords. There are the three here, the Green, White and Blue Dragons identified by an emerald, diamond, and a blue sapphire respectively. Arthur Slayne carries the Black Dragon, which has a lustrous black pearl in the handle."

Gang paused, stroking his chin. "And then there is the fifth sword, the Red Dragon, marked with a dark ruby the color of blood."

"Who has it?"

"The vampire Armitage."

"Why on earth does she have it?"

"The Red Dragon was given to the Emperor of Japan in 1676, apparently the Imperial family gifted it to a traveler in 1897."

Anton shook his head in disgust. *How does she do that? She has everything she needs.* He frowned, took a deep breath and suggested, "You expect I will need this sword to fight her."

"It's inevitable. She has some dark purpose of her own that involves you. Why else would she leave you alive? We need to thwart her purpose, and you need a weapon that is the equal of what she carries to stand a chance against her."

"Well, unless her purpose is to see a lot of dead vampires, I don't see how my being a member of the Order of Thoth is going to work out well for her."

Gang shook his head and advised with a voice filled with cautious tones, "She is subtle, very subtle. In all things remotely associated with her, you must be fully aware of what the consequences are." The table fell silent. "One more for the road," Gang said, pouring each of them a final shot of sake.

They downed their drinks and Gang ordered, "Now everyone to bed, breakfast will be at 7:30 in the garden. It will be our last breakfast here, so don't be late."

Anton and Li both gave their assent and went to their rooms. As they walked down the hallway together, Li suddenly turned and hugged Anton fiercely. She stood on tiptoes, whispering into his ear, "Thank you, Anton, for looking after us tonight."

She kissed him quickly on the cheek, then broke away and went into her room closing the door behind her.

"Uh, sure, no problem—" Anton said half-dazed, and then realized sheepishly that he was speaking to an empty hall. He went to the bathroom, and then to bed. He found himself staring at the ceiling, his mind replaying Li's embrace, and his cheek tingling with the sensation of her kiss.

And with that in mind, Anton drifted quietly into sleep.

* * *

Chloe Armitage met privately with Cornelius Crane in his chambers on the 104th floor of the Vampire Dominion citadel.

She said confidently, "The Boston cell will run later today. Their current position is no longer tenable."

Crane arched a quizzical eyebrow and inquired, "You believe they will seek Mirovar, and draw him and his followers out into the open?"

"Yes, Cornelius."

He smiled. "It is good to see you are still on track with the promise you made in Jerusalem."

"Yes, I will have this wrapped up within the week."

"Francis Mirovar and his team are no easy marks, what is your plan?"

"We will track Gang and Li Wu to ground, and create a perimeter with Shadowstone forces. We will keep our vampire forces nearby, and then attack once Mirovar arrives."

"You will be fighting on a ground of their choosing," Crane said with a frown. "That suggests a tactical disadvantage for our forces, have you accounted for that?"

"The ground must be chosen by the Order," Chloe said. "Mirovar will not step into an obvious trap, we have to give them the ground to create confidence and foster the belief they have the initiative."

"'... 'And therefore, those skilled in war bring the enemy to the field of battle and are not brought there by him.'" Crane declared.

"Sun Tzu, from the Art of War. You see my strategy here?" Chloe asked rhetorically.

Crane frowned. "Of course, but there will be losses. How many of my praetorians do you plan to sacrifice on this mission?"

Time to ask for what he will not give. Chloe shook her head and said, "I cannot guarantee that any engagement with the Order will be without casualties. To ensure success, I will need twelve praetorians, four to engage the Wu family and eight with me to engage Francis Mirovar and his team."

Crane stared at her for a long moment, and then stated decisively, "You will have six of my best. I can spare no more. We both know how you excel at combat. I expect to see blood on your blade when you return to my citadel."

Chloe responded, "Yes, Sir."

"Furthermore," Crane continued. "I'm concerned with the use of Shadowstone forces in an Order of Thoth engagement. Their primary purposes are surveillance and maintenance of operational security. Their involvement in this mission risks their unnecessary deaths and exposure of the secrets of the Vampire Dominion."

Why are these men so important to you? Chloe asked herself. Crane could and had seen millions die without blinking.

Crane frowned again and directed, "If necessary, to maintain secrecy – I will not hesitate to cleanse them all. But I warn you, do not put me in the position of having to make that choice."

"Yes, Sir."

Crane leaned toward her. "You must keep our Shadowstone operatives out of futile engagements with the Order of Thoth. Such battles are currently beyond their capabilities—"

Aha, currently beyond, but not in the future? UK Shadowstone enhanced operatives deployed to Jerusalem. Arthur Slayne conducts an operation against Crane in Brazil. Crane's network of distributed labs and research centers are working on secret projects with a single overarching goal. Chloe's mind raced as she integrated all the evidence she had before her. *He has a plan for Shadowstone super soldiers able to directly combat the Order of Thoth and the Red Empire during the day. How far away is he from completing this plan and how does he propose to control such men?*

"—I expect you to manage this engagement for victory with minimal losses."

"Yes, Sir," Chloe replied, not missing a beat while her mind spun through the implications of Crane's secret super-soldier program.

"Now there is fresh food on the 105th. I suggest that you get a bite to eat and rest up in one of our studios here. You can leave with the praetorians later this evening."

Chloe nodded. "Will do, Sir."

Crane clapped her on the shoulder and grinned wolfishly. "Good hunting General."

"Yes, Sir." Chloe stepped back, gave a small bow, turned and left his chambers. She smiled slyly as she walked down the corridor to the vault-like doors that were the only means to exit the floor. *Only six praetorians that leaves me under-resourced for this mission. A sharp defeat so close to home and a sudden attack by the Red Empire will drag Crane's attention away from the Metaframe artifacts, and give me a free hand to address matters in the northeast. As for his super-soldiers, I will bide my time and wait to see where the most fruitful path lies.*

Chloe's new plan began to come together as she left Crane's quarters.

* * *

Gang strolled through the garden at the back of his home.

He inspected his roses along the back fence for the last time. They had not received much attention over the last five weeks due to the heavy training schedule with Anton and Li. He leaned over one of his favorite plants. A Rugosa rose with a set of strongly perfumed pink flowers, he gently sniffed one of the blooms. *Beautiful, just beautiful. Who will look after you when I am gone?* Pulling back from the rose, he noticed a small object wedged against a brick on top of his back fence. It was a short cylinder that merged with the silhouette of the brick and trailed a short lead the color of aged mortar behind it. On the front of the cylinder, he could clearly see a lens.

Shadowstone! Gang's heart froze, but he kept moving. He sniffed a second and a third flower. He murmured approving comments as he spent another three minutes thinking furiously while strolling around the back yard.

He berated himself bitterly. *I have been lax! I have allowed the issues around Anton's arrival and the Hu Shizu to distract me. God knows how much Shadowstone have learned.*

Gang went into the house, catching up with Anton and Li in the kitchen. He tapped them both on the shoulder, before writing a quick note on a piece of paper. It read, 'Stay silent, we are compromised.'

Anton and Li, stared at him, shock flashing across their faces.

Gang wrote another note which read, 'Get your gear, we leave now.'

Anton and Li, immediately left for their rooms.

Gang went out to the garage and opened a safe there. Inside was a thick wad of cash and a short-barreled Glock 9mm in an ankle holster with a spare magazine. Next to the gun were a pair of incendiary grenades modified with ten-minute timers. He pocketed the cash and strapped the Glock to his ankle. He carefully synchronized the timers on the two incendiary grenades with his wrist watch. He armed and placed the first of the grenades in the trunk of the car, right next to the fuel tank. Picking up a metal jerry can of fuel, he left the garage. He carried the can into the kitchen where Anton and Li were waiting for him.

Gang put the can of fuel on top of the kitchen table. He set the timer of the second incendiary grenade to a half second behind the first grenade, armed it and strapped it to the jerry can with duct tape.

He checked his watch. *Six minutes and forty-five seconds before all this blows.* Gang mouthed, *wait.*

Anton and Li both shot worried looks at the timer on the grenade before nodding.

Gang went to his room, and fetched the backpack he'd prepared earlier that morning. Picking up the White Dragon in its traveling case, he went back to the kitchen. He reached into the backpack, pulling out an old Nokia cell phone and switched it on. As it powered up, he wrote two notes for Anton and Li. On the notes was the same message, 'Split up, be indirect and meet at this address in two hours.' He wrote the address beneath the instruction.

He scanned the timer on the grenade, it was now reading under three minutes. He picked up the Nokia and dialed 911. He got an operator and described a fire and gas explosion at his home address. He abruptly hung up, put the old cell phone next to the jerry can, and turned the gas on full on all the cooktop hobs in the kitchen.

Gang indicated with a sharp movement of his thumb that it was time to leave and they all went to the front door. He got there first, tapping his watch, he held them back. After another minute, he opened the front door. They could all hear the wailing of sirens in the distance. He held up his hand again, before nudging Li to the threshold. Anton stepped in behind her.

"Get ready," Gang whispered. "Split up and walk down the street, when you hear the first explosion, Ramp and run – you will have half a second – make the most of it to get some extra distance."

Li and Anton wore hoods, peaked caps and sunglasses. They had backpacks slung over their shoulders and carried their swords in long narrow travel cases.

Gang held up his hand, counting down the last five seconds with his fingers. His fist clenched for zero. Li exited the front door, followed by Anton. All three of them reached the street and went in different directions.

Anytime now.

The car went off first with a loud thump which blew the garage to smithereens.

Gang ramped, moving forty yards down the street. Half a second after the car, the kitchen exploded, smoke and debris from the house erupting into the air. The noise was deafening as bricks, burning wood and plaster flew into the street.

Within seconds, a fire engine rounded the street corner in front of him. He could see the grim faces of the firemen, the leaping fire and billowing smoke reflected in the truck's windshield as it passed him by. Moments later, the fire engine screeched to a stop out front of the remains of his home.

Gang slung his backpack over his left shoulder. Pulling his hat and hood tighter over his head, he held the White Dragon carry case in his right hand, and walked off down the street. He was determined not to look back.

His feet came to a halt as if they had a mind of their own. He paused, shook his head and turned around. Li and Anton had disappeared, and the fire was spreading to the Noodle House. He watched for a long moment as smoke rose high into the summer sky.

It's over now. It's really gone. Tatsu, Qiang, our home is gone.

Gang turned with a heavy heart, hurrying away to make the rendezvous with Anton and Li.

Chapter Five

Section 14.4.1 False Flag Media Posts

Summary: Normalcy bias and the poisoning the well logical fallacy.

[1] This tactic is based on exploiting the cognitive normalcy bias, and the poisoning the well logical fallacy. It relies on the target population's susceptibility for belief in the content of mainstream and authoritative belief systems, and resistance to change once a belief has been established.

[2] Secured facts that must be kept secret are published into the mass media in forms that will produce mainstream derision and rejection of their central tenets.

[3] Published secured facts should be altered in small details to enable the disassociation of belief from similar ideas and memes to ensure that whole tranches of secured discourse become mainstream taboos.

[4] There will always be a small subset of the target population who will believe the posts. The small population of believers adds to the strength of the tactic as they are able to be labeled as "fringe" and "other" in mainstream discourse. Thus, reinforcing the rejection of the central tenets of the secured facts by the target population.

[5] In this way, the target population is inoculated from ever believing that the secured fact is true, and will continue to act as if the secured fact is false.

Detail: Definitions and worked examples

The details of this tactic with worked examples is described below.

[REDACTED]

– Excerpt of Section 14, Strategic Influence and Information Disruption, Shadowstone Covert PSYOPS Manual

* * *

Boston, June 11th, 08:17

James Haley twitched, spilling his coffee as the sharp bang of a nearby explosion reached his ears.

Across the street, the Wu family garage was the center of a bright glare, reflexively James began to twist away. The Wu residence exploded in a ball of flame, with smoke and debris rising high in the air. He dived away, turning like a cat, and was face down on the floor when the windows facing the street shattered. A glittering mist of razor-sharp fragments filled the space where he'd been standing.

Higgins was neither quick nor lucky, bearing the brunt of the flying glass as he looked up from his computer console as the windows in front of him blew into the room. Rolling out of his chair, he lay screaming on the floor, blood flowing from numerous cuts across the top half of his body.

"What the hell!" James shouted, pushing himself upright and surveying the street. The fire was already leaping across to the Noodle House, and a big red fire engine was pulling to a halt in front of the Wu residence.

James pointed at the fire engine and declared in a voice dripping with derision, "You've gotta be kidding me! How long ago were they called? This is no accident!"

Higgins was still screaming when Wesson and Johnson ran back into the room. Rushing toward Higgins, Wesson shouted, "Don't pull it out!"

The warning came too late as Higgins dragged an inch-wide shard of glass from the side of his neck. The glass had missed his trachea but had caught his carotid artery. The wound began to spray blood. His eyes went wide with terror as he clutched his throat and blood sluiced around his fingers.

Johnson grabbed a hand towel from a bench, pushing it hard against the wound as Higgins lay back down on the floor.

Chaos filled the array of consoles in front of James. Half were registering static, the rest were showing fire, smoke and the arrival of a second fire engine. The one useful display was the main screen showing the Panopticon reference maps, it displayed a cluster of green contacts at the front gate of the Wu residence and along the street in both directions.

The targets had split up. *So, where and when are they going to meet again?* James watched the contacts change from green to yellow flags as they became stale. The most recent Panopticon contact on any of his targets was now older than a minute. He growled and snapped, "Damn this smoke and fire! We've just lost contact. Damn it, our targets have escaped."

"Looks like Higgins is gone," Wesson said flatly.

James looked down at the floor. Higgins lay still. Johnson grimaced as he pressed a blood saturated towel on Higgins' throat, a red pool spreading in a circle around Higgin's head and shoulders.

Johnson sighed once and stood up; his lips pressed tightly together. He turned, holding his bloodied hands away from his clothes and retreated to the bathroom.

"Wesson, get him cleaned up and ready for action," James ordered.

"Yes, Sir."

James flipped open his laptop. It was still operational; it was the machine providing the Panopticon feed on the surviving main screen. He initiated a fresh top priority search focused on the Boston region. The Panopticon would harvest feeds from every available camera, searching for Li and Gang Wu, and Anton Smith.

Slayne was so well hidden, even the Panopticon didn't know his real name. *How did they do that?* The Order of Thoth's ability to compromise the Panopticon was an unsolved mystery. One he didn't have time to solve.

A minute later, Wesson and Johnson returned from the bathroom. He now wore a fresh shirt and his hands were clean.

"What now boss?" Johnson growled.

"Okay, the three of us will have to re-establish contact with the targets ASAP," James directed. "Johnson, clear this equipment back to the van and clean all our tech from this site, including the feeds on the back fence of the Wu residence. Wesson, call in your team. Get the whole of Green-4 to Boston now."

"Yes, Sir," Johnson replied.

"Sir, what equipment mix?" Wesson asked.

"Combat surveillance operations. Bring in the nightfalcons."

"Yes, Sir, we can base the helicopters out of Logan Airport."

"Do it."

Wesson nodded, dialing her Shadowstone smartphone.

James stared at the Panopticon screen which was now a sea of red, orange and yellow, his hands reflexively clenching into fists. *They're Order of Thoth, and they're not going to get away from me.* He took a deep breath, relaxed his hands, and went to the nearby secured room. He opened his smartphone and voice dialed General Armitage.

The phone rang eight times before she picked up the call. Her voice was flat. "Yes?"

"There has been a development."

"You've lost them haven't you," Chloe said sardonically.

How did she know that? "… Yes, Ma'am."

"You will find them again before sunset tonight," Chloe commanded with absolute certainty.

A shiver went up James' spine, it was clear that failure was not an option, and he replied, "Yes, Ma'am."

"I will be there tonight with a special forces team, now remember – do not engage the Order of Thoth. The mission is to identify them, track them, and if they go to ground, put a cordon around the site and stop them escaping again. Is that clear?"

"Crystal clear, Ma'am."

"Excellent."

The line went dead.

James Haley was not an easily frightened man, but he felt a disturbing unease as he put his phone away. *I must find these Order of Thoth terrorists or else.*

The 'or else' remained chillingly undefined.

* * *

Li Wu dodged adroitly through the traffic and crossed Bedford Street in the Boston suburb of Charlestown.

Ducking beneath a row of trees she came up against a rusty and weathered security fence. Beyond lay an apparently unused industrial site fronting onto the Mystic River. She tracked the fence for twenty yards before finding a split in the wire where it had come away from a post. Peeling the wire back another foot, she slipped through to the other side. A minute later, she'd crossed the deserted parking lot and was up against the corner of the front wall of a large warehouse.

The building was easily two hundred yards long and half that wide. Its front had two enormous steel doors spanning openings twenty yards across and half that high; both doors stood closed. Above the doors were large gantries constructed from thick steel frames with rails and access walkways, they looked worn but solid. The back third of the warehouse sat on a finger of land jutting out into the river.

Where she stood, at the front right corner of the building, Li could see a solid stone dock running forty yards past the far end of the warehouse. The whole above-ground structure comprised gray masonry stone, which up close gave the building an ambiance of solid, industrial permanence. A cold war era designed building, built to survive heavy bombardment, and possibly nuclear attack.

Li pressed her back up against the wall, cutting her silhouette to a minimum. A steel door opened a dozen feet away along the side of the warehouse. Her father poked his head out and called to her, "Li, I'm in here."

Li darted over, joining Gang in the cool dimness of the warehouse. She asked urgently, "Has Anton arrived?" She took off her sunglasses and looked around, there were numerous shipping containers on the floor and a pair of huge rolling cranes just under the ceiling, but no sign of Anton.

Gang shook his head. "No. However, it's still early, he should be here soon."

She hoped so.

"While we wait for him, we have much work to do," Gang directed with a grin. "This place is a treasure trove."

"Yes?"

"I will show you. Come this way."

Li followed her father as he walked between organized rows and lines of shipping containers stacked in pairs to make walls nearly twenty feet high.

It's like a maze in here, I wonder what Father has found.

* * *

Sergeant Detective of the Boston Police Department Homicide Unit, Luke Walker, drove his Ford SUV along Bedford Street Charlestown. He saw a young man on the sidewalk apparently waiting for a break in the traffic so he could cross the street.

Luke was about sixty yards away from him and closing quickly. He slowed his car down from thirty miles per hour to give himself another couple of seconds before he passed him by. There was something about him that piqued his curiosity. The forward tilt of the cap, the broad sunglasses, the gray long sleeve hooded top, the backpack and a long, slim case carried as if it held something precious.

Whoever he was, he was hiding something. Luke felt a sudden sense of familiarity and his 'Hunch Meter' red-lined. He was certain he should know who the young man was but he was equally sure he'd never met him before.

Recognition flooded through him and his SUV screeched to a halt directly opposite the young man. They stared at each other for a second, then the young man turned away, walking briskly along the street toward the nearest intersection.

An evidence photograph he'd resented having to hand over to the FBI and the memory of a brutal unsolved murder flashed through his mind.

Anton Smith!

Slapping a portable police light onto his dash, he switched it on. Just as someone tooted him from behind. Luke was already rolling forward to keep pace with Smith, he glanced in the mirror and saw the driver of a Toyota Corolla already backing off now that his police lights were flashing. He looked forward again, glimpsing Smith as he went around a corner and disappeared from sight.

He swore loudly, "Damn!" and floored the accelerator. His SUV lurched forward. He made a hard-left turn into the side street the fugitive had fled down. Parked cars lined the one-way street and numerous narrow alleyways branched off it. It was more than a hundred yards to the end of the street. There was no sign of Smith anywhere. He'd vanished into thin air.

Luke rolled slowly down the street, his head swiveling left and right, looking for Smith. Swearing under his breath he pulled his car over as he came to the end of the street.

"Damn it all to hell, where is that boy?" Luke growled as he shut off the police light and dialed the duty desk to call the sighting in. *What the hell, it's been more than five weeks, what is he doing still walking the streets? What on Earth are the FBI doing with this case? After all, they took every last shred of evidence from my crime scene. What are they doing with it – sitting on it?*

Luke fumed in silence as he waited for the duty desk officer to answer his call.

* * *

James Haley's laptop chimed as the Panopticon alerted him to a hit on one of his targets.

The transcript of a phone conversation of a Sergeant Detective Luke Walker of the BPD flashed onto his screen. James read the conversation in seconds, absorbing all the salient details. Walker had called in a sighting of a fugitive, named Anton Smith, wanted by the FBI in connection with a terrorism investigation.

James shook his head. Well, not actually the FBI, he would have to make some calls and squash this thing all over again. Noting the location of the sighting, James used the Panopticon mapping service to display it. The Panopticon provided real-time map data in extraordinary detail. He zoomed in on the reported location, the corner of Bedford and Mallston streets in the Boston suburb of Charlestown. The transcript stated the detective witnessed Anton entering Mallston Street before disappearing.

James whispered to himself, "If he was running away from the police, then where was he going before he was spotted?" He zoomed away from the street so that he could see for half a mile around the street corner. Slayne could have run into some of the narrow inner suburban streets with abundant hiding places. On the opposite side of Bedford Street was a broad industrial park that fronted onto the Mystic River. He ran an infrared filter across the satellite imagery, carefully scanning the park, about half the park was active, filled with operating businesses. The rest looked empty, except for a warehouse with two very faint human contacts in it.

The building was heavily shielded. Only two people were in the building. Could it be Gang and Li Wu? Was this their rendezvous point? James set about finding out. He flipped off the filter and zoomed in on the warehouse. The Panopticon supplied situational metadata that streamed alongside the images on the screen. The US Navy originally commissioned the building into service in 1958. An armory for repairing heavy ship equipment, but decommissioned after the fall of the Soviets when Congress slashed budgets in 1991. Ownership of the building shifted to a company named Clayton Holdings, registered in Massachusetts, which was a wholly owned subsidiary of another company registered in the Cayman Islands. The local company had a managing director, a Mr. Paul Roberts, and no other staff. The utility bills and taxes were all paid on time from an account owned by Roberts. Roberts even had a rarely accessed Facebook account and looked like a genial fiftyish white male with a wife, two grown up children and a cocker spaniel.

He considered the options in front of him. The original military purpose and cold war era construction explained the shielding. However, he wondered if Mr. Roberts was a real person or just a digital phantom conjured up to cover the identity of the building's true owners.

James zoomed in on the area around the building. There were untended weeds growing in the cracked asphalt of the parking lot, but no fresh engine oil spills. He used the Panopticon to search electrical power utility logs. The site normally used only a minimal amount of electricity, yet usage today had spiked much higher than normal. Further examination quickly confirmed the building was normally deserted.

And yet there were two people in there, today of all days, and a lone detective had spotted Anton Slayne within five hundred yards of the building.

James didn't believe in coincidences.

His smartphone rang. Louise Wesson was calling him, he answered it.

"Sir," she said. "The van is fully packed; Higgins is bagged and Johnson is ready to roll."

"Good, get Johnson moving and meet me at my car. I will be there in two minutes. We have somewhere to go."

"Sir?"

"I will tell you in the car."

"Yes, Sir," Wesson replied before hanging up the call.

James looked around at the remains of the stakeout. The floor where Higgins had bled out was now the cleanest part of the room. The room reeked of too much bleach mixed with smoke from the morning fire across the street. Late morning sunlight streamed through the broken window frames, illuminating dust motes floating in the air.

James stood up, closed his laptop and slotted it into a carry case. He hung back from the front wall, glancing out through the broken window frames. The Noodle House had lost half its structure and what remained looked ready to collapse. The Wu residence was a steaming pile of wet ash. Surveying the room for the last time, he was confident his small team had eliminated any connection between the recent events in this building and Shadowstone. He sincerely hoped he would never see this dump again.

James strode from the room, descending downstairs to where he'd parked his car. Louise stood on the opposite side of his vehicle, a combat surveillance kit bag at her feet. James flicked the lock and got into the car.

Lobbing her kit bag onto the back seat, Louise sat down in the front passenger seat and turned to face him, a quizzical look on her face.

"Yes, I've found them," James declared. "Now we move."

Louise smiled. "Yes, Sir."

"What is the status on the Green-4 spectrum team?"

"They've arrived in a nightfalcon helicopter with a combat operations mission fit out, and are waiting at Logan Airport. They can be anywhere in Boston in less than fifteen minutes."

"Good. Put Red-1 and Blue-5 teams on ready alert for combat operations. What is the flight time from Fort Dix?"

"Green-4 got to Boston in seventy-five minutes."

"Wait, no, that's too long. Get those teams into the air and forward base them with Green-4 at Logan. That will give us three combat helicopters, and forty-eight troops to use at short notice."

"Sir, that would be forty-six, Green-4 is down two men, Higgins, and Johnson."

"Forty-eight counting us – I think we can expect to get our hands dirty tonight."

"Sir, there is one more thing." Wesson said, arching an eyebrow.

"Yes?"

"We also have a four-man squad from Indigo-6 in town. They have an armed rigid hulled inflatable boat we can put on the river."

"An armed RHIB, outstanding, make it so."

"Yes, Sir. Do we have new orders?"

"If we can get all three Order of Thoth in the same location, then we have to deploy a cordon and keep them there. General Armitage will be coming tonight with a special forces team to deal with them."

"I would like to see that."

"So, would I," James agreed, starting the car and driving off toward the warehouse.

Wesson opened her smartphone and started giving orders to the other teams of Shadowstone operatives. They would soon marshal at Logan Airport and along the Mystic River.

Pulling out onto the main road, the ten seconds of scrubbed video of the previous night's fight replayed in James' mind. General Armitage's special forces troops would surely be a damn sight better than the Chinese thugs that took on the Wu family and Slayne. James had no doubt the last day in Li and Gang Wu, and Anton Slayne's lives had dawned. He reflected, *Just how good are these Order of Thoth operatives? Well, we'll soon find out, my men are far better trained and armed than those triad wannabees were. I'm sure that if needed they can do the job. Vampire Dominion? They're fucking insane.*

James chaffed at the restrictions General Armitage had placed on him. This was an opportunity for real action against the enemies of society. It was why he'd signed on to Shadowstone in the first place – to make a difference in the world.

James unloaded his growing frustration on the car's accelerator, gunning the car, and speeding off down the road.

* * *

The mid-afternoon summer sun blazed in a bright blue sky.

Anton Slayne stood in the shadows of an abandoned house facing onto Bedford Street. Across the road was a disused parking lot and a large warehouse jutting out into the Mystic River. Anton carefully studied the surrounding area. He'd been watching it for hours. He hadn't seen anything that might be an indication of active surveillance. He'd identified visible traffic cameras, their orientation, and paths that would avoid them.

But what about satellites? He couldn't allow Shadowstone to find him again, but he had no way to be sure he'd hidden himself properly. He reflected on the morning, what terrible luck to run into the detective from the night Armitage murdered his mother. As soon as he'd broken visual contact by turning into the side street, he'd ramped for about two seconds, covered thirty yards, then ran down a side alleyway and hid behind a dumpster. Through a crack between the dumpster and a brick wall, he'd watched the Ford SUV trawl its way past the mouth of the alley.

Anton was certain the detective had recognized him, there was no doubt he would call in the sighting. He'd decided to stay in the area, and a few minutes searching had discovered the abandoned house he now stood in front of. He'd waited patiently; however, nothing had happened, no police cars, no helicopters, nothing at all. The secret keepers were hard at work. He didn't need to worry about the Boston Police Department, they were not the real problem. Shadowstone, their pervasive surveillance system, and the vampires they guarded were the real problem.

Anton had waited hours before risking any movement. Gang's note had said to meet at the address of the warehouse by mid-morning, he was now more than four hours late. The growing tension made him feel sick to his stomach. Four hours was a long time, Gang and Li would be worried. He hoped they would stay put and not try and look for him.

It was time to make a move. He would just have to take his chances with the satellites. A break appeared in the Sunday traffic. Anton pushed off from the wall of the house, leaped over the front fence, and walked calmly across the road. A minute and a half later he was through the boundary fence, across the parking lot and up against the corner of the warehouse.

He saw movement to his right as a steel door opened an inch and he readied himself to Ramp.

"Anton, finally you're here," Gang remarked. "Quick come inside before anyone sees you."

Anton ducked inside and Gang pulled the door shut behind him. Li regarded him with a steady gaze, her arms folded across her chest. A wave of relief washed through him. Gang and Li were safe.

* * *

James Haley watched his laptop screen.

The Panopticon satellite feed showed a third figure hurrying across the open parking lot toward the warehouse. He dialed Louise Wesson, she immediately picked up her smartphone.

"Sir?" Wesson queried.

"Was the target sighted?"

"Yes, Sir. He has just reached the warehouse."

"Good work, call in your helicopters, we will rendezvous in the parking lot. Put Green-4 on the dock, and the other two in the parking lot near the front fence. Get the RHIB to sit a hundred yards off the dock in the middle of the river."

"Yes, Sir. The helicopters will be on site in about ten minutes, and the RHIB in about fifteen."

"How long will it take you to get to the parking lot?"

"I will be there when the nightfalcons arrive."

"Excellent," James replied and hung up.

James put his laptop down and started the engine of his car. He welcomed the air conditioning, as he'd been waiting in his car for the last four hours. He'd parked about a mile back on Bedford Street underneath the shade of a large tree. He'd sent Wesson into a nearby industrial park with a suite of surveillance gear to get a clear sight of the area near the warehouse. He considered the Panopticon all well and good, but often it was best to have human eyes on the target.

A surge of relief washed through him. He'd confirmed Gang and Li Wu and Anton Slayne were in the warehouse. In less than half an hour he would have a cordon around the site that no one could escape from. He noted his unusual feeling of relief. He realized he was responding to the attitude of General Armitage. She seemed to have more than a professional interest in the operation.

The thought concerned him. He'd been reporting to General Armitage for the last eight years, and for all of those years he'd prided himself on his professionalism and skill in executing the role of Head of the United States arm of the Shadowstone organization. But this mission was different, it felt like the General had a personal agenda in play.

There was a dangerous undercurrent beneath the mission and he wondered if he fully understood what was going on. James shrugged of the momentary doubt. He put the car into gear, rolling forward into the Sunday afternoon traffic and proceeded down Bedford Street toward the warehouse.

"Time to nail this mission," he declared to himself. He spotted a shady tree just near the entrance to the parking lot and decided that would be a perfect spot to park and wait for the Shadowstone forces to arrive and deploy.

Yeah, he thought with sudden enthusiasm. *Time to pin their Order of Thoth hides to the wall.*

* * *

Stepping away from the steel door, Anton entered the cool of the warehouse.

Gang drove a thick steel bolt home to lock the door. Smiling broadly, he clapped Anton on the shoulder. Li threw her arms around his neck, crushing herself against him.

Li released him a moment later, and stepped back. Her hand flashed forward and hit him hard on the shoulder.

"Ow!" Anton exclaimed.

"What took you so long?" she demanded.

Anton grinned ruefully. "Li, you really know how to make a guy feel welcome."

Li's eyes tightened and her lips pressed into a thin line.

Anton rubbed his shoulder and said, "I had a run in with the BPD and had to make sure they weren't following me. I'm pretty sure I gave them the slip."

Li tilted her head, unimpressed with his excuse.

Anton sighed; she'd get over it. Gang and Li, were both dressed in army surplus combat fatigues, with webbing for modern weapons and a scabbard for their swords slung over their shoulders. Happy to get the conversation off his late arrival, he asked, "Looks like you're expecting company?"

"Yes," Gang answered. "We've been preparing since we arrived here. When you were late, we suspected Shadowstone must have found you. You may have evaded the Boston police today, but it is highly unlikely you have evaded Shadowstone. They almost certainly know we're here by now."

Anton pursed his lips with disappointment.

"Don't blame yourself," Gang advised, "there was only a slim chance we would get away cleanly once we were discovered at the Noodle House."

"If Shadowstone and the vampires arrive in force, isn't this place a death trap? Why don't we move out while we can?" Anton asked. "We could keep moving and escape the city."

"We already have an agreement with Francis Mirovar to meet here tonight. Moving during the day exposes us in multiple ways to detection by Shadowstone. If they catch us out in the open, and there is a pitched battle, a lot of innocent people could be hurt or killed, and you know the principles of the Order."

"Don't kill the innocent."

"Yes, exactly." Gang said firmly, "We are the aware ones. We have the ability to make an informed choice to put ourselves in harm's way. They do not."

Anton nodded and resolved to make the best of the situation. Stacked shipping containers hemmed them in. Hanging from the ceiling thirty yards above his head was a heavy framework of steel girders. The massive frame supported a crane. Steel cables, giant hooks – and a fully loaded container dangled twenty yards above the concrete floor. He followed the line of the rails the crane ran on, and they went to the very ends of the warehouse, exiting through the front and back walls.

Along the long wall and above the side door he'd just come through were a set of mezzanine levels, with offices, utility rooms, and bathrooms. Halfway along the wall was a diesel-electric power backup plant. Sets of steel stairwells rose up to the mezzanine floors, and from the top level, maintenance walkways spanned across the roof and gave access to the crane.

Realizing he might have to fight here, Anton inquired, "Okay Gang, so how does this place work?" he pointed to the mezzanines. "What's the view like from up there?"

"Excellent questions," Gang said. "Follow me. Li and I have been busy." He led Anton and Li up the stairs to the first mezzanine level. As they ascended, Gang pointed out the various equipment and utility rooms, and the backup diesel power generator on the ground floor beneath them and stated, "The US government built this warehouse during the Cold

War. It has backup supplies for power and water, and the walls and roof are steel reinforced stone masonry."

From the first mezzanine level, Anton could just see over the top of the stacked containers. There was a second crane running on identical rails parallel with the first crane, but able to cover the far side of the warehouse. It too supported a large container. He also saw that at the front end of the warehouse were a pair of massive sliding steel doors aligned with the cranes. If they'd been open, they could easily allow two semi-trailers to sit side by side for loading with shipping containers by the cranes.

"Let's go up to the next level," Gang directed. "You will be able to see precisely what we have done while you were playing with the BPD."

"Yeah, Okay," Anton agreed, following Gang and Li up to the next level. They walked along for about twenty yards before they came to a series of offices. One had lights on and an open door.

Gang led them to it, turned and waved broadly toward the warehouse floor. "Look at the floor and tell me what you see?"

Anton looked out and down across the warehouse. There were hundreds of the big steel shipping containers. The containers were stacked in pairs, one on top of the other to create a massive maze of nineteen-foot-high steel walls. The longest straight lines were about forty yards. He exclaimed, "It's a giant maze!" He pointed at the two containers suspended high in the air by cranes near the main entrance and said, "Looks like they would fit neatly into holes in the maze."

Gang acknowledged Anton's observations. "Well spotted. If dropped at the right time, we can box some people into some very tight corners."

"It won't stop vampires."

"Yes – it won't stop them or slow them down. They will simply run along the top of the maze. Which brings us to the gantry cranes and the maintenance walkways." Pointing out several key intersections in the maintenance walkways that tracked the gantry crane rails, Gang said, "There at the front, halfway along, and just before the exits at the dock are excellent locations to place a variety of tricks to distract our foes."

"What sort of tricks?" Anton asked.

"Pyrotechnics mostly – good for hazing the battlefield."

Anton's jaw dropped open.

"This whole site is a honey trap for vampires," Gang said. "This is an Order site, designed by your grandfather and developed and maintained since the mid-1990s for the purpose of collecting a large group of vampires into one location and then destroying them."

"Can we do the same with just the three of us?"

"That's not the aim today. We only have to survive long enough for the Order to arrive so we can exfiltrate with them." Turning away, Gang led Anton into the nearest office. Li sat at a desk, her fingers flashing skillfully over a keyboard. In front of her was a wide rack of eight separate monitors showing camera feeds from the outside of the warehouse and a pair of monitors displaying command line computer screens.

"Is this where you control the cranes? Isn't that going to lock you into one spot?" Anton asked.

Li turned toward Anton and smiled. She lifted her smartphone and pressed some icons on its surface. Anton heard the nearest crane rumble and he spun around – it was already moving.

Li said, "They're on an internal network with a secured WIFI router we can ping with the phones. I rewrote the SCADA code controlling the cranes. They will drop their loads based on a WIFI connect request. I select this command on my mobile, and a tenth of a second later the container on the right will drop. If I select another command, the one on the left will drop. Father's mobile is set up the same way."

Gang smiled wickedly, waving his smartphone.

"You can write SCADA code?" Anton asked.

"I've just graduated from MIT, Maths and Computer Science, I started an accelerated study program at sixteen."

"That's awesome," Anton enthused, impressed by her achievement. He reflected momentarily; *I've been wasting my time. Li and I are almost the same age, and she's already finished her first degree.* He declared, "I spent my time playing sports, collecting varsity letters and getting an Icy Hockey scholarship. What you've done is amazing."

Li smiled, blushed and laughed. "Thanks, Anton, let me show you what this system does."

Taking a seat next to her, Anton listened carefully as Li explained the details of how the warehouse operated and the locations of the various traps littering the building.

* * *

Louise Wesson pushed up from her prone position after the call from James Haley ended. She packed her scopes into her combat surveillance kit bag with practiced efficiency.

She'd mounted the industrial fuel storage tower to attain her current observation point overlooking the abandoned warehouse and had sweltered in the summer sun for the last three hours.

Louise had changed into urban camouflage patterned combat fatigues before mounting the tower. Her infiltration of the site hadn't involved killing anyone, but there was one security guard who would probably lose his job for drinking alcohol on duty and falling asleep at his post. The drugged dart she'd fired into his neck was completely biodegradable. It would soon disappear with the only remaining trace of its existence a blood alcohol reading that was similar to drinking a bottle of whiskey in an hour. When the guard recovered consciousness a day later, his memory of the twenty-four hours before the dart would be a black hole. The darts were just another trick that Shadowstone had up their sleeve to maintain operational security.

She voice activated her smartphone. The phone dialed a voice conference number for the troop leaders within the three nightfalcon helicopters waiting at Logan Airport. Once the call connected, the men identified themselves.

Louise commanded, "The mission is on. Get yourselves in the air now. Red-1 and Blue-5 bring your teams into the parking lot just before the fence line on the city side of the warehouse. Green-4 take the end of the dock on the Mystic River and hold it. Gentleman, this is a cordon operation. We take and hold a position, and enforce a line that no one crosses, is that understood."

"Yes, Ma'am," the men replied.

The Green-4 troop leader asked a question, "Ma'am, what are the rules of engagement on this operation?"

"Standard engagement model for a cordon, don't shoot unless the targets fire first."

"Yes, Ma'am."

"Any other questions?" she asked.

"No, Ma'am," they all answered.

"You have your orders," Louise declared and disconnecting the call.

With her kit bag packed, Louise carried an FN P90 submachine gun slung over her right shoulder, and a Glock 9mm holstered at her hip. Wiping away the perspiration from her forehead, she adjusted her cap over her straight brown hair, put on mirrored sunglasses and descended the long metal staircase that spiraled down and around the tower. In ninety seconds, she'd reached the ground. Hefting the kit bag over her shoulder, she lifted her speed, making for the parking lot half a mile away. She anticipated arriving at the parking lot entrance in less than five minutes.

Loping easily through the industrial estate, Louise reflected on the last twenty-four hours. Events were coming to a head. She was still alive. James Haley hadn't purged her, and he hadn't even looked like he was about to take action against her – which was a good sign. The Order of Thoth operatives were in the warehouse, which with three heavily armed nightfalcon gunships and nearly fifty fully armed Shadowstone operatives inbound looked like nothing less than a death trap for them.

A trace of doubt lurked at the back of her mind. The Order of Thoth operatives were exceptional. She was honest enough to admit she knew almost nothing about them, or their combat techniques. A quote from Sun Tzu's, The Art of War, came to mind on the topic of knowing your enemy.

'If you know others and know yourself, you will win every battle; if you do not know others but know yourself, you win one and lose one; if you do not know others and do not know yourself, you will lose every single battle.'

She understood the capabilities of the Shadowstone operatives coming to the warehouse, but of the Order of Thoth, she knew next to nothing. *We are about to flip a coin, and the outcome will be uncertain.*

Louise hated uncertainty.

She ran on, reaching the edge of the parking lot. Haley's car sat under the shade of a large tree near the entrance to the site. He was standing next to his vehicle, still wearing his suit, smoking a cigarette and carrying a full military spec assault rifle with a red dot laser sight and an under-barrel grenade launcher.

Louise slowed to a walk to cover the final few yards. She scanned the horizon. In moments, three black specks resolved into view and rapidly expanded into the oncoming nightfalcons. Shadowstone had armed each helicopter with eight laser-guided Hellfire III and eight Stinger II missiles, an M134 Minigun at the waist, and a pair of triple-barreled GAU-19B .50 Caliber machine guns on fixed mounts beneath the cockpit. Each craft carried a full troop of sixteen fully armed Shadowstone operatives, all highly skilled ex-members of various special forces, the CIA, and the NSA. A heavily armed, superbly equipped, tough, skilled and disciplined para-military force. She frowned, and silently wondered, *How many are going to survive tonight?*

The heavy roar of the helicopters' jet turbines shattered the afternoon air as they split formation to come into land. Two came to a halt in the parking lot and the third came to rest at the end of the dock on the far side of the warehouse.

Louise shielded her face from the backwash of the rotor blades. Darkly armored Shadowstone operatives streamed from the helicopters in four-man squads. They deployed rapidly to form a perimeter around the warehouse. In less than three minutes there was a ring of armed men ready to kill anyone who might attempt to cross their line.

Louise glanced at Haley, he grinned confidently at her, his face lit with a fierce desire. She turned and studied the forbidding massiveness of the warehouse. *This place reeks of secrets — we will be lucky to survive tonight.*

She checked her P90 submachine gun, ejected the standard clip and loaded a fifty-round strip of high-velocity, armor-piercing rounds from her kit bag. She added three spare clips of the same premium ammunition, and four anti-personnel fragmentation grenades to pouches on her combat webbing. She checked the communications links with the four spectrum teams on site and the red, blue, green and indigo squad leaders all reported in.

A sardonic smile curled her lips, her eyes becoming flint like. *If tonight is going to be my last, let's make sure it's a memorable one.*

* * *

Li heard it first.

"Helicopters," she murmured, swiveling in her chair to face the direction the sound was coming from.

"… Yes," Gang agreed. "Nightfalcons."

"Shadowstone?" Anton asked.

"Yes," Gang replied calmly. "They're here."

The monitors linked to the external CCTV cameras provided a clear view of the warehouse surrounds. They watched the helicopters land and the Shadowstone troops begin to deploy to form a perimeter.

"Why haven't they taken out our cameras?" Anton queried. It was the first thing he would have done.

"A good question," Gang acknowledged. He paused for a moment, studying the displays. "Looks like a cordon. They're here to stop us leaving. They're probably forbidden from attacking us – for now."

Li turned away from the monitors and reported, "Three helicopter gunships and nearly fifty troops, all in combat armor and carrying assault rifles with grenade launchers. There are at least three snipers with .50 caliber rifles. From what I can see, the helicopters have two fixed, heavy caliber miniguns in the hull, a waist mount M134 minigun, and Hellfire and Stinger missiles."

"I've not heard of Shadowstone doing this before," Gang said with a frown. "They're armed for war."

Anton shook his head with disappointment. "They followed me here."

"Spilled milk," Li said with a shrug.

"Don't worry Anton, we're prepared for this possibility," Gang advised him. "Li, please stay here and keep watch. I'll show Anton what I showed you earlier." Gang beckoned Anton with a wave of his hand. "Follow me. Now is the time for you to pick up arms." He led Anton back down to the warehouse floor and over to an open shipping container. Nearby were thick chains and an open heavy padlock that was half a foot across.

"Anton, this was prepared by your grandfather. He gave me the key to this container when I last saw him and he told me about its contents. Now, wait here," Gang said, and entered the shipping container. He rummaged about for a long moment, and then emerged with a large military grade lock box which he sat down on the floor in front of Anton. He flipped open the lid and directed, "Look here."

Inside the box were five multi-barreled grenade launchers. Someone had daubed each weapon with a paint stripe across the barrel: two were blue, two were red, and the last one was white.

"These are modified Milkor MGLs, they carry six 40x46mm caliber grenades and have an auto-fire mode that will shoot at a rate of three grenades per second. The blue ones hold grenades with a hundred and ten pure-silver flechettes. They're an excellent weapon to use against vampires at close range. It's a lot like firing a giant shotgun round without the recoil. The red ones carry a standard high-explosive round with a shaped charge. They're best against a vehicle, but you can use one against humans or vampires in a pinch. The white is a thermobaric round – big explosion, lots of heat, and absolutely lethal within the blast radius."

"Wow! Which one should I use?" Anton asked excitedly.

"Oh my God! None of them," Gang declared. "You don't have enough training for these." He walked back into the container and came out carrying a long thick barreled gun with a large magazine in one hand, in his other hand he held a much smaller submachine gun. He gave both weapons to Anton.

Gang pointed to the large gun and said, "This is an AA-12 automatic shotgun with a thirty-two-round magazine. It's good up to about a hundred yards, and is excellent in this sort of environment."

Gang pointed at the submachine gun. It had a red-dot sight on top of the barrel, and a short magazine, and instructed, "This is a Heckler and Koch MP7 A2 personal defense weapon with a twenty-round magazine. It has a high rate of fire like the MAC-10s the Hu Shizu used in the Noodle House, but is a far more accurate and reliable weapon. It's loaded with high performance rounds optimized to deal with human body armor."

Anton studied the guns and asked, "Which is best against vampires?"

"Neither, the plan is to be out of here before the vampires arrive. In a pinch, you can use either gun against a vampire, but you need to be up close, and it is best to shoot them from behind, or else they will dodge. In fact, with all the weapons I have shown you, it is always best to shoot a vampire from behind and up close."

Gang frowned. "Except of course the grenades, you need some distance there."

Anton smiled wryly. "Makes sense."

Gang scratched his ear and said, "However, for the silver flechettes, you can use those up close as there is no explosion."

"There are a lot of exceptions."

Gang nodded, shrugging his shoulders. "What can I say – they're vampires – fighting them is a difficult business."

Anton nodded. "Clearly, but what is your best advice?"

"The trick is getting yourself in the right position to attack them. What makes that so difficult is that their senses are extraordinary. However, we can haze them with sensory clutter. Too much noise, odd smells, and lots of smoke can temporarily throw them off and give you a chance to make an effective attack. Just what the interior of this warehouse will be like tonight."

"What do you mean?" Anton asked.

Gang grinned. "I will show you shortly."

"If the environment is full of clutter, won't we be affected just the same?"

"We have less sensory power to lose, it will level the playing field."

"Okay, how do I use these guns?"

Gang proceeded to give Anton a five-minute lesson in how to hold, point, fire, reload and flick the safety switch on both weapons.

"Don't worry about learning to shoot straight, use your Ramp awareness and focus on pointing the weapon exactly where you are looking and accuracy will look after itself. We will place ammunition reloads at precise locations so you can move from one position to the next without running out of ammo. Our speed will act as a force multiplier. Anton, this is the key to survival, rely on your speed and the natural cover within the warehouse. Once combat starts, keep moving, and never stand still."

Gang looked at his wristwatch. "It's nearly six hours to sunset. That's when the Order will arrive."

"And the vampires too?"

Gang nodded. "Unfortunately, most likely."

Anton felt a mixture of fear and excitement as he chambered a round into the automatic shotgun. The weapon made a satisfying click as it became armed. It felt completely natural in his hands as if made for him. He trained the weapon on a far corner of the warehouse and sighted along the barrel. A shiver ran up his spine and he turned to Gang. "Whose gun is this?"

"It was your grandfather's, one of his favorites."

Lugging a large box from the container labeled, 'Warning: Pyrotechnics: Keep away from flame.' Gang said, "Anton, please help me with these tricks, we have some preparations to make before our guests arrive."

Fireworks, Anton noted to himself, and replied, "Sure." He stepped over to help Gang unload the box. He smiled grimly as he worked with Gang to set a range of traps around the warehouse. It was time for some payback.

* * *

The mid-afternoon summer sun beat down upon the city of Boston.

James Haley assembled the troop and squad leaders under the shade of the trees near the site entrance. He wore a discrete headset that used his Shadowstone smartphone to link with his laptop, the Panopticon, and the communication links of the assembled combat leaders. Beside him, Louise Wesson stood, wearing her own combat gear and her 'game on' face partially hidden behind her mirrored sunglasses.

The eight Red-1 and Blue-5 combat leaders all wore matt black combat armor and tactical helmets provided with an extensive suite of sensors and communications links. They carried their weapons easily and waited patiently, alert, relaxed and ready for action. The Green-4 squad leaders remained at their post on the dock; networked in by the tactical communication links.

James stood in front of the group and addressed his men, "This cordon has to be airtight. I don't want anyone or anything crossing it until we're done. Our task is to ensure that the three Order of Thoth terrorists in that warehouse," he thrust his finger at the massive building, "stay there until General Armitage arrives tonight with her special forces to deal with them."

"Sir?" One of the squad leaders asked.

"Yes?"

"I think we're attracting some unwanted attention," the squad leader remarked with a nod toward the street where small huddles of people stood watching the proceedings.

James glanced around, snorted derisively, looked at his watch, and directed, "The BPD will be providing an outer perimeter, they should be here in five minutes. Our cover is simple; this is a counter-terrorism exercise. The BPD will play ball and keep the locals from getting in the way."

James turned to his senior team leader and asked, "Wesson, what's the status on the RHIB, they're not showing up on my network comms."

"It's on station, a hundred yards off the dock."

"What's on it?"

"A single squad from Indigo-6. The RHIB itself is a thirty-six-footer. It carries a fore mounted Mk-19 grenade launcher, a rear mounted M2 .50 caliber heavy machine gun, and a quad mount FIM-92 Block II Stinger surface to air missile system amidships."

"You could start a war with that. Make sure they keep moving up and down the river and they keep a lookout for anything that could assist a river exfiltration. These Order terrorists didn't choose this site by accident. Make sure your men have their heads on a swivel, and get them connected to my comms link."

"Yes, Sir."

James faced his men and demanded, "I need two snipers and an electrical power expert. We need to take out all their external CCTV cameras and cut the power to the warehouse, who is available?"

The squad leaders responded quickly, issuing commands across secured links and five men dropped out of the cordon. Two men in pairs took up positions on either side of the warehouse. In less than twenty seconds, eight single shots rang out, reducing eight CCTV cameras into mangled lumps of twisted metal and sputtering power cables.

The fifth man ran to the Blue-5 nightfalcon, and extracted a kit from the helicopter. He went to a nearby electrical power distribution pole. Scaling it with a special climbing rig, he selected and cut some key wires. Turning, he gave James a thumbs up, before descending to the ground and returning to his position in the cordon.

James consulted the Panopticon satellite view of the warehouse, switching on a specialized filter to examine what he expected to be a dead zone of zero electrical activity. In the distance, a diesel engine came online. A soft thrumming from a hundred and fifty yards in front of him. He frowned, looking down at his screen. The warehouse was a spaghetti maze of electrical cables – all alive. He switched filters, there was a plume of hot exhaust escaping a three-inch pipe jutting out of the roof midway along the right side of the warehouse.

James grinned wryly and muttered, "Damn. Well, okay, you have a backup generator but not for long." He signaled one of the Red-1 squad leaders, gave him some quick instructions, and a minute later the Red-1 nightfalcon was lifting off from the parking lot.

James noted that half a dozen BPD cruisers and vans had shown up on Bedford Street, more than twenty police officers were setting up temporary roadblocks and police line tape to keep the public away. He sighed, *they will certainly get a show, I will need a PSYOPS crew to come in and spin this operation for general consumption*. The Red-1 nightfalcon took up a position facing the right-side wall, a hundred and twenty yards away from the warehouse. He slaved the helicopter's combat system to his laptop and fed in the Panopticon supplied location of the diesel generator. It sat on the ground level of the warehouse, butting up against the wall. The Panopticon specs for the building indicated the walls were three feet of steel-reinforced stone masonry.

The helicopter veered slightly to the left, settling about ten yards off the ground, its nose down at a slight angle. The men in the cordon backed away and gave the helicopter plenty of space.

James smiled, and gave the order to fire.

Showtime!

Beneath the cockpit of the nightfalcon, two multi-barreled heavy machine guns opened fire with the unique sound that Gatling guns make, like a thickly woven mat being torn in half overlaid with an electric whirr. The sound started and didn't stop. Gray smoke streamed from the mouths of the guns, swirling away in the wash from the helicopter's rotor blades. Spent casings dropped like confetti from beneath the spinning machine gun barrels. The bullets flashed into a mark two yards in diameter at the base of the wall, every fifth round a bright tracer, the rest comprised depleted uranium penetrators.

The stone masonry of the wall started to ablate and flake away. Disintegrating before the ferocious barrage of the twin guns. Giant sparks flew as thick reinforcing steel cables wilted under the titanic hammer of the heavy fire. Grit and dust spewed from the hole in a billowing cloud. Suddenly the bullets were through and the diesel generator exploded and a ball of flame shot out through the gaping hole in the wall.

The guns fell silent. Veering to the left, the nightfalcon made its way back to its original landing spot in the parking lot.

James heard cheers from the onlookers. They were crowding the police line and waving American flags. He momentarily considered the idea of simply letting them stay and get their minds blown away by what would go down this night, then thought better of it. He called out a quick command, "Wesson, get those BPD clowns to clear the street and the houses back to the end of the side streets. I want a clear perimeter out to a mile until we're done."

"Yes, Sir. On it," she replied, jogging off toward the police line and the BPD Officer in Charge.

James returned to his laptop, the Panopticon satellite feed with an infrared filter showed a sizable fire raging against the right wall. As he watched, the fire started to die, first slowly, and then quickly.

"A fire suppressant?" James murmured. This site was proving to be quite resilient and he mused to himself, *These guys have a lot of tricks.*

As the fire died, three faint human contacts came back into view, spread out on the far side of the warehouse. He noted silently, *Well, now you're blind and when night comes you will be sitting in the dark. Let's see what you do while we wait for General Armitage to arrive.*

* * *

Anton, Gang, and Li regrouped in the middle of the warehouse.

Acrid smoke tinged the air, but the quick response of the fire suppressant system around the diesel generator had prevented the warehouse from becoming a smoke-filled death trap.

Gang gripped both their shoulders and instructed in decisive tones, "Their strategy is clear, they want to make us powerless and keep us here until sunset; when no doubt the vampires will arrive in force." He glanced

152

at his watch and thought for a moment. "Sunset is about twenty minutes past eight which means that we have five and a half hours before they arrive."

Anton said, "With the power out, we're not going to be able to use our crane traps."

"And once it gets dark, it's really going to be to the vampires' advantage rather than ours, it would be much better to have lights," Li remarked.

"Is there any way we can fix it?" Anton asked.

Gang frowned. "Not that I know of."

Li's face lit up and she declared with an excited smile, "Father! The fire suppressant system was operating while the generator was on fire and the main power lines were cut. What's its power source?"

"I'm not sure. Let's look."

The three of them moved through the maze, coming to the right-side wall where the diesel generator lay in ruins. They moved cautiously around to make sure they were not presenting any opportunities for a sniper to get a shot through the gaping hole in the wall where the diesel generator had stood.

They reached the wall to the left of the ruined generator. There was an array of eight silvery-gray rectangular cabinets along the wall. Each one was about eight feet high, three feet wide and about two feet deep. Heavy cables ran above them and connected at the top of each cabinet. Anton looked down the wall toward the dock, the cables ran the distance of the wall and there was another array ten yards further along.

Anton suggested, "I think this equipment runs the length of the wall."

"That's a lot of battery power," Li said.

"Anton, this is typical of your grandfather – he believed in defense in depth," Gang remarked.

"They're always watching," Anton said. "We'll need to be able to test this without letting them know that we still have power."

"Speaking of which," Li stated decisively, pressing a red button near the array. "Now they're all disconnected. They will hold their power, and not show up on some Shadowstone operative's fancy surveillance system. But testing this without giving the game away will take time, I'll have to inspect the power cables, and I can run micro-currents through the system to see that the circuits are still complete."

"Good girl," Gang declared with a grin. "You start on that. Anton and I will continue with prepping the tricks, traps and general mayhem for our much-anticipated guests."

Li left to collect the equipment she needed. Gang pulled Anton aside and suggested, "I think we should make a call; this phone of mine is not so dumb. Francis was able to send me an app, which I installed, it provides an encrypted text capability beyond the capacity of Shadowstone to decipher."

"Cool."

Gang sent a text message using the secure app, which read, 'We are at the Boston Warehouse and Shadowstone are here. Gang.'

About twenty seconds later a reply came back which read, 'We have seen it. They have you surrounded. We have a long way to come, we will be there after sunset. I will text details before we arrive. F.

Anton read the message over Gang's shoulder, and remarked sarcastically, "So, they will arrive with the vampires – wonderful."

Gang shrugged his shoulders helplessly. "Well … there is nothing to be done to speed their arrival, or slow the passage of the sun."

Anton lifted his hands and queried, "Does the Order have a problem with daylight operations?"

"Everyone has a secret to keep,' Gang replied. "We're the same as the vampires in that respect."

"Wouldn't it be better for us to simply 'out' the truth about the vampires?" Anton suggested.

Gang smiled wryly. "Do you think you would be believed?"

Anton's shoulders slumped, then he straightened. "There must be a way to convince people of what is going on."

"The vampires own, through layered proxies, all the major media outlets. They'd squash the truth, and paint the Order as Nazi loving, death worshiping, satanic child-thieving cannibals out to drown the world in blood. They'd turn everyone against us, and we can't fight everyone."

"Then why haven't the vampires tried that?"

"They have, are you aware of the witch craze in Europe and North America from the 15th through to the 18th century."

"Yes."

"The so-called authorities of the day murdered a lot of innocent people, including some members of the Order. The vampires orchestrated the whole thing. It was a great cover; they could go into a village pretending to be witch finders, kill any Order members in the village, and then depopulate it to hide what had actually happened. The local authorities would then thank them for it."

"Vampires were behind the witch hunters?"

"One of Crane's early experiments with social control."

"Why don't they try the same tactic now?"

"Society has moved on; fewer people would believe it. I think Crane is simply weighing the risks. A public campaign against the Order risks his own exposure, so he has more to lose than to gain by such a strategy. So, both camps live in the shadows and fight our battles in secret."

Anton nodded. "It's a pretty messed up world we're living in."

"That it is," Gang agreed. He looked at his watch. "Time's getting on Anton, let's get these fireworks in place on the maintenance walkways. I also have some claymores to set up around that hole in the wall and throughout the maze, and we still have to set up our ammunition reloads so they're easy to pick up."

Anton smiled and agreed, "You're right, we can solve these problems another time – perhaps over a beer."

Gang smiled and winked.

The two men set to work.

* * *

Anton lined up the modified M18 claymore mine next to the base of a container and spooled out a net of thin electrical fibers in front of it.

The net stretched forward from the bottom of the mine, blending in with the concrete floor of the warehouse. The tripwire net created an area ten-feet wide and twelve-feet deep in front of the claymore where anyone making a single step would fire the mine on a three second 'Sneaker' delay – designed to allow more than one person to enter the area of deadliest effect. Anton circled around the net, reached down and flicked an arming switch on the mine.

He took a step back from the armed mine. It covered a square forty yards on a side surrounded by stacked shipping containers. There were two other entrances into the trap that would funnel anyone entering the square toward where Anton stood. This was the last of twenty mines he'd positioned in accordance with a map provided by Gang.

He stood between two containers, a ten-foot-wide gap in the maze wall. He prepared himself, ramped, making a vertical leap that brought his feet to the top of the first container. He pushed off again, landing in a crouch on top of the opposite pair of containers. In two vertical leaps, he'd ascended nearly twenty feet.

He rose up from his crouch and adjusted the fit of the automatic shotgun he carried diagonally across his back. The weapon rested next to the scabbard for the Blue Dragon sword. At his hip, he wore a holster for the H&K MP7 A2 submachine gun.

He looked for Gang, finding him on the second mezzanine level. The mezzanine was still accessible by stairs from the floor. The stairs had survived the partial destruction of the first mezzanine level when the diesel generator had exploded more than three hours earlier.

"Gang, I'm done," Anton called out. He only had to raise his voice a little for Gang to hear him across the warehouse.

"Good work. Meet me at the front doors."

"Sure," Anton agreed, jogging along the top of the maze toward the front of the warehouse. In moments, he arrived, jumping down to the ground below. Gang showed up a few seconds later with two of the Milkor MGLs, the ones with a splash of red paint across their thick barrel.

Anton felt his excitement rise as he recalled Gang's words. '*The red ones carry a standard high-explosive round with a shaped charge that is best against a vehicle, and can also be used as an anti-personnel weapon versus humans or vampires.*' He asked excitedly, "You need my help with one of these?"

Gang tilted his head quizzically and frowned. "Those men out there are someone's son, if they die today at our hand, it's not a cause for excitement."

"What?" Anton blinked, nonplussed by Gang's attitude. "Are you sure of that? Look at the choices they've made. As bad or worse than those triad thugs that attacked the Noodle House."

Gang shook his head and instructed, "I would be happier if you were calmer. The ideal is to find a center of peace in the midst of combat. Your excitement borders on lust for their deaths."

"A center of peace?" Anton hissed. A tight ball of fury ignited in the depths of Anton's soul. He pointed fiercely past the gates at the front of the warehouse. "What the Hell! Those bastards covered up the torture and murder of my mother and the abduction of my father to some crazy fucking insane vampire torture. They all volunteered at some point to wear those uniforms. They deserve whatever punishment I can give them."

Gang stroked his chin and then wagged his finger in Anton's face. "Shortly after I first met you, we spoke briefly about vengeance and justice. Do you remember? I see now that nothing has changed."

Anton frowned, his eyes narrowed in barely controlled rage, and he snapped, "Something about walking in the shadow of vengeance and the light of justice."

"Something like that," Gang said quietly.

"I don't see anyone else stepping up to the plate to deliver justice for my parents. It will have to be me."

Gang stepped in, clapped Anton on both shoulders and pulled him close with enough strength he couldn't resist if he wanted to. "Anton, there is no room for a personal vendetta on this journey. You must let this anger and hatred go."

"They destroyed my family. I have every right to feel this way. I promise you. I will not stop until I have destroyed Armitage, Shadowstone, and the Vampire Dominion."

Gang sighed, and his grip relaxed. "Perhaps it would be best if you were not here."

Anton shrugged off Gang's hands, stepping back, his face filled with shock. "You would send me away?"

"For your own sake – yes."

Anton's anger melted away. Gang and Li were the closest people to a family he had now, he would rather die than lose them. Working past a knot in his throat, Anton asked, "Why would you send me away?"

"Anton, you are a good man, perhaps a very good man with a great capacity for love and courage, but right now, your life is on a moral knife-edge and you could either step into the light or fall into darkness."

Gang waved at the warehouse. "Why are we here today? Why is Shadowstone assembled for war out there in broad daylight? It's unheard of. The vampires are coming tonight, and so is the Order of Thoth. There has not been a major battle in the last twenty years. What's different Anton? It's you, it's your presence here, the hidden Slayne, perhaps the last Slayne. You had a direct male line ancestor that lived in the time of Hakron the Scribe, who was part of the original post-Ahknaton Order of Thoth. Hakron entrusted your ancestor with the protection of the Papyrus of Hakron the Scribe, and it remained in the safe keeping of your family up until a few short weeks ago. Life is a strange mix of fate and choice, and I think the next few hours will be more about you and your choices than about anyone else."

A poignant sadness almost overwhelmed Anton and he asked, "You truly believe that my choices matter that much?"

Gang nodded and declared with quiet certainty, "More than you can understand."

Ashamed by his outburst in front of Gang's steadfastness, Anton said quietly, "What do you need from me?"

"Your help."

"You've got that anytime you want it," he declared solemnly.

Gang pointed to where the rails of the cranes passed through holes in the front of the warehouse and said, "The maintenance walkway up there will give you a sight on the Shadowstone positions in the parking lot. We need to thin these guys down before night falls, or else, we will have all of them and the vampires to fight at the same time. We need to take out their helicopters, they're a key asset for them, and so that's what we will use the MGLs for."

Gang gave one of the MGLs to Anton and showed him how to operate the simple weapon. He directed, "Now you take the right-hand side, and I will take the left. Watch my angles, I will show you before I fire. Fire the first three rounds only, that will take a second, then immediately pull right back to our first defensive position, they're bound to fire back at you. We have the element of surprise, but that's only good for the first shot, Li will cover our rear at the dock."

"Will do," Anton agreed, following Gang back to the mezzanine stairs. Ascending to the top level, they were able to access the maintenance walkways that spanned the roof of the warehouse. Anton took up position on the walkway next to the right-side crane rail at the front of the warehouse. He spotted Li as she took up a position on the maintenance walkway at the river end. She carried a large sniper rifle, two of the MP7 submachine guns holstered at her hips, and the Green Dragon in its scabbard over her shoulder.

Anton wanted to be at her side, but she'd her job, and he had his. He focused on the task at hand. He glanced across at Gang, who was sliding backward on his belly from the gap in the warehouse wall. He stood up, signaling Anton with a thumbs up, and pointed to his MGL, which he held at an angle up from the horizontal.

Anton mimicked his position and readied himself to Ramp. He would have to move forward, sight the target, pull the trigger, and once the first three rounds had fired, pull back off the maintenance walkway to the top of the maze below. He watched as Gang held up his right hand, counting down the seconds with his fingers, first holding up five, then four, then three, then two. Anton ramped, watching Gang move in slow motion as he held up his last finger, then Gang ramped, flashing forward. Anton moved a fraction of a second later. He came to a halt level with the gap in the wall of the warehouse. In front of him were two of the nightfalcon helicopters, the one on his side was spooling up, its rotors spinning faster and faster. In his peripheral vision, he saw a grenade shoot out from Gang's position toward the other helicopter, the noise of the shot reaching him a moment after he saw it. He raised his MGL to the same angle as Gang had demonstrated, lined it up on the helicopter and pulled the trigger. The grenade sailed away from him with a solid 'choof' sound, the revolver like barrels of the MGL began turning and a second and a third grenade quickly followed the first.

Gang's words rang in his mind. *Then immediately pull right back to our first defensive position.* Anton waited. He wanted to make sure he'd hit the target. The first of Gang's grenades struck the helicopter on the left. Its fuel tank exploded and it vanished in a huge fireball. The second and third grenades bracketed the exploding helicopter, adding to the mayhem amongst the men nearby. He saw the first of his grenades just miss the top of the helicopter, and then the second and third followed to land harmlessly along the edge of the parking lot.

What the hell? He'd missed everything. Anton's ramp stuttered, the world flicking back into normal motion.

More than a dozen Shadowstone operatives responded to the threat, swinging their weapons toward him and the other walkway. Gang had already disappeared back into the warehouse. He was safe.

He dived back into silence and his ramp took flight. The first of the muzzle flashes from the assault rifles started popping along the cordon. He lowered his weapon slightly, pulling the trigger of the MGL. It fired a fourth grenade toward the remaining nightfalcon. A couple of bullets whizzed past his head. A dozen more shattered the stone near his shoulder, sending splinters into the left side of his face. Twisting away, he leaped back along the walkway and out of the line of fire. Behind him, he heard another large explosion out in the parking lot.

"Got it!" he exulted.

There was a trickling wetness on the left side of his head. He dragged his hand across his face as he moved to the first defensive position. His hand came away covered in blood and tiny stone fragments. He blinked; both his eyes were still okay.

He laughed and exclaimed, "Hell, I got worse on the Hockey rink!"

* * *

James lit a cigarette.

A 40mm grenade looped out of the front of the warehouse and crashed into the Blue-5 helicopter. The nightfalcon exploded in a blinding glare. A wave of heat and pressure blowing over the men nearest the helicopter. Another two grenades followed, adding their destructive power to the mayhem amongst his forces.

He whirled; more grenades flew at the Red-1 helicopter which was preparing to take off for a low-level reconnaissance run around the area. They all passed over the spinning rotors, exploding harmlessly along the parking lot's fence line. His men returned fire and a swarm of 5.56mm rounds reached toward the two gaps fifteen yards up the face of the warehouse. The man who had destroyed the Blue-5 nightfalcon had already disappeared. The second man fired a fourth grenade that looped directly at the Red-1 nightfalcon. James' heart sank as it smashed into the front of the helicopter which promptly exploded in a bright ball of flame. He had to turn away, shielding his eyes from the glare. When he looked back at the warehouse, the second man had vanished.

A name rushed into his mind. *Anton Slayne – alias Smith – you're a dead man.*

"Wesson, get the Green-4 helicopter airborne, get your team back here, and move the RHIB back fifty yards."

"Already happening, Sir," Wesson replied, sprinting over to stand next to him.

"Damn MGLs," James growled with disgust.

"If they have those, they could have anything."

"Teams report," James growled into his comm links.

A rapid succession of reports flowed in. There were four dead aircrews; pilots and co-pilots. Red-1 had lost two men to flying debris from the helicopter explosion, and another two men were too wounded to fight.

The Blue-5 team had operatives closer to their nightfalcon, as it had been stationary. They had lost six men from the three grenades and another two wounded and out of action. That left twenty operatives from the two spectrum teams' original strength of thirty-two men.

"Wesson, reform the teams into five squads of four, position the wounded back here and give them some first aid and water."

"Yes, Sir," Wesson responded. She rushed to comply, issuing directives through her headset.

At the other end of the dock, the Green-4 nightfalcon completed spooling up. Taking off, it veered violently away from the warehouse. It bristled with guns as the operatives on board trained their weapons on the open gates at the river end of the warehouse. Half a minute later the helicopter had parked in a deserted Bedford Street, beyond the range of the MGLs. The Green-4 operatives streamed from the nightfalcon and it took to the air once more. In moments, it had risen to a position six hundred yards above the ground and the same distance back from the front of the warehouse.

The Green-4 operatives marshaled before her. Wesson made three squads of four men and one squad of two. She assigned the three squads to join the main Shadowstone force with James and assigned the remaining half squad to herself. She turned to James and reported, "The men are ready."

"Outstanding," James acknowledged with a growl. "I want the RHIB to move into a position where it can fire on anyone coming out of the rear of the warehouse. It's got a .50 cal, and a belt fed MGL, that should be able to supply enough firepower to block any escape. Take your squad of two and block the right-side entrance, and the hole in the wall where the generator was. Make sure that no one escapes from that side."

"Yes, Sir," Wesson agreed. Turning away, she gave directions over the tactical link to the Indigo-6 squad manning the RHIB. Her two-man squad followed her, checking their weapons as they jogged after her.

James addressed his remaining men. "You know our orders. We have to hold these bastards here until the damn cavalry arrives."

The men grumbled and swore.

"I know exactly how you feel. Our standing orders are that we do not fire unless fired upon. Well, we have been well and truly fired upon." He shook his head and thrust his finger at the warehouse. "And I'm not giving these rat bastards another chance to kill us."

He stood in front of his men, his hands on his hips. He leaned forward and declared, "Now here's what we're going to do. We're going to use the remaining nightfalcon to blow the front doors off with Hellfire missiles and then take a position over the river."

He drew a circle in the air with his right index finger. "Then all of us are going in via the front door." He slapped his right fist into the palm of his left hand. "We will be the hammer and the RHIB and the nightfalcon will be the anvil."

He stood tall, his eyes flashing. "We will go in there and kill them or push them out onto the dock where the RHIB and the nightfalcon will take them apart. Now there are thirty-three of us going in, and only three of them. If they don't surrender, kill them. If they do surrender – kill them. We take no prisoners today!"

The men shouted, "Yes, Sir!"

The Shadowstone force moved out as one. Dispersing across the parking lot, they readied themselves to move forward toward the warehouse without making a target of themselves.

James tossed his laptop into his car, and picked up his assault rifle. He'd already swapped his dark gray suit jacket for a bullet proof vest. He wore combat webbing to carry extra magazines and grenades for the M203 launcher on his rifle. He cocked the assault rifle and loaded a grenade. He opened his comm link to the Green-4 nightfalcon, ordering it to destroy the front gates of the warehouse.

The helicopter barely moved, only enough to tilt its nose toward the giant steel doors on the front of the warehouse. Two seconds later a pair of Hellfire III missiles launched from their pylons to the left and right of the helicopter's cockpit. They streaked toward the steel doors, detonating with a pair of thunderous explosions and a white thermobaric glare. The heavy steel doors evaporated, the crane gantries above the gates disappearing into a cloud of flying steel fragments.

Before the smoke and dust could begin to clear, the heavy machine guns under the nose of the nightfalcon opened up. They sprayed the interior of the warehouse with a sustained barrage of .50 caliber rounds. After ten seconds and a thousand rounds, the firing stopped. The helicopter veered away to take up a new position over the Mystic River.

"Go! Go! Go!" James shouted. Sprinting with the assembled operatives toward the cavernous openings in the front of the warehouse.

In less than ten seconds they were all through the entrance.

* * *

The giant hammering of the nightfalcon's machine guns abruptly stopped, silence rushing in to fill the vacuum.

Anton lay prone on top of the maze wall about fifty yards back from the front of the warehouse. He lifted his head, just enough to sight the billowing smoke and dust obscuring the smashed entrance. Missiles had vaporized the great steel doors. Late afternoon sunlight backlit the swirling haze. The play of sunlight, smoke, metal and stone dust against the emerging torn remains of the warehouse gates and tangled crane gantries, left Anton filled with an eerily surreal awe.

The haze suddenly eddied, swirling as men clad in black body armor, carrying assault rifles, streamed over the rubble and into the warehouse. They came in pairs, their heads in combat helmets swiveling this way and that as they looked for targets. They held their rifles high, red-dot laser sights on top of the guns tracking their lines of sight. He wriggled backward, hugging the cold metal of the container. The Shadowstone operatives disappeared from view, obscured by the maze wall.

Anton glanced across at Gang, who held a similar position beneath the crane rail on the other side of the warehouse. Above and behind him, he saw that Li had left the rear of the warehouse and was lying prone on the uppermost mezzanine level near the maintenance access walkways. She had her smartphone in her hand, working it intently.

Six grappling hooks trailing solid black lines appeared over the maze wall thirty yards directly in front of Anton. Another set of grappling hooks appeared on Gang's side of the warehouse. The lines went taut as the men below began scaling them. In a couple of seconds, they would be up on the maze wall with Anton and Gang.

"Damn it!" Anton muttered. They were supposed to go through the maze, not over it. He rose to one knee, aiming the MGL at the top of the container where most of the lines were. The first of the black helmets appeared, and he pulled the trigger. The grenade flew toward them where it exploded, ripping open the top of the steel container like tearing tinfoil, and slashed through the black lines. The other operatives spotted the shot and ducked away. Anton pointed the MGL into the space where the black lines ran down, firing his last grenade which disappeared below the edge of the maze wall before exploding in a bright glare.

Someone screamed for a moment and then fell silent.

There were more choofs of launching grenades. Gang fired a volley of them across the front line of the maze, then dropped his empty MGL and ran back about twenty yards.

Anton ramped, running back across the maze toward the middle of the warehouse as Gang's grenades exploded and more screams and shouts emanated from the ranks of the operatives along the front of the warehouse. *Gang's grenades should drive those guys forward and deeper into the maze.*

The warehouse fell silent. Anton strained to hear and see anything moving in front of him. *They're not moving!* He placed the empty MGL at his feet. Pulling the automatic shotgun off his back, he trained it on the area where he expected the operatives would emerge.

Grappling hooks sailed for a second time over the container walls near Gang. More hooks and lines followed, landing forty yards in front of

Anton. The black lines stretched taught, but no black helmets appeared. Instead, a dozen slim grenades flew over the maze wall, and wherever they landed they stuck as if glued to the metal containers. One landed a yard in front of where Gang stood, he ramped, blurring backward more than a dozen yards.

Anton reflexively turned his head away. All the grenades exploded in blinding glares and thunderous reports. Even though he'd looked away, Anton found himself dazzled as gray spots flew before his eyes, and his ears rang as agonizing pain shot through his skull. Staggering backward, he stumbled over the MGL at his feet and slipped off the maze wall. As he fell, he managed to reach out wildly with his left hand, grabbing a vertical metal rail along the side of the top container. He slid down, coming to a halt with his arm outstretched above him, and his feet dangling inches above the webbed network of a trip wire for one of his own claymore mines. His eyesight was beginning to return as he looked up to see his MGL teetering on the top edge of the container above him.

Gunfire erupted in the warehouse. Staccato three round bursts from the assault rifles, interspersed by the high-speed rips of Gang's MP7s, ripped through the air.

They're on the maze wall! I have to get back up and help Gang and Li. Anton swung backward to get some momentum and then launched himself upward as a stream of rifle fire burst through the air above the container. A stray bullet hit the MGL, knocking it flying over the edge. Anton kept swinging upward, letting go as the MGL passed him on the way down to the concrete floor of the warehouse and the waiting web of tripwires for the claymore mine.

His maneuver threw him a yard over the top edge of the container. He rolled as he landed. Springing to his feet, already ramped, he ran directly toward six Shadowstone operatives five yards away on the wall.

The three operatives at the front all began firing at the same time. Anton leaped into the air, a massive ten feet up and over the flying bullets and their heads. He pulled the trigger of the automatic shotgun which answered the rifles with a fusillade of heavy shot that knocked one of the operatives off the maze wall and into the space that the MGL had fallen into. The man was still flailing in midair when the claymore mine fired – tripped by the MGL that had fallen seconds before. The man instantly disappeared in a hail of lead and gray smoke.

His following shotgun rounds struck another two operatives. Blown backward by the force of the hits, they slipped over the edge of the maze wall.

Twisting in mid-air, Anton landed on his feet facing the three remaining operatives who were sliding to a halt and spinning around to follow him. The one on the right allowed himself to fall backward and twist around, his gun was the first to bear on Anton. He dodged hard left as a three-round burst ripped past his right arm. He fired his shotgun again; a pair of rounds struck the front of the operative's tactical helmet and he dropped immediately. The remains of his shattered visor covered in blood.

The remaining two operatives stepped backward to give themselves room to bring their rifles up. Anton ran into them ramped, clubbing one in the side of the neck with the butt of his shotgun. The man silently falling backward, disappearing over the edge of the maze wall.

The last operative turned, lashing at Anton with his own rifle butt. Anton leaned backward; the rifle butt swung past over his face. Anton sprang back erect. He swung his shotgun butt up, catching the man underneath his chin. The force of the blow lifted the operative clear of the container, throwing him off the maze wall.

Anton's head swiveled around. On the other side of the warehouse, Gang was reloading his MP7s. In front of him two black-clad bodies lay limply on the maze walls.

There were no more live Shadowstone operatives on top of the maze walls. The front quarter of the warehouse exploded in multi-colored flashes, and silver sparkles. Loud whistles erupted as rockets launched and streamed down and across the warehouse from row upon row of boxes and cylinders strapped to the maintenance walkways. The warehouse became a crazed Fourth of July as light and sound battered the Shadowstone operatives in the front quarter.

Anton took advantage of the momentary chaos to back deeper into the warehouse and move to the right. Gang, having completed reloading his MP7s, did the same. He looked around for Li, she'd vanished from the mezzanine level and he could not find her anywhere.

Fear and worry for her was a cold clamp on his chest. *Damn it, where is she?* He dropped to one knee to lower his profile. Reloaded the shotgun with a fresh magazine from his combat webbing and sighted along the weapon toward the front of the warehouse which still flashed, smoked, banged and whistled with colored, sparkling mayhem. Moments later the fireworks bled dry as a final lonely rocket shot across the warehouse, exploding with a loud whistling bang in a streamer of green sparkles.

One of the operatives called out in a disgusted growl. "You've gotta be kidding me?" The warehouse went silent, and grappling hooks once again sailed over the container walls. *They're not buying it. They know we're up here now and they're going to fight us here.*

Gang signaled with his hand. The lights on the cranes came on; the right container plummeting to the floor with an earsplitting bang, a half second later, the left container followed it down. A scream of horror suddenly cut off as the second container slammed onto the concrete floor of the warehouse. Li had dropped the containers, which could only mean the operatives were now in the claymore kill zones.

The grappling lines went taut again on both sides of the warehouse. This time, Anton had to wait until the operatives leaped and rolled onto the top of the containers. Men in black body armor appeared on top of the wall on both sides of the warehouse. Gang's MP7s ripped into action. Anton started firing his shotgun. The weapon barked and stuttered. The lead operative wore a suit, a bulletproof vest, and a snarl on his face. He rolled forward and sideways with cat-like reflexes. The heavy blasts of shot striking the next operative in the chest who staggered backward and fell off the wall.

It was the suit from the night of his mother's murder. The head of the secret keepers. Rage rooted Anton to the spot, before Gang's earlier instructions ripped through him – 'keep moving.'

Anton ramped hard, moving to the right as return fire lanced past him on the left. He felt bullets whiz past his head, the suit was still firing at him with uncanny accuracy even as he blurred away. Before Anton could fire back, another two operatives fell backward in quick succession, struck by heavy caliber rounds fired from above and behind him.

It was Li, his guardian angel with a sniper rifle.

The remaining two operatives on Anton's side of the warehouse followed the suit as he led them off the top of the maze wall.

They were breaking. Anton moved again, this time backward and to his left, zig-zagging across the top of the maze. Gang's MP7s fired again as he traded streams of bullets with the operatives that had scaled the wall on his side of the warehouse. The operatives had spread out and Gang had multiple dispersed targets. He blurred, fired, blurred and fired again. Two of the operatives spun around, dropping to the floor below, another two followed them as Li claimed their lives with her heavy .50 caliber sniper rifle.

Suddenly two of the claymore mines went off, one to the right, near Anton and the other to the left near Gang. The explosions rang through the warehouse. The crash of hundreds of ball bearings smashing against the steel containers preceded the screams of the wounded and dying men caught in the blasts.

Anton ramped, backing deeper into the warehouse, Gang did the same. They both took up positions mid-way along the maze. Gang signaled Anton with his hand, pointed to his eyes and then at the rear of the warehouse. Turning, Anton jogged along the top of the maze toward the river end of the warehouse.

When he got near the river end, he took up a position where he could see the dock entrance. There was no one on the dock. In the distance, he could see a RHIB patrolling the river, above him, he could hear the distant sounds of a hovering helicopter.

He rested and kept watch, as silence descended upon the warehouse, broken only by the cries of wounded and dying men.

* * *

The injured man stopped moaning, lapsing into unconsciousness as the powerful narcotic took effect.

Each of the Shadowstone operatives carried a kit with syringes, filled with stimulants, painkillers, and other useful compounds. James threw the used syringe to the floor. Squatting, he picked up the fully armored man, throwing him over his shoulder like a two-hundred-and-fifty-pound sack of potatoes. He carried him back to the front of the warehouse where he laid him down with the other three wounded. The three remaining active operatives, Rigby and Hansen from Blue-5, and Boorman from Green-4 stood guard. They stood dispersed in a line just inside the front of the warehouse. Their rifles on full auto, scanning the maze wall for any sign of attack.

James turned away from the wounded men. He stared with flat eyes at the steel containers, now peppered with holes from the initial nightfalcon strafing, and scorched from the Hellfire missiles that had blown apart the great steel doors at the front of the warehouse. Containers that now hid the bloody remains of twenty-five of his men. All killed in a firefight that had lasted less than three minutes. He scratched his head with both hands, rubbing his scalp hard, forward and back. His mouth was a thin slash in a face that had gone tight and pale. His hands clenched into fists and then unclenched, he brushed them on his blood-splattered trousers. He lifted his hands and glared at them; the blood of his men covered them with streaks of gore.

He took a deep breath and let it out, tapped his earpiece and growled an order, "Wesson report."

"Sir, exits are secure at the river end, and on this side of the warehouse, no one has escaped," Wesson stated, her voice flat in his ear.

What a damn nightmare. James looked at his watch, it was 18:05, it would take close to a hundred minutes for more spectrum teams to get ready, and reach Boston with their nightfalcons. That still left him, at least another half an hour to re-establish the cordon before General Armitage and her special forces team arrived after sunset.

"Wesson, who is left on standby at Fort Dix?"

"The rest of Indigo-6 are available. One nightfalcon and three squads. Orange-2 and Violet-7 are on international deployment in South America, and Yellow-3 is in reserve at Fort Dix, it would take three hours to get them here via helicopter and nearly six hours by van."

"What about our forces from the other three sectors in North America?"

"Too far away to get here in any sort of meaningful timeframe, Sir."

"Get Indigo-6 here ASAP, and fire up Yellow-3 and get them to mobilize cleanup and PSYOPS crews. We'll need everyone tonight."

"Yes, Sir."

James spat on the ground in disgust. Turning to his remaining men still standing, he directed, "Move back to the parking lot entrance. Help me with the wounded, if they had wanted to kill us, they would have done it by now."

The men slung their rifles. Each man picked up one of their comrades and followed James back to the far edge of the parking lot, the big shady tree, and the original four wounded men.

James laid his man onto the thin grass under the shade of the tree. The sun was nearing the horizon and shadows were beginning to reach their dark fingers toward the front of the warehouse. He rubbed his chin, shook his head, keeping his thoughts unspoken before his men. *What a disaster. We were completely unprepared for this fight. Years of training, combat experience, and superb equipment meant nothing in that death trap. What the hell does General Armitage expect to achieve with her damn special forces when they arrive?*

James turned, inspecting his wounded, and discovered that one of them had just died. He couldn't stop himself from doing the math.

Make that twenty-six dead from the warehouse assault.

* * *

The elevator doors swished aside; overhead lights gleamed off Chloe's all-black nightfalcon as it sat in the middle of the citadel roof-top hangar.

Before the machine stood six of Crane's handpicked praetorian guards. Each wore matte black Shadowstone body armor, and combat helmets modified to protect and facilitate vampire senses. They all carried M249 light machine guns with one hundred round drum magazines, half a dozen hand grenades attached to combat webbing and an assortment of personal edged weapons composed of various long bladed swords and heavy battle axes.

She emerged from the elevator, dressed in the same style of armor and combat webbing as the guards, but instead of an M249, she carried the Red Dragon sword belted to her left hip. She strode with determined grace toward her personal nightfalcon. The guards tilting their heads in deference, parted before her. She led them on board, taking a seat facing back into the cabin behind the vampire pilot. The praetorians filed into the cabin, the last one pulling the door shut.

The helicopter's twin turbines spooled up with a low whine. In seconds, the rotors were spinning and gathering pace. Red lights strobed throughout the hangar. A klaxon sounded a steady ululation and other vampires cleared the space as the bay doors began rapidly winding back. The late afternoon sunlight slashed through the air above the nightfalcon and gleamed off the domes of the citadel's advanced air defense systems as they emerged above the roof line of the massive tower. The twin turbines roared like bound demons composed of bright steel and blue fire. The black nightfalcon leaped through the gap in the roof, speeding away to the northeast, its polished skin sparkling in the setting sun.

Chloe surveyed her troops. Each of the praetorians had been alive for more than a century, some for more than two centuries. Crane had carefully selected them from the near-dead on battlefields across the world. Their long years of service to him honing unparalleled skills in combat and warcraft. Crane had saved them all from death at the very last moment of their mortal lives and they were to a man, determined to serve their immortal master for eternity. She'd provided them with an extensive briefing of the site and the mission in a ready room off the hangar bay. She smiled quietly at them as they sat relaxed, confident, and ready to deal death once more. One particular thought ran on a path of certainty through the field of her mind. *None of you will survive tonight.*

She glanced to the side, looking through the dark transparent armor of the canopy at the hard, luminous ball of the sun descending toward the horizon. It was moments like this, from behind heavy shielding, that she could look at it without fear of crumbling to dust.

Chloe stared at the sun, shivering with a deep, heartfelt longing.

One day I will bathe in your rays again and the world will tremble before me.

* * *

Anton clicked the last shotgun round into the magazine. Ramming the full load into the automatic shotgun, he chambered the first round.

He held the gun tightly and noticed his own knuckles were white against the dull gray of the weapon. Smiling wryly to himself, he slung the gun over his shoulder, flexed his fingers and took a couple of deep breaths. He needed to ease up and get frosty.

Anton looked over to where Gang was standing on a ladder, duct taping one of the blue paint splashed MGLs to the end of one of the top-level shipping containers. The MGL lay positioned just out of sight to allow easy access by anyone running along the top of the maze who knew it was there. It was one of the vampire specials, loaded with explosive canisters of silver flechettes.

"First the Triads, then Shadowstone, and now the Vampire Dominion. It's been a busy couple of days," Anton remarked.

Gang studied Anton for a moment, grinned broadly and declared heartily, "You know what – we have been so busy that we have forgotten to eat – which is appalling." He backed down the ladder and picked up his backpack. Rummaging around inside it for a moment, he brought out a large thermos flask and three large plastic mugs in a stack, and laid them out on top of a metal ammo can. He poured the contents of the flask into the mugs which steamed lightly and filled the nearby air with a delicious aroma.

"Hmmm, I thought I could smell something good," Li said avidly, jumping lithely down from the maze wall.

"It's vegetarian, I don't recommend meat – too heavy just before a battle," Gang said.

"And no sake as well," Li queried hopefully.

"Just so, which reminds me," Gang replied. He reached into the backpack, and pulled out a polished steel hip flask. "The last of Tatsu's family reserve, we will share it together when tonight is done." Gang grinned. "Now who can I trust to look after it?"

"C'mon," Anton said, spreading his hands in a wide embrace. "That would be me."

Li blurred forward, plucking the flask from Gang's hand. "Family rules."

"Okay – can't argue with that," Anton remarked.

Li put the flask away in one of her belt pouches.

Anton picked up the mug of soup. It smelled wonderful, a thing of beauty in the midst of the blood-stained warehouse. Anton put his fingers around the mug, feeling the warmth of the soup flowing into them. He sipped the soup, discovering the delicious flavors and textures of cream, fennel, spinach and asparagus.

"This is fantastic, but I don't remember it being on the Noodle House menu."

"Well, the style of the Noodle house was a selection of authentic northern Chinese cuisine, but my personal style has always been a fusion of Chinese, Japanese, and Western flavors."

"Do you think you'll do it again?" Anton asked, wiping a stray drop of soup off his top lip.

"What, a restaurant?" Gang reflected. "Well, I would love to – I still have a passion for food and I love to cook. We'll just have to see how all this pans out. But yes, if I get a chance, I would like to do it again. But next time, not with such a low profile, more a full expression of the natural fusion of flavors from eastern and western cuisines."

Anton sniffed, drinking the aroma; and then swallowed some more of the soup which was just at the right temperature to be comfortably drunk. He said, "Gang, have you considered you just might be a genius cook?"

"Well …" Gang stroked his chin contemplatively, took a hearty slurp of his soup and laughed. "You could be right."

Li turned to the south, her face a study in concentration and declared decisively, "Another helicopter."

"Reinforcements – and not yet dark. How many?" Gang asked.

"… just one."

"How do you do that?" Anton asked. "Your hearing is so good,"

"Just lucky I guess."

"Are we prepared?" Gang inquired glancing from his daughter to Anton and back.

"The second set of pyrotechnics are in place."

"Good work Li."

"Will they work?" Anton asked. "The last set didn't seem to impact the Shadowstone forces."

"They gave you time to reload, didn't they?" Li said.

Anton nodded, conceding the point.

Gang advised, "Vampires are natural night hunters – their senses are optimized for operating with minimal light – we can turn that strength into a weakness."

"How many will come?" Anton asked

"They know there are two or three Order here – they would aim for two to one odds. They will show up with four to six vampires. Not a big force."

"How many is a big force?"

"More than six."

"What if they know that Francis Mirovar is coming?"

Gang frowned and declared, "Then we have far bigger problems. It will be sunset soon. I don't think that the vampires will wait. This battle will be decided within an hour. Now I'm not going to give you some big speech to bolster your courage like," and Gang flourished one hand dramatically, orating in deep tones. "'Once more unto the breach, dear friends…'. As I would rather you simply survive and keep your freedom. I won't gloss over the very real danger of fighting vampires. I want the two of you to stick together, look after each other and don't play the hero."

Gang grasped both of their shoulders and stated firmly, "Just remember, tonight is all about surviving to fight another day."

Li nodded.

Anton promised, "All of us, or none of us."

Gang nodded. "Yes – we all make it out."

"Shall we check what they're doing?" Li asked.

"Yes, let's use the access walkways – just don't get shot."

Anton smiled wryly. "Great advice."

"I'll check the river," Li said, ramping away.

Anton looked at Gang, and glanced toward the west. They both ramped at the same time, blurring away to the front of the warehouse. A handful of seconds later, they were inching their way to a position that overlooked the parking lot. They watched the new nightfalcon as it dropped off its troops and immediately took to the air, with an operative remaining in the cabin, manning the waist minigun. It joined the other helicopter as both began circling the warehouse at a distance.

Anton squirmed backward, turned to Gang and asked, "How long can they keep circling like that?"

"Long enough. We need to get to our positions. They're now simply waiting for the vampires to arrive."

Anton followed Gang back into the midst of the warehouse and found his place on the right side. He stood facing the front of the warehouse. He held the automatic shotgun with both hands. The MP7 submachine gun sat holstered on his right hip and the Blue Dragon rested in its scabbard over his shoulder.

His breathed slowly and was surprised to discover how calm he felt. There was only one thing left to do; *Wait for the storm to break.*

* * *

Louise Wesson carried her military lock box away as the Indigo-6 nightfalcon roared into the air.

The box sported her name in bold letters on the lid. Her thumbprint unlocked the box. She flipped open the lid, smiling grimly as she peered inside it. In moments, she pulled off her boots and started to strip off her combat fatigues. She noticed the appreciative glances of the other operatives, and shouted a sharp command, "Eyes front." They immediately turned away, and she completed the removal of her outer clothes.

Louise pulled a matt black carbon nanotube jumpsuit from the box and put it on. It covered her sleek form from ankle to wrist, and to the top of her neck. She followed it with a matt black combat vest. The combination provided an excellent capability to stop penetrating wounds and disperse impact shock. She completed the transformation by adding additional, elbow, hip, thigh, knee, and shin guards, and a pair of gauntlets. She used the box as a stool to put her combat boots back on. Picking up her tactical helmet, she pushed her fine brown hair back from her forehead and put it on. A heads-up-display automatically activated as her visor guard came down, covering the top half of her face. A moment later the helmet reached out, connecting with the Shadowstone tactical networks and her command links to the remaining squad leaders came online.

She commanded, "Squad leaders report in."

"Green-4 Alpha in position, Ma'am."

"Blue-5 Alpha in position, Ma'am."

The three Indigo-6 squads all reported in, followed by the fourth squad manning the RHIB on the river, as did the two nightfalcon pilots circling the warehouse at a radius of a thousand yards.

Red-1 wiped out, Green-4 and Blue-5 cut to ribbons, the operation to cordon off the warehouse and contain the Order of Thoth had become a debacle. Events had vindicated Louise's earlier reservations. However, she took no pleasure in being right. She'd spent the last six months working very hard with these men, and while a cold-blooded killer when the job demanded it, she was also naturally loyal to the team. She felt the losses of her men like a knife in the guts. A knot of quiet anger burned within her. She'd only one question. Who was more responsible? Gang and Li Wu and Anton Smith for killing them, or James Haley for leading his men into an obvious trap.

Flicking her visor up, she added her P90 submachine gun, Glock 9mm and four hand grenades to the holsters and webbing on her armor.

She jammed the last grenade into position with a half-voiced snarl.

Maybe it's time to frag the boss.

She sighed, her anger loosening its grip as she restored her professional demeanor. She turned, walking over to where Haley stood watch on the warehouse.

"Sir, we have fourteen Hellfire III missiles on our nightfalcons. We could simultaneously fire the missiles into the interior of the warehouse from both ends and flatten it. The targets inside would have no chance of survival."

Haley snorted, stared down at her and said derisively, "An admirable plan Wesson, except for one small detail – that's not our mission."

It wasn't our mission two hours ago either – and that didn't stop you. "… Sir, we—"

"Enough!" Haley growled. "We hold the cordon until the General arrives. Then it's her problem." He stepped toward Louise, leaned in toward her face and snarled, "Is that clear?"

"Yes, Sir," Louise replied without blinking.

"I'm sure you've got something to do, the General will be here in thirty minutes."

"I'll check the men."

"Good," Haley snapped, turning back to stare at the warehouse.

Louise turned away and began to inspect the men in the cordon. She reflected briefly; *I'm really beginning to dislike that guy.*

* * *

Chloe scanned the report.

The Red-1 team had twelve dead and four wounded, Green-4 had twelve dead, Blue-5 had eleven dead and three wounded, and two nightfalcons lay in ruins with their crews. She arched an eyebrow in measured respect. *Two Order of Thoth and a rookie did all this. The Wu family may have been living quietly for twenty years, but they obviously haven't been idle.*

She read further, the Indigo-6 team were on site with their nightfalcon and a special forces RHIB. The Green-4 nightfalcon was also available. Counting James Haley, and Louise Wesson, there were seventeen operatives on the ground and another four on the river. An active police cordon had been in place for most of the day and had held the public back a mile from the site. Chloe smiled. *Crane will be furious. This is precisely the sort of defeat that will deflect his attention, ensuring that he keeps me here in North America.*

Her nightfalcon swooped in to land on Bedford Street at the entrance to the site's parking lot. The street lights had come on with the onset of twilight and they gleamed off the helicopter's black skin. The cabin door opened. The six praetorians stepped down from the machine, making two lines to the left and right. Chloe was the last to emerge, walking between the praetorians as they waited for her.

James Haley and Louise Wesson stood twenty yards in front of her. Beyond them, the men of the cordon stood watch over the warehouse while the two nightfalcons circled slowly a thousand yards above the site.

Chloe pivoted, addressing her praetorians in quiet tones, "When you assault the warehouse, flush the Order to the dock where I will be waiting." She tapped a tall redhead and a lithe African-American on their chests and commanded, "Hendricks and Smithson, your target is Gang Wu – kill him." She flicked her gaze across the rest of the praetorians. "Run Li Wu and Anton Slayne out onto the dock where I will complete the engagement. Be aware the Mirovar force team is in the vicinity, we expect to draw them out with this battle. They will not be able to resist saving their own. Is that clear?"

The praetorians nodded their assent.

Chloe's eyes narrowed for a long moment as she weighed the foreseeable outcomes. *I must risk Anton's life, if he falls here, he would never have defeated Crane and I must plan anew, else I will continue with this scheme.* She turned from the praetorians, striding to where James Haley stood, she ignored Louise Wesson and took a position a yard in front of Haley.

She stared hard into his face and declared, "You disobeyed my orders!"

"We were fired upon, our standing orders—"

"Are preempted by my orders."

James stood straighter and answered, "Yes, Ma'am."

"My orders were explicit. You stated that they were, 'Crystal clear,' – did you not say that this morning."

"… Yes, Ma'am, I did say that."

"Did you understand my orders?"

James frowned briefly and then conceded, "Yes, Ma'am."

"Then please explain to me which part of, 'The mission is to identify them, track them, and if they go to ground, put a cordon around the site and stop them escaping again.', implies a frontal assault on a well-defended position?"

James' face paled in the street lights. "When they attacked it could have been a prelude to escape."

"Did they try to escape at any time today?"

"… No, Ma'am"

"Correct, they did not try to escape, and you had no justification to lead your men to be slaughtered."

"Ma'am, no one could have known they would have been so effective against us."

Chloe stepped forward. Leaning in close, she whispered tightly, "You saw the Triad attack on the Noodle House, did you not learn anything from that?"

"Ma'am? … Yes, Ma'am."

Chloe stepped back, staring at James for a long moment, everyone within earshot stood still and waited for her words. "You underestimated your opponents. You set the cordon too close to the warehouse within the range of man-portable weapons. That resulted in the loss of two nightfalcons and eight of your men. You then compounded that error by launching an ill-considered attack versus a prepared defensive position that has decimated three spectrum teams."

Chloe stared at James with her hands on her hips and declared flatly, "Given your choices and your lack of effective preparation that result was predictable."

"Yes, Ma'am."

"What you should have done after the destruction of the nightfalcons, was pull back and reset your cordon out of range of their weapons."

"Yes, Ma'am."

Chloe looked past James at the warehouse beyond and said quietly, "You are most fortunate that tonight's mission is not yet concluded, and I still need you and your men."

"Ma'am?"

"I'm a forgiving soul," Chloe said with a sardonic smile. "I will forgo punishing you for your errors of judgment today, pending your discretion and diligence to your duty tonight." She leaned in close and whispered for his ears alone, "Your redemption is still possible — make sure that you do everything necessary."

"Yes, Ma'am. I will."

Chloe smiled icily. "Of that, I'm sure."

Now he is correctly motivated, time to move forward with the main plan for tonight.

* * *

James watched as General Armitage turned and strode back to her waiting special forces troops.

They made a huddle; she gave quick sharp orders beyond his power to hear. She gave a final command and they split past her like a wave going around a lighthouse. They passed James in a quick walk, exuding confidence, purpose, and power. He turned, watching as they took up a position in a loose line a hundred yards before the front of the warehouse.

James wondered why they carried swords and battle axes, and why were they all armed with light machine guns? What were they going to do — hose the place down with lead?

He felt his skin crawl over his back. He twisted around; General Armitage stood before him again.

"I have fresh orders for you and your men."

James stood to attention and barked, "Yes, Ma'am."

"Assemble all the remaining operatives on land. When my special forces move, follow them immediately into the warehouse. Do not hesitate, the Order will fall before them or run. We will flush the game to the docks and I will kill them there."

James was shocked. *Did she just say that she would kill them?*

"Ma'am, we have the RHIB and now three nightfalcons to guard the—"

"Unnecessary — I will be there."

James felt adrift and said candidly, "They just killed twenty-six of my men, how will you kill them? It's not possi—"

A shining blade appeared an inch before his nose, gleaming in the streetlights. For the first time in his life, James felt his guts freeze in a moment of existential terror as the hairs rose up on the back of his thick neck and goosebumps rippled over his skin. *Who is she? She's faster than the eye can follow.*

General Armitage moved the Red Dragon a hands width aside. Leaning in toward James, she declared softly with supreme confidence, "I will be there." She raised an eyebrow quizzically. "Do you understand your orders this time?"

James answered, "Yes, Ma'am. Understood."

"And one final word – at the end of this, there must be no witnesses."

James frowned, pausing for a moment before nodding. "Yes Ma'am. I will see it done."

She held his gaze and nodded once. The General's nightfalcon was already spooling up. She turned away from James, strode toward it and stepped into the cabin bay. In moments, its engines reached full power, launching the helicopter into the night sky.

Beneath her soaring nightfalcon, James tapped his comms link and called his men in to form a loose rank behind the General's special forces unit. The General's men stood with a preternatural stillness. They stared at the warehouse like waiting lions with their eyes locked on a herd of nervous antelopes – just waiting for one to move before attacking with deadly effect.

James marshaled his troops. He watched as the General's nightfalcon hovered momentarily over the river end of the warehouse, its skin reflecting flood lights that had come on over the dock.

The Order operatives had restored electric power.

He saw the General's black armored form leap with superhuman power and grace from the cabin of the helicopter and disappear from view. *That's a forty-yard drop to the dock or twenty-five to the crane – who can do that?* James shook his head, whispering in sudden bewilderment, "What on Earth am I looking at here?"

Vampires? No – of course not! It couldn't be?!

A creeping sensation of dread slithered up his back as he led his men after the advancing special forces.

What the hell happens next?

Chapter Six

Sky Roman @ SkyRoman133 – 3m

'Explosions in Boston! What's happening? #Crazy #Nightmare'

John Smith @ JohnSmith1249 – 3m

'I'm on my roof. Just saw a helicopter crash and burn. #Bombs #Terrorism'

Trusted Reporter Boston @ TrustedReporterBoston – 3m

'It's a tragic accident. Training exercise gone wrong. #PublicSafety #Tragedy #Official #News.'

– Consecutive Twitter posts.

* * *

Boston, June 11th, 20:26

Anton sat back on his heels, resting on the maze wall on the right side of the warehouse.

Twenty yards to his left, Gang held a similar position. They faced the front of the warehouse a hundred yards away. Above and ten yards behind them, Li rested on the maintenance walkway with her .50 caliber sniper rifle facing forward, and the white-daubed MGL holding the thermobaric grenades beside her.

Gang fidgeted, a moment later he was reading a message on his smartphone. He glanced at Anton and Li, and reported urgently, "Francis is nearby – he says make for the dock."

Anton looked up at Li. Her eyes widened as she immediately ramped, swiveling the sniper rifle after a target. The rifle was already barking as Anton launched himself to the right. A stream of bullets and dull reddish tracers appeared where he'd been standing. They followed his movement like a stream of water from a fire hose. Before he'd moved three yards a second stream of fire reached out from the front of the warehouse, cutting through the air barely three feet in front of him – he was running straight into it. It'd cut him in half.

177

Collapsing, he rolled onto his front, the two streams of fire crossing above him. The burnt metal of the tracers reeked as the bullets ripped through the air above him. He pushed himself off the container. Leaping upward and to the right as the lines of fire started to swing back toward him. Pointing the barrel of the automatic shotgun toward the sources of the firestorms he pulled the trigger, his shotgun burst into action and a stream of spent shells filled the air to his left. Rising into the air, he caught sight of his assailants, three vampires in Shadowstone combat armor were rushing along the top of the maze in a reverse V formation, two in front and one behind. They broke formation as he fired at them, spreading out across the maze walls.

I can only fire on one at a time and the other two will kill me. Reaching the apex of his leap, he drew the MP7 with his left hand, aimed it at the vampire on the left and pulled the trigger while he continued to direct the shotgun at the other two vampires. The vampire watched him taking aim, and darted further left as the high-velocity rounds streamed through the space he'd just vacated.

The rearmost vampire leaped into the air, landing on the maintenance walkway. Running toward Li, the barrel of his M249 smoking as fire lanced along the length of the walkway.

Li rolled off the walkway, dropping toward the maze wall below. She fired her MGL as she fell, thermobaric grenades streaking toward the walkway and the vampire whose line of fire was swinging toward her.

"Li!" Anton screamed as he landed back on the maze wall.

The vampire attacking Li, leaped off the walkway, which promptly exploded in a blinding glare. He disappeared from sight, dropping the full distance onto the floor of the maze.

Anton started zig-zagging his way toward Li and the river, while emptying his magazines at the pursuing vampires.

A second later the fallen vampire appeared back up on the maze wall, joining with the lead vampire running forward on Anton's left, firing their M249s as they blurred along the maze wall.

"There are too many," Anton yelled, dodging violently aside as bullets and tracers whipped past him.

Gang called out, "Fall back!"

Suddenly, another set of pyrotechnics flooded the warehouse. *Li! Giving us cover,* Anton thought furiously, barely able to keep pace with events. Everything was happening too quickly to follow.

The nearest vampire, now only ten yards away on Anton's right, put his gauntleted hand up to shield his eyes. Anton pointed both of his guns at him, pulling the triggers – they both clicked on empty.

The praetorian dropped his hand and barked a short laugh. The vampire was a heavy-set blond man with a battle axe at his hip and a sword over his shoulder. He stood an equal distance with Anton to the only section of the maze wall that gave access to the river. Anton had run past it and was in danger of the vampire cornering him against the wall of the warehouse.

Snarling, the blond vampire raised his light machine gun. Anton stared down the barrel, watching the vampire squeeze the trigger, he ramped aside. The M249 fired, spitting two rounds which whizzed past Anton's head, and then ran dry. The vampire cursed, dropping the gun. Dragging his battle axe and sword from their scabbards, he blurred toward Anton.

I have no time. Reaching the junction on the maze wall at the same time as the vampire; Anton wheeled around, with the Blue Dragon in his hands. He parried the blond praetorian's attacks and stepped back along the container.

Time slowed; his sensory awareness snapping into overdrive. He felt the way he had in the kitchen at the Noodle House when surrounded by the four Tiger Clan gangsters and their Mac-10s. Suddenly calm, the Blue Dragon arced up through the air, flicking left and right just like he'd trained with Gang and Li, each time it moved it deflected a slashing strike by the vampire.

The vampire's booted left foot slammed out, catching Anton in the gut. He found himself flying through the air, back a dozen yards before crashing down onto the containers. The landing jarred the Blue Dragon from his hand. He groaned with anguish, when the bright blade flew over the top of the maze wall, dropping to the floor below.

The blond vampire blurred toward him again. Behind him came the other two vampires on his side of the warehouse firing bursts from their M249s which whipped past him.

There's a claymore mine down there, and less than three seconds before it fires.

Li screamed, "Anton! No!"

He dived over the side after the sword. He rolled as he hit the ground. There were still fireworks streaming across the roof of the warehouse, and the Blue Dragon gleamed on the floor. Across from it, the claymore stood on its squat tripod legs staring right at him. Snatching up the sword, he ran at the side wall of the nearest container butted up against the warehouse wall.

I have to get higher — now!

* * *

Gang dropped the MP7s as they ran dry.

The vampires sprinted forward, letting go of their empty M249s. They reformed into an A formation, one in front and two behind. The lead praetorian, a huge, powerfully-built man with flowing black hair, carried an oversized double-bladed battle axe. He swung it back and forth as easily as Gang could swing a bamboo Shinai training stick.

The praetorians closed. Gang flipped backward, his hands disappearing into a six-inch wide space at the end of the container. He came back up to his feet, pointed the blue-daubed MGL at the onrushing vampire, and fired from point blank range. The grenade spat from the muzzle, immediately expanding into a fist sized cloud of razor sharp, silver flechettes that carved through the chest armor of the praetorian. He froze in place as the other two vampires, a tall redhead, and an athletic African-American blurred past him. They slashed at Gang with their swords.

Drawing the White Dragon free in a flash, Gang deflected the first blows of the vampires' weapons. He blurred backward, calling out, "Li!"

Li fired her MGL, a thermobaric grenade struck the paralyzed vampire. The heavy explosion rocked the maze wall. The praetorian, now a seven-foot-tall flaming torch, toppled over, falling off the wall.

She's a good girl.

Gang's heart swelled with pride.

* * *

Chloe stood poised on top of the crane gantry, accelerating her mind and extending her senses to their limits.

A hundred yards above, her nightfalcon hovered. The other two nightfalcons circled the warehouse, their waist miniguns manned and tracking the perimeter of the site. The RHIB stood fifty yards off the side of the dock, the men on board manning their weapons and watching all directions around the boat.

The warehouse was full of pyrotechnics, the sounds of gunfire had ceased, and the clash of metal on metal had begun. The Shadowstone tactical comm links were thick with shouted commands as James Haley and Louise Wesson led the remaining operatives into the warehouse.

The praetorians and Chloe maintained a separate channel that ran on their voice prints, cutting the Shadowstone operatives out of the vampires' communications.

"Spengler is gone," Hendricks reported grimly.

Chloe smirked, *feeling your mortality, are you?* She snapped out a quick order, "Keep pushing them toward the dock."

Chloe turned, scanning the perimeter, there was no sign of Francis Mirovar and his team. *We left all the communications systems open around this site, surely you know that this battle is happening? If you wait too long, it will all be over.* Staring into the black depths of the Mystic River, she frowned and hissed, "Where are you hiding? Are you down there in the water?"

Her long-range plan against Crane hinged upon the prompt arrival of the Mirovar force team.

She couldn't afford for them to be late.

* * *

Anton ramped to maximum speed, racing along the side wall of the container.

He climbed to the warehouse wall, and then to the opposite container, literally wall running his way up to the top of the Maze. All three vampires moved onto the containers around him. A thermobaric grenade exploded within the warehouse, all of the vampires looked away, and two blurred out of sight. The blond vampire remained; his face twisted with hatred. He glared at Anton, shouting, "Come to—"

The claymore mine detonated.

Anton felt something pin his right foot for a moment, but he ran on gaining the final yard up the maze wall, stepping out onto the top of the maze. He ducked to avoid losing his head, a sword slashing through the air above him. Parrying the praetorian's second attack with the Blue Dragon, he turned aside the vampire's battle axe, which instantly embedded itself into the warehouse wall. The vampire halted, momentarily slowed as he dislodged his axe.

Blurring past him and away from the warehouse wall, Anton again moved back and sideways toward the river. On the other side of the warehouse, Gang and Li wielded the White and Green Dragons as they fought the other four vampires.

The last of the pyrotechnics faded away. There was a shout from the front of the warehouse as Shadowstone operatives clambered onto the top of the maze wall. They immediately began running toward the river end of the warehouse.

Anton wheeled around again to defend himself from the blond vampire who rushed upon him, slashing at him with a combination of sword and axe attacks. He was five yards to the right of where Gang and Li fought the other vampires. He backed away under the blond praetorian's onslaught and the two melees merged into one.

Outnumbered, Anton, Li and Gang gave ground to avoid the five vampires and the onrushing Shadowstone operatives surrounding them. In seconds, the battle spilled out of the warehouse. Anton found himself next to Li, trading blows against three vampires and edging backward along the floodlit dock. Gang had become separated and was underneath the nearer of the two crane gantries where he fought furiously with the remaining two praetorians.

* * *

Chloe watched from above as the battle spilled out onto the dock.

Anton and Li Wu were fighting Calley, Senna, and Hato while Gang Wu stood beneath the second gantry fighting with Hendricks and Smithson.

She looked once more out at the river, searching for the missing Mirovar force team. Sighing, she dropped lithely down to the dock.

She landed, drawing the Red Dragon from its scabbard. She whispered in soft acknowledgement of her life, "And so it progresses, as it must – to blood and ruin."

* * *

A figure clad in black, dropped with superhuman agility from the top of the crane gantry. They landed beyond the vampires fighting Gang near the butt of the dock.

Anton struggled to stay alive against the sudden and powerful attacks launched by the three vampires. Li blurred next to him, but so did the vampires as blades crashed again and again. He hoped the figure in black was Francis Mirovar. They needed a savior – and fast.

The Blue Dragon drew sparks as it ground along the blond vampire's sword until the two hilts clashed and Anton found himself inches away from the vampire's face. The praetorian pushed back hard, Anton half fell, half leaped back. The vampire struck again, Anton twisted violently away to the left, ducking under the vampire's battle axe as it swept vertically down. He dragged the Blue Dragon through an arc that would have gutted the praetorian except that he also turned and moved, just fast enough that the blade scored his body armor without penetrating it.

Anton spun, bringing the Blue Dragon to guard position. Attacks came from both sides, even though ramped to maximum, he was unable to avoid getting slashed across the right shoulder by the razor-sharp tip of another vampire's sword.

Anton's blood splashed. The sword wielding vampire grinned, snarling, "I will drink Order blood tonight."

The blond vampire shouted, "Senna, the Order pup is mine."

Anton blurred forward. Swinging his blade low, he dived and rolled to his feet on the other side of the blond vampire.

Screaming, the blond vampire turned away. Hopping on one foot as the Blue Dragon had sheared through his other foot.

The other vampire rushed after Anton, who met him with the gleaming meteoric iron of the Blue Dragon. Their swords clashed in a shower of sparks as Anton's blade sheared along the edge of the vampire's sword.

Anton's perception spontaneously accelerated, time slowing to a crawl, his Ramp fluctuating wildly beyond his control. The vampire in front of him leered at him with a face filled with hate. The blond vampire was steadying himself, rushing back into the battle. To his left, Li was engaged in a lethally fast war of blades with a Japanese vampire of samurai heritage who wielded a shining black handled katana. Beyond the melee, praetorians, a big red-haired one, and a lithe African-American were fighting a terrific battle with Gang beneath the nearest crane gantry. Shadowstone operatives were swarming out of the warehouse. They held their rifles high, red dot sights crisscrossing the dock in a crimson web.

His heart jumped. Chloe Armitage stood beneath the far crane gantry. Remnants of the vision at the homeless shelter flashed before him. *Armitage stood alone, her dark hair, long and flowing, a delicate golden crown on her head. She beckoned him with her outstretched hand, her eyes locked with his. Wild emotion surged, lightning crackled across the night sky, the Blue Dragon became an arc of bright, vengeful flame.* The shadows and the lights flickered – swapping places, back and forth. The momentary vision disappeared, reality reasserting its dominion.

He blurred forward, then suddenly dodged back to avoid the vampire named Senna cutting him in half with a slashing horizontal strike.

Armitage stepped forward, shouting at the operatives, "Hold your fire!"

The Shadowstone operatives pulled to a halt, their guns remaining fixed on the three targets of Li, Gang, and Anton. The five praetorians continued to press their attacks.

Why doesn't she order us shot? Anton asked himself, nonplussed. The three praetorians continued to push hard against Li and Anton's defenses. The Blue Dragon, once again bright steel, snapped left and right in his hands.

Armitage! What's inside my head? He stopped thinking, devoting himself to keeping Li and himself alive for as long as he could.

* * *

Chloe caught James Haley's gaze and shook her head.

The barrel of his gun dipped. A scowl briefly crossing his face before he hid his disappointment.

She turned back to stare at Gang as he fought the two praetorians. Both vampires had cuts, Hendricks more than one – Gang was unharmed.

They cannot touch him – how interesting. Intrigued, Chloe waited, watching as Gang Wu fought the two praetorians, she'd sent against him. Behind him, the other three vampires pressed hard against Anton and Li Wu. Her senses expanded to their maximum; she accelerated her mind to its full extent. The world slowed down and she watched Gang's techniques in detail, absorbing every nuance, learning every move.

Experiencing the moment with every fiber of her being, she consumed everything she witnessed. Without effort, she would be able to repeat Gang's techniques perfectly. This was the second of the powers she kept hidden from her master, Cornelius Crane; the power of muscle mimicry.

Fascinating, he is a beautiful exponent of the katana. I have not seen such mastery since I fought Arthur Slayne in the secret vault beneath St Peter's Basilica.

The diamond on Gang's sword drew her attention as she focused on the blade's familiar, perfect form. Her breathing quickened. *He has the White Dragon.* An electric thrill shivered along her spine. Smiling broadly, her body and soul sang with the opportunity. *This is a challenge, a test of mastery – who will survive tonight? He is one of Slayne's students, the innovations, clarity and purity of technique is a signature of the master's influence.*

A genius worked his magic with the blade before her. A rare excitement rose within her, anticipation edged with fear – she would attempt to take Gang Wu's life tonight – but there was a shadow of doubt as to who would be the victor.

"How rare," she whispered.

* * *

Li had begun her training on her third birthday.

Drawing on everything she'd mastered over the last fifteen years, she beat back the samurai vampire's sword with a set of flashing strikes, forcing him to give ground. With the vampire on the back foot, she reversed direction, charging toward Anton and the two vampires that had him surrounded. The blond vampire was preparing to plunge a chrome bladed battle axe into Anton's head. With every ounce of power she possessed, she launched a flying kick at the base of the praetorian's skull. Connecting with a sickening crack, the vampire flew limply through the air, landing with a mighty splash in the Mystic River.

Li landed on her feet, deflecting a slashing, overhead strike by the Japanese vampire who had followed after her. Rushing past him, she slashed hard, but he managed to roll over the Green Dragon and avoid Li cutting him in half.

Li found herself back-to-back with Anton, as all four combatants simultaneously paused as if taking the time to consider options after the removal of the blond vampire from the fight.

Anton and Li circled in place, the two vampires stalking them just beyond striking distance.

"You're bleeding," Li said. "I thought I taught you better than that?"

Anton grimaced. "Thanks. I'm sure I needed reminding."

"And your foot as well—"

"Huh?" Anton grunted, glancing down in surprise.

"Don't look down," Li hissed.

The vampire named Senna was in front of Anton. He arched a waxed eyebrow, and promised confidently, "Don't worry young fellow. In moments, I will free you from your wife."

"We're not married," Anton and Li shot back in unison.

They struck out at their opponents, and the fight rejoined as they fought back and forth across the dock.

* * *

Squad Leader Harvey West commanded the rigid hulled inflatable boat and his small team of Indigo-6 operatives.

It'd been a long day, cruising up and down the river opposite the warehouse, making sure no one crossed the perimeter in either direction. They'd all watched the battle unfold. Jacked in with the Shadowstone tactical comms links they'd heard everything their fellow operatives had said. His fingers itched to aim his assault rifle and take a shot at the terrorists now fighting on the dock. He could see them clearly in the warehouse's flood lights. It seemed crazy to him the fight was still ongoing. Why were they fighting with swords? There were three nightfalcons armed with heavy weapons – just lay down a barrage on the dock and kill them all.

He'd been excited earlier in the day to discover they'd cornered a team of Order of Thoth terrorists, and then shocked when the first engagement had destroyed two helicopters, killing their crews, and another eight good men. Then there'd been the ill-fated assault on the warehouse where another twenty-six had died. What a disaster, nothing like that had ever happened before in the history of Shadowstone.

"What the hell!" Harris shouted from the bow of the boat where he manned the Mk 19 automatic Multi Grenade Launcher.

West watched as a blond Shadowstone special forces soldier flew end over end to land in the river with a splash.

"How did she do that?" Martinez demanded at the stern, his hands on the .50 caliber machine gun, swinging it to aim at the melee on the dock.

"Who knows? Some sorta crazy Kung Fu," Jenkins said from amidships next to the quad mount FIM-92 Stinger missile system.

West growled, "Stow that crap, and keep your eyes peeled – our job is to keep watch – not provide a damn sports commentary."

West checked that his safety was off, surveying the shoreline about five hundred yards opposite the warehouse. The police had evacuated the park beyond the shoreline. The Boston Police Department enforced a cordon to make sure no one would approach from that direction. He'd a strong suspicion that if the rest of the Order of Thoth were as capable as the handful of terrorists fighting on the dock, then the BPD would be pretty much useless in this fight.

The RHIB rocked for a second.

Harris yelled, "What—"

West looked forward to the bow of the RHIB. Harris was falling limply into the river.

There was a loud splash and he twisted back to the stern. Martinez had vanished.

Jenkins stood up, pointing his rifle at the river, firing and screaming, "They're in the water!"

West swung around lifting his gun. Something flashed through the air, striking Jenkins in the back of the head. It was a knife; Jenkins fell forward, toppling over the edge of the RHIB and into the river.

"Oh my God!" West whispered, pulling the trigger on his assault rifle, firing blindly around the boat into the water. He emptied his magazine and the gun clicked dry.

There was a sudden pressure on West's back, and a bloody blade erupted from his chest as pain flared through his body. There was a powerful push from behind and he fell forward off the blade, pitching head first into the river.

Underwater he could hear a dull roar as the throttles on the RHIB's engines surged to full power. The boat disappeared as a darkness far greater than the murk of the river overwhelmed him.

* * *

Gang's sword crashed against the praetorian's blades.

The praetorians fought with skill and power, they pressed hard against Gang and he had to give ground, shifting backward toward the melee along the dock. A dozen yards away, Chloe Armitage waited with glistening eyes, her attention focused on him. The Red Dragon lay naked, its point carried in perfect stillness an inch off the concrete surface of the dock.

First these two, and then Armitage. Gang reassessed the battle, as the two vampires circled around him, probing his defenses without success. *I can't allow her to get to Li and Anton – they're not ready to face her – I must protect them.*

Plunging his mind deeply into silence he became one with space, flow, and time. Power surged through his body, the White Dragon arcing through the air, shearing through the red-headed praetorian's sword in a shower of brilliant sparks. The vampire's eyes widened in terror as Gang's blade continued past his shattered defenses, driving deep into his chest. Gang drew the White Dragon back, cutting the vampire's heart in two.

The second praetorian's blade whispered through an overhead arc toward Gang's head like the hammer of a dark god.

Blurring with blinding speed, Gang continued the motion of drawing the White Dragon from the dying vampire. Sweeping it through a horizontal arc and striking the second praetorian beneath the armpit. The White Dragon continued easily through ruptured armor, flesh and bone before exiting in a spray of bright red blood.

The vampire, his mouth gaping with shock, slid off the lower part of his body, crumpling into a writhing heap.

The sound of sincere applause erupted ten yards away and Gang looked up, straight into the vivid blue eyes of Armitage. She declared sincerely, "Such mastery of the blade. I've not seen it's like since I fought Arthur Slayne."

Walking toward her, the White Dragon moving in slow arcs in front of him, Gang declared in tones of absolute conviction, "You have nothing to say to me – vile filth."

Armitage smiled again, but her eyes hardened into azure ice. She flourished the Red Dragon and blurred forward.

Shadows blurred; Gang and Armitage faced each other barely eight feet apart. They each held their swords with both hands poised over their shoulders. A mirror image study of purity and purpose. For a long moment, stillness reigned. Two great masters facing each other in perfect silence.

Armitage leaned forward slightly, whispering in heart-felt tones, "Gang Wu, I see you."

Gang's eyes flashed without a trace of mirth. "And yet, you understand nothing."

Both moved at the same time. Their blades flew through elegant arcs, crashing against each other with utter fury and power. The uncanny meteoric iron comprising the White and Red Dragon's blades flexed and shivered, and withstood forces that would have shattered any other weapon. A moment later, having neatly traded places, Gang and Armitage faced each other again. Both were untouched, their defenses equal to the task before them.

Gang's mind plunged once more into deep silence. The future and the past dissolved as he became one with the moment. The Ramp flowered into crystal being, golden light coruscating along every nerve and muscle fiber. He surrendered to the effects of long years of dedicated training, engaging Armitage in mortal combat without regard for safety, hope or deliverance.

Gang wielded the White Dragon with dazzling mastery, the blade glimmering in the floodlights over the dock as he struck blow after blow against Armitage's formidable defenses. Time and again they blurred and shifted position, engaging in a deadly dance of razor-sharp metal. In the depths of his sinews and nerve fibers, Gang began the unique sequence of moves he'd developed over the last twenty years for this one specific task. This would be the test of his life's work. A test of his ability to innovate beyond the martial gifts of Armitage and claw away her life with a blood-soaked blade.

A test whose result would be determined before the passing of another minute with either her death or his own.

* * *

James Haley let the barrel of his gun drop down, and took a puzzled step backward.

Next to him, Louise Wesson lowered her P90, a quizzical look on her face as she also took a step back. The rest of the Shadowstone operatives maintained their positions, their guns held high, a net of red dot sights focused on the available targets. Li and Gang Wu, and Anton Slayne.

James took a deep breath and slowly exhaled. The battles on the dock continued to evolve. In a sudden movement, Gang Wu killed two of the Shadowstone special forces operatives, and Chloe Armitage rushed forward with her blade. In moments, they'd engaged, their blurred movements impossible to track.

"This is insane!" Wesson exclaimed. "Look how fast they move, all of them – this is why we were slaughtered in the warehouse."

"It's like the Noodle House, but this time, we have special forces that match them."

"It's another world," Wesson whispered.

"It is, isn't it?" James agreed.

Something caught his eye out on the river. The RHIB was under full power, charging toward the end of the dock. It was about sixty yards away and approaching fast – something was very, very wrong. He reflexively pushed Wesson aside, diving to the left. He shouted, "Incoming!"

The Mk 19 MGL on the bow of the RHIB started firing grenades toward his men. James and Wesson fell to the ground, the grenades fell amongst his men, exploding with devastating effect. In less than two seconds a dozen grenades destroyed his team.

James lifted his head, looking out at the battle, his hand on his assault rifle. The RHIB stopped at the far end of the dock, five Order terrorists leaped from the boat and blurred along the dock firing MP7 submachine guns. One of the special forces soldiers fighting Li Wu froze. She blurred past him, her sword flashing through a high arc. The man's head flew off his shoulders and rolled along the dock. Bizarrely, the man's headless body remained stiffly upright. *What the fuck? What the hell was going on?*

Stinger missiles fired from the quad mount in the middle of the RHIB, streaking up into the night sky toward the circling nightfalcons.

Damn the orders. James got to one knee, swinging his rifle up to his shoulder. Sighting down the barrel along the dock, he looked for a clear target. *This mission has gone to hell. I've got to do something to fix it.*

Chapter Seven

"Flavor is a universal language understood by everyone." – Chef Gang Wu, the first and last lines of the Noodle House Menu

"If you love others, life will of necessity be tragic, beautiful, but tragic." – Gang Wu, father, husband, and widower

"Effective innovation is the child of mastery of both technique and self." – Gang Wu, Ramp master, wielder of the White Dragon

* * *

Boston, June 11th, 20:29

The grenades boomed, and cracked.

The Shadowstone troops fell away in disarray, annihilated by the surprise attack from the RHIB. Defensive flares streamed through the night sky as the circling helicopters attempted to evade the missiles streaking toward them. First one, and then another helicopter exploded in balls of flame, falling from the sky in showers of burning debris. One helicopter survived as both missiles simply stopped working within a thirty-yard radius of the black nightfalcon, before tumbling harmlessly away.

Anton scrambled to defend himself, parrying, blocking and backing slowly along the dock as he dodged the rain of blows from the praetorian facing him.

The vampire reversed, moving backward, as two men in combat fatigues and carrying long katanas rushed past Anton to engage him. The vampire's eyes flattened with grim determination, he picked up his pace as he furiously defended against the two Order warriors. In a moment, Anton found himself able to take a breath and assess the broader battle.

In the brief respite; he took in the RHIB at the end of the dock, a single warrior moved from the bow where the grenade launcher was to the stern where a heavy machine gun stood ready for war. Near the RHIB, three Order members and a dripping blond praetorian with a battle axe in one hand and a sword in the other traded blows.

I thought he was dead – he's back.

Above the crane gantries, the surviving Shadowstone helicopter hovered, its waist gun unmanned. Beneath it on the dock, Gang and

Armitage were blurring around each other in a display of awesome mastery.

Li walked away from the strangely upright, headless body of the Japanese samurai vampire. The Green Dragon was red with his blood. Flicking her sword, she cleaned it, while heading toward where her father fought Armitage.

Before the gates of the warehouse lay the smashed remains of a score of Shadowstone operatives. However, one was upright on one knee at the edge of his fallen men. It was the suit who had led the Shadowstone team on the night Armitage murdered his mother. Vengeful fury flooded Anton's soul.

The man pointed his assault rifle down the dock, his head tilted to sight his targets. The under-barrel grenade launcher fired and the assault rifle smoked as the operative followed the grenade with a withering burst of fire.

Anton yelled, "Grenade!"

The grenade exploded at the end of the dock, bullets streaming toward the RHIB, the Order warriors, and the blond vampire.

I can take him out, then join Li and Gang against Armitage — we can kill them both tonight.

* * *

The General's helicopter swooped down, looming above them, as Gang Wu and Chloe Armitage continued their one-on-one combat.

Gang rested deeper into the silence as his sequence of attacks and defenses neared their ultimate expression. The world shrank, the smoke and the screams of the wounded and dying drifted away, and time slowed to a crawl. The White Dragon met the Red Dragon in another clash of blades and the White Dragon's blade slid down to the Red Dragon's Guard.

Gang stepped back and they broke away from each other. Armitage raised her sword up, revealing the intended gap, and Gang drove through it with the White Dragon.

This is it.

The White Dragon pierced Armitage's black armor just below her left breast. The blade drove deep into her, its point erupting in half a dozen blood-soaked inches from her back.

The first strike would not kill her, but with the edge of the White Dragon facing next to Armitage's heart, the reversing cut as he pulled the blade free would fatally slice her heart in two.

Gang began withdrawing his blade. Pulling back on the White Dragon, it began to bite further in toward Armitage's heart.

In a sudden movement that blurred before his eyes. Armitage's left hand fell from her sword's handle, grabbing his left wrist before he could continue to pull on his sword.

The bones in his wrist instantly gave way before Armitage's titanic strength. He ignored the agony of her crushing grip, focusing all of his power on completing a fatal cut.

His movement halted, frozen in place.

Swinging his free hand wide, he knew he'd lose his left hand.

The Red Dragon flashed before his eyes, instantly severing his hand.

The sequence was over – it had failed.

Ignoring the shock that raced up his arm, Gang crouched, sweeping with his foot. Armitage leaped over the attack, drawing the White Dragon from her chest as she flew over him.

Lightning quick, Gang rose, turning and leaping backward a dozen feet.

Armitage was faster; flying through the air, she landed in front of him, lunging forward with the White and Red Dragon swords.

Gang grimaced as the blades sheared through his chest, pushing out through his back in a spray of blood. He tried to gasp but wheezed as blood rushed into his lungs.

Armitage and Gang stared at each other in a moment of deadly intimacy and then she drew the blades out. He fell backward and lay still on the cold concrete of the dock, his blood rapidly pooling around him.

Armitage staggered, a trickle of blood breaking past her lips. Dropping the White Dragon, she clutched at her chest. Above her the nightfalcon hovered lower, its rotors perilously close to the top of the gantry. With inhuman speed and power, she leaped upward into the open cabin of the helicopter. The nightfalcon's engines roared, it veered up and away from the battle.

* * *

Li screamed with horror.

Anton spun back around. His rage evaporating, he dashed forward toward her. In front of him, Gang slid off two sword blades as Armitage staggered back, dropped the White Dragon and then leaped upward into the cabin of her hovering nightfalcon. A hard knot engulfed his chest, choking his throat.

He ran forward silently, bullets zipping past his head. The surviving Shadowstone operative was retreating back into the warehouse, firing short bursts of covering fire as he left the dock.

Above the gantries, the black helicopter's turbines roared under full power as it leaped upward, veering away over the Mystic River. He got a glimpse of Armitage standing alone within the cabin bay, blood covering the left side of her chest armor. She was staring at her gauntleted right hand pressed tightly under her left breast.

Gang had got her?

A line of tracers erupted from the .50 caliber machine gun on the RHIB. They sparked off the armor of the helicopter and with them appeared a row of holes, stitching along the hull of the nightfalcon from nose to tail. The armor piercing bullets struck Armitage just as she looked up and she vanished in a cloud of pink mist.

The helicopter's engines stuttered, black smoke pouring from their sides. It dropped like a stone into the Mystic River, landing with a huge splash, and sinking beneath the surface in seconds.

Anton's throat loosened, he exulted, "She's dead! She's dead!"

He ran over to where Li cradled her father's head, dropping to his knees opposite her.

Blood soaked Gang's chest. Anton's heart sank, his throat constricted again. The nightmare of losing his parents rolled back over the horizon and swallowed his world.

Steepling his hands over his nose and mouth, he whispered, "Oh no!"

* * *

Li cradled her father's head. She gently stroked his face with blood-stained hands as tears streamed from her eyes.

Gang blinked, gurgling as blood trickled from the edge of his mouth. He whispered weakly, "Lift me up."

"Father, lie still, stay with us," Li pleaded.

Gang snorted, coughing blood, and smiled wanly. "Always the disobedient one."

"Father! Don't leave us," Li cried, bending her head over her father and crying with terror.

Gang began to push himself up, grimacing with pain. Li and Anton both reached beneath him, bringing his shoulders up so that he was almost sitting. Anton moved his knee behind him, supporting him with his thigh as Gang reclined back. His face was pale with blood loss. Dragging in a breath, he turned to face Li and smiled at her, his eyes glistening in the flood lights.

The sounds of combat on the dock faded away as Li trembled with shock. Old memories flooded her mind. Of a thirteen-year-old girl holding her father's hand with too tight a grip. Of the coffins of her mother and older brother standing on rails before her. Of attendants removing the supports and the coffins descending into graves cut from the snow-covered ground. She remembered tears freezing on her cheeks before they could fall. The cold of that day was a pale echo of the frigid depths of sorrow that now brushed her heart with icy fingers.

Gang struggled to breathe. Each breath was harder than the one before, and each gap longer before he drew the next breath. He stared at his daughter's face, never moving his gaze.

He lifted his right hand, stroking her cheek, his eyes were moist as he whispered, "My beautiful daughter, you are everything I could wish for in a child. I'm so proud to be your father."

Li's heart broke in two, tears rolling down her cheeks. Her father's hand wrapped gently around hers and squeezed. "Don't worry little one, Tatsu and Qiang are waiting for me." His eyes blinked, focusing past her shoulder, he whispered, "I can see them now."

Gang shivered. With his right hand, he held her shoulder with a grip that was an echo of his former strength. He whispered, "I'm sorry Li, I wasn't enough. Don't face her alone … she's fast … faster than anyone."

Li sobbed. "Father … Father … no!"

Gang coughed again, fresh blood spilling past his lips. His eyes lost focus again, he whispered something that Li could not hear.

She tilted her head, bending closer so that her ear was only an inch from his mouth. Gang whispered again, his voice faint, "There is … a letter."

He drew in another ragged breath. She could feel the agony radiating from him as he struggled to tell her something. Gang breathed out, saying at the last, "With a … friend."

His head lolled back, his hand falling limply away.

Li howled with inconsolable grief, her arms wrapping around her father's body.

* * *

Anton stroked Li's back, kneeling tensely beside her. Black storm clouds thundering behind his eyes.

The two remaining praetorians fell to the blades of the five Order warriors. Silence descended on the dock, only broken by Li's quiet sobs. She cradled her father's body, rocking back and forth as Anton rubbed her back. He looked across the river, there was no sign of the black helicopter. He looked up. A tall, lithe man with long dark wavy hair tied back in a wet ponytail, a short mustache and a close-cropped beard was striding toward him. He flicked blood off his sword, sheathed it, stood a yard from Gang's feet and looked down.

His lips pressed into a thin line and his brown eyes tightened with heart-felt loss. He said softly, "Vale well my old friend."

He looked at Anton. "I am—"

"Too late!" Anton snapped, putting Gang down and leaping to his feet. "If you had arrived five minutes earlier, Gang would still be alive."

The tall man declared calmly, "We arrived as fast as possible. There is no time for these ... accusations – we must act quickly." He put a gentle hand on Li's shoulder. "Li, we must pick up your father and go."

Li looked up at him, her face wet with tears and whispered, "Francis ...?"

Is he serious? "Hang on a second," Anton interjected. "There's another Shadowstone operative back in the warehouse. I saw him run in there. We haven't finished the job."

"Yes, it is. We're not here to hunt down random humans."

Li stood up. The men around her fell silent as the rest of the Order team approached. She declared decisively, "Francis, we will go with you." Turning to Anton, she asked, "Could you please help me with my father's body?"

Anton blinked; his heart torn in two for Li's loss. If Li needed him to crawl across broken glass right now, he'd do it. He nodded and conceded, "Of course." He picked up Gang like he weighed nothing and cradled him in his arms.

Li walked over to where the White Dragon rested on the ground, its blade covered in her father's blood. She stared at the blade for a moment, suddenly turning back to Anton in horror. "Father!" she screamed. Rushing over to Anton, she felt for a pulse on her father's throat.

"What is it?" Anton asked.

Francis frowned, placing his hand on the handle of his katana.

"Her blood was on the blade before she stabbed him, he could be transforming now."

"Unless there is too much damage, in which case the vampire blood will not take," Francis said, but he also felt for a pulse on Gang's throat. "No. ... Thankfully he is truly gone."

"Better dead than a vampire, but better alive than dead," Anton said darkly, staring at Francis.

"Look," Francis stated, a spark of indignation flaring behind his eyes. "I put my whole team at risk to be here tonight, on a mission that looks a lot like a trap. Now I came here to extract Gang, Li and yourself – but if it means so much to you, go and find that fellow that ran off into the warehouse. I don't need you to come with us."

Li turned to Anton and declared, "Leave it, Anton, come with us."

Sighing, Anton conceded, "Li, if you're going, then so am I."

"Are we all sorted now?" Francis inquired, with a hint of annoyance in his voice. "It's time to move before vampire reinforcements arrive."

"Reinforcements?" Anton queried.

"They're already on their way. The Panopticon monitors praetorian life signs, and it is standard procedure to intervene in force when they die. They will come out of New York. They will be here within an hour."

Francis turned, striding back down the dock toward the RHIB, the rest of his team following him.

Li scooped up the White Dragon, ramped and flicked it so all the blood on it flew away. A moment later she was walking beside Anton, reaching out, she put her hand on her father's head.

Anton followed Francis as the team formed into a group around Li, and himself. The Order members held their MP7s ready, scanning the horizon for any activity.

"How can you be sure more praetorians will come?"

Francis glanced at Anton. "Brutal experience." He suddenly stooped, picking up a smartphone off the dock, he frowned, fingering a slash across his left chest pocket.

"That was close," Francis said.

"Yeah, you nearly lost your phone," cracked a burly, heavyset man with thick red hair, who looked like he would fit in perfectly as a linebacker in any leading NFL side.

Francis raised a quizzical eyebrow, his lip curling wryly. He put the phone into a thigh pouch on his combat fatigues and continued forward.

They reached the RHIB, and everyone climbed on board. Anton gently laid Gang down on the floor of the RHIB just in front of the operator console and sat next to Li.

She picked up her father's hand and cradled it with her own.

Francis directed, "Peter, take us to the pickup point, it's time to go home."

The burly man replied, "Sure, Boss." Pushing the throttle forward, he steered the RHIB into the river.

And where is home – really? Anton studied the team, while slowly rubbing Li's back.

I have no home.

* * *

James Haley emerged from the shadows of the warehouse.

The RHIB had vanished along with the Order of Thoth. The wreckage of the two nightfalcons continued to burn where it lay in two piles on the edges of the site. Since there had been no order to lift the BPD cordon, the Boston Fire Department would not attend. The third nightfalcon had fallen into the Mystic River and presumably was on the bottom of the river.

And General Armitage with it?

James checked the bodies of his men first. They were all dead, killed by the grenades from the RHIB. He was thorough by nature, he double checked, finding one of his team still alive – Louise Wesson.

She was still breathing, but with few visible marks on her body. He assumed the explosions had concussed her. He rolled her over, placing her into the recovery position. He picked up her smartphone, as his own had lay smashed by a piece of shrapnel from the grenade attack. It accepted his thumbprint as all North American Shadowstone phones did.

James dialed the lead operatives from the Yellow-3 spectrum team at Fort Dix and the Shadowstone PSYOPS crews. He confirmed a massive cleanup operation on the Boston warehouse site. It would be a piece of work to clean up the physical mess and spin what happened tonight for the media. No one in Shadowstone would be getting any sleep in the next twenty-four hours.

Once the gears of the Shadowstone machine were in motion, he returned to check on the special forces operatives that had arrived with General Armitage. The closest were the two killed by Gang Wu. They were obviously dead, especially the African American, who lay cut in half through the chest. The other, a large red-headed man lay on his back, his jaw agape in apparent shock.

In the warehouse floodlights, something odd with the red-head's mouth drew James' attention. He crouched next to the body, checked the upper teeth, and exclaimed with shock, "What the hell?!" *He's got canines like a dog or a wolf.*

James stood up, his breathing accelerated, a very unfamiliar shiver of dread racing up his spine. He deliberately took a couple of slow, deep breaths, turned and checked the special forces operative chopped in half. *He's got fangs too.*

James checked the other three bodies on the dock. There was the weird one that still stood upright. He circled warily around it. Some blood had leaked from the headless neck. It struck him that there should have been a lot more – then he laughed out loud with a touch of hysteria, quickly stopped and shook his head. *What's stranger? The lack of blood or not falling down?* He pressed on the corpse's chest, pushing the body over. Blood sluiced from the open neck wound like a tipped bucket, spreading out in a pool. *Was the heart stopped? The body was stiff from the get go – paralyzed.*

James checked the severed head and the other two bodies. They all had a pair of prominent one-inch canines that were clearly not human. His mind whirled, he felt dizzy; his world spinning out of control. *Superhuman speed and strength. Why did we have to wait until night for them to arrive? Have I ever seen General Armitage in daylight?*

James rubbed his chin, and muttered to himself, "Looks like I'm not in Kansas anymore."

No witnesses — now that makes a lot of sense. He looked around. *There are still our wounded in the parking lot, there is another one of these — vampires — still in the warehouse. There is the nightfalcon in the river and its pilot who is probably also a vampire, and where is General Armitage?*

"At the bottom of the river? Still alive or dead?" he whispered. James frowned, his disciplines kicking into gear, his voice raised to normal volume and he declared, "I'll have to do something about this. I can't leave these bodies here for anyone else to find."

James walked back to the dead Shadowstone operatives and collected a satchel of hand grenades. *These should do it.* He stared at the closest of the dead vampires. He pulled a pin on a grenade, lobbing it so that it rolled to a stop next to the vampire's head. The grenade exploded, obliterating the head, leaving no evidence of anything inhuman.

Yes, that will do.

James pulled the pin on a second grenade.

* * *

Memories flashed through Chloe Armitage's mind.

The violent impact of the heavy machine gun rounds as they tore through her torso, throwing her backward in a mist of her own blood. The edge of the cabin door smashing into the side of her face as she fell out of the helicopter. Her combat helmet coming free as she hit the surface of the river. The dreadful sight of her own nightfalcon coming straight at her, and finally the concussive force of the armored front of the helicopter as it smashed her into oblivion.

Now she was awake, half buried in the mud and drowning in the dark. Panic rose within her, driven by the hemorrhaging from the two .50 caliber bullets that had drilled holes beneath her lowest left rib, and through the bottom part of her right lung. The sword cut that ran through her upper chest burned, adding to the blood loss. Her heart raced. She closed her eyes, willed herself to relax to quell the panic and shock. She slowed her heart to a level that would stem the flow of blood leaking from her body. The world collapsed around her as her perceptions shrank to a single focused point. Her left leg lay trapped beneath the nose of the helicopter — she must move it or die.

She drew upon the ancient training of the Order of Thoth and ramped. She activated the third of the three secret powers that she possessed. The power to achieve a supreme Ramp, a level of capability above that achieved by the Order of Thoth and the Red Empire in the last five thousand years. Time slowed precipitously, her heart pausing between beats. New energy exploded from the base of her spine, flooding through her body. Sinews like steel cords responded, bone stronger than iron bore forces that would crush any other vampire. Stiff, unyielding fingers punched through the metal armor of the nightfalcon and with a single convulsive movement she ripped the nose of the helicopter apart.

With her leg free, she swam upward through a murky darkness that could defeat even the vision of a vampire. She slowed as she reached the surface. Letting only her face break out into the night air, she expelled the bloody water in her lungs and took a single ragged breath. Allowing herself to sink back down, she turned, swimming away from the remains of the battle toward the far shore of the Mystic River.

The pain grew, threatening to overwhelm her, but she crushed it with her will. She covered five hundred yards underwater in just under five minutes. Her head emerged out of the river. She took a shallow breath, then another, and another. With each breath, she expanded her lungs a little further. She gritted her teeth, hissing in agony on each exhale. She glared and spat blood. Her wet hair clung to her scalp. Her eyes were black and bloodshot, and a dark bruise shadowed her right cheek.

Wading slowly through the mud to shore, she staggered out of the river and onto an open expanse of well-maintained lawn and trees. The park was clear of people except for two Boston Police Department cruisers sitting with their lights strobing at opposite ends of the grassy reserve.

She gravitated toward the nearer of the two vehicles. She could already smell the delicious aroma of the men inside; they were both young, fit and fresh. Her throat burned with thirst. A desperate desire filled her body, threatening to overwhelm her mind.

Behind her, she heard the distant crump of an exploding grenade. She glanced backward. James Haley rolled another grenade next to the head of one of the fallen praetorians. It promptly exploded, erasing the visible evidence of vampirism from the corpse.

She'd been right not to kill him.

Chloe turned back toward the police cruiser. It was only twenty yards away and both of the officers had emerged from the car. They seemed unsure of what to do.

Was she friend or foe? They couldn't know. With her damaged body armor, she looked like a wounded special operations soldier, who was clearly in need of help.

The vampiric thirst was upon her. She needed blood or she would die of her wounds within minutes. Her hand brushed past her sword scabbard and found nothing there. A pang of loss ripped through her. *Damn ... the Red Dragon – it's back in the river.*

She staggered, dropping to one knee, putting out her hand in supplication. She implored the young officers, "Help me. Please help me. I've been shot."

The officers both moved forward, in a moment they were beside her, each taking an arm to support her.

"Who are you?" the first one asked.

"What happened? Where are you shot?" the other said.

"'What are you?' would be a better question," Chloe remarked coldly. Snapping both of their necks before they could react. A second later she plunged her fangs into the throat of the nearest of the men as he lay slumped on the ground and proceeded to drain his blood. He died of blood loss before his fractured neck and severed spinal cord could kill him.

She stood up, her body feverishly processing the fresh, hot blood. Immediately she felt better, stronger, refreshed. Pushing a finger through one of the bullet holes in the front of her body armor, it came to a halt against her flesh knitting beneath the ceramic plates.

She looked longingly at the expanse of black water. The Red Dragon sang a siren song in her mind. She considered swimming back out and retrieving it from the bottom of the river.

Did she have time to get it?

She looked across the park, the other police cruiser still waited. With the cruiser's flashing lights stealing their night vision, and given the distance, the police officers probably didn't know their colleagues were already dead.

She would have to make sure.

Her smartphone vibrated, she laughed with surprise. Pulling it from its pouch on her combat webbing, she opened it up. There was a message from Marcus Drake that read, 'The Red Empire have attacked and destroyed the Jerusalem Shadowstone facility, only Haras Mosule and I have escaped. M.'

"Excellent," she whispered, closing the phone and putting it away. She took a deep breath and let it out, her lungs felt whole again.

Chloe looked down at the fallen officers, searched them and found the car keys and their Glock 9mm handguns. Carrying the men to the cruiser, she stuffed them into the trunk. She had to bend and break their bodies in several spots to make them both fit into the available space. She went to the cabin, ripped out the camera system and crushed it with her bare hands. She smashed the GPS, and all other systems that could track the vehicle. She then got into the car and drove it to where the other police cruiser waited on the other side of the park.

She could see the two men in the car looking at her without seeing her. With both police cruisers running their strobe lights, it was impossible for a human to see into the cabin past the reflection on the windscreen.

Chloe stepped out of her car with a Glock pistol in each hand, emptying both clips as fast as she could pull the trigger into the cabin of the police car. For good measure, she pulled a pair of grenades from her combat webbing, lobbing them through the shattered windscreen and into the cabin of the BPD cruiser.

She was already back in the stolen car, pulling away with a roaring engine and screeching tires when the grenades ripped the second police cruiser apart.

There would be no witnesses.

Chloe plotted a course to the Boston Shadowstone facility housing the R.I.S.C front company. It had a small permanent staff who could be relied upon to dispose of the police cruiser and a pair of bodies. It also had a helicopter pad on the roof of the building that would allow for easy transport to the Vampire Dominion citadel in New York City. She pulled her smartphone out again, set it to hands-free, and voice dialed James Haley. There was no answer. She then voice dialed Louise Wesson's phone, and James answered it.

"Yes?"

"You recognize my voice?"

"Yes, Ma'am. I'm glad to see you're still alive."

Chloe laughed sardonically, "I'm sure you are."

"Ma'am?"

"Status report."

"Gang Wu is dead. All the other Order of Thoth members have escaped with his body. I have already initiated a cleanup detail using the Yellow-3 spectrum team and I have activated a PSYOPS crew. They will be on site in about two hours. In another five minutes, there will be no witnesses. Do you have any new orders?"

"It is imperative you clean up properly. Get divers into the river. There is a nightfalcon on the bottom. Use the GPS logs from the Panopticon to recover the craft and the pilot. You will also find a sword nearby. I must emphasize, do not stop looking until you have the sword, once you have it secured, call me immediately on my personal line."

"Yes, Ma'am," James answered.

There was only one reason why he would be dropping grenades onto dead praetorians – he knew the truth – dead vampires do tell tales.

"James, you have done well to survive tonight. Keep doing your job, ensuring you wipe all evidence clean and recover my sword, and I'm sure your career in Shadowstone will continue to prosper."

"Yes, Ma'am. Thank you, Ma'am."

Chloe heard a trace of uncertainty in James' voice, it was clear he was still coming to terms with his discovery of vampires.

She hung up the call and relaxed, setting a tiny fraction of her mind to operate the police cruiser while she reflected upon her plans. With the battle done, it shocked her how closely she'd come to dying. Death had brushed her in the past, more than once, but this was the closest she'd ever come to her own end.

Gang Wu was a genius with the blade, he almost had her. Then the helicopter, if she'd stayed unconscious a little longer, she would have drowned or bled to death.

It was a shame to kill someone who handled a blade as beautifully as Gang Wu did. She'd felt something like regret at the end when she drew the blades out. Such a waste, but what were her options? The plan must progress.

She sniffed and then laughed out loud. The past was gone. She'd watched Anton and Li during the battle, they had fought hard to protect each other. Love? Or something close to it.

Chloe smiled, factoring the possibility of using Li Wu as another lever with which to move Anton toward her own desired goal.

Anton is now with the Mirovar team, he will most likely find a place within it. His skills and power will increase. I must keep the pressure on, I do not have time to waste. I feel certain Crane will have done with me once he has all the Metaframe artifacts or discovers my plan. I must be certain of the relationship between Crane and the Order, is Ramin Kain a traitor as Gang Wu believed, and if so, how can I turn that to my purpose? I must make best use of the Red Empire agent within Francis Mirovar's team; the Raven must be put to work.

With the Red Empire attack in Jerusalem, and this defeat by the Order so close to home, Crane will be distracted and off-balance, he will not see the subtle agency of my plan.

Chloe shivered in anticipation; her pulse quickened. *There is a reason for my gifts, a purpose beyond my life. Crane will be defeated and a new order will come to this world, an order based on the truth that I will reveal.*

Her eyes glistened as she drove the police cruiser into the basement parking garage of the R.I.S.C building.

Time to go to the citadel, I must manage Crane's fury and turn it to my advantage.

* * *

James pulled his Glock 9mm from its holster at his hip, and crouched next to the unconscious Louise Wesson.

No witnesses. The General's orders had been explicit, and he wouldn't fail her again. He put the Glock against Wesson's temple, his hand trembling slightly. He pulled the gun away and took a breath. He then placed the gun back to an inch from her ear and now it was steady as a rock. He began to pull the trigger.

Her eyelids fluttered and she moaned. "What … happened?"

He lifted the Glock away, placing his left hand gently over her head and asked softly, "What do you remember?"

"Owww," Wesson moaned. Her hand came up and rubbed her forehead. "The teams … Red, Blue and Green … they've just arrived. Where am I?"

"On the dock. There's been a battle. It went badly for us. We're the only survivors."

James stood up, holstering his gun.

Wesson convulsed, vomiting the contents of her stomach, the mess splashing across James' boots.

He sighed; took off his flak jacket and made a hard pillow for Wesson's head. He directed, "Rest here, I'll be back soon."

Wesson murmured an answer he couldn't make out.

James strode away. He pulled a silencer from a pouch at his belt, fitting it to the barrel of his Glock. He walked around the warehouse and back out to the parking lot.

The wounded men, patched up as much as they could be, waited patiently for medical extraction.

James strode up to his men as they rested under the big tree near the site entrance. They looked at him with curious eyes. He hid the silenced Glock behind his back.

Another seven good men who will have to make the ultimate sacrifice.

James pulled his gun up, firing until the twenty-round magazine lay empty.

He shook his head, turning back toward the warehouse and Louise Wesson. Fragments of the recorded conversation from the previous morning flitted like ghosts through his mind, the words of Gang Wu prominent amongst them.

Who the hell am I really working for? The Vampire Dominion?

* * *

It was a clear summer night as the RHIB powered along the Mystic River.

With his emotions grinding their pitiless way through his soul, Anton looked up at the stars, questions hurtling through his mind. His wild ramp on the dock, visions in the midst of combat, a crowned Chloe Armitage. There were no answers, only the raw emotions of loss and a driving need to act. *Gang was like family. No – he was family. He treated me like a son and now he's gone.*

Rage struck him, a red wave that rocked him to his core. He glanced at Li, she sat next to him, her hands resting limply in her lap. She'd arranged Gang's remaining hand over his chest, his other arm lay along his side, hiding the fact that it ended just above the wrist. His eyes lay closed, someone had put a jacket over his chest. He looked peaceful like he was asleep – except for the deathly pallor of his skin.

Anton wrapped his arm around Li. She shivered and he pulled her closer. She turned her head, crying quietly into his chest.

She's torn to pieces.

Anton clenched his teeth, a dark fury boiling within him.

Li put her arms around him, turned her head on the side in his lap and squeezed him tightly. He stroked her hair, brushing it away from her forehead. He felt the dark fire within wither and retreat. His eyes filled with tears, he bent his head forward, weeping quietly.

A slender woman with dark, wavy hair approached and suggested gently, "Your shoulder needs suturing and I think we should check your right foot, there is definitely something wrong there."

Anton looked up, wiping his face with his hand and said, "Thanks, I'm Anton."

She nodded. "I know. I'm Juliette Mirovar."

Anton looked at her more closely. "Are you, his wife?"

"Yes," she replied with a warm smile. "We make quite a team."

Anton undid his combat webbing and pulled off his top without disturbing Li, who continued to rest her head in his lap. He grimaced as he pulled his shoulder clear of his clothes, dropping them to the side.

There was a nasty gash on his right shoulder. Juliette opened a black case and pulled out a pre-filled syringe.

Anton frowned and asked, "What's that?"

"Painkiller. We can do this without it if you would like."

"No, that's okay, go ahead."

Juliette put a LED headlamp on her head and with its light shining on Anton's shoulder she used the syringe to inject Anton several times around the wound site. She counted ten seconds and then rapidly set to work stitching the edges of the cut back together with black thread. Two minutes later she completed the task by tying off the thread and applying an antiseptic herbal salve.

She smiled at Anton, moving to sit opposite him.

"That was quick and painless, you're a bit of a miracle worker."

"I've done battlefront tours with Médecins Sans Frontières, do you know about them?"

"Yes, Doctors without borders."

"So now you know a little something about me. Let's have a look at your foot."

Anton lifted his right foot up, placing it on the seat opposite. He'd not checked it before, but now that he did, it looked a mess. Something had gone through the top of his combat boot.

"I didn't really feel anything. I think it may have been a steel ball from a claymore mine."

"Well, we'll soon find out."

Juliette undid the straps of his boot, gently peeling it away from his foot. She cut away the sock with a pair of scissors, revealing a raw puncture wound that'd penetrated the instep of his foot and exited just behind the ball of his foot. She picked up the syringe, applying more of the painkiller around the wound entry and exit sites.

"You could have some foreign material in the wound, we will have to make sure it's clean."

Li sat up, staring at Juliette as she pushed a sterilized probe through the hole in Anton's foot.

"Does it hurt Anton?" Li asked.

"I can just feel it – like pressure."

"Our medications are very effective, and now that you can Ramp, your physiology is changing. Your capacity to heal is accelerated, nowhere near as fast as a vampire, but much faster than a regular human. Now you have completed your mastery of the Ramp, your body has completed the physical transformation. You will heal in a day what would normally take ten."

Li shook her head. "Anton is still mastering the Ramp, he only started six weeks ago."

Juliette shook her head, momentarily perplexed. "I'm sorry – what did you say?"

"Six weeks, my father used the pressure point technique for switching on the Ramp capacity of Anton's body."

Juliette paused for a moment, frowning at Anton, and then her face relaxed into a broad smile. "Well, you're a very lucky young man, it is rare for anyone to survive the process, which is why we rarely use it. But still, you were holding your own against Crane's praetorians when we arrived, you must have mastered the Ramp."

Li shook her head again and said, "No he hasn't, his speed fluctuates, but sometimes he is very fast."

"You've never mentioned this before," Anton said.

"Instability is typical of a student, but you must have been consistently operating at a mature top speed to be able to survive against vampires, especially skilled and experienced fighters like praetorians," Juliette declared. She picked up her needle and thread, and started sewing the wounds in Anton's foot. She pursed her lips in thought and then said, "It is highly unusual to be so fast with only six weeks for the body to transform, you should be only about halfway there. Perhaps you have a talent."

Peter leaned over from where he was steering the RHIB and remarked, "Don't tell him he's got talent. He's just survived a fight with half a dozen vampires and the Witch Queen herself, he'll get a big head."

Francis sat down next to his wife and said, "Stay with us, fight with us, and if you do well, I will sponsor you at the next Order Conclave."

Anton glanced at Li, she stared back at him with a look on her face that said, 'don't say no.' He looked within his own heart, feeling a resonance as he looked into the faces of Francis and Juliette Mirovar.

These people are honest and good.

"Thank you," Anton replied with a nod. "I will join your team."

Francis put out his hand, and Anton shook it. Francis had a firm, powerful handshake.

Anton let go, the RHIB slowed, pulling into a pier. A nondescript van waited there. Two men stood next to it. They wore black overalls and balaclavas to cover their faces.

"Order helpers," Juliette said softly to Anton and Li.

"We're here," Peter stated, leaping onto the pier and lashing the RHIB to a bollard with a stout rope.

Everyone got out of the RHIB, with Anton carrying Gang's body in his arms, they moved over to the van. The two Order helpers gave Francis the keys to the van, and got into the RHIB, driving it away from the pier and back out onto the river.

Francis and Juliette got into the front of the van. Anton got in the back with the rest of the team, laying Gang's body gently to the floor of the van. In moments, the van was on its way.

"Where are we going?" Anton asked.

"To a safe house," Peter replied.

Anton suddenly felt a wave of fatigue overtake him. He realized just how tired he was as he fitted a seat belt, put his head back and closed his eyes. As he dozed, a thought kept recurring to him.

How can anywhere be safe when the vampires are in charge of the world.

The van sped off on its way and Anton drifted into fitful sleep.

* * *

The Raven sat in the back of the van, studying Anton Slayne and Li Wu.

They'd recognized Anton immediately for who he was. Their Red Empire instructors had briefed them extensively on the key figures of the Order of Thoth and the Vampire Dominion. Anton's striking resemblance to his grandfather had given his identity away. The Raven reflected upon these new members of the team. *Who is Anton Slayne? The grandson of an outcast with no place in the Order, and Li Wu, someone who has hidden away from the fight for years, and yet they both survived the praetorians and it would seem — Chloe Armitage herself. What difference can they make to my mission?*

The Raven sat with the other team members in the back of the dimly lit van. The van cruised along route I-95 past Salem, toward New Hampshire, Portsmouth and the state of Maine. They held a smartphone; the screen was dark as if the phone was off. The Raven had taught themself how to operate the phone with the screen dark through memory and touch alone. The phone was the same as the rest of the quantum encrypted smartphones that the Order team members all carried, except for one thing – it hosted a set of Red Empire applications written by a deeply hidden cell of the Red Empire operating out of the city of San Francisco.

The Vampire Dominion and their Shadowstone lackeys have no awareness of the presence of the Red Empire on this continent. Now to test the trojan inserted into Francis Mirovar's phone during the chaos on the dock. The Raven had been waiting months for a chance to access Francis Mirovar's smartphone, seizing the opportunity the moment it had arisen.

The Raven's fingers ran lightly over the dark surface of the smartphone, activating a specialized Red Empire application. The software ran for three seconds, in that time, it compromised Francis Mirovar's smartphone. In another two seconds, it decrypted the contents, filtered the accounts and delivered the quantum signature of Ramin Kain's smartphone to the Raven's smartphone. The Raven attached the contact details of the Head of the Order of Thoth to an encrypted message and sent it to the smartphone of Shabbah al Ahmar's secret ally. Questions burned within their mind. *Who is Shabbah al Ahmar's other operative? Who is his ally?* The Raven didn't know. The Red Ghost had forbidden it.

With another critical step in the mission accomplished, the Raven put the smartphone away in a waist pouch and rested with their eyes closed.

The Raven had found the years of hiding within the Order difficult. Inserted as a child and only partially trained, it had been a risk for the Red Empire that the Order would not accept the Raven, or given their young age, they would in time transfer their loyalty to the Order.

Shabbah al Ahmar himself had decided the Raven had all the right pre-requisites to fulfill the mission and become a highly placed agent of the Red Empire within the Order. He'd taken steps: constructing a detailed background identity, assembling a fake family, creating a plausible and believable story to wrap around the Raven's arrival on the Mirovar's doorstep. The Raven had baited a hook – a hook swallowed by the Order.

From the day of their arrival, the Raven had excelled at blending into force leader Francis Mirovar's team. They'd grown to adulthood within the team, absorbing all the Order had to teach them, blending the Order's training with the intensive early instruction provided by Shabbah al Ahmar and the best instructors of the Red Empire.

Shabbah al Ahmar expected the Raven to rise to become the Head of the Order, and from that position, to subvert the operation of the Order to his will.

The Red Empire know me as Al Ghurab, the Raven, and one day, perhaps one day soon, I will bring the Order to its knees before the rulership of Shabbah al Ahmar and together, the true children of the way of the Ramp will conquer the Vampire Dominion.

It was a noble cause, which fueled a passionate fire within the Raven's heart. *Our cause is both right and just, we will prevail over our enemies.*

Prologue – A Traitor's War

Port-au-Prince, Haiti, December 24th, 1857, 20:25

The scent of aniseed laced rum filled the air as drunken revelers spilled out of the port tavern. The foul odors of sweaty, unwashed bodies clashed with the salt tang of the ocean and fought battles with the reek of bales of goatskins and mahogany stacked in piles along the docks of Port-au-Prince. The lush warmth of the night fed the ambiance of celebration as children carrying oil lamps sang carols in the street, and people sang, danced, drank and feasted.

Pools of light from taverns, shops and warehouses illuminated the packed earth of the street, and the people moved through the soft lights and dim shadows as they mingled, shouted in semi-delirium and loved wildly.

The people of Port-au-Prince celebrated Christmas Eve. Above them, an entirely different ceremony was well advanced in the top floor suite of the Ivory Moon hotel. The hotel's staff had cleared the rooms of furniture the week before, the bare floorboards lay exposed, and thick black curtains draped the windows.

Jean Philippe Allemande, Voodoo Sorcerer, and his student sat opposite each other within the confines of a magic circle. The circle was three yards across and drawn in fresh human blood. Both men had stripped to the waist, wearing simple dark cloth trousers. They were wet with perspiration. A fine sheen that glowed like gold in the candlelight covered the student's pale skin, long limbs, and lean musculature. Jean Philippe's mahogany skin, burnished in the candlelight, dripped sweat onto the floorboards where it soaked into the dry wood. The air was thick with the scent of black candles wrought from the fat of human cadavers. Flat copper bowls of slowly congealing blood lay at the eight cardinal points around the bloody diagram on the floor.

The student had arrived in the winter months of 1846. They'd struck a bargain. They'd swap power for immortality. In the following years, the student had visited, time and time again. Participating in training his mind, body, and soul to confront the Divine Engine of Thoth and draw from it a tiny fraction of its true power.

The student's agents had delivered Jean Philippe to the Americas, the Far East, Turkey, Europe, and England, where he'd aided the student in the acquisition and binding of a circle of five servants of great power. Tonight's service would be the last one that he would provide, and it would bring him a step closer to the fulfillment of his greatest desire.

Jean Phillipe's craving for the Key of Ahknaton threatened to break his deep concentration. The wondrous artifact that granted full access to the Divine Engine was often in his thoughts. It was why he sought immortality, a gift the student bore within his blood. With immortality, he would have the time to find the Key of Ahknaton, and with the Key in hand, he could remake the world in his own image.

Jean Philippe had explained the ceremony to his student. The protections were necessary to defend themselves from the raw power of the Divine Engine. It was only with strict adherence to the rules that the precautions would work. The slightest misstep would bring utter catastrophe. The student had insisted that despite the risks, they should proceed, and finally, the time had come to complete the greatest sorcery that Jean Philippe had ever attempted. From bitter experience, he understood the boundaries of what he could ask of the Divine Engine. He'd brushed against those limits once before and had spent many months cowering in madness before a semblance of sanity had returned.

Jean Phillipe watched his student intently. He speculated on the power the student had asked for. He wondered what might happen if the powers of the Divine Engine were set against each other. Would an irresistible force meet an immovable object? He admitted to himself that he no longer had the courage to attempt such a thing. He thought it best to keep his concerns to himself lest the student leave without making payment.

The student was ready – residing in a place of perfect stillness. Jean Philippe tightened his concentration to a single point. The air shimmered within the confines of the circle, like summer heat rising off sunbaked stones. An awesome presence filled the room. The candles dimmed, the shadows thickened, and a glimmering rainbow flickered in the center of the magic circle. The rainbow solidified, resolving into a swirling mass of multi-colored lights the size of a melon hovering two feet off the floor.

He uttered a single phrase, "Grant the power of foresight."

Gleaming dust motes halted in their flight before Jean Philippe's eyes and time itself seemed to pause, then the Divine Engine disappeared.

Intense disappointment cut him like a knife. The promise of limitless power remained tantalizingly out of reach. Without the Key of Ahknaton, all he could practice were petite sorceries, and he could never satisfy his lust to consummate a union with the Divine Engine and become one with the gods.

He glanced at his student. A terrible wonder lit the vampire king's face, his eyes focusing on empty space a yard in front of him.

"Mr. Crane, what do you see?"

"The many future paths before me."

"That is a potent gift."

"Agreed."

"I have delivered what I promised, five binding curses and an unlimited sorcerous power for you."

"You shall have your reward."

The student's mouth trembled. He smiled hungrily, fangs gleaming wetly in the candle light. He lunged forward, sinking his razor-sharp teeth into Jean Philippe's throat.

With his blood rushing out of his body, Jean Philippe's gaze lit upon the lone spectator to the ceremony. A young woman, her body warm and luxurious, struggling frantically against her bindings, her eyes wide above the cloth gag filling her mouth. Her companion lay dead on the floor, his blood used to draw the magic circle and fill the copper bowls. She would be his first true meal, the fruit of the earth, destined to satisfy his immortal needs.

A succulent fruit, the first of many he would savor on his island home.

Chapter Eight

Progress Report – The Day Guard Program Phase V

Report#: 134
Date: June 11th

Summary begins:

The development of the Day Guard serum has now entered its final stage. The success rate is now more than 50% (50.4%), with enhanced effects proving persistent beyond thirty days without degradation. We conclude that administration of the serum will produce permanent enhancements without side effects within 3 hours in one of every two healthy, adult subjects.

Current averaged measured results across the twelve successful test subjects are as follows,

- Strength increases by 304%
- Motor speed increases by 315%
- Agility increases by 294%
- Endurance increases by 515%
- Reflex speed increases by 324%
- Pain tolerance increases by 312%
- Healing rate increases by 524%
- Motor skill increases by 378%

These results represent a doubling in activation of the System Zero epigenetic factors when compared with the Phase IV subjects, yet still fall about 50% short of the theoretical maximums.

The symptoms of serum failure continue to manifest as berserk rage, followed by progeria, and catatonic depression with onset 24 to 48 hours after the administration of the serum with inevitably fatal results within two days of the onset of the symptoms.

All test subjects have been terminated using the TEF-4 neurotoxin. Final wrap up of this program has commenced and can be expected to be completed within two weeks. All technical details for the design and production of the Day Guard serum, the TEF-4 neurotoxin, and their associated delivery systems have been committed to secured data vaults on the Panopticon cloud.

The primary active ingredient of the Day Guard serum is derived from the *Ophiocordyceps diabolicus* fungus. A substantial quantity of the fungus has been harvested from the Amazonas region of Brazil – sufficient to compose five hundred doses of the Day Guard serum.

The fungus has been sent by secure courier to Shadowstone Research Facility #19, Fort Dix, New Jersey.

Summary ends:

– Quantum encrypted email from Shadowstone Research Facility #34, Brazil.

* * *

Boston, June 11th, 20:53

General Chloe Armitage ran her fingers through her damp hair.

She glanced into the police cruiser's rear-view mirror. The heavy bruising on the right side of her face had disappeared, her eyes were clear, and she glowed with health. Feasting on a young Boston police officer would do that for a vampire. She drew her hand down her face and nodded – pleased with her perfection.

Her wounds from the pair of .50 caliber bullets, katana chest thrust and the nightfalcon helicopter crash occurring less than half an hour before had healed completely.

Exiting the car, her smartphone vibrated with the arrival of a text. Drawing the phone from her pocket, she read the message, 'Ramin Kain – quantum signature attached.'

Only one person could have sent that message: the Raven.

Chloe grinned broadly, filled with exhilaration. She put the phone away. With the quantum signature of Ramin Kain's phone, she could penetrate his information defenses. She was certain it would not be long before she would know everything there was to know about the Head of the Order of Thoth.

She determined to ensure that Shabbah al Ahmar's agent within Francis Mirovar's force team never discovered who she was. The Raven was too valuable a prize to lose and finding out the supposed second agent of the

Red Empire in North America was general Chloe Armitage of the Vampire Dominion would do exactly that.

Chloe took in her surroundings. She was standing in the first level parking garage of the Boston Risk Investigation Security Consultants building. There were two stairwells, one elevator, another lower-level parking garage, and eight cameras, two of which pointed straight at her.

The nearest stairwell echoed with the quick footsteps of men rapidly descending toward her. Pausing next to the police cruiser, Chloe sardonically saluted the nearest camera. The stairwell door burst open, three Shadowstone operatives dressed in suits and carrying FN P90 submachine guns fanned out into the parking garage.

"Halt!" shouted the lead operative.

The second operative demanded, "Put your hands up."

The third operative moved sideways. The barrel of his gun aligned perfectly with the middle of Chloe's chest. His gun's red dot sight sitting steady on the matte black of her battered and scarred chest plate.

Chloe turned toward the lead operative, arched an eyebrow quizzically, and inquired sardonically, "Which is it, halt or put my hands up?"

The men suddenly recognized her, a flash of confusion shadowing their faces like clouds passing over the sun. They quickly lowered their weapons.

The lead operative stepped forward; his face stiff with fear. "My apologies, Ma'am. We didn't recognize you wearing combat armor and with all the chaos tonight—"

Chloe frowned. "Don't justify your overreaction, I expect better from Shadowstone operatives."

"Yes, Ma'am. What are your orders, Ma'am?"

"Do you have a nightfalcon?"

"No, Ma'am. We have a light transport chopper."

"It will have to do," Chloe conceded. "Order the pilot to begin immediate pre-flight checks, I need to be back in New York as soon as possible."

"Yes, Ma'am. It should be ready for take-off in ten minutes."

"Let's make it five."

"Yes, Ma'am," he replied, tapping his earpiece and giving urgent commands to scramble the R.I.S.C helicopter.

"One other thing," Chloe noted, glancing back at the car.

"Yes, Ma'am?"

"Dismantle that police cruiser and dispose of the two bodies in the trunk."

"... Two bodies? ... Dismantle a police cruiser?"

Chloe pushed her shoulders back and glowered at the lead operative. "Are you going to make me repeat myself?"

"Ah, no, Ma'am," the lead operative averred, his Adam's apple bobbing as he swallowed nervously. "I will make sure it's done."

"Tonight – no delay."

"Yes, Ma'am."

Chloe dismissed the men with a nod. Turning she entered the stairwell. Once out of sight, she blurred upward before any of the operatives could follow her. In moments, she reached the top of the R.I.S.C building and stepped out onto the helipad. The helicopter rested in front of her, a sleek, black, civilian model, with R.I.S.C written in bold white letters on its side. The letters sat beneath a red lightning bolt that arced to the nose of the craft. The helicopter's pilot was sitting in the cockpit, rapidly flicking switches. The single turbine switched on, started to spool up and the rotors began slowing spinning. She bent low, jogging over to the open cabin door, climbed in and sat down directly behind the pilot.

She tapped him on the shoulder.

He jerked half out of his seat, twisted around and yelled, "HELL!"

Chloe tilted her head slightly, smiling at the pilot with quiet amusement. "New York – The R.I.S.C Tower."

The pilot slapped his chest a couple of times. His eyes wide, he managed to state, "I assume you're the VIP Carter told me to scramble for."

"You assume correctly."

The pilot hesitated for a second, clearly perplexed. He turned back to his controls, muttering under his breath, "How did she get up here so quickly."

Relaxing back in her seat, Chloe strapped herself in. She considered her options, composed a brief message on her smartphone, and sent it to Cornelius Crane.

* * *

The boardroom dominated the north side of the 101st floor of the R.I.S.C Enterprises Tower. It was here that Cornelius Crane, King of the Vampire Dominion, played the part of the mysterious and reclusive owner of the privately-owned R.I.S.C Enterprises Corporation. The public face, hidden amongst thousands of ordinary corporations, that masked the Vampire Dominion and Cornelius Crane's Citadel.

Cornelius stared out of the boardroom windows at the brilliantly lit skyscrapers of midtown Manhattan and the dark swathe of Central Park beyond them. The windows resembled regular commercial glass but were composed of transparent armor that could stop a direct hit by a 30mm anti-tank round. The windows were slightly darker than normal, hiding a broad-spectrum electromagnetic shield laminated within the armor. An information cloak proof against any known method of spying encapsulated the boardroom.

He blinked and sighed, pressing a button on a hand-held remote as he frowned at the vibrant city laid out before him. It had been decades since he'd witnessed such losses in the west. The Red Empire had killed four praetorians, and destroyed the Shadowstone facility in Jerusalem. An agent or agents unknown had killed two more praetorians in Brazil, and now the Order of Thoth had slaughtered six of his best in Boston.

Cornelius turned and studied the large monitor and multiple screens filling the far wall. He watched the wreckage of a suddenly hot war burn in silence. He'd muted the sound to help himself think. He glanced at the bottom right-hand screen, dominated by several digital timers. There was one in red, just ticking over eighteen minutes. An hour ago, it was registering over nine years of continuous, uninterrupted operation of the Panopticon.

Cornelius cursed out loud, "How the hell did they haze all the nearby cameras and the satellite over Boston. I've got a seventeen-minute black hole three miles wide centered on that damn warehouse, and during that time everything goes to shit!"

For the first time in decades, an unsettling sense of creeping chaos wormed its way into his mind. The sudden and severe loss left him staring incredulously at the screens. The initiative had clearly shifted to his opponents, and he vowed silently to get it back.

The door into the boardroom clicked open, and Cornelius inhaled the familiar scent of a subtle perfume.

"Sir?" A feminine voice asked.

Cornelius looked toward the voice. His executive secretary stood in the doorway; petite, blond, beautiful and superbly efficient.

"Ursula, organize the immediate recall of the Orange-2 spectrum team to Fort Dix. Violet-7 must remain on deployment at research facility number thirty-four in Brazil until the current phase of the Day Guard program is complete, then they are to return to Fort Dix as well."

"Yes, Sir. Should I liaise with General Armitage?"

"No. Pass my orders directly to the Shadowstone troop commanders on the ground."

"Yes, Sir. Is there anything else, Sir?"

"Has Ramin Kain arrived at our meeting point?"

"He has signaled that he expects to be there at 21:15."

Cornelius nodded. "Good, ten minutes from now. That will be all."

Ursula smiled briefly. "Yes, Sir."

Cornelius watched her slim form depart the boardroom, the door closing behind her. He turned back to face the muted screens on the wall opposite from where he stood.

Multiple real-time drone and satellite feeds of the Boston warehouse site dominated the main screen. All the important objects on the monitor had streams of Panopticon metadata associated with them. Flashing red star and stable white cross markers littered the warehouse and dock. The Order of Thoth had killed six vampire praetorians and over sixty Shadowstone operatives. The wreckage of four nightfalcons lay in piles around the site, two were still burning, the other two had almost cooled to the level of the background environment. A fifth helicopter lay under the surface of the Mystic River, its vampire pilot also dead. A Shadowstone RHIB burned a half mile along the Mystic River, destroyed by the Order of Thoth after using it to escape.

One screen showed a civilian R.I.S.C helicopter rushing toward his Citadel. Crushing the remote in his bare hand, Cornelius slowly shook his head and declared, "How did this happen? I'll have her head if she is responsible for this!"

A row of picture-in-picture views along the bottom of the main screen remained dedicated to events off site. Two nightfalcon helicopters were inbound from Cornelius' Citadel, each carrying eight fully armed vampire praetorians with an ETA at Boston of 21:50. Another nightfalcon from Fort Dix was circling to land at the Boston warehouse with half the Yellow-3 spectrum team. The rest of the Yellow-3 team raced from Fort Dix to Boston in Shadowstone OPSEC vans; they would arrive in another three hours, just after midnight.

Three vans sporting the livery of major news channels were racing along the I-91 highway from New York City to Boston. Shadowstone PSYOPS crews were due to arrive on site in less than an hour to shape the public news feeds. Their colleagues in the Shadowstone PSYOPS directorate were already hard at work in the offices of a Manhattan public relations firm, wholly owned by R.I.S.C Enterprises.

There was a view showing two Shadowstone operatives still alive on site, the metadata next to the blue markers read James Haley and Louise Wesson. The woman's vital signs indicated she was suffering from a concussion.

Cornelius shook his head again, disgusted at the waste of good, useful men. He didn't care about them individually; it was the fact that they would have made excellent candidates for his Day Guard program that hurt the most. The sixty men would have provided thirty loyal fighters he could have used in daylight operations against his enemies.

Cornelius smacked his hand down on the table. "What the fucking hell has she done? I explicitly told her not to waste my Shadowstone men against the Order."

Cornelius looked down at a printed email resting in an open buff-colored cardboard folder on the boardroom table. It described the final results of the Day Guard Phase V program. His own initiative, designed to produce an enhanced super-soldier, capable of engaging the Order of Thoth and the Red Empire in daylight. They would provide the edge that he needed. His opponents would not be able to rest. Pursued by the Day Guard during the day and his praetorians at night. It was the one bright spot in an otherwise disastrous night.

His lips curled into a sneer as he silently vowed to wipe the Order of Thoth and the Red Empire off the face of the Earth.

Cornelius flipped the folder closed. Noticing the crushed shards of the remote that littered the boardroom table, he used the folder to sweep the fragments into a nearby waste bin.

He put the folder into a disposal chute on the wall, where with a slight whirr, the paper and plastic turned into confetti and dropped down to a basement incinerator. He strode over to a rack in the corner of the boardroom and selected a hat and a light coat. He spoke a sixteen-digit alphanumeric code. There was a brief hum, a seam appeared along the long axis of the boardroom table, and it separated into two perfect halves. They glided apart to reveal a hole a yard wide in the floor, its interior a blend of chrome and shadow.

Cornelius stepped forward, disappearing down the hole.

* * *

Cornelius Crane wore a light weight, dark-gray coat over his suit, and a matching fedora with a barely discernible white and gray feather in the band. He glided on his long legs up the stairs toward the East Balcony of Grand Central Terminal. As he came onto the upper level, the doorman of the Gilded Tea Club greeted him.

Unknown to everyone in the discrete and fashionable Gilded Tea Club, Cornelius owned the establishment through a set of front companies, and Shadowstone swept the site for surveillance systems on an hourly basis. It was a public place where he could hold a secure and anonymous conversation without revealing the location of his citadel to whomever he was talking with.

Cornelius nodded politely to the doorman; a sudden bead of perspiration appeared on the man's brow as Cornelius strode past him. Entering into the warmly lit interior of the cafe, the rich aromas of premium tea and coffee, aged oak, fine leather and the sharp, coppery scent of the blood of more than thirty humans surrounded him.

He moved amongst the people like a force of nature. A pathway leading to where he wanted to go opened up. People paused in their conversations, suddenly lost for words. Others stumbled aside or mumbled confused apologies. In moments, he reached a sheltered cubical in a back corner of the room farthest from the entrance.

Behind him, the room rushed back to normal, like a ship righting itself after a rogue wave.

Cornelius sat down opposite a man of above average height and solid build. The man could pass for early forties in age with a sprinkling of gray in his dark hair. He had the charismatic face of a successful politician and wore a dark-blue suit. They stared at each other for a couple of seconds as the background noise of the cafe returned to its usual modest volume.

Ramin Kain nodded in greeting, and said with a note of irony in his voice, "I heard on the news that a counter-terrorism exercise in Boston has devolved into catastrophe. Apparently, a helicopter had a major weapons system malfunction and shot down four other helicopters before plunging into the Mystic River with massive loss of life." He tilted his head slightly. "Or so I'm led to believe."

"Indeed," Cornelius noted, his mouth tightening into a grimace.

"The Boston Police Department are also missing two officers. Apparently, they went rogue, killing two of their colleagues and absconding with a cruiser." Leaning forward, Kain arched a quizzical eyebrow. "And you know what? They're still missing. So, what happened? Is the Red Empire now operating in North America or was it a masterful display of Shadowstone incompetence?"

Cornelius stared at the man impassively. He'd met men like Kain before; intelligent, vain, ambitious, overconfident and – in the end – dead. He always outlived them, and he fully expected to outlive Kain.

"The Order of Thoth as it turns out," Cornelius stated, watching carefully as Kain's grin evaporated from his face. "Combined action by the Wu family and the Mirovar force team."

"The Wu family? They opted out ..." Kain rubbed his top lip and then snapped his fingers. "Two decades ago! They must have been associated with the Slaynes." He spread his hands wide. "But this is a small price to pay for what I give you."

Cornelius kept his face impassive as anger and disgust flared in hidden depths.

The two men stared at each other; one with studied patience, the other with feverish ambition.

"Why did you call this meeting?" Cornelius asked.

Kain leaned forward, and demanded conspiratorially, "I need a new coven of vampires, I need to get results to impress the force leaders and keep them in line. I provided you with the Slaynes, you owe—"

"I owe you nothing," Cornelius snapped. "Our arrangement exists at my pleasure, should I recall my forces from the rest of the world and bring them here. I could easily extinguish the Order of Thoth once and for all."

Slapping the table with the palm of his hand, Kain leaned forward and asserted forcefully, "And you would have the Red Empire at your back. I gave you the Slaynes. I virtually gave you the Papyrus of Hakron the Scribe, all you had to do was send someone around to pick it up."

"... Yes, and now you have much less to offer me," Cornelius observed disdainfully.

For a long moment, Kain looked up at the ceiling before flicking his eyes back toward Cornelius. "The detente has served us well. You have a quiet front here in the west, and you keep your senior vampires alive. While I rule the Order of Thoth without challengers."

Cornelius leaned over the table, his hands apart on the dark wooden surface, his face a thin veneer of control over restless passions. "Served us well, has it?" he shook his head, pointing a long finger at Kain's face. "No – not at all. You will fix it, and you will fix it soon. Get your force leaders in line. I tell you now, Mirovar must die."

Kain blinked uncertainly, his mouth moved as if he was about to speak, but he remained silent.

Cornelius sat back and remarked matter-of-factly, "I will provide a new coven. Allow two months for the fruit to become ripe."

Kain nodded.

"One more thing. Two survived the battle on the dock. One was the Wu girl, who was the other? I must know who the other person was and you will find out for me."

"Yes, of course," Kain vowed.

Cornelius straightened out of his chair, stepping away from the table. "Excellent, I believe we're done here."

"Yes, we are."

Cornelius turned and walked briskly out of the cafe without looking back.

* * *

Cornelius blurred out of the hole in the floor, appearing in the middle of the R.I.S.C Enterprises boardroom. He spoke the code words again, and the two halves of the table glided back together to form a seamless whole. He returned his coat and hat to the rack in the corner of the room.

He turned to the windows, extended his senses to their vampiric maximums and silenced his mind to a still point of concentration. He became a tall, lean statue, preternaturally still while passions flowed through nearly a thousand years of memory. He began the process of activating the precognitive power sourced from the Metaframe sorcery of Jean Philippe Allemande.

Mekra; her touch had been pure electricity, her passions like storms as powerful as they were unpredictable. She'd found him in the Levant in 1096, Baron Cornelius de Grue, a noble of Brittany and a General in the first Crusade. She'd told him she wanted a military leader to stand at her side and quell the chaos of the vampire world. Her offer had fallen upon fertile ground. Cornelius had grown weary of the internecine struggles between various factions of the Order of Thoth and the Red Empire. The constant wars to gather together the three artifacts of the Metaframe to a single hand. He'd forsaken his oath to the Order of Thoth and Mekra had made him a vampire.

Memory continued to unfurl, rolling past the diamond-like focus of his mind. The chaos of centuries of war of all against all, his eventual rebellion and assassination of Mekra, and the destruction of the cult of her devotion. The discovery of the voodoo sorcerer Jean Philippe Allemande in Haiti. The realization that magic was very real, and based on a partial, incomplete access to the Metaframe. Training with Allemande and using the sorcerer to bind five generals to his service during the 1850s. Four exceptional men and one unique woman who were unable to harm him, and unable to defend themselves against him. With the generals in place, the Vampire Dominion had become the unquestioned power amongst the surviving vampires, and the time of chaos had ended.

Chloe Armitage flooded his mind. They shared a common heritage; both born into the Order of Thoth, both Ramp masters before their conversion into vampires, both heirs to rulership. Desire, admiration, and regret flooded his soul, warring amongst themselves without resolution. Of the five generals, she was the best, and the closest to what he'd sought in a protégé.

The power of prevision bloomed within him. The near future came into view, as the momentum of past events spread out into a multi-dimensional matrix of possible events aligned to his own life. Bright lines anchored in the certainty of the past, whipped through the nodes of the matrix, linking the most probable future paths. Other lines, fading from bright to dull, indicated the less probable through to the least likely events.

There were no nodes where Chloe could attack, or kill him. The curse of Jean Philippe Allemande continued to bind her and the other generals, making it impossible for them to harm him. It was an inescapable trap, born from the same source that gifted him his precognitive ability.

He noted a new line, barely illuminated, leading directly from the events on the Boston docks to spear through a new node of his own death. There was a small chance that within a year, his long life would end. A new threat had been born on the docks, closely associated with the Wu family and now waiting to grow to realization. Cornelius had foreseen such events before and had taken action to thwart them. He noted the possibility and anticipated he would again be victorious. He would watch the event gain form, he would identify who was shaping it, and he would kill them before the possibility of his death could become a certainty.

He searched through the matrix for pathways leading to the acquisition of the Interpretive Codex. A line of moderate strength led through General Haras Mosule. Chloe was now absent from all pathways that would bring the Codex into his possession. He emerged from the previsionary meditation and reflected upon what he'd learned.

Something has recently changed, her growing ambitions blind her, she is no longer looking for the Codex. It is slipping away from me. First, we must quell this petite rebellion and then refocus our efforts on recovery of the Codex. Chloe will be the key to both goals, I must restore her motivation to the tasks at hand, she is the most valuable piece on the chessboard. And now there is a new threat, Chloe has messaged me of her victory over the Order grand master Gang Wu, but what of his daughter and his apprentice? Either of them could be the origin point of the new threat line. I need to know more about what happened tonight.

Cornelius paged his secretary. A moment later the boardroom door opened and Ursula inquired, "Sir?"

"Any news?"

"Sir, General Armitage has just arrived on the external helipad in a R.I.S.C helicopter."

"Bring her here, I'm not meeting her in my private quarters tonight." Cornelius shook his head emphatically. "But first – bring me my sword."

"Yes, Sir," Ursula replied and left.

Cornelius continued to watch the details of the recovery and cleanup of the Boston warehouse site, the main screen illuminating his face with colored lights and shadows.

He mused out loud to himself in the empty boardroom, his voice filled with dreadful intent, "I've spent centuries mastering information and knowledge. I built my library, mastered more than a dozen languages, I commissioned the Panopticon and even acquired a secret Metaframe inspired pre-cognitive ability, and yet I couldn't see that it was a trap. Someone set a trap, and caught us in it – but a trap set by whom, Francis Mirovar, Arthur Slayne or Shabbah al Ahmar? Chloe had better have an exemplary excuse for tonight, or by God, I will bathe this room in her blood and take the Interpretive Codex from the dead hand of Shabbah al Ahmar myself."

* * *

Chloe stared at the smooth chrome of the doors as the elevator descended from the external helipad to the 101st floor. Crane had never asked her to attend an audience in the corporate boardroom. That was where Crane dealt with humans, not with his generals. He was deliberately insulting her. Chloe sighed once; her lips pressed into a thin line as she considered the possibility, she'd misjudged Crane's response.

She'd taken off her body armor in the R.I.S.C helicopter, stripping down to her form-fitting black jumpsuit. The nanotube suit was already dry, she stood comfortably in her bare feet waiting for the elevator to reach Crane's public executive suite. There was no point in trying to protect herself from her king; Allemande's curse ensured that she would not be able to defend herself should Crane choose to attack her. In her left hand, she carried her chest and back plates by their straps; the puncture marks and bullet holes clearly visible on them. The body armor damage matched similar blood-stained holes in her jumpsuit.

The body armor was her primary evidence to explain what had happened and to drive home the risks that Crane now faced.

Chloe considered her tactics. *A bold approach is best. The truth is my ally, the more he knows, the better to demonstrate my loyalty and competence in the face of a tactical defeat. There is but one key fact I must keep secret — the existence of Anton Slayne.*

The elevator pulled smoothly to a halt, the door swishing open. Chloe walked into reception, approaching the main desk. Sitting primly behind it was Crane's executive secretary Ursula Zielinkski.

Ursula smiled coldly, her blue eyes lighting up with anticipation. "General Armitage, you're expected. He is waiting for you in the boardroom."

Chloe ignored her, walking confidently into the boardroom. Closing the door behind her, she dropped her body armor onto the top of the boardroom table where it clattered against the fine wood and leather.

"Six praetorians you gave me — I needed twelve!" she declared forthrightly.

Crane blurred across the room toward her. Chloe reflexively stepped back, there was neither room nor time to avoid him pushing her hard up against the wall. The point of Crane's broadsword punched through the fabric of her jumpsuit, slicing through the skin over her sternum and grinding through the bone beneath. For the second time this night a sword blade rested inches from her heart.

Crane's left hand clamped down on her right shoulder, holding her against the wall. He held his sword flat and level as he leaned in, his face inches from her own.

A cold fury erupted deep within Chloe, she stared hard at Crane as he straight-armed her up the wall, her feet dangling half a foot off the floor.

Crane glared at her with tightly held rage, and demanded, "The truth Chloe."

Chloe blinked, for a second the world closed in upon her. The hand holding the sword in her chest was rock steady, terrifying in its stillness, matching the resolve writ large in Crane's eyes.

The urge to fight flowed strong and clear through her soul and Chloe's hands clenched into fists. She conceived the attack in a moment, she would take a deep cut as she pushed Crane's blade out of her chest with her left hand, while her right broke his hold upon her shoulder.

Chloe dropped into a supreme ramp and blurred.

Lightning crackled through the boardroom, playing along her skin, icy fire ripping along her nerves.

"Allemande's curse!" she gasped past gritted teeth, her limbs as limp as a rag dolls. The lightning ebbed; her mind raced, *I'm trapped, but the truth is still my ally.*

Crane barked a single harsh laugh. "Tell me the truth!"

Chloe looked steadily into Crane's eyes, and explained around gasps for air. "The ground proved more treacherous than anticipated. The Order used the river to advantage and approached with stealth. Our forces failed to discover them."

Crane shoved her hard against the wall, the plaster cracking behind her. "I warned you about giving your opponent the choice of ground for the battle. It was clearly a trap, and you walked into it like a novice."

"Mirovar would never have appeared without the ground, he is not stupid," Chloe observed; managing to hold onto her composure. "I had to give them the ground to draw them out, and it worked – they showed up in force."

"Well, we lost. So, someone was stupid," Crane said, glaring at her. "I wonder if it was me for trusting the promise you made in Jerusalem."

Chloe shook her head. "We needed the extra praetorians. If we had twelve, we would have won."

"I've always respected your integrity," Crane said, his voice silky soft, "You've always kept your word."

A wet patch spread out from the cut in her chest as blood oozed past the blade. She braced herself, she'd seen Crane in this sort of mood before where he would praise quietly before—.

Crane twisted the sword blade a quarter turn, speaking with tightly controlled fury. "But now you falter, now you fail."

The metal grinding against raw bone sent jagged bolts of pain through her body.

Chloe gasped out past gritted teeth, "I asked … for twelve … you insisted … I go with six."

"Six would have been enough if you had not lost our Shadowstone forces before the battle started," Crane snapped.

Chloe's eyes widened. "You advised me to keep Shadowstone out of it – and now you claim that they were essential for victory?"

Dragging his sword clear, Crane threw her down to the floor.

Catching herself before she fell flat, Chloe crouched and looked up at him, her face an unreadable mask.

Crane frowned, shaking his finger at her. "Do not dare put this on me. We have worked together for more than a century – I know your tactics – you should have won."

Chloe stood up, the wound in her chest began to close. Nodding contritely, she said, "Normally I would have. This time was different."

"I wonder if you held back. I wonder if your heart is still in this fight. Are you still willing to take the battle to our enemies or," Crane said, then thrust his long index finger at her, "are you playing your own game?"

Chloe tilted her head and declared incredulously, "I am stunned that you would ask that of me."

"Something happened in the last twelve hours that cost us victory tonight. You are the most powerful piece on the chessboard. What happened? Why did you fail?"

Chloe shook her head.

Crane stared at her. He remained silent, forcing her to continue.

"We underestimated Gang Wu, he was a genius with the sword," Chloe attested, pushing a finger through the sword cut on her jumpsuit. "He nearly killed me; his blade was against my heart." She thumped her chest. "I only just managed to get my hand down in time to prevent him dragging his sword out and cutting it in two."

Crane's face twisted into an incredulous leer, he stepped close, pushing his fingers through the hole in Chloe's black jumpsuit.

"He would have been fully ramped," Crane observed decisively, his eyes darkening with suspicion. "You're very fast, but that is extraordinary, even for one of us."

"I was lucky, I started moving as he thrust."

Crane sniffed skeptically, stepping over to the boardroom table, he fingered the bullet holes in Chloe's chest plate. ".50 cal if I'm not mistaken."

"Depleted uranium, hurt like hell and pushed me out the side of the helicopter."

"You didn't see them firing at you?"

"Not this time."

"I don't see how someone, as experienced as you are, could miss a machine gun firing at them."

"I'd just been stabbed!"

Crane pursed his lips, dropping the chest plate on the table. Turning away from Chloe, he looked out the windows at the metropolis shining in the night.

"Then what happened?" he asked irritably.

"Machine gun fire struck the engines of the helicopter, and it followed me into the Mystic River. It crashed on top of me, knocking me unconscious and pinning me in the muck on the bottom."

"... Clearly, you got out."

"The nose cracked open on impact with the river bottom. Luckily, I was off to the side and not directly underneath it. I was able to wriggle my leg free and get back up to the surface before I drowned or bled to death."

Crane turned back from the window. He stared hard at the wrecked body armor, frowned, and studied it closely.

He is listening – success.

* * *

Cornelius stroked his chin thoughtfully.

Chloe had almost died. If his best warrior was almost overwhelmed, he must have underestimated the threat. Obviously, Kain did not have enough control over the force teams and especially the Mirovar team. Was the Order resurgent? The shift in probable outcomes could easily have resulted from actions by the Order. Was it the doing of Mirovar, Gang Wu, or the new fellow from Boston? He decided he'd relied too much on the secret detente with Kain.

"We have become complacent but not anymore," Cornelius declared. Reaching out, he flicked a switch on a console in the middle of the table. The room filled with the open communications from the praetorians at the Boston warehouse site.

Cornelius and Chloe looked up at the main screen. He manipulated the console and one of the satellite streams on the screen expanded to fill it. It showed a floating crane positioned about sixty yards away from the dock. Thick black cables ran down from the crane into the Mystic River, they snapped tight, the barge tilting under the load.

A tall praetorian stood on the dock, blond hair escaping from underneath his tactical command helmet. Looking up at the Vampire Dominion drone hovering two miles above the site, he tapped his comm link and inquired, "Sir, are you watching this?"

"Yes, Centurion, give me your report."

"We're in the process of recovering General Armitage's nightfalcon and her equipment."

"Can you confirm casualties?"

"Yes, Sir. I can confirm Spengler, Hendricks, Smithson, Calley, Senna, and Hato are dead. We have also recovered the pilot's body from General Armitage's nightfalcon."

"Were the bodies sanitized?"

"Yes, Sir. The Shadowstone lead operative has used grenades to keep our secret."

Chloe said quickly, "James Haley cleaned up the evidence."

Cornelius' eyes flicked toward Chloe, and he whispered, "So he knows."

She nodded once.

"And the status of the site, what of the humans?" Cornelius asked.

"Sir, we have secured the site and bagged the bodies. Shadowstone PSYOPS are providing media coverage."

"Good. Ensure full handover to Shadowstone by oh four hundred and return to the Citadel."

"Yes, Sir," the Centurion replied. The audio dropping back to mute as he turned away and began giving orders to his troops.

Cornelius frowned, turning back to Chloe he directed, "It is clear that Haley knows our secret, and even though he has done the right thing, he and the Wesson woman must be dealt with."

"Yes, Sir. I've watched Haley closely over the last eight years, and I would recommend him for advancement into our ranks. He has highly intuitive combat skills and would make a fine vampire warrior."

"Haley's conversion is approved but what of Wesson?"

Chloe's eyes flicked back to the main screen, and she suggested, "From the data, looks like she's got a concussion, I will confirm what she remembers. If she doesn't know our secret, she will assist us with rebuilding Shadowstone. She is a highly capable operative and excels at forming teams. I will need time to assess how best to induct Haley, and I will verify Wesson at the earliest opportunity."

"Be careful how long you take with Haley."

"We will need to allow time to provide an effective cover story and to groom a replacement for him. I would recommend holding off for now – especially given the current state of the Shadowstone organization, Haley is critical to rebuilding it."

Cornelius frowned. "You will be held accountable for his actions."

"I can guarantee his discretion."

"See that you do."

"Yes, Sir."

Confident of his safety and the effectiveness of Allemande's curse, Cornelius turned away from Chloe. Stepping toward the broad windows, he surveyed the city before him. The boardroom lay reflected in the transparent armor; to his right Chloe moved up, and stood a couple of yards back from his shoulder.

Cornelius studied the city-lit nightscape and said confidently, "I believe that the Red Empire has commenced operations in North America. The attack in Jerusalem and this event in Boston have occurred too close together not to be part of a coordinated plan."

"I agree," Chloe conceded. "It would not surprise me to discover that Shabbah al Ahmar has a secret agent in Francis Mirovar's force team – it would allow for a coordinated action just like this."

Cornelius stared at Chloe's reflection in the boardroom windows incredulously. "You suggest that the Red Ghost has co-opted Mirovar."

"Not with Mirovar's knowledge, just someone on the inside who he trusts. Someone who is able to provide information at the right time and make Mirovar a cat's paw for the Red Empire."

Cornelius stared out the window, his voice thoughtful as he said, "Well as unlikely as that may seem, if you live long enough, you will see all manner of improbable things come to pass."

"Yes, Cornelius – our enemies surround us on all sides."

"The Order have lost respect for our power and we must teach them a sharp lesson. You have carte blanche for operations against the Mirovar force team in North America. Fulfill the promise that you made in Jerusalem and bring their heads to me. First, we must quell this pathetic rebellion and then refocus our efforts on recovery of the Interpretive Codex. Never forget, securing access to the Metaframe remains our primary goal."

"Yes, Sir, understood."

"Set Haley, and Wesson – if we can trust her – to rebuilding Shadowstone, and do it quickly. I want Shadowstone back to full strength within three months. Focus on recruiting special forces, we need warriors more than we need intelligence operatives. The state of play between the Ramp Masters and the Vampire Dominion is evolving rapidly."

"Cornelius?"

Cornelius stared at her reflection in the window. "You know what you need to know."

"Yes, Cornelius, and what of the praetorians?"

Cornelius smiled grimly. "I will personally select and recruit them. I will call on you when the time is right. I will need more than one vampire to help me convert as many as I need."

"Yes, Cornelius." Chloe smiled slightly. "Of course, I will render every possible assistance."

Cornelius turned to her and said without hesitation, "I am sure that you will."

Or else you will discover that my patience with you has worn out.

* * *

Carte blanche, Perfect. Chloe thought triumphantly.

Crane believed the might of the Red Empire was on the move. Chloe determined to leverage that belief in full. She mastered the impulse to smile broadly, keeping her face calm and her expression alert. Her body completed healing itself from the trauma of Crane's recent attack and the ripping forces of Allemande's curse. She waited patiently for the meeting to end.

Crane stroked his chin contemplatively, tapping his index finger against his lips. He pointed his finger at Chloe and declared, "There is one more thing."

"Yes, Cornelius?"

"There were three Order of Thoth operatives in Boston; Gang Wu, his daughter Li and someone else. I've reason to believe the Wu family were closely associated with the Slaynes. I need to know who that other person was. Whoever he is, he survived a battle with six praetorians and yourself, and he has appeared from nowhere. It's imperative we find out precisely who he is and determine the risk he presents to our operations."

Chloe's heart froze. Crane was so close to the truth. The smallest misstep and her plan would come undone.

"Cornelius, the Panopticon identified him as Anton Smith, he is young, he must have been trained in secret by Gang Wu."

"I want a comprehensive report on my desk by tomorrow night."

"Yes, Sir. I will start immediately."

"Good work, you are dismissed."

Chloe nodded, bowed respectfully and departed the boardroom.

James Haley had best be awake, she thought furiously. *He has work to do. And what of Ramin Kain, if he is the traitor in the Order, he could reveal the truth to Crane. I can't let that happen.*

Chloe entered the elevator, ascending to the external helipad on top of Crane's Citadel. The pilot and the R.I.S.C helicopter were still there.

"Move it! Now!" Chloe shouted, running over to the helicopter cabin. The pilot started the engine. In moments the sleek, black and red helicopter was aloft. She gave him directions to her Manhattan penthouse; they would be there in minutes.

She had to move quickly. There was too much evidence in the Panopticon. They would have to hide it immediately.

* * *

Chloe rushed into her penthouse suite. She sat down at her desk, opened her personal laptop, and logged into the Panopticon.

She opened her smartphone, dialed Louise Wesson's phone and set her phone down on her desk with the loudspeaker on. She expected James Haley would still have Wesson's phone. James was essential to her plan. She needed his knowledge of Shadowstone and his ability to act in daylight.

James will respond to trust with loyalty, she thought. *I must exploit that weakness.*

The phone rang three times before James answered it. "Ma'am?" James asked, a slight tremor tinging the edge of his voice.

"James, I have a critically important task that only you can do."

"... Yes, Ma'am. What is it?"

"We need to reset the history of Anton Smith away from his parents and his family home in Jamaica Plain. There can be no connection between the Anton Smith in the Panopticon records and the identities of William and Anna Smith. They must become childless, and Anton must have a new set of parents. We should also position him as close to the Noodle House as is practically possible."

"The identity of Anton Smith is already a fake."

"Indeed, it is, James. Well done. We'll have to take this another step forward. It will be a fake of a fake, the second level of misdirection."

"This will be messy," James warned. "There will be physical records, such as photos, that we will not be able to reach."

"That doesn't matter, we simply need to ensure that the Panopticon does not link Anton Smith to his real parents in any way, shape or form – is that clear?"

"Yes, Ma'am. When do you want it done?"

"Immediately. You must complete this work before dawn."

James paused for a long moment. "That's impossible."

"No, it's not – don't disappoint me – use the R.I.S.C building in Boston. It's only minutes away from where you are. You can access the Panopticon from there without interruption."

"I don't have the right privileges to do this. I'm going to have to dig through a multitude of systems."

Chloe tapped her keyboard. "You do now – I've elevated you to my level for the next eight hours, make the most of it."

"... Yes, Ma'am," James paused again, his voice steadying. "There is a way this could be done."

"Yes?"

"No parents at all, we can make him a foundling orphan, a ward of the state. I can easily access all the state records. All the public elements of his life will remain untouched: schools, sporting teams, online accounts, everything. We just insert him into the right records, it will do the job, a lot less complicated than putting him into another real family."

"I knew that I could rely on you James, now make it so."

"Yes, Ma'am will do."

"… While I have you – what of my sword – has it been recovered?"

"Yes, Ma'am. The praetorians have it. I asked them for it, but they would not release it to me," James answered, his voice betraying his disappointment.

"Don't worry about that. The praetorians will bring it to me, that task is complete. I need you to focus on the new mission."

"Yes, Ma'am," James confirmed, his voice steady for the first time in the call.

"Send me a text when you are done, and get a new phone, I can't be calling Louise Wesson all the time."

"Yes, Ma'am."

"By the way James, how is Ms. Wesson? I am a little surprised she is still alive."

"She is concussed; she has no memory of the battle or knowledge of vampires."

"James," Chloe said warmly. "I am sure you will manage the risk. You are on a new path now, embrace it, and all will be well."

"Yes, Ma'am … yes, Ma'am, I will."

"Send me a text when the work is done."

"Yes, Ma'am."

Chloe hung up the call and put the smartphone down.

The Panopticon system data streamed down her laptop monitor. Chloe accelerated her mind, her fingers flashing over the keyboard faster than a human eye could follow. The computer responded, the images and command line text becoming a blur. After thirty minutes of dedicated work, she'd erased all evidence that could personally link Anton Slayne (alias Smith) to herself. Especially the conversation recorded the morning before in the garden behind the Wu residence, where Gang and Li Wu revealed so much about the Slaynes. Now there only the task of restructuring the false identity of Anton Smith, which James would complete before sunrise. She relaxed, leaning back in her chair and allowing her mind to float freely.

She surprised herself with an unladylike snort of laughter.

Anton Smith 2.0 is about to be born.

"Now to focus on dismembering the schemes of Ramin Kain," she whispered to the empty room.

* * *

231

It was a cloudless night, the sky was crystal clear, dominated by a full moon and a massive river of stars.

Anton stood in an open field, a short distance in front of him was a wooden fence, painted white like the ones used to corral horses. There was an awful insistent murmuring behind him, and a dreadful feeling crept through him. His breathing was suddenly shallow, his lungs tight; he forced himself to turn around.

A writhing mass of naked humanity lay before him; the crowd of people seethed and heaved, stretching away into the distance as far as the eye could see. Above the people, hovering mere yards away from Anton, was a creature beyond nightmare — his eyes widened, instinctively taking a step backward and lifting his arm up as if to ward off an attack.

Its body was leech-like, easily thirty yards long and about two yards across. Its pale, translucent skin glistened wetly in the moonlight. The creature's internal organs were dark shadows, visibly writhing beneath its skin. Its large, saucer-shaped eyes were blood red, with vertical irises like a cat. Its lipless mouth reflexively gaped open, revealing rows of needlepoint teeth. Its tail ended in a foot-long sting; scalpel sharp and slick with venom.

The creature glided over its host, its head bowing low over one particular specimen, a healthy young fellow who moved with more vigor than the rest. Slit-shaped nostrils flared, the monster's tail quivered, lashing forward, the sting plunged into the man's back. A pouch directly above the sting violently contracted, injecting venom, and inducing a sudden lethargy in the man.

In plain sight of Anton, the man slumped to the ground. His plight ignored by the crowd of humanity instinctively moving away from him.

The head of the creature swung lower, red eyes gleaming with wet hunger, it fixed its mouth onto the man's abdomen with an unbreakable grip. The man's eyes stared blankly, venom coursing through his veins, he was unable to grasp what was happening to him.

Anton froze with terror — panting — unable to move.

The parasite extended a proboscis from within its throat into the man's abdomen, flushing his body with digestive fluids. The corrosive liquids rendered the man's organs into a dark mush, rapidly drawn up into the hovering monster. Anton watched in horror as the monster consumed the man from the inside out. In a handful of seconds, his body collapsed into a dried husk, the crowd surged back, and he disappeared beneath the living, his loss unnoticed by those around him.

Anton rose high into the night sky as if lifted on the hand of a giant. The air rushed past him until the curve of the Earth stretched before him. Beneath him, the surface of the world lay crisscrossed by white fences, and within each corral, there was a mass of humanity attended by a hovering parasite.

To the east stood a single tower, rising high above all else. It gleamed in the moonlight, on top of it floated the largest of the leeches, surveying the world below with a tireless intelligence.

Anton flew helplessly toward the tower with tremendous speed, and in a moment the tower filled his vision. It was taller than it first appeared and he rose upward until he reached the marble platform of the ruler of the world.

The monster turned to face him, its baleful gaze boring deeply into his soul.

Anton shivered as the creature's insatiable hunger flowed over him in an icy wave. Its mouth gaped open, its fangs gleaming in the bright moonlight, its harsh voice cracked through the air like thunder.

"You are mine!"

The monster lunged forward.

Anton awoke in a cold sweat, his throat dry, and his heart pounding.

A hand with fathomless strength grabbed his shoulder, and a deep voice asked, "Hey buddy – are you okay? You were screaming like a girl."

Anton's eyes focused, and he recognized the burly form of the man named Peter. He sat opposite Anton in the van as it drove smoothly through the night. He glanced around the dim interior of the vehicle. The rest of the members of the Mirovar force team sat in their seats looking at him with quizzical expressions on their faces, only Li and Peter evidenced any concern.

"We're farmed like cattle," Anton muttered.

Peter snorted, slapping Anton on the shoulder. "You've woken up – good."

Anton gave him a dark look.

"We're almost home," Peter enthused. "You'll feel a lot better once you get something to eat."

A wave of nausea gripped Anton's stomach.

Everything is wrong, he thought. He swallowed hard against a sudden reflex to vomit.

* * *

The wheels of the van crunched over a gravel yard before pulling to a stop.

An athletic young man with dirty-blond hair and a close-cropped beard slid the side door open and leaped out of the vehicle. In moments, most of the team followed him, leaving Anton and Li in the cabin.

Seconds later, the rear doors of the van opened, and the bearded young man directed, "Bring his body out now."

Under the interior lights of the van, Anton looked down at Gang's body, now wrapped in a black, plastic tarp. Li maneuvered over to the other side of her father's corpse, and he nodded when she caught his eye. Together they gently lifted Gang's body and carried him out of the back of the van.

Once clear of the van, Anton adjusted his hold, lifting Gang's body by himself. Li let go, ducking back into the van to retrieve their dragon swords.

The cool night air struck Anton like a jolt of caffeine. He took a deep breath and a small surge of energy sparked along his limbs. There was not much left to draw on, the last thirty-six hours had taken their toll. Someone switched off the van's engines and killed the lights. An ocean of brilliant stars lit the sky. He paused, drunk on their beauty in stark contrast to the mute sadness of carrying the lifeless body of Gang Wu.

In the distance was a very faint glow, a small rural town a handful of miles away. The yard was big, easily a hundred yards across, the boundaries dominated by a pair of large wooden barns that stood opposite each other, and an even larger haystack. At the head of the yard, a large two-story house loomed, several ground floor windows lit by interior lights.

Peter and Francis flicked on flashlights, and Li returned with their swords.

Francis waved his flashlight toward the far barn and commanded, "Peter, take them into the main barn and set Gang's body on a table. We will bury him tomorrow afternoon."

"Sure, Boss. Anton and Li, follow me," Peter called back over his shoulder, as he strode toward the barn.

They followed him. In a minute, they were inside the barn, and Peter was clearing a space on a large wooden table with easy familiarity.

"You've done this before?" Anton asked.

"There are occasional casualties, we always have a place to put people before burial."

"Right."

Anton placed Gang's body onto the table. Adjusting the tarp to ensure there were no gaps leading into the body. Li put her hand on the tarp and bowed her head. Anton did the same, feeling flat, drained, and numb. The adrenaline from the battle at the Boston warehouse had completely worn off, leaving him mentally and physically exhausted.

Peter stood back from the table, waiting patiently. When they looked up, he said, "Time for our debrief. Hopefully, the Jorgenson's have catered for our arrival."

"The Jorgensons?" Anton asked.

"This is a working farm, John and Mary Jorgenson are order helpers who live here. The farm makes a small profit, pays taxes and provides a perfect cover for what we really do here."

"Order helpers, like the two guys that were with the van back in Boston?"

"Yes. Not everyone in the Order is at the tip of the spear."

Anton nodded.

"Follow me," Peter directed. He led them from the barn. Once back out in the night air, he shut the barn door behind them and strode toward the house.

Anton and Li fell in beside him, and Anton asked, "No locks?"

Peter smiled. "Not needed. We have some sensors. He'll be safe tonight."

"Oh," Anton grunted.

They approached the house. It rose out of the darkness, a large, two-story affair with a pair of wide wings left and right. Warm light leaked through curtained windows, spilling in soft pools in front of the house. The building was a classic and well-maintained rendition of New England architecture dating from a previous century.

Peter led them inside. Voices murmured mere yards away; in moments, they joined the rest of the Mirovar force team in a large room. An oval table, surrounded by a dozen, mostly empty chairs, dominated the chamber. A pair of trays laden with sandwiches, bottles of water and glasses sat in the middle of the table.

The room held a lot of empty space and four thick wooden columns supported the ceiling. Peter leaned toward Anton and whispered, "Ex-dojo. We replaced it with the barn. You'll see where we train tomorrow."

Anton nodded.

Peter smiled, sitting down opposite the trays of food and declared gustily, "Perfect."

Anton and Li followed, sitting down next to him.

Francis stood in front of a large whiteboard, jotting down notes with a blue marker. There was a list of abbreviated bullet points on the board: penetrate police lines, capture RHIB, attack Shadowstone on the dock, kill nightfalcons. Juliette sat nearest to him, a laptop open in front of her, her fingers occasionally flashing over the keyboard as she took notes.

The serious-faced young man with roughly cut, dirty-blond hair from the van reported, "The stingers just dropped dead like hitting a wall about thirty yards back from the black helicopter."

"Electronic warfare; must have been her personal nightfalcon," Juliette Mirovar noted.

Peter snorted. "Definitely not standard issue tech."

Francis frowned at him, and Peter adjusted his position in his chair as if he could not find a way to sit comfortably.

A young woman with long coppery hair tied back into a ponytail and warm blue eyes, sitting next to the first speaker reported, "We fired as we landed on the dock and managed to hit one of the praetorians." She glanced at Li and continued speaking matter-of-factly, "The one that Li was fighting froze, and she took his head off."

A smile flitted across her face. "A praetorian came out of the river, catching us by surprise, and then one of the Shadowstone operatives fired a grenade and emptied his clip, but everyone evaded, and no one got hurt."

"Ahh…" Peter uttered, scratching the side of his head. "I beg to differ; I caught a piece of shrapnel."

Juliette looked up from her laptop and inquired with a frown, "You didn't mention this before."

"Well, I thought it would be okay – it's really just a scratch."

"I'll be the judge of that," Juliette declared, reaching for the medical kit bag at her feet.

All business, Juliette stood up and walked briskly around to where Peter continued to squirm uncomfortably in his chair.

"Where were you hit?"

"… In my butt."

Juliette blinked, raising her eyebrows she asked, "Which side?"

Francis sighed. "Okay everyone – take five minutes."

While Peter submitted to the attentions of Juliette, the rest of the team started on the sandwiches and water. Anton realized how hungry he was, helping himself, he bit into a ham, cheese and tomato sandwich with gusto. Anton thought to himself, *I need some names here, everyone already knows Li, and I'm at a loss.* Finishing the sandwich, he determined to introduce himself.

"Hi guys," he stated. They all stopped talking amongst themselves and looked at him. "I'm Anton Slayne."

Silence dropped over the room, and everyone stared at him.

Okay – what? Have I suddenly grown a second head?

* * *

Jay Creeley dropped his half-eaten sandwich back onto his plate. Putting his hands on the edge of the table, he pushed his chair back hard and stood up. He smacked the table with an open hand, and it shook fit to break.

"Jay!?" the copper-haired young woman next to him half-shouted in sudden alarm.

"If I'd known we were picking up a Slayne tonight," Jay ground the words out with barely restrained fury. "I wouldn't have bothered."

"Steady on Jay, he's not committed a crime," Juliette asserted as she closed her medical kit bag.

"Not yet. But why should we give him a chance?" Jay asked incredulously.

"He's fought bravely against vampires, he is one of us," Li declared.

"He's not a member of the Order," Jay spat the words angrily, "and neither are you."

"Not yet, but we both will be," Li promised, fire igniting behind her eyes.

"I've got nowhere else to go. I know too much. What do you expect from me?" Anton asked, his face filled with shock and dismay.

"I'm sure a second grave can be dug tomorrow," Jay declared with a sneer.

"Enough!" Francis roared – his voice cutting through the room like a knife. "Jay Creeley, I have invited Anton to join us and prove his worth to the Order, and that is the end of it."

Francis looked directly at Anton. "I realized who you were as soon as I met you, you're the spitting image of your grandfather when he was younger."

Jay stared at Anton, his face flushed, his mouth a grim slit.

Francis looked at Li. "I was a little mystified as to why your father didn't mention Anton's family name in his communiques."

Li shrugged her shoulders.

Francis turned to Jay and said, "Now I know why. Jay, I understand your feelings, but you have to let this go. Anton is not his grandfather."

Jay's eyes flicked back and forth between Anton and Francis, and Francis stared back – a hard uncompromising light behind his eyes.

Jay lowered his gaze. "… Yes, Sir," he conceded flatly. His face rigid, his mind burning with righteous anger. He would rather die than see a Slayne confirmed in the Order.

* * *

Maybe I should just leave.

A sudden nausea gripped Anton's guts; his emotions churning chaotically.

Francis called the meeting back to order. Li sat down on Anton's right and Peter on his left.

Francis addressed the young woman with coppery hair sitting next to Jay, "Yvette, please continue your report."

"Well, there were two vampires left on the dock – both wounded at that point. I saw Jay clean up the one that you had slashed as you ran past him, then Juliette and I killed the blond one that came out of the river. They were all dead, except for a Shadowstone operative who disappeared back into the warehouse."

Anton wondered what happened to the suit leading the Shadowstone forces. He hoped he'd stepped on a mine as he escaped back through the warehouse. But there had been no explosions.

He probably got away. Anton thought bitterly.

"Thanks, Yvette," Francis said. He turned his attention to another young woman with lustrous dark wavy hair, olive complexion, and large brown eyes. "Chiara, what have you got to report."

Chiara reported, "I was first on the RHIB. I manned the MGL and later the .50 cal. I was the one who shot Armitage. I watched her helicopter drop into the river. I'm sure that it landed on top of her."

Francis nodded. "Very good, Chiara."

"Did she die?" Anton asked hopefully.

"Without a body – we can't be sure she's dead," Francis observed.

Anton murmured in pain, and everyone in the room looked over at him.

"Anton, you have something to add?" Francis asked.

"No … nothing," Anton noted. His heart sank, certain that against all hope – Chloe Armitage was still alive.

Jay snorted disdainfully.

Francis looked around the group, and addressed the team, "Thank you for your work tonight. We lost a great warrior in Gang Wu, but we have won a victory against the Vampire Dominion. Get some rest, we start a new training cycle tomorrow at 08:00. I expect to see all of you in the training barn fit and ready. Is that clear?"

"Yes, Sir," the team members chorused. Anton and Li assenting a moment later.

"Peter and Chiara. Anton and Li can share your rooms. That is all – good night."

The team dispersed around the house. Li smiled briefly at Anton before she got up to leave with Chiara.

Peter tapped Anton on the shoulder and directed, "Hey, Anton, follow me."

Anton followed Peter down a hallway and up a flight of stairs. At the back of another hallway was their shared room. Inside the room were a pair of wardrobes and double beds.

"Our bachelor pad, not much to it. The bathroom is down the hall on the right, just before the stairs and your bed is that one over there," Peter instructed pointing to a neatly made bed with a simple, gray cover. He pointed at the wardrobe nearest to Anton's bed. "You can put your stuff in there."

"Li and I have nothing, just our swords and the clothes we are wearing." He thought of Gang lying in a pool of blood on the dock and sighed quietly. "We lost everything in the fight."

"We have spare clothes here, I'm pretty sure we will find some that will … kinda fit you. Li and Chiara are very similar in build; Chiara will have some clothes to share. As for equipment, we can always get more, that's not a problem."

"Thanks," Anton said, slumping down on the bed. His shoulders sank forward, and he asked, "Do I belong here?"

Peter cocked his head, sitting down on his own bed opposite Anton. "That depends on you."

"Are you sure of that?"

"I'm certain."

Anton looked down, brushing his right hand through his thick dark hair and rubbing the back of his neck.

"Trust me – things will improve," Peter said.

"I can't help who my grandfather is."

"Precisely – which is why Jay will come around. He's not stupid. Besides which, Francis more or less endorsed you. He would not have invited you to join us if he didn't believe that you could make it."

"Why would he endorse me? He doesn't know me. Why would he care?"

"Francis has never said a bad word about your grandfather, mind you, he has never said a good word about him either, but Arthur Slayne was his force leader and his weapons instructor. There must be some sort of bond between them. Given that you look just like your grandfather it's no surprise that he recognized you. Now I've never met Arthur Slayne or even seen a photograph, so who you are was news to me. But I don't care about your past. I'll make my own judgments based on what you do, and you fought vampires tonight which is good enough for me."

"Thanks, but you know what? I don't think I killed any vampires tonight. I think at most, I chopped half a foot off."

"Better than me, I didn't hit anything." Peter shrugged his broad shoulders and grinned broadly. "I just got hit in my butt."

Anton half grinned.

The room fell into silence. Peter looked thoughtful for a moment, then said, "It kinda begs the question you know, who else is going to recognize you? Anyone who knows your grandfather will see the similarity and are likely to draw the obvious conclusion that you're related."

"Not much I can do about it."

"Except be prepared for more reactions like Jay's."

Anton nodded. "Sure."

"Look, you're probably feeling a bit lost with everything that has happened, so I'll fill you in with a bit of history about us all. The Red Empire killed my parents when I was ten years old. Francis and Juliette took me in and raised me as a member of their family. I still remember my parents well, and of course, I still love my parents and miss them, but the Mirovars are like a second set of parents to me, they're family."

"What of the others?"

"Well, there's Jay Creeley, his father has been dead for a long time, his mother was killed at the same time as George Madison – apparently by your grandfather."

"So that's why he's so pissed off at me," Anton said quietly.

"Yep, then there is Yvette Mirovar."

"Their daughter?"

"Adopted. Unknown assailants killed her parents when she was eleven. She has been with us ever since; she is a year younger than I am."

"How old are you?"

"Twenty, and you?"

"Eighteen."

"We're a young crew. Jay is the eldest at twenty-four."

"So, he would have been about five when his mother died – and his dad was already dead. It's harsh, no wonder he's angry, I get it."

"Everyone has lost someone they love."

"What about the last one, Chiara?"

"Ahh… the lovely Chiara Romano. Italian-American heritage, a runaway from an abusive family. She started her training late. She would have been about nine when she arrived, which is pushing it to start Ramp training. But she has progressed really well, a quick study, a strong talent. You wouldn't know she only started at nine. She is very good, especially with edged weapons, almost as good as Jay."

"How good is Jay Creeley?"

"Every force team has a premier warrior, someone who is the best, baddest, most dangerous fighter – in our team – that is Jay Creeley."

"He's better than Francis?"

"Just a touch better, he will be a force leader one day, and a great one at that. The Order is grooming him for the role."

"Great. I have really dangerous people wanting me dead."

Peter shrugged. "Look, Jay's a good man. Give him time, he'll come around."

Anton muttered dejectedly, "What if he is right? What if my grandfather was a murderer and a traitor? I don't know what happened back then."

Peter paused contemplatively for a moment. "Why don't we set out to find the truth."

"Can we?"

"I'm sure of it. I will help you find out what really happened on the night George Madison died."

Peter put his hand out, and Anton shook it. Peter's handshake was powerful, there was clearly a reserve of strength within Peter beyond anything he'd met before. He assessed his roommate with fresh eyes; Peter was perhaps an inch taller, about six feet two with a shock of red hair adding another inch of height. Built like the proverbial brick wall. He was thick of calf and thigh, with a low center of gravity through the hips, broad shouldered, deep chested, with long muscular arms that ended in big powerful hands. However, there was no hint of being musclebound or overdone in the easy, confident way he carried himself.

Peter chuckled. "So, you noticed."

"Just how strong are you?"

"Sometimes you will find someone in the Order who has a capability beyond what is normal for a Ramp master, some are faster, some are stronger. I'm stronger – a lot stronger."

"You look like you could go hand to hand with a vampire."

"Yes," Peter smirked. "But it's not recommended."

"Is there anyone else like you?"

"Just one, Justin Blake. He's the force leader covering the South West of the US. He's a true badass. You will meet him when we get to the Order conclave for your confirmation."

"Cool."

"Look, it's been a long night. Time to get some sleep, we have a big day tomorrow."

"Right, thanks for filling me in."

"No problem."

Anton and Peter made their preparations for going to sleep. Anton managed a quick, hot shower in the bathroom down the hall and in minutes was lying in his bed in a darkened room. He sighed, no longer tired. He tossed and turned for close to an hour, his head buzzing with thoughts before he finally began to drift off. His mind ebbed away with a fading sense of indignation, unfairness, and loss.

Gang is dead, and she's alive.

These thoughts continued to disturb him as he fell into a restless sleep.

* * *

James looked at the clock, it read 06:30. He'd been awake for over a day, and there was still work to do. Yawning fit to dislocate his jaw, he rubbed his eyes and stared harder at the large computer screen a foot in front of his face.

He tapped fluently at the keyboard, hesitated, backspaced with a flurry of clicks and tried again.

"C'mon, almost done," he whispered.

James hit the enter key, and the computer responded with a stream of command line outputs across multiple windows on the screen. He glanced at the large coffee mug to his left, its interior stained brown from use. There was no decision to make, he stood up, walked to the nearby kitchenette and refilled it from a pyrex jug filled with lightly steaming filtered coffee. When he got back to his desk, the computer windows were still scrolling text output.

He blew gently on his hot coffee before taking a sip. He put the cup down and checked a written list of tasks on an A4 pad to the left of his keyboard; he'd ticked most of them off. Three tasks remained: verify the new Anton Smith ghost identity, purge the main physical backups at the Panopticon hub in Utah, and purge the offsite backups at Fort Dix.

James stared at the list, feeling decades older than his thirty-eight years.

The act of swinging his Glock 9mm up from behind his back and leveling it at his wounded men haunted him. He'd emptied the clip before they could properly react. Their expressions were vivid, the shock, the terror, the hate – some had lived just long enough to hate him. His years of training and specialized skills had meant quick deaths for them all, but he knew that he would never forget their faces.

Murderer, he accused himself.

The shocking self-accusation quickly succumbed to a wave of bitter acceptance. The light in his soul was fading, and in its place, a creeping darkness had begun to take hold.

He rubbed his scalp hard with both hands, his short dark hair was slick, grimy with old sweat. In front of his eyes, the screen continued to writhe with lines of output as windows opened, ran their programs and exited. The work recruited a tiny fraction of the quantum processors of the Panopticon. They processed their commands at the speed of light. Other, much older systems out in the world beyond Shadowstone responded far more slowly. The programs ran, traversing networks, subtly altering data, and transforming the original identity of Anton Smith in place.

The windows on the screen all came to a halt. James started a Panopticon verification program, and twenty seconds later it displayed a dashboard covered in green ticked checkboxes. The old Anton Smith had become a forgettable memory, in his place was a new doppelganger, a ward of the state of Massachusetts with no connection to Anna and William Smith.

He crossed off the third last task on the A4 pad, only the purging of the physical backups at the primary site in Utah and at Fort Dix remained to complete.

The image of shooting his men flooded his mind again, and he violently shook his head.

Slamming his fists into the desktop, he cursed, "Fuck it! The job is hard. I did what I had to do. How many more would die if there were no one to maintain stability? Millions? Billions? The world is a fucking nightmare."

The weight of recent events weighed heavily upon him, he momentarily shivered, and the darkness crept closer. He reached for options the way a drowning man would reach for anything to cling to. He could create a new ghost identity. Someone with money, not too much but enough. A ghost living a long way away – somewhere like New Zealand.

He lifted his coffee mug, taking a full mouthful, his eyes unfocused as his mind spun away.

I could escape and remain … human.

He frowned, putting the mug back down onto the desktop. At the Boston warehouse, Chloe Armitage's sword had appeared in her hand faster than the eye could follow. Certain death had stared him in the face – she was a vampire, one of many, and sure enough, they would hunt him down and kill him.

He had courage to spare in any fight where his own skills could make a difference, but in a fight against the Vampire Dominion, there was no chance of victory. His eyes dropped, his shoulders sagged, and he sighed loudly as all vestiges of hope fled from his life.

Chloe Armitage's words echoed in his mind. *'You are on a new path now, embrace it, and all will be well.'*

He barked a single bitter laugh.

The light within him died. A spiritual candle snuffed out in a winter storm. The desire to serve his country that had inspired him to join the US Army, the CIA and finally Shadowstone, died silently. He'd wanted to make a difference. He'd wanted his life to matter. He'd dedicated his life to being the best at whatever he turned his hand to – now none of that seemed to matter – none of it at all.

The creeping darkness engulfed him.

James spent the next five minutes staring silently at the computer screen. Once the screen saver came on, he stood up. He looked around, spotted a long couch, walked over to it, laid down upon it, and was asleep in moments.

He screamed once in his sleep, his arms flailing wildly – but no one was there to hear it.

* * *

Chloe stood before the full-length windows of her Manhattan penthouse apartment.

The windows were composed of the same dark transparent armor of the nightfalcon canopies. The heavy shielding of the transparent armor, the only thing protecting her from swift death. She could see the ball of the sun, rising into the mid-morning sky. With a deep, longing to walk in open sunlight coiling quietly within her soul, she considered her options.

Chloe mentally ticked the items off in her mind. One, find out where the Mirovar force team's safe house was so she could keep an eye on Anton Slayne. Two, find out the details of the Crane-Kain detente, and three, do it quickly before events got away from her.

With the quantum signature of Ramin Kain's smartphone, she could make a single, full access call to his phone. As soon as he realized someone had compromised his phone, he would surely destroy it. There would be precious seconds where she could use the phone's own systems to record voice prints, take photos and video. A treasure trove of useful information she could give to James to seed Panopticon searches with.

Once found by the Panopticon, it would be a relatively simple matter to hunt him down and disrupt his plans, or even kill him. However, James would have to conduct all searches secretly. Chloe would not be able to justify how she knew who Kain was without revealing too much about her own capabilities to Crane. With the Crane-Kain detente almost a certainty, Crane would not forgive such a step against his own carefully cultivated plans. He would likely reward her with a suicide mission against the Red Empire.

Today would be Kain's final test. She would capture the information she needed from his phone. She would then use the Panopticon to track his location. She was sure that he would lead her to the current safe house of the Mirovar force team and Anton Slayne.

Chloe's eyes glittered like burning coals. Crane wanted to know who Anton Smith was. If Kain was the traitor, then Crane would have asked Kain to investigate from within the Order of Thoth. As soon as Kain found out that Anton Slayne existed, he would no doubt conclude that Anton Smith was a cover identity, but which name would he give to Crane, Smith or Slayne?

Chloe retraced the brief that she'd received for the recovery of the Papyrus of Hakron the Scribe. Her eidetic memory enabled perfect and certain recall. There was no mention of the name Smith anywhere in the brief, it was only about Anna and William Slayne and the residence in Jamaica Plain.

It was her own mission preparations that had revealed the Smith cover identity and the existence of Anton Slayne. It was an unresolved mystery as to why the Smith cover identity was not visible to the Vampire Dominion. A fact she was thankful for; if Crane knew that Anton Smith was really Arthur Slayne's grandson, her own plans would become next to impossible.

The only real possibility was that whoever informed on the Slaynes knew them by sight, and in their own mind never thought of them as other than Slaynes. Such a person would have reported the existence of Anna and William Slayne to Crane without mention of a cover identity that had nothing to do with the presence of the Papyrus of Hakron the Scribe.

It was clear that for some reason Kain had missed the existence of Anton Slayne.

If Kain told Crane that the other survivor was Anton Slayne, then her plans would be in tatters as Crane would seek out Anton and destroy him. Even worse, Crane could easily conclude that either the cover identity had duped her, or she'd deliberately lied to him. Most likely, he would decide that she'd deceived him and there would be a long wait in a silver coffin in her future or summary execution.

She stood in perfect stillness. Staring through her window, she stopped breathing. It would be necessary to put the knowledge of Anton Slayne's existence at risk to find out more – there was no other way. Her eyelids closed as she calculated the risks. She resumed breathing; the decision made.

Chloe opened her eyes. It was essential that she was able to track Kain's movements as soon as possible, and Anton Slayne would make the perfect bait. She picked up her smartphone and placed a call using the stolen quantum signature.

* * *

The beautiful Monday morning sunshine beamed out of a bright blue sky, gracing Midtown East Manhattan with a relaxing summer ambiance.

Ramin Kain adjusted his 24kt gold aviator Ray-Ban sunglasses for a slightly better fit on his nose. He used a fork full of the last of his Atlantic salmon to chase down the final bit of yolk from a pair of poached eggs. The rest of his plate held the half-eaten remains of rye toast, smashed avocado, grilled tomatoes, and mushrooms. He'd ordered an espresso instead of a cafe latte since recently committing to watching his waistline.

Opposite him sat Samuel Luther, his lean frame neatly attired in a new suit. He'd scraped his plate clean, and he was already drinking his second, long black coffee. Even sitting still, he always struck Ramin as a man possessed of excessive nervous energy or a mind-blowing coke habit. Ramin was thankful he'd found Sam. He was an excellent and able junior partner in his ventures. They shared the same values, politics, and predilections. If Sam had been a woman of even average good looks, Ramin would have seriously considered marrying her.

Pushing his breakfast plate back, Ramin sipped his espresso. He savored the flavor of an exclusive Costa Rican blend and soaked up the pleasant ambiance of an early summer Monday morning.

Ramin's smartphone rang. He waited for it to buzz to one less than the maximum six before it would divert to voice mail. He looked at the screen and picked up the phone. He realized at the last moment that the caller was unknown and he stabbed at the answer button.

"Hello, who's calling?" he asked brusquely, curiosity flooding through him.

"A friend," declared a wonderfully modulated feminine voice with a dash of upper-class English polish.

"A friend, eh?" he said skeptically. "You must be a genius or insane to ring this phone."

The woman laughed briefly. "Is there a difference?"

Ramin tapped his fingers impatiently on the table top, and he asked in a low tight voice, "Who the hell are you and what do you want?"

"It's not who I am that matters, it's what I know."

"Don't play games with me girly. This is a private number; how did you get it?"

"Let's just say that a little bird told me and leave it at that."

Ramin growled, and snapped, "I told you not to play games."

"No Games. There is something that you should know."

"What?"

"Anton Slayne is with the Mirovar force team."

Ramin froze. The fine breakfast he'd just enjoyed, suddenly a dead weight in the pit of his stomach. A moment later the call disconnected.

Ramin looked at his phone with horror. He stood up, moving briskly outside he smashed it to pieces on the sidewalk. Sam rushed after him.

"Who was that?" Sam inquired urgently.

"I don't know?" Ramin replied, frowning as he ground the phone into fragments with his heel. "Get the valet to bring the car around."

"Sure, RK, where are we going?"

"Maine – but first, I need a new phone."

Oh hell, Ramin thought with growing dismay. *The other survivor at the Boston warehouse was Anton Slayne. How did I miss the fact that Anna and William Slayne had a son? I'll have to deal with this immediately.*

* * *

Chloe mused, *should I assassinate the Head of the Order of Thoth?*

She lowered her smartphone. She'd only spoken with Ramin Kain once, and already she didn't like him. He'd made her wait as long as he could before he'd picked up the phone, he was clearly self-important. Studying the images stripped from his smartphone while he was speaking, she noted his gold sunglasses, the expensive suit, the upmarket cafe. His vanity and pride were on full display. He'd arrogantly called her 'girly.' She smiled ruthlessly, Kain had some obvious weaknesses that she would enjoy exploiting as she crushed him.

She grasped and rubbed her jaw. She considered killing Kain tonight. Just to be sure he couldn't interfere with her plans, and damn the risk of discovery.

Looking at the rack on her wall that held her swords, the Red Dragon was conspicuous in its absence. A pang went through her soul. She missed her favorite blade. She consoled herself with the knowledge the praetorians would return it soon.

Staring at the gap where the Red Dragon normally rested. A realization struck her. Kain's recent words roared through her memory. His pride, vanity, and arrogance would not allow him to ever admit he'd done anything wrong. No one else knew his darkest secret, not even the flunky who was having breakfast with him. She hummed with satisfaction. The only option that Kain had was to tell Crane that it was Anton Smith who was with the Wu family on the Boston docks. Kain would confirm her own story.

Chloe went to her desk, opened her laptop and logged into the Panopticon. She pulled up all the available data on the identity that matched the photos of Anton taken by CCTV outside the Noodle House. She quickly accessed the new cover constructed by James Haley. Anton Smith's parents remained listed as 'unknown,' and had abandoned him days after his birth. The local authorities made him a ward of the state of Massachusetts until his eighteenth birthday on April the twenty sixth of this year. He'd then left the orphanage and lived on the streets for a short while before Gang Wu took him in. His history matched the new identity, his schools, and sports teams remained the same, even library cards, bank accounts, and social media all reflected the new identity, every reference to parents pointed back to the state, the home address was always the orphanage.

Chloe considered the problem of Anton's Ramp skills. She reasoned Gang Wu must have used the pressure point technique for Ramp activation. She knew Crane would accept it as an explanation for Anton's skills and his sudden appearance from nowhere.

She ran a second search on Anna and William Smith. Anna came back as deceased, a victim of an unsolved murder. William was still missing, and there was no reference to a child. James had scrubbed Anton from all online photos, and then extrapolated and filled in the backgrounds as if he'd never existed. Even subtly modifying gestures and body language to ensure the images still made sense. He'd then followed with inserting pitch-perfect images of Anton into relevant online photos from the orphanage.

Chloe was impressed; the work was without flaw.

She returned to the previous query on the doubly fake identity of Anton Smith. She drew down what she needed to compose a report for

Crane. The report would be perfect and just as she'd promised, would be on his desk tonight.

She picked up her smartphone and dialed Louise Wesson's phone. She knew James had Wesson's phone, his own destroyed during the battle in Boston. The phone rang out and went to voice mail. Chloe tried again with the same result.

Chloe frowned and remarked disdainfully, "Humans – what's a vampire got to do to get something done?"

* * *

James woke up. Someone was shaking his shoulder.

"Sir. Wake up, Sir," the operative said, almost shouting in his ear.

James opened his eyes; he was lying on a couch in the Boston Shadowstone offices at the local R.I.S.C building. He blinked, swung his legs down and sat up. The man shaking his shoulder stepped back as James rubbed his face with both hands. He looked up at the man standing in front of him. The operative wore a fresh suit, was clean shaven, bright eyed and thoroughly energized.

James wanted to vomit. The taste of stale coffee filled his mouth. He desperately wanted a cigarette but had run out the night before. This day was starting as badly as the previous night had ended.

"The boss rang," the young operative reported. "She wants you to ring her ASAP."

James rubbed his ears and his cheeks. His head clogged up and fuzzy, seemingly stuffed full with mush. He sniffed once and muttered, "Yeah, Okay. I got it."

"Yes, Sir."

"Dismissed Rose. Good job," James stated, blinking and frowning.

The young man quickly left the room.

James got off the couch, went to the kitchenette and drank a couple of large glasses of water. He returned to his desk, picked up Louise Wesson's phone and dialed Chloe's smartphone, it rang once before she picked it up.

There was a moment of silence before James inquired, "Ma'am, you asked me to call?"

"Yes James, you owe me a text," Chloe reminded him.

"My apologies Ma'am. The lapse is inexcusable."

"I'm going to overlook it this one time."

"Yes Ma'am."

"I've checked your work. It is precisely what I was looking for, immaculate, very well done."

"Thank you, Ma'am."

"Now that task is completed, I need you focused on a new mission."

"Yes, Ma'am," James replied. "What do you need?"

"I have a new target for you named Ramin Kain, I want you to track his whereabouts, and if possible, record his communications. However, I also want this done off the Panopticon record. Make immediate offline copies of the material and scrub the online records."

"I will need your level of security access to be able to do that."

"Granted – the privileges that I gave you last night have been extended indefinitely."

James paused for a moment digesting the implications of her words. Chloe Armitage was trusting him enormously.

"Is the target using quantum technologies?" James asked, his interest flaring like a new flame.

"Yes."

"Do you have his quantum signature?"

"No, but I have excellent photos, his voice print, and I know he will be traveling from New York today. I've just sent you the details, if you act quickly, you should be able to pick him up."

"When do you want reports?"

"Daily – by physical drop at this address," Chloe instructed, providing a dead drop location in Manhattan.

"Yes, Ma'am. Why is this target so important?"

"Kain is the Head of the Order of Thoth," Chloe declared.

"… Yes, Ma'am," James replied with quiet intensity. His heart surged with new life. Here was a real purpose that he could sink his teeth into.

"You are the only person that I can trust to get this done," Chloe said, her voice glowing with approval.

James' chest swelled with pride.

"Yes, Ma'am, I will see it done."

"I'm sure that you will," Chloe declared confidently.

"Is there anything that I should be on the lookout for?" James asked.

"The Mirovar force team safe house. I expect that Kain will lead us to it."

"That's fantastic, operational safe houses have been extremely difficult to find."

"This opportunity is the best we've had in years. That's why I'm entrusting it to you – I know you will not fail me."

"I'm your man, Ma'am," James attested.

"Indeed, you are," Chloe said.

The phone call disconnected, and James put the phone down. He logged into the Panopticon and began searching for Ramin Kain, the Head of the Order of Thoth.

* * *

The morning sunlight streamed through the open windows of the barn. Hay bales lined the walls and packed earth comprised the floor. Whereas the main barn opposite was a real working farm barn, this one supported the training of a small specialized team of fighters.

Peter nudged Anton's arm. "We work with time-honored principles such as, 'No Pain, No Gain,' better get used to it."

"I know how to train," Anton declared confidently, arching his back with his hands held high up in the air. There was a loud click behind his shoulder blades. "Geez, I feel like crap."

"You're new to the Ramp, and you spent a lot of time ramping in the fight last night. I overheard your conversation with Juliette on the RHIB, your body must still be adapting, it's no wonder you're hurting."

"Humph," Anton grunted. Turning his head left and right, he tried to loosen up.

Peter grinned. "But it's a good hurt you know."

"How's your butt?" Anton asked with a wry grin.

Peter laughed and replied, "Almost healed up."

Anton considered the injuries he'd sustained eleven hours earlier. A sword cut to the right shoulder and a ball bearing through his right foot. Juliette Mirovar had expertly cleaned and stitched both wounds, and in half a day they had shown the healing progress of five days. They were nearly ready for the stitches to come out.

The foot wound was the more serious of the two, but the steel ball had miraculously missed the bones and passed straight through. Anton tried jumping lightly up and down, testing the foot and everything seemed to hold together nicely. He felt ready for anything that the team could throw at him.

Everyone was kitted out in loose, light clothing and had runners on. Anton had borrowed his own, very loose clothing, from Peter. He was barefoot, as he didn't have shoes that fit him yet and his combat boots hadn't survived the fight at the warehouse. Peter had promised him that he would go into the nearby town of White Hill and get all the necessary essentials. When Anton had pointed out that he didn't have any money, Peter had told him not to worry as the Order would pay for it.

Yvette and Jay were pushing against each other to warm up and studiously ignoring Anton's presence. Li had dropped into the splits and was touching her right shin with her forehead. Chiara was hanging from the ceiling of the barn, suspended twenty feet upside down on a rope. Francis and Juliette walked into the barn carrying buckets filled with crushed ice and towels.

Peter nudged Anton again and grinned. "The ice is for injuries, and to cool us down – high intensity – it's the name of the game."

Anton shook his head. "How long are you going to keep up with these clichés?"

"We never give up – we make the other guy give up."

Francis addressed everyone in the barn, "Listen up team, we have new members in Anton and Li. So, we will start a new training cycle to embed them into our ways and means. Is that clear?"

Everyone chorused, "Yes, Sir."

"Excellent," Francis declared. He cast his gaze up toward the ceiling of the barn and commanded, "Chiara, drop down and lead us in a warm up. One of your specials to iron out the kinks of battle and freshen us up."

Chiara let go of the rope. Twisting acrobatically through the air, she landed perfectly on her feet in front of the group. "Okay everyone," she ordered. "Form a circle around me with a spacing of ten feet between you and your teammates beside you."

The team moved, and in moments they were ready.

"Let's start," Chiara directed. "Please follow my lead."

Chiara began with short sequences of standard exercises, each one running for twenty or thirty seconds before she replaced it with a different exercise focused on different muscle groups. All the exercises were dynamic, there was no static stretching.

Anton's body loosened up. Then the exercises got harder, squat leaps, one armed pushups, and inventive exercises that Anton had never seen before. This continued for another fifteen minutes without rest.

Chiara stopped and instructed them. "Shake it off, folks."

The break lasted fifteen seconds.

"The next move requires a partial ramp," Chiara explained, expertly assuming a handstand which she held with perfect poise.

Everyone did a handstand and held their form steady.

"Hold it," Chiara commanded.

Chiara had positioned herself directly opposite Anton, and they spent the next five minutes facing each other in silence. Chiara had plaited her long wavy hair into a thick ponytail that snaked down to the ground beneath her head. Her eyes were large, brown and filled with hidden depths, her body was an exquisite balance of sensuality and athleticism.

She stared at Anton with quiet intensity.

Anton stared back. He held his position. He could feel the perspiration rolling over his face before disappearing into his hair. The partial ramp required to hold his form created a slowly intensifying burn in his torso, shoulders, and arms.

Chiara appeared to hold her position with ease, Anton started to feel the strain.

"Fingers now," Chiara directed. Pushing off her palms and balancing on her fingers.

Anton followed suit.

"Right hand," Chiara directed. Shifting her weight slightly, she supported herself with one hand.

Twenty seconds later she directed, "Left hand."

Everyone shifted to their left hand.

Another twenty seconds passed, and Chiara grinned and commanded, "Right thumb and hold."

Anton lifted his focus. The ramp increased, a line of heat flowing from his thumb through his whole body before exiting out of the soles of his feet. A drop of sweat ran into one of his nostrils, and a sudden urge to sneeze made him squeeze his eyelids tightly shut for a second.

"Control," Chiara urged. Her eyes crinkling slightly as if she was laughing inside.

The Ramp burned through his body.

"Left thumb and hold," Chiara commanded.

Anton shifted his focus, transferring his weight to his other hand, supporting himself on his left thumb.

Chiara watched him with a slight smile.

The burn continued to mount, he wanted to gasp but controlled his breathing.

"Release," Chiara instructed. Flexing her thumb, she returned to an upright position on her feet in a single graceful movement.

Anton collapsed onto his face, before rolling out and back onto his feet.

Chiara stepped forward and whispered, "We will have to work on your dismount."

"Yeah," Anton agreed sheepishly, brushing straw and dust off the front of his body.

"Take five minutes and re-hydrate," Juliette instructed, and the team walked around, drinking water and talking in quiet tones.

The time flew by.

Francis stepped forward and commanded, "Okay team, time to move onto sword drills."

Everyone got a metal training sword from a pair of racks. Jay and Yvette paired up, and Anton nodded toward Li, who stepped toward him.

"You four," Francis declared, indicating Jay, Yvette, Li, and Anton, "can swap."

"Huh?" Jay grunted, then moved to stand opposite Li.

Francis moved over to him. Took his left arm and pulled him into position in front of Anton, and directed, "Get used to it, you're on the same team."

"This is a mistake!" Jay said incredulously.

"No arguments."

"… Yes," a hard grin flashed across Jay's face, "Sir."

What's he thinking of doing? Anton questioned silently, staring into Jay's blue eyes while preparing to defend himself.

Francis and Juliette stood to the side to watch the combat form of the team members.

"Open sparring, normal sparring rules apply, no ramping," Francis instructed.

Anton threw a quizzical glance at Francis. Jay immediately attacked, Anton barely managed to get his sword up, but Jay's blade went through his defense like a hot knife through butter, nicking his chest. Jay stepped back; the very tip of his sword smeared with Anton's blood.

"You're dead," Jay noted, a touch of relish creeping into his voice. "You need to pay attention."

Anton's eyes widened with momentary dismay.

"Why don't you give it your best shot," Jay taunted.

Anton began a series of attacks. Jay danced aside, batting his blade away each time, after the third deflection, he riposted and again nicked Anton on the chest, an inch away from the first cut.

"You're dead again, how the hell did you survive last night?"

"I was trained by a master."

"You're kidding me."

Anton lifted his focus without ramping. "Gang was a genius."

Jay slashed left and right. Anton deflected the attacks away, but when Anton riposted, Jay's blade met his early and easily deflected it aside.

"Gang was a true master, everyone knows that. Too bad you didn't learn anything."

Jay launched an attack high, which Anton moved to defend against, then Jay went low with his body, sweeping Anton's legs out from under him. Anton found himself on his back. Jay's blade nicked his throat, no worse than a shaving cut. Anton leaped back to his feet, his sword ready, but Jay was already out of reach.

"Once more you're dead," Jay remarked with a mirthless grin. "Gang wasted his time on you."

Anton glanced at Francis and Juliette, who were watching all three pairs train.

Jay tracked his gaze and said darkly, "They're not going to save you – no one can. Sometimes people die in training."

Both men paused for a split second. Silence overwhelmed Anton. Suddenly Jay was moving, the tip of his sword thrusting toward Anton's heart at full Ramp speed. Jay's blade was set to skewer him like a piece of meat.

Anton's Ramp blossomed as he stepped aside, turning, bringing up his sword in a desperate defense. His Ramp echoed his experience fighting the blond praetorian the night before and against the last of the gangsters in the Noodle House kitchen. The Ramp was wild, time slowed, Jay adjusted his movements, automatically tracking Anton's defenses as the two swords clashed and ground against each other in a shower of sparks. Anton barely pushed Jay's blade aside.

Jay continued to attack, too close now to use his sword effectively, his right fist flashing forward at Anton's face, a killing blow at such speed.

Anton's right hand appeared before it, catching Jay's fist inches in front of his nose. There was a loud clap as Jay's fist stopped as if it had hit a brick wall.

Jay's right leg jack-knifed like a machine, his kick catching Anton on his left ribs and propelling him thirty feet across the barn.

Anton landed hard, slid across the dirt, and rolled on the ground, winded and struggling to breathe.

Jay grunted with pain and dropped his sword. He twisted away and plunged his fist into a nearby bucket filled with an ice slurry.

"Stop!" Francis shouted. He stepped between the two men who were too busy hurting to put up any more fight. Juliette, Chiara, and Li all went to Anton. Yvette went to Jay, who dragged his fist out of the water long enough to groan at the damage before plunging it back into the ice.

Anton started to sit up, and firm hands pushed him back down.

"Lie still, Anton," Juliette commanded, expertly assessing him for damage. "I saw that kick."

Anton winced as she prodded his abdomen and his ribcage. He could see for himself a wide bruise already spreading on the left side of his chest.

"Li, bring me an iced towel from my bucket," Juliette ordered.

A moment later, a freezing cold towel was soothing the pain of his ribs.

Anton looked around him, there was the professional concern of Juliette as she held the ice-cold towel in place. Li and Chiara kneeled beside him to his left and right. Both girls looked at each other with the same quizzical, annoyed, 'what are you doing?' expression on their faces.

Juliette hauled Anton to his feet. "Up you get, soldier."

Francis, stepped back so that he could see both men at the same time. With tightly checked anger he declared, "You were both warned not to Ramp. What are you trying to do – kill each other?"

Jay and Anton looked at each other, a dark promise passing silently between them.

"The vampires would love this dissension in our house. That is who you are serving with this behavior. You're a disgrace, the pair of you," Francis declared coldly, giving them both a withering look. "Well, neither of you are fit for training now. Show up ready tomorrow. Li, stay here and work with Peter."

Francis looked at his wife, and she nodded with understanding.

Juliette ordered, "Okay you two, come with me. Chiara, I will need your help."

"Yes, Ma'am," all three replied, following Juliette from the barn. Jay hugged a bucket of icy water with his left arm, his right fist resting in the slurry. Anton walked gingerly a few yards to his right with an ice-cold towel pressed to his ribs.

Anton and Jay glanced at each other. Looking at Jay was like staring at an unyielding glacier.

What a mess, what a great big mess, Anton thought despondently to himself.

* * *

Anton lay face up and stripped down to his shorts on a padded table in a well-lit room.

The Order had converted two former ground-floor bedrooms into a clinic for Juliette to practice her medical skills in. She was tending to Jay's broken hand in the room next door.

The sharp medicinal odor of herbal balm cut through the room. It was the same balm Gang had used. It brought back sad memories that cut through the residual resentment of the fight. Anton had no desire for a war with Jay Creeley. He understood how Jay felt, he was increasingly familiar with the desire for revenge, and could not condemn in another what he felt so strongly himself.

Gentle, careful hands dabbed the balm onto the skin of his chest. They brushed it down the left side of his torso from just below his chest muscles to the top of his hip, gliding over his smooth skin in confident strokes.

It never felt like this when Gang slapped on some of his healing balm.

Chiara had a focused look on her face, which broke into an easy smile when she realized Anton was watching her. Her touch had an unreal quality about it. Her fingers stroked his skin, applying almost no pressure, and yet they were touching an inch beneath the surface.

It was mesmerizing and unlike anything he'd experienced before.

Chiara completed the application of the balm and directed, "Please sit up, I will strap your ribs."

Anton sat up, expecting stabbing pains across his chest, but only a muted ache remained.

Chiara approached him with a rolled-up bandage and strips of strapping tape. She gestured for him to raise his arms. Anton lifted his arms up and out. Chiara moved in carefully, and efficiently applied the strapping tape, following with the bandage.

With each loop of the bandage, she reached around Anton's torso, getting up close and almost hugging him. Anton couldn't help but notice how good she smelled. They had been working out for nearly an hour, and yet she had a fresh, delightful scent.

She applied the last of the strapping tape to hold the bandage in place and advised, "Keep that in place for two days, and you will be ready to go, but no training for the next forty-eight hours."

"Two days."

"Three cracked ribs, two days to heal, the wonders of the Ramp in action, all we have to do is strap and bandage."

Anton moved to get off the table.

"Not so fast," Chiara warned, placing her hand on his chest.

"What?"

"Show me your hand."

"Oh." Anton held out his right hand.

Chiara took his hand. Turning it over, she squeezed it. Anton squeezed back.

She shook her head. "That's amazing. Jay's broken half a dozen bones in his hand and will be out of action for a week, and you got off Scott free – how did you do it?"

"I honestly don't know."

"I don't think anyone knows how you did that, and I'm not the only person here who noticed it. Your hand didn't move when Jay hit it. I've never seen anything like it."

Chiara sniffed quizzically, then patted him on the shoulder. "Well, all done here."

She watched him as he dressed and then shooed him out of the room. She called to his back, "I have to write notes for Juliette."

Anton paused at the door and looked back over his shoulder. "Thanks for all your help."

"Not a problem," Chiara said with a smile.

Anton nodded and left the room.

* * *

Anton sat on an ancient wooden porch seat next to the front door.

He was resting while his ribs healed, and waiting for the rest of the team to complete the preparations for Gang's funeral. He watched calmly as a car emerged from the lane leading from the main road to the safe house.

The silver Bentley sedan rolled smoothly over the yard before pulling to a stop in front of the safe house. The driver exited first. He was of medium height with a lean build, and short dark hair. He stared intently at Anton through a pair of sunglasses. He held his face still, impassive, like a poker player but his taut stance screamed raptor ready to attack.

The passenger exited the other side of the car and walked purposefully around the front of the Bentley. He was taller and heavier than the driver, with a hint of gray sprinkled through his dark hair. Both men wore finely tailored dark suits, Italian shoes, and sunglasses that gleamed in the late afternoon sunlight slashing across the yard.

The passenger grinned as he approached Anton and the driver fell into step behind him.

Who are these guys? Can't be vampires in daylight, Anton thought warily to himself.

Smiling warmly, the passenger walked toward Anton. He extended his hand to shake and asked pleasantly, "Hi, and you are?"

"Anton," Anton replied, lifting his hand to grasp the stranger's hand.

"The resemblance is striking," the stranger observed, dropping his hand before making contact with Anton. "You really do look like your grandfather when he was young." He stepped adroitly to his right. Behind him, the driver held a Glock 9mm pistol aimed for the center of Anton's chest.

Anton automatically began to ramp. His senses snapping into razor sharp overdrive.

The driver's finger pulled the trigger.

Anton shifted violently to the right.

The muzzle flashed. A spent brass casing flipping away to the left. The bullet ripped through his left lung before punching a hole out of his back.

Anton jerked backward with the momentum of the hit. A second bullet followed the first, smashing through his ribs a couple of inches to the left of the first wound. He started to build up speed as a third bullet crashed through his left arm, breaking the bone before exiting.

The driver began ramping hard, his pistol tracking Anton's movements.

Anton ducked low and blurred to the right. The first three gun shots echoed across the yard. A fourth bullet slashed through Anton's shirt from behind, taking a chunk out of his right shoulder. Blood splashed from his chest, back, and arm, and he could feel his lung begin to collapse, but there was almost no pain, just a growing sense of pressure. He leaped hard over the porch rail. He flew twenty feet out into the yard, landing near the back of the Bentley and rolling on his left shoulder.

The driver fired twice more, the bullets zipping past Anton's head as he ducked behind the car.

Anton twisted around, lifting his head up just enough to stare through the car's windows at the front of the house. He needed to get sight of his enemies if he was going to find a way to defend himself.

The front door burst open, a fully ramped Peter Lamb blurred past the passenger, tackling the shooter and taking hold of his gun arm. There was a loud crack as the shooter's pistol arm snapped like a twig. Grunting loudly with pain, the shooter dropped the gun.

Peter turned in an instant, throwing the disarmed shooter directly at the passenger, knocking him to the ground.

The shooter rolled away with a moan. The passenger leaped back to his feet and shouted, "How dare you interfere with Order business – stand down!"

Francis and Juliette appeared on the porch, poised to fight.

"Ramin Kain?" Francis asked, mystified.

"He's shot, Anton!" Peter yelled.

"Everyone stop," Francis commanded.

"Where is he?" Juliette demanded, stepping off the porch and scanning the yard.

"Here … I am," Anton called out between gasps. He waved his left hand just above the trunk of the car. His legs gave out, his shoes slipped across the gravel, and he sank back out of sight.

Juliette rushed around the rear of the car and appeared at Anton's side.

Kain stepped around the front of the Bentley, drawing a silvered Glock 9mm from a shoulder holster under his jacket. "Step back everyone," he commanded, waving his gun around, "I'll finish this cleanly."

Jay, Yvette, Chiara and Li rushed into the yard from the training barn.

Anton slumped back against the side of the car and wheezed a question at Juliette. "Who … are they?"

"The Order," Juliette said in tight hard tones, staring up at Kain. She assessed his wounds in a moment. Grabbed his right index finger and jammed it straight into the first bullet wound in his chest, and ordered him, "Hold this still."

Anton gasped. Li and Chiara appeared next to him, crowding in, applying pressure to his wounds.

Juliette stood up, facing Kain across Anton's splayed legs. Her voice cut through the air like a sharp knife as she stated with absolute conviction, "I declare sanctuary on Anton Slayne."

Everyone stopped, and all Anton could hear was his own wheezing.

Kain staggered back a step as if slapped. His pistol hand dropped to his side, and he objected, "You can't do that."

"Whoa," Peter declared from the front of the car. "She just did."

Kain spluttered. "This is outrageous. It's the law."

Francis promised in cutting tones from the porch, "Harm my wife, and I will have your head on a platter."

Juliette put her hand on Anton's head, and a sad peacefulness swept through him. Li looked at him, her face filled with horror. Chiara's face was serious and tense. His breathing was horribly labored, his heart racing. He coughed hard, blood spraying in a pink mist. Broken ribs, a ruptured lung, and his broken arm erupted into fiery agony. It was like someone had pulled a pin. A floodgate loosed and pain washed through his body. He gritted his teeth and attempted to bear it, but a low agonized groan escaped his lips.

"Peter come here," Juliette ordered. "We need to get him into my clinic now."

Peter appeared next to Anton. Lifting him effortlessly, Peter carried him inside the house and down the halls to the medical rooms. He put him gently onto a table. The lights were already on, they were terribly bright, and Anton clenched his eyes shut.

"Stay with us Anton, I'm going to have to operate, and fast," Juliette directed.

The world closed in, and he fell away into darkness.

* * *

The Bentley was brand new. Its sophisticated onboard electronics allowed the car to drive itself. Its powerful headlights cut through the night as the car raced along the I-95 toward New York City.

Ramin sat in the driver's seat deep in thought. There was a movement on the edge of his vision. He looked across at Sam, his partner was carefully cradling his right arm close to his chest. The break had been a simple one, Ramin had set it, and used Sam's tie and his Glock pistol as a simple splint.

Sam looked at him and declared incredulously, "He's faster than anyone I've ever seen."

"It's not your fault, Sam."

"He's faster than anyone has any right to be, he ramped straight out of the blocks."

Ramin nodded. "Yes, he is very fast and very lucky."

"Then there was Lamb, he broke my arm – who are these people."

"Dinosaurs."

"RK?"

"On the way to their own extinction."

"Well, he's probably dead."

"Maybe, maybe not – we can't assume that."

"Oh, I hope he's dead. The Slaynes are such a threat to what we're trying to achieve."

"Unfortunately, Juliette Mirovar is a crack combat surgeon."

"I got him twice in the chest," Sam said despondently. Attempting to poke his own chest with his right hand. He winced, lowered his broken arm, and swore under his breath.

"And good shots they were too, Sam."

"Surely, he's dead, he would have bled out."

Ramin frowned in the shadows of the cabin. "Until it is proven otherwise, we have to assume that he has survived."

"I screwed up. I should've put the first one in his head."

"Don't worry Sam, there will be another chance to put this right."

"What are your plans?"

Ramin smiled briefly. "Oh, I'm sure that another opportunity will present itself soon enough."

"We can't just go and shoot him again. Juliette Mirovar has declared sanctuary on him."

"Yes." Ramin paused for a long moment. "Direct action is off the table. We will have to ... do something else."

"Is she crazy, why did she do that?"

"She's a traditionalist, just like her husband."

Sam shook his head. "Madness."

"Quite so," Ramin said sagely. "Attachment to the past is a form of insanity, and in the end, it will get them all killed."

"I hope so."

Ramin faced forward, staring into the distance. He let the conversation lapse, there was nothing new to speak of. Sam understood his plans to transform the Order of Thoth and bring it into the twenty-first century. It was good to have a loyal confidant who fully understood the need to centralize power and control with a single capable leader. If the Order was truly united underneath a single commander, he could wield it as a real force against the vampires.

Once the transformation of the Order was complete, then Crane would discover just who was playing whom.

Ramin's face froze as he burned with old resentments. *Mirovar. Mirovar! MIROVAR! He's a dinosaur. He's everything that has to change in the Order if we are to move forward.*

Ramin rubbed his right temple, he could feel a headache coming on. Today's events had gone badly. He'd lost the opportunity to kill Anton Slayne under the remit of protecting the secrecy of the Order. Possibly, the young Slayne was still alive, a living threat who could undermine his rulership of the Order. While everyone continued blaming Arthur Slayne for the deaths of Mary Creeley and George Madison, no one was looking for the truth, but Anton Slayne could change all that – if he survived.

Anton Slayne was now sheltering underneath Juliette Mirovar's wings. He must do something about that, but first, he had to give Crane a name. He couldn't tell him about Anton Slayne, Crane would wonder why he never mentioned him to start with. Ramin had recognized William Slayne at a public lecture at Boston University. He'd found out that he was calling himself William Smith, but Ramin always thought of him as a Slayne, and that was what he'd reported. After all, it had always been the Slaynes who possessed the Papyrus of Hakron the Scribe and that was what Crane was really interested in.

If Crane knew that Arthur Slayne had a living grandson, he would investigate him. He would be very interested in Anton Slayne, after all, Arthur Slayne was still out there, and the last thing that Crane would want would be a return of the Slaynes to leadership within the Order.

There was already an identity in play – Anton Smith – he decided to give Crane that name. Most likely he would look no further. It would be a disaster to have someone with Crane's powers look too closely at his past relationship with the Slayne family. Crane's investigations could lead him back to Ramin, and he couldn't let that happen. The last thing he wanted was for anyone to find out he'd killed Mary Creeley and George Madison. No one must ever know what really happened.

Oh my God! The leverage Crane would have if he knew the truth.

Ramin opened up his smartphone, held it so that Sam could not read the screen, typed in a message and sent it to Cornelius Crane.

* * *

The smartphone's screen lit up with a message, 'The other survivor at the Boston dock was Anton Smith.'

Cornelius' lip curled skeptically. Both Ramin Kain and Chloe Armitage claimed that the other survivor was Anton Smith.

He sat by himself at his desk in his library. In front of him was an open folder holding a freshly printed copy of Chloe Armitage's report. Turning the last page, he closed the folder.

There was a laptop on his desk, he used it to log into the Panopticon.

Cornelius ran searches on Anton Smith, Gang Wu, Li Wu, William Slayne and Anna Slayne. After twenty minutes of careful work, there were several clear conclusions. Gang Wu and Anna Slayne were dead. According to the Panopticon, William Slayne was missing, but Cornelius knew that William Slayne was a vampire interred in silver at the secret facility on Rikers Island. Li Wu and Anton Smith had disappeared. Crane surmised that they had gone to ground with the Mirovar force team at a safe house. He hungered to know where they were now, but the Order continued to evade the Panopticon.

Cornelius glanced at the closed report next to his laptop.

There was no connection between Anton Smith, and Anna and William Slayne. Gang Wu had likely switched Anton Smith on with the pressure point technique. It was a risky process, and he was lucky to survive it. However, it was the explanation that best fit the facts.

Cornelius sat back in his chair, slowly stroking his chin.

Everything seemed to check out, there is no way that Chloe and Kain could be colluding on anything. The Panopticon confirmed that Anton Smith was an orphan who had recently been closely associated with the Wu family and now he'd disappeared with the Mirovar force team.

The story, around this young man who had appeared from nowhere, checked out neatly.

Cornelius paused mid-thought. *Perhaps too much so.* There was a single thought, like a splinter in his mind, working its way deeper and deeper into a festering wound. *Chloe Armitage and her ambitions.*

Leaning forward, Crane opened the intercom and instructed his executive secretary. "Ursula, please recall General Clayton Maze from Nairobi. I want him back in New York City within three days."

"Yes, Sir," she responded.

It was unsafe to assume he'd mastered all the information. Boston had taught him the dangers of complacency. It would be best to bring in another set of eyes of proven loyalty. He would set a wolf to watch a fox and make sure that Chloe Armitage was not playing any games.

* * *

Louise Wesson lay in her Massachusetts General hospital bed, with her eyes closed and her ears open.

While she appeared to be sleeping, she was wide awake, her mind on fire, processing the events of the previous night. She was fully aware of the young, armed, Boston Police Department officer sitting outside her room. The city had assigned him for her protection. The Boston police force saw her as an agent for a Federal Government anti-terrorism task force, but she knew better.

She was expecting a visitor, someone who would tie off loose ends. She'd secreted a dinner knife under her sheet, it wasn't much, but in her hands, it was far more dangerous than it appeared. There was a rustle outside her door, the slight scrape of a chair across a linoleum floor as the BPD officer stood up. There was a brief conversation followed by a light knock on the door.

"Ms. Wesson. May I please come in?" queried a voice she immediately recognized.

Louise pushed herself up into a sitting position and replied, "Of course, General Armitage, please come in."

The door opened, and Chloe walked into the room. She nodded at Louise, indicated a nearby chair and asked, "Do you mind if I sit?"

"Please, make yourself comfortable."

"Thank you," Chloe said. Repositioning the chair so that she could sit within easy reach of Louise.

The two women looked at each other calmly for a moment, neither giving anything away.

Chloe leaned forward slightly. "I wanted to personally thank you for your service last night. It is clear that you have acted with honor and bravery under the most trying circumstances, and it has not gone unnoticed."

Louise drew upon a decade of specialized training to master her autonomic responses. She harnessed her sympathetic and parasympathetic nervous systems and put pupil dilation, heart rate, perspiration rates, capillary response and breathing under conscious control. Her long history as an elite CIA spy hunter and assassin equipped her perfectly for this moment.

"I only wish the outcome had been different," Louise declared earnestly.

"Don't we all. However, every defeat is an opportunity to learn," Chloe replied sagely.

"That's true."

Chloe leaned further forward, resting her hand lightly on Louise's wrist, her face lit with concern. "I'm glad you survived, I was impressed with your work at the Noodle House, you're very insightful, and Shadowstone needs you." Chloe looked into Louise's eyes. "... We need you. We need someone who is sharp and decisive as the head of the North American arm of Shadowstone, and I believe that is you."

"Are you offering me the job?" Louise asked with surprised interest.

Chloe smiled. "Not yet. Mr. Haley still has some work to do. But I believe the position will become available in the near future."

"I'm honored," Louise acknowledged.

"You've earned it."

"Thank you."

Chloe's smile faded away.

"In the meantime, there is much work to do. It's a shame you're still here," Chloe noted, frowning with concern. "How is your concussion?"

"Good," Louise answered. There was the slightest increase of pressure on her wrist under Chloe's hand. "I should be out of here tomorrow morning."

"Excellent, and your memory?" Chloe asked, watching Louise steadily.

Louise shook her head and replied, "I still feel like I've been on the wrong end of a Shadowstone sleeper dart. All I've got are flashes of the nightfalcons arriving in the early afternoon, after that – it's a black hole."

Chloe nodded and said, "Perhaps it's for the best. You don't want to be carrying all that ... slaughter with you for the rest of your life."

Louise nodded and said, "Yes. It's a memory I don't need."

Chloe let go of Louise's wrist. Standing up, she directed, "Thank you for your time. When you discharge tomorrow morning, go to Fort Dix and report in. Shadowstone needs rebuilding, and you will play a critical part in that process."

"Will do, Ma'am."

Chloe nodded once, turning away, she left the room. The BPD officer poked his head into the room with a quizzical look on his face. Louise tilted her head, he backed away and closed the door.

Louise reflected on her experience at the Boston warehouse, she remembered everything up to the point where James Haley had pushed her aside and shouted 'incoming' and the grenades had starting exploding through the troop of Shadowstone operatives. She remembered throwing up on Haley's shoes and watching him walk away while fitting a silencer to his Glock 9mm. She remembered everything with the trained precision of a highly experienced CIA black-ops operative at the top of her game.

She bit her bottom lip pensively. *I'm working for vampires, and they don't know that I know.*

Louise was suddenly sick to her stomach and almost gagged before her training mastered the automatic responses. She took a couple of slow, deep breaths as determination nourished from deep within herself welled forth. With razor sharp clarity she began to plan her response to the existence of vampires. A small smile caressed her face. She always felt at her best when she believed in her mission.

Chapter Nine

"Behind every unquestionable belief is a system of control." – Juliette Mirovar, loremaster of the Order of Thoth

* * *

White Hill, Maine, June 12th, 22:30

A dull light leaked through Anton's eyelids.

He blinked a couple of times, before squeezing his eyes shut again. He was lying on a table. There was a nearby machine whispering away, and there was something hard and uncomfortable in his throat.

There's a tube down my throat.

Anton tested his fingers and toes; he could still wiggle all of them. There was a dull ache across his chest, especially on the left side and his left arm was in a cast. There were people nearby speaking with quiet voices.

"He only just made it. I had to repair a mass of blood vessels just to the left of the heart. It was a mess in there, it's a miracle he didn't bleed out. The first bullet did most of the damage. The second was almost as bad. The third broke his left arm in the middle of the humerus, but that will heal up fine. The fourth was just a superficial wound on his other shoulder."

"He would have needed blood, how much have we got left on site?"

Anton realized that the speakers were Juliette and Francis Mirovar.

"We're out," Juliette noted. "We had to give him multiple transfusions. Fortunately, he's progressed far enough through the physical transformation to be a universal receiver, and some of the team helped out with live donations."

"Who supplied it?" Francis asked.

"Jay and Peter."

"… Well, Jay would have liked that," Francis observed ironically.

"He didn't complain," Juliette said calmly. They approached his bedside. "He's waking up."

Firm hands held his head steady as someone pulled out the tube in his throat. He almost gagged as it slid out of his mouth, the nauseous feeling passed immediately, and he started breathing without the tube.

"It's been five hours since he was shot," Francis stated.

"Equivalent to two days healing, he's doing well."

Anton opened his eyes.

Francis let go of his head. Moving to stand next to his wife. He asked, "How are you feeling?"

"Smashed … but I'll live," Anton replied, his voice quiet and raspy.

Francis smiled slightly. "Good man."

Anton lifted his head to sit up, thought better of it and rested back down. Juliette put a cup of water with a straw in it near his mouth, he tilted his head slightly, sipping the throat soothing water in careful swallows.

Anton looked at Francis and inquired, "What happened? Who were they?"

"Ramin Kain, and—"

"His lackey, Samuel Luther," Juliette interjected. "What?" she glanced at her husband, her eyes flashing. "You know I've never liked either of them."

Francis nodded. "The Head of the Order of Thoth, and one of his staff."

"They tried to kill me, why?"

"That's a good question," Francis sighed. "And I'm not sure what the answer is."

"He shouldn't have shot Anton, it's outrageous," Juliette declared fiercely.

Francis said, "Yes – attacking someone who is already training with a force team – it's just not done. Any disciplinary matter is always referred to the force leader." He shook his head. "Never has the Head of the Order attempted the blatant assassination of an unconfirmed member of the Order."

"So, why?" Anton asked perplexedly.

"Technically he is entitled to defend the secrecy of the Order." Francis said.

Juliette titled her head, her lips curling skeptically. "And it's what he claimed he was doing."

Francis frowned. "Yes, he went on about it at length."

"I'm no threat to the Order?"

"Of course, you aren't," Juliette agreed, placing her hand calmly on his forehead.

"Are they still here?"

"Long gone," Juliette smirked. "Kain stormed off, with Luther scuttling along behind him."

Francis put his hand gently on Anton's left shoulder. "Don't worry, they know better than to try something like that again."

Memories flashed through Anton's mind, and he asked, "Sanctuary – what is it?"

"The heart of our tradition," Francis declared seriously.

"Anton, you're a guest with us until the Conclave," Juliette stated serenely. "There is no way that I would allow a guest to come to harm, not while I draw breath."

Francis' mouth worked momentarily, and he looked away. When he looked back, his eyes were glistening. "You're under my wife's protection, that means that you are under mine as well."

Francis' emotion washed over him in a wave. Its power shocked him to his core. Two things were crystal clear, Francis Mirovar loved Juliette more than life itself, and he hated the fact she'd taken on the risk of protecting Anton.

Juliette put her arm around her husband's shoulders. Leaning in, she kissed him on the cheek and whispered, "Always the emotional one."

Anton was embarrassed by the display of private intimacy between Francis and Juliette and glanced up at the ceiling.

"Harrumph," murmured Francis. He fixed Anton with a steely glare. "Don't imagine that our protection is a pass on training, combat or acceptance by the Order. Get well soldier, I don't want you falling behind."

"... Yes, Sir. Thank you, Sir."

Francis nodded, squeezed his wife's hand and left the room. Juliette continued to work with Anton, adjusting equipment and monitoring his vital signs for another fifteen minutes. She gave him an injection to help him sleep. As he started to drift away, a question gnawed at his mind.

The Head of the Order of Thoth wants me dead, and I don't know why. What the hell is going on?

* * *

The afternoon sunlight cut through the glade, dappling the grass and freshly turned soil. A solemn quiet ruled the spaces between the trees on the hill. The members of the Mirovar force team stood around the open grave. There was no music, no fanfare, only the silence of the woods near the safe house farm.

Li lifted the flask that contained the last of her family reserve sake and poured it over the grave. She shook out the last drops, turned away in silence, her face streaked with tears.

Francis stated softly, "May his heart be as light as a feather."

I've had enough of this, Anton thought.

He nudged Peter's thigh with his right forearm and whispered harshly, "Give me a hand."

Peter leaned down and supported Anton as he lurched out of the Vietnam war vintage wheelchair, he'd been sitting in. He stood on unsteady legs for a second or three, wobbled a bit, and then straightened up.

"Gang was the best man I ever met. The best teacher and the best friend. I will never forget him."

The group murmured their assent.

"The world is poorer for his passing. I'm not going to sit in a damn wheelchair feeling sorry for myself when I'm damn sure that Gang wouldn't do the same. Goodbye … Gang … you'll always be in my heart." Anton's voice caught on Gang's name. "… I'm done here."

Turning, Anton pushed past Peter and started walking the half mile back to the safe house.

Juliette appeared beside him, and declared hotly, "Don't be stupid Anton, it's been less than twenty-four hours since you were shot."

Anton faced her. Wearing a reckless grin and glistening eyes. "This world is hard – I'm going to be harder."

"Well, don't waste my efforts dying on the way back," Juliette insisted in nettled tones.

Anton turned away, declaring, "I won't," over his shoulder, and led the team back to the safe house. He walked slowly and steadily. About halfway there, Li came up and nudged herself in under his right arm.

"You're really starting to wobble," she whispered.

"I'm going to kill her," Anton vowed.

"Not by yourself."

Anton looked down at Li, her face was still, her gaze was intense.

"Agreed."

Anton pushed on but had to admit to himself, it was only the presence of Li that got him the last fifty yards to the safe house.

* * *

Li found Francis alone in the library. A cozy room on the lower floor, opposite the briefing room. Bookshelves filled with an eclectic array of books and folios covered the library's walls. She hesitated for a moment at the doorway, pensive with a rare indecisiveness. She carried the White Dragon before her with hands that threatened to tremble.

Francis looked up; his eyes widened. He put aside the book he was reading. Indicating another lounge chair next to his own with a wave of his hand, he said, "Please sit with me."

Li walked over to the chair and sat down. The White Dragon resting in its scabbard across her knees. She looked directly at Francis for a moment, then lowered her eyes. After a moment, she looked at him again and declared baldly, "I want you to have the White Dragon."

Francis' eyes glistened. "Are you sure? It's a family heirloom."

Li paused for a long moment. "I am the last of my family."

"You may have children one day."

Li smiled wanly. "Perhaps, but who knows when."

"If you keep the sword, you can pass it down when the time comes."

Li stood up decisively, presenting the White Dragon to Francis. "No, the time is now. There is no one else who is more deserving of this sword. No one else who shares the same commitment to the goals of the Order as my father did."

Francis stood up and bowed toward Li. Receiving the White Dragon, he said sincerely, "You honor me with this priceless gift."

Li shuddered as grief, and helpless longing coalesced within her. The gift of the sword carried with it the final acknowledgment of the death of her father. With the memory of his burial fresh from the morning, tears rolled down her cheeks, and she sobbed once. Francis put the sword aside. He wrapped his arms around her. She buried her face against his chest.

Francis tenderly stroked the back of her head. She sobbed again and again. There was a timeless moment when she felt protected and safe. Taking slow deep breaths, her sadness retreated enough to allow her to speak.

"Thank you," she whispered.

"Thank you, dear child," Francis said softly, loosening his arms.

Li pushed back and looked up into Francis' face. There was only acceptance and fatherly love there. Her heart overflowed. Her breath caught for a second, she stepped back further, bowed formally and left the library.

* * *

The sun was peeking over the horizon, its light washing across the farm yard.

Anton had been up for fifteen minutes, it was a week since Gang's funeral, and he hungered to start training. Juliette had finally given him a medical release. He'd healed up enough to join in without risk of doing any more damage. The scars remained, puckered marks and suture lines running across his ribs just below his left nipple. His arm was free of its cast, and he rotated his shoulders to loosen up. The team waited in the training barn. Someone had thrown the doors wide open and a light morning breeze washed steadily through the building.

Francis ordered, "Peter, lead us in."

"Sure, Boss. Okay everyone, form a line. It's time to feel the burn."

Someone had arranged a set of stations throughout the barn. Tractor tires, thick ropes attached to the ceiling, heavy kettlebells, and thick rubber bands.

Peter stood in front of Anton, leaned forward and grinned. "I'm going to introduce you to the concept of active rest."

"Right, sounds like fun."

"That's the spirit."

Peter stepped back and addressed everyone, "Okay – we're just getting older standing around, Francis and Juliette, start with the tires, Li and Chiara on the ropes, Yvette and Jay on the kettlebells, and Anton and I will start with the bands. One-minute rotations, no stopping."

Peter checked his watch, set a timer and got into position next to Anton. He picked up the thick rubber band, stepping onto it with both feet shoulder width apart. He grabbed it with both hands palm down, lifted and pushed it up as if lifting a barbell. Anton watched Peter and did the same.

"Okay. No ramping – Go!" Peter shouted.

A familiar competitive urge rushed through Anton's soul, he desperately wanted to match whatever Peter could do.

The exercises continued without rest. Peter's watch pinged loudly every sixty seconds, and the pairs would swap to another station. Anton and Peter rotated through the kettlebells, lifting the twenty-kilo weights repeatedly up to their chests. Followed by climbing the ropes as fast as they could hand over hand and then reversing back down them. Then it was the tractor tires, flipping them over, running around them and flipping them back. After four minutes, each pair returned to their original station, and the cycle began again and continued throughout the morning. Peter spiced up the cycle by adding sprints up and down the length of the barn and then added squat jumps, pushups, and burpees as well.

At two hours and fourteen minutes into the workout, Anton pulled to a halt at the end of a sprint, doubled over and repeatedly dry retched for about fifteen seconds.

Peter paused next to him, and looked down at the bare ground at Anton's feet. "No blood, that's a good sign. Now try and keep up."

The session continued for another sixteen minutes.

"Good work everyone," Peter called out. "Get some water and come back in five."

Anton picked up a water bottle, and it shook in his trembling hands. He concentrated on stilling them and took a long swig of water. He stretched his chest, his ribs on the left were tight and raw. He breathed deeply, sure that his full powers would come back in time.

Li patted his shoulder. "Are you okay?"

"Yeah, sure."

"Good."

He followed her back to where Peter stood. Peter led them through twenty minutes of stretching, demonstrating that he possessed amazing flexibility for a big man. The session ended with a gut-busting plank where they held a position face down, supported on their toes and elbows for ten minutes. Anton made it to the seventh minute and then began collapsing onto the ground.

Peter appeared beside him, his finger just beneath Anton's chest. Peter pushed up slightly, supporting Anton's body weight. He whispered into Anton's ear, "C'mon Anton, you can make another couple of minutes."

Anton drew on every resource that he could call on and lifted himself back off Peter's finger.

"Awesome. C'mon Anton keep it going."

Sweat dripping from his face, his body trembling, Anton wore the pain and moved deeper into the intensity of the effort.

"Thirty seconds."

Anton vowed to go harder.

Anton's body dropped a fraction of an inch, brushing Peter's finger, and immediately jerked back up into position.

"Ten seconds."

White noise roared through Anton's body.

"Stop."

Anton refused to stop.

Peter's hand pressed into the middle of his back, and he collapsed forward onto the hard-packed dirt of the barn floor. He rolled over and lay there, sucking air into his lungs. Peter and Li stood over him, grinning.

"First session back – not bad," Li observed.

"Awesome work, Anton," Peter said. He hauled Anton back to his feet and handed him a fresh water bottle. "Time for a shower and breakfast."

Anton nodded and started walking slowly toward the house with Peter and Li. Before they left the barn, Francis called them over. Juliette was standing next to him, smiling happily.

Francis put his left hand on her shoulder. "Li, we need an understudy for the roles of loremaster and netmaster, Juliette will help you with that."

Li looked shocked. "I'm honored."

"You're a natural," Juliette said. "It would be a terrible waste not to train you."

"Thank you," Li said.

"Li and Anton," Francis directed. "You need driver and flight training. Peter will teach you."

"Sure, Boss," Peter agreed. He looked at Juliette. "Is it okay if I get them both into the simulations after breakfast."

"Yes, Peter, that will be fine," Juliette replied. "Li and I will start together this afternoon."

"Good. Then everyone knows what they're doing," Francis declared with a short nod.

Peter, Li, and Anton made their way across the yard to the safe house.

Anton looked across at Peter and Li, and asked, "What's a loremaster?"

"Someone who keeps all the recorded history of the Order of Thoth," Peter explained. "Juliette is a loremaster, there are only six alive in the world. The Order operates on tradition and precedence. The loremasters know everything there is to know about the Order of Thoth, they keep our traditions alive. They maintain the soul of the Order."

"How do they do it?"

Li grimaced. "By oral history and severe memory training – I think."

Peter looked hard at Li. "Yes – there is a lot of hard work involved as I'm sure you will soon find out."

Anton nodded. "Li, I'm not surprised they picked you. I'm sure you will do well."

Peter laughed, grabbing them around the shoulders and pulled them in with a hug as they walked toward the safe house. "Yeah, she'll be great, now let's get something to eat. My stomach thinks my throat's been cut. Then we can see how many helicopters you can crash before lunchtime."

"Helicopters?" Anton asked.

"Flight Sim – very realistic. I hope that you don't get airsick."

"I should be okay."

Peter chuckled. "I'll make sure that we have a mop and bucket handy, just in case."

"Right," Anton drawled as he followed Peter and Li up the steps and into the safe house.

The smells of the kitchen reached him in the hallway. His stomach growled and his mouth salivated like a broken faucet.

Eggs, bacon, toast, mushrooms, tomatoes, and sausages – great.

* * *

The classroom was located in the basement of the safe house.

There was a simple wooden table with a laptop on it in the middle of the room. There was a white pull-down screen, a projector, half a dozen desk chairs, and a pair of dual-sided whiteboards on stands. Soft downlights in the ceiling lit the chamber.

Juliette sat opposite Li, and inquired, "Was there anything worth noticing as you came down here?"

"There are metal contacts on the door," Li noted.

"Indicating?" Juliette asked.

"There's a Faraday cage around the room."

"Good, why would we build a room this way?"

"Electromagnetic shielding for security."

"Is it perfect?"

"No. But it is much better than nothing."

"Correct. This is the most secure location for a conversation on this site, and that is why we're here."

Li nodded, ready to hear whatever Juliette had to say.

Juliette paused for a long moment, looking steadily into Li's eyes as if probing her character.

Li relaxed, confident in herself.

"There is no obligation to accept the role of loremaster. If you wish, you can remain a warrior with full honor," Juliette noted, smiling softly. "In addition, loremasters are excluded from the roles of force leader and Head of the Order. If you go down this path, you'll never be in either of those two roles."

"Are any of the others training with you?"

"No. They were all offered the role, but they all turned it down."

Li hesitated for a second. "What's the issue?"

"I must share with you enough information so that you can make an informed decision about this," Juliette declared seriously. "Anything less would be unacceptable. I'm not interested in a student who doesn't understand the commitment they have to make to be loremaster."

Li was uneasy for the first time at the safe house.

"I overheard your comment to Anton and Peter earlier this morning. Yes, the loremasters maintain an oral history and undergo severe memory training. It is clear that your memory is excellent, in time, it will become perfect."

"You can train for an eidetic memory?"

"Yes. Furthermore, we can elevate your use of memory to become a powerful tool for integrating diverse information and finding obscure, but real, patterns. Using your memory this way, is known as a 'mind palace.'"

Li was intrigued and leaned forward. "That sounds cool."

Juliette glanced down at her hands before looking back at Li. "It comes at a price; I haven't spelled out the full role yet."

"Oh."

"We use technology too, and a nanotech implant right here," Juliette explained, indicating a location on the inside of her right forearm about three inches back from the wrist.

Li sighed softly, anticipating that the downside was coming up. "What does the implant do."

"It hooks through software on your laptop to quantum encrypted storage on the Cloud with a wetware interface directly into your nervous system."

Li's eyes widened. "... Oh my God. What does that feel like?"

"Both glorious and terrible. The loremasters can communicate with each other using quantum communications via the implant, and it feels like someone is talking inside your head."

"That could get weird," Li noted. "Can they read your mind?"

"Only what you're willing to share."

"Well, that doesn't sound too bad," Li conceded with a frown. "There must be something else."

"There is. This is critically important," Juliette instructed. "The quantum communications networks work alongside the regular networks, and—"

"Of course," Li interrupted, her mouth forming an O of surprise. "You can see everything on the regular networks, everything would be available."

"Yes."

"How do you filter it, there must be an enormous amount of junk data of no relevance to us."

"Through training, you learn to filter, but it's not the junk that is the issue." Juliette reached across the table and gripped Li's hands. "The darknet is also open to you, you will see every horrible, evil thing that human beings can do to each other and post online."

Li looked at Juliette in silence.

"There will be things you will see that you can't unsee," Juliette said emphatically. "It's corrosive. It can get to you and destroy your willingness to put your life at risk, or see your friends and loved ones put their lives at risk to protect humanity. It can make you give up. It can make you despair."

Li shook her head and stared at Juliette. "That won't stop me."

Juliette stared back. "There are loremasters that have killed themselves, two in the last decade. One in four loremasters have committed suicide."

Li shrugged her shoulders. "Suicide is not my thing."

Juliette looked hard at Li, as if peering into her soul. She remarked in a low voice, "There is one more risk, which is ... difficult to explain. If it eventuates you can always remove the implant before you are damaged."

Li arched an eyebrow and queried, "Hard to explain?"

"Yes. You have to experience it to know what it is. Not many become affected by it. You can still back out if you want to."

Li thought of her father, *what would he do?* She nodded and declared firmly, "When do I start?"

"Now."

* * *

It was an hour and a half before midnight.

Dillon Browne was just about as happy as he could be. He had a nice wad of cash and good quality Colombian cocaine in his shirt pocket. His crew was with him, it was the fourth of July in Boston, and it was time to party. Like every Friday night, they would walk half a mile to the Four

Corners/Geneva railway station. They would catch the next train into Boston city. The nightclubs were their playground. They could have some fun and do some business hooking people up with whatever they needed. He liked the train. Cops didn't stop trains to test people on them for drugs like they did with cars. In the twenty-five years of his life, no cop had ever pinned Dillon for anything more serious than a parking fine, and he intended to keep it that way.

The night sky was clear. The air was fresh. Dillon walked with a jaunty air of confidence bred from total familiarity with the rules of how to get by in Dorchester. He was a big deal in the suburb. No one dealt drugs on his turf without his say so, and if anyone broke the rules, then his crew would punish them – permanently.

The sidewalk they were on curved past the entrance to a forested park. Streetlights normally lit the trees, but some idiot had vandalized the lights over the entrance. Now, shadows cloaked the park in a near impenetrable gloom.

As he approached the stone archway of the park entrance, Dillon's left hand slid over the rounded hip of his latest girlfriend. She wore a tight leather skirt, a see-through net top, high heels and little else. She was hot, hot, hot and he wondered if she would last more than the typical three to four weeks. He kinda hoped that she would. She responded to his touch by pushing in close underneath his muscular left arm.

A deep voice behind him declared, "I love fireworks, we'll see some great fireworks tonight."

Dillon looked over his left shoulder at Caleb Moore, his chief enforcer. Caleb was scary big and wide, a coulda, shoulda, woulda been NFL forward who never quite made it out of Dorchester and who was the longest serving member of Dillon's crew.

Dillon scrunched up his nose, grinned broadly, and swore happily, "They'll be fu—"

His left arm jerked hard, and his new girlfriend vanished.

Her younger brother, Gabriel Williams, who was tagging along for the night, pointed into the park and screamed, "Aaliyah."

Dillon whirled, his left arm ached like it was nearly dislocated, he reached behind his back with his right hand and dragged a Colt .45 automatic from the back of his pants.

He stared into the park. He could just see the outline of a tall, slim man gliding backward into the enveloping darkness. He was carrying Aaliyah like she weighed nothing, her feet dangling a foot off the ground. One of his pale hands was over her mouth. She was struggling but couldn't make a sound. A moment later they disappeared into the shadows.

A shiver of nameless dread prickled the skin at the back of Dillon's neck. He couldn't process how fast Aaliyah had vanished into the dark. It didn't make any sense. A part of his mind sat dumbfounded by what had just happened, the rest boiled with fury.

Ethan Jones, the third member of his crew, pulled a MAC-10 9mm from within his coat. He stepped up beside Dillon and snapped, "Some cracker stole your girlfriend."

Caleb Moore grunted in agreement, pulling out his own MAC-10 which looked tiny in his big fist. He waved the barrel toward the park, looking expectantly at Dillon.

Dillon growled, his anger boiling away the dread. His fist tightened around the pearl handled grip of his .45. "That fool is going to be in a world of hurt. No one takes what's mine."

He walked confidently forward, leading the other three men into the darkness.

* * *

Cornelius Crane cinched the heavy belt tight and locked it.

The young man, little more than a boy, stared at him wide-eyed without really seeing him. Cornelius stepped back from the boy to survey his handiwork. There was a faint diffuse light amongst the trees. The park was a night lit wonderland of luminous colors, rich scents, and faint rustles. Cornelius was perfectly aware that for the five young people trying to see him, he was little more than a dark nebulous outline.

The boy's face gleamed with the sweat of fear as he struggled vainly against the thick belt.

This one is named Gabriel, how like an angel he looks behind his terror. Perhaps too beautiful and too innocent to condemn to this immortal life.

Cornelius sniffed, his eyes narrowing. The five humans, four men, and one woman reeked of the familiar stench of terror. He'd strapped them upright to the trunks of old trees, their mouths covered with gray duct tape. They struggled and wriggled but could not escape their bonds.

Before each of his candidates, he'd laid out a similarly trussed and silenced homeless man.

Cornelius went to a nearby black duffel bag and extracted a thick leather binder the size of an A4 folio. He placed it on the grass and opened it. Inside was a set of six syringes, and a razor-sharp nine-inch knife. He picked up the knife and slashed the inner thighs of the five candidates. The cuts were deep, expertly severing the femoral arteries. The candidates moaned and whimpered behind their silenced mouths. Air rushed through their dilated nostrils. Their hearts, already beating fast, accelerated toward their maximum capacity.

The blood sluiced down the candidate's legs, pooling at their feet. Selecting five of the syringes, Cornelius filled them in turn with his own blood. He approached the first candidate, plunging one of the syringes directly into the left ventricle of his heart and emptied it. He repeated the process with each of the other candidates. When finished, he neatly packed his gear back into the duffel bag and closed it. He cleaned the knife, tucking it unsheathed behind his waist belt and waited patiently with his long arms crossed over his chest.

Vampire conversion takes a variable amount of time, but typically around five minutes. The first to complete was the second candidate he'd injected: the young woman. She stopped writhing in agony, a few seconds later she burst through the heavy leather belt and tore off her gag. Cornelius appeared next to her, his hand on the back of her neck, guiding her down to the throat of the homeless man lying in front of her. She needed no further help, tearing into his flesh with her new fangs and instinctively wrapping her mouth over the gushing wound. The sound of her ravenous sucking was loud in the otherwise silent park.

A moment later, the second belt burst and Cornelius assisted the huge man named Caleb to his first victim. Caleb crushed the man's skull with one big fist in his urgency to get to his throat, but a second later he was gorging on the homeless man's blood.

In the next handful of seconds, the other three completed their conversions. Cornelius blurred around them, making sure they reached their designated victims. He stepped back and waited for their feasting to finish.

He did not have to wait long. Moments later, Dillon Browne and his crew stood to face him, their terror gone, replaced with shock and wonder.

"What the hell just happened? Who are you?" Dillon asked.

"Hey man, we're vampires. He must be that guy, ah, Dracula," Ethan asserted.

Cornelius stepped forward and said calmly, "I promise you; I am not the figment of someone's fevered imagination, but yes – you are now immortal vampires, you will not age, and you need not die. As for my name, it is not important, what is important is that you obey my rules."

"Obey your rules." Dillon shook his head, sneering incredulously. "Your rules, cracker? We don't have to do anything that you say. This is our turf, I rule here, I say what happens in Dorchester."

Dillon growled, lunging at Cornelius. Ethan and Caleb blurred forward, moving with him to tackle Cornelius.

With nearly a thousand years of combat experience, Cornelius easily evaded Dillon's forward rush. He trapped his arm and threw him hard, face first onto the ground. He dealt with Ethan and Caleb in the same manner, throwing them on top of Dillon. Cornelius blurred forward, slapping Aaliyah unconscious and trapping the young Gabriel in an unbreakable hold. He turned, holding Gabriel a foot in front of him as Dillon, flanked by Caleb and Ethan bounced back to their feet.

Cornelius stared at them, a ferocious light in his eyes. He growled softly, almost a murmur, but certain that they could easily hear him. He declared in cold tones, "You will obey me because I can do this."

Pushing Gabriel toward them, Cornelius whipped the knife from his belt. He passed it through the young man's neck with such violent speed that it splashed blood across the faces of the three shocked men a dozen feet away. Gabriel's body took another step forward on its own before crumpling to the ground. His head rolled forward end over end, coming to a halt, a foot in front of Dillon's boots.

The fight drained from Dillon and his crew. They were predators through and through, they respected strength, and they instinctively understood that they were in the presence of the greatest predator they had ever seen.

"Okay," Dillon muttered. "Your rules."

"Yes, my rules. They are simple. Stay in Dorchester. You can hunt Boston but do not leave this city. If I find you outside of Boston, I will kill you. Do not attempt to make more vampires or I will hunt you down and kill you. Do not move in daylight as sunlight will kill you."

Cornelius paused for a long moment to let his words penetrate their minds. "Are there any questions?"

"Why? Why us?" Dillon asked.

Cornelius' lip curled into a half smile. "It's your lucky day, someone has to be immortal."

Dillon and his crew watched him in silence.

Cornelius glanced at Aaliyah who was waking up and commanded, "Tell her what I told you." He pointed at the bodies. "And dispose of the trash, don't leave it lying around for anyone to find. Keep yourselves secret or else I will come back and kill you all slowly."

He watched as Dillon frowned, sucking indecisively on his lower lip.

Time to disappear – that will really put the fear of God into them.

Cornelius flourished his long coat dramatically, throwing a short-fused flash-bang grenade to the ground. It burst into blinding light with a crash like thunder. By the time the new vampires regained the use of their senses – he was gone.

* * *

Cornelius Crane drove his personal black Mercedes toward New York City.

He left the autopilot off. He enjoyed driving, confident his own enhanced senses and reflexes were superior to the technology delivered with the car. After all, he considered, sometimes the autopilots crash the car and kill everyone inside. He anticipated that maybe in another fifty or hundred years they would get the technology right – he could afford to wait.

He mused about the night's events. *What's a cracker? I will have to look that one up, sounds derogatory.*

Shadowstone had fitted the car with an array of communications technology. It was a simple matter to conduct fully scrambled voice calls, and send and receive encrypted text messages driven only by voice commands.

"Compose text message to The White Pawn," Cornelius stated in a calm, steady voice. The White Pawn was an alias for the quantum address of Ramin Kain's latest smartphone. The quantum address was the sub-section of the full quantum signature, used to connect any two quantum communication devices in a traceless call.

Cornelius said to the machine, "There are four targets in Dorchester, Boston. End text message."

The system responded with a ping as it delivered the message.

Now the ball was in Kain's court. He needed to deliver on the Mirovar force team.

Cornelius grinned, with the Mirovar force team caught between operations from Kain and Chloe, their doom was certain.

The car pinged with an automated message from the Panopticon.

Cornelius frowned and commanded his vehicle's console, "Display."

The car responded by projecting a translucent image of live satellite footage onto the interior of the car windscreen. Cornelius' eyes widened, and his jaw dropped. There was a smoking crater surrounded by burning buildings and thick Amazonian jungle. As he watched in growing horror, the center of the remaining buildings suddenly exploded, sending debris high into the air. Thick black smoke billowed in great clouds over the site.

A red message repeatedly streamed along the bottom of the screen, '*** Brazil-34 *** No Communications ***'.

Cornelius snarled. He was certain who was behind this attack. "Fucking Arthur Slayne!"

Cornelius paused for a second before speaking through gritted teeth, "Broadcast voice message, list alpha. Activate the war room and meet me at the Citadel immediately. End Message."

The vehicle's communications system instantly sent the message to a list of first responders in his force of praetorians. Cornelius put his foot down, and the car surged forward.

"Damn it, how much of the fungus do we still have? Enough for five hundred doses, that's not enough for my plans."

Cornelius Crane spent the rest of the journey considering options to recover his Day Guard strategy.

* * *

The stream meandered its way down the hillside. The warm mid-morning sunlight speared through the thick canopy of Maples, Beech and Birch trees, dappling the rough stone and dirt trail that followed along the edge of the stream.

Anton ran alongside Francis Mirovar. They were both kitted out in running shoes, socks, loose shorts and sports singlets; newly bought for Anton and worn down with wear and tear for Francis. Francis wore an old, black peaked cap with a French flag on the front of it. His long hair tied in a ponytail hanging out the back of the cap.

Anton dragged his hand down his face, and it came away slick. They kept a good pace; it had been uphill for over an hour, and he was still feeling good and strong. His breathing was even and his movement fluid. It had been over three weeks since the shooting, the physical trauma had fully healed, and the scars were beginning to fade.

The hill became steeper, and the path ended on a set of stairs cut into the rock. The stream became a waterfall, falling from about fifteen yards above them. Anton moved to go up the stairs, and Francis tapped his arm.

"No Anton, this is where we stop," Francis noted, stepping off the trail and taking his shoes, socks, and singlet off.

Anton did the same and followed Francis as he moved to the edge of the stream. They leaped onto a boulder, moving nimbly over a slew of rocks to a position a yard out from the waterfall. The spray of the waterfall caught the sunlight, reflecting a crisp rainbow for a moment before Anton got too close, and the bright colors melted away. After the run, he cupped his hands, filling them with water and slaking his thirst. The water was wonderfully refreshing, clean and crystal clear.

The two men stood on separate boulders, relaxing in front of the waterfall. Anton looked steadily at Francis, who was rubbing his hands dry on the back of his shorts.

Francis looked across at Anton. "Your Grandfather was my teacher before my confirmation in the Order, and he taught both Gang and myself this practice which I will pass onto you today."

"What's that?"

"Watch and learn," Francis directed with a brief smile.

Francis centered himself, dropping into the silence of the Ramp. His fists blurred forward in rapid combinations that twisted and turned in the waterfall, but there was no disturbance of the flow of water. As quickly as it started, it stopped. Turning toward him, Francis opened his hands and displayed them – they were dry.

"Now you try Anton, ramp and punch through the water without getting wet," Francis instructed, watching Anton intently.

Anton confidently expected that there was an easy trick to the technique.

He nodded, turned and silenced his mind. He dropped away from anticipation and memory, allowing himself to flow with the moment. The Ramp flowered within, time slowed, the waterfall started to break up into streams of separate droplets. Anton's fists blurred forward and immediately splashed through the waterfall. Frowning, he dropped out of the Ramp, shaking the water off his hands.

"It's harder than it looks."

"Yes," Francis observed. "And that surprises you?"

Anton looked sheepish for a second. "Well, yes."

Francis studied Anton for a moment and promised, "Master this technique and your combat ability will be a notch above what it is now."

"Yes Francis, but what am I doing wrong."

Francis tilted his head. "There's no snatching in this – you're snatching at the spaces between the drops."

"… I hope that you're not about to tell me to 'be one with the waterfall,'" Anton remarked, rolling his eyes.

Francis rubbed the side of his nose. He suddenly tapped Anton on the chest, just hard enough to make him lose his balance. Anton slid off the rock and into the stream. He twisted in the air but hit the water before he could recover, making a big splash as he disappeared beneath the surface of the water. A moment later his head bobbed back up to the surface, and he swam back to the rocks.

Anton shook his head, his eyes narrowing slightly. He put his hand up for Francis to help him out.

Francis put his hands up in front of his shoulders. "I'm not falling for that, you'll just pull me in. You climb back out yourself."

Anton clambered out onto the boulder. He stood up, running his hands back through his thick, dark hair to clear the water from it. "Okay, I suppose I deserved that."

Francis threw him into the stream again.

Anton's head broke the surface of the stream again, and he swam briskly back to the boulder.

How did he do that? I never saw it coming.

Anton climbed out of the stream, taking his position on the boulder next to Francis' rock. They stared at each other for a moment, and Francis arched his right eyebrow.

"Do I need to push you in again or are you ready to learn?"

"Ready to learn."

"Good, then start with learning that cynicism is not wisdom, there is no place for it in my force team, do you understand?"

"Yes, Francis."

"Good, do you have any questions?"

"Yes, how were you able to throw me in the water the second time? I get the first happened because I was surprised, but the second, there was no warning at all. You didn't telegraph anything at all, it just happened, and then I was falling back into the stream."

Francis paused for a moment, then leaned forward slightly. "Because I can punch water without getting wet."

Anton bit down on saying *right*, and instead stared at Francis for a moment and nodded his acceptance.

"So, let us begin," Francis directed.

An hour later, a thoughtful Anton was tying up his shoelaces. The waterfall skill was wickedly difficult. It almost seemed like magic the way that Francis could do it at will. He'd assured Anton there was no magic involved, none whatsoever. It was persistence, method, and correct instruction, followed by deep insight, and more persistence. He'd spent the session splashing water with every punch, and it seemed he'd made no progress.

Gang knew this technique, but Armitage still killed him, how easy would it be for Armitage to kill me?

Anton vowed to himself, *I must master this skill, and soon ... and then go beyond it.*

Francis nudged his shoulder and said with a half-grin, "It's ten miles back home, let's see if you can beat me."

"Are we allowed to ramp."

"Yes."

"What if someone sees us."

"They won't, not today. Juliette checked the satellite positions – we have an open window until lunchtime."

"Okay then – I'll be waiting for you when you get back old man."

Anton blurred away, Francis blurred with him, and the two men hurtled down the track.

* * *

The barn was set up for unarmed combat. The central space was dry packed earth, swept clear of dust and straw. There were buckets of iced water and wet towels. Chiara, Peter, Li and Anton stood in a loose half-circle facing Juliette.

Chiara glanced at Anton, and thought, *this will be interesting.*

Juliette caught Anton's and Li's gaze and said, "Li, Anton, the Order has been perfecting unarmed combat for thousands of years and what we have now has influenced, and been influenced by every style in existence. We have distilled everything down to two key principles; does it work, and is it fast."

Anton and Li nodded, Chiara and Peter were both familiar with Juliette's instruction and stood relaxed, waiting for the physical part of the lesson to begin.

"Li, I know you have benefited from your father's instruction for many years, and can be considered fully trained, but Anton, it's been less than three months since you started, so we're going to focus on progressing your skills as fast as possible."

"Sounds good," Anton noted. "I'm ready."

"Ready to lose," Peter observed, grinning.

"Boys!" Juliette declared sternly. "Pay attention. Anton, we're going to test you hard for the next two days. This is an immersive training system, and mostly it's done while ramped. It will be grueling, and I can guarantee that by the end of tomorrow you will not think it was fun."

Juliette stepped close to Anton, her face looking up, inches from his own. "It will be three against one at all times. Peter with his strength is equivalent to a vampire at close quarters, Li and Chiara are equivalent to Red Empire assassins."

Anton glanced at Peter and said, "Gang always told me that it was a good idea to avoid hand to hand combat with vampires."

"He was right," Juliette agreed. "You should avoid grappling with Vampires, their superior strength makes it a low probability option."

"Why do we bother?"

"We don't always fight vampires. There is also the Red Empire."

Chiara grinned, and declared, "Deadly assassins."

"And in actual combat with edged weapons," Juliette explained, frowning slightly at Chiara. "Unarmed combat skills remain an essential part of our fighting system."

"Okay – what do I need to do?" Anton asked.

Juliette guided him to the center of the barn and stepped back. Peter took a position a couple of yards in front of Anton. Li and Chiara stood a similar distance away from Anton on the other corners of a triangle.

"I've already briefed Li on this training form, so everyone is ready," Juliette stated. She pulled a black hood from her belt and handed it to Anton.

"What's this?" Anton asked, looking at the hood.

"Vampires don't fight in daylight mate," Peter said dryly.

"I'm doing this blind?"

"Yes. You will be blind throughout the training," Juliette acknowledged.

Taking a deep breath, Anton sighed and put the hood on, pulling it down over his face.

"Focus on the silence within, Anton, find the still point of calm in the midst of chaos, and you will know what to do," Juliette instructed from the sidelines.

The attack started without warning. Peter leaping forward with a combination of blows, that he pulled at the very last moment so that they would not be penetrating. Anton's hands flashed up, blocking the attacks and he started to move left toward Li, who promptly swept his feet out from under him, and he fell backward. Chiara helped him to the ground with a lightning-fast kick to his chest.

He jackknifed off the ground like a click beetle on a summer night. One outstretched hand almost catching Chiara's foot as she launched a second kick which she instantly pulled to avoid getting trapped.

My God, he's fast and intuitive.

Chiara paused for a moment, circling, as Peter and Li engaged with Anton, carefully watching his every move.

How attached is Anton to Li? She wondered.

The training continued in two-hour blocks broken with fifteen-minute breaks for the rest of the day and repeated the next day.

* * *

Jay walked along the corridor to the front door of the safe house, putting his hand out to push it open.

Something dropped onto the porch in front of the door with a heavy half-muffled clunk. On a sudden intuition, Jay pulled to a halt just inside the door, placed his left hand up on the wood, leaned his head forward slightly and listened.

Francis' voice came from the porch as he asked, "How's your training at the waterfall progressing?"

"Still getting wet," Anton answered with a sigh.

Jay stepped back from the door. He turned to face an oil painting of a revolutionary war scene on the wall and pretended to study it.

"It's only been ten days since you started," Francis said. "Not everyone progresses at the same pace. Continue to persist, you'll get there in the end. Focus on the silence, and arresting your attention in the present moment. You will discover that silence is a spectrum where there is no end to how deep you can go. It is there, in the eternal quiet, that you will find the mastery that you seek."

"Yes, Francis."

"I have something else for you," Francis noted. "We'll spend a week on wilderness survival skills. You'll learn about fishing and hunting, water and shelter, making traps and snares, and how to move stealthily to avoid detection."

"I can learn all that in a week?" Anton asked incredulously.

"You will learn enough to make a difference, consider it a crash course, and there will be a test in three weeks' time."

"Where are we going?"

"About fifteen miles, due west, toward Mount Washington."

"Great, when do we start?"

"Now."

"Oh, is my gear in that backpack?" Anton asked.

"No, that is my gear."

"Do I have any gear?"

"Just what you're wearing."

"Oh ... Okay."

"Let's move it," Francis directed. "... Wait a second, you're the one carrying the backpack."

"Oh, sorry, ah, your gear and all ... yes, Francis."

The floorboards in front of the door squeaked as the heavy backpack rose off the porch. Two pairs of footsteps tramped away from the front door. Squeaking porch floorboards replaced by crunching gravel before the footsteps receded into the distance.

Jay ascended to the upper floor and the room that he shared with Yvette. He kept a fully stocked backpack ready in his wardrobe at all times. After changing clothes to suit a wilderness expedition, he grabbed the pack and started downstairs.

Yvette stood at the foot of the stairs. Looking up at Jay as he descended, she inquired, "Where are you off to in such a hurry? We have a training session in just under an hour."

"I've gotta get away for a week."

"A week! Are you crazy? What for?"

"I really need time away, this whole thing with Anton Slayne showing up has thrown me for a loop. I need to get away and clear my head."

"Have you told Mom or Dad?"

Jay shook his head. "No, it's a spur of the moment thing."

Yvette frowned. "I hope this isn't about getting at Slayne? You know Mom has put a sanctuary on him."

"Yes, I know," Jay said, looking away. "This isn't about him."

"Well, I certainly hope so. I know how you feel, but going after Anton Slayne would be going way too far."

"Sure." Jay nodded. "I've just gotta get some time away and get my head around this."

Yvette moved to stand in front of him. They stared at each other for a brief moment. She reached up, throwing her arms around his neck and kissed him hard on his lips. Jay kissed her back.

"Don't forget that I love you, you big lunk."

Jay hugged her tight for a moment, whispering in her ear, "How could I ever forget." He kissed her again. "Love you too."

"So where are you going?"

"Just the forest, I won't be too far away," Jay said, gently moving past Yvette and making for the door.

"Okay, bye then," Yvette said, her voice betraying a mix of concern and annoyance.

"Bye," Jay said over his shoulder, and pushed the front door open. He strode across the porch and into the bright morning sunlight. He squinted for a moment from the glare, and then put a pair of sunglasses on before setting off for Mount Washington.

Anton's tracks would be easy enough to follow, and come the test – he would be waiting.

* * *

Old fluorescent tube lights attached to the ceiling illuminated the training barn in a soft pale light. The air was still and humid. The shutters along the walls lay open but gave little relief from the evening mid-summer heat.

Peter punched a pair of big steel hooks into a hay bale and twisted them so that they sat behind a slim rope that bound the hay together. He'd attached two ropes to the hooks. Anton held one of the ropes, and Peter joined him at the end of the other rope. Together they pulled on the ropes, dragging the hay bale across the floor of the barn. Once they got the bale to the other side of the barn, they worked together to flip it onto its long end. They repeated the same operation another nineteen times, constructing an eight-foot-high wall of hay around the barn, and leaving one corner bare.

Anton brushed the sweat off his forehead with his forearm. He pointed at the newly exposed door in the floor of the barn. "Hey, Peter, what's down there?"

"Our armory," Peter answered, brushing straw off the front of his faded New England Patriots T-shirt. "Now that you're finished being chased by bears in the woods, I've got some cool things to show you."

The door comprised two steel panels, clasped shut with a thick bolt. Peter dragged on the bolt which opened smoothly. Anton stepped around to the other panel, and grabbed hold of the handle opposite the one Peter held with his right hand. Peter nodded, and they lifted together.

Anton's panel barely moved, and he watched as Peter dragged his up and let it down slowly, so it didn't crash.

"Sure, you're not really a terminator from the future?"

"Yes, I'm sure." Peter shrugged. "Give it another go."

Anton repositioned to effectively use his thighs to help with moving the door, he also dropped into silence and activated the Ramp. Power flowed through his body as he pulled on the handle, the door moved up and over, and he quickly repositioned to guide it down to the floor.

"Good work Anton, we don't really need locks if a regular person has to use a winch to open the door."

Peter stepped into the open doorway and descended a stairway into the armory. Anton followed directly after him, his eyes wide open, taking in everything that he could see. By the time they were halfway down the stairs, a set of lights in the basement automatically switched on.

The space beneath the barn was huge. It was composed of cinder block walls and concrete floor, with a fifteen-foot-high ceiling, and long racks of equipment. Anton was amazed at the array of equipment. There were NBC and Ghillie suits, personal communication rigs, packs of dehydrated rations, water purifiers, combat armor, edged and blunt handheld weapons and long racks of military style guns. Peter led Anton between the racks, pointing out the equipment as they walked.

"Milkor MGLs are over here, next to the fire-retardant blankets and anti-smoke/gas rebreather masks."

"I've used the MGLs before," Anton noted. "What rounds do you have for them?"

"The usual. Silver flechettes, standard high-explosive shaped charge, thermobaric and unarmed training rounds."

Peter grabbed a pair of buckets, labeled M67 training grenades. Handing them to Anton, he said, "We'll need these later."

They came back down the other side of the rack. Anton read the labels on the equipment packing the rack: plastic explosives, detonators, live grenades, and rows of Heckler and Koch 416 assault rifles, and the larger H&K 417 Recon rifles.

Peter walked past the rifles and picked up a single H&K VP9 pistol and a couple of spare magazines loaded with 9mm rounds.

"I haven't seen that gun before," Anton said.

"It's very accurate."

"Don't we need two?"

"Nope, just one will do."

Anton stopped walking. "I have a sneaking suspicion about where this is going."

Peter raised his eyebrows and shrugged his shoulders. "I don't know what you mean."

"I haven't seen a gun in the last six weeks, and I hope that I'm not at the wrong end of target practice."

"Don't worry about it." Peter grinned wickedly and began ascending the stairs. "We'll mostly be playing around with the grenades tonight."

Peter and Anton picked up half a dozen variable lengths of five-inch rainwater downpipe. Someone had welded the pipes to foot-wide square steel plates.

Anton lifted one of the pipes and indicated the weld with a flick of his head. "Is this your work?"

Peter grinned. "Sure is. You know, everyone loves to practice their fighting skills, but someone has to know their way around a machine shop or absolutely nothing would work around here."

"I'm glad someone is looking after our gear."

"Thanks," Peter said and pointed to a location on the floor. "Now put that one over there."

Anton did as Peter asked, and moments later, they'd arranged the tubes in a wide circle around the barn.

"Okay, let's start," Peter directed. "Pass me a grenade."

Anton picked up a training grenade from a bucket and tossed it to Peter. He caught the grenade, dropped it over his shoulder, and kicked it with his heel. It flew in a loopy twenty-yard arc, dropping directly into a down pipe.

Anton burst out laughing and called out, "That's bloody awesome."

Dusting off his chest with his knuckles, Peter said dryly, "Stick with me kid, and one day, you too can be a certified genius."

Anton and Peter spent the next thirty minutes practicing trick shots with grenades. With each move, they would call out, "Three, two, one. Bang!" training reflexes to manage the timely throw of a grenade.

Peter clapped his hands together. "Time for some batting." He moved to collect grenades from the downpipes, putting them back into the buckets.

"Batting?" Anton asked, moving to help.

"Yeah. Stand over there," Peter directed, pointing to the middle of the barn.

Anton moved into position, surrounded by the circle of downpipes and the hay bale walls.

"Be prepared to Ramp – they will be coming in fast."

"Sure, okay, I'm—"

Peter blurred, a bucket tucked under one arm, he threw grenade after grenade directly at Anton. It was like a semi-automatic gun firing, there were three grenades in the air before the first one reached Anton.

Anton ramped, his hand whipping up to deflect the first grenade away. He swayed left and right, his hands blurring in front of him. Peter leaped into the air, throwing grenades straight at Anton. Anton stepped left, then back, then right, ducking and batting the grenades away. Landing, Peter ran out of grenades and came to a halt.

"Well, I started with twenty, how many are in the pipes."

"I counted fourteen in, and six out," Li observed.

Whirling around, Anton demanded, "Where did you come from?"

"Peter asked me to drop by about 9:30, he said you needed some extra motivation."

"Motivation?"

"Yeah. Next round of the game," Peter explained. He handing the now loaded H&K VP9 pistol to Li and picked up the second bucket of training grenades. "She shoots at you, while I throw grenades and we see how many you can get into the downpipes."

Li lined the gun up on the center of Anton's chest in a single smooth motion. He shivered, feeling sick to his stomach.

Anton took a deep breath. Li and Peter were watching him intently, both suddenly serious.

Get a grip, he told himself. *I've gotta deal with this, and better sooner than later.*

Anton grinned wryly. "Do me one favor, start with a grenade, and I'll ramp on that."

Li winked. "Got it."

Peter's hand blurred, and the first grenade flew toward Anton.

The H&K VP9 pistol barked, the bullet zipped through the space that Anton had just vacated.

The H&K VP9 had a fifteen-round clip. Li emptied the gun three times in the next ten minutes. After she'd fired the last round, there was a resounding cheer as all the grenades were in the downpipes.

Euphoria surged through Anton, and he grinned crookedly.

I'm back. I'm really back.

* * *

Francis handed Anton a hunting knife.

"The objective is clear," Francis declared. "Don't get caught. The rest of the team will be looking for you. You have an hour head start. Meet us back here in two days' time at sunset."

"What happens if I get caught?" Anton asked.

Francis frowned. "We send you straight back out for another two nights, and we start again."

"So, unless you like eating raw food and sleeping on the ground ..." Peter observed dryly. "You'd better get on with it."

Anton drew the knife from its sheath, turning it left and right. It gleamed in the early morning light, sharp and deadly. He replaced it back into its sheath and tucked it into his waist belt. He nodded. The force team had assembled in the forest clearing. Jay and Yvette both stood impassively, almost disinterested. Chiara looked back, her eyes twinkling with hidden thoughts. Peter and Li were both smiling like tigers about to go on a hunt. Francis and Juliette would drive the van back to the safe house. They would be back late on Sunday afternoon to pick everyone up.

The rest of the team wore comfortable clothes and practical shoes. They carried small backpacks, filled with food, water, medical supplies, and other useful items. Anton had the knife, a pair of loose pants, a black T-shirt and was barefoot.

Five versus one, an hour head start, don't get caught ... simple.

Anton studied the glade, it was deep in the White Mountain forest, a couple of hours slow drive from the safe house, there was an old, mostly overgrown track that disappeared deeper into the forest. It was the same territory that Francis had led him through during survival training two weeks before. He had a handful of ideas and options in mind for where to go and what to do.

He needed to stay hidden from just after eight on Friday morning to sunset on Sunday evening. He planned on not using the Ramp, it would be a marathon, not a sprint. Not wanting to give anything away, he jogged casually toward the overgrown track.

As Anton hit the edge of the glade, Peter called out, "Don't embarrass us by getting caught by tourists."

Anton called back over his shoulder, "Thanks, I'll keep that in mind."

"Just being helpful," Peter shouted.

Anton smirked for a moment as he ran, and then his smile faded. It was time to put some serious distance between himself and the team.

He moved onto the track proper, and in moments, the glade disappeared behind him. He accelerated his pace, narrowing his focus on gaining distance, and not leaving tracks. He considered his strategy as he ran. What would he have done if he was doing the chasing? Guard the water sources and wait for the target to show up. Water was a basic consideration for a sixty-hour stay in the forest. He didn't know if they would work as a coordinated team, or as sub-teams or singly. He knew that he would have to allow for any of those strategies.

The trees whipped past, and Anton made the most of his natural running ability to penetrate deep into the wilderness. He focused on using everything he'd learned from Francis nearly three weeks before about stealth and wilderness survival. With his mind buzzing with thoughts of what to do, Anton pushed toward the nearest mountain. The first hour flew past, and a single note from a gas-powered horn rang out far behind him.

It was time to mix it up. Anton changed course, making for a second mountain beyond the first.

The hunt had begun.

* * *

The waxing moon, just shy of being full, sailed on a river of night toward the horizon. Its pale light gleamed in the golden eyes of a Great Horned Owl. A mature female, her head rotated this way and that, watching the forest floor beneath her perch. She suddenly called out in high-pitched alarm, "Hoo, hoo, hoo, hoo, hoo." Then with a sudden movement, she spread her wings and swooped noiselessly away. Giving her territory to another predator who glided over the forest floor in near perfect silence.

Chloe Armitage, dressed in matte black combat fatigues, walked smoothly into the open glade. She paused for a moment in the center of the clearing. Listening carefully and sniffing the air. She stared at a mass of branches and leaves. Anton's camouflaged lean-to was directly in front of her. Anton's breathing was quiet, his heart beat slow and steady. His smell was distinctive and familiar to her senses. It was clear he'd been living and sleeping rough for more than a day.

Chloe had been in the forest for hours. She'd discovered the positions of five other Ramp initiates. She whispered, "I've found you but what are you doing out here?" she tilted her head quizzically. "Is the Mirovar force team hunting you? Hmmm, not quite. No, you're in training."

The nearest member of the Mirovar force team was more than six miles away. Too far away to help if Anton should scream. Chloe frowned, her eyes darkening. She whispered, "But why should you scream?"

She took a step closer to Anton's lean-to. She stared hard at the rough shelter. Anton lay beneath the branches. His chest slowly rising and falling. Hard muscle curving across his shoulders. The moonlight dappling his dark hair. He'd grown since the Boston docks. He was stronger, more powerful. Her nostrils flared, the scent of him was delicious. Ancient urges stirred in the back of Chloe's throat. A warm tingling rose from low in her body, filled her chest, and flared into urgent desire.

Chloe found herself on her knees, inches away from the edge of the lean-to. The air vibrated slightly with each of Anton's breaths. Her heart instinctively accelerated as she carefully and silently picked at the lean-to. She separated the branches and removed individual leaves. Her actions were quick and precise. In moments, there was a hole a foot and a half across in the lean-to. The moon was behind her, its light streaming through the hole and falling onto Anton's chest. She gazed longingly at his smooth skin, luminous with life, rich with throbbing veins filled with blood, energy, and power.

Oh my God, I have left it too long since I last fed. She shuddered with need; her eyes widened. Her blue eyes, dark as the ocean in the moonlight. Her fangs descended into their attack positions. Her left hand snaked forward through the hole and hovered over Anton's throat. Her thirst was a torrent. She could feed on him now. The beauty of his life, so rich and abundant, so succulent, so tempting.

Chloe's hand descended to an inch above Anton's throat. The warmth of his flesh radiating like a furnace. Her senses, alight and roaring in response to the life force she could feel within him. Desire sang through every fiber of her being. An urgent need to feed rushing through her. An exquisite agony that stormed and raged through her soul.

Her hand trembled slightly, she shuddered again, drawing in a quick breath. She had almost no time left before her thirst would overwhelm her.

Chloe stared at Anton, her eyes filled with intense purpose riding over rampaging need, she whispered passionately, "Crane is my enemy. Crane ordered the murder of my parents. Crane is my enemy."

Anton stirred, frowning in his sleep.

She exhaled a slow sigh. Her hand moving instinctively, sliding her index finger over Anton's cheek, from the edge of his full mouth to the corner of his right eyebrow. Her skin tingled with the touch, a current flowing from Anton, through her hand, and deep into her body.

Chloe blurred backward to the center of the glade, her eyelids fluttering, her mouth an open circle. She shivered with unfamiliar terror and desire. She shook her head once as if to clear it. Turning away from Anton and the distant Mirovar force team members, she faced decisively to the west. A distant flashlight flickered on the edge of her supernatural vision. Murder filled her soul, extinguishing all other lights.

"Tourists! What a dreadful fate! Dismembered by a bear!" she whispered harshly.

She vanished into the forest.

* * *

A quick seven-mile run and I will be back at the pickup point.

Anton ran at a brisk pace down a stone track, the late afternoon sun warm on his back. To his left, old growth forest composed mostly of red pine hugged the side of the mountain, to his right, open ground led to a cliff edge and a sheer drop.

I can use this track to cut past the glade and come in from the far side, I will be able to approach parallel with the vehicle access track. The rest of the team will be pulling back by now. We're going to crowd the pickup point. I will have to—

A shape blurred out from behind a thick tree trunk and tackled him hard from the left. The momentum of the hit carried both men to the cliff edge, pushing Anton into the open air. He reached back hard toward his assailant, but he deflected Anton's hand away. With nothing to hold on to, Anton began dropping down the sheer rock wall.

Surging fear ripped through him, freezing his mind. Fighting vampires armed with the Blue Dragon was one thing, falling helplessly was another. His arms started flailing. Reaching wildly for the rock wall, his fingertips brushed over smooth rock which began to accelerate past him.

His fear morphed into rage. A diamond-hard light exploding behind his eyes. He ramped wildly. Time slowed to a crawl. His eyesight clarified, the rock wall a yard in front of him snapping into razor sharp detail. The rock face was smooth, his hands brushed over it, once, twice, three times without finding any purchase.

Beneath him stretched a long, deadly fall, hundreds of yards onto bare rocks.

A thin shadow appeared opposite his knees. A fine horizontal crack in the rock, rushing upward past him. There was a single chance. He punched forward with his right hand; his fingers hard and tight like a knife. They penetrated into the inch-high space to the end of the second knuckle. His body kept falling. Anton put everything into holding his grip on the rock face. Heat surged along his arm. His hand fixed in place within the rock wall. With a crack, he thumped into the sheer rock face. A jagged jolt of agony ripped along his arm, but his grip held.

Drawing a shuddering breath, Anton held onto the rock face with the four fingers of his right hand, he scrabbled about with his left hand for something else to hold onto, finding nothing.

"Damn it, you're still alive." Growled a voice above him.

Anton looked up.

Jay peered over the cliff edge at him. His face frozen with grim determination. He turned away and disappeared.

Anton glanced down and to both sides, the rock wall was almost completely sheer. The little hole he'd filled with his fingers, a rare imperfection. Footsteps approached, and he looked up. Jay launched a rock the size of a basketball directly at his head.

The stone rushed toward him with tremendous speed.

Anton ramped again, wild, powerful, fast. His left hand swept up, deflecting the rock harmlessly past him.

"Why won't you die?" Jay cried out; his voice filled with frustration.

"Jay, you don't want to do this, you're not a murderer."

A hard smile twisted Jay's face, and he snapped, "Don't speak to me."

"I know you think my grandfather murdered your mother."

Jay vanished, his voice lingering above the cliff edge. "I don't think it, I know it."

Damn it, he'll be getting more rocks or something worse.

Anton envisioned Jay returning with a thick tree branch. A solid branch would wipe him off the rock wall like a windscreen wiper cleaning off a crushed bug.

Jay reappeared at the edge, and a volley of rocks the size of oranges flew down at Anton. He ramped again, batting and deflecting, but his position remained horribly exposed, and the last stone got through his defenses, glancing across the side of his head. Pain flared through his skull, and he groaned loudly.

Jay laughed bitterly.

Yvette's voice called out from some distance away, "Jay, what's holding you up, we're running out of time."

Anton looked up. Jay's face was torn with indecision. He called out, "Jay, I'm not my grandfather!"

Jay's face hardened. "The Slaynes are murderers, you'll kill us all one day." He turned and moved out of sight. His footsteps ran down the track and faded into silence.

Blood trickled down the side of Anton's neck from the cut in his scalp. Since he couldn't do anything about it, he ignored it.

Anton looked around himself again. The stone wall above him was smooth, unscalable, there could be no escape that way. He looked below him, after a handful of seconds, he spotted another hole similar to the one he was holding onto with increasingly numb fingers. It was fifteen yards below him and about four yards to his left. He was beginning to lose his grip on the rock wall. He pushed with his left and swung back to get some momentum. Launching himself diagonally across and down the rock face, falling and twisting he struck out with his left hand and gripped the hole. He thumped hard into the rock wall with the left side of his body.

He flexed the fingers of his right hand, he had to rest them for half a minute before he could make his next move. As they recovered, he scanned the rock wall below him and spotted more handholds. He decided on his next move, twelve yards down and three to the right. He took it, leaping and catching the handhold and again thumping hard into the rock face.

He paused for a moment, breathing deeply. He could feel the blood running down his neck from the scalp wound. He took another huge breath; he could see his way out. Seven minutes later, Anton reached the bottom, bruised, sore, but alive. He judged the way back to the glade from where he was. He smiled, there was a way to sneak in from this angle that most likely remained unguarded. Jay had inadvertently done him a favor.

Anton took off his black T-shirt. Folding it diagonally, he made a rough bandage. He wrapped it around his skull, covering the cut on his scalp over his right ear. Pulling the knot tight, he loped off through the forest toward the pickup point in the glade.

Jay is going to be very surprised when I show up on time. But what on Earth am I going to do about him? He wants to kill me, even though he knows it's wrong. I've got to find a way to get through to him. I can't let this continue to fester, or one of us is going to kill the other one.

Chapter Ten

Where are the homeless disappearing to?

By Ralph Crawley | Mercury Correspondent AUGUST 5,

Anecdotal evidence continues to mount that something is happening to the homeless of Boston.

We have empty rooms in our shelter, I have never seen that before, said Samantha Laney from the Lighthouse Center Homeless Shelter in a phone interview on Friday night.

Quite a few of the people that we normally help are simply no longer there, said Jordan Rumsey of the Boston chapter of Meals for the Needy in a phone interview Saturday morning.

There has been no increase in missing person reports, but we are continuing to monitor the situation, said Boston police spokesman, Harold Jacobs in a phone interview Saturday afternoon.

It remains to be seen if the homeless of Boston are simply moving on in search of better opportunities, or if something more sinister is occurring. Only time will tell, but whatever happens, it will be faithfully reported by this newspaper.

– Boston Mercury Newspaper article on the Internet.

* * *

Dorchester, Boston, August 6th, 23:00

It was eight weeks since Ramin Kain's meeting with Cornelius Crane, and just over a month since the arrival of the text message alerting him to the creation of a new coven of vampires in Boston.

Ramin had waited for the reports to begin. The rumors of missing persons on social media. The sober news reports of disappearances in the mainstream media and the hysterical accusations on the Internet of UFOs, alien body snatchers, vampires, bogeymen and government conspiracies. The atmosphere in Boston had taken a turn for the worse. There was an air of uncertainty. People would pause and hesitate. They would look a second time for a lurking danger. There was a loss of confidence. A reluctance to be out alone at night. A nervous fear of an unknown threat.

The fruit provided by Cornelius Crane had ripened and was ready to harvest.

Ramin glanced at his watch, it was an hour before midnight. He sat in the driver's seat of a nondescript, gray Ford sedan. A one-way dark film that made it difficult for anyone, man or vampire, to see into the interior covered the car's windows. Next to Ramin, sat Samuel Luther. They wore casual clothes, wrap-around light amplifying night glasses, and wireless headphone sets. Their heads slowly scanned left and right as they hunted for vampires in a neighborhood that was falling rapidly into ruin.

Ramin turned a knob on a black metal box sitting on the dashboard and inquired, "Did you hear that?"

"No," Sam averred. "Wait ... yes, what is it?"

"Digging! We need to move."

Ramin kicked over the engine and took off slowly. Gently accelerating, he drove about four hundred yards before pulling to a stop at a crossroads. He turned the knob on the box again, listening intently.

"We got em."

The box displayed coordinates in green writing on a small LED screen.

Sam entered the numbers into a program on his smartphone and declared quietly, "They're half a mile from here."

"They could notice the car. We'll leave it here and approach on foot," Ramin directed. He killed the engine and punched a button to unlock the car's trunk.

Ramin and Sam exited the car and circled around to the back. Ramin opened the trunk, revealing an extensive cache of equipment. They put on broad-brimmed hats. Strapped swords at their waists. Fitted Glock 9mm pistols loaded with silver bullets at their belts, and put on long dark coats to hide all the weaponry. Sam picked up a solid black case and Ramin softly closed the trunk. They turned as one, crossed the road and headed off down the street.

Five minutes at a brisk pace put them two hundred yards short of their target location. They slowed down to a gentle walk. They wore stealthy padded-soled boots, their clothing was neat and tidy, with their equipment held close to their bodies. They moved with barely a rustle along the deserted street.

Abandoned houses and derelict apartment blocks littered the street. The flotsam and jetsam of a decaying suburb. Only one in three street lights still functioned, their wan yellow light barely illuminating the sidewalks beneath them.

Ramin went to put his foot down and suddenly halted. Pushing backward, he maintained his balance. Sam sidled up behind him. Ramin stepped around a handful of spray paint cans and a black tote bag lying on the sidewalk. He studied the wall briefly, an unfinished graffiti mural of ghosts rising from tombstones covered half of it.

Not half bad, Ramin thought. *Too bad you picked the worst place in Boston to practice your art.*

Ramin turned to Sam. He pointed at the artwork on the brick wall and then at the cans, before silently making a two-fingered stabbing motion at his throat.

Vampire attack!

Sam nodded. Frowning, he looked at a map displayed on his smartphone. Lifting his right hand, fingers stiff, he pointed across the street toward a large five-story apartment block. The target building lay shielded by a thick line of trees and a row of shorter two-story buildings facing onto the street. The target was a hundred yards away. Beyond it was the Neponset River and an expressway. It looked like it would be a maze of rooms and a difficult target to attack.

Ramin continued forward, looking for a good location to stake out the target. He ducked down a side street that passed the near end of the target building. He jogged toward a water tower rising over the suburb. Ramin and Sam reached the base of the tower. They could hear the faint hum of the pumps. The water tower was still functional. They checked the ground-level entrance and a thick padlock secured the door. Ramin examined the padlock for a moment, the hint of a smile curling the edges of his lips. The tower could prove to be very useful.

Three yards to the right of the door, a weathered set of metal stairs started ten feet off the ground and snaked upward around the tower. Ramin glanced at Sam, nodded once, ramped and leaped up onto the stairs. Sam followed and in a handful of seconds they were at the top of the tower.

The location was perfect. The top of the water tower was fifteen yards across, surrounded by a four-foot-high parapet. In front of them squatted the derelict five-story apartment block. Behind them was the expressway, running with sparse, late Sunday night traffic. The expressway bridged the Neponset River.

Ramin stared intently at the decrepit building. He was certain it harbored a fresh coven of newly turned vampires within its rotten bowels.

Sam placed the black case quietly on the concrete top of the tower and opened it. Inside was an array of high-tech surveillance equipment. Three minutes later he had a suite of sensors arrayed on the top of the parapet. In a handful of seconds, the microphones and spectrum analyzers had picked up noises in the depths of the apartment block, providing a visual representation of the noise locations on a small six by nine-inch screen. Sam twirled a knob and the image on the screen resolved into ghostly human forms. Metadata appeared next to the forms in small red letters and numbers that read, 'Sub-37 Vampire.'

Ramin whispered, "Map it."

Sam nodded, adjusting the equipment. A minute later he packed the equipment carefully back into the case. They descended the water tower with gentle steps and crept away.

A quarter of an hour later they were driving toward New York City, all their equipment stowed in the car's trunk.

"They're burying their victims in the basement," Ramin observed sagely. "We've found four vamps."

"Definitely four," Sam agreed.

"It's a big coven. We haven't had a find like this for over a year."

"You're a genius RK." Sam gushed. "Where would the Order be without you?"

"Quite so, Sam. If everyone had the wit to see it your way, my job would be a lot simpler."

"Who will you send?"

"Mirovar, it has to be Mirovar's team."

"It's about time they did something useful."

"Yes, Sam – quite so – it is time for them to do something useful."

A slow smile crept across Ramin's face as the car rushed away from Boston.

* * *

Ramin Kain locked the front door of his Manhattan penthouse. He glanced at his watch, it read 04:04. He rubbed his forehead, sighing deeply. It had been a long night driving back from Boston.

Kicking off his boots, he walked in his socks to a climate-controlled cabinet. He opened it and spent half a second making a decision. He selected a vintage Shiraz, pulled the cork and poured himself a large glass of wine. He went to a long lounge and sat down in the middle of it. Sniffing the wine deeply, he took a full mouthful, swished it around in his mouth and drank it down. He sighed again and drank a second mouthful. Setting the glass aside, he lay back on the lounge and opened his smartphone.

The old bloodsucker should still be awake. He dialed Cornelius Crane's smartphone.

"Ramin Kain," Crane answered, his voice carrying the barest hint of interest. "To what do I owe the pleasure at this late hour."

"I've found the Boston coven, and I will use the Mirovar force team to wipe them out."

"And this matters to me?"

"I am willing to provide you with the exact time of the attack by Mirovar's team."

"Indeed … and what will this information cost me?"

"Nothing at all, this is pure mutual advantage. We both need Mirovar out of the picture. He is a thorn in your side and an embarrassment to me."

"Go on, is there anything else."

"Anton Smith, he is a favorite of Mirovar and a born troublemaker. He has to go."

"The boy who was at the Boston dock, why him in particular?"

"He's dangerous, he loves Mirovar and will take everything that Mirovar stands for forward. They both have to go at the same time. With them out of the way, I can disperse the rest of the Mirovar team amongst force leaders of proven loyalty, and the virus of Mirovar's traditionalism will die out."

"Ramin, I'm surprised. Surely you can clean your own house without my help?" Crane observed sardonically.

"This is not a matter of house cleaning," Ramin retorted.

"Then what is it?" Crane inquired; his voice laced with curiosity.

"Smith! … Juliette Mirovar has given him sanctuary."

Crane laughed. "Oh, well, that does change things. Why did she do that?"

Ramin rolled his eyes and snapped, "Hell, I don't know. A moment of madness?"

"Well, he is out of range now, touch him, and you touch her. More than half the Order would be baying for your blood. She's a legend in her own lifetime," Crane noted, chuckling wickedly for a long moment.

Ramin scowled, drinking another mouthful of Shiraz, suddenly the wine tasted sour in his mouth, he grimaced and swallowed it quickly.

"How long would you last?" Crane asked rhetorically between chuckles. "What? Less than twenty-four hours I would think."

Crane burst out laughing.

The bastard. The fucking bastard.

"Can't we focus on the deal?" Ramin growled bitterly.

Crane continued to laugh as if captured by some great mania.

Ramin fumed as Crane slowly regained his composure.

"Okay, okay … you've come to me to sort your problems out," Crane observed dryly, his voice filled with delight.

Ramin sighed, he knew this part of the deal was going to hurt.

"Shutdown your operations in the northeast, pull everyone back west of Michigan and south of Illinois."

"That's too much!"

"You can do this without me?"

Ramin paused for a long moment, thinking furiously about how he could sell such a large loss of territory to the rest of the Order. A desperate plan came to mind. There would need to be a rebuilding phase. A tactical withdrawal to consolidate forces after the tragic and untimely loss of Francis Mirovar.

Ramin's eyes widened. "I agree to your terms."

"Then, we have a deal. However, I will offer you a caveat."

"Yes?"

"Bring me the head of Arthur Slayne, and I will grant you back your territory."

"Done," Ramin snapped eagerly.

"Indeed – we have an agreement, now to tactics."

"I will send you details of the attack once they're known," Ramin said. "I will be in a position to directly tip off your forces."

"I will provide you with a quantum address to use to send messages to my praetorians," Crane instructed.

"Agreed."

"We're done. Goodbye Ramin," Crane declared, hanging up the call.

Ramin smirked, and declared to the empty room, "Well, that was expensive, but I'll be rid of Francis Mirovar and Anton Slayne. I can disperse the rest of the Mirovar team throughout the Order."

Ramin leaned back on the lounge and proceeded to finish the bottle of Shiraz, dreaming of consolidating control of the Order of Thoth within his hands. His desire for power and control was so fierce that he could taste it. He reached for a remote, and flicked a switch, a moment later, the crystal-clear sounds of Beethoven's Ninth Symphony, fourth movement filled his penthouse. He waved his hands to the music as if conducting an Orchestra, careless of the half-filled glass of red wine in his right hand.

Vintage Shiraz spilled across the carpet. Ramin, his eyes closed, swayed in silence, drunk on his ambitions.

* * *

Cornelius hung up the call and chuckled again.

He hadn't laughed like that for decades. What an ass Kain was. Such a temporary little man filled with vainglorious ambition.

Cornelius leaned back in his chair and stroked his chin. Kain was desperate over something. It had to be something critical to him to put a whole force team at risk. Was it about the boy from Boston? Kain had tried to hide the introduction of the assassination of the boy as if it was an afterthought – clearly, it wasn't. He'd worked up to the boy, asking for the lesser thing first. In fact, the boy's death was more important to Kain than Mirovar's death.

Why would Anton Smith be so important to Kain?

Cornelius considered his options. He reached toward a panel on his desk and flipped a switch. "Ursula, please place a call to Centurion Rawlings, I will need three praetorian sniper teams for insertion into Boston at short notice."

"Yes, Sir," his secretary responded immediately.

Cornelius grinned wolfishly. Here was the perfect opportunity to take out the whole of the Mirovar force team in one operation. It would balance the ledger after the losses at Boston. With surprise and tactical awareness of the ground on the side of the vampires, victory would be swift and certain. Kain had clearly failed to understand the shift that had occurred after the delivery of the Slaynes and the Papyrus of Hakron the Scribe. He'd warned Kain he had less to offer, but he hadn't adjusted his strategy.

Kain was a fool who expected the future to be like the past.

Cornelius was not willing to risk failure. He contacted his secretary again. "Wait, Ursula, ask Centurion Rawlings to take personal command of the mission."

"Yes, Sir, three sniper teams commanded by Centurion Rawlings, the message has been passed on."

"Thank you, Ursula, that will be all for tonight."

Cornelius pursed his lips, struck by a disturbing thought.

Anton Smith's secrets will die with him, but even a dead man's secrets can come back to haunt us all.

The uncertainty around Anton Smith remained unresolved. It nagged at his mind, draining his good humor at Kain's obvious discomfort.

Pushing back his chair, Cornelius stood up and stepped away from his desk. His gaze lingered on the array of books within his great library. He walked to the stacks, selecting one of his privately commissioned works. Over the centuries, he'd selected authors to write unique works. There would be a single copy, and he would be the sole owner. It was time to revise a masterwork.

Cornelius smiled grimly as he walked to his bedroom with 'The Discovery of Betrayal' by Sir Francis Walsingham, spymaster for Queen Elizabeth the First.

* * *

The early August pre-dawn light promised a bright day to come.

Anton walked to the training barn for the next session of physical conditioning. Juliette fell in beside him. She handed him a glass bottle filled with a dark brown fluid. Anton took hold of the bottle. It steamed lightly, stinking of rotting vegetables and burnt mushrooms.

302

"What is it?" Anton asked. Sniffing dubiously at the concoction. "I hope you're not going to ask me to drink it!"

"It's a restorative," Juliette asserted. She smiled, gesturing a 'bottoms up' motion with her right hand. "You've only had one night to recuperate from your long run. This will help a lot."

Anton scrunched up his nose. "It smells foul."

Juliette grinned. "It tastes terrible but is incredibly effective. Just drink it quickly."

Anton frowned for a second, shrugged his shoulders and drank the bottle to its last dregs. The fluid was hot, thick and sludgy, and a pervasive warmth began spreading out from his middle.

"Oh my God, that's disgusting!" Anton declared, handing the empty bottle back to Juliette.

Anton looked at his hands. "My fingers are tingling, is that normal."

"Sure," Juliette said, patting him on the shoulder. "That effect will only last a few seconds."

Anton shook his hands as if drying them. Licking his lips, he said with a shrug, "Yeah. It's gone now, and so is the taste."

"Excellent."

Anton moved to go into the barn where the rest of the team were limbering up. Juliette pulled him aside and said, "A quick word Anton, I just wanted to say that you have been progressing really well, which is great to see."

"Thank you."

"You know, you're much like your grandfather."

"Is that a good thing?" Anton asked doubtfully.

"Arthur Slayne was my teacher, he has skills that I haven't been able to master. He is an exceptional man, and the man I know is not a murderer. It is good that you take after him."

"You have a lot of faith in him."

"More knowledge than faith," Juliette said with a soft smile. She looked intently into Anton's eyes, speaking with quiet conviction. "Arthur Slayne is a great servant of the Order of Thoth. You have every right to be proud of him."

A long silent moment passed between them. She reached up, hugging him tightly, and whispered, "You'll be okay Anton, it'll all work out in the end."

Anton hugged her back, a soft warmth flowing between them. His eyes moistened. Letting her go, he stepped away, a crooked grin playing at the edges of his mouth. "I better get to training."

"Yes, Anton. That's best," Juliette agreed with a warm smile.

Anton walked into the training barn. He grinned broadly as he saw his teammates. A rush of euphoric joy exploded through his chest. They were all such great people, much more than friends, they were brothers and sisters in arms. He knew without a shadow of a doubt that he would rather give his own life than see any of them come to harm.

Anton looked at Li and really saw her beauty, grace, and wisdom. Peter was standing next to her, with his easy-going grin, courageous, generous and loyal. Jay, poker-faced, stood to the side, his mind sharp and fast like his sword work, a natural leader carrying a dreadful wound. Yvette, standing at Jay's side, lovely, purposeful, and protective. Chiara, next to Yvette, sensual, mercurial, and mysterious.

Anton's emotions surged, swirling around in a chaotic vortex.

I'm all over the place, why is that?

Suddenly his knees wobbled, the ground rose up to meet him, and his world faded to black.

* * *

Anton awoke into darkness.

It was pitch black. Someone had jammed cloth into his mouth and bound it there with gaffer tape. A thick hood completely covered his head. Strong hands dragged him across the yard. He could feel the gravel tearing at his feet. He tried to move, twisting and bucking against the powerful grips holding him. His feet and hands were bound with what felt like rope and try as he might he could not break free.

What the hell's going on? There are two of them, one on each side. I've got to do something quick.

Stilling the surging panic in his mind, Anton fell into silence. He tucked his feet under himself and ramped. Pushing hard, he jackknifed upward. The grip on his right loosened, his heart leaped with hope, but the grip on the left tightened like an immovable rock, and he crashed back to the ground. A third assailant grabbed his ankles, and lifted him aloft. Unable to gain purchase and leverage, his captors rendered him helpless.

Where is everyone? He screamed silently.

The trio carried Anton another thirty yards and threw him down. He expected to hit the ground, but there was nothing there. He kept falling for another couple of yards before crashing onto something solid. Sucking air into his lungs, the earthy scent of wet clay assaulted his nostrils. He thrashed about, the smell got stronger, a terrifying realization cut through him as he dropped out of the Ramp.

Oh, my God, I'm in a pit.

Something landed on his back. Shovels struck the ground above him, an unnaturally fast staccato rhythm. Great clods of earth fell on top of him, pummeling him like fists.

They're burying me alive.

More earth, clay, and soil landed on top of him. In moments, the weight of the soil became oppressive. He could feel the hood closing in around his face.

I'm going to suffocate. There is no time. I must break this rope!

Anton took a breath, the hood dragging in close to his nostrils. He knew it was his last breath inside the pit. Closing his eyes, relaxing his muscles, his heart slowed. Silence rushed into his mind. Cold silvery fire surged from a point three inches in front of the base of his spine and arced along his limbs. He rested deeper into the silence. Time gave way, slowing down as his mind accelerated to a level he'd never reached before. Energy flowed through his body. His skin tingling as power coiled like a thousand forged springs tighter and tighter. He relaxed further, and terror fled. There was only the present moment, the pressure of the earth above him, and the power of the Ramp.

Anton flexed, energy unleashing like a bolt of lightning throughout his body.

There was a thunderous crack, like a shotgun firing next to his ear — something had broken.

His hands and feet were free.

Staying deep within the Ramp, power flowed, inexhaustible and pure. He pushed hard against the earth, and the mass of soil above him rose up. He scrambled in that split second where the earth and clay, seemingly ignoring gravity, floated above him. Getting his feet beneath him, he kicked as hard as he could. Reaching up he pushed through the loosened earth. He struck out blindly, his right hand reaching the lip of the pit, his fingers clawing into the gravel and clay. A moment later, his left hand went past it and found purchase as it dug into the ground. Surging violently upward, the soil above him flew into the air as he burst out of the pit.

Dragging off the hood, he ripped away the gag. He landed in a half-crouch on the familiar gravel of the yard, facing away from the safe house. His eyes blazing, his nostrils flaring, sucking in air, he whirled around.

Anton's heart froze.

"Oh, no!" he moaned in anguish.

* * *

It was deep night, a full moon sailed high overhead. A single light globe over the front door of the safe house competed with the moon to illuminate the yard.

In front of the safe house, Li, Peter, and Chiara lay in pools of blood, surrounded by their weapons. Peter had the tail end of a crossbow bolt jutting out of his forehead, his face unrecognizable beneath the gore. Li and Chiara lay face down on the gravel, their clothes bloodied and torn.

Beyond them, stood two praetorians in full combat armor and tactical helmets. Their mirrored visors were down, cruelly reflecting the broken bodies lying on the ground. They were carrying FN P90 submachine guns, and swords strapped to their waists. The smaller of the two praetorians fired first. The submachine gun ripping into life, smoke issuing from its barrel in gray blooms as each round cracked through the night.

Already fully ramped, Anton twisted his right side back, watching the first rounds fly past. The vampire responded by tracking his movement. Anton blurred forward veering to his left, tracers and bullets zipping through the air on his right.

He ran to where Li lay face down in a pool of blood, the Green Dragon lying naked next to her. Voiceless rage flooded through his soul like a freight train from hell. Moving instinctively and beyond all reason. He cartwheeled over the Green Dragon, picking it up and throwing it at the vampires in a single motion.

The Green Dragon gleamed in the sparse light. A silvery whirling shaft of edged death spinning toward the vampires like a divine scythe. It cut through the gun smoke which eddied and swirled around it. The praetorians violently fell away to the left and right. Blood splashed in the grim light. The blade clipping the taller of the two vampires on the shoulder.

The wounded vampire recovered immediately. He dragged his weapon up, stepping forward he fired at Anton. The second vampire regained their balance, running further to Anton's right, straight-arming their submachine gun and firing single handed. Bullets were flying at Anton from both directions. He leaped, tumbling and rolling past where Peter lay. Peter's sword and battle axe were on the ground, dropped from his dead hands. Positioned between the vampires, Anton picked up both weapons and threw them in opposite directions at the same time. The shooting stopped as the vampires dodged aside. Anton blurred to where Chiara lay face down on the gravel, scooping up her sword in a single fluid motion as more bullets began to whip past him.

With Chiara's sword in hand, Anton blurred forward in an arc, ending back near the pit. The move put the smaller of the two praetorians between the other vampire and himself. Advancing upon the closer vampire, he realized from their body shape that they must be a woman. She dropped the empty FN P90, swiftly dragging out her sword. Anton pressed his attack, he only had a moment to defeat her before the second vampire repositioned to attack with gun, blade or both.

Ramp and rage combined, barely holding back a storm of grief. Anton couldn't think the words, 'Li is dead.' He hurled himself forward, silence flooding his torn mind like a tidal wave through a broken dam wall. Power surged through his body, Chiara's sword moving so fast it was barely visible. The vampire retreated, blurring backward, her sword dancing, blocking, parrying – defending with everything she had – it was not enough. Anton lunged through her defenses, his strike piercing through her sword arm, her blade flying away from suddenly nerveless fingers.

She took another step backward, her arm coming free from his sword. Anton stepped forward, his blade blurring again, lunging straight for her heart. She started a desperate, madly defensive open hand parry of the sword blade.

A second blade caught his sword in a shower of sparks, the two blades pushing up, high into the air. The other praetorian was between them, his armored fist flashing forward, expertly catching Anton on the side of his head.

Thrown to the side, Anton fell once more into darkness.

* * *

Anton snapped awake to icy cold water splashing on his face. He was lying on the bare ground of the training barn floor. He blinked for a moment, his eyes stinging from the freezing water and the sudden glare of the overhead lights. Wiping his face once with his hand, the horror came back with a rush.

Li is dead! The thought ripped through his soul.

His heart skipped a beat before razor sharp claws of outraged grief shredded it.

Not again.

He blinked, something big moved above him, shadowing his face from the lights, it resolved into a familiar form.

"Peter?!"

"Hey, Anton," Peter greeted him, grinning broadly.

Anton leaped to his feet and whirled around. Li and Chiara were standing side by side in torn clothes soaked in blood. They looked at him with concern written all over their faces. Peter grinned at him; his face edged with traces of blood as if he'd given it a half-hearted wipe with a wet towel. The back six inches of a crossbow bolt stuck out from the front of his forehead. Under the bright lights, Anton could see the thin, flesh-colored straps holding the bolt to Peter's head.

Francis stood opposite Peter; his face impassive.

For a long moment, Anton was speechless, his mouth opening and closing like a beached fish. His emotions swirled and roiled before relief won through and he pushed past Peter, hugging Li for all he was worth.

Li hugged him back, sweet silence filling the spaces between them, and he whispered, "Oh my God, please never do that again."

"Never, I promise," Li whispered back.

Anton let Li go, turning to face Francis he stated with quiet intensity, "A test?"

"Yes."

Anton sighed. He knew that he just had to deal with it. Whatever was necessary to take down Chloe Armitage, the Vampire Dominion and especially – Cornelius Crane.

Anton asked curtly, "Did I pass?"

A faint smile curled the edges of Francis' mouth. "That remains to be seen."

Anton shook his head. "Juliette gave me a drug, didn't she?"

"Yes," Francis agreed.

"It wasn't a restorative?"

"Correct. It was a psychoactive compound that makes it easier for you to believe in what you are seeing. The effect has worn off now."

Anton bit back a snark-filled comment. He took a deep breath, released it and said, "Okay. Okay, I get it. I'm the new kid, so this is just typical stuff that everyone has to go through."

Anton looked at the faces around him, they were quietly shaking their heads; even Peter was frowning, his face speaking volumes.

"Your kidding – this was just for me?" Anton asked incredulously.

"Anton," Francis explained calmly. "You're a special case, we had to do—"

"I'm a special case?" Anton interrupted, his efforts at remaining calm starting to fray.

Francis put up his hands and shook his head. "Yes. Few people are switched on with the pressure point technique. Everyone else here has over a decade of training and are well known to us, you're not."

Anton stared at Francis. "C'mon Francis, you know me! I'm not keeping any secrets, I'm an open book."

"I believe in you, Anton, but I don't know you fully. We had to test you before you go into combat with the team."

"I can fight."

"That's clear Anton, but that's not the question."

"What's the question?"

"Will you keep your head—"

"While those about me are losing theirs?"

Francis nodded. "Precisely."

Anton realized that Francis was worried about him cracking up under pressure.

"Now please take off your shirt," Francis directed, indicating Anton's clothes with his right hand.

Memories of Gang hitting his chest to switch on his Ramp capability flooded Anton's mind. He took off his shirt and was surprised to discover a dozen white dots the size of his thumb, stuck to his skin. They had tiny red lights in their centers that blinked steadily with the beat of his heart. He was starting to get the picture. He sighed and asked expectantly, "You had me wired?"

"Monitored," Francis corrected. Moving in, he peeled the dots from Anton's skin.

"Turn around please."

Anton turned, and Francis collected another dozen patches.

"Done," Francis declared, tapping Anton on the shoulder. "Now have a shower, drink plenty of water and get some sleep, it's past two in the morning."

Peter clapped Anton on the shoulder, and said, "You aced it mate, nothing to worry about."

Anton gave him a dark look for a moment, then sighed. "What the hell. I'm starving."

"We have some pork fillets I picked up from the White Hill butchers this morning."

"Of course," Anton looked hard at the traces of blood on Peter's face, "pig's blood?"

"Yeah. A couple of big buckets worth."

"I don't want to know," Anton noted. Reaching up, he ripped off the fake crossbow bolt, which came free with a snap.

"Hey!" Peter yelped.

"Suck it up, princess. I think you owe me one for this."

Peter laughed, pushing Anton playfully toward the barn door. Li and Chiara were already halfway across the yard with Francis. Anton and Peter followed them.

"Where's everyone else?" Anton asked.

"Jay and Yvette are getting patched up by Juliette," Peter observed.

"Oh," Anton grunted. "Jay's going to be pretty upset with me stabbing Yvette in the arm."

Peter shrugged his shoulders. "He knew the risks, he volunteered for the role."

"Probably enjoyed shooting at me."

Peter pulled Anton abruptly to a stop and declared firmly, "He's not allowed to shoot you. Remember the impact of the drug. They were deliberately shooting past you, just close enough to allow you to believe it was real. They both shed blood tonight to allow Francis and Juliette to test your responses under stress. I suggest you think about that."

Peter turned back to the safe house, and said with a lighter tone, "Let's get inside, I've a delicious Cajun spice that will be great with the fillets."

"Sure," Anton agreed, his stomach growling and his mind buzzing with thoughts. It was one shock after another. He felt stupid to allow himself to feel comfortable at the safe house. Could he trust Juliette and Francis? He had to, there was no one else. They would not have done something this extreme unless they believed it was absolutely necessary. The fact that they had done it said a lot about how bad the threat must be.

Anton stood still for a second. Struck by the question – *am I the risk?*

Nameless emotions overwhelmed him. He clenched his fists, then relaxed them, taking a couple of deep breaths. Peter was a step ahead, pushing through the front door and didn't see his reaction. He was suddenly very much alone.

Mom, Dad, Gang … I miss you all … I miss my old life.

* * *

Francis sat opposite Juliette in the briefing room. The doors stood closed and locked, ensuring they remained alone. Juliette's fingers flashed over the keyboard of her laptop, projecting a graph onto a white screen hanging on the wall.

"What have we got here?" Francis asked, frowning at the graph.

"It's extraordinary," Juliette declared, using a red laser pointer to indicate an early section of the graph. "Anton goes off the chart right here, when he's buried in the pit."

"Li confirmed that Anton was switched on by Gang on the fifth of May," Francis noted. "It's now the eighth of August, he's completed the physical transformations of the Ramp."

"This is more than physical transformation, there were over fifteen hundred pounds of soil on top of him, and he's pushed it aside like it wasn't there."

"Hmmm … where does this place him relative to Order norms?"

"Top ten percent on a sustained basis, and top one percent on bursts."

Francis stared at his wife. "There is also the incident where he stopped Jay's fist in the first training session, what's that all about?"

"We don't know, and notice this," Juliette advised, replacing the graph with a video playing in slow motion. It was the point where Anton ran around Yvette to position her between Jay and himself. Even with the video running in slow motion, it was clear that Anton was moving visibly faster than Yvette.

"Yvette's got the best defensive sword skills in our team, and he cuts through them in the first engagement, if Jay hadn't intervened the test would have been a disaster."

"How is he doing it?"

"It's a very good question." Juliette displayed another graph. "These are his emotions, normally when ramping people get calmer, not Anton – not this time. Really strong emotion was flooding him. It's surprising that he wasn't screaming in a heap on the ground. I can't be sure what he was specifically feeling, the type of emotion is not measurable with our equipment, but given the context, I believe it was rage and grief, look at his face."

Another video replaced the graph. Anton's face stood frozen as he moved in slow-motion, his skin pale, his teeth gritted, his eyes fixed in an unblinking stare.

Francis watched the video play out in stunned silence.

"How stable is he?" he asked in dismay.

"I don't know. This is new, I've not seen anything like this before. It's not part of our Order lore. It looks like he has another way of doing a Ramp."

"A second way?"

"At least. Possibly more. Now, Anton's opened the door – who knows where it leads?"

An unsettling disquiet gnawed at Francis. "What happens if his emotions lead him somewhere else?"

"Anything could happen. He's unpredictable."

Francis sighed. "Yes, we will have to keep a careful eye on him."

"He reminds me of his grandfather," Juliette observed, then mused, "I wonder if there's a family trait, something that skipped a generation?"

Francis shrugged. "Unknown and probably unknowable."

"Honestly, Anton could become dangerous."

Francis nodded. "Very dangerous."

"It's a good thing he's on our side."

"Yes, very good. If we can manage him," Francis asserted doubtfully.

Francis and Juliette stared at each other for a long moment.

"Best invite him in," Francis suggested.

Juliette nodded. She pushed her chair back, stood up and opened the door leading to the hall.

Anton was waiting on a chair outside.

"Please come in, Anton," Juliette invited with a warm smile.

Francis thought to himself, *how best to phrase this? Hmmm, emphasize the positives, yes, that will do it.*

* * *

'The supreme art of war is to subdue the enemy without fighting.'

Well, that would be a nice trick wouldn't it, Anton thought sourly.

Anton was resting on the wooden porch seat next to the front door of the safe house. It was late evening with the sun close to setting, and long shadows stretched across the yard. He was finding it hard to focus fully on what he was reading, still mulling over the meeting with Francis and

Juliette that morning. He put down Francis' worn copy of Sun Tzu's, 'The Art of War,' and replayed the meeting in his mind.

I was right about it last night. They're frightened that I'll crack up under pressure.

Anton shook his head, a slow burn of indignation oozing through him. *That's crazy, I didn't lose it in Boston at the warehouse or on the docks. They know that I can fight, they were clear about that, no problems there, but I'm too emotional, they're not sure if I'm ready for combat operations. They think that I'm a risk to myself and the team.*

Anton shook his head again; it wasn't making any sense.

Francis made a special point that I haven't mastered water – does it really matter, I'm getting faster and stronger, and my skills have really improved. I'm sure I'm ready, but how do I convince them of that without having a chance to prove it in combat?

Something caught his eye, and he looked up. Sunlight glinting off metal flashed again. A car was coming down the lane leading to the safe house. Anton stood up to see what it was. A familiar silver Bentley sedan emerged from the trees surrounding the mouth of the lane, and rolled smoothly over the gravel, before pulling to a stop in front of the porch. Anton's guts tightened, his eyes narrowing as he stared at the car. Ramin Kain and Samuel Luther exited the sedan and started walking toward the safe house.

Anton prepared himself to Ramp at a moment's notice, keeping a careful eye on both men as they walked up to the front door.

Kain took off his sunglasses, catching Anton's gaze. A smooth smile spread across his face. "Mr. Slayne, I hope that you're ready for battle tonight, the Order needs you."

Anton did a double take. He was unwilling to trust a word that came from Kain's mouth, but his heart leaped at the thought that there was a chance to prove himself against the vampires. He stayed silently impassive as Kain shrugged, stepping past him into the safe house. Luther followed, giving Anton a cold glare and a grin that wavered between a fake smile and a snarl.

Before the front door could swing shut, Anton dashed forward, following the men into the main hall. They had already veered left into the briefing room, and he caught the edge of the conversation as he approached the doorway.

"—of four vampires," Kain explained.

"That's a sizeable coven," Francis observed. "The Vampire Dominion usually don't let that many vampires operate in the same location, so I presume they're young and haven't been there for long."

"They're new, but their existence was obvious."

Anton watched Francis stare at Kain for a long moment. Francis' eyes flicked over to Anton at the doorway, he frowned and directed, "Anton, please go find Jay and send him in, and close the door as you go."

Anton nodded, Francis, Kain, and Luther watched him as he pulled the door shut. He wanted to stay and listen to what they said but frowned briefly as loyalty overwhelmed his curiosity. He dashed up the stairs to the first floor. Walking up to Jay and Yvette's room, he knocked on the door. There was a brief rustle and steps approached from within the room.

Opening the door, Jay looked at Anton and asked brusquely, "What?"

"Francis wants you in the briefing room, Ramin Kain and Samuel Luther are here."

Jay smirked and said, "That must have been fun for you seeing them again."

Anton stepped back to allow Jay to get through the doorway, and said as Jay pushed past him, "There are vampires."

Jay's demeanor immediately shifted, a stillness came over him, a smile curling the edges of his mouth. He glanced at Anton and said, "Good, I'm getting sick of nursemaiding you."

The two men stared at each other for a second, before Jay turned away and strode down the hall.

Something stirred on the edge of his vision, and Anton looked back into the room. Yvette was lying on top of the bed, dressed simply in jeans and a white T-shirt. Her long coppery hair lay in a loose fan on the pillows. Her left forearm resting across her flat stomach was bound with a white bandage. She regarded him with curious blue eyes, quizzically arching her left eyebrow.

"Yes?" she asked.

Anton nodded toward her forearm. "Sorry about that."

"That's okay, the training was necessary," Yvette replied calmly.

"Oh, good." Anton nodded. "I'll be on my way then," he stated, pulling the door shut.

Maybe they're starting to get used to me being here, Anton thought as he walked back down the hall to the stairs. He needed to retrieve the book he was reading from the front porch, and wait and see what eventuated from Francis and Kain's meeting.

* * *

Francis, Juliette, and Jay, sat opposite Ramin Kain and Luther around the oval table in the briefing room.

Jay listened carefully as Ramin used his smartphone to display a video filled with ghostly images onto a white screen hanging on the wall.

Ramin said, "We caught them burying their kills in a basement beneath an abandoned apartment block." He locked gazes with Francis and declared, "The mission is clear, you must assault the site and kill all the vampires. There are four hostiles, you will need every available member of

313

your team to ensure that none escape and you minimize the risk of casualties."

"Thank you for your concern," Francis said, a faint hint of irony in his voice. "But the last time I looked, I was in charge of the tactical disposition of my force team, not you."

Luther frowned sourly, Ramin smiled thinly and said, "Of course Francis, I was just making the point that the site is littered with tactical difficulties. As Head of the Order, I fully recognize your authority over your own team, I only seek to assist by providing the benefit of my detailed knowledge of the target environment."

Juliette leaned forward slightly and inquired, "How did you find these vampires?"

"He's a genius," Luther blurted.

Juliette inclined her head and said dryly, "Well, of course, he is. That makes all the difference."

Ramin's eyes flashed darkly for a split second. "I track Internet chatter and news feeds. The signs are obvious if you know what to look for. The mood in Boston has taken a turn for the worse, and the presence of a coven of vampires was a simple conclusion."

"Simple," Luther stated, glancing knowingly around the table.

Jay sat quietly to the right of Juliette and Francis, and opposite Luther. He kept his expression neutral while he wondered why Ramin put up with such a sycophantic prat like Samuel Luther. While admittedly arrogant, it struck Jay that Ramin was an effective and capable leader of the Order of Thoth.

"This is getting us nowhere," Francis observed, frowning. "We need a full copy of your data for analysis."

"Of course," Ramin agreed. He handed a data stick over to Juliette who placed it next to her laptop.

In moments, the data transferred across. Juliette scanned her screen and nodded. She pursed her lips and said, "It's a beast of a site." A 3-D schematic of the building projected onto the wall screen and rotated around its midpoint axis. "Five long floors above ground, and one below. At night, vampires could leave from any direction. This should really be a daylight raid to ensure they don't escape."

"Impossible," Ramin declared. "It has to be at night, we can't risk exposure of the existence of the Order."

"Our rules of engagement are clear," Luther declared pompously.

Juliette shook her head slowly. "It will increase the risk that one or more vampires will get away."

"That is why you must take everyone you have," Ramin observed sagely. "Including your novices, Li Wu and Anton Slayne, they have already proven their worth in Boston. They will allow you to close this mission out successfully."

Francis and Juliette glanced at each other, a silent question passing between them. Juliette nodded, and Francis declared, "We will take the mission, and we will commit our whole team."

Francis leaned forward, turning to Jay. He commanded, "Jay, prepare everyone for a raid – we go to Boston tonight."

"Yes, Francis," Jay responded, rising and striding from the briefing room. He mused to himself as he strode up the stairs to where the team members were resting, *maybe Slayne will make some newbie error and get himself killed – one can only hope.*

* * *

The dark-gray van stood in front of the safe house. Its engine idled as the Mirovar force team prepared for combat.

The team members were all dressed in combat fatigues. Slashes of dark grays and browns suitable for blending into an urban environment at night dominated their clothing. They wore hoods, belts, and webbing to hold a multitude of edged weapons and submachine guns. They checked each other's gear and climbed into the van.

Peter pushed his kit bag into an overhead locker and declared loudly, "Someone's gonna get spanked for making vampires, it's well known that Crane hates unsanctioned vampire creation. It's suicide for a vampire to do it."

"So why would any vampire do that – surely, they know the rules?" Li asked, taking her seat in the back. The Green Dragon resting in its scabbard between her legs.

Anton sat down in the seat next to Li. "I suppose we'll never know."

Peter laughed. "We usually don't spend much time chatting with them – maybe we'll make an exception tonight just for you Li."

Li stared at him, and Peter grinned as he stepped back out of the van and got into the driver's seat.

Chiara, Jay, and Yvette filed into the van, taking seats opposite Li and Anton.

Jay leaned forward and whispered, "Hey newbie, Kain insisted that you be a part of this mission, so please do us a favor and don't get us all killed."

Anton stared back silently. *Bastard!*

Jay leaned back; a smirk just visible on his face for half a second. Then all business, he opened a small case. He extracted five sets of tiny earbuds and handed them around the team. "Put these in your ears, you'll have secure comms and still be able to hear everything around you."

Anton put the earbuds into his ears.

There was a short hum as they booted up, powered by his body heat.

"Okay everyone, listen up," Juliette stated over their earbud comm links. "I can see that everyone is hooked in and green across the board. I will be conducting net overwatch from the safe house. I will be in the background monitoring the Panopticon feeds, providing situational awareness and blocking identification by the Vampire Dominion."

Anton looked across at Jay and asked, "You've hacked into the Panopticon?"

Jay pulled out his earbuds, leaned forward and snapped, "It's not all about you Slayne. We had missions before you showed up, we didn't sit around with our thumbs up our butts. Of course, we've taken action to disrupt the operations of the Panopticon."

Anton leaned forward, pulled his own earbuds out and snapped back, "Right! I got it."

Both men sat back against the walls of the van. Jay re-inserted his earbuds, and Anton followed suit.

The comms system came back online, and Juliette inquired briskly, "Jay, Anton, are your earbuds loose, you both dropped out for a couple of seconds."

"It's all good Ma'am," Jay responded quickly.

Anton's lip curled, and he said, "Yeah, we're good Ma'am. Ready to go."

The van moved off toward Boston. Francis directed from the passenger seat next to Peter, "Okay team, game faces on. We have good intel on a coven of four vampires operating out of an abandoned apartment block in South Dorchester. The target building is next to the Neponset River and the Southeast Expressway. Anton and Li, you're new, I want you working with Chiara throughout the operation. Stick close to her and stay out of trouble. Jay and Yvette will form the second team, and Peter will work with me. I will spell out the details of the mission and assess contingencies as we drive there. So please pay attention as there will be no time for repeats. Is that clear."

"Yes, Francis," the team chorused together.

Anton looked around the van, there was a palpable sense of tension and excitement within the team members.

Just like a championship game.

Anton loved it, he'd been waiting for an opportunity to kill vampires since Boston, and now it was here. Energy snapped and crackled along his nerves and excitement flooded his soul, but from the back of his mind, from a place beaten into existence by recent traumas came a voice of caution, *take care, Kain hates me. For some reason, he wants me dead, and he insisted that I be on this mission tonight. Gang believed that Kain is colluding with the Vampire*

Dominion. Where did these vampires come from? They're so close to the safe house. Of course, it would be the Mirovar team that would deploy.

Anton looked at Li. She put her hand out. He reached across and gripped it. She stared at him for a long moment in the dim light in the van, smiled softly and nodded.

Yes, we'll fight them together, but I'm keeping my eyes open, it could be a trap.

* * *

Chloe Armitage's smartphone pinged.

She glanced at the screen. There was a message from the Raven, the Red Empire agent within the Mirovar force team. The message read, 'Ramin Kain has ordered an attack on a vampire coven in Boston. The whole of the Mirovar force team will be engaged tonight.' A date-time stamp, and a set of GPS coordinates followed the message.

Chloe opened her laptop and logged into the Panopticon. She entered the GPS coordinates into the Panopticon's map system and examined the site. She opened a Panopticon sub-system and retrieved a list of the current whereabouts of the praetorians. The system listed seven as en route to Boston from Crane's Citadel.

Chloe recognized the names and said quietly to herself, "Three sniper teams and Centurion Rawlings. Crane already knows about this operation, and he didn't invite me – I'm cut to the quick."

Chloe used the Panopticon to make further checks. A military satellite would be over the site in three hours. Whatever was going to happen, the satellite would record it with high quality broad-spectrum cameras, but no sound. The clock on her laptop displayed 21:11.

She thought quickly. *General Clayton Maze will be watching me like the faithful hound that he is. Crane is suspicious, and with all the overwatch, a helicopter is out of the question. A hire car is cutting it fine to be there on time, but a hire car will have to do.*

Chloe prepared a long, black duffel bag with some recently imported gear, including an electrically heated body suit. She looked across to a finely crafted wood stand that held the Red Dragon in its scabbard. The priceless katana retrieved by the praetorians from the Mystic River and returned three months past.

"Not tonight my thirsty friend," she stated with a wistful smile. "You're a little too recognizable."

She reached for two shorter blades of Red Empire design, flourishing them with practiced ease before placing them into the bag with the rest of her gear. Zipping the bag closed, she hefted it easily over her left shoulder before picking up her car keys and leaving the penthouse.

She descended in her personal elevator to the parking garage in the building's basement. She'd long ago fixed the internal camera on the lift to a continuous loop that hid her current activity. She opened the bag. Beginning with the close-fitting powered body suit, she fitted her disguise. The lift reached the basement, quiet excitement stirring within her.

Filled with intent, she mused silently, *time to go hunting.*

In the parking garage below Chloe's penthouse, the Panopticon recorded a car hired to a Mr. Jason Harcourt, drive out of the building at 21:15. Mr. Harcourt appeared to be just under six feet tall, wearing a long dark coat, and a broad-brimmed hat that hid his face.

He had a long, black duffel bag on the car seat next to him.

* * *

Cornelius Crane sat alone. He was at the head of a long table, in his most secure command room on the 103rd floor of his Citadel. Unlike the operations center on the same floor, he'd dedicated the war room to the most secret operations of the Vampire Dominion. Multiple screens depicting direct feeds from the Panopticon, as well as views from the helmet cams of the seven praetorians engaged in the current mission dominated the opposite wall.

Cornelius sat in perfect stillness. He ignored the screens, his mind far away, contemplating the threads of probability that ran through the next few hours of his life. In his experience, short term prevision was the most accurate. He confirmed for himself that victory remained highly likely, bordering on a certainty. He checked that his generals in the United States, Clayton Maze, and Chloe Armitage, would have no impact on the outcome of the mission. Both showed dark lines, indicating zero probability to influence events. His prevision confirmed his expectations of his generals. They remained unaware of his secret mission against the Mirovar force team.

There remained a low probability line, glimmering just above darkness, passing through the Mirovar force team leading to his own death. He expected tonight's engagement would extinguish that line forever.

Cornelius dropped out of his previsionary meditation. He leaned forward slightly, pressing a touch screen built into the top of the table, he opened up a single, secure comms link.

Looking back up at the main screens, he inquired, "Centurion Rawlings, are your men in position?"

The Centurion responded with a crystal-clear voice, "Yes, Sir."

"Confirm your tactics."

"We have triangulated the site; two of three teams can cover each approach."

Cornelius checked Rawling's words against the Panopticon feeds displaying real-time satellite and drone data on the wall of screens.

"Good work, Centurion."

"Sir, we're waiting for the Order team to arrive."

"Expect a vehicle, such as a van," Cornelius instructed, glancing at the clock, it was nearly midnight. "Expect them to arrive within the hour."

"Yes, Sir. Once we have a clear shot, we will take them out. We will catch them in a crossfire from at least two SAWs and two sniper rifles."

"Wait – allow the Mirovar force team to engage with the vampires in the apartment block first. They should not exist, and if any are still alive after you have destroyed Mirovar and his team, kill them all."

"Yes, Sir. Anything else?"

Cornelius declared without hesitation, "No, Centurion. Nothing, except good hunting."

"Yes, Sir." Centurion Rawlings responded enthusiastically.

The line automatically muted itself. Cornelius sat back, steepled his hands in front of himself and focused on the screens on the far wall.

Now it is time to strike a blow against the Order of Thoth, he thought with quiet, confident anticipation.

Chapter Eleven

BODY

- -

SHADOWSTONE, PSYOPS DIRECTORATE ANALYSIS
REPORT, FINAL ANALYSIS

- -

COUNTRY: (U) UNITED STATES (USA)

SPECIFIC OBSERVATIONS AND RECOMMENDATIONS:

A. (O) THERE HAS BEEN INCREASED CROSS MEDIA REPORTS
OF PARANORMAL ACTIVITY SINCE THE LAST REPORT.

B. (O) THE BOSTON INCIDENT OF JUNE 11 THIS YEAR HAS
PRODUCED HIGH LEVELS OF CONSPIRACY IDEATION.

C. (R) THAT TACTICAL OPERATIONS AVOID HEAVY WEAPON
USAGE IN URBAN AREAS UNTIL CURRENT CONSPIRACIES OF
WEREWOLVES, VAMPIRES, ALIENS, AND SECRET
GOVERNMENTS HAVE BEEN DISCREDITED.

D. (R) THAT ADDITIONAL PSYOPS RESOURCES BE
ALLOCATED TO ONLINE INFORMATION SUPPRESSION AND
DISRUPTION UNTIL MEDIA REPORTS OF CONSPIRACY
RETURN TO THEIR FREQUENCIES PRIOR TO JUNE 11.

~~TOP SECRET/FGEO~~
RQ
#5404

NNNN
CLASSIFICATION: ~~TOP SECRET~~, SECRET

– Content from a partially declassified Shadowstone PSYOPS analysis
report.

* * *

South Dorchester, Boston, August 9th, 00:30

The dark-gray van slowed to twenty-five miles per hour as it crossed into South Dorchester.

A wary, nervous energy shadowed Anton's excitement at the impending raid. He worried about the possibility of a trap. He didn't want his new friends and teammates to get hurt or killed. Taking a deep breath, he sighed noisily.

"What's up?" Li asked, patting his thigh.

Balancing the Blue Dragon on the point of its scabbard, Anton nervously flipped it from hand to hand. "I just have a feeling this is a trap."

Li's hand paused on his thigh. She leaned closer, frowned and asked, "A trap. How?"

Jay sitting opposite Anton, overheard. Tilting his head quizzically, he declared, "A trap! The only people who know we're here are members of the Order of Thoth. What are you saying – there's a traitor in the Order, someone who would sell us out to the vampires?"

Anton shrugged his shoulders.

Jay rubbed his face with his right hand, and stated incredulously, "I can't believe I'm hearing this. Who are you to question us? You're not even a member of the Order. Why are you here? You don't belong—"

"Quiet!" Juliette commanded over the comm links.

"Ma'am?" Jay responded. "But—"

"You heard me. Focus on the mission."

"Yes, Ma'am," Jay agreed flatly, his eyes flashing with controlled anger.

Anton stared at Jay, and thought to himself, *keep calm, Juliette is right. Don't let Jay get under my skin before we go into combat.*

Anton leaned forward so that he could see out the windscreen of the van at the streets they were passing through. They almost lay completely deserted. They passed one corner where a trio of young men faced each other in a huddle.

Is that a drug deal going down? A couple of miles away are four vampires, and those guys are oblivious to what is happening.

He shook his head cynically.

Juliette directed, "Commence stealth operations, no talking unless absolutely necessary. Jay, please pass out the night glasses and ensure that Anton's and Li's fit perfectly. GPS logs indicate there is still vehicle traffic along the streets near the target building so we can approach closely without seeming out of place. You're twelve minutes to the drop off point."

Anton leaned back, stilling his nerves. He closed his eyes, his right hand on the Blue Dragon. His left resting on top of an FN P90 submachine gun loaded with a fifty-round magazine of high-velocity silver bullets.

Only a few more minutes, this waiting is the hard part, he thought silently to himself.

* * *

The late summer night was warm and sultry. The waning moon was pushing up into the night sky. A light breeze, occasionally gusting, matched the patchy clouds that drifted languidly across the sky.

The vampire adjusted his squat position behind the parapet of the water tower. From where he crouched, he could see a black van parked three hundred yards away on his left, up on the near edge of the southeast expressway overlooking the apartment block. His commander, Centurion Rawlings, and the Alpha team were in the van. Their position allowed them to cover the whole of the south and west sides of the target environment.

He scanned the north and east approaches, the night was alive with silvery moonlight, and soft shadows fell everywhere. There was a background hum from the laboring machinery of the pumps beneath his boots. Rustles, drips, and knocks drifted up on the cool, night air. He sniffed, there was a trace of the unmistakable stench of rotting corpses emanating from the apartment block. His mouth twisted into a sneer. He hated untidy vampires with a passion and considered the coven below to be nothing but low life scum he should eradicate like vermin.

As he squatted behind the parapet, he wondered who was stupid enough to violate King Crane's edict against vampire creation. He stared at the apartment block. The whole situation remained a mystery to him. Every vampire alive knew it was certain death to create another vampire without the express approval of King Crane. They all knew the praetorians and the generals would come for them and that there could be no survival against the military elite of the Vampire Dominion. And yet, the coven existed, and had apparently done so for months.

The vampire shook his head slightly, mystified by the circumstances of the mission. He scanned the approaches again, there was no sign of the approaching Order force team.

He opened his tactical comms link, and reported, "The northeast approach is still clear, Sir,"

"Roger that Beta One," Centurion Rawlings replied. "Keep your eyes open. We're expecting a dark-gray van. I'm broadcasting an image."

"Yes, Sir," The praetorian scanned his heads-up display. An image of a dark-gray van appeared. It rotated through three-sixty degrees and displayed the number plate. There would be no mistake made in identifying the vehicle. "Image received, Sir."

The comms link returned to silence.

Beta One hungered for revenge. He relished the thought of slaying the Order operatives who had killed so many praetorians in the recent battle at the Boston docks. He sighed, wishing they could simply drop a two-thousand-pound bomb on the site and be done with it. But the directive to only use personal weapons had come from Crane himself, and the vampire had not survived the last century by disobeying the king's orders.

Beta One's .50 caliber sniper rifle sat next to him, and his spotter, Beta Two, kneeling two yards away, carried a standard issue M249 light machine gun with an uprated two hundred round drum magazine. The two vampires of Beta team stared at the north and east approaches to the nearly deserted apartment block and waited for the Order team to walk into their carefully prepared trap.

* * *

Jay lifted up his open hand, thumb and fingers taut.

Five minutes, Anton thought to himself, adjusting the fit of his new night glasses. They appeared to be simple, wrap-around sunglasses, with an elastic strap around the back of his head to fit them securely to his face.

He leaned forward, looking out the front windscreen at the boarded-up buildings, and deserted streets. The night glasses provided by Jay amplified and filtered the available light, making the world appear as if it was still early twilight. They passed three cars, stripped and burnt out, standing in a line like a skeletal parking lot. The street lamps were a uniform sickly yellow. More than half stood shattered, leaving pools of deep shadow, resting like lesions on the asphalt and concrete.

The urban landscape breathed desolation and decay like a bloated corpse lying in an open sewer.

Anton shook his head with wonder, and thought, *how did Kain find these vampires? Important vampires don't live in slums.*

He remembered Gang Wu speculating that Kain had a deal with Crane. A deal for throw-away vampires Kain could find and kill for show.

And yet I'm here despite the risk this is a trap, as Kain insisted that I be on this mission. Anton pursed his lips, *and anyway, I jumped at the chance to prove myself.*

A digital clock on the wall of the van read 00:44. The van started to slow down.

A tight wariness surrounded Anton like a blanket, it didn't matter to him if it was a trap, he would fight anyway. There was no going back, there was nowhere to go back to. There was only the team, he pushed away his concerns and focused on the mission – killing vampires.

* * *

The two praetorians of Gamma team heard the approaching van before they saw it. They repositioned to the northeast corner of the two-story building, standing between the five-story apartment block and the north side street. From their position, they could create a crossfire with the Beta team on the water tower, but they no longer had visual contact with Centurion Rawlings and the Alpha team in the black van on the southeast expressway.

The vampire smiled as he watched the dark-gray van approach, it matched the visual image Centurion Rawlings had supplied ten minutes earlier.

"I have visual on the target vehicle, they're coming down the street from the east," he reported. His tactical helmet comm links broadcasting to the other two teams of praetorians surrounding the apartment block.

"Copy that Gamma One," Centurion Rawlings stated. "Maintain visual contact and keep reporting. The damn Panopticon can't see them. An Order netmaster is blocking it."

"Beta team should be able to see them any second," Gamma one declared. "Damn, the windows are covered in a reflective material – I can't see inside."

"Hold your position, Gamma one. Maintain visual contact and allow them to engage the vampires in the apartment block."

"Yes, Sir."

The two praetorians in Gamma team assumed prone positions on the roof of the two-story building, keeping their weapons trained on the slowly approaching van.

* * *

The lightly thrumming pumps of the water tower hummed in the darkness. Ramin Kain crouched next to the second-floor window overlooking the northeast approach to the apartment building.

Earlier, he'd shrunk backward, when two fully armed praetorians had mounted the stairs spiraling around the water tower. They hadn't noticed him, his presence masked by the background noise of the nearby pumps, and the heavy-duty construction of the tower's walls. He'd sighed with relief as they passed him by, moving to the top of the tower.

He adjusted the fit of his Order night glasses and stared at the northeast approach. He checked his gear as he waited, his sword was ready, and his Glock 9mm remained loaded with silver bullets. He didn't expect to use his weapons. No one knew where he was. Even Cornelius Crane would only know that he was able to view the site, but would not know precisely where he was. If he had to use his weapons, it would only be to save his life and would mean that his mission had almost certainly failed. He checked his smartphone and ensured that it was on full silent mode. He returned it to his chest pocket. He'd used it fifteen minutes before to send an image of the Mirovar force team van to the praetorians, using the quantum address provided by Cornelius Crane.

A thin edge of fear hovered in the background. Ramin took a slow deep breath and wished for the arrival of the Mirovar force team. He stared through the window, there was a glimmer of street lamp light reflecting off painted metal.

It's the van, they're here, he thought excitedly.

A dark-gray van paused at the mouth of the lane way as if teasing him. All it needed to do, was roll forward about a hundred yards, and it would pass directly in front of the water tower. A perfect position for an attack from above. If not taken there, the van would loop around an abandoned parking lot, and past the main entrance of the apartment block.

Please come down this side, he begged whatever gods might listen.

With his breath passing through gritted teeth; Ramin waited in nervous anticipation for the murder of Francis Mirovar and Anton Slayne to begin.

* * *

The van rolled to a stop. Everyone inside waited in silence for the spectrum analyzers mounted on the front dashboard to scan the target building.

Francis' voice came in over the comm links, he stated, "We have them, four hostiles and two civilians. They're on the ground floor. They've probably just hunted and are now about to feed. We need to move fast if we're going to save those two people."

Juliette reported, "There is heavy counter-cyberwarfare occurring, the window of coverage of the Panopticon on site is not more than fifteen minutes and could be less."

Jay got up, moving to the back of the van. He opened the rear doors and jumped lithely out onto the street. Yvette followed him, they carried swords, and FN P90 submachine guns.

Chiara nodded at Anton and Li, and directed softly, "You two with me, stay close."

Anton and Li followed Chiara out of the van and onto the street. Yvette and Jay were already on the move, walking stealthily along the sidewalk toward the apartment block. Chiara signaled with her hand, running across to the near wall of a two-story building, Anton and Li quickly followed her.

Francis' voice came over the earbud comm links, he ordered, "Our targets are currently in the middle of the building on the ground floor. There are building entrances out the front and on the back corners. Team one, Chiara, take the northwest corner. Team two, Jay, take the northeast corner. We will move the van to the front of the building. That will attract their attention and then you will hit them from behind on my command."

"Yes, Sir," Jay murmured.

"Yes, Sir," Chiara whispered.

Anton carried his FN P90 low, as he fell into position, jogging lightly just behind Chiara and next to Li. He'd slung the Blue Dragon across his back, the handle jutting up over his right shoulder so that he could easily draw and slash in a single movement. Now he was moving, the nervousness fled. He grinned, a pale-yellow street lamp momentarily illuminating their faces and giving them all sallow, jaundiced looks.

"Time for some karma," he whispered.

"Cut the chatter," Juliette broadcasted over the comm links.

Absolutely, Anton thought to himself. He shifted gears, lifting the intensity of his focus and plunged into silence.

In the distance, a stray dog barked dolefully. A breeze rallied into a gust, sending a half-crumpled coke can scuttling along the laneway, and the team froze for a moment before proceeding on.

Chiara led them past the two-story building, through a stand of trees, and along a path to the far corner of the apartment block. To their left, Jay and Yvette positioned on the near corner. The van trundled toward the front of the building, disappearing past the edge of the apartment block.

* * *

Someone laughed heartily in the gloom.

Dillon Browne exulted with unrestrained bloodlust and power. He flicked a wall switch, and the overhead lights came on. He enjoyed seeing the food realize what was really happening to them. Huddled together in front of him, were a young woman wearing gold hot pants, a silvery mesh halter top and impossibly high platform shoes, and a thin young man with a waxed mustache, wearing a dark brown pin-striped suit.

Dillon blurred forward, taking the young woman by the jaw and lifting her upright. Her dark eyes were wide. Wet mascara ran in dark streaks down her cheeks. She tried to lean away, moaning with terror. The thin man, backed away, his shiny black shoes tapping on the cold linoleum of the floor, his head whipping around like a child's toy. Caleb Moore loomed behind him; the thin man froze, his eyes darting left and right, a thin line of spit hanging from his bottom lip.

Dillon's eyes flicked left and right toward Aaliyah Williams and Ethan Jones, he nodded toward the thin man.

He watched as Caleb's hand lashed forward, grabbing the man on the left shoulder, holding him fast. The thin man whimpered, trembling with fear. Aaliyah grinned, baring her fangs. Ethan snarled like a wild animal, his long canines gleaming in the overhead lights.

Dillon twisted the girl around, holding her tight, forcing her to watch what was happening.

She screamed, a full-throated, high-pitched, keening wail.

Dillon clapped his left hand over her mouth. Pulling her close, he declared mockingly, "Hush now, that sort of noise could wake the dead."

"Wait!" the thin man pleaded. "I can get you things, I can get you anything."

Dillon laughed, and the other vampires joined in.

"I can bring you people, boys, girls, anyone you need," he said. His eyes darted desperately from face to face. "Please, just let me go." Pointing at the girl, he declared enthusiastically, "There are plenty more just like her."

Dillon's mouth curled into a grin and he asked derisively, "Do you think we need your help?"

"Everyone needs he—"

Dillon's free hand blurred forward. A straight razor slashed across the thin man's mouth, cutting deeply through both cheeks. The thin man squealed; his tongue split in two wriggled obscenely. Blood began streaming down the sides of his chin to splatter in fat drops on the floor.

"I don't like big mouths," Dillon observed flatly and nodded again.

The three vampires attacked, tearing the thin man to pieces. Blood sprayed wildly. The vampires latched onto body parts and greedily sucked on the open arteries. The thin man's entrails fell to the floor where the vampire's feeding frenzy kicked them around.

The young woman looked on. Dillon clasped his hand tightly over her mouth, muffling her screams. Above his hand, a look of horror overtook her eyes, like an eclipse of the sun, all hope vanishing into eternal darkness.

Dillon could feel the young woman's heart beating like a bird trying to escape its cage. Lust to feed rose within him. He leaned her head to one side to expose her neck, his canines descending into attack position. He started to rear back his head for the final plunge forward when he jerked to a sudden stop.

Dillon looked around for a moment, his ears wiggling as he searched for what had disturbed him.

"There's someone out front," he hissed.

"Huh?" Caleb grunted, dropping a leg torn off at the hip.

"It's a van pulling up outside, get your guns," Dillon ordered with a snarl, holding the young woman tightly in front of him.

The vampires pulled out MAC-10 submachine guns and turned to face the entrance of the apartment block.

* * *

"Stow your guns, there is still one human left alive – swords only," Francis commanded.

Grinning crookedly, Jay slung his FN P90 over his shoulder. Drawing his katana, he looked at Yvette who had done the same. They stood opposite each other at the northeast side entrance. One door hung half off its hinges, and the other was gone completely. Before them stretched a long corridor, unlit except for a pool of light close to a hundred yards away that flooded from a large room into the hall.

"Four hostiles and one civilian are still in the main room in the middle of the building," Francis whispered over the comm links.

Jay nodded once, standing ready to enter the ground floor of the apartment block through the side entrance.

"Go!" Francis commanded.

Jay sunk into an immediate ramp, blurring through the entrance and down the long hall. Yvette ran beside him, her naked sword held above her left shoulder.

They reached the lit area and burst into the main room. Opposite them were four vampires and one terrified girl. The vampires were already whirling about, raising MAC-10 submachine guns. The girl began to shriek, thrown hard through the air toward Jay and Yvette by the vampire who had held her. They both moved to dodge her, Yvette veering left, while Jay went low. He put his left hand down and started to slide underneath the girl's body, angling his sword away to the right to protect her.

9mm rounds started flying as the vampires opened fire. Yvette cursing in alarm as she twisted violently and blurred away.

Jay's left foot ran into something slippery, and he lost purchase on the linoleum. He watched in sudden horror as blue and gray-white pieces of gut looped around his foot and he slid on his hip through a puddle of blood and human entrails toward a pair of vampires, one a hulking brute of a man and the other a snarling gangster.

His mind raced as he struggled to regain his balance, *where the hell is everyone else?*

* * *

Centurion Rawlings watched the Order van pull to a stop outside the front entrance of the apartment block. Two men leaped from the van, equipped with slung submachine guns and drawn edged weapons. They blurred toward the building as gunfire erupted inside. He checked his Panopticon feeds, the van was not visible, hazed into invisibility on his screens. The rest of the site was in view. His teams clearly marked on the screens with steady red stars.

"Gamma team reposition to cover any escape."

"Yes, Sir," Gamma One responded.

"Beta team, prepare to engage with crossfire on the kill zone between the van and the building. We'll get them as they exit."

"Yes, Sir, we're ready!" Beta One replied enthusiastically.

"Watch my mark Beta team, I will open up with the minigun, and I want both of you firing from your position."

"Yes, Sir," the praetorians of Beta team chorused together.

Centurion Rawlings slid the side door of the van to the left, exposing a gap a yard wide facing the apartment block. He hefted the Dillon Aero M134D-H minigun and pointed it directly at a point halfway between the Order van and the entrance of the building. His ears twitched as gunfire stuttered in the lobby of the building. He expected the Order would soon win the little battle inside the building against the worthless trash vampires. He grinned broadly, all he had to do was wait, and a whole Order force team would soon cease to exist.

He was supremely proud to be the instrument of their execution.

* * *

A bellowing laugh split the air.

Anton rushed into the lit room. Chiara and Li fanned out to his left. In front of him, a female vampire charged toward Yvette, who was dodging 9mm gunfire from another vampire near the entrance.

He took another blurring step, twisting to his right. Looming before him was a huge vampire holding Jay a foot off the floor by his throat and his right wrist. The vampire's shoulders bunched, preparing to tear Jay apart. Jay's face twisted in agony and horror, his body spread-eagled, his feet thrashing as he attempted to break free of the terrible grip. His one free hand, blurring forward, again and again, to beat at the hand at his throat.

The vampire holding Jay bellowed again, his laughter booming through the room like thunder.

Anton drove the Blue Dragon through a short, deep arc. The big vampire's head toppled forward as bright red blood fountained into the air. His body crumpling to the ground, dragging Jay with him in a tangle of arms, legs and spraying blood.

Snarling, the second gangster vampire leaped forward, somersaulting over Anton's head, striding momentarily along the ceiling as he lined his MAC-10 up on Anton's head.

Anton's Ramp went wild, he twisted, blurring to the left, as the vampire's MAC-10 billowed gray smoke just above him and a line of bullets raked the floor. Linoleum puffed upward, and blood splashed as stray bullets ripped into the headless body of the huge vampire.

The vampire landed, his gun running dry. Turning, he fled.

Anton started to run after him. A gleaming axe tumbled past his shoulder, shearing through the back of the vampire's head before embedding in the wall. The vampire flopped to the ground, twitching, and jerking. He pulled to a halt, twisting back to face the room. Peter and Francis rushed through the open front doors.

To his left, the female vampire wailed once, falling silently to the floor.

Yvette stepped past her body, flicking her katana clean.

Everyone evaded as another volley of bullets raked the room. The final vampire's MAC-10 clicked on empty, and he cursed loudly, "Fuck you—"

Francis beheaded him from behind with the White Dragon. His body slumped to the floor, his head rolling to the nearest wall. Blood gushed forth in a spreading red pool from his neck.

In the sudden silence, Jay pushed the big vampire aside and stood up, vampire blood dripping down his face. Breathing heavily, rubbing the red, raw marks on his throat, he declared in disgust, "I'm covered in this shit!"

Jay stared at Anton for a long moment. His face clouded with strong emotion, then he broke eye contact and looked away.

* * *

"Less than ten minutes of Panopticon cover left," Juliette broadcast over the earbud comms.

"Quickly now, clear the dead," Francis commanded. "Li keep watch, Yvette help Jay clean himself up, and Chiara, check the girl."

Peter caught Anton's attention, nodding his head at the gangster vampire he'd killed with a throwing axe. They went to grab the body, and it twitched violently, starting to push itself upright.

"Damn!" Peter growled, twisting the skull and snapping the spine. His muscles bunched again, and he tore the head free of the body. Blood fountained from the headless body onto the floor.

"Make sure that you've got a true kill," Francis warned. He started dragging the huge beheaded vampire by his boots toward the front doors.

In less than a minute, Francis, Peter, and Anton cleared the room of the various vampire body parts. They lined them up on the ground, a handful of yards outside the main entrance to the apartment block. Sunlight would flood the south facing entrance at dawn, and the bodies would flame to ash in seconds.

They returned to the main room. Chiara was helping the girl stand on unsteady feet. She began hyperventilating and shivering, Francis stepped forward and waved a thimble sized vial under her nose. She immediately collapsed, Chiara, guiding her gently to the floor.

Francis picked her up like he was carrying a sick child and commanded, "Back to the van now! We can run past an emergency room and drop her off on the way home."

"Won't she remember everything that has happened?" Anton asked.

Chiara remarked, "No way. Not with a dose of 'Lethe.' She won't remember anything from the last twenty-four hours."

"Focus everyone, guns back on, keep your eyes open until exfiltration is complete," Francis instructed, striding through the doorway with the limp young woman in his arms. Jay a step behind him, his FN P90 held up, scanning the environment. Anton, Li, Chiara, Yvette, and Peter followed them, weapons up and on the lookout for any more hostiles.

The team exited the apartment block. They descended the front stairs where the bodies of the four dead vampires lay and headed for their waiting van.

* * *

The praetorian, call sign Beta One, sighted along his .50 caliber sniper rifle. The magazine held six rounds of high velocity, hollow point ammunition. He targeted the lead Order member carrying a young woman in his arms. He focused the crosshairs onto the center of the man's chest, a single round would blow a hole through the man's body that he could push his fist through without touching the sides.

Breathing slowly, he mastered his excitement. His spotter lined his M249 light machine gun on the center of the group of Order operatives behind the first two. The kill zone was only 150 yards away from the top of the water tower, almost point-blank range for their weapons.

"This will be a turkey shoot," Beta One whispered.

His spotter chuckled softly before whispering back, "Fucking A."

Beta One tapped his tactical communications link and broadcast, "Sir, I have the lead Order operative in my sights right now, ready to take the shot, waiting for your mark."

...

"Sir?"

* * *

Ramin Kain stared through his Order night glasses at the Mirovar force team as they exited the apartment block and made their way to the van.

Any second now, he thought, his mind seething with expectation, his fists clenching spasmodically.

One of the team members toward the back of the group looked up, directly at the top of the water tower, as if they had seen something that grabbed their attention.

Hell, one of them has seen the praetorians above me!

Hell, fucking hell, when will someone start shooting?!

Ramin's eyes widened as he watched the Mirovar force team walk into the sweet spot in the middle of the kill zone between the van and the entrance to the building. The one who had looked up, glowed in his amplified night vision, their body temperature rising rapidly.

They're ramping!

"C'mon!" he whispered with desperate urgency. "Kill them!"

* * *

Beta One sighted along his sniper rifle, let his breath out, waiting for the pause between heartbeats. The shot would be perfect; the lead Order operative was about to die. Beside him, his spotter was ready to simultaneously fire his M249 light machine gun into the mass of Order operatives in the middle of the kill zone.

Where's Centurion Rawlings? They're smack in the middle of the zone right now. Must be a communications failure, more Order cyberwarfare, his mind raced. *I'll have to take the shot.*

Beta One started to squeeze the trigger.

A searing pain burst from the base of his skull. A blood-drenched blade rammed out through the space between the bottom of his nose and his top lip. He shuddered, his nerveless finger trembling uselessly next to the trigger. The blade twisted to the right, before whipping down to the left, carving its way through his jaw, spine and a mass of blood vessels in his neck.

Whoever attacked him blurred away toward the spotter.

Beta One's body slumped forward, his helmeted forehead bouncing off the parapet before settling back down upon it.

A wet gurgle came from his right. Facing the parapet, he could just see the sole of one of Beta Two's boots. The boot twitched twice and then lay still.

He rested there, unable to move, his head barely connected to his body. Blood flooding from his throat pooled at his knees. Locked in a pose that resembled someone praying, he began the final death.

Before the eternal darkness claimed him, a vast regret for the failed mission washed through him. Behind the emotion rolled a wave of all-consuming nothingness.

* * *

Flicking the two Red Empire swords clear of blood, general Chloe Armitage shrank back into the shadows on top of the water tower.

She surveyed the area around her. The nondescript black van parked three hundred yards away on the southeast expressway brooded with a ghostly silence. Its interior painted with the blood of Centurion Rawlings and the Alpha Team praetorians. Recent memory flooded her mind. Flashing blades, punctured metal, and bloody flesh. The praetorians had died in silence. Their deaths so quick, they had no time to draw breath, let alone scream.

From where she crouched, she could see the squat two-story building between the apartment block and the street to the north. On its roof, lay the broken remains of the praetorians of Gamma Team. They had been the first to fall to her blades before she'd swung around the far side of the apartment block to take the vampires in the van from behind.

Chloe sheathed her short swords in their scabbards at her hip, pulling a dark Red Empire cloak around her. An assassin's hood covered her hair. A dark veil covered her face from the bridge of her nose down. Only her vivid blue eyes and pale complexion showed in a thin strip above the veil.

She sidled up to the parapet, glancing down at the Order van, the last door closed and it started to pull away. She watched it pass beneath her, rolling out into the street and disappearing from view. She waited until she could no longer hear the engine of the van, and the entire site lay reduced to the background noises of nature and the mechanical sounds of the pumps beneath her boots.

Chloe prepared to leave when something clicked unexpectedly beneath her. She looked briefly over the parapet, and the door at the base of the tower pushed outward. She stepped back from the parapet, her mind racing. Someone had been watching.

Her lips parted with a knowing smile. She wondered if she would be surprised by who the watcher was. She flipped over the edge of the far parapet and clung on to the outside of the tower. She blended into the shadows; her Red Empire garb perfectly suited to her needs. The parapet extended out from the tower by about two feet. With fingers like forged steel, Chloe hung onto the crevices between the bricks. Her core strength allowed her to hold her position flat beneath the parapet for as long as she needed. The external metal stairs gave slightly, as someone jumped up on them. As they advanced up the stairs, she scrambled silently around the tower and remained out of sight. She could hear his heartbeat, it was slower than normal, that and the ten-foot leap to the stairs told her that it was a Ramp Master approaching.

Chloe continued to scuttle silently along. Hiding in the thick shadows beneath the parapet, placing the tower between herself and the stranger as he ascended the stairs.

* * *

Ramin Kain stepped onto the top of the tower, faltering momentarily as he took in the scene.

He braced himself for a second on the parapet, then stepped forward, careful not to leave any marks of his presence. The first praetorian knelt upright. Face down on the parapet, positioned like a wax figure in a grotesque display. The nape of the praetorian's neck lay exposed, a blade had entered straight through the brain stem, before tearing out most of the vampire's throat. The second vampire lay spread-eagled on the floor, his heart separated from his chest and resting half a dozen feet away. Ramin skirted the pools of blood around the praetorians and made his way to the center of the tower's roof.

Whoever had done this, was very fast, stealthy, expertly skilled, and had taken the two vampires completely by surprise.

His scalp itched terribly. Ramin rubbed both hands through his hair beneath his broad-brimmed hat. He looked around, shocked, disbelieving what he was seeing.

"What the fuck happened?" Ramin whispered. His voice trembling, so much had hinged on this mission.

Ramin looked around again, his head jerking left and right. His night glasses gave him excellent night vision, but he could see nothing out of the ordinary, except for a brooding black van parked on the expressway and two corpses lying yards from him. He strained to hear anything, but there was only the silence of the night and the faint noises of the tower's pumps.

A shiver went up his spine, he was horribly alone and exposed. Whoever had slaughtered the praetorians could still be around. He pulled his Glock 9mm and drew his sword. A dreadful sense of malevolent eyes watching him shivered across his skin, but he could not see from where or by whom. He ramped, hard and fast. Blurring away from the top of the tower, he descending down the stairs in a flash to the ground below.

Ramin promptly disappeared north along the laneway to the streets of South Dorchester.

* * *

Chloe pushed herself away from the brick wall beneath the parapet, dropping lithely to the bottom of the water tower. For the benefit of any watching cameras, she sank into a deep crouch, before standing up. The drop was a decent jump for a vampire but a mighty leap for a Ramp master.

She stared at the fleeing form of Ramin Kain. Smiling beneath her dark veil, she whispered to herself, "The wicked flee when no man pursueth: but the righteous are bold as a lion."

So, you were watching, and now you are running away as if pursued by the devil himself. Well may you fear a pursuer but not tonight, for tonight you are safe. You and I will meet again and then you will discover a fate beyond the limits of your imagination.

Snorting once, Chloe shook her head. *This damnable heated suit is horribly uncomfortable, time for this fake Red Empire Assassin to disappear for good. After all, it is wise to never repeat a specific tactic.*

She blurred along the laneway to the north as if pursuing the fleeing Ramp master, and disappeared into the desolate slums of South Dorchester.

* * *

The van accelerated away from the accident and emergency entrance of the hospital and merged into the street traffic.

"All onsite cameras were offline for the drop-off," Juliette reported calmly over the earbud comm links. "We will have continuous cover back to the safe house."

"Good work everyone," Francis added from the front seat. "That's one more innocent life the vampires didn't claim tonight."

Relief surged through Anton, everyone had survived, not even a scratch. He'd been certain that there would be a trap, and he still had a lingering feeling of a narrow escape. He looked around the team, everyone sat relaxed in the van, comfortable, variously happy or calm, discussing the night's events and actions the way that victors do, with a natural confidence and ease.

He felt oddly out of place like he was looking at a big jigsaw puzzle and a single pivotal piece was missing. There was something, an idea or a notion, that was tantalizingly out of reach, just beyond the boundaries of his mind. He tried reaching for it, but it was like groping in pitch darkness for something that wasn't there.

The sensation of missing something became painful, and Anton remarked, "Wasn't that too easy?"

The team quietened down, and Francis replied, "I don't think so, Anton. Chiara, Li and yourself came in late, and Jay nearly died. We also didn't save all the people, there was one casualty tonight."

Jay tilted his head and asked, "Yes, what slowed you guys down?"

"What was your entrance like?" Chiara asked Jay.

"Our doors were shut," Li noted. "We didn't open them until Francis gave the call to go."

Yvette nodded and reported, "Ours were off their hinges, we had a straight path in."

"That's enough to account for the gap," Francis observed.

Anton frowned, sighed and stated uneasily, "Okay, there's a tactical issue there, but apart from that, it felt too easy. It still feels too easy, like there's something missing."

Francis directed, "Anton, we will debrief in full when we get back to the safe house, see if you can clarify your thoughts by then."

"Boojums?" Peter remarked from the driver's seat.

Anton shrugged and frowned.

Jay caught Anton's gaze and grinned tentatively at him.

Anton leaned forward slightly in the gloom of the van's interior.

Jay put his right fist up in a lazy loop. Anton did the same, and they gently fist punched.

Jay leaned forward and said contritely, "You saved my life tonight. This doesn't change how I feel about your grandfather, but I understand that you are not him. I apologize for how I've treated you; it was horribly unfair."

An intense wave of relief washed through Anton, and he replied, "No problem, forget it."

Jay looked at Anton quizzically for a moment, whispering tightly, "I tried to kill you."

Anton grinned crookedly. "Well, you're not the only one."

"You're taking it well."

"Jay, I'm just glad we're on the same side."

Jay nodded and declared, "For sure, we're on the same side."

Finally, some progress, Anton thought.

* * *

The Raven strove to understand the night's events.

They had seen the break in the silhouette of the parapet along the top of the water tower. The Raven was sure it was two praetorians, armed with a sniper rifle and a light machine gun. The Raven had ramped without breaking stride. Their senses going into overdrive just as a new figure appeared from the shadows on the tower top. Cold metal had gleamed for a brief instant in the moonlight, and then the slaughter had begun.

The action on top of the tower was over a moment later. The figure shrinking back into the shadows. The Raven had breathed in the night air, letting it out slowly, allowing their Ramp to die to a cool ember. The two short swords, cowl, and long cloak were unmistakable; the figure had been a Red Empire assassin.

The rest of the team had not noticed the fight, their attention elsewhere at the critical moment. As no one else had reacted, it was obvious that only the Raven had seen the two praetorians and their mysterious killer. The Raven was shocked, what were the praetorians doing there in the first place? Did they know about the mission? Or were they simply staking out the coven, waiting for any members of the Order to arrive?

Anton, Li, and Jay had talked about the mission being a trap. Anton had proposed the idea and Jay had dismissed it, but it had turned out that Anton had been right.

An uncomfortable feeling of disquiet crept through them as they considered what had happened. Anton was quite insightful to see a trap which everyone else had dismissed. The Raven added it to the list of odd abilities that Anton had. The hard defense that broke Jay's hand and his wild speed under desperate conditions. One day Anton may have enough awareness to see through the Raven's disguise.

The Raven shook their head gently, beset with uncertainty. The mission had been a trap. There were two options. The first was that the Vampire Dominion had created the coven as bait, and then the praetorians had staked it out until the Order of Thoth showed up, and the second was that there was a traitor in the Order who had betrayed the Mirovar force team to the vampires.

The only people who knew of the mission were the Mirovar force team, Ramin Kain, and Samuel Luther. The Raven had grown up with the other team members. They were much-loved, albeit faithless heathens, who had not yet seen the truth of the way of the Red Empire. The Raven believed that they would all come willingly to the Red Empire in the end. It was the Raven's sacred duty to guide them to the truth, and God willing, it would be so.

The Raven considered it impossible that any member of the Mirovar force team had betrayed them, that left only Kain, or Luther, or both, in the role of traitor.

What were the possible responses? It was safer to assume that Kain and Luther were both traitors until proven otherwise. Although, they couldn't rule out that the coven was simply a lure designed to catch and kill them all.

What about the Red Empire assassin? Who was it? Perhaps their childhood instructor Taipan, a true master of Red Empire Ninjitsu, or another who had come of age since the Raven's insertion into the Mirovar force team. The Raven concluded that the assassin had to be the Red Ghost's other agent in North America, the same person on the end of the messages that the Raven had sent. The only one the Raven had told of tonight's mission and they had intervened against the vampires.

Why had the other Red Empire agent broken their cover to protect the Mirovar force team? The Raven considered the possibility they had come to observe and fortunately discovered the praetorians before they could attack. Could they also be secretly protecting the Raven? They could ensure that the Raven would fulfill their own mission of rising to the top of the Order of Thoth. From that high position, the Raven could bend the Order to the will of Shabbah al Ahmar until the Red Empire absorbed the Order.

Then all the Ramp Masters would unite under one glorious banner against the Vampire Dominion.

The following conclusions remained: they could not trust Kain and Luther and they may have betrayed the Order of Thoth to the Vampire Dominion, and Shabbah al Ahmar's agent in North America was willing to risk all to protect the Mirovar force team.

The Raven's eyes hardened. The Vampire Dominion may be willing to create covens of vampires simply to bait a trap with. Anton was brighter than people gave him credit for and his ability to reach the correct conclusion before others did may one day be a threat to the Raven's mission.

The Raven smiled slightly, barely visible in the gloom inside the van. They would have to ensure that Anton could never suspect them of having a mission beyond the Mirovar force team. They would have to take special care to manage their relationship with him.

The van sped through the darkness, chasing the twin cones of bright illumination that lit up the trees beside the road. The trees loomed over the road like giant watchmen, silent guardians of the boundaries of the highway leading back to the safe house.

The Raven relaxed in their seat. Something teased at the edge of their awareness. They wanted to ignore it, but it wouldn't go away, so they reached for it, and it rushed through them like an ice-cold knife.

What if Shabbah al Ahmar's agent in North America was a double agent or worse a member of the Vampire Dominion?

A sick feeling bloomed in the middle of the Raven's gut. The question was shocking, the level of betrayal almost beyond imagining, and yet – it felt right. It would mean Shabbah al Ahmar's agent had been playing the Raven to achieve their own ends. But what could be their agenda? If they were also working for the vampire dominion, why would they intervene and kill the two praetorians waiting to ambush the Mirovar force team? It didn't make any sense.

The sense of truth faded away into the surrounding darkness. The Raven groped after it, but it was like trying to grasp mist and shadow. In the end, they had nothing left beyond an uneasy feeling of having missed something critically important.

The Raven worked hard to remember in detail what they had seen on top of the water tower. The masked figure was briefly visible while the Raven was ramped, time had slowed, the assassin's techniques were pure Red Empire Ninjitsu and executed with stunning speed.

The assassin wasn't Taipan. Not even the Raven's premier instructor was that fast. It could have been a lone wolf, someone with a rare talent for speed, and their own agenda. Someone who knew of the Vampire Dominion and the Mirovar force team's plans.

Hell, it could have been a rogue vampire warrior dressed up as a Red Empire assassin.

The thought sent a shiver along the Raven's skin, and they remained troubled by thoughts of betrayal for the rest of the journey back to the safe house.

* * *

General Clayton Maze leaped from the hovering nightfalcon helicopter to the top of the water tower.

He landed on his feet, in a minimum crouch, his vampire physiology absorbing the impact of the twenty-yard fall without harm. His nostrils flared. The air reeked with the scent of recently congealed blood, and the whiff of decay from the apartment block opposite the tower. His eye's widened as he took in his surroundings. He noted the precise methods used to kill the two praetorians.

"Clearly an expert," he observed without irony.

Two praetorians equipped with body bags, dropped from the helicopter, landing beside him. They moved forward to recover the remains of the Beta team.

Clayton had already seen enough to confirm the video record he'd watched in the nightfalcon. The Panopticon had harvested imagery from a US military satellite during the mission and the two praetorians had died at precisely 00:52:34. He was not surprised by his failure to detect any sign of the assailant. He'd spent over a century at war with their ilk. His lips curled with distaste. He hated the Red Empire with a passion bordering on fanaticism.

He went to the parapet and looked over. Better able to judge the distance to the ground from where he stood than by watching satellite images in a helicopter. It was quite a drop; not too difficult for a vampire, but a long way for a Ramp master – a very long way. Was the assailant human? Anyone could don the garb of a Red Empire assassin, but no one could fake the combat effectiveness on display.

A brief gust pulled at the dark suit jacket that he wore. The air was moist, the first hint of rain. He stood with his hands on his hips and surveyed the site. Another team of praetorians had commandeered the black van on the expressway and were driving off with it. A second nightfalcon hovered over the two-story building to the north, picking up the remains of Gamma team.

His final team was bagging the bodies of the coven vampires arrayed by the Order of Thoth in front of the apartment block.

Clayton was troubled. There was the telltale heat plume of the Ramp in the satellite view, easy to detect with an infra-red filter. It appeared there was a very talented Red Empire assassin conducting operations in North America. He shook his bald head slowly – the facts seemed to fit a Red Empire assassin. But he'd never encountered one this effective and that left room for doubt.

Clayton reviewed the video footage in his mind, the assailant had appeared out of the abandoned houses on the north side of the main street at 00:52:06. They had blurred across the road to the base of the two-story building where they had ascended the outer wall. They had surprised and promptly dismembered the Gamma team on the roof at 00:52:13. They had then moved on, descending down to the trees and the path that wound its way around the western end of the apartment block.

Cornelius Crane had issued his abort mission command to Centurion Rawlings at 00:52:19. Rawlings never got the chance to pass the message onto his teams.

The assailant had reached the expressway over the Neponset River at 00:52:20. The van's rear door had been torn from its hinges, and the assailant had entered the van, exiting two seconds later at 00:52:23. They had then covered the three hundred yards from the van to the tower top in ten seconds. The Beta team praetorians had died a second later.

Clayton leaned out over the parapet and saw there was enough room for someone to hide underneath it. Provided they could hold onto the edges of the bricks. A vampire or a Ramp master could do it.

The assailant had paused for a while on top of the tower, before hiding out of sight underneath the parapet while another Ramp master had ascended the tower and investigated the dead praetorians before disappearing away from the site. The assailant had dropped from beneath the parapet to the ground. They had paused briefly, and according to their infra-red heat signature had remaining ramped. They had blurred away, disappearing into the nearby abandoned houses bordering South Dorchester. For man or vampire, it would be an easy matter to break contact with the Panopticon and escape. The camera coverage in South Dorchester had decayed with the rest of the suburb.

"Who was the other Ramp master?" Clayton asked, there was no answer from the rising wind.

The praetorians completed bagging the dead and retrieving their equipment. The nightfalcon swung lower to allow them to leap on board. Clayton shook his head as he surveyed the site one last time. He sensed the distances involved and evaluated the speed of the attacks, especially the assault on the van. He touched his right ear, where a Shadowstone quantum communications earbud rested. It filtered out ambient noise and allowed for easy conversation even within the howl of the helicopter's downwash.

"Sir," he said. "I don't think we're dealing with a normal Ramp Master here. They're faster than anyone I've seen, powerful too, most likely some sort of super Red Empire assassin."

There was a brief pause on the link, then Cornelius Crane answered, his voice tight and controlled, "It's too early to draw conclusions. Wrap up your operations and return to the Citadel."

"Yes, Sir," Clayton replied. Closing the link, he leaped up into the nightfalcon. He took a seat, looking out at Boston as the ground shrank away from the soaring helicopter, a question hammering at his mind.

General Chloe Armitage, where are you tonight?

Chapter Twelve

> 05:45:12 Init Transcript Program..........
> 05:45:12 Init Source Anonymization..........
> 05:45:12 Init Traceless Call..........
> 05:45:13 Call...1...2...3...4...5...6
> 05:45:19 Init Redial
> 05:45:20 Call...1
> 05:45:21 Call Connect [Sergeant Detective Luke Walker] [LW]
> 05:45:22 [LW] "What? Who is this?"
> 05:45:25 [ANON] "An informant."
> 05:45:27 [LW] "I have to tell you that it's an offense to make a false report."
> 05:45:32 [ANON] "You need to hear this."
> 05:45:34 [LW] "Hear what?"
> 05:45:39 [ANON] "A ring of serial killers has been murdering the homeless in Boston for the last two months."
> 05:45:39 [PAUSE]
> 05:45:42 [LW] "You can back this up?"
> 05:45:44 [ANON] "Check out the basement at [REDACTED]."
> 05:45:49 [LW] "[REDACTED]?"
> 05:45:53 [ANON] "Yes."
> 05:45:55 [LW] "Who are you?"
> 05:45:57 End Call..........
> 05:45:58 Move Transcript to
../../../Investigations/ChloeArmitage/[datestamp]/Transcripts..........
> 05:45:58 Set Privacy for Generals Eyes Only [FGEO] [General Clayton Maze]
> 05:45:58 Init Erase..........
> 05:45:58 End Transcript Program..........

– Content from a partially declassified Panopticon transcript.

* * *

The War Room, 103rd floor, Crane's Citadel, Manhattan, August 9th, 05:00

Chloe was fascinated by a throbbing vein on Cornelius Crane's left temple. She'd seen such things many times before on her opponents or her prey, but never on her king.

She'd disposed of the Red Empire assassin disguise in the sewers of Boston. The evidence burned beyond recognition with a white phosphorous grenade. She smiled inwardly. The sudden appearance of a terrifyingly capable agent of the Red Empire, the deaths of seven praetorians and the subsequent disappearance of the agent would create a mystery that would further confound her king and aid her cause.

Chloe had just returned to her penthouse when she received the call from Crane to come to the Citadel for an emergency meeting. She attributed the gap in time between the events in Boston, and the call, to the necessity of Clayton Maze investigating the site and then returning to Manhattan. It had allowed her time to change into a fashionable black pinstripe pants suit, offset with a scarlet red chiffon blouse and red shoes.

Chloe stared at Cornelius as he shouted at Clayton and herself. She brought her attention back to his words as he continued to rant, sweeping a bloody helmet off the war room table to the floor.

"—it's outrageous! Nineteen praetorians killed in seven months. What the fucking hell is going on?" Cornelius shouted.

The praetorian tactical helmet bounced and rolled to a stop in front of Clayton and Chloe. They stood to attention, staring resolutely forward. Neither allowed the helmet and the stale reek of dried vampire blood to distract them.

Cornelius shook his finger at both generals and snapped, "The two of you will find out what is going on, or I'll put you both in silver for a year and see if that sharpens your ability to follow orders."

Turning back to the war room table, Cornelius punched a button on a console. The screens at the opposite end of the room displayed a composite picture of a world map. More than forty red stars blinked repeatedly, spread throughout Europe, Asia, Africa and the Middle East. There was a single red star in North America; squatting by itself in New Jersey. Praetorian losses over the last twenty years, each one marked with a date-time stamp and a name.

"The status at the end of last year," Cornelius stated irritably, punching another button.

The screens refreshed, the original red stars stopped blinking, fading to a dull orange. Nineteen new red stars flashed into existence, four in Jerusalem, six in a tight cluster in Boston, two in Brazil, the first in Rio de Janeiro, the second in the Amazon, and another seven stars blinked in a second tight cluster in Boston.

"Boston has become a death trap," Cornelius declared.

"Clearly, the Order is increasing its activity," Chloe observed calmly, pointing at Boston on the map. "I know of these deaths on the Boston docks, I was there, and Arthur Slayne is the likely Order operative in Brazil. But what of these last seven? Where were they killed exactly? Can we expand the resolution of the map?"

Cornelius stared at Chloe for a moment before silently pressing another button. The map expanded, Boston, spreading across the screen. In moments, the map displayed the seven dead praetorians in three separate clusters, three on an expressway, two on a water tower, and the last two on the roof of a two-story building. Each site was approximately three hundred yards from the other two, describing the points of a rough triangle centered on a large apartment block.

Chloe read the metadata next to each red star, did a double take, and asked incredulously, "Centurion Rawlings is dead?"

"That's what it says." Clayton sneered.

Chloe stared at Clayton for a moment, tilting her head slightly. She looked back at Cornelius and asked, "Why were they there?"

"They were on an operation under my direction against the Mirovar force team."

Chloe leaned forward on the balls of her feet. "I thought that I was in charge of operations in the northeast?"

"I grew tired of waiting for you to fulfill your promise to deliver their heads," Cornelius stated flatly.

"Sir, I could've helped," Chloe declared passionately.

"Perhaps, but you may have met your match."

"Why, what happened?"

"Watch this footage," Cornelius commanded. Tapping a button on the console.

The main screen displayed full satellite video of the attack of the mysterious assailant. Clayton stood impassively; he'd clearly seen it earlier that night. Chloe watched the screen intently. The video finished with the assailant disappearing into the desolation of the South Dorchester slums.

Chloe looked at Cornelius and arched one eyebrow quizzically in an unspoken question.

"It appears that the Red Empire have unearthed a talent," Cornelius observed, shaking his head slowly. "A new Ramp master with extreme speed, strength, and skill."

"The Red Empire are ruthless killers," Clayton declared.

Chloe smiled slightly, and remarked, "Just like us."

"Nothing like us," Clayton snapped. "They're vermin."

"Enough!" Cornelius roared. He paused for a moment then continued in level tones, "Your petty rivalry bores me. Focus on the task at hand."

"This is unprecedented," Chloe noted. "Are we sure it's not a rogue vampire pretending to be a Red Empire assassin?"

Clayton glanced across at Chloe and said, "It's not beyond the realms of possibility."

"What of the operative that emerged from the tower?" Chloe asked, frowning. "Clearly, he hid carefully and watched everything. He must have been there before the praetorians arrived. Otherwise, they would surely have seen him. Who was he?"

"Unknown, there is insufficient visual or audio evidence for the Panopticon to identify him," Cornelius explained.

"Clearly, he was another Ramp master, but of the Order or the Red Empire?" Chloe asked.

"Also, unknown," Cornelius noted.

"What of the helmet cams," Chloe inquired, "did they record any pertinent features?"

"There was a tenth of a second of video from within the van," Cornelius advised. "Centurion Rawlings turned his head just before a blade ripped through his helmet. It took out the camera on the way through. It's a blurred image. The agent was moving very fast."

Chloe frowned intently, and asked, "Can Shadowstone clean the image up? Perhaps we could get enough detail to get a match."

"It's already happening," Cornelius stated. "A team at Fort Dix is processing the video. Looks like a face shot, someone covered with a veil, and a hood."

"Classic Red Empire garb," Clayton observed confidently.

"Interesting. At least that's something. When will we have a clear image?" Chloe asked.

"By tonight," Cornelius advised.

"Excellent," Chloe said, smiling.

"What are you so happy about?" Cornelius snapped.

"I love a challenge – they're obviously good with a blade," Chloe observed. She glanced sideways at Clayton. "I don't often get a challenge."

Cornelius stared at her for a long moment before grinning fiercely. His fangs descended into attack position, and he commanded, "Both of you have two days to find out what is going on. I will have a full report here, on Friday at 23:00. I expect results, do not fail me."

"Yes, Sir." They chorused together.

"Now get out of my sight," Cornelius ordered.

The two generals bowed low, backing away before turning and exiting the war room.

* * *

Chloe followed Clayton through the door and into the operations center. Over a dozen vampires staffed the main operations room; all busily at work for the Vampire Dominion.

Clayton turned to her and asked suspiciously, "So, where were you five hours ago?"

"I was in my Manhattan penthouse."

"Can anyone back that up?"

"I was alone – am I under investigation?"

Clayton stared at her for a long moment.

Chloe hissed. "What are you going to do? Accuse me of the murder of seven praetorians – are you mad?"

Clayton wrinkled his nose, and declared, "I have to investigate all options."

"You think!" Chloe replied sarcastically.

They paused for a moment; the operations center had fallen into silence. All the other vampires were staring at them. Chloe's eyes tightened with a thinly veiled threat.

Clayton sniffed and said in a low voice, "I don't have time to bandy words with you, I have a mess in Boston to clean up."

Chloe's eyes momentarily flashed with seething hatred as she watched Clayton turn away and stride from the room. The other vampires in the room had quickly returned their attention to their monitors, and sheaths of paperwork. She waved at them and called out in steely tones, "Stop faking that you didn't notice anything. Now get back to work everyone, the show's over."

The vampires buried themselves deeper into their work.

Chloe assumed a neutral expression on her face and walked calmly over to the elevators, the night was getting late.

The doors slid apart, she entered the elevator and punched the button for the basement parking garage. As the elevator descended, she worked through the problem of the helmet cam video. The video would reveal her eyes, and Crane and the rest would surely recognize her. She determined to ring James Haley as soon as she was in her penthouse. He was the only resource she had positioned to intervene. The mission would reveal to James her role in the deaths of the praetorians. He would know enough to destroy her by revealing her actions to Crane. If she took no action, failure was inevitable, she had to use James, but she would need to ensure his absolute loyalty.

Chloe smiled briefly, calculating how much time remained before dawn.

A phone call won't do; I'm going to have to pay James a visit. It's a good thing that he lives in New York.

* * *

Cornelius dropped out of a previsionary meditation. He continued to sit in the war room. His generals had left the room ten minutes before. He remained troubled, although the meditation had drained his anger away. The probability line toward his own death had strengthened during the night. The failed mission against the Mirovar team had increased the risk from someone within the force team. The probability line went all the way back to the Boston docks, and anchored in Li Wu or Anton Smith.

Cornelius steepled his long fingers and rested his chin upon them. It was clear he'd lost the initiative on the night of the battle on the Boston docks. He'd attempted to regain it with the lure of the vampire coven, and the complicity of Ramin Kain but his plan had failed. The mission was a disaster. His lead praetorian, Centurion Rawlings, was dead, along with another six of his elite vampire soldiers.

And now the threat to my life has increased. The thought rolled around his mind like an alien artifact, strange and dubious.

Cornelius pressed his lips into a thin line of determination. He'd not survived nearly a thousand years by giving way to fear, doubt and uncertainty. The situation was fluid, but he'd survived far worse threats than that posed by two children of the Order of Thoth.

His fingers dropped, and he rested his chin on his clasped fists, staring silently at nothing, his mind far away. He mused on the fact that his prevision had shown victory before the mission had begun, and yet comprehensive failure had occurred so quickly once the mission had commenced. It was clear that the assailant, Red Empire agent or not, was a personage of true power. Able to shape events at will, and beyond his capability to anticipate with his ability to see the future.

In the long years since the ceremony with Jean Philippe Allemande, he'd discovered that the precognitive ability was tightly bound to the results of his own choices and actions. The interventions of others could shape the results with sudden effect. Anyone with a persistent ability to impact his life, he had either eliminated or co-opted, but life goes on, new people are born, and new threats could always arise. He'd adapted to the limitations of his prevision and maximized its value.

The disappearance of the assailant troubled him. It was as if they had simply ceased to exist. There were no probability lines leading from the events of this night to another encounter with the agent who had worked so effectively against his plans. He'd never seen anything like it before.

Cornelius determined that he would get to the bottom of the mystery of the assailant. The first attempt to recapture the initiative from the Ramp masters had failed, he would adapt his tactics and try again. He leaned forward and used the command console on the war room table to place an encrypted call to Kain's smartphone. The phone rang three times before Kain picked it up.

"… Oh, it's you," Kain answered.

"What did you see?" Cornelius inquired.

"Someone killed your two vampires. I saw the fresh remains – there's a third player – and they knew what was happening."

"There's a leak in the Mirovar force team. Likely from a Red Empire agent, and they have a friend, someone powerful who killed my praetorians."

"The Red Empire does not have an agent in the Mirovar force team! That's impossible!" Kain declared incredulously.

"I know that my praetorians didn't leak the information. That leaves an agent within Mirovar's team, or it was you."

"Well, it damn well wasn't me."

"Are you trying to screw with me?"

"Of course not. What would I gain? I asked you to help me get rid of Francis Mirovar and Anton Smith. Why would I sabotage my own mission?"

"Which means the leak came from within the Mirovar force team – accept it – it's the only option left."

There was a long pause on the line.

Kain said, "Damn, you must be right."

"Of course, I am," Cornelius stated matter-of-factly. "So, do something about it."

"Oh, I will." Kain hissed. "Don't you worry about that."

"Once you find your spy, keep them alive, and in place, we need to find their accomplice, the one who killed my praetorians."

"Obviously."

"Keep me appraised of your progress on this topic – it affects us both. It would be harmful to our agreement for you to start keeping secrets on this issue."

"Yes, of course."

"Don't take too long."

"Yes," Kain agreed impatiently.

Cornelius stroked his chin and declared, "We're done then?"

Kain said, "Yes."

Cornelius hung up the call and smiled slightly. He always enjoyed it when Kain was under pressure. It was clear that Kain had not seen the insertion of the Alpha and Gamma teams at the mission site. He must have been close to the water tower, or even inside it when the Beta team had positioned themselves on top of it. Obviously, Kain was the other Ramp master captured on video fleeing the site.

Cornelius speculated that Arthur Slayne had returned to North America, and was now in Boston. He'd witnessed firsthand Arthur Slayne's fighting ability in the secret vaults and passageways beneath Saint Peter's Basilica. Slayne was capable of the deeds done tonight. The problem with Slayne's involvement was explaining how he knew of the mission. Cornelius sighed, no, there was no evidence linking Slayne to the events tonight. It was most likely someone else, someone as powerful and dangerous as Slayne.

Cornelius admitted to himself that Kain had said it best – there's a third player. He got up from his chair and made his way through the operations center to his personal quarters. It had been a long night, and he needed to rest.

As he lay on his bed, Cornelius contemplated the option the assailant came from the Red Empire, and was not human. He had to admit the final possibility that there were one or more rogue vampires within his own organization. He vowed to himself to find out if there were any traitors within his ranks. He was certain that Hell would be a place of love and kindness compared to the fate that he would visit on any who had betrayed him.

* * *

Ramin Kain shook his head incredulously as the smartphone call disconnected.

It had been another long night, and it had ended in disaster. He remembered with perfect clarity the moment when one of the Mirovar force team looked up and saw the praetorians on top of the water tower. Was it by chance? Were they simply scanning for threats, or did they know what to look for? The options were dizzying, Ramin's stomach churned and knotted.

There was something deeply wrong with Mirovar's team. The idea, forcefully provided by Crane, that there was an active Red Empire agent embedded in the team had shocked him. Current events forced him to admit that it was the only viable possibility. He drew on his memory of who was in the team. The agent would be someone young. Francis and Juliette Mirovar were beyond question. Jay Creeley's history was well known. That left only Yvette Mirovar, Chiara Romano, and Peter Lamb as the possible agent unless somehow it was Li Wu or Anton Slayne.

Ramin snorted derisively. Anton Slayne in the guise of Anton Smith was a true nobody, it was clear why Arthur Slayne had hidden his grandson. There was no chance the Red Empire had co-opted the young Slayne. The same went for Li Wu, a traditionalist like Gang Wu would not have raised a daughter who would spy for the Red Empire. No, the Red Empire agent had to be one of the other three.

Then there was the problem of the Red Empire agent's accomplice, the one who had surprised and killed the two praetorians on the water tower. Ramin reluctantly admitted to himself, that he didn't have the skills to creep up on vampires and suddenly kill two of them. The accomplice was clearly very skilled, powerful and dangerous.

Ramin rubbed his face with both hands. Having to deal with all this scheming by other players was a right royal pain in the butt. Why didn't people simply defer to his obvious genius? He shook his head again, still incredulous at the sudden turn of events. Victory had been certain, the plan had been perfect, and yet Francis Mirovar and Anton Slayne were still alive.

It was as if divine intervention was on their side, and whatever gods there were, were laughing at him as they destroyed his plans.

"Fuck it." He swore. "I'm going to have to find this damn spy, their accomplice and destroy Mirovar and Slayne as well."

Ramin vowed to himself to find a way to cut through all these difficulties and seize victory. There was no other way to transform the Order of Thoth into an efficient fighting force. The Order must be under his direct and total command. It was the only way to win against the vampires.

He toyed with the idea of getting Sam to simply kill Anton Slayne and Francis Mirovar. He could say that Sam had gone mad, and acted on his own. A crazed lone wolf attack. It would be best for Sam to die in the mission so he couldn't have any second thoughts or tell any tales. Ramin weighed his options. He wrinkled his nose, sucking air through his teeth. Sam was just a little bit too valuable to burn in a suicide mission. He needed another way, and he needed it quickly. Anton Slayne was getting more powerful every day. How long would it be before he was as capable as his grandfather? Another loose cannon with the ability to split the Order of Thoth down the middle and not only threaten his own position as Head of the Order but also his life.

However, the assassination of his enemies would not solve the complication of the Red Empire agent or their deadly accomplice.

Ramin racked his brain.

The pathway forward became clear, he needed an Order traveler. Not just any traveler but one of proven loyalty to himself. Someone who was aware of what Ramin stood for, and was truly committed to the transformation of the Order of Thoth. There was one man he could trust to do the job, Deon Lamar. A man whose particular talent had required Ramin's utmost skills to cultivate and co-opt.

A slow grin spread across his face. Ramin picked up his smartphone and dialed Sam Luther. He knew Sam would be up at this early hour, training with weapons. The phone rang twice before Sam answered it.

"Hi RK, what can I do for you?"

"Do you know where Deon Lamar is?"

"Deon Lamar? He's in Australia, Sydney, I think. Evaluating a new novice with the local Force team. Why?"

"I need him in Maine."

"You want him to investigate Mirovar?"

"Not him. A member of his team."

"Anton Slayne?"

"Hold your horses, Sam. I'll explain."

"... Sure RK."

"It looks like there is a Red Empire agent within the Mirovar force team."

Ramin imagined Sam shaking his head in disbelief.

"... That's shocking."

"Yes, quite so. Now, I need my best spy catcher on point for this mission, and that's Lamar."

"For sure, Lamar is our best man. He's also very switched on politically."

"True, he's very intelligent – precisely the sort of man that we want on this mission."

"Do you want me to contact him?"

"Yes. Get him over to Maine at the earliest opportunity. Warn him about Anton Slayne, and Li Wu. They're likely accomplices of any Red Empire agent in the team."

"Anton Slayne, a Red Empire spy? ... Sure RK, will do."

"Sam, don't underestimate the Slaynes, they have their fingers in all sorts of pies. They're the very heart of deviousness. We have to be clever if we are to defeat them."

"Sure RK, I understand perfectly. I will instruct Lamar on what to expect. Is there anything else?"

"Yes. Most importantly, impress upon Deon the necessity to identify the spy without giving away the fact he's discovered them. We need to find the spy's accomplice in the US. Is that clear?"

"Yes, RK. Crystal clear."

"Good work, Sam. I knew that I could trust you to understand the gravity of the situation within the Mirovar force team."

"I wish we could disband them."

"Quite so."

"Is there anything else?"

"No Sam, just keep me in the loop as things progress."

"Yes, RK."

Ramin hung up the line and put down the phone. He smiled grimly. *I may be able to manage this so the same net that captures the Red Empire agent also captures Anton Slayne.*

His smile broadened into a wide toothy grin.

* * *

There were a pair of knocks on the front door of James Haley's apartment. At the same time, his smartphone pinged with a text message. He rolled out of bed and glanced at the smartphone's screen. The message was from Chloe Armitage and read, 'Knock, Knock.'

"Oh my God, what's she doing here?" James whispered to himself as he pulled on a pair of shorts and tracksuit pants. He didn't have a clean shirt handy, and he walked bare-chested down the hall from his bedroom to the front door of his New York apartment.

James opened the door. Chloe stood before him. She wore a black pinstripe pants suit, a scarlet red chiffon blouse, red shoes and a slight smile.

Tilting her head slightly, her smile broadened. "It is customary to invite a guest in."

James hesitated for a split second, wondering if the old myth that vampires could only enter your home if someone invited them in held any water. In the same moment, he decided, *fuck it*, and replied, "Yes, Ma'am, please come in."

Chloe stepped across the threshold, approaching to stand directly before him. She smiled again, put her finger gently on his lips. "Please, call me Chloe when we're alone together."

She stepped past him, walking slowly down the hall, looking at photos on the wall. One caught her eye, and she paused in front of it. "Looks like Afghanistan?"

"Firebase Cobra, Oruzgan Province," James noted. His mind buzzing with questions. The chief among them – *why is she here?*

Chloe looked back along the hall and stated, "US Army 3rd Special Forces Group, 1st Battalion, Captain James Haley, Operational Detachment commander. Awarded two silver stars during your tours in Afghanistan. Then you joined the 902d Military Intelligence Group within US Army Counterintelligence. You served another two years there, mostly based in Washington DC, before moving to the CIA."

James nodded; the personal history lesson meant nothing to him anymore. Those events had happened to someone else. Someone who had wanted to make a difference in the world. Someone who didn't know vampires ruled the world and treated people as disposable cattle.

Someone who hadn't murdered his own men.

"Then Shadowstone of course. Quite a distinguished career you have James, we will have to see what happens next."

"And what would that be?" James asked flatly.

For nearly two months James had been actively tracking the Head of the Order of Thoth, Ramin Kain. He'd picked up his close associate Samuel Luther. He now had physical data files an inch thick on both men. He knew where they both lived, what their habits were, and most importantly – the location of an active Order safe house in Maine. The rush of enthusiasm he'd felt at the beginning of the new mission had faded over time. The desolation after the defeat on the Boston docks had come back to haunt him. Only his professionalism kept him moving forward.

Chloe looked at him for a long moment. "I understand your pain, James."

James frowned but remained silent. They stood in the hallway a couple of yards apart, but seemingly separated by a million miles.

"Patience James, a very long game is being played here, and don't underestimate your part," Chloe advised. "I promise you; I have the solution for your suffering."

"What? Vampirism?" James asked in dark tones.

"No," Chloe answered. "Nothing as blunt as that."

"Then what?"

"The truth."

"The truth?" James asked doubtfully.

"Yes, the truth, the whole truth and nothing but the truth."

"So, help me God?"

"So, help me God."

James frowned, his face frozen with suspicion.

Chloe said lightly, "But first, a shower and a shave. We need to get you ready for work."

"Yes, Ma'am," James replied automatically. He'd never seen Chloe act this way, so informal, it was – unsettling.

"Chloe." She corrected him softly.

"Yes, Chloe."

She followed him into the bathroom, and James had a sudden and disturbing vision that she was about to join him. Instead, Chloe grabbed a double handful of white towels, and said, "Meet me in the kitchen in five minutes, and don't bother shaving."

James ran himself through a quick shower and dried himself hurriedly. Five minutes later, with a bath towel wrapped around his hips, he walked into the kitchen. There was a pot of steaming water on the stove, wet towels in the sink and one of his stools in the middle of the kitchen.

On the bench, glistening like a wet mirror in the overhead lights, was an old-fashioned straight razor. It looked brand new; he'd never seen it before.

"Please take a seat, there isn't much time, and I need to explain a few things," Chloe invited with a warm smile.

James approached the stool, turned and sat down with his back to Chloe.

She put both her hands on his head, he almost flinched but managed to stay still.

"Relax James," Chloe advised and began to massage his scalp.

James found the experience surreal. Why was the most powerful vampire on the planet massaging his head? Despite himself, he started to relax. She was really good at it. He closed his eyes.

A minute later she wrung out the towels, and gently placed a hot wet towel on his face. The heat was right on the upper limit of what was comfortable. She gently massaged his face through the towel. She followed the towel with the application of lightly scented shaving cream.

A moment later, there was the first touch of cold steel against his temple. Chloe expertly drew the razor down his left cheek toward his throat. She finished by wiping the blade against a towel on the bench and re-positioned the blade to make her second swipe.

"You mentioned the truth?" James asked dubiously.

"There is a lot to tell you about the Order of Thoth, the Red Empire, and the Vampire Dominion. You need to know everything. You need to understand that your life matters."

James jerked forward, and Chloe whipped the razor away from his face. His eyes flashed, and he declared incredulously, "Matters! How does it matter now?"

Chloe put her hands on his shoulders, guiding him back into position, she leaned forward close to his right ear and whispered, "Trust me, James. It will become clear soon."

James sighed, sat back and asked, "What about vampires?"

"Vampires have only existed for a little over five thousand years," Chloe explained, continuing the shave, moving the blade perfectly to ensure that James could speak without injury.

"How did they come about?"

"By accident," Chloe observed matter-of-factly.

"You're kidding me?"

"It's the truth," Chloe said. "There were two princes in Southern Egypt. They had access to a system they called the Engine of Thoth. One of them, Ahknaton, tried to use the Engine to resurrect his dead wife. She came back as the first vampire and killed him. The other prince, Hakron, survived and recorded what happened."

"What's the Engine of Thoth?"

"We call it the Metaframe today. It's at the foundation of reality. It defines the rules of the universe, such as gravity is an attractive force, time moves forward instead of backward, and that vampires exist."

"That's insane."

"You're used to the idea that the laws of the universe are immutable. It's always a shock to find out they're not."

"Do you have proof of this?"

"Is it that big a stretch for you? How long ago was it you didn't believe in vampires?" Chloe inquired, lifting the razor away from James' throat.

James frowned.

"I can provide proof in time but not today," Chloe advised.

"So, the Metaframe is what this is all about?"

"Yes, James," Chloe stated approvingly. "The Order of Thoth, the Red Empire, and the Vampire Dominion are at war over who controls the Metaframe."

"Who's winning?"

"No one. My boss, Cornelius Crane has organized the vampires for nearly two centuries but it hasn't made a difference. The war is in a deep stalemate between the three factions. In fact, there is an active, secret alliance between Crane and Kain."

"That's corrupt. From what I know of the Order, they would never ally with the vampires."

"True, they shouldn't. Kain and Crane are both traitors, but their respective betrayals are not the main issue."

"What is?"

"Who protects the Metaframe and for what purpose."

"Who does protect the Metaframe?"

"No one. The war protects the Metaframe by keeping the capability to access it separated amongst the factions. Crane is in the dominant position as he has the Key of Ahknaton and the Papyrus of Hakron the Scribe. All he requires now is the Interpretive Codex which is in the hands of his arch-enemy, Shabbah al Ahmar, the head of the Red Empire."

"The Red Ghost?"

"Yes. You know Arabic? ... Of course, I remember now ... it's in your file."

James nodded. "What's the Key of Ahknaton?"

"Honestly, no one knows. Ahknaton invented or acquired it. It allows absolute access to the Metaframe. Hakron described what Ahknaton did when he used it, and the Papyrus is the only guide we have."

"What's the Interpretive Codex?"

"Hakron encoded the Papyrus, the Codex explains how to read it. Hence why Crane wants the Codex."

"No one can break Hakron's code?"

"It's gibberish. The Codex is essential."

"You've read it?"

"Both of them."

"Then you understand how to access the Metaframe?"

"Yes. I just need the Key."

"What will you do once you have it?"

"Protect Humanity."

"From what?"

"Everything."

"What do you mean?"

"I mean everything. Overpopulation, global war, climate change, resource depletion, asteroid impact, plagues, famine." Chloe stepped back and waved her hands expansively, the razor gleaming in the kitchen lights. "Everything."

"How?"

"Through a single use of the Metaframe to empower the true rulership of vampires over this world."

"So, vampires would rule?"

"Yes. Vampires have an absolute vested interest in the survival and health of the human population. Our immortality provides stability. Our rule will usher in a new world order of lasting peace and prosperity balanced with the long-term survival of the planet."

A new vista opened up in front of James.

"James – I need people at my side who are committed to really solving the problems that have plagued humanity for thousands of years. I believe that you are one of those people. James, your life matters enormously, your choices and actions are absolutely critical to the success or failure of this vision. I know you better than you know yourself. Let me tell you what your true purpose is. It is to become an immortal protector of humanity, a guide, and shepherd of the flock. A man with the power and the will to ensure that humanity survives and prospers."

James could see the sense of Chloe's words, but he said, "You're still vampires, living off the lives of people."

"We'll eliminate war, crime, illness, starvation, all the usual sources of early death. In comparison, the small harvest that vampires make on the human population will be trivial."

"Do you know where the key is?" James asked, belief growing in the tone of his voice.

"Yes, I know exactly where it is."

"What's stopping you from taking it?"

"A sorcerer placed me under a magical curse that forbids me from directly harming Crane. An impact of the curse is that seizing the Key of Ahknaton would kill me. I can't touch it while Crane lives."

"Sorcery? Magic?"

"It's real, and associated to the Metaframe."

"You're trying to get rid of Crane?"

"Yes, the long game that I spoke of earlier."

"What do you need from me?" James asked, his eyes flashing with fresh interest.

"There's blurred video footage of me at Fort Dix that needs to be managed."

"In what way?"

"Doctored, so that it doesn't look like me. Shadowstone is working to clarify it today."

Chloe made the last swipe with her razor and swished it clean in the hot water in the sink. She placed a hot towel over James' face and gently wiped the last traces of shaving cream away.

James stood up and declared, "I'll get it done."

"Thank you, James. I will stay here today. It's too late in the morning for me to move around outside."

James nodded. "Of course."

"Once the task is done, come back here."

"Yes, Chloe."

Chloe moved in close, leaned up and kissed James once on the mouth. She stayed close and whispered, "You're special James. Never forget that."

James stared at her for a moment, stepped away and went to his bedroom to dress. Ten minutes later he was in his car and heading to Fort Dix.

James considered what had just happened. Chloe really trusted him. Her words rang true. She'd told him everything. There was a great war of powers underway, and it was time to choose sides. What Chloe was fighting for made sense. The world did need protecting, humanity needed protecting. There was a real chance to make a difference of historic proportions. Chloe's ideas and ambitions were compelling. The choice was clear and easy to make.

James made his decision, embraced his future, and there was no more doubt.

* * *

The video conferencing system of the war room displayed three of the generals. Shen Zhen from Beijing. Dieter Franz from Berlin, and Haras Mosule from Jerusalem. In the war room, facing the main screens, sat Cornelius Crane, flanked by Clayton Maze on his left and Chloe Armitage on his right.

Zhen, Franz, and Mosule had completed their reports. In the last three months, there had been an increase in Red Empire activity across all world zones. They'd wiped out a Chinese Shadowstone cyberwarfare unit and stolen their cyberweapons. They'd embezzled tens of billions of Euros from several Italian, French and German banks. A Russian submarine armed with nuclear demolition munitions had mysteriously failed and sunk beneath the Arctic ice. The nuclear weapons remained missing, presumed lost to the Red Empire.

Clayton had provided his report detailing the parameters of the assailant who had killed the praetorians in Boston. The Shadowstone team at Fort Dix had completed their work on the fragment of video that captured the assailant's face. He was male, brown-eyed, with a small mole next to his left eye. Based on satellite footage. His physical capabilities for speed, agility, and strength exceeded the upper end of the scale of a praetorian vampire. Clayton finished his report by concluding that there were two likely options. The Red Empire had managed to convert one of their own elite warriors into a vampire and send them on a mission, or there was a rogue vampire of great skill and power operating against the Vampire Dominion.

Crane rubbed the bridge of his nose and looked to his right. "General Armitage, your report."

"Sir," Chloe began her report. "I spent last night scouting the sewers of South Dorchester. I focused on the area directly north of the battle site where the assailant escaped to. I discovered a day old white phosphorous grenade scorch and this," Chloe placed a congealed blob of metal on the table.

Crane frowned curiously at the scorched metal. "What is it?"

"Based on chemical analysis it corresponds to the remains of a power unit for an electrically heated body suit."

"Someone wore a suit to artificially raise their body temperature?" Crane inquired.

Chloe nodded. "To simulate the Ramp."

"It had to be a vampire," Crane deduced.

"Yes, Sir," Chloe agreed confidently.

Clayton declared, "This confirms my results."

"A vampire is working for the Red Empire," Chloe asserted. "I double checked the video footage. The assailant is a master of Red Empire Ninjitsu. There are no vampires in the Vampire Dominion with that skill set apart from Haras Mosule, and he's accounted for."

"And yet," Crane frowned, "they destroyed the heat suit."

"They must be planning to change disguises," Chloe advised. "It makes good sense not to repeat tactics."

"So how did they know about the mission?" Clayton asked?

Crane and Chloe exchanged a glance. Crane stared at Clayton. "There is reason to believe a Red Empire agent is operating within the Mirovar force team."

Clayton did a double take. "Sir, when were you going to share that with us?"

Crane shrugged his shoulders. "It wasn't confirmed."

"It is now," Clayton declared. "The agent within the force team would have tipped off the Red Empire operative, and they showed up and protected the team. The Mirovar force team must be a cat's paw for the Red Empire."

"It would seem so." Crane allowed.

"If I may continue?" Chloe asked with a touch of exasperation.

Clayton nodded.

"In summary," Chloe stated. "My report confirms that a vampire is working with the Red Empire and is protecting the Mirovar force team. The vampire's skill set indicates they originated from within the warrior elite of the Red Empire. I suspect that he is a volunteer, once his mission is complete, he'll walk into the sunlight and destroy all evidence of his existence."

Crane said, "Excellent work General Armitage."

"Thank you, Sir."

Crane studied his generals for a moment. "General Armitage suggested the possibility that the Red Empire have an agent in the Mirovar force team back in June. Events have proved her to be correct. She has demonstrated initiative, perceptiveness and an admirable ability to integrate diverse pieces of evidence. The rest of you would do well to emulate her methods."

The other generals kept their faces impassive, as they replied, "Yes, Sir."

"Humph," Crane grunted. "The policy is clear – regain control over your territories and push back hard on Red Empire operations."

"Yes, Sir." The generals chorused more enthusiastically.

"Dismissed."

The conferencing system automatically shut down the remote screens.

Crane turned to Clayton and directed, "You have a new mission."

"Sir? What of my current mission?"

Crane nodded. "Your current mission is complete."

"Yes, Sir."

"I will brief you in two hours. Take a break and come back then."

"Yes, Sir. Very good, Sir."

Clayton collected his notes and left. The door automatically closing behind him.

Crane leaned forward and gently held Chloe's left hand. "Chloe, we need to talk."

"Yes, Cornelius."

I wonder what he's got in store for me now?

* * *

Cornelius looked steadily into Chloe's eyes. His previsionary experiences demonstrated that she could have nothing to do with the recent reversals. The probability lines for her and the other generals were always dark. He was impressed by her recent identification of the threat of the Red Empire co-option of the Mirovar force team and the revelation that an elite Red Empire assassin had become a vampire. The Red Empire agent in the Mirovar force team was working closely with the vampire assassin. The Red Empire was on the move around the world. He needed his best general at his side and well informed of current operations.

It was time to tell her about the secret detente with the Order of Thoth and his strategic plan. He declared matter-of-factly, "There has been an agreement between the Head of the Order of Thoth, and myself for nearly two decades."

"What?" Chloe asked incredulously. "You know who he is?"

"Yes. His name is Ramin Kain."

"What's the deal? It must be good to justify such a bizarre relationship."

"Chloe, I'm a practical man. The detente is a temporary convenience. It has allowed me to focus on operations limiting the Red Empire and to complete my Day Guard program. The Day Guard program is all but ready to execute. I have enough super-soldier serum to create a force of two hundred and fifty soldiers. Soon I will be in a position to conduct twenty-four-hour operations against the Ramp masters. The Day Guard will eliminate their key strategic advantage: the ability to operate effectively during the day. When I'm ready, I will crush the Red Empire and the Order of Thoth."

"Who will lead the Day Guard?" Chloe asked.

"I will assign operational command of the Day Guard program to Clayton. It will be his job to see it through to completion. We will start with the first group of two hundred and fifty this month and build our tactical methods."

"Will the Day Guard be integrated with Shadowstone."

"Yes. They already are, in the UK."

"Indeed." Chloe nodded. "I remember you assigning a force from the UK to Jerusalem about two months ago when I was there."

"The Phase IVs in the UK are an advanced prototype of what we have now perfected."

"You will need a human interface between Shadowstone and the Day Guard," Chloe said. "I would recommend Louise Wesson."

"You have verified her?"

"Yes. She checked out fine."

"What of James Haley's replacement?"

"Wesson again. Allow her to select her team. She has the capability to manage both organizations."

Cornelius paused for a moment. "Granted. I will instruct Clayton of the organizational changes."

Chloe leaned forward slightly and asked, "You always emphasized the need to acquire the Metaframe artifacts. How does that fit with this strategy?"

"As always, the artifacts remain our primary goal. I need to hold the dynamics of the conflict steady while I build the weapon that can crush our enemies once and for all. The Day Guard is the weapon, and once in play, it will prove decisive."

"So, what happens now?"

"We are at a late stage in my strategy. These recent reversals threaten it. Stability is the key to completing my strategy."

"What do you need from me? How can I help?"

"I need Ramin Kain kept alive and in place as the Head of the Order of Thoth until I'm ready to act. He is a self-obsessed fool who imagines he is a great strategist. In reality, he is a conniving schemer with very real political skills but poor military ones. The last thing I need is for someone who would be militarily effective, such as Francis Mirovar or Justin Blake to replace him. Kain has become unreliable. He's deeply attached to killing Francis Mirovar, and for some unknown reason, Anton Smith. To stabilize the situation, we need to destroy the Mirovar force team and ensure Kain remains safely at the top of the Order."

"I'm sure it can be done."

"It is essential. There have been further reversals. Someone destroyed my research facility in the Amazon five weeks ago, most likely Arthur Slayne. I've begun the process of rebuilding it. But it has put the Day Guard program back by at least a year, perhaps two. Two hundred and fifty soldiers are not enough, I planned on having ten times that amount. I need to ensure that we have another year to complete the new research facility in Brazil. Once we have more serum, we can build a force of two and a half thousand fully equipped Day Guards. With such a force we can destroy the Order of Thoth and the Red Empire."

"It is a stunning strategy sir."

Cornelius studied his best general. Was she being sarcastic? The moment passed, there was no trace of deceit in Chloe's face.

"Humph," he grunted. "Be that as it may, it's not done yet. There are other risks we must manage. The new Red Empire vampire assassin, chief amongst them. I want you to focus on finding and destroying him."

"I will need resources," Chloe stated, spreading her hands wide. "There are many threads here. Find and destroy the Mirovar force team. Find and destroy the Red Empire vampire. Keep Ramin Kain safe. I can't be everywhere at once."

"What of James Haley, have you converted him yet?"

"No. He is still too useful as a human, and for this mission, I would like to keep him that way. Instead, I need Marcus Drake to return, and I need a specialized Shadowstone combat team."

"Granted. I will replace Marcus once I've recruited new praetorians."

"When will that be?"

"Tomorrow. You need to feed tonight and prepare for a trip to Syria. We will leave in five hours' time."

"Targets?"

"A US Black Ops team is on the ground. A much larger Syrian government force is about to swamp them."

Chloe raised her right eyebrow quizzically. "Which side are you playing?"

"Both."

"How many recruits?"

"A dozen to start with. I'll get eight to ten after we account for loyalty issues. It will provide a new force with modern tactical and weapon skills."

"Where will you use them?"

"Jerusalem, they can back up General Mosule, and you can have Marcus Drake back."

"Excellent."

"You mentioned a specialized combat team. What did you mean?"

"A small tactical unit equipped with blackwidow gunships."

"How many, and for what purpose?" Cornelius asked.

"Three, and I will use them against the Mirovar safe house when I find it."

"That's the spirit of old. I like your confidence."

"I'm sure that we will find the safe house, there are some good leads that suggest it is up in Maine. Another two weeks and we will have it for sure. Once identified, I will vector in the blackwidows and destroy them."

Cornelius leaned forward. "You can only use the Widow's if the target is outside an urban area. We must not risk another Boston incident."

"Yes, Cornelius," Chloe agreed, smiling confidently. "I will make sure of that."

"Another thing."

"Yes."

"This secret is known only to Ursula, yourself, and me."

"Understood."

"Shadowstone cannot be made aware of this arrangement."

"How will I keep tabs on Ramin Kain without engaging Shadowstone."

Crane smiled. "I'm confident you will find a way."

Chloe frowned. "Yes, Sir."

"That's what I like to hear," Cornelius said. He reached forward and patted Chloe's knee. "Now go and feed."

"Thank you."

Cornelius watched Chloe rise, bow and leave. Throughout the meeting she'd been attentive, responsive, genuine – the old Chloe was back.

* * *

The Raven's smartphone vibrated silently beneath their pillow. They woke up on the second vibration, grabbed the phone and got out of bed. They glided silently over the floor, wrapped a bathrobe over their shoulders and stole from the room. The other person they shared the room with remained blissfully asleep.

The Raven had participated in the deployment of the sensors that watched the area around the safe house and the barns. They had ensured there was a single narrow path through them to the haystack. The Raven used all their Red Empire Ninjitsu skills to navigate their way past the sensors. They moved around to the far side of the haystack, out of sight of the safe house.

The Raven read the text message. 'Request Contact.'

It was the other Red Empire agent. The Raven sent the next check message in the list they had memorized as a child. 'A red blade flies in the shadows.'

A few moments later, their smartphone vibrated with the response. 'And finds its intended mark.'

Satisfied with the response. The Raven dialed the quantum address. The agent answered the call on the first ring.

The agent, their voice depersonalized and masked by the software declared, "I have two tasks for you."

"Yes, I'm ready."

"Ramin Kain is now in play. Bug his phone with a tracker at the earliest opportunity. It is critical you ensure that other members of the Mirovar force team are aware of the bug and are able to track his movements. Send me a text when you have done it."

The Raven considered their options. There was a way they could do it. "Understood."

"I need you to place an immediate conference call to Shabbah al Ahmar using your phone as a node."

The Raven realized the agent did not have the capability to contact the Red Ghost directly. The agent had to be a third party and not a true member of the Red Empire. A shiver crawled over the Raven's shoulders.

"Of course," the Raven agreed. "I will place the call now."

The Raven completed setting up the conference call. Their phone vibrated once and became silent, excluding the Raven from the conference call. The agent would talk with the Red Ghost in unbreakable privacy. Three minutes later, the conference call ended with another vibration.

The Raven stared at their smartphone for a long moment. What were the agent and the Red Ghost planning? How would the Raven be involved beyond the bugging of Kain's phone? What would be the impact on the Mirovar force team? Who was the agent?

Filled with unanswered questions, the Raven made their way stealthily back to their bedroom. Five minutes later, they were under the covers of their bed, their mind still buzzing with questions. One loomed over the rest, leaving the Raven feeling sick to their stomach. Was the agent a rogue vampire?

They had no answer.

* * *

Half a dozen or more AK-47s fired on full auto, the bullets ripping through the wooden crates in the Aleppo warehouse. Cemal, the team's Kurdish guide, rocked backward and slumped to the ground; the top half of his skull splashed across the crates.

Captain John Tilson and his team of special forces operatives crouched behind whatever cover they could find, pinned down by the Syrians in the warehouse. The Syrian Army had shown up ten seconds ago and had opened fire immediately. He was already two men down. The rest of his team dragging Carter and Woodstock back. They had come in by truck from the town of Reyhanli, forty-five miles away, across the border in Turkey. There had been rock-solid intelligence the warehouse held a chemical weapons cache. The mission was simple, identify and record the weapons, and then destroy them.

That mission had gone straight to hell. The new mission was equally simple – survive.

"Back to the truck," John shouted. His men didn't need any urging. They fought their way back to the other end of the warehouse where the truck waited, engine idling.

Sargent Smith, John's 2IC, pumped a grenade toward the Syrians and followed it with a burst from his H&K 416 rifle. The grenade exploded. Men shrieked and cursed, and the hail of bullets from the Syrians lessened for a moment.

"Call in a drone strike," John commanded. He loaded a fresh mag, and zig-zagged back past another crate, bullets whizzing overhead.

Smith ducked, ran beside him and swore bitterly, "Damn comms are down."

"What the hell?" John asked.

"We're being jammed," Smith declared, his face bleak.

"It's a fucking trap," John called out. He twisted up and over the crate next to him and emptied his clip at the advancing Syrians. Two collapsed, and the rest dodged to the sides.

Smith cursed, "What a clusterfuck!"

John shook his head with dismay. "Someone's trying to get us killed. The mission's compromised, we need to exfiltrate now."

The truck's wheels smoked as it lurched backward toward the team. It smashed through crates of dry goods, spilling bags of rice across the concrete floor.

"Quickly now," John called out, urging his team forward.

Two of his men carried the wounded over their shoulders to the back of the truck. The rest of the team covered their retreat. Smoke bloomed from the hot barrels of their assault rifles and grenades cracked and boomed. The Syrians paused in their advance, taking cover where they could. John and Sargent Smith were the last to reach the back of the truck.

A rocket-propelled grenade zoomed over them, striking the cabin of the truck which promptly exploded in a yellow glare, killing the driver instantly. Machine-gun fire erupted from the side of the warehouse and raked the back of the truck. John watched in horror as a stream of bullets cut his team to pieces. He turned back toward the approaching Syrians and fired again, taking out the nearest with a head shot. A hail of bullets returned, some hitting his body armor but three more went through his lower gut.

John fell backward onto the floor. Sargent Smith stepped over him, his H&K blazing as his bullets ripped through the Syrians. Smith jerked backward, slumping to the side, his H&K clattering to the floor. His hands gripped his throat where a round had slashed through it, blood pouring past his fingers.

The firing stopped.

The Syrians advanced, their boots making heavy footfalls over the warehouse floor. A Syrian Army officer crouched next to John, pointed a 9mm pistol at his face and asked in passable English, "So Yankee, what in Allah's name are you—"

A shining sword blade appeared through the officer's skull. The tip dripping blood for a fraction of a second before the blade disappeared. John could hardly believe what he'd seen. It had happened so fast. The officer's body started to fall toward him. It stopped in mid-air, a handspan above him, and then flew backward like a broken toy across the warehouse. Wild shooting and panicked screaming erupted nearby. The shooting stopped first, and then the screaming a couple of seconds later.

A stunningly beautiful brunette appeared over him. A guardian angel with cold blue eyes, dressed in black combat fatigues. She put her sword down and knelt on one knee beside him. She pulled a thick syringe filled with red fluid from her belt and thrust the needle into the side of his heart.

"What … are … doing?" John managed to ask.

"Saving your life," she declared.

Behind her stood a tall, slim man, armed with a longsword. Figures blurred in movement at the edge of John's vision. He took another breath. That was when the gut shots faded into the background, and the real pain began.

* * *

It was late on Sunday night when James Haley's smartphone rang. The caller ID indicated, 'Chloe Armitage.'

He picked it up and asked, "Chloe?"

"Yes, James," Chloe answered. "I have a new mission for you."

"What do you want me to do?"

"You need to pack your bags. I've organized a private jet for you out of JFK airport at 02:00 flying direct to Jerusalem."

"A R.I.S.C jet?"

Chloe laughed briefly. "No. It's off the books. I'll text you the specifics."

"Okay. What's the mission objective?"

"We're going to assist the Red Empire to capture General Haras Mosule."

James smiled; he loved the audacity of Chloe's plans. "Captured, not killed?"

"Captured. It is essential we keep him alive. I just need him on ice for a while."

"How do I contact the Red Empire?"

"The Red Empire will contact you via my associate, Marcus Drake. He is in Jerusalem and will be a key ally in this mission."

"Do we have any Shadowstone assets on the ground?"

"Yes. However, they must never find out what is really going on. There is a mobile Shadowstone annex in operation. We have four agents there right now. Your Shadowstone contact on arrival in Jerusalem is Gareth Nightingale. I will send through all the necessary quantum addresses, and I will ensure that all your contacts are aware of your arrival."

"Is there anything else?"

"After the capture of Haras Mosule, I need you to escort Red Empire assassins into the UK and the US."

James blinked with surprise. "… Where in the UK and the US?"

"There is a private airstrip outside of Whitby in Yorkshire, and the US site is Logan International Airport in Boston. You will need to manage customs and border controls in both countries."

"Sure. I have ghost ID templates in the Panopticon. I can use them to set up internationally viable identities that will pass inspection by any US or UK government agency."

"Excellent. That's why you're on this mission. You're perfectly placed to make it work."

"Why do we need these guys."

"For use against the Mirovar force team."

James nodded. "Understood. Is there anything else?"

"There are detailed briefing notes on the plane which should answer any other questions you may have."

"Yes, Chloe."

"Good hunting, James."

"Thanks, Chloe."

The call disconnected. James consulted his watch. The flight would leave in three and a half hours. Plenty of time to get ready and make his way to the airport. He relished the idea of getting into the thick of operations on the ground. It was what he excelled at. No more herding clean-up squads and conducting endless evidence suppression. In the last four days, he'd let go of the shame he'd felt over killing his own men. Their deaths now served a far greater purpose, the protection of humanity. It was a purpose he'd grabbed with both hands, like a drowning man clutching at a life raft in the middle of an ocean storm.

James got his suitcase out of his wardrobe and opened it up on his bed. It was time to pack.

* * *

The Red Empire assassin lay crucified on an X-shaped frame. The raw steel frame stood within a bare open space. The floor was polished concrete, the ceiling and walls lost in darkness. A single modern lantern resting a dozen feet in front of the frame provided illumination.

The assassin's eyes flickered open as he regained consciousness. He gasped in pain. Metal spikes pierced his feet, knees, elbows and hands, pinning him to the frame like an exotic butterfly to a piece of corkboard. But unlike an insect in a collection – he was still very much alive.

General Haras Mosule emerged from the shadows and said calmly, "I see that you have returned to us."

He carried a squat, gray, ceramic urn. It was fat bodied with a narrow neck. He placed it on the floor next to the lantern. "I've grown tired of hunting you and your ilk. You are the unlucky one caught just when my patience has become exhausted."

"Traitor! I will give you nothing," the assassin shouted.

Haras frowned at him. "We will see if an ancient pet of the Red Empire changes your mind."

The assassin's gaze focused on the urn. His skin paled, his eyes widened, and he whispered incredulously, "Olgoi Khorkhoi?"

"Yes, Al Far," Haras answered. "A Mongolian death worm."

Al Far shuddered on the cross. His hands clenching spasmodically. Fresh blood dripped from his wrists and splattered on the concrete.

Haras smiled briefly, shaking his head gently. "I've recently fed; you will not distract me with such a display."

Al Far rallied, his eyes flashing with a trace of hope. "It's a trick. That urn is too small to hold a worm."

"You are right," Haras agreed, nodding. His eyes gleamed in the lantern light. "It's too small to hold even a young juvenile worm."

Haras pulled a thick, black, rubber glove from behind his belt and stretched it over his right hand. The glove reached up to his elbow, he flexed his fingers in front of his face, making sure that the glove fitted perfectly and was free of holes. He knew exactly how dangerous a Mongolian death worm was to human or vampire. The venom of an adult worm could kill a man in seconds and a vampire in minutes. Just touching the skin of a death worm was hideously painful. The larval form was without deadly venom, but its touch was as agonizing as an adult. For the purpose of interrogation, the larval form was far more useful than an adult worm.

Haras unlocked the lid, lifting it slowly and carefully off the urn. His gloved hand blurred down into the urn's neck. His arm vibrated and thrashed as he hunted the worm with all his vampiric speed and ancient Red Empire knowledge. Fine sand sprayed across the concrete floor as he jerked his hand free. In his grip writhed a pale worm, an oversized maggot, two inches thick and nine inches long. Its maw gaped open, revealing a trilateral arrangement of curved black fangs. Lines of smaller teeth disappeared in rows down its throat. Its tail ended in a hard nub, the immature form of a deadly sting.

Haras approached Al Far, putting the worm a hand span in front of his eyes. The larva responded by straining in Haras' grip, repeatedly lunging at the man's face.

Haras leaned in and whispered, "A freshly hatched larva."

Al Far moaned, pulling his head back as far as he could.

"This one is hungry," Haras stated, staring at Al Far with an avid gaze. "He hasn't fed for days. I think he's quite starved, the poor thing."

"Tanin al Layl – you and the vampires will never win."

Haras snorted. "You know my old name. No one has called me the Night Dragon for more than a century."

Al Far ground out between gritted teeth, "The Red Empire never forgets."

Haras snorted. "And yet nearly two centuries have passed without reprisal. The Red Empire's memory is nothing but an empty threat."

Al Far stared at Haras, and vowed, "And we never forgive. We will punish you for your betrayal. You should have greeted the dawn on the first day you discovered you were a vampire, rather than live in shame."

Haras smiled grimly. "You should worry about yourself first." He pushed the worm closer, to within an inch of Al Far's eyes. "Where is the location of the Red Empire Citadel? Tell me now, and the worm goes back in the urn."

Al Far shook his head, his lips pressed tightly together.

"I will kill you quickly."

The assassin shook his head again, then snapped, "I do not fear death."

None of us fear death," Haras agreed. "It's the dying that's the problem." He hummed, shrugged his shoulders and took a step back.

Al Far glared at him in silence.

Haras ripped Al Far's tunic open, baring his chest and stomach. He dangled the worm in front of Al Far's abdomen and declared, "They like the soft flesh best. It takes a longer time to die when they enter there."

The worm writhed and twisted. Its powerful muscles rippling under its skin. It turned and snapped at Haras' fingers. He jerked his hand back. Grinning ruefully, he re-established a sure grip on the larva.

Haras promised, "You will tell me in the end."

"Never," averred Al Far.

Haras slapped the worm onto Al Far's stomach. In less than a second fresh blood splashed on the floor and the worm disappeared into the assassin's abdomen. Al Far's eyes rolled upward, and he screamed in agony.

Haras stepped away. The bare skin over Al Far's torso writhed, several ribs cracked loudly as the assassin's body bucked on the frame. The bloody head of the worm emerged for a moment, its maw working, clearing meat and gristle before looping over to burrow back into the man's body.

Haras allowed the worm to feast for another ten seconds as Al Far shrieked and cried out. His hand blurred forward like a knife through the first entry wound and with a loud sucking sound he pulled the blood drenched worm free from Al Far's body. The worm, slick with blood, whipped back and forth in Haras' iron grip, its maw snapping open and shut in abject lust for flesh.

Al Far gasped and moaned in relief.

Haras leaned in close and whispered. "Where is the Citadel or it goes back in?"

Al Far whispered a handful of words and then convulsed, blood pouring from his mouth. Haras grinned, a hard light in his eyes. He now knew where the Red Empire Citadel lay hidden. His long search was at an end.

He replaced the death worm larva back into the urn and closed the lid, carefully locking it tight. He reflected upon his mission. *We must act immediately before the Red Empire discover we have compromised the location of their citadel. It is time to use the newly recruited praetorians against them. We will see how their modern weapons and tactics go against our ancient foe.*

Haras picked up the urn and disappeared into the darkness. He left the pinned corpse of the Red Empire assassin dripping blood onto the cold concrete floor.

* * *

Al Far's handful of words had led Haras Mosule to the location of the Red Empire Citadel.

Months of fruitless searching of Jerusalem, both above and below ground, had left Haras with two things; a burning hunger to come to grips with his enemies and a very detailed map. Al Far's information had neatly filled in a blank space on Haras' map. A space near enough to a main sewer line to provide a remarkable opportunity.

It had taken sixteen hours to mobilize a team of workmen to cut a path through concrete and raw stone from the sewer into the Citadel's main air duct. The final breakthrough into the duct had taken an hour of careful work to muffle the sound and vibration.

Haras' eyes gleamed in the darkness, and he smiled. This was a rare instance where pure brute force was preferable to subtlety.

The breach in the main air duct bypassed the duct outlets. The outlets to the surface were too small for anything approximating a human to pass, and useless as a means to enter or exit the Citadel. Without doubt, the latest Red Empire technology would scan the pipes and lay traps against any feasible intrusion. Autonomous drones with motion detectors would randomly travel along the ducts, setting off alarms over anything larger than a mouse. The drones would also traverse the main air duct but with so much territory to cover the chances of meeting one this far into the Citadel was greatly reduced.

It was a calculated risk Haras was willing to take.

He'd donned the traditional garb of a Red Empire assassin, the better to confuse his opponents in the event of a fight. The workmen were all dead. The last drained of his blood to sate Haras' appetite and maximize his ability to heal from any wounds.

His ear bud communication device whispered in his ear. Marcus Drake and the new praetorians were heading toward the staging point within a secured warehouse. Haras turned from the hole and blurred through the sewers. It was time to organize a diversion to hide his stealthy mission into the heart of the Citadel. Soon he would have the Interpretive Codex in his hands.

* * *

Facing an array of computer screens, James Haley sat alone inside a shipping container and considered recent events.

The flight from New York to Jerusalem had taken five hours. Chloe's off the books plane had turned out to be a supersonic Spike 512 business jet. James had taken the opportunity to get a nap during the flight before landing at 14:00 local time. Gareth Nightingale, the local head of the Shadowstone annex had met him at the airport and introduced him to the mobile command center in a shipping container on the trailer of a Ford rig. Nightingale had familiarized James with the mobile command center operations and provided him with an initial brief on the tactical environment in Jerusalem. He'd then declared he had no further part to play in the operation and had left just before sunset.

The Ford rig had driven from the airport and pulled into a nondescript warehouse. The driver had exited the cab and made a beeline for the exit. The truck would remain stationary in the warehouse during the operation. Ten minutes later James had met with the Vampire Dominion force.

They had emerged from the sewers, ten of them, led by General Haras Mosule. They wore typical Red Empire combat attire, but most carried modern weapons. One who looked like he could have a role as Thor in a Hollywood blockbuster had introduced himself as Marcus Drake.

Drake had then introduced an eight-man combat team led by Captain Tilson. They were heavily armed with modified M249 light machine guns fitted with two hundred round magazines and an under barrel experimental X41 rocket launcher. They also carried an array of white phosphorus grenades and thermobaric rockets.

James had nodded to himself. The focus on area of effect weapons made sense against fast moving opponents. He'd looked closely at the men, one of them had grinned at him, his fangs clearly visible in the gloom of the warehouse. They were all vampires, and by their modern bearing and speech, newly recruited. James had helped fit helmet cameras and strapped tactical communications rigs to their heads. The command center would act as a secure communications hub and would provide a control point for an array of autonomous ground and air vehicles, and a pair of high-flying surveillance drones.

The General had given the team their orders and emphasized the necessity of acting quickly. The General's information would grow stale as soon as the Red Empire realized their enemies knew the location of their secret citadel. One of the new praetorians had remarked wryly about "Nuking the site from orbit," and the General had simply stared at him until the young man looked away. He'd ended the briefing by giving James his orders. The team then left the warehouse, blurring away to the sewers.

That was just under thirty minutes ago.

Marcus Drake's deep voice cut through James' headset, and he declared, "Our men are in position."

Unleash the drones, James thought.

His fingers flew over the keyboard and one of the screens divided into twenty smaller views. Each mini-screen displayed a feed from a tiny camera mounted on a scurrying autonomous ground vehicle. The views were green lit, light amplified data feeds of the sewers near the Red Empire citadel.

"Crawlers are away," James broadcast to the team.

"Copy that," Marcus replied.

The vehicles rolled along the access paths next to the sewers, scanning for threats, identifying cameras, traps and automated weapons. Whenever they found something, they would fire an infra-red laser at it. The laser was small, but so were the hidden motion sensors and cameras. The twenty machines converged in a rough circle through the sewers toward the target. The Red Empire would know they were under attack as they lost sensors and cameras, but they could not be sure who was attacking or what size the force was.

The circle of drones contracted to the point where it was a mile across. James waited for the inevitable response. A handful of seconds later sentry guns opened fire. Bright bursts of light bloomed in the green tinged views. The data feeds from the autonomous ground vehicles started to go dark as the defenses shot the individual drones to pieces. They'd expected sentry weapons. The ground drones were expendable. Every drone that 'died,' identified the location of an automatic weapon.

James flicked a switch and broadcast, "Fliers are away."

"Copy that," Marcus replied for the second time.

The second wave of drones, held behind the first wave of crawlers, swept forward through the sewers. Each of the second wave drones was a mini helicopter, the size of a tennis ball equipped with an explosive charge. The fliers flew erratically toward the sentry guns. Bullets flashing past them. A counter in front of James switched down from a 100 to 99, 98, 94, 91, 90, 86, paused for a second as three mini-views went dark in green flashes indicating successful detonations. The drones swarmed forward; the vampire assault team close behind them. The advancing drones came into contact with more sentry guns, the counter dropping rapidly into the 70s.

The sound of gunfire came through the helmet comm links as the praetorians pushed up behind the drones. The circle contracted to a thousand yards across. The counter dropped past 50. The fire from the automatic sentry weapons intensified as the circle contracted past five hundred yards. In seconds, his drones advanced another hundred yards, and the flier counter dropped to 24. The praetorians pushed in closer. They wanted to be right on top of the front door of the Citadel when they ran out of drones. Their job was to kick it down, push in hard, kill anyone they found, and then draw the assassins out of the citadel by retreating back into the sewers.

James vectored a reserve force of fliers past the praetorians. The drones zipped past Captain Tilson's soldiers and threw themselves at the remaining sentry guns. The counter momentarily rose to 48 with the commitment of the reserves and then rapidly dropped back below 30. The circle contracted to two hundred yards across, and the praetorians pulled to a halt.

They were close enough to see the entrance of the Red Empire Citadel. The counter was down to 9 fliers. They died in the next two seconds, taken apart by a pair of belt fed M134D-H miniguns. The automated guns tracked left and right, searching for targets as gray smoke curled from their barrels.

Captain Tilson's soldiers blurred forward as a coordinated unit, eight thermobaric bombs rocketing toward the sentry guns. The men maneuvered backward as a well-drilled team. The explosions whited out all communications. James scanned the monitors. The head cams all came back online a second later. The team blurred forward again, rockets flying from the launchers under their gun barrels. The rockets exploded against the main doors, evaporating the entrance to the Citadel.

The force disappeared through the smashed doorway. Their head cams went dark. A single line of white text, 'No Signal,' appeared in the middle of each head cam view.

James frowned and demanded, "Captain Tilson, report in … Marcus Drake, report in … anyone?"

The only response was utter silence.

"Recording comms down at 20:16:34."

He shook his head with dismay. Every monitor viewing a location within a mile of the Citadel was dark. Only the views from the high-flying drones overhead were still working. It was as if everyone in the team had simply vanished.

He considered the mission's true objective and wondered if they'd captured the target.

Where was General Haras Mosule?

* * *

The air duct was three feet in diameter, and Haras had nearly flown along it.

He came to an abrupt halt. A foot in front of him spun a metal fan. He pulled a device from his belt. A very short-range industrial cutting laser, good for a single shot. He drew it close to the center of the blades and pressed the trigger. The laser gleamed like a living ruby in his vampire vision as it cut through the fans. He nimbly caught the blades as they separated from the hub and put them quietly aside. A moment later, he was past the fan and rushing along the air duct.

Haras came to a screened vent. He peered through it and listened carefully. His vampire senses extended to their maximum capability. He could hear the beating of six distinct hearts within fifty yards of his position. He crouched closer to the screen, the tip of his veiled nose an inch away from it. His brown eyes swiveled left and right. There were four Red Empire assassins in the immediate vicinity. They were standing still, waiting in the typical assassin guard pose. Relaxed, alert, and neatly balanced on their feet. He could burst through the screen with ease, but they would be on him in a moment.

He frowned. He was confident that he could defeat any two Red Empire assassins at the same time, but four at once would tip the odds in their favor. He waited; the first phase of his strategy was due to start any moment.

The explosions at the entrance of the citadel reverberated through the complex. The guards in the room all became preternaturally still. The lights in the ceiling of the room switched to a slowly strobing red. The Citadel was under attack. Haras grinned, soon at least some of the guards would have to leave to deal with the soldiers attacking through the front door.

There was a soft whirr. A metal shield began descending over the vent.

Haras' mind raced, *a lock down system!*

His eyes widened, he thrust with all his might at the vent's screen. It exploded into the room. He quickly followed it, catapulting forward through the vent and landing on his feet in the middle of the chamber. The four Red Empire assassins immediately blurred forward, their curved swords gleaming wetly in the red emergency lighting.

Haras dropped into silence, ramped, drew his swords in a flash, and fought for his life.

* * *

The crawler adjusted its position. Easing back past the blast debris before the front entrance of the Red Empire Citadel. Its motion detector red-lined. Its tracks spun, and it whirred backward at maximum speed. Its light intensifying camera continued to face the dark entrance. Its microphone, at full sensitivity, registered an outrush of air through the doorway.

A tall, blond vampire was the first to emerge from the darkness. His left arm hung limply at his side as he blurred past the crawler. A moment later, another four vampire soldiers erupted from the gloom, rushed past it, and disappeared from its scopes.

A second later a pair of rockets zoomed out of the doorway, whizzing over the crawler and vanishing around the sewer corners. A fraction of a second later there were massive explosions, and fire rolled back through the sewer pipes. The crawler lay flat against the ground as the edge of the flames blew over it.

The crawler started to rise, then flattened again. Red Empire assassins blurred above it. Booted feet fell to the left and right of the crawler as it hugged the concrete floor. In a moment, the assassins were gone.

The sewer was quiet, then gunfire erupted in the distance. There was the crump of explosions, magnified in the confined space of the sewers.

The crawler rose slowly, pivoted 180 degrees on its tracks and rolled forward. Its communications with the command center had failed at 20:16:34. It had waited sixty seconds for the comms to come back online. The default protocol kicking in after the re-connect sequence had timed out. The crawler scanned the space in front of it for threats. It was time to preserve itself, leave the Red Empire Citadel behind, and find its way back to its origin point.

The crawler moved off into the pitch darkness.

* * *

There was a loud crack.

Haras let go of the fourth Red Empire assassin's throat, and the man collapsed limply to the floor. Haras winced and looked down at his waist. A polished hilt and leathered handle jutted out from his stomach. The blade had pierced all the way through, courtesy of the dying effort of the assassin. He flicked his remaining sword clean and sheathed it at his belt. With both hands, Haras pulled the short-bladed sword from his gut and dropped it on the floor. He held his fingers over the wound for a few seconds, he could feel it knitting back together.

Haras stepped over the fourth assassin's body. His second sword lay embedded in the skull of the third assassin. He pulled it free, flicked it clean and sheathed it next to the first. He walked calmly to the first assassin to die. An officer of the Red Empire. His head lay severed from his body, and Haras picked it up by the hair. With the officer's head in hand, he strode over to a large, steel door in the wall opposite the chamber's entrance. Next to the door was a retinal scanner. He pried open the head's right eyelid and positioned the eye in front of the scanner.

"This had better work," he whispered.

A green light appeared above the retinal scanner.

Haras could taste victory. The Codex would be on the other side of the door. The Red Empire never changed the architecture of their citadels. The Codex vault was always located at the geometric center of the building. Only the defenses around it had evolved over time.

Something slammed behind him. The lights switched from dull red to a bright white glare. Dropping the head; Haras whirled around, shielding his eyes with his hands. Gray spots danced in front of him. He blinked, the spots cleared and he dropped his hands. There was a great polished steel door across the exit. Another steel sheet covered the vent he'd used to enter the chamber. The vault door behind him remained still and silent.

Stones ground above him, a thin sprinkle of dust falling from the ceiling. Hundreds of tiny holes appeared above him, and a gleaming mist of metal dust puffed into the room. Haras' heart sank. The cold, sharp, stench was unmistakable. He coughed as the first particles struck his face. His mouth went numb. He collapsed face down on the floor before the full effect hit him.

In moments, his body lay paralyzed, but his mind remained active. *Silver!*

The far door slammed again. Footsteps, dulled by the paralytic effect on his hearing, approached.

A triumphant voice spoke, sounding as if it was a long way away, "Wrap him in the silver net and transport him to the real Citadel."

"Yes, Shabbah al Ahmar."

"Remove our honored dead from this illusion and detonate the charges. Erase all existence of this place."

Helpless rage burned through Haras as strong hands lifted him and carried him away.

Al Far managed to lie to me, Haras thought incredulously. *He was bait. This whole site was a trap.*

* * *

The mid-morning sunlight bathed the private Jerusalem airfield. Four black Chevrolet Suburbans sat on the tarmac. In front of them rested a dart-shaped white and blue, Spike 512 supersonic business jet.

James Haley stood at the base of the stairs leading up to the cabin. Beside him was a simple fold away table with a cardboard box on it. The last two men in the line moved in front of him. There was a single parcel left in the cardboard box. He looked at the assassins in front of him. One he recognized from the data Marcus Drake had provided him. Nasr al Dam, the Blood Eagle, team leader of the group destined for the USA. Marcus' data had listed sixteen Red Empire assassins organized into two teams. James had spent all his available time over the last two days preparing a cover identity for each of the men. He'd handed a package to each of them before they boarded the plane.

James gave the final package to Nasr al Dam and indicated the plane with a slight nod of his head. Nasr nodded once, mounted the stairs and disappeared into the body of the plane.

The final assassin moved forward to stand directly in front of James. The man was of medium height and athletic build, with a touch of gray at the temples and in his neatly cropped beard. He carried himself with the casual ease of a skilled operator. It was clear this was a man who stood high in the ranks of the Red Empire. They spent a long moment staring at each other. A slight smile of studied indifference curled the edge of the man's mouth, and he said, "I am Thueban Kabir. You may call me Taipan."

"Okay," James replied, arching an eyebrow. "You have something to tell me?"

"Yes. You have delivered us our traitor, and in return, we have kept our word. These men will serve your master unto death, or if she orders them to attack each other or the Red Empire – whichever comes first."

James nodded once.

Taipan turned on his heel and strode over to the closest car. He quickly got in, and the suburbans pulled away.

James made a note to himself to remember everything that he could about Thueban Kabir or given a literal translation of his name, the Great Serpent. He'd given James the name Taipan. A snake species with the most toxic venom in the reptilian world. A single bite could kill a hundred people.

James asked himself, *is Taipan the most dangerous assassin in the Red Empire?* He believed it was a question he would one day have to answer. He walked up the flight of stairs and entered the crowded interior of the plane. The first Red Empire operatives to board had taken all the seats, and the rest filled the aisle. He grunted, then shrugged. He could stand – it would be a quick flight. First stop would be Whitby in Yorkshire, where he would drop off most of his cargo and four of the assassins. Then it would be another quick flight over the Atlantic to Logan International Airport in Boston. The final twelve assassins were for a mission in New England.

Time was fast running out for the Mirovar force team and their safe house in Maine.

* * *

Haras Mosule sat in utter darkness. He extended his vampire senses to their maximum power. The susurration of air through a vent far above him was the only thing he could hear.

The floor was hard and smooth. It felt like polished glass, as did the walls. He'd measured the dimensions of his cell. It was a cylinder, three yards across and an unknown number deep. The Red Empire had descended with him via a rope ladder. They had removed the silver net and wiped off the silver dust. They had used the rope to climb out of the hole. The rope had disappeared into the darkness and minutes later the silver paralysis was gone.

He had no way to judge the passage of time, but given how famished he was, it was at least two days since his capture.

A thin green slit appeared above him. Haras blurred to the center of the cylinder directly beneath it.

The light disappeared for a moment, and a hard voice snapped, "Here you go bloodsucker."

The green strip appeared twice more. There was movement above him. Something was falling toward him. He stepped aside and adroitly caught a soft plastic bag. Moments later, he caught two more. His nostrils flared with a familiar scent. He plunged his face into the first bag. His fangs ripping through the plastic and warm blood splashed into his mouth. He gulped and sucked, finally twisting and squeezing the last drop of blood from the bag. He dealt with the second and third bag in the same manner.

"Shabbah al Ahmar wants to keep me alive," Haras stated to the empty cell. "But for what purpose?"

Haras' mind flashed back to the capture of Al Far. Marcus Drake had led him to where he'd discovered Al Far. Not obviously, but through hints during the night. They had captured Al Far together after a chase. The rising sun had nearly beaten them. Marcus Drake had knocked Al Far unconscious and grinned at Haras in triumph.

The whole sequence of events over the two days before Haras' capture stank of treachery.

Marcus Drake had captured Al Far, what if the Red Empire had deliberately given Al Far to Drake. That would mean that at the very least Drake was a traitor, and most likely so was Armitage.

The parts clicked together – Chloe Armitage and Marcus Drake had betrayed him to the Red Empire. He couldn't imagine any reason for the Red Ghost to keep him alive. His imprisonment must serve another's purpose. The only other person with enough power to deal with the Red Empire was Chloe Armitage.

Haras shook his head. Crane and the Vampire Dominion were in deep danger, and there was nothing that he could do about it.

Chapter Thirteen

BREAKING: Explosion Reported in Jerusalem.

There are reports of a massive explosion south of the Old City.

Published 08/14 14:05 EST

Witnesses report that a massive crater has formed a mile south of the walls of the Old City. Initial reports from Jerusalem authorities attribute the explosion to a gas leak in the sewers. The explosion occurred minutes ago just after 11PM local time.

– Breaking News article for The New York World site on the Internet.

* * *

White Hill, Maine, August 19th, 17:45

Everyone lies.

It was a truism Deon Lamar lived by. Fate had seen fit to gift Deon with the ability to see through lies. To discern falsehood and unravel webs of deception. To uncover spies and traitors. It was a rare talent amongst the Ramp initiated, and Deon was a master of it.

He'd vowed to fulfill his mission to investigate the Mirovar force team. The identification of the Red Empire agent would only be the first step. He would follow with the co-option of their means of communication, the laying of traps and the capture of their accomplice. In the end, he would charge with treason all those who had betrayed the Order.

A fiery righteousness burned brightly within him. He visualized the agent and their accomplice bound in chains before an inquisitorial court. The judges would make their stern and immutable judgments. He would take the guilty to a place where he could easily dispose of their bodies. It would be his honor to deliver swift and impartial justice with the executioner's sword.

It was a joyous mission, a true exercise of his gift. It was his calling to be an Order traveler. A spy hunter reporting directly to the Head of the Order. A man Deon revered as a living genius. A man with the vision to bring the Order into a state of perfection. The one man who had always acted with perfect integrity in his presence. The only man who was the exception to the rule. The man who had never lied.

Ramin Kain.

The deep, low-throated roar of the motorcycle's engine was unmistakable. Deon's Harley-Davidson, downshifted through its gears, rolling smoothly into the safe house yard. Deon was a thick-set man of medium height. He kicked the bike's foot stand into place, parking the bike in front of the house. Taking off his helmet, he put it on the bike seat. The late afternoon sunlight gleamed off his silver rimmed sunglasses. Taking them off, he rubbed his short, tightly curled hair with his free hand.

He'd arrived unannounced. All the better to begin his investigation with a surprise first impression. The yard was still. A lone farm tractor chugged away in the distance. The Order team stood in the shadows of the barn, watching him, hands still holding training weapons. A smile curled the edges of his lips, and his dark brown eyes narrowed with concentration. Amongst the group of young men and women was a Red Empire assassin pretending to be a member of the Order of Thoth.

His heart swelled with pride. He relished the opportunity to root the spy out and crush them. Samuel Luther's instructions came to mind. Twinging inwardly, his smile vanished; such satisfactions would have to wait. He was in the service of the Order of Thoth, reporting directly to Ramin Kain. Luther had been adamant about Ramin's directives. He must first identify the spy and then leave them in place to allow for the capture of their accomplice. The sublime righteous joy of delivering punishment to the wicked would have to wait.

And so, it would be. No matter how much he might chafe at such restrictions, the day of satisfaction would have to wait while a longer game played out to its inevitable conclusion.

Deon walked purposefully toward the team. It was time to get to work.

* * *

The man approached the force team like he owned the safe house farm and they were his guests.

He smiled confidently and declared forthrightly, "Francis, Juliette. Good to see you are both well. How is everyone?"

"All good. Thank you," Francis replied.

Juliette half smiled. "You're just in time for dinner, Deon. I'm sure that Mary and John can set another place."

Who do we have here? Another Order goon? Deon … who? Anton thought warily to himself.

Deon looked past Francis and Juliette. Catching Anton's gaze, he said, "I see you have some new members in your team."

Anton stepped forward slowly, his hand outstretched to shake Deon's hand. "Yeah, Li," he indicated Li with a quick nod, "and I are new. I'm Anton Slayne."

Deon took his hand and shook it firmly. He clasped Anton on the shoulder with his free hand and declared, "My God, you're the spitting image of your grandfather as a young man."

"Yeah, I get that a lot."

Deon stared at Anton for a second, then grinned broadly. He turned, offering his hand to Li.

Li looked at his hand as if he was offering her a stale fish. Nodding once, she stared hard at him, and said, "Hello, Mr. Lamar. My father spoke of you."

Deon pulled his hand back, scratching nonchalantly behind his right ear. "All good I hope."

Li shrugged.

"Well then, let's not stand on ceremony. Please everyone, call me Deon."

"Great," Peter said. "Pleased to meet you again." He shook Deon's hand quickly. "I can smell Mary's cooking from here, and you know she doesn't like people coming late to her table."

There was a general assent, and everyone started moving across the yard toward the safe house.

Anton tugged on Li's elbow, and she slowed down. Chiara dropped in on Anton's other side.

"So, who is he?" Anton asked in a tight whisper.

"A traveler." Li and Chiara whispered back at the same time.

"That doesn't help."

"A spy catcher," Li explained.

"A walking lie detector," Chiara said. "He's only a problem if you have something to hide."

Anton shrugged his shoulders. "So, no trouble then."

Deon cast a glance over his shoulder at the three of them. For a fraction of a second, he stared directly at Anton. A slight smile curled the edges of his mouth before he turned to enter the safe house.

Anton sighed. He was beginning to wonder if there was anyone in the Order beyond the Mirovar force team that wasn't out to get him. Mounting the steps before the front door he asked himself, *it's not paranoia when they really are out to get you is it?*

* * *

Deon Lamar had tested the Raven at the last Order Conclave.

Afterwards, Francis Mirovar had formally accepted them into his force team and confirmed them as a full member of the Order of Thoth.

They had met other travelers over the years within the Order. Each time they had mastered their sympathetic and parasympathetic nervous system responses and kept their cover intact. The presence of the traveler could mean only one thing. Ramin Kain was investigating the Mirovar force team.

But what had prompted the investigation? Only Ramin Kain could assign a traveler to investigate a force team. It was clear that Kain had it in for Anton Slayne. The purpose of the investigation could be to find something that would allow Kain to eliminate Anton while he was still an unconfirmed novice. Even with the sanctuary of Juliette Mirovar in place, an Order Inquisition could possibly trump her sanctuary and reach Anton. But given Juliette was a loremaster and her husband a senior force leader, pitting an inquisition against Juliette sounded like a poor strategy.

If Anton wasn't the target of the traveler, then who was?

The Raven sighed softly. Kain must suspect there was a Red Empire spy in the Mirovar force team. If they knew who it was, the Raven would be in chains already or consuming false information to disrupt the plans of Shabbah al Ahmar. Since no one in the Order had revealed anything important to them, their cover most likely remained intact.

Therefore, Lamar was on a fishing expedition. The task at hand was to avoid the cast of his net.

The Raven needed a decoy. Someone to throw into the path of the traveler, ensuring they would become the focus of his investigation and not the Raven. It would have to be something major to distract a traveler. But it couldn't be anything that would hint at the Raven's mission or current assignment to insert a tracker on Ramin Kain's phone. It would also need to be a crime that would easily stick to the target. And above all else, it needed to be believable.

There was no apparent solution. The Raven was momentarily at a loss as to how to proceed. They shook their head slowly. They would have to wait, watching carefully until an opportunity presented itself.

Then they could pounce upon it.

They shook their head again. The Raven loved the other members of the Mirovar force team as if they were family, as well as brothers in arms. Whomever the Raven selected as a decoy; it would not be an easy decision.

The bonds of loyalty lay twisted within them. A knot of anguish tightened at the thought of sacrificing one of the other members of the Mirovar force team to serve their own mission.

They pushed the pain away. Disappointed with the presence of such weakness. What would their master Taipan think? What would Shabbah al Ahmar think? They couldn't tolerate such feelings. If they must sacrifice an innocent to advance the cause of eliminating the curse of vampires, then they must accept the sacrifice.

It was the Red Empire way.

The Raven steeled themselves, vowing to do what they must to succeed. The one positive of the presence of the traveler was Ramin Kain would not be far behind in paying a visit to the safe house. Their arrival would allow the Raven to plant the tracking software on Kain's phone. That would satisfy the last directive from the other Red Empire agent. They could use the opportunity provided by the discovery of the decoy to ensure that Kain's phone was properly co-opted. The Red Empire software would hide itself and the phone would continue to operate perfectly.

No one would be the wiser. But it was essential that other members of the force team could find out how to track the phone. That would be trickier. How to provide that information without giving away that they were also the source of the tracking software.

It was an unsolved problem, but the Raven was sure they would be able to manage it. Time was short, events were pressing, and they would have to take risks.

The Raven always lived with risk.

* * *

Peter Lamb held out a fist filled with straws.

Yvette, Jay, Chiara, Li and Anton stood in a semi-circle in front of him.

"Pick one. Whoever draws the short straw gets sober duty."

Anton waited until there were only two straws left, Peter's and his. Everyone else had picked a long straw. He shook his head and picked one at random, it was the short straw.

Peter sucked air through his teeth and clapped him on the shoulder. "Tough luck, mate. We'll really miss you at the party, but someone's gotta stay sober and keep watch. Can't have everyone on their ear if a bunch of vamps show up."

"What's the chance of that?"

"Pretty much zero," Peter stated with a shrug.

Anton sighed. "Catch you later." Picking up a tall glass of orange juice, he walked outside to the porch.

It was nine o'clock on a Saturday night in the middle of August. It was a beautifully clear and moonless night. There was the lightest of breezes flowing through the farm yard.

Anton sipped his orange juice, made a face and put it down on the porch. He walked over to the training barn and pulled a bale of hay from inside the wall. He positioned it a dozen yards back from the barn, lay down on top of it with his hands behind his head, and looked up at the stars.

His mind drifted for a few minutes, before picking up a current like a small boat captured on the edge of a whirlpool. The fateful events of April the 28th circled around him. His mother's torture and murder, and his father's abduction. He hadn't done enough since then. Chloe Armitage and Marcus Drake were still alive. His father was now a vampire imprisoned in silver, an undeserved half-life of torment.

He knew he would have to kill him. There was no coming back from being a vampire. It was the only way to free him, but God only knew where he was. A terrible sense of dismay attacked him, corroding any experience of peace.

How do you kill your father?

It was a horrible idea. It was something that had been lurking in the background. He'd pushed it aside, focusing on the training, learning everything he could and surviving the Order's boot camp. But now, during a quiet moment in the most peaceful of settings beneath a beautiful New England night sky, it had all come rushing back like some dreadful curse.

Anton exerted himself. Drawing upon his training, he evaporated his thoughts, falling into silence. The baleful images of the past disappeared like banished ghosts.

There was the barest whisper of movement nearby. A cool, gentle hand came down over his eyes, and he sat up with a start.

"Not much of a watchman, are you?" Li observed wryly. She was smiling mischievously with an eyebrow arched in a mock query. She balanced a tray with her other hand, supporting a glass jug filled with ice and a dark colored drink, and a pair of tall glasses.

She declared with a wave of her free hand, "I've made some iced tea."

"Great," Anton said, mildly disappointed. "I could really use something stronger."

Li frowned. "… Bad memories?"

"Yeah. I just feel … like I'm not doing enough."

"You can't rush it, Anton. You … no, we'll only get one chance at this."

There would be no second chances in a fight with Chloe Armitage. Anton remembered what he'd glimpsed on the Boston docks. Gang was a genius with a blade and she'd still beaten him. He asked, "When will we be ready if not now?"

"We're not ready," Li answered.

"You're sure?"

"Absolutely."

Anton sighed and shook his head. "How do we beat her?"

"… I honestly don't know," Li declared. She put the tray on the hay bale and sat down next to Anton. "You know what Father would do right now? He would pour some tea, and think about it."

Anton sat up, and Li positioned the tray between them. She took the jug and poured a glass for Anton and one for herself. Anton picked up his glass and Li did the same.

"Tea?"

"Yes."

"Not one of Juliette's specials?"

"No. Of course not."

Anton nodded. "Thanks."

"You're welcome."

Anton and Li sipped their tea in companionable silence. A mild fragrance from the tea filling the warm night air.

They emptied the glasses and Li moved the tray aside. In the moonless night, the shadows were deep, almost pitch black. The lights from the house were far behind them.

They both reached for each other at the same time. The silence of the night enveloped them. Anton's arms wrapped around Li and she moved in close. Li put her head against Anton's chest. He rested his chin on top of her hair. They held each other for a while, neither moving.

Li suddenly sobbed.

Anton's eyes were moist.

"Father," Li whispered in trenchant grief.

"I know."

"I miss him."

"I know."

Anton held her tight and Li wept quietly into his chest.

* * *

A slight breeze tickled the rooster-shaped weathervane, and it creaked as it rotated a lazy quarter turn.

The weathervane sat on a miniature version of the barn atop the safe house working barn. The blocky support was two yards long, a yard high and a yard wide, and provided a marvelous hiding place on a moonless night.

At least, that was how Chloe Armitage judged it. She sat in the thick shadows at the bottom of the weathervane on top of the barn. She stretched her long legs out in front of her with one ankle over the other and leaned back against the thick wooden base of the weathervane. She had used information provided by the Raven to carefully infiltrate the defenses of the safe house farm and had been sitting there for fifteen minutes.

Anton had emerged from the house, setting himself up on a hay bale near the training barn. Li Wu had joined him. She'd watched with interest as they shared tea and then quietly embraced each other.

Chloe frowned. If they had sought temporary oblivion in sex, she would have been happier. Instead, they had comforted each other in their mutual grief and cemented commitment to a shared purpose.

Emotional intimacy was dangerous. Emotional commitments could drag Anton away from her purpose. She could not allow such forces to persist in Anton's life.

She needed to remove any supports in Anton's life apart from those that would advance his combat skills. Li was a pillar who was restoring Anton's balance by giving him someone he could care about and relate to.

Li Wu was dangerous, she had to go. Chloe's eyes hardened. *Li Wu must die.* Li Wu's death would drive home Anton's sense of loss, horror, and need for revenge. She needed Marcus to be involved in the process. It couldn't be a random death. Li Wu's death needed to reinforce Anton's focus on Cornelius Crane and his original orders to seize the Papyrus of Hakron the Scribe and destroy Anton's family.

Events were in motion. Forces were on the move. Soon Li Wu must join her father in an unmarked grave. She was certain Li Wu would be dead within days.

Chloe waited for Anton and Li to return to the safe house. Once she was alone, she dropped down to the ground on the far side of the barn. She used her perfect memory to retrace her steps past the sensors to the outer perimeter of the farm.

Well away from the farm lights, she looked up at the clear, night sky. She stretched her senses to full awareness. The stars above glowed in an achingly beautiful river across the sky. The night sang with the rustles, clicks, and chirps of insects and night birds. A faint breeze caressed her face, ruffling her hair.

The beauty of the world filled her to overflowing, her heart aching with it. She could not bear to lose such beauty. She could not allow risk of harm to her world. Chloe vowed to herself to save all the beautiful things.

She was the only one who could.

* * *

Early morning sunlight speared through the kitchen windows.

The weekend was over. It had been two nights since the arrival of Deon Lamar, the Order spy hunter. Francis and Juliette had gone around the team and quietly advised them to be themselves and allow the traveler to do his work. They trusted their team and were confident that any inquiry was groundless and that Lamar would eventually leave empty handed.

Anton speared a sausage with his fork, spread some mustard on it and wolfed it down. Workouts that involved the Ramp burnt calories like a freight train, and he needed fuel. The sausage joined four fried eggs, three slices of toast, fried tomatoes, spinach, half a dozen rashers of bacon, honey, jam, buttered crumpets, a big glass of fresh whole milk with the cream settling on top of it and a pair of fresh, ripe oranges.

Across from him, Peter pushed his second plate away and tapped his taut stomach with both fists. "Damn that was good."

"Peter Lamb! No swearing. Not in my kitchen," Mary Jorgensen commanded, her gray eyes flashing.

Dismay flashed across Peter's face. "Sorry, Ma'am."

"You will be. I need a new load of firewood cut. Please see to it today."

"Yes, Ma'am. I'll see it done after lunch."

"Good."

Peter sighed and turned his attention back to Anton. He stroked his chin, his eyes gleaming mischievously. "I think we should all have code names when we go on missions."

"Yeah," Anton said, "such as?"

"Well, I would be Axeman, Li would be Bladestrike and Chiara would be Deathtouch."

"And what about me."

"Oh, … I think you would have to be Tiffany."

"Tiffany?" Anton said, pulling a face.

"C'mon – what's wrong with Tiffany? We could call you Tiff for short."

Anton rubbed his face, and then stated baldly, "Go for it. I'll be the most," Anton dropped his voice to a whisper, "bad-assed," and then raised it again, "vampire hunting, Tiffany on the planet."

"Speaking of," Peter mouthed, *bad-assery*, "it's time for more helicopter sims."

"Boys," Mary declared in exasperated tones. "I'm neither deaf nor blind. You've had your fill, now get out of my kitchen."

"Yes, Ma'am," Anton and Peter chorused together.

Anton got up from the table and asked, "What's the point of these sims? We don't have any helicopters."

Peter tilted his head. "You've heard of thievery, haven't you?"

Anton grinned. "You've stolen a nightfalcon?"

"Not yet. But I'm prepared to at the first opportunity."

Anton smiled and remarked sardonically, "I can just see it. It will work really well," he waved his right hand through a pair of figure eights and then smashed it into his left hand. "Until you run into something."

"Well let's test that out. You either shoot me down today, or I'm calling you Tiffany for the rest of the week."

Anton grinned and punched Peter's fist. "Done."

"That's the spirit," Peter enthused, clapping Anton on the shoulder. "Let's get to it."

"Sure," Anton followed Peter from the kitchen.

Lamar watched them leave, his face impassive as he nursed a cup of coffee.

* * *

There are no vampires in New Zealand.

The members of Justin Blake's extended family kept the islands clear of any bloodsuckers. Those were his mother's brothers and sisters, and his cousins on the Maori side of his ancestry. A family for whom the Order of Thoth and Ramp mastery seamlessly integrated with their ancient Maori beliefs.

His father, a US citizen, had brought his young Maori bride back to the west coast, and Justin had been born a year later. He'd lived most of his life in the US. Initiated into the Order at seventeen years of age, he'd taken command of his own force team at the young age of twenty-eight.

Now ten years later, he was on a personal mission for an old friend. He carried with him, tucked in a pocket inside his leather jacket, a letter. A letter addressed to Li Wu from her father. Gang had charged Justin to deliver the letter in the event of his death.

The engine of Justin's Harley-Davidson motorcycle rumbled as he pulled the bike to a halt in the farm yard. Motion to his right caught his eye. There was a lithe figure practicing with a katana in the shadows of a barn.

He parked his Harley and pulled off his helmet.

There was a squeal of delight. "Uncle. You're here!"

Suddenly there was a young Asian-American woman spread across his chest with her arms around his neck. He'd first met Li when he'd spent time training with Gang. She'd shyly asked him his name and he'd said casually to just call him, 'Uncle,' because Gang was like an older brother to him, and the pet name had stuck.

He hugged her back, a broad smile spread like sunshine across his face and he said, "Li, you've grown so much since I saw you last."

Li wrapped her legs around his flanks. She was a bundle of fierce enthusiasm in his arms. He placed one broad forearm under her hips and rubbed her back with his free hand. He whispered gently, "I know what happened. I share your loss. Gang was a great friend."

Li turned her head so that she could see his face. "You've been gone so long; why didn't you tell me you were coming?"

"Because it's a secret," Justin answered, pulling his head back and staring at her seriously.

Li scrunched up her nose and slid off him like a puma dropping off a tree.

Wrapping an arm around his lower back, Li looked up at him and asked, "What secret?"

"Have you somewhere we can talk?"

Li frowned. "How secret do we need to be?"

Justin shrugged his massive shoulders. "Just needs to be private."

"The library. It's normally deserted this late in the morning. Let's go there."

"Lead on."

Li stepped forward toward the safe house. Justin following her, shedding his black biker jacket. He wore a black T-shirt like a second skin. His heavy muscles rippling beneath the fabric as he followed Li into the house. Ducking his head reflexively as he walked through the door, his thick, dark curly hair still brushed the lintel. In moments, they were down the hall, and Li was showing him to a comfortable lounge chair in the library.

Justin started to sit down. Li reached out, grabbing his arm and declared, "I'm a terrible hostess. Can I get you something to eat or drink? You must be thirsty after your ride."

He smiled. "Just some cold water for now. I'll join you for lunch later."

"Sure, I'll be back in a moment."

Li ducked out of the room.

Justin looked around the library. He'd been at this safe house many years ago, before he'd become a force leader. He'd helped stock the armory under the barn. Justin had trained with the members of the Mirovar force team. Ticking off names in his head, most of them had survived. There had been some attrition, but less than most of the other teams. Only his own team maintained a better kill/casualty ratio. He glanced at the shelves lining the walls. The books looked worn and he recognized most of the titles. There was only a handful of new books; not much had changed in over a decade.

Li came back into the room with a tray which she placed on a low table in front of him. On the tray were a plate of dry crackers smothered in smoked trout pate, thick slices of aged cheddar, a large pitcher of ice water, and a pair of glasses.

Justin grinned. "You can take the girl out of the restaurant ..."

Then he faltered. Li sat down in a second lounge chair next to his. He saw memories of Gang in her eyes. Her grief was still quite raw. He reached over, picking up his leather jacket from where it lay draped over the back of a desk chair. Opening it up, he pulled a thick, double-folded, buff-colored, A4 envelope out of an inside pocket and gave it to Li.

"Your father wanted you to have this," he stated simply.

Li took the envelope and sat quietly for a long moment, staring at it.

Justin waited patiently.

She opened the envelope and pulled out a sheath of typed pages. Pinned to the top of the sheath with a paper clip was a hand-written note. She flicked her gaze from the note to Justin and back, and then began reading it out loud, "'I hope this letter finds you well little one. I wish I could be there with you, but I know that if you have survived to read this note, then my life has not been in vain, and my death was not a waste. The letter is all my research on the comings and goings of Ramin Kain and Samuel Luther. I only told you a fraction of what I found out. I didn't want you to lose all faith in what the Order stands for. The bearer of this message is a man who I would trust with your life. He, like the Mirovars and the Slaynes, understands the true soul of the Order. He lives for the protection of the innocent and come what may I would be pleased if he is with you.

BTW, I know you had a huge crush on him at fourteen.

Always your father.'"

She faltered for a moment on the last line. "'Gang Wu. The luckiest father in the world.'"

A tear fell onto the page, smudging the ink of Gang's name.

Li thrust the papers away. Wiping her cheeks with her hands, she sniffed, squeezing her eyes shut for a long moment. Taking a deep breath, she shook her head, her long hair swinging across her shoulders. She took another big breath, sniffing once more and composed herself. She picked up the pages of the letter. Separating the hand-written note from the rest, she placed it carefully back into the envelope. As she did so, something caught her eye. It was a tiny data stick the size of her thumbnail inside the envelope.

She fished it out and quickly moved to the desk in the corner of the room. On the desk was an open laptop. She logged in and accessed the data stick. A program ran, and map after map flashed up onto the screen. All marked with red path-lines.

Justin stood up, moving to stand behind her. He asked, "What is it?"

"I don't know yet," Li noted. Turning to the body of the letter she began reading the first page.

* * *

The Raven recognized Justin Blake.

They had first met at the last Order conclave. Blake had been too young for the Red Empire to establish a file on him while the young Raven had still been in training.

Blake was a concern for the Raven. The young force leader's career had risen like a flaming meteor streaking across the sky. His ascension established on the foundation of the loyalty he inspired in his team mates and his personal abilities for strategy, tactics, and combat.

He was an obvious rival for the position of the Head of the Order of Thoth. One day, the righteous would sweep the Kain/Luther cabal and their soulless supporters away. If Francis Mirovar didn't take the position of Head, then Blake would be the next logical choice.

The Raven stood in the shadows of the training barn. Li welcomed Blake like a long-lost brother, and they whispered something the Raven couldn't hear. They made a decision and went into the house. The Raven moved closer, spying on them through one of the library windows.

Blake gave Li an envelope. What did it contain? Was this the opportunity the Raven had been waiting for? Li was by far the least well known of the Mirovar force team. Li would be the easiest to sacrifice.

Where was Lamar?

The Raven went in search of the Order traveler, passing Li in the hallway as she headed toward the kitchen.

They nodded to each other in friendly greeting.

She looked happy. She looked to be happier than the Raven had ever seen her. The Raven's guts twisted. It was wrong to tip off Lamar, they pulled to a stop near the end of the hallway.

They ground their teeth in indecision. Their mission could not fail. They would honor their sacred duty regardless of personal feelings.

There would be no more weakness.

They walked through the back door. Lamar was meditating in the backyard. It was a practice that he did each day before lunch. The Raven walked up behind him. In minutes, they'd ensure Lamar's whole attention was focused on Li Wu.

The Raven prayed silently, that whatever Blake had brought Li would cast her in the worst possible light before the Order traveler.

* * *

Li finished reading the last page, quickly turning back to the laptop.

"The letter is a summary and a guide," she remarked. "The real information is on the stick, and it's dynamite."

Justin squatted down beside her so that he could see the laptop screen clearly. "Like what?"

"Father spent time tracking Luther and Kain over the last decade. However, most of the data is more than five years old." Li sucked on her bottom lip for a second, her eyes narrowing. "He stopped after Mother and Qiang died."

"He wanted to focus on you."

Li nodded. "I suppose that makes sense."

"Hmmm, what did he find out?"

"Kain never made a mistake when he looked for vampires. Every time he searched for vampires, he found them."

Justin frowned and asked incredulously, "How does anyone do that?"

"Father tracked him fourteen times in six years. It's here on the maps. The red path-lines show exactly where Kain and Luther went based on Father's own GPS as he followed them. Each time he went straight from New York to the lair of the vampires."

"Show me the maps."

Li flicked through the images, and Justin studied each of them.

"They're all over the United States, and even in Canada and Mexico," he said, his voice rumbling in his chest like distant thunder. "These three here," he pointed at the screen, "in Los Angeles, Phoenix and Mexico City. My team handled those targets. All three were small covens of new vampires."

"They're all new vampires, less than six months old. And there is no evidence of these new vampires spawning other vampires."

"Following instructions, were they?" Justin asked, half suspicious, half joking.

"… It's very odd. Young vampires are notorious for being undisciplined. They must have been frightened of something to keep them in line."

"Or someone?"

Li stared at Justin for a long moment and whispered, "Crane?"

Justin nodded. "Who else could get away with it. Unsanctioned vampire creation would have Chloe Armitage and the praetorians hunting the vampire down. All this evidence points to consistency and planning, and an ability to get away with it."

"There is nothing linking Kain to Crane. Father mentioned it several times. All the evidence is circumstantial."

"With quantum technologies, they could be communicating with text messages, and no one would know."

"Yes."

Justin shook his head. "This is bad."

"It's terrible. Kain's in league with the Vampire Dominion."

"That's not what I mean," Justin declared and shook his head once. "What I really mean is that there is not enough here to impeach Kain with. It paints a horrible picture, but it doesn't nail him to the wall."

A hurt look shadowed her face, and Li asked, "Why didn't Father tell me about this?"

"This is dangerous information, he probably wanted to keep you safe," Justin replied. "He's kinda tossed you a live grenade with the pin pulled out."

They looked at each other quietly for a long moment.

* * *

The door to the library burst open. Deon Lamar rushed into the room.

"Treason!" he shouted. "Conspirators! Traitors! Criminals!"

He blurred forward, reaching for the pages of Gang's letter lying on the desktop.

Li's heart skipped a beat.

Justin caught Lamar's hand before it reached the desk. He blurred to the side, dragging Lamar with him and away from Li. A moment later they separated, Lamar flying to the opposite side of the library.

Li ripped the data stick off the table, stood up and moved to the side. Lamar regained his feet. The air in the room crackled with menace as the two men faced off.

Lamar snarled. "Stand down. Force leader or not, you have no right to obstruct an officer of the Order."

Justin raised an eyebrow and moved into the center of the room. His eyes gleaming, his voice rumbling as he said, "You lack manners."

"Manners!" Lamar shouted, stepping toward Justin. "Sedition is at work in this room, and you talk of manners. Are you mad?"

Justin stared down at Lamar and declared flatly, "Are you calling me mad?"

"I'm not frightened by you," Lamar cried out, his eyes flashing. "The Order of Thoth stands behind me."

"Actually," Li observed with a nod of her head. "It's the Mirovar force team that's standing behind you."

The room shrank around Lamar as the Mirovar force team swarmed into the room.

"What on earth is going on?" Francis demanded.

Lamar's head swiveled left and right. He focused on Li, thrust his hand out, his finger pointing stiffly at her face and declared, "Li Wu is a traitor to the Order."

An incredulous murmur spread through the room.

Juliette laughed. "Poppycock."

"It's true," he declared with utter conviction. "I heard her incriminate herself."

"What's going on?" Anton growled, moving to stand next to Li. Peter and Chiara moved to join him a moment later.

"A false accusation I would think," Juliette observed with an arched eyebrow.

"Not false. And you," Lamar claimed, pointing a finger at Juliette, "a loremaster – should recuse yourself immediately. How else can you officiate at an inquisition?"

Lamar looked at Li and demanded, "Hand over the data stick and the letters. I know you're hiding them."

"Don't do anything Li," Anton advised.

Francis stepped forward and commanded, "Everyone stand down. You too Deon. This must be some sort of misunderstanding."

Lamar declared flatly, "The law will have its way."

"Indeed, it will," Francis said. "Juliette, please take everyone out of the room apart from Li, Deon, and Justin."

Anton squeezed Li's hand before he joined the others leaving the room.

Francis shut the door and turned back into the room. His face was flat and serious as he demanded, "Li first, what's going on?"

"Justin brought me a letter from my father," Li declared.

"A document filled with lies," Lamar snarled.

"Enough Deon. Let her speak," Francis ordered, his eyes flashing with tightly held anger. "Go on Li, what was in the letter."

"It was about Ramin Kain," Li said firmly. "It looks a lot like he's in league with the Vampire Dominion."

Lamar sucked air through his teeth and declared triumphantly. "Sedition from her mouth. She self-incriminates."

Francis looked at Lamar as if seeing him for the first time.

Justin stared hard at Lamar. "If you make a spurious accusation against Li," he rumbled. "You'll answer to me for it,"

"You can't threaten me. I'm an officer of the Order."

"The laws of the Order still maintain the right of challenge."

"You wouldn't dare."

"You think so … we'll see who makes the first bone to break and you know as well as I do that there is no limit on which bone gets broken."

Lamar's face twisted into a snarl. "And we can impeach a force leader. You're not above our laws. Be careful you don't find yourself in chains before this day is over."

Justin snorted dismissively. "Did you bring metal thick enough to hold me?"

Lamar stared up at Justin and declared hotly, "You will conform with the law or be outcast. The choice is a simple one."

Justin stared back, his eyes flat and steely. "The first thing you've said that makes any sense. It's always been a simple choice."

"What do you mean by that. Do you seriously place Li Wu's life over the Order? You're not fit to be a force leader."

Francis came to an inevitable decision and commanded, "Enough! There will be no challenges here." He turned to Justin and demanded, "Justin Blake, force leader of the Order of Thoth, do you accept the charge of inquisitorial guardian of Li Wu, novice of the Order?"

Justin looked like he would rather do anything else as he said, "Yes. I do."

"Deon Lamar, Order traveler, do you accept the charge of inquisitorial prosecutor?"

Lamar's eyes gleamed with triumph as he declared proudly, "Yes. I do."

"Li, hand over the letter and data stick to the prosecutor," Francis demanded.

Li looked at Justin, and he nodded his head once. She handed the papers and the data stick to Lamar and said, "Look at what's in there. It's damning."

Lamar's lip curled derisively. "Yes, I'm sure it is."

"Open your mind," she snapped.

Lamar took a step forward. "You presume to instruct me?"

Francis put his hand flat on Lamar's chest. "Call the Head of the Order. Do what you must."

Lamar turned, hurrying from the room.

Francis looked back at Li. "I hope your position is defensible."

"What have you done to me?" she asked.

"What I had to do as a force leader," Francis declared, his voice hard. He turned away and left the room.

"Uncle, what's happening?"

"An inquisition," Justin observed gloomily.

"You'll be my guardian though won't you."

"Not that way. I'm to guard you to ensure you don't escape."

The world seemed to shrink around her, the library suddenly becoming horribly claustrophobic.

She looked at Justin, her eyes large with worry. "How do I fight this?"

"I don't rightly know," he said softly. "Tracking the Head of the Order and accusing him of being in league with the vampires without rock solid proof of his guilt ... and you're a novice ... it's not good Li."

Li sat back stunned. Her father had never discussed the intricacies of an inquisition with her – they were so rare.

What was going to happen now?

She had no idea.

Chapter Fourteen

"Humility and wisdom walk hand in hand; there are no wise zealots." – Quote from The Way of the Faithful, a book of Red Empire lore

* * *

Boston, August 21ˢᵗ, 11:45

James Haley's smartphone pinged. A moment later so did his laptop as a Panopticon message appeared on the screen.

James scanned the text with a glance. Ramin Kain and Samuel Luther were on the move. Predictive algorithms presented their most likely destination. A red line snaked across a map from New York to a spot just south of a small village in Maine.

The Order safe house.

He vectored cameras along the route immediately in front of Kain's current position. He drove past in his Bentley, followed by a white Chevy Suburban with four male occupants.

The implications of the second vehicle were obvious. Kain had a security detail with him. James had never seen these operatives before, and he mentally noted the new information. He used the cameras to capture sufficient details to identify them again.

James backed up the new data onto a small, portable hard drive, and then purged the information from the Panopticon. The current search on Kain and his associates evaporated, the Panopticon screens vanishing like ghosts.

He pocketed the hard drive.

Opening his phone, he deleted the duplicate Panopticon message and dialed Chloe Armitage. She picked up the call before the first ring had finished.

"James?"

"Yes, Ma'am. The package is in motion toward the Order safe house."

"Any pertinent details I should know about?"

"Kain has a four-man security detail."

"… Initiate the plan. I will meet you at the staging location outside White Hill."

"Yes, Ma'am."

"Good work James. Tonight, will see an important step forward toward our goals. It is critical the Red Empire assassins are in place on time. Will there be any issues?"

"No, Ma'am. The plan is ready to execute."

"Excellent. I will see you after nightfall."

"Yes, Ma'am."

The call disconnected.

James sat back in his chair in his office at the Boston R.I.S.C building. His mind abuzz with thoughts, his heart filled with keen anticipation. A dozen Red Empire assassins waited in a set of suites on the floor below. He pushed his chair back, stood up, grabbed his coat and strode to the elevator.

Fifteen minutes later, three black Chevy Suburbans drove out of the building's parking garage and took off down the street.

* * *

Chloe put the phone down on the marble bench top.

In front of her rested six plastic bags of 'O positive' blood. She'd been so busy lately she hadn't had time to hunt properly. The bags came from an emergency supply she kept in her fridge. She'd warmed them up in a pot of water set to ninety-seven degrees Fahrenheit.

She picked up a bag, tossing it toward her guest.

Marcus Drake caught the bag and remarked glumly, "Thanks."

"Yes, I know. Not perfect, but it will do. Time is pressing, and we must make do with what is available."

Marcus cut the bag with his teeth, draining it dry in a second.

Chloe picked up a bag and followed suit.

A few seconds later, all the bags were empty, and Chloe put them neatly away into a bin.

She walked into her living room, Marcus following behind her. Elegant lamps lit the chamber with soft, indirect lighting. She'd drawn heavy curtains across her full-length windows against the midday sun. There would be no sunbathing in the presence of Marcus, or any other person. Her longing to walk in sunlight would forever be her secret.

They sat down opposite each other on a beautiful and elegant couch of modern design.

"And what of Jerusalem?" Chloe asked.

"It's a disaster for Crane. He is there now, personally supervising the evacuation with general Maze."

"And the target?"

"Captured by the Red Empire and disappeared."

Chloe smiled. "General Mosule is currently held in the Obsidian Prison. It's a holding facility for vampires the Red Empire constructed back in the late '90s. He cannot escape."

"What happens to him now?"

"Nothing. He cools his heels in that black hole until I see fit to free him."

"He will blame me for his capture. He'll link the assassin that passed on the location of the fake citadel to me."

"Don't worry about him. By the time he is free, you will be beyond his power to harm."

Marcus nodded. "And the mission tonight?"

"You have one objective, the safe abduction of Ramin Kain."

"And what of the boy?"

"If you have to kill him to defend yourself, then do it. If he can't survive tonight, he was never going to be any use against Crane."

"You know that I would kill Crane for you."

"Yes. But you know that I want it. Your knowledge is a hook that links you to me and Allemande's curse. If you attack him, you kill me first."

Chloe looked away from Marcus, her eyes growing distant. "The attack against Crane must remain hidden, unexpected, and utterly self-motivated. The young Slayne is growing in power. One day he will match his grandfather and then ... we put them together. Anton Slayne and Cornelius Crane. I'm sure that will be the day that I will once again be free."

"And I will be by your side."

Chloe turned back to Marcus; her eyes warm. "Yes, Marcus. At my side forever."

Marcus smiled.

Chloe's eyes hardened. "But first we strike tonight. With Crane's attention focused on Jerusalem and the Red Empire, we will be able to act without interference."

Marcus nodded; his eyes fierce.

Chloe stared at Marcus intently. "Victory will be ours."

"Yes, Chloe," Marcus agreed. He moved closer, Chloe leaning into his embrace.

She rested her head on his shoulder, wondering how many more days he had left to live. She held him tight.

There was little time left with Marcus, and she'd spend none of it on regret.

* * *

James Haley pulled the Chevy Suburban to a halt halfway along the main street through White Hill.

The Red Empire assassins driving the other two cars pulled dutifully in behind him. He turned to the man sitting next to him and directed, "Keep your men in the cars."

Nasr al Dam, the leader of the Red Empire troop, nodded and touched his earpiece, speaking a short command in Arabic.

James exited the car, walking over to the nearest street corner. The local post office dominated the street, and he slapped a device the size of a postage stamp on the wall of the building. A quick glance assured him the device remained securely attached and his actions unnoticed by any of the locals attending to their personal affairs.

He turned away from the wall, walking casually back to the car. The bug carried a tiny fish-eye camera and a radio transmitter with enough power to run for another twenty-four hours. James had programmed it to watch for Ramin Kain's Bentley. Kain's car would have to turn on this corner to head toward the Order safe house. Once it did so, the device would alert him instantly without leaving a Panopticon trace.

James glanced at his watch as he approached his car. Kain should be passing through White Hill in about two hours. He still had plenty of time to secure the staging area and prepare for battle. He got back into the car and drove off to the local airfield.

His eyes were flat as he led the suburbans through the airfield's entrance. The Red Empire assassins would assist with the bloody work of clearing the airfield and locking it down. He'd guaranteed Chloe there would be no witnesses to the night's forthcoming action.

He could not afford mistakes or errors. The stakes were too high. He would do whatever was necessary to ensure the success of the mission.

The three Chevy suburbans pulled to a stop next to each other in the airfield's parking lot. The doors flew open, the assassins blurring out of the cars. They all carried a simple dagger for work such as this, and in less than a minute the only people left alive on the airfield were those who had arrived in the black SUVs.

James opened his phone, sending Chloe a text message which read, 'The airfield is secured.'

He surveyed the carnage. His eyes flat. All these people had died for a great purpose. At least their lives were not wasted.

* * *

Chloe Armitage's smartphone pinged.

James Haley had sent another text message, it read, 'Kain has just passed through White Hill.'

She replied with, 'Our ETA is two hours from now.'

"Time to move Marcus," she ordered.

Marcus flourished his Red Empire swords and plunged them back into their sheaths across his broad shoulders. The dark cape he wore had a pair of slits that accommodated the blades positioned in an 'X' across his back.

"You know I would prefer a mace, flail or axe," he said with a grimace.

Chloe smiled briefly, gave him a pair of sais, and adjusted the fit of his tunic. "Tonight, you need to blend in. Now don't forget your hood and veil. It's very important."

"Yes, Chloe," he replied, tucking the sais into his belt.

She stepped back from him. She wore simple dark-gray combat fatigues and a matching cap; the Red Dragon belted at her left hip.

The edge of a smile curled her lips, her eyes gleaming with anticipation. "Follow me."

Chloe turned, leading Marcus up the stairs in her penthouse to her private, shielded helipad. A brand-new nightfalcon, as black as night, stood in a covered bay just large enough to hold it. She slid the side door back and bounded into the cabin. In a moment, she was in the pilot's seat and flicking switches.

Marcus sat down in the seat beside her.

Above them, heavy steel doors rolled back into hidden recesses. The late afternoon sun slashed across the rotors of the helicopter. The engines roared into life. The rotors blurred, the nightfalcon leaping into the air like a caged eagle suddenly set free. It soared away. The sunlight glinting off the darkened, transparent armor of the helicopter's canopy.

Chloe booted up the nightfalcon's combat system and sent commands to a flight of blackwidow helicopters stationed at Fort Dix. The attack helicopters had been waiting on hot standby for the command and immediately took off. Their engines hushed with stealth technology; they sprang into the air with a low rumble before rapidly dwindling to specks in the sky.

James Haley would log the whole operation as an aerial attack on an Order of Thoth safe house. There would be no reference to a troop of Red Empire assassins, and he would carefully manage the Panopticon record of events to back up the story.

Chloe flicked on the autopilot and leaned back in her chair. All the pieces were in motion. There was nothing left to do but wait.

She reflected upon her plans. The abduction of Ramin Kain was in play. She would spirit him out of the country. She would squeeze him of all useful information on the operations of the Order of Thoth.

It would be an utter disaster for the Order. They would try to rescue him. The only team in position to act would be the Mirovar force team. With Kain as the lure, she could set a trap that would ensnare Li Wu and drive Anton further along the path toward the assassination of Crane.

Chloe frowned. It was a good plan, but nothing was certain. The battle at the safe house could see any of the principles killed. She had to take the risk. There could be no stinting on the forging of a weapon to bring down an adversary as powerful as Cornelius Crane, King of the Vampire Dominion.

Anton would survive tonight's battle, or he would prove himself unfit to fulfill the purpose Chloe had for him.

It was entirely possible Anton would die, perhaps even probable. There were many ways her grand plan could stumble this night. But she had hope, a bright, shining hope. Crane's entrapment of her in his cursed web would blow up in his face. She planned to be there when it happened.

She wanted to be at his side when he died. To watch the light fade from his eyes. To hold his hand, not in comfort, but in a final intimacy to let him know just how badly he'd failed against her.

It was only fitting for someone who'd completely robbed her of her liberty.

* * *

Ramin Kain stared through the front windscreen of his Bentley without seeing what was in front of him.

What the hell has Lamar done?

Ramin desperately wanted to talk with Lamar. Preferably alone, in a quiet room with a baseball bat, or even better, in a hidden location in a trackless forest where a body could rot away without possibility of discovery.

Lamar was supposed to identify the Red Empire agent and hold back so that they could discover their accomplice, and if possible, link Anton Slayne to the agent. What on earth had prompted him to accuse Li Wu of sedition?

Anton Slayne wasn't even in the frame.

Ramin was flabbergasted by just how pear-shaped Lamar's mission had become in just a couple of days. It was bizarre. In his near twenty years in position as the Head of the Order of Thoth, he'd never seen anything like it.

The Bentley barreled along the country road. A white, Chevy Suburban a handful of seconds behind it. Sam slowed the big car, turning into a laneway. They had arrived at the safe house.

Now was the time to find out what had actually happened to precipitate this disaster.

The Bentley pulled to a stop in front of the house. Francis and Juliette Mirovar stood on the porch. A half step in front of them and to Francis' left stood Lamar. His face lit with an enthusiastic excitement.

Ramin got out of the car, walking around the front of it toward the safe house.

Deon came down the steps to meet him and declared, "Sir. I have uncovered a plot to destroy you."

"Very good, Deon," Ramin stated smoothly, shaking Lamar's outstretched hand. "We must not jump to hasty conclusions. The inquiry will reveal all."

Lamar blinked. "But Sir. The evidence is irrefutable."

"Deon, I fully appreciate your endeavors and your commitment to the Order, but we must allow the inquiry to run its full course. We must ensure that justice is not only done but is seen to be done."

"Yes, Sir," Lamar agreed, standing aside. "Of course, Sir."

Ramin checked his sympathetic and parasympathetic nervous system controls – they were still in place. He radiated confidence, certainty, and maturity as he walked past Lamar and proceeded up the steps to where Francis and Juliette Mirovar stood patiently.

"We have a serious situation on our hands," Ramin declared with a frown.

"Yes, we do," Francis agreed flatly.

"The prisoner, where is she?"

"With Justin Blake," Juliette observed. "She is safe."

Ramin leaned forward a fraction. "We need to make sure that remains the case."

"Of course," Francis replied, frowning. "It goes without saying."

"Quite so," Ramin noted.

The Mirovars did not move aside, and the scuffle of feet across gravel sounded loud in Ramin's ears as Sam, and his personal security detail moved into position behind him.

"Do I need to be invited in like a vampire?" Ramin asked incredulously.

Juliette laughed briefly. "Of course not, that would be ridiculous."

Francis stepped aside, and swept his hand back. "Please come inside."

Juliette took a step back, making space for Ramin, Sam and their men to enter the safe house.

"The security detail," Juliette inquired as Ramin approached. "Is it strictly necessary?"

Ramin paused in front of her and declared, "I'm here in my official capacity. Of course, they're necessary."

"Are you implying that the Mirovar force team is a source of threat to your personal safety? That we would violate our oaths to the Order?"

Ramin blinked, frowned, and said, "Of course not." He glanced to his side at Francis who stared at him with a look of utter distaste that could've killed an ox at ten paces. "I mean no offense. There is no reason to impugn the honor of a loremaster."

Juliette smiled warmly, putting her hand casually on his shoulder. "I'm so happy to hear that. I would hate to see an 'honor challenge' made over an ill-considered insult."

Ramin's lips pressed together for the briefest of moments before he regained control of himself. Juliette Mirovar had just threatened him in broad daylight in front of witnesses, and there was nothing he could do about it.

He had no illusions. A single match between Francis Mirovar and himself would end in only one way. With himself gutted like a pig in an abattoir. He loathed the ancient traditions of the Order with a passion but there was nothing he could do about it; an honor challenge was a very real possibility.

Ramin grinned at Juliette like a politician who has just kissed a baby with a full diaper and declared forthrightly, "There will be no honor challenges while I'm Head of the Order of Thoth."

Juliette looked into his eyes, and Ramin quailed inside. The woman was unnerving. She was outrageously self-confident, it was infuriating. She could say more with a moment's silence than many could with a long speech.

Ramin drew upon every resource he had, every ounce of training in the arts of manipulation and control. Speaking smoothly with an air of mature professionalism he said, "Let's move this unfortunate situation forward. There is no reason to be standing on this porch."

Juliette nodded. "Yes, let's get this done."

Turning she led Ramin and his retinue into the safe house.

Francis followed after them.

Ramin walked a step behind Juliette, his mind racing. She'd just made it absolutely clear he must take care to avoid any opportunity to turn this into a personal challenge. Mirovar and his blade would be ready, and his personal security detail would stand down in the face of tradition and the Order's senior loremaster. He would be defenseless. Perhaps with the exception of Sam, but even he would not last long against Mirovar.

He must avoid an honor challenge at all costs. Damn Lamar and his precipitous actions. He still didn't know all the details of what Lamar had accused Li Wu of. Such knowledge would have to wait until the inquiry.

What have I walked into here? It feels like a trap. A damn ugly trap.

He had to find a way to prevail. Perhaps he could salvage the situation. He could provoke Anton Slayne into a rash action that even Juliette's declaration of sanctuary could not save him from.

A glimmer of hope remained; he could use Slayne's inexperience, youth, and attachment to Wu against him. All Ramin would have to do was keep pushing on Anton's need to protect Wu. He wouldn't be able to help himself. He would do something stupid and get himself killed.

Hope bloomed in his heart, as his plans turned on a dime. It was all he could do to avoid smiling as he entered the library.

It was time to up the pressure on Anton Slayne.

* * *

Li stood in the middle of the library. The door was open, Francis, Justin, Kain and his men stood in the room while the rest of the Mirovar force team crowded the hall outside.

"I relinquish my charge to the Head of the Order," Justin declared solemnly, stepping away from Li's side. He moved to the side of the room, his eyes watchful, his face a dark, inscrutable mask.

Kain's men moved forward, surrounding Li.

She put her hands out in front. There was a solid click as steel shackles locked around her wrists.

Kain approached with Luther a step behind him and stood before her. They stared at each other for a moment, Li wondering why Kain hesitated.

"Li Wu," Kain began in formal tones. "You are charged with suspicion of insurrection against the Order of Thoth."

The room was utterly silent.

Li's heart was loud in her ears. *How do I fight this?*

Kain didn't wait for a response. "You will be given the drug, Truther. You will be taken to a chamber of inquiry and put to the question. The truth or falsity of the charge will be laid bare by your own testimony in front of a panel of judges. If the charge is found to be false, you will be freed, and no record of the inquiry will be laid upon you. If the charge is found to be true, given your status as a novice, you will be taken from the chamber of inquiry and summarily executed. Is that clear?"

Li looked around the room. Impassive, serious men surrounded her. She wished she had her sword with her. The Green Dragon would give her a fighting chance of survival and escape, but it lay in her room.

I'm trapped! Li looked at Justin, his eyes stared at her, dark with pain. He frowned slightly and gave the barest of nods. She glanced at Francis who stood near the door. His jaw was tight as conflict raged in barely hidden depths.

If she didn't go along with this, where would Francis and Justin end up standing? Would they side with her against Kain and his men? Two powerful force leaders allied against the Head of the Order. It would tear the Order of Thoth apart.

There were currents far deeper than her own life at stake here.

Li nodded and replied solemnly, "Yes. I understand."

Kain nodded once. "Samuel, please administer the serum."

Luther reached into his coat, withdrawing a small leather folder. He flipped it open. Inside was a syringe filled with a clear liquid. He took the syringe, stepped in close and jammed it into the base of Li's neck, depressing the plunger slowly.

Li stared at him. Luther stared back; his eyes gleaming with something that chilled her heart.

A cold fire spread out from the injection site, racing along her veins.

Luther pulled the syringe clear and stepped back. A faint smile flitting briefly across his face.

Li's eyes flashed with sudden indignation. "Is he allowed to enjoy this?"

Kain ignored her and ordered, "The prisoner will be kept in this room for the next two hours to enable the serum to reach full effect. The Chamber of Inquiry will be made ready, and we will convene there at," he paused to consult his watch, "twenty minutes past eight."

Kain turned away and left the room. The others followed until only Li, and the four Order operatives remained in the library.

She assessed the men. They wore suits, in-ear tactical comm links, and from the bulges, in their jackets, they carried Glock 9mm handguns. Each had a katana sword with a scabbard belted at their hips.

Li frowned and sat down, her shackled hands in her lap. There was nothing she could do except wait.

She turned inward, calming herself and preparing herself to act.

You never know when an opportunity would present itself, and she vowed silently to be ready for anything. She was willing to die to preserve the true spirit of the Order, but she wouldn't lift a finger to preserve Kain's corrupt rule of it.

* * *

Peter Lamb and Anton Slayne stood opposite each other in their shared room on the first floor of the safe house. The last vestiges of sunlight drifting through the windows managed to lift the illumination in the room to a dull gloom.

"This is nuts," Anton snapped in a harsh whisper. "If anyone should be on trial, it should be Ramin Kain."

Rubbing his hand through his thick, red hair, Peter declared without irony, "Kain has all the characteristics of a Bond villain and none of the charisma."

"What the hell is Truther?" Anton asked.

"A truth serum. Li will spill her guts. She's going to write her own death sentence."

"You're kidding?"

"No. The Order will end up killing her."

"That's crazy."

"It's how it works."

"What do you mean?"

"She's still a novice. She hasn't been confirmed as a full member at a Conclave. Kain can order her killed to protect the secrecy of the Order."

"What about sanctuary? Couldn't someone offer her that?"

"Not during an inquisition. It's the one, and only time, sanctuary can't be offered. She's in a very dangerous position – she could easily be killed tonight."

Anton shook his head. "We can't let that happen."

"It won't happen," Peter averred.

Anton thought back to what had happened to his grandfather and his family. Being innocent offered no protection from injustice. He asked, "Are you sure?"

Peter paused for a moment, indecision flashing over his face.

Anton made his decision. "If Kain is going to kill Li, then fuck the Order. I don't want to be a part of it."

Peter frowned. "You'll get yourself killed too."

"I remember you promising to help me find out the truth."

"… Hell … that I did. I wasn't expecting that particular promise to get me killed or outcast."

Anton looked at Peter in silence.

Peter shook his head, smiling grimly. "Don't worry, I don't forget my promises."

"We have to stop this trial – the wrong person has been accused. It should be Kain that is stuffed full of truth serum and put to the question."

"Maybe we don't have to stop anything. She could be found innocent, Francis and Justin are part of the judging panel, surely sanity will prevail."

"I'm not taking any chances."

"Okay then, but we do this my way. We'll hide our weapons in the briefing room and keep some flash bangs handy. If we need to rescue Li and make a break for it, we will."

"And afterward?"

"Well, that's going to be a negotiation with the Order."

Shaking his head, Anton looked at Peter. "I shouldn't involve you in this. It's too much to ask."

"Not really. Kain got up my nose when he had you shot down like a mad dog. I've never felt anything good about him. He's a creep, and the fact that he is Head of the Order is a mockery of everything I stand for."

Anton nodded. "I'll get the Green Dragon from Li's room. She'll need it if we have to rescue her."

"I'll grab my axes. I've also got a bag of flash bangs under my bed."

"Under your bed?"

"Of course, where else would you keep a satchel of explosives?" Peter asked with a mock incredulous grin.

Anton smiled briefly, then turned to his wardrobe, the Blue Dragon rested on top of it. He pulled it down, it always felt like it belonged in his hands and he was certain he would need it tonight.

"I'll bring a blanket," Peter said. "We'll need to keep everything out of sight … you know what? Maybe I should get some guns."

Anton arched an eyebrow.

"Nah, probably overkill."

Anton nodded, and clapped Peter on the shoulder. "Thanks. I couldn't do this without you.

"Hey, I'm doing it for Li. She's real cute."

Anton stopped for a second, staring at him.

"Hey – that got a reaction. I know you're keen on her."

Anton shook his head. "It's not like that. It's complicated."

"Sure."

Anton sighed.

"Don't worry, your secret is safe with me."

"We have work to do," Anton declared, giving his sword to Peter.

"For sure – see you back here in a minute."

Anton nodded, he needed to see if Chiara was not in the room, she shared with Li. He had to find the Green Dragon. Li would need it when they escaped.

Sanctuary with the Order, Anton thought bitterly, *what a farce.*

* * *

The Raven walked casually along the hall. The briefing room was empty.

They ducked through the doorway, blurring to the far side of the oval table. There were three high backed wooden chairs behind it, the judges' chairs. Ramin Kain as Head of the Order would sit in the middle chair.

The Raven moved behind Kain's chair.

The device they held was tiny. Dome shaped, with a half-inch-long stem. The Raven drove the device into the back of the chair, halfway up on the left-hand side. They had observed that Kain was right-handed, and right-handed people often kept their phones on the left side of their body.

The Raven fully understood that it wasn't the best plan in the world, but it was the best they could come up with at short notice. The device would activate when Kain's phone was within a foot of it. It wouldn't need long, a matter of seconds to co-opt Kain's phone and insert the tracking software.

They assessed the plan as a fifty-fifty proposition.

They blurred to the doorway. Reaching the hallway, they dropped back to a stroll and made their way into the kitchen. They had one proximity bug left, and they started working on a plan B.

They poured themselves a drink of water and were shocked when they almost dropped the glass.

Their hands had never trembled before – why now?

The Raven sighed, a wave of confusion flooding through them.

Suddenly nothing made sense.

Nothing at all.

* * *

The dark of night washed across the sky, pushing the last vestiges of twilight over the western horizon.

Chloe Armitage's nightfalcon swooped into land at the regional airport outside of White Hill. She checked her scopes. The three blackwidow attack helicopters were still en route with an ETA of 20:10.

She smiled, she'd fifteen minutes to address James Haley and the Red Empire assassins before the helicopters arrived. That would be plenty of time to get the men organized.

She switched the engines off.

Marcus pulled the helicopter's side door open. She stepped lithely down to the ground. Standing well back from the helicopter in a tight semi-circle were the Red Empire assassins. They had already changed into their combat gear. Each one wore a pair of lightly curved short swords, and an array of throwing stars and daggers. She studied them for a moment, more than half were barely into their beards. The Red Ghost had sent her a young crew. People he wouldn't miss.

James Haley stood next to them, dressed in his usual suit.

All eyes were upon Chloe as she approached the semi-circle of men facing her.

She lifted her voice and declared firmly, "Tonight we take a decisive step against our mutual enemy – the Order of Thoth."

The men stared at her with avid attention.

"We will abduct their leader – the Head of the Order. We know for a certainty that he is at a nearby safe house. Protected by a single force team and a handful of guards."

A murmur spread through the assassins. The Head of the Order of Thoth was a target equal to the Red Ghost. His death or capture would bring great honor to their names.

"Your purpose is his safe capture. Kill all who stand in your way, but do not waste time pursuing the operatives of the Order. This is a lightning mission; speed is of the essence. Once we have the Head of the Order, we will leave this location behind. Shadowstone attack helicopters will cleanse the site. Do not fall behind or remain behind forever."

The men nodded. A few smiled grimly.

Chloe indicated James with a wave of her hand and said, "My aide will introduce your target."

James moved amongst the men with an open laptop, Ramin Kain's face displayed on the screen. Each man took a close look at the rotating pictures, memorizing his features.

Chloe indicated Marcus with a glance. "Marcus Drake will lead you in your approach."

The assassins variously nodded and gave their assent.

"Is it clear? Any questions?"

The leader of the Red Empire troop stepped forward and tapped his chest. "I am Nasr al Dam, the Blood Eagle, we of the Red Empire will do our duty against the weaklings of the Order."

Chloe nodded once and ordered, "Marcus Drake will lead the assault. I command you to obey your oaths and follow him."

Nasr al Dam nodded once. Chloe stepped in close and addressed him directly, "Take your best men to capture Kain. Use the rest to cover your actions and keep the rest of the Order away from your target. Marcus Drake will back you up."

Nasr al Dam grinned, indicating four men to his left. "These are the 'Fist,' the best of my troop. We will not fail in our mission."

Chloe studied him for a second. "Excellent."

She stepped back, nodding at Marcus.

Marcus moved forward. "We leave now," he commanded. "We have three miles to cover to reach the target."

The thirteen men turned away as a group, blurring from the airport.

James approached, standing patiently at Chloe's side.

In the distance, three lights resolved in the night sky. The attack helicopters were arriving from Fort Dix.

She turned to him. "You will fly in one of the blackwidows. Create a perimeter and watch my lead. The Order will fight back, take care and expect substantial losses." She glanced after the distant Red Empire fighters. "Did you notice how young most of them were?" She sniffed, not waiting for his answer. "Guard my exfiltration with Kain and allow the Order to escape."

"Ma'am?"

Chloe smiled briefly. "There is a larger purpose in play tonight beyond the elimination of a handful of Order operatives." She looked off into the distance. "… It's a shame the Head of the Order of Thoth is about to be caught up in the destruction of an Order Safe House by Shadowstone." She clicked her tongue and shook her head. "Who could've predicted such an unfortunate turn of events. Crane will be most displeased when he hears of this latest reversal."

Glowing with an ebullient mood, she turned back to James. "It's such a great time to be alive. So much is happening. Tonight, is a pivotal moment where we begin to seize the initiative from Crane and Kain."

James nodded, his eyes narrowing.

Chloe dismissed him with a look. No one could possibly understand the future she saw for the world. Not until she'd actualized it. It was too much for them to grasp.

The attack helicopters circled the airport, swinging into land around the black nightfalcon.

A familiar pre-battle excitement began to build within her. She looked toward the safe house farm. Soon she would have Kain; forcing the Mirovar force team to follow after him to a battlefield of her choosing.

A battlefield where Li Wu would die and she'd push Anton Slayne toward his inevitable confrontation with Crane.

She shivered with excitement. Everything was at risk. As it must be to achieve great things.

If Anton or Li died tonight, it would be disappointing, but she had time to plan anew.

Oceans of time.

The ultimate realization of her vision was inevitable.

* * *

The briefing room had become a chamber of inquiry.

The main table stood near the back of the room, clearing a wide space in the middle of the chamber for the prisoner.

Li sat in a simple wooden chair facing the table and Francis, Kain, and Justin who sat behind it. Her wrists remained shackled, with a second, thick chain looping around the metal braces and hobbling her ankles. She calmly, a side-effect of the drug coursing through her system. She knew she would tell the truth. She wanted to tell the truth. Her inhibitions and sense of self-control had vanished on the Truther's tide.

The world was bright and shiny. She tried ramping and failed miserably. The drug affected her capacity to be silent. Her internal voice chattering incessantly; she was losing all her filters. It left her feeling naked, vulnerable and somehow – clumsy.

She looked around the room, everyone was there. She ached with sadness. What would her father think of her now, chained and alone in an Order inquisition? The lights dimmed, the gloom settling in like a clinging shroud around her. Where was the light? How could everything be so dark?

Why did people have halos?

She could see auras. *This was new*, she thought to herself.

Nausea worked slowly through her system. *People had colors, who knew?* Was this another side effect of the drug or was something else going on?

Luther and the four members of Kain's personal security stood in a group near the judges. A dark cloud shot with swirls of murky greens and reds moving through them. Kain sat between Francis and Justin, covered with the same murk as his men, but also crowned with a ring of red fire.

Though separated by half the room, Francis and Juliette were wrapped in brilliant golden cords with flashes of silvery light streaming between them. More of the same covered Jay and Yvette.

Lamar stood alone, wrapped in turbulent yellow and black mists. Chiara, Anton, and Peter stood against the front wall. Chiara limed in a hot, red glow, while bright blue and green lightning played and sparked furiously around Anton and Peter.

Justin sat at the judge's table, a purple cloud around his head, his eyes boring into her soul. He lifted his right hand and golden rays speared forth.

A woman's voice cut through the air. The words ringing through the chamber like the voice of an angel. Li's head whipped around to face the speaker.

"—inquisition is called to order."

Kain declared, "The judges acknowledge loremaster Juliette Mirovar – keeper of our law."

"Three are met, force leaders true," Juliette declared. All eyes in the room turned to her. "May the great Thoth guide their judgment with wisdom and fealty to the law."

A bell tolled three times. Incense burned, filling the room with its musky aroma.

Juliette's voice rang throughout the chamber, "The guardians of the law are in place; may justice be swift and sure. The Inquisition of the Order of Thoth has commenced. May no man stand against it, rebuke its judgment or stand forsworn before the great Thoth."

Juliette stepped to the side. Her eyes dark with hidden emotions.

Kain nodded toward Lamar and declared, "The inquisitor shall stand and begin their inquiry."

Stepping forward, Lamar stood a yard in front of Li. He focused fully upon her, his eyes staring into her face.

"What is your name?"

"Li Wu."

"Who is your father?"

"Gang Wu."

"Is he alive or dead?"

"Dead."

"Are you a woman?"

"Yes."

"How old are you?"

"Nineteen."

"Are you a novice of the Order of Thoth?"

"Yes."

"Have you answered any of these questions falsely?"

"No."

Lamar stepped back and announced to the panel of judges sitting behind the table, "The Truther is in full effect."

"Continue your inquiry," Kain declared matter-of-factly.

Lamar turned back toward Li, a slight smile curling his lips. Mustard and charcoal clouds stormed around his head. Red sparks crawling like ants over smoldering embers, filled his eyes.

Li stared at him. She loathed him and yet desperately wanted to tell him anything, as long as it was the truth.

Lamar stared back at her. He reached inside his jacket and pulled forth the envelope in which her father's letter had arrived. His eyes glowed with a fevered light as he regarded Li for a long moment.

He started to circle around her, his voice asking questions about the providence of the letter.

* * *

The blackwidows zoomed off toward the safe house.

Chloe Armitage's nightfalcon flew twenty seconds behind them. She sat in the pilot's seat and flicked a switch to provide a heads-up display of her combat team. Ghostly images played across the windscreen. Metadata streamed next to GPS locations for each of her men. Her command links were open, the soft voices of her team whispering with perfect clarity in her ears.

"The safe house sensor arrays have been disarmed," Marcus reported. "We're in position."

"Hold your position. Our ETA is two minutes," Chloe responded.

She expanded the view from a helmet cam strapped to Marcus's head. He was facing a curtained window at the front of the house. The infra-red filter showed a room full of people. The arrangement of the glowing forms hinting at an ancient memory.

Chloe's mind raced.

Kain had arrived with a personal security unit. He was here on official business. Three people were behind a table. One sat in front of them while a fifth person slowly circled the seated person.

Was it a court? *Yes. An inquisition.*

"Marcus, Kain is the middle man of the three behind the table."

Marcus broadcast the details to the Red Empire assassins.

"Our ETA is ninety seconds. We'll cut the house in two. Time your move with our attack."

"Yes, Ma'am."

"Good hunting Marcus," Chloe whispered to herself.

The three blackwidows broke formation and began to circle the safe house in decreasing circles. Two were circling clockwise, the third, with James Haley on the gun controls, circled in the opposite direction.

Chloe brought her nightfalcon to a spot a little above the blackwidows and eight-hundred meters off to the side. All she had to do now was wait and hope that the Raven had managed to bug Ramin Kain's phone with a tracker.

If the bug failed, she would need a plan B for leaving a believable trail for the Mirovar force team to follow.

* * *

It remained a peculiarity of an Order Inquisition that the inquisitor would withhold the evidence from the judges prior to the event. Only the charge would be known. In this way, the judges would be free of prejudice when presented with the evidence against the accused.

A peculiarity Ramin vowed to get rid of once he assumed the absolute rulership of the Order of Thoth.

Deon Lamar pulled Gang Wu's letter, and the data stick from the envelope. He laid the pages down on the table with a flourish and declared, "Here is the evidence of the lie. A seditious lie designed to tear the Order apart. A lie propagated by traitors claiming Ramin Kain is in league with the Vampire Dominion."

Ramin stared at the pages and data stick in front of him. His heart froze with fear. His mind clouded with a storm of doubts. *What the fuck is this?*

"That's outrageous," Sam shouted, his eyes flashing with indignation.

Juliette called out, "There shall be order in the court Mr. Luther, or must you be removed?"

Luther's head rocked backward as if he'd been physically slapped and he took a step back.

Lamar waved his hand theatrically around the room, declaring loudly, "I have examined the data stick carefully. It is a series of maps where the traitor Gang Wu—"

Anton Slayne hissed. "Bastard."

"Order Mr. Slayne," Juliette declared. She captured his gaze with a hard stare, and his face paled.

Lamar studied the audience for a long moment and then said, "Outlined Ramin Kain's sterling work discovering covens of young vampires."

There was a long silence.

Francis leaned forward slightly and asked, "And?"

Lamar turned to Francis and stated incredulously, "He deduced that Ramin's one hundred percent success rate on searches could only be the result of collusion with Cornelius Crane."

Ramin's armpits and the small of his back became wet with fear. His face flushed as decades of self-taught training deserted him. He whispered hoarsely, "You idiot."

A look of puzzlement flitted across Lamar's face. A low murmur spread through the room.

Justin Blake's hand appeared around Ramin's left wrist.

Ramin looked at it with shocked incomprehension, and then shouted, "Guards!"

His personal bodyguards drew their katanas free as one, moving to stand opposite Blake.

Their leader leveled his blade at the massive force leader, and commanded, "Let him go."

"Make me," Blake growled. A dreadful smile curling his lips while his eyes were as dark and flat as river stones on a moonless night.

The room fell into absolute silence.

The Wu girl, her face filled with sudden intent, called out, "Quiet, someone's here."

"What on Earth are you talking about?" Ramin snapped.

A look of recognition seized her face. "Helicopters. Stealth shielded."

"What?" Francis asked.

Straining at her chains, she shouted, "We're sitting ducks."

The low rumble of dampened turbines filtered into the room.

"Oh, fuck," Ramin whispered.

Chapter Fifteen

"For those who die with honor, the touch of death is simply the unlocking of a door between this life and the next."

— Quote from The Way of the Faithful, a book of Red Empire lore.

* * *

White Hill, Maine, August 21st, 20:27

Peter dragged the gray blanket away from the cache of weapons.

Anton snatched up the green and blue dragons. A pair of double-bladed axes appeared, like a magician's trick, in Peter's hands. Anton blurred forward to stand next to Li, the twin dragon blades crossed in front of him, his face filled with frightful intent.

"This stops now," Anton declared to the room, his eyes scanning the boundaries of the chamber.

Peter moved to the other side of Li where he grinned at everyone in front of him while circling his razor-sharp axes back and forth.

Luther screeched. "How dare you come armed—"

"See! See!" Kain shouted, leaping to his feet. His left wrist, still immobilized in Justin's iron grip, left him half tilted to the side. He pointed at Anton with his free hand. "Slayne is the traitor. He—"

The front door burst in. Windows shattered. The back door crashed open. Tan and black-clad forms blurred into the chamber. Each wielded a pair of gleaming curved blades. The night beyond the windows erupted into a thunderous firestorm as stealth gunships opened up on the safe house and the surrounding buildings. Twenty-millimeter cannon fire tore through the side of the house, evaporating everything it touched.

Chaos overwhelmed the room.

* * *

The room went to hell.

Justin dropped Kain's wrist. The side of his wooden chair shattered into a cloud of splinters as he blurred toward the one door out of the briefing room.

There was a swish to his right, a hidden katana appeared in Francis' hands, its blade mirroring the golden lamps and flickering candles in the room. Francis, his face a white mask, blurred right, interposing himself between two Red Empire assassins who were rolling to their feet and his wife, Juliette. Man-made lightning flashed beyond the shattered window behind the assassins as cannons thundered overhead.

The four men guarding Kain, their blades already drawn, swiveled around to face the threats rushing in from all sides. Their faces stilled as they descended into silence. Kain stood behind them, his mouth agape.

Justin picked up the remains of his chair with his right hand, swinging it through a tight arc at a knot of Red Empire assassins heading directly toward Kain. In the crowded space, the closest assassin could not escape the path of the chair, taking one leg across his chest and the other across his face. He flew across the room in a cloud of splinters, crashing into the far wall.

Justin surged through the opening and the doorway beyond.

Behind him, the wave of Red Empire assassins who had come through the front door, hit the four Order operatives guarding Kain, blades clanging and crashing in desperate combat.

Weapons. Justin blurred into the front yard where his Harley-Davidson stood. Above him, blackwidow helicopter gunships wheeled through the night sky, streams of fire lancing toward any available target. Their hammering cannons and whirring miniguns cutting across the low rumble of their muffled turbines.

Justin only had moments before their crews saw him and turned their devastating weapons against him.

He tore open the saddlebag on the back of his motorcycle. He reached inside. Grinning tightly, his dark eyes flashing, he drew forth his weapon of choice.

A line of 7.62mm rounds from a minigun speared into the ground, racing toward him.

Justin dove into silence, blurring to the side.

The blackwidow shuddered through the air, wheeling toward him, hunting him with its cannon and miniguns.

Thunder and fire bloomed around him.

Fuck!

Was there no escape?

* * *

Shattered glass littered the floor.

A pair of Red Empire assassins leaped to their feet, swords slashing toward Jay and Yvette.

Stillness reigned in Jay's mind. He blurred forward at maximum ramp, stepping inside the arc of the first blade. His right shoulder slamming into the assassin's chest as his hands slapped together around the hilt of the second blade. The assassin had just enough time for his eyes to register surprise as Jay spun a hundred and eighty degrees, wrenching the blade free of his grasp.

Jay used his grip on the unbalanced assassin's right hand to lean him forward with his own momentum. Jay's left foot lashed out, crushing the man's right knee. He pivoted back the other way, plunging the stolen sword through the assassin's skull, painting the nearest wall with a thin ribbon of blood.

The man fell limply to the floor, his other sword sliding across the polished hardwood.

Jay spun around. Yvette was dodging the flashing strikes of the second assassin, the pair of them rotating through a blurred and deadly dance. He reversed the sword in his hand, throwing it toward Yvette.

She reached for the blade.

Jay dashed for the second blade on the floor.

Is there enough time?

* * *

"What the hell," Luther shouted, backing away and dodging the strikes of the nearest Red Empire Assassin.

A second assassin flourished his swords, advancing on Chiara.

She fell into silence, time slowed down. The assassin ramped, rushing forward. She twisted away to the right as he went past her. She took in the room as she turned. Justin had vanished through the doorway. Five Red Empire assassins were rushing the Order guards in front of the judge's table. Francis engaged two more on the far side of the room as Juliette sought safety behind him. Jay ran past a blood-soaked corpse for a fallen blade. Yvette caught a thrown sword, turning furiously toward her opponent.

Chiara leaned back hard as blades passed over her head.

Li remained chained to her chair. Peter and Anton blurring around her, a ferocious wall of bright metal and desperate intent.

Lamar stood in no man's land, outside Anton's and Peter's defensive ring, his head swiveling, his face rigid with shock. Kain disappeared beyond the swarm of blades and bodies as the four Order guards stood firm before the onslaught of the best of the Red Empire troop.

Chiara leaped, flattening herself face up on the ceiling as the assassin lunged beneath her.

Weapons?

The glass on the floor glittered in the lamplight. She pushed back off the ceiling to land near the front wall. A gray blanket lay crumpled on the floor. She snatched it up, sweeping it over the glass toward the onrushing assassin.

The glass came alive. A glittering mist of shards flying through the air. She let the blanket go. It flew toward the assassin, spreading out like a sail in the wind. The assassin began to dodge aside but the glass was moving too quickly, and the blanket was too wide. The glass struck first, then the blanket wrapped over his front, covering his face and torso from the waist up.

Chiara followed, both her feet striking him in the chest. She rebounded back, the man flying across the room, crashing into the far wall.

She grinned. He'd dropped one of his swords. She scooped it up, twisting around, the sword snapping up into a defensive position in front of her.

An assassin, his leather veil knocked away, blood streaming from his crushed nose, came at her from the front corner of the room. He ramped and lunged. Chiara ramped and defended. His first attack got past her defenses, scoring a cut across her shoulder.

She grimaced, giving ground. This one was a better fighter than the first.

Where was Luther? He'd vanished. There was no help from that quarter. She dodged again. A second assassin, the one who had first struck at Luther, advanced upon her from the opposite side.

It was two against one, and all she had was one Red Empire sword to defend herself with. She vowed to sell her life at a high price. She plunged deep into silence, becoming one with the moment, energy surging through every fiber of her being.

The assassins struck, whirling past her.

She was alone.

She fought.

Blades ground against her sword. Sparks flew, glittering as they drifted away in slow motion. Reflected in the mirror-like shards of glass remaining on the floor. Her dark hair floated around her as she moved through the narrow spaces between the assassins' shining weapons. Candlelight gleaming in her eyes. Four blades against one, her only hope was for one of her opponents to make a mistake.

The first to do so would die.

She held no illusions – she had to fight perfectly.

She'd had practice at that.

* * *

The shock passed, evolving into outrage.

His mind on fire, Deon Lamar took stock of his surroundings. Anton Slayne and Peter Lamb had brought weapons to an inquisition in clear violation of the law. Even worse, Francis Mirovar, a senior force leader of the Order of Thoth had hidden a katana beneath the judge's table.

The violation of trust was more than he could bear. He screamed in inarticulate rage. He stood in a pocket of space devoid of violence, except for the righteous fury burning within his soul.

"Criminals!" he shouted, pointing at Francis. His face flushed, pointing at Anton and Peter, he screamed, "Criminals! Traitors! Spies!"

He spun around.

A Red Empire assassin blurred into the doorway. A straggler, the only member of the troop to enter the house via the back door. Their eyes locked on each other. The assassin rushed forward, his swords flat edges of shining metal at chest height.

As an Order traveler, Deon's training emphasized unarmed combat against armed opponents. All the better to arrest a spy or traitor alive so he could interrogate them before the inevitable execution.

He had an unassailable belief he could survive this encounter. With exquisite timing he pivoted to the side, taking control of the assassin's right arm, he flipped him forward, face-first onto the floor. A sharp crack resounded through the room as the man's face caved in on the polished hardwood.

Deon stepped back, the assassin's limp body lying in perfect stillness at his feet.

The man's death was a deserved death. The Red Empire had split from the Order twenty-three centuries ago. A rebellion that could end in only one way – destruction and death. He thrilled with the knowledge he'd assisted, even if in only a small way, with the destruction of the Red Empire.

Slayne shouted at him, the words lost in the wild noise of battle.

His heart filled with triumphant exultation. He turned and shouted, "Victory is—"

A pair of blades, their points soaked with his blood, appeared in front of his chest. The blows picked him up, carrying him forward to the front wall. The points of the blades drove into the drywall, pinning him like a bug on a cork board.

The swords dragged down and out, shaving through half a dozen ribs on either side of his spine. The world turned, he slumped backward, crashing to the floor.

Deon looked up, for the briefest of moments, his assailant loomed above him.

He flailed feebly with one hand, once, twice.

The world grayed out, and darkness swept in.

* * *

The Blue Dragon flashed through the air, and sparks flew to the left and right. The chains binding Li's wrists dropped to the floor.

Li's eyes flicked between Peter, Anton and the chaos swirling through the room, she snapped, "I can't Ramp."

"It's the Truther," Peter said, his battle-axes held ready and his eyes searching for foes.

Anton shouted, "We've got to get her out of here."

"Where?" Peter asked. "There's helicopters everywhere."

"Damn it."

The Red Empire were all over the chamber. Only half the Order in the room had weapons. Francis wielded the White Dragon, Jay, Yvette and Chiara had managed to capture blades from their opponents, but Lamar, Kain, Luther, Juliette and Li stood unarmed or unable to fight.

A battle boiled mere yards from where Anton stood as the four elite Order guards held off the core of the Red Empire troop. Lamar slammed an assassin face first into the floor. The man's head caving in on contact with the polished hardwood.

The largest of the Red Empire assassins, hanging back from the fight with the Order guards, peeled away to his left. He headed straight for Lamar.

Anton shouted, "Behind you."

Too late – the big assassin plunged his swords through Lamar's back. Blurring forward, he lifted Lamar off the floor and pinned him against the front wall. Dragging his blades out with a downward draw cut to maximize damage, he stepped back to get out of the way of the falling body.

The assassin turned around and faced Anton. Their eyes met – it was Marcus Drake.

"What the fuck?!" Anton swore.

A sick feeling surged through his guts. His breathing stuttered. His father's words, '*I will make you pay,*' slammed like a freight train through his soul. The edges of his world whited out – there was only Marcus Drake and the memories of April the 28th.

Drake strode forward. His booted feet reverberating across the floorboards. His dripping swords snapping up into an attack-defense position, the forward one low, the rear one high.

Anton stalked forward, the Blue Dragon in his right hand, the Green Dragon in his left. For a brief moment, they stood ten feet apart, staring at each other in silence as individual battles raged throughout the room and helicopter gunships rumbled like fire-breathing dragons overhead.

"Where's my father?" Anton demanded through clenched teeth; his voice low with tightly-held hatred.

Drakes' eyes tightened, he snarled once then declared, "Beyond your reach."

"You know where he is?"

"Of course," Drake stated, grinning broadly.

"Tell me," Anton demanded.

Drake's face froze with hatred and he shouted, "Never!"

A red mist descended. Something snapped within Anton. Anguish surged up through his chest. His face paled, his hands stilled to stone-like immobility. Energy coruscated from the base of his spine, flooding muscles, nerves, and bone.

Silence rushed through him, swirling around a pillar of agony transfixed in the middle of his soul.

He ramped instantaneously.

Drake blurred, his swords arcing forward like the scythes of the angel of death.

Anton snapped his blades diagonally up and down, catching Drakes' strikes. The Red Empire metal ground against the genius-forged meteoric iron of the Dragon swords. Splintering in silvery shards, they shattered into thousands of burning pieces. Blooming into twin clouds of glittering metal.

Drake kept coming. Closing to grapple where his overwhelming strength would be a decisive advantage.

Anton's right foot lashed out. All the explosive power of his Ramp flowing through a simple front kick performed with perfect timing. Drake folded around it. All of his forward momentum arrested and reversed. He flew backward, smashing a hole in the wall and disappearing into the front yard of the safe house.

Anton followed him through the gap and into the night.

* * *

Justin leaped straight up the front of the safe house.

Streams of minigun fire ripped through the spot he'd been standing in. The two Harley-Davidson's parked in front of the safe house were torn in half, falling away in crumpled heaps of burning metal.

"Now that hurts," he remarked, landing on the roof in a crouch. He pointed the Milkor MGL he'd taken from his motorcycle's saddlebags at the blackwidow and pulled the trigger. The launcher chuffed, a bloom of gray smoke trailing the grenade arching toward the helicopter.

The blackwidow's sensors detected the incoming threat, incandescent flares streamed from the underside of the helicopter, lighting up the yard. Chaff bloomed to the left and right in glittering, silvery clouds.

The blackwidow's technically advanced defenses were optimized to deal with smart weapons with sophisticated seeker warheads. The 40mm grenade heading toward it was a 'dumb' weapon that relied on the skills of the person firing the launcher to aim it accurately.

The grenade sailed through the flares, ignored the chaff and slammed into the lower left side of the helicopter. Its warhead exploded, sending a molten copper whip slashing through the armor and into the body of the machine.

Blurring to his left, Justin leaped from the roof to the top of a steel water tank next to the house. Mini-gun fire immediately cut through the tank, water sluicing around him. He dropped down to the yard, blurring forward with his right hand holding the MGL outstretched toward the helicopter. He pumped the trigger, the barrels rotating as he ran. Grenades looping toward the blackwidow.

The Helicopter turned on the spot. The mini-gun on the near side and the main cannon chasing him, 7.62mm and 20mm rounds stitching their way across the yard. A stray tracer round nicked the side of a diesel bowser next to the farm's working barn.

It blew up, fire and black smoke fountaining into the air. The blast wave struck Justin from behind and blew him over, the MGL rolling from his fingers. He turned over onto his back. The Helicopter was about fifty yards above him, rocking to the side as the same blast hit it, brilliant flares and glittering chaff steaming from its sides. The first grenade scored a great slash across the nose, the second slammed into the middle of the near engine which promptly started sparking and giving off great puffs of black smoke. The third grenade missed it entirely, looping harmlessly away.

"Fall, you bastard, fall," Justin growled.

The helicopter stuttered. Vents on the second engine opened, the far-side turbine suddenly roaring at full power – all pretense at stealth dropping away. The blackwidow righted, backed and pivoted, turning nose down toward him. Its main armament – the 20mm cannon lining up on him.

Justin scrambled back to his feet, diving back into silence, the Ramp flowering within.

A big, Red Empire Assassin smashed through the front wall of the house. Taking out the rail around the porch, he landed on his back in the front yard. The MGL was three feet back from his right shoulder, within reach if he saw it.

The assassin shook his head once. Blurring upright, staring fixedly toward the house. He pulled a pair of sais from his belt and flourished them, poised to attack or defend.

Anton blurred out, the Green and Blue Dragons in his hands.

Justin rushed forward, scooping up the MGL.

The gunship's cannons remained silent, smoke and a dark fluid leaked from a rent in the armor just above them. The pilot grimaced, the blackwidow sliding to the left. The near side minigun pivoting around toward Justin cued to the gunner's helmet – it pointed where he looked. The crew on the helicopter focused on him alone. They ignored the others brawling in front of the house, it was the man with the MGL that was the immediate threat.

Justin blurred again, firing another round at the middle of the blackwidow's cabin.

The gunner in the helicopter stared at the incoming grenade. The minigun on the same side swiveled around and up. Fire burst from its spinning barrels. A golden stream of tracers lit up the night sky, intersecting with the grenade, which promptly exploded twenty yards short of the target.

"Shit," Justin hissed between clenched teeth.

He had one grenade left.

Justin blurred through the space where Anton and the big assassin fought. Dodging past them, he fired his last grenade vertically up through the floor of the blackwidow. The grenade disappeared through the armor into the middle of the cabin.

A bright flash lit the interior of the blackwidow. The inside of the canopy immediately painted with a dark crimson wash.

The second engine died, and the helicopter dropped like a stone.

Justin, Anton, and the big assassin scattered.

The shadows of the night lurched forward as the blackwidow crashed into the yard before fleeing as the helicopter erupted into a huge fireball.

* * *

Marcus Drake and Justin had vanished.

The flaming wreckage of the blackwidow gunship burned in the middle of the yard. Unspent ammunition randomly exploded. A Hellfire missile cooked off, the front half of the helicopter evaporating in a blinding glare.

The edge of the blast knocked Anton flying into the wall of the training barn. He fell forward onto the ground. Sparks fell all around him. Several sizzled through his shirt, burning his chest and shoulders.

He jumped to his feet, patting himself off. The barn was on fire, flames leaping through it. It was already half gone. The hay bales lining the walls burning like dry kindling. The air lay thick with smoke.

Two more blackwidows flew concentric circles around the safe house. They were bearing in on the yard at the same time from opposite directions. Mini-gun fire opened up from the left and right, golden streams leaping along the ground toward where he stood.

Anton blurred backward into the barn and hit the deck.

The heat in the barn hit him like a sledgehammer. The smoke enveloping him and stinging his eyes, he could barely see. Bullets ripped through the side of the barn, whizzing over his head. He hugged the ground. He held his breath. He had to do something about the helicopters – no one was getting out of this alive while they were still flying.

Scrambling to his feet, he blurred to the armory door. It stood shut, waves of heat washing through the air above it. Anton ripped off his shirt, and wrapped it around his hands. Grabbing the door handles, he ramped and dragged the armory door open. It fell to the side with a reverberating clang.

Smoke immediately curled down the first step.

Anton dashed down the stairs into the darkness.

* * *

The room was a riot of colors. The Truther coursing through Li's veins was in full effect.

Without being able to Ramp it was almost impossible to follow what was happening around her.

She was desperate to tell someone the truth. Anyone would do, but no one was asking any questions. It was a horribly uncomfortable sensation.

Li shook her head. Anton had run off after some assassin. What was he thinking? She didn't need Truther to tell him precisely what she thought of his priorities. Thankfully Peter was steadfast, staying close – no one had even tried to come near them.

A spray of blood jetted across her face.

One of the Order guards fell to the floor, blood gushing from his headless neck.

A second guard stumbled to the side, three blades converging through his body. They were gone again in a flash. He fell to the ground, his eyes catching Li's for a brief moment before they glazed over.

The line of guards was breaking.

Luther blurred from the side. Scooping up one of the fallen katanas, he leaped into the fray.

The two assassins who had been probing Francis' defenses without success backed away, turned and rushed toward Peter and Li. Francis repositioned to best protect Juliette. His sword held defensively in front of him, ready to gut the first assassin to come near.

"About bloody time," Peter declared grimly, his axes flashing through the air. In moments, he was a whirl of silvery metal as he clashed against the assassins.

Li lay exposed on the other side where Jay, Yvette, and Chiara fought against three opponents, including one from the core group who Justin had wounded with a chair.

Jay swept with his left foot, unbalancing the nearest assassin. Yvette attacked high with a flashing kick across the man's chest. He fell back hard, sliding across the floor toward Li.

Ramped or not, Li's physiology was ramp conditioned. Her bones, muscles, and nerves were harder, stronger and faster than any normal human could hope to match. She leaned forward, grasping the man's head and with a quick, simple motion – snapped his neck.

He immediately went limp.

"Swords?" she asked, indicating with a nod.

Jay and Yvette grabbed another fallen blade each. Jay stayed to assist Peter, while Yvette rushed toward Chiara.

"That felt good," Li declared with a smile, sitting back within the circle defended by Peter and Jay.

After all, she could only speak the truth.

* * *

The Raven fought in tandem with another Mirovar force team member against a pair of Red Empire assassins.

They were horrified by the attack. What were the Red Empire doing here? The only other person who knew about the safe house outside the Order was Shabbah al Ahmar's other agent. The voice on the other end of the calls. The one who had asked them to bug Ramin Kain's phone.

The one who could be a rogue agent?

But the Red Empire never moved in numbers this great without authorization from the Red Ghost.

The Raven blurred, artfully defending against a flurry of attacks. They knew their team mates well, having trained with them for years. Fighting in tandem with any of them was a seamless process.

The floor was becoming treacherous with the blood and bodies of Order and Red Empire dead. The Raven fought for their life and their mission. The Red Empire assassins in the room were either ignorant of or indifferent to, the presence of a Red Empire spy within the Mirovar force team. The Raven considered the former to be the most likely option. They fought blindly against their own colleague, and if they died by the Raven's hand, it was for a good cause.

A large Red Empire assassin appeared at the door.

Reinforcements?

The man's cowl had fallen away, his face veil hung in tatters. He held a pair of sais. His fair skin stood out, his blue eyes flashed, his blond hair lay cropped short next to his scalp.

The Raven almost died as memory flooded through their Ramp. Red Empire blades slashing past their throat. Years of childhood training and dedication to the craft of edged weapons just barely managed to save their life.

It was Marcus Drake.

Their instructors had schooled the Raven on every important opponent, and the chief lieutenant of general Chloe Armitage was near the top of the list.

Sheathing his sais at his belt, Drake picked up a fallen katana, leaping into the fray in front of the table. A pair of Order guards and Luther were fighting like madmen against the main strength of the Red Empire troop.

Beyond them, Francis waited with Juliette, the White Dragon a vision of lethal stillness in his hand.

Kain, his eyes darting left and right, stood with his back hard up against the wall.

The Raven threw themselves back into the fight. Their soul raged. They had been deceived beyond their worst nightmare. The Red Ghost had allied themselves with the hidden voice in an act of supreme treachery. The secret voice, the killer of the praetorians on the water tower, the agent who was not of the Red Empire. The one who had played the Raven for a fool. The pieces of the puzzle clicked neatly into place; the voice could only belong to general Chloe Armitage.

Shabbah al Ahmar was in league with the vampires.

Interposing themselves between their team mate and the assassins, they struck with all the righteous fury of the betrayed.

Nothing could withstand the full force of their true faith.

The Raven burned with a horrifying light, and their opponents burned before them.

$* * *$

Peter blurred forward, Yvette dove into the fray, and Chiara launched a ferocious attack.

...

Peter's left axe caught an assassin's right sword. His right axe trapped the man's left sword. He pushed outward, spread-eagling his opponent. Stepping in close, his head jerked forward, his forehead crashing into the assassin's face.

The assassin went limp on his feet. Blood fountaining from his smashed nose, he started to fall.

Peter's axes flashed in and across each other. The man's head sailed away. His body, jetting blood from the severed vessels in his neck, crumpled to the floor.

...

A dozen feet away, Yvette's left foot lashed out catching her opponent's hand, his blade spinning away.

The assassin lunged forward with his remaining sword.

Batting the blade to her right with her left hand, she stepped within his strike as it went past her shoulder. Her right hand flashed up, her blade disappearing under the man's ribcage. The point erupting in a spray of blood at the base of the man's neck.

He shivered on her blade, his eyes bulging from his head.

Yvette hissed through clenched teeth. Twisting the blade, she ripped it up and out of his chest, slashing through his ribcage, heart, and lungs.

The assassin fell at her feet, dead before he hit the floor.

...

Chiara flew through the air, her feet blurring into her opponent's face.

He blurred away, taking at most a glancing blow.

Another assassin, his face slashed and bleeding blurred forward to replace the previous one. He carried a single sword, the twin of her own. Grimacing with rage, he attacked furiously.

She feinted aside, then ducked under his strike, before driving her sword up and under the man's chin. The point sliced up through the assassin's skull and he shuddered for half a second before she pulled the blade free.

She stepped aside as he fell to the floor, blood pumping from the wounds beneath his chin and on top of his head.

...

Peter dashed back into guard position next to Li and Jay. His axes dripping gore. His face speckled with blood and random flakes of bone. His eyes filled with deadly intent. Yvette, flicking her swords clear of blood stalked the room like an angel of death. Chiara, her face a mask of avenging fury joined her.

* * *

Suddenly three assassins died.

Ramin Kain's heart leaped with hope. The tide was turning; he may yet survive this catastrophe.

Sam fought with the Order Guards, his last line of defense. Good Sam, loyal Sam, perhaps Sam would save him, he could certainly fight.

A large, Red Empire assassin, his cowl thrown back, revealing close-cropped blond hair, and wielding a stolen Order katana pushed into the battle. His sword flashed forward just as one of the Order guards defended himself from another strike. The blade shot through the gap, ripping open the man's chest and he fell backward against the table before slumping to the floor.

The leader of the Red Empire troop lunged forward, the point of his blade beating past the deflection of the last Order guard. A line of red appeared across the guard's throat. He reflexively reached for it. Before his hand could land on the wound, a pair of blades gutted him. He gurgled, blood sluicing past his fingers as he fell forward over the bodies of his comrades.

Two elite Red Empire assassins stalked Luther, who backed away toward Francis.

The blond assassin and the troop leader grinned at Ramin and leaped across the table toward him. Two more assassins, one sporting a broken nose followed after them.

Enough was enough. Clearly, the tide had not turned.

Ramin blurred to his right, fleeing past Francis, Juliette, and Luther. Leaping through the broken window, he disappeared into the night.

Six assassins followed after him.

* * *

Justin picked himself up from where he lay on the gravel next to the porch.

He'd been a fraction too close when the Hellfire missile had cooked off and had been dazed for a few moments. A pair of blackwidows rumbled overhead. The clash of blades rang out from the house. A smoky haze mixed with the sharp tang of burning metal shrouded the air. Both barns and the haystack were alight, the flames turning the yard from night into day. Cannon fire had blown half the safe house away.

There was no sign of the big Red Empire assassin or Anton Slayne.

His MGL was empty, all the rounds expended taking down the first blackwidow. He looked around. He needed a weapon, anything would do. Half his motorcycle lay a couple of yards away. On the edge of the wreckage was the drive chain, one end lying in the gravel.

The helicopter gunships circled overhead – currently ignoring him. He assumed their crews hadn't yet seen him move. He didn't expect that to last and had no desire to tangle with them again – especially without weapons.

Justin was brave, but he wasn't suicidal. He blurred forward, stripping the chain from his motorcycle wreckage in a single smooth motion. Turning, he rushed back into the house toward the briefing room.

Passing through the doorway, the room resembled an abattoir. Blood and bodies littering the floor. A Red Empire assassin advanced on Peter.

Beyond Peter, Li looked up at Justin and smiled. Jay circled past her, and Yvette and Chiara advanced toward Francis' position. Beyond them, a knot of Red Empire assassins rammed past Luther, Francis, and Juliette toward a broken window.

Ramin Kain had vanished.

Justin leaped forward, whipping the chain with all his strength through a diagonal slash across the nearest assassin's back. The rugged metal blurred forward, faster than anyone could follow. The chain ripped through the assassin's body from above his right shoulder to the top of his left hip. Everything in between, in a strip an inch wide, reduced to bloody pulp.

The man slid apart as he crumpled to the floor.

Justin stepped forward, looked at Peter and Li, and said in a low rumble, "What did I miss?"

* * *

Ramin Kain had disappeared through the window and into the night.

The Red Empire assassins followed after him.

Francis knew that he would have to rescue the head of the Order. There was no way they could allow Kain to fall into the hands of the Red Empire. He knew too much about the operations of the Order of Thoth.

The last of the Red Empire assassins, his nose still bleeding from an earlier crushing wound delivered by Justin with a chair, headed for the window – his attention focused on pursuing Kain.

The White Dragon blurred out. The man didn't have time to register surprise as the blade passed effortlessly through his neck. His forward momentum took both his body and his head through the window, and onto the porch where he fell in a heap, his head rolling out onto the gravel of the yard.

One less opponent to thwart Kain's rescue. They'd cleared the room of assassins. They needed to evacuate the house immediately. With no 'friendlies' on site, there was no reason for the helicopter gunships not to flatten the property with a pair of Hellfire missiles.

Francis commanded urgently, "Juliette, Li, Yvette, Chiara, run for it out the back and head for the western tree line. The rest follow me."

"What about Anton?" Li asked.

Francis shook his head. "There's no time – move it."

Francis blurred toward the window in pursuit of Kain and the Red Empire assassins. A half second later the room was empty; except for a set of lamps, a number of guttering candles, and the dead.

* * *

Chloe pivoted the nightfalcon.

Ramin Kain fled from the safe house, pursued by Marcus Drake, Nasr al Dam and the three surviving members of the elite Fist team. She was not surprised to see that only the strongest had survived the encounter with the Mirovar force team.

She signaled the blackwidows and commanded, "Cover the escape of those men heading south and meet me at the tree line. Expect immediate pursuit from ground forces."

"Yes, Ma'am," answered the pilots.

She opened a second comms link directly to James Haley, operating as a gunner on the helicopter gunship swinging around behind the safe house. "James, you will need to eliminate these crews. They've seen too much. See to it after this engagement."

"Yes, Ma'am," James answered flatly.

There could be no witnesses.

Chloe dropped the nightfalcon like a stone, diving down to a position well in front of Kain.

So far, everything had proceeded to plan. She frowned. Now was the critical moment where success or failure hung in the balance. She'd done everything she could to ensure the former, but there was always a chance of something unexpected occurring.

She scanned the horizon, the only potential threat to her objectives was from the Mirovar force team. She extended her senses, favoring them over the high technology of the nightfalcon.

Four members of the team were heading slowly toward the western forest. The rest were in close pursuit of the Red Empire assassins and Kain.

There was no sign of Anton Slayne, his distinctive Ramp signature was absent.

"Where's Anton," she murmured.

It had always been a risk that he would not survive to become the weapon that she desired.

There was nothing she could do but wait and see if he turned up.

* * *

Ramin Kain sprinted across the field.

His feet barely touched the ground. Arms pumping, knees lifting high, head still, eyes focused on a tree line a mile away. He ran like the devil pursued him, and he wasn't far wrong.

He glanced back over his shoulder. Five figures blurred behind him, silhouetted against the burning farm. Their faces hidden in shadow, they sprinted after him, their blades faintly reflecting distant fires. Above the farm, two blackwidow gunship helicopters wheeled about, setting a new course toward him.

They were coming for him. Everyone was chasing him. Ramin centered himself in his running. If he could make the tree line, he could disappear into the forest. The Red Empire assassins would have been ramping at maximum during the combat in the inquisition chamber. He'd stood back, waiting for his opportunity. He remained rested. There was a good chance that he could out run them. After all, vampires were not chasing him.

He glanced back again.

A second set of figures pursued the assassins. Sam, and the rest of the Order. Brave Sam would save him. He just had to stay alive long enough for them to catch up.

The Red Empire assassins would be looking over their shoulders soon, and they would discover the hunters had become the hunted.

Hope flared in his heart.

A sleek, black nightfalcon emerged from the night sky. It swooped down, hovering a dozen feet off the ground in front of him. The canopy reflected the distant fires raging at the farm. It rested a hundred yards before the tree line, like a great black insect or predatory bird waiting for him and him alone.

Ramin zigged to the right.

The nightfalcon slid in the same direction.

He zagged to the left.

The nightfalcon moved again, blocking his path.

A shiver shot up his back, his anal sphincter puckered and shrank. The assassins were surely making ground as he attempted to evade the black helicopter. He couldn't tell without looking, they'd conducted their pursuit in near silence.

He didn't dare risk slowing down for another look back.

The blackwidows rumbled louder as they approached from behind.

"Damn it, Sam," he snapped in desperation. "Where are you."

He was running out of time.

* * *

Anton emerged from the burning training barn.

He wore a thick, gray blanket like a cape, pulled tight over his head. It smoked, tongues of flame struggling to consume it in a dozen spots. He shrugged it off, and it fell at his feet. He lifted a pair of Milkor MGLs, one in each hand. A bandolier of high explosive armor piercing grenades ran across his naked chest. The Green and Blue Dragons lay strapped in an 'X' across his back.

Half the available Order team members were blurring over the fields in pursuit of the Red Empire and Ramin Kain. A pair of blackwidow's converged toward a spot near the south tree line. A black, nightfalcon hovered there blocking Kain's path.

"First Drake, and now Armitage," Anton said, his eyes flashing. He sank into his Ramp. Power surged through him. He blurred forward at maximum speed. The nearest blackwidow was still within range of his MGLs. He lifted his right hand, pumping the trigger as he ran. The final shot was 'chuffing' away on a trail of gray smoke as the first of the grenades triggered the helicopter's automatic defense systems. Rows of brilliant flares jetted to the left and right, clouds of chaff bloomed above the flares, reflecting their light like so much silvery confetti.

The first of the grenades sailed past the blackwidow, which began to frantically turn away. The second, third, fourth and fifth grenades stitched a line of explosions across the rear of the helicopter. The nose dipped down. The tail broke away. The body of the machine began spinning wildly as it continued to lurch toward the tree line.

The fuel ignited. The helicopter exploded into a huge fireball. Secondary explosions disintegrated the blackwidow into a rain of flaming debris.

Anton dropped the empty MGL, blurring toward the hovering nightfalcon.

The last blackwidow flew in from the far side of the field. Its cannons and miniguns blazing, tracers slashing across the field. The Order team members took evasive action, scattering before the firestorm.

Anton ran on.

The Red Empire caught up with Kain. He disappeared behind their bodies as they converged on the nightfalcon. They leaped up the dozen feet necessary to reach the helicopter's cabin. The nightfalcon roared into the night sky.

Anton shouted, "No." He strove to his utmost. Swinging his second MGL up toward the nightfalcon, he pulled the trigger. The first grenade zoomed away. Anton kept pulling the trigger until the MGL clicked on empty.

Turning away to the east, the nightfalcon disappeared into the night as the grenades all fell short of the target.

"No, damn it, no." Anton dropped the MGL, fell to his knees, hiding his face with both hands. After a moment, he sighed. Picking himself up, he retrieved the MGL at his feet and headed toward the Order operatives. They were already returning from the field, heading for the remains of the safe house. There would be another chance.

While he was alive, there would always be another chance.

* * *

Marcus Drake moved forward to take over the flying of the nightfalcon.

Chloe Armitage moved into the main cabin, she wanted to meet her guest. Ramin Kain lay on the floor of the cabin, bound with chains. There were plenty of empty seats along the walls of the cabin. She took one where she could easily look into his face.

Someone had hit him hard; he was unconscious. His eyes flickered once, and then again. He woke up with a start.

"What the hell," Kain swore, his eyes darting around the cabin at Chloe and the four Red Empire assassins.

"Hello Ramin," Chloe stated airily, unable to hold back a smirk of delight. "Do you know who I am?"

"Crane's whore," Kain snarled.

Chloe's eyes went flat, her hand flashed out, and Kain's head rocked to the side. He shook his head, staring at her with naked hatred flashing in his eyes, the outline of her hand a red print on the side of his face.

"Who am I?" Chloe asked softly, just loud enough for him to hear over the helicopter's engines.

"General Chloe Armitage."

Chloe smiled, but her eyes remained flat.

"That's better," she observed evenly. "Now you've found a civil tongue in your head."

"What game are you playing at?" Kain demanded. "Crane would not have sanctioned this. You're completely out of bounds."

"Indeed."

Recognition flashed across Kain's face. "You're the other player – you killed Crane's vampires on the water tower. You called me that morning months ago to warn me of Anton Slayne – you played me!"

Chloe studied him silently.

Kain leaned his head forward, his gaze darting over the four Red Empire assassins, then it flicked back to Chloe. "What strange bedfellows? I see you needed help to capture me. What? Couldn't do it on your own?"

Chloe smiled, her eye's twinkling. "If you're expecting a 'gloat speech' where I reveal the details of my plan to prove how superior I am." She lashed forward with her fist, catching Kain on the chin, his head snapping back hard against the floor.

He quivered momentarily before his eyes glazed over.

"… You're talking with the wrong girl."

Chloe patted Kain's pockets, found his smartphone and fished it out. It was still fully operational. She went back to the front of the nightfalcon and sat in the co-pilot's chair. She plugged the phone into an available charging socket.

It wouldn't do to have it run out of power.

She looked across at Marcus. "Call Logan Airport and get our aircraft ready. We'll be coming in hot. There is no time to waste."

The Order was sure to follow, and follow hard and fast. They couldn't afford to leave the Head of the Order in the hands of their enemies. Their pursuit was a certainty.

Chloe was counting on it.

Soon Anton, Li and the rest would be in the middle of her trap.

It was inevitable.

* * *

Francis picked up the White Dragon's scabbard from where it lay taped underneath the briefing room table. Once it was free, he slid the White Dragon home and returned it to the belt at his hip. He fished around under the table for a second and stood up with a Glock 9mm in a holster. He attached the holster to his belt on his right hip.

All the survivors had returned, the house lay damaged beyond recognition, but it still stood. It hadn't caught fire the way the barns had. They were still burning, but the peak of the fires was over as they had collapsed in on themselves.

"Two minutes, just the essentials," Francis commanded.

Peter walked into the room, shaking his head sadly. "John and Mary are both dead. Caught by cannon fire."

Francis nodded grimly. The farm family had been loyal Order helpers all their adult lives. They knew the risk and had volunteered anyway. Brave, kind people, he vowed never to forget them.

"Quickly now. Shadowstone will return to eliminate any evidence," Francis directed. "We don't want to be here when they arrive."

"Why not?" Anton asked grimly, Li at his shoulder. She was holding the Green Dragon in its scabbard at her side.

"We don't have time. We have to rescue Ramin Kain."

"What the hell for."

"He's the Head of the Order," Luther spat.

Anton snapped back, "He's a traitor."

Luther shook his head, stepping in close to Anton. They stared at each other, a few inches apart.

Francis pushed between them. "Stand down. There is no time for this. Anton – we have to get Ramin Kain back before whoever took him pumps him for everything he knows."

Anton blinked and nodded, stepping back.

Luther sneered silently and stepped back as well.

434

Anton looked at Francis and declared loudly, "It was Armitage and Drake."

"What?" Francis asked in surprise.

"It was Armitage and Drake who took Kain. I recognized him tonight. He was the big, blond assassin. I kicked him through the damned wall."

Luther snarled, shaking his finger at Anton. "You're still running with this insane conspiracy crap."

"It's true. It was Marcus Drake. I'm sure of it."

Luther implored Francis, "Why are we listening to this crazy kid?"

"I know exactly what I saw," Anton insisted.

"And what did you really see?" Luther sneered. "Just another man."

Anton spread his hands wide and snapped, "What do you want from me? I'm telling the truth."

"What does that mean when you're a Slayne?"

"Enough!" Francis commanded, stepping between the two men. "Enough of this bickering. It would be safer to assume Anton is correct until proven otherwise."

Luther started to speak, then stopped himself.

"Marcus Drake wouldn't be working with a Red Empire troop without Chloe Armitage's permission," Juliette observed calmly, putting the strap of her laptop satchel bag over her shoulder. "Vampires, Red Empire assassins and Shadowstone all working together. Chloe Armitage must be running her own operations behind Crane's back."

Luther shook his head once, his eye's narrowing.

Francis and Juliette exchanged a glance.

"We need to move," Francis declared. He waved his hand around his head and called out, "Everyone, listen up. We're heading for rendezvous point number one. We'll split up to make sure they don't catch us as a group on the way there. Jay, please take Luther, Yvette, Justin and Chiara. Peter, take Anton with you. First hit the demolitions and then follow after us. Li, you'll come with Juliette and me."

Everyone nodded.

"Let's go."

The team streamed away from the house.

Anton turned to Peter with a quizzical look on his face. "Demolitions?"

Peter shrugged his shoulders and nodded. "Yeah. I've got the place wired. It'll only take a minute to arm it."

"Right," Anton noted, following after him as he tracked through the site.

Three minutes later they were at the south tree line. Peter looked back at the safe house, frowned for a second and then pressed a stud on the top of a silvery cylinder in his right fist. The safe house erupted. A fraction of a second later the first explosion was dwarfed by the armory under the training barn going off. The ground shuddered. The northern horizon over a mile away darkened and then a bright flash ripped away the night. Six seconds later a thunderous boom rolled over them.

"What the fuck was that," Anton asked in awed tones.

"A fuel-air explosive," Peter answered glumly. "The only one I had."

Anton wasn't entirely sure what saddened Peter the most, the loss of the safe house or the loss of the bomb.

"I'd plans for that one," Peter whispered as he turned to the forest. He looked across at Anton and grinned ruefully. "Follow me."

Anton ran after him.

Chapter Sixteen

THE METEOR THAT NEVER WAS!

August 21 | Permalink | Comments: 87

By **Chief Tinfoiler**

Categories: Secret Government, Aliens, Extra-terrestrials, Signs

Well, Tinfoilers, gather around and listen up. This is big. No this is HUGE! No, this is **GINORMOUS!** I know it's all over the corporate-state owned "mainstream media." The Meteor, the Star Rock, The Sky Hammer. The fake news of the rock that fell just short of the sleepy hamlet of White Hill in western Maine – well, there was no rock.

I REPEAT – THERE WAS NO ROCK.

Read on to find out how a secret government agency destroyed a nest of extra-terrestrials using advanced tactical weapons not available to our military. That's right, the extra-terrestrial menace is lurking out there and hiding in sleepy hollow.

 – Blog post snippet on the Internet

* * *

South of White Hill, Maine, August 21ˢᵗ, 20:37

Light flashed at the horizon behind them. Fifteen seconds later a thunderous detonation washed over them from the north.

Francis led Juliette and Li into a clearing. There was just enough moonlight to navigate the paths through the forest. He suddenly stopped and swore in harsh French, "C'est un foutu bordel!"

He turned to Li, held out his hand and demanded, "The Green Dragon, pass it to me."

Juliette, her eye's wide, asked, "Francis?"

Li stared at Francis for a moment and then handed her katana to him.

Francis whipped his Glock 9mm out, putting the barrel against Li's temple.

"Francis!" Juliette shouted in alarm.

"Merde! Mon amour. I must know."

Juliette, her eyes flashing, declared earnestly, "Francis. You don't need to do this."

Francis ignored Juliette and asked, "Li, are you a spy for anyone?"

Li shook her head and stated hoarsely, "No."

"Are you wholeheartedly committed to the Mirovar force team."

"Yes."

"No reservations?"

"None."

"What of the Order of Thoth?"

"It has its problems."

Francis sighed and frowned.

"Do you know of anyone else who is a spy?"

"No."

Francis jerked the gun away from Li's head. "I'm sorry Li."

He holstered the Glock and gave the Green Dragon back to her. She took her sword and stepped back, her face pale in the moonlight, her eyes glistening as she stared at him.

"Satisfied?" Juliette asked in annoyance.

"The sensor array was bypassed. There must be a spy in our team!"

"Well, it's not Li."

Francis glanced back at Li; anguish flitted over his face. He turned back to Juliette and declared, "The only person above suspicion is you. If you are the spy, then the team is already dead."

"I could have told you it wasn't Li."

"Your mind palace is a powerful tool, but it couldn't predict this attack, nor tell us who the spy is. I had to take action."

Juliette grimaced. "Li, you're on the inside of this now. Your training with me means it's inevitable that you will know. There is a Red Empire spy within our team. It's one of Peter, Yvette or Chiara. Lamar's arrival two days ago indicated it and tonight's attack confirmed it."

"I had to clear you as well," Francis addressed Li. "To make sure you hadn't been co-opted in any way."

Li stared at him.

"I have to defend this team."

In a voice filled with shock, Li asked incredulously, "By putting a gun to my head?"

Francis dragged his right hand down his face and looked at Juliette. Naked panic threatened to overtake him. Juliette was unarmed in the middle of a fight against a superior force. It was a miracle that so many of his team had survived. If the Red Empire dedicated themselves to killing them, rather than capturing Ramin Kain – they would all be dead. Someone had completely compromised the security of the safe house. The

Order was in disarray, and the Mirovar force team was hanging in the wind.

The situation was intolerable.

"Yes. Yes, absolutely," Francis declared wholeheartedly, his eye's glistening in the moonlight. "And you, you wonderful, loyal young woman with a true heart passed with flying colors."

He bowed low. "My sincere apologies. The Order has horribly abused you in the last few hours, and it tears my heart that I've added to your burdens. But know this, I will declare for you at the next Order conclave, and you will always have a home in the Mirovar force team should you desire it."

Li shut her eyes for a long moment. The clearing seemed to hold its breath. Something indefinable flitted across her face.

Stepping forward, she put her hand on his shoulder, and said softly, "Apology accepted." She glanced once at Juliette before staring into his eyes and whispering, "We all must serve unto death and death will claim all who we love."

Francis' breath fled. He stood up; his heart filled with horror. He nodded once, glancing at Juliette and directed in devastated tones, "Follow me."

Juliette, her eyes wide, whispered. "Of course, mon amour."

They ran from the clearing toward the rendezvous point.

* * *

Anton followed Peter through the doorway and into the log cabin.

Everyone else was already there. Justin loomed in a corner talking quietly with Jay. Yvette had just finished suturing Chiara's shoulder, and they were comparing combat moves. Juliette had her arm around Li's shoulders and was talking with her in quiet tones. Francis and Luther were standing apart, apparently lost in their thoughts.

There was a bucket of water just inside the door filled with wet towels. Peter grabbed two and handed one to Anton before scrubbing dried blood from his face.

Francis looked up as Peter and Anton arrived and declared, "Good, everyone is here now."

Luther looked up, lifting his smartphone to show everyone else in the room. "Look here. I have a track on Ramin's phone."

Everyone stared at him for a second. Juliette moved to stand next to him. Luther turned the phone to show Juliette. "See."

"That's incredibly lucky."

"He's trying to help us find him. He's managed to turn his phone into a GPS beacon."

439

"Or Armitage is trying to lure us into a trap," Anton snapped.

"Not this again?" Luther snarled, pushing past Juliette to stand in front of Anton.

"ENOUGH!" Francis roared.

Everyone stopped and stared.

"Samuel Luther, stand down," Francis ordered. Whipping around he pointed his finger at Anton and commanded, "And you be quiet."

Anton blinked and stepped back.

"It's clearly a trap," Juliette observed knowingly.

"They could've wiped us out with missiles," Francis said. "Instead, they took losses to snatch Ramin Kain."

"We have to get him back," Luther demanded.

"Of course," Francis agreed. "We can't allow him to remain in the hands of our enemies. He knows too much."

Francis looked at Justin. "Will you join us for this mission?"

"No. I have to leave," Justin advised with a frown. "I have to prepare the next conclave ... most likely we need to elect a new Head of the Order."

"Don't be so sure of that," Luther snapped. "Ramin is a living genius and a hero of the Order. Mark my words, I'll be proven right in the end."

Anton glanced at Peter, who shrugged his shoulders. He held his tongue.

"Be that as it may," Juliette conceded without a trace of sarcasm in her voice. "We will proceed on this mission as if it is a trap. We do not know the agenda of those who abducted Kain. But it is obvious they would expect us to pursue him. The availability of Ramin Kain's phone as a GPS beacon to follow is too convenient. They want us to follow him. Soon we'll know where he is going. As to why?"

Juliette left the question hanging and flipped open her laptop.

"We'll have to find out – the hard way," Francis answered directly. "We have two SUVs parked here and ready to go. Juliette, do we have a track on Kain's beacon."

Juliette scanned her screen. "Heading directly to Logan Airport. They'll arrive in ten minutes. From there, they can go anywhere."

"We're three and a half hours away from the airport. Three hours at best," Jay advised.

"Five minutes, everyone," Francis directed. "Peter and Jay, you're driving. We're heading to Logan Airport as soon as possible."

Anton nudged Peter with his elbow and asked in a whisper, "Will Kain reveal what he knows?"

"He'll squeal like a pig," Peter whispered back.

"Peter, your hands are idle – prep the vehicles," Francis ordered

"Yes, Boss. Anton give me a hand."

"Sure."

Anton followed Peter out, and around to the back of the cabin, where a carport shielded two late model Ford SUVs.

Peter declared, "Let's get to work."

Anton nodded. He helped Peter get the cars ready. In minutes, they would be on their way.

* * *

Samuel Luther stepped out of the log cabin and walked about twenty yards into the forest.

He looked around, making sure no one had followed him. He pulled out his smartphone and dialed a number from memory. The phone rang twice before it was answered.

"Samuel?" A voice asked.

"Calvin, we need to talk."

"What the hell is happening over there. There's talk of a major meteor strike all over the media."

"That's just fucking Shadowstone PSYOPS. The Red Empire with help from Shadowstone have abducted Ramin."

There was a long moment of shocked silence on the other end of the line. "This is a disaster."

"Tell me about it. Mirovar is incompetent and a coward. There was a full-on battle. He just stood around on the fringes of it like he didn't want to get his hands dirty."

"That's disgusting."

"It's well known he is a liability who has risen far above his actual ability."

"So, what are you going to do."

"I'll be leading the rescue mission to get Ramin back."

"Is he still alive?"

"He has to be. He's turned his phone into a GPS beacon to allow us to follow him."

"A stroke of genius."

"Absolutely. God only knows what he's going through at the hands of those fiends."

"We have to get him back. He's central to our movement."

"Oh, we'll get him back. Even if I have to sacrifice every member of the Mirovar force team to do it."

"Good approach, they're expendable."

"Completely. By the way, Blake is on the move."

"Blake? What?"

"He'll begin organizing the next Conclave – he wants to unseat Ramin and put Mirovar or himself in charge."

"God help us. What a nightmare."

"We'll have to block any initiative either Mirovar or Blake put in place. You'll have to look after it. I'll be too busy making sure Mirovar doesn't fuck this up."

"Don't worry about it Samuel, the rest of us will look after the political end – just get Ramin back."

Samuel nodded and declared vehemently, "I'll get him back or die trying."

"Good luck."

"Won't be necessary," Samuel promised, hanging up the call.

He walked back to the cabin, and whispered to the night air, "Hold on Ramin, we're coming to get you."

* * *

Outwardly the Raven appeared calm and focused as they helped the team prepare to leave the cabin.

Inwardly, their world was chaos. They were almost ready to make a run for it. To slip away, escaping into the forest. To leave everything behind until they worked out what the hell was really going on and what they really wanted to do about it. But they couldn't leave their friends on the eve of a battle. That was beyond the pale.

The very same loyalty that would have seen them obey a direct order from the Red Ghost to kill everyone in the Mirovar force team now worked to bind them to the team. The link to the Red Empire lay broken. Loyalty could not remain in the face of betrayal.

The foundation of the Raven's world had been torn away the moment they understood the Red Empire had allied itself with vampires. Such an act was unforgivable.

The Raven smiled briefly at something one of the others said. They turned back to their work, cursing Luther for discovering Kain's GPS beacon. The beacon the Raven had managed to put in place with a Red Empire bug on Kain's chair.

If they had been able to stop the beacon, they would have. They wanted nothing more to do with 'the plan' instigated by the Red Empire's other agent – none other than general Chloe Armitage of the Vampire Dominion.

A light switched on inside them. Armitage didn't know the Raven had unmasked them. She still expected the Raven's loyalty. The Raven grinned. They could secretly work against her plan.

A thrill flushed through them, wiping away their distress. They had a new mission – same as the eternal mission – defeat the vampires.

Armitage was in the Raven's sights, and they would do everything within their power to thwart Armitage's trap.

That will be the first step. And then my father, Shabbah al Ahmar, I will bring you to justice.

* * *

Chloe's smartphone pinged.

It was a message from the Raven which read, 'They have taken the bait. The team is pursuing the GPS beacon.'

She continued up the stairs into her Spike 512, supersonic business jet. Marcus Drake, carrying the limp form of Ramin Kain, followed her.

Back on the tarmac, James Haley and the surviving blackwidow pilot walked up to Nasr al Dam, and the rest of the Fist. A second later, the pilot slumped to the ground. Nasr al Dam turned to the side, cleaning a dagger with a black cloth.

Reaching the top of the stairs, she paused, glancing out through the main hangar doors at an Embraer business jet taxiing toward the runway. It had a single passenger. A well-charged smartphone that was behaving exactly like a GPS beacon. The plane's manifest defined a charter by a New York businessman named Ramin Kain, bound for London.

Chloe smiled briefly; events were tracking to plan. James would stay behind with the surviving Red Empire assassins. They still had work to do tonight, especially James to manage the content of the Panopticon. There would be well-constructed video footage of Kain boarding the Embraer business jet and the battle site would need to be cleansed of any remaining evidence. Although it appeared, the Order had done much of Shadowstone's work for them by detonating a fuel-air explosive at the safe house.

She entered the cabin, checking her phone as she took her favorite seat at the front of the luxuriously and stylishly appointed cabin. It was 21:30, she was at least three hours in front of the pursuing Mirovar force team. But there was no time to waste; they would be traveling east toward the sunrise and needed to beat its arrival over the northeast of England. The Spike 512 could fly to the UK in three hours, which would put the local time at 05:30 on landing. A couple of minutes short of half an hour before sunrise.

Soon, she would be back at her ancestral family home – Armitage manor.

She would take off after 'Kain's' Embraer jet. She would honor Crane's command to keep him safe by traveling to the UK after him, 'just to keep a close eye on him.'

Shadowstone had delivered a victory against the Mirovar force team by destroying an active, safe house, albeit at the loss of two blackwidow helicopters and three crews. The battle provided its own distractions. Already Shadowstone were spinning a web of deception over everything that had happened.

James Haley was proving invaluable.

There was plenty of time to sow doubt and muddy the water of the evidence trails. By the time James completed his work, the only narrative Crane would be able to find would be the one she was in control of.

She hit the intercom button. Her family retainers piloted the plane. Loyal humans who knew precisely what she was but didn't care. Another little secret carefully kept from the view of Crane.

"Home, Derek. There is no time to waste."

"Yes, Ma'am," The pilot responded.

The outer doors closed automatically, and within a minute the plane was taxiing out of the hangar.

Chloe relaxed back in her seat, closing her eyes. Anton had survived the fight. He had even tried to shoot her down with grenades at the end of the battle. She'd recognized his Ramp heat signature as he ran across the field.

She was pleased he'd made it, and Li as well.

All the pieces were falling into place to drive home his belief in revenge.

So much was happening, it was a thrilling time to be alive.

Soon, in less than forty-eight hours, her plan would take another major step forward.

She was sure of it.

* * *

The Day Guard lab facility sat on the third underground level beneath Fort Dix.

The two levels above it were also pure Shadowstone. The US army operated the entire above ground site, and the US taxpayer funded everything. The Shadowstone facility seamlessly integrated with the military base as a para-military government/private contractor partnership under a framework agreement signed by a US president several decades in the past.

When a relationship has been in place long enough, everyone forgets how it came to be, and no one questions it.

Unless, of course, you're Louise Wesson. She stood in front of a line of twenty fit young men dressed in simple white slacks and T-shirts. All volunteers, recruited from a diverse cross-section of US special forces teams for a 'special assignment.' Apart from their common backgrounds, they also shared very high levels of native physical ability and had proven themselves under combat conditions.

They were natural warriors. They were the first batch to receive the Phase V Day Guard serum. She'd selected these men personally. She regretted the fact that ten of them would be dead within two days and they didn't know it.

Louise had worked hard to find the best men, not just to fill Crane's quotas, but to maximize their individual survival rates under the serum. The research notes provided to her were crystal clear about the effects. Full physical transformation would normally complete within three hours, but it took one to two days to be sure the subject would survive. The symptoms of failure were specific and consistent; berserk rage, rapid aging, catatonic depression, and death. Once the rage started death was inevitable.

Four lab techs walked in front of the men. The first handed out mouth guards. The second carefully injected a specially encoded RFID chip with a microcapsule of TEF-4 neurotoxin next to their brain stem. The third injected a measured dose of the Day Guard serum into the side of their necks. The fourth guided each man to a low stretcher on the floor behind them.

Louise noted the date and time on a simple notepad, '21:31, Monday, 21st August.' Underneath a penciled in and thickly underlined heading, 'Super Hero Program Day 1.' It had been two months and ten days since she'd woken up to the existence of vampires and their secret rule over humanity.

She watched calmly as the first of the subjects began to quiver on their cots, biting down hard on their mouth guards.

Rule by vampires didn't sit well with her oath to '… defend the Constitution of the United States against all enemies, foreign and domestic; …' and the rest. The idea of the subjugation of humanity to a tribe of blood-sucking predators revolted her on a deep level.

The situation was intolerable, and she was not going to put up with it.

The vampires had ordered her to build them an army. She would do that. The next step was to wrest control of that army away from the vampires and use it to kill them.

The trick was in staying alive long enough to do it.

She needed to stay hidden while watched by apex predators with super-sensory abilities.

It was the biggest challenge of her life.

A slight smile curled the edges of her lips.

Where else would you rather be?

Epilogue – A Traitor's War

An infamous historical figure discovers the Vampire Dominion ruthlessly enforces their laws.

Greifswald, Northern Germany, May 1st, 1945, 23:05

The former *Führer und Reichskanzler* of the Third Reich, Adolf Hitler stared at the passing streets of Griefswald as he made his way through the town toward the docks.

Adolf seethed with rage. The Red Army occupied the city. *Gifted to the communists intact by that ridiculous traitor Petershagen. The sniveling coward who gave the city away without a fight.*

Turning to his companion. Adolf's rage retreated into the background, replaced with something akin to adoration. Dieter Franz, his savior, his mentor, a beautiful Aryan god he'd first met on the blood-soaked mud of Passchendaele in 1917 – his youthful blond hair and blue eyes unchanged in twenty-eight years.

An immortal who had admitted him into the ranks of the divine the night before in the bowels of the *Führerbunker.*

On the night of the 30th of April, Adolf admitted to himself that all had been lost. He'd written his last will and testament. Then it was to have been a poison pill and a 9mm round from his own Luger. Better honorable suicide than the humiliations the Slavic hoards of the Red Army would visit upon him.

Then, against all hope, Dieter had arrived. A colossus towering over the other men within the bunker. He'd locked the door behind him, knocking Eva Braun unconscious with a slap and then attacked him.

Adolf felt ashamed of his display of primal terror, whimpering as Dieter bit deeply into the side of his throat. The pain of having his throat slashed open and feeling his blood draining away in seconds was nothing compared to what came next.

Dieter laid his forearm open with his gleaming fangs. Pressing the gushing wound directly against the holes in Adolf's throat, his divine Aryan blood had mixed with Adolf's own. The excruciating agony of the ravenous fire of Dieter's immortal blood cleansing all human weakness from his body. While his flesh writhed in torment, his mind exalted in triumph over death, and victory over time.

As the pain ebbed away, Adolf had been surprised to discover how the overwhelming lust for blood had a deeply familiar feel to it. He realized he'd felt this need all his life and only after this divine transformation could he fully embrace his deepest predatory need with immediate frenzied feeding.

Eva Braun awoke just long enough to register terror on her face as he lunged at her. Pinning her to the ground with hands like iron. Latching hold of her throat with an unbreakable grip. His fangs lacerated her arteries, blood pouring into his mouth. He drew on new internal muscles, creating a vacuum effect, accelerating the flow and in seconds she ran dry.

Leaning back from Eva's limp body, Adolf sat down on the floor. Drunk with blood, his head whirling, exhilarated beyond measure.

Dieter dragged him to his feet and declared, "Time to go."

Rage suddenly flared, *how dare he touch me*, then immediately settled back to a quiet hum as Adolf followed Dieter from the bunker.

Of course, no one stopped them, he was Adolf Hitler, and the tall, powerfully built Aryan god marching in front of him added an extra layer of intimidation. In moments, they cleared the bunker, striding together through the ruins of Berlin. Fires lit the horizon, smoke tinged the air, and shells whistled and crumped in the distance.

Adolf looked up at Dieter and asked, "What of the Russians?"

"We will go through their lines. I have transport waiting north of Berlin, follow me to safety," Dieter instructed. He threw his coat to the ground, revealing a longsword belted at his waist. He drew the blade, the razor-sharp metal gleaming with a crimson hue in the light of the surrounding fires.

Adolf's mouth twitched incredulously, halfway between a snarl and a smirk. "What use is a sword against tanks?"

"Have faith – it will be all we need. Now make sure you keep up."

Adolf watched in wonder as Dieter rushed off through the ruins of Berlin with superhuman speed. He followed after, wonder giving way to exhilaration. He reveled in the speed and power of his new divinity.

Dieter cleared the way before them. None could stand in his way; he was too fast for the Russian soldiers to react. Blurring through their ranks like a scythe through a field of wheat. He steered Adolf past rows of advancing tanks and together they broke through the Red Army lines. They quickly covered nearly eight miles to an abandoned house surrounded by ruins.

Waiting in front of the house were a dozen heavily armed young men dressed in civilian clothes. They jumped to attention and saluted as soon as Adolf approached. Their youthful faces lit with pride to be part of the mission to save the *Führer*. Discarded uniforms of the 1st SS Panzer Division littered the front yard of the house. The men were members of the *Leibstandarte SS Adolf Hitler*, his personal bodyguard.

Adolf smiled, pleased to see these young flowers of Germanic youth. He knew they would do their utmost to serve him and he was certain he would require nothing less.

Across from the house brooded three powerful armored saloons. The exclusive Mercedes were the color of night and stood ready to fly down the roads. The men piled into the first and last of the cars, with one of the men sliding behind the steering wheel of the middle car and the last man holding open the passenger door for the *Führer* and his companion.

"Our transport," Dieter stated calmly, indicating the middle car with a nod of his head.

Adolf climbed into the plush accommodation of the rear seat of the saloon, and Dieter followed him in, storing his sword and scabbard on the floor well. The last SS man got into the front of the car and the powerful engines of all three vehicles fired into life. Moving forward as a column they disappeared into the night and escaped Berlin.

Morning arrived as they reached the outskirts of Greifswald, and Adolf discovered why thick black curtains covered the middle vehicle's windows. He was intensely disappointed to discover this weakness. This terrible vulnerability to sunlight and his expression remained sour until they had taken refuge in a barn.

Dieter quietly explained while they waited that when evening came, they would enter the port town of Greifswald, making for the docks and a waiting submarine. The Type IX U-boat would take them through the Baltic Sea, then across the Atlantic to South America and a new life in Argentina. The twelve unsuspecting young men of the Waffen SS would join the submarine's crew – as additional food – to sustain them during the weeks of travel. By the time they reached South America, the submarine would be a ghost ship without a crew, but the two immortals on board would survive and flourish in a new land.

The sun had fallen and they'd left the barn. The way into Greifswald had meant crossing the paths of units of the Red Army. Adolf had joined Dieter in combat. Using his bare hands, he'd fallen upon the Russians as a wolf amongst sheep, reveling in bloodlust and death. Not a single soldier they encountered had survived their divine wrath.

Adolf reflected on his new abilities. *A new base of operations to create a foundation for a new Reich, superior to the third Reich, an amalgam of the irresistible alloys of the Aryan race and yes, I must admit it – vampires. I will rule forever. None can resist my power; I am a true Übermensch.*

Suddenly the first car pulled to a halt, and Adolf's mind returned to the present with a jolt. There was a roadblock, four of the Waffen SS exited the front Mercedes, more men came out into the street from the car at the rear. One of the men at the front shouted commands, the men started firing their 9mm submachine guns. In moments, the guns at the front fell silent, their harsh voices replaced with swishing sounds and wet thuds.

Adolf struggled to see what was happening from within the confines of his armored saloon. The men at the back of the column started firing wildly into the air. He thrilled to the rising panic of men beset by terror as something leaped over his Mercedes.

A terror that would never touch him again. *I am the new god of death — all will worship me and die!*

"There is a problem," Dieter declared, grasping his sword and blurring away. The car door spinning into the street, torn from its hinges as he exited the vehicle.

Adolf followed him, flushed with his new powers and supremely confident that whatever the challenge, victory would be his. He blurred out of the saloon and onto the street. Dieter stood twenty yards away. The Waffen SS men lay about on the ancient cobblestones — all dismembered, all dead — their blood pooling in the gutters.

Opposite Dieter stood a tall, young woman of exquisite beauty. She was clad in loose black clothing, carrying a long gleaming sword with both hands like one of the occult assassins that Himmler had been so fond of. She flicked her head, her long dark hair flowing across her shoulders. Glancing past Dieter, she stared directly into his eyes and something passed between them — a recognition of inevitable destiny.

A shiver of dread raced up his spine, his confidence evaporated as his guts curdled and suddenly cramped. Without thinking, he took a step back, raising his hands as if to ward off an impending attack.

Turning slightly toward Dieter, a slight smile curled her sensual lips as she chastised him in sardonic tones, "You have been a very naughty boy."

"He is under my protection. You have no authority here!" Dieter declared.

She laughed coldly. "There are standing orders from Crane himself, you know what must happen now."

"I know no such thing, witch!" Dieter thundered, blurring forward.

They clashed in a shower of sparks. Even with his new abilities, Adolf could not follow how quickly they fought as their flashing blades rang out through the night. He took another step back, a dreadful foreboding freezing his heart.

Suddenly, Dieter's sword shattered into half-melted shards. The dark-haired woman's sword passing through it to cleave off his right arm above the elbow. She blurred again, taking off his legs above the knees. Dieter flopped to the ground in a jumble of separated limbs and spraying blood.

The woman immediately turned to him. Their eyes locking on each other for the briefest of moments before she leaped over Dieter's writhing torso toward him.

Adolf didn't wait for her to land. Turning, he fled down the street. Becoming a dark blur in the shadows. Hurtling toward the docks and the sanctuary of the waiting submarine.

If I can only get inside, I can get away from her. She cannot follow me into the open sea.

The buildings whipped by. Adolf strained to hear the sounds of pursuit, but there were no noises discernible as his pursuer. There was the drip of dank water in nearby gutters, the scuttling of rats lurking in the sewers, the murmurs of frightened townsfolk accustomed to staying inside if there was trouble on the street.

He lamented silently. *Why am I alone? Why is there no one left to die for me?*

He darted into an alleyway and came to a halt. He backed himself up against a wall, looking, listening – his heart beating rapidly – even for a vampire. His head swiveling left and right. *Where is she? Where is the witch?*

There was no sound of pursuing footfalls. There was only a slight whistling. A shadowed hint of a breeze. A glint of reflected moonlight from somewhere above him, and then her sword, an ancient Japanese katana made by a 17th-century genius slicing through his neck.

Adolf felt his head topple from his shoulders. It bounced painfully off the cobblestones of the laneway before rolling into a filthy gutter. He was still conscious, a ring of agony engulfing his throat, an even two inches below his jaw line.

Something smeared over half his face. Stinging his eye, squishing into his nose, seeping into his mouth which soundlessly opened and closed like a beached fish. Its horrid taste magnified by the superb acuity of his vampire senses. It was unmistakable for a man who loved German Shepherds more than he loved people. His mouth brayed silent words, *Dog shit! I have dog shit in my mouth! And its been ill! Mein Gott! What has it been eating?! It's in my eye!*

The experience of life began fraying around the edges. A finely leathered boot tilted his face up slightly. He saw the woman peering at him as a scientist might stare at an obscure butterfly pinned to a corkboard. She wrinkled her nose in physical disgust, her beautiful blue eyes narrowing as hidden emotions bloomed behind them.

"I loathe wannabees," she declared fervently.

Suddenly, she stepped away. He rolled back into the wet dog shit; which again seeped into his mouth and pushed up into his nose.

She called out, her voice betraying her exasperation, "Dieter! Stop trying to escape – or do I have to take your remaining limb as well?"

The darkness closed in. His senses left him one by one, sight, hearing, touch. The last two lingered for a long moment, smell and taste. The most ancient senses and the last to go as his vampire vitality ebbed away.

Adolf's mind echoed a single pungent word repeatedly as it finally collapsed into oblivion, *shit, shit, shit*—

Prologue – The Dragon's Den

The Armitage Manor, England, July 5th, 1856, 22:25

A single shaft of moonlight cut through the summer air. It glimmered through an open bedroom window, caressing the curves and angles of two lovers entwined on white sheets. One was an exquisitely beautiful young woman; the other was something that was ancient before she was born.

He stilled, his skin becoming hot to touch. He was ramping. Chloe followed his lead, dropping into silence and accelerating her mind. Time slowed. Exquisite bliss bloomed throughout her being. The silence deepened, her joy intensified, and surface reality evaporated away.

He was a fiery, golden light, shuddering in rhythmic waves and she became the same. All sense of corporeal reality disappearing completely, like the night giving way to the dawn.

There was only golden light, a steady drumbeat of time, glorious bliss and union.

Then hot kisses on her throat. A sudden gasp of air into oxygen-starved lungs. Her fingers plunged into his long dark hair, bringing his head up. Their mouths met for a long, lingering kiss.

She moved slightly, turning and resting her head on his shoulder, holding him gently.

"Oh my God!" she whispered. "What just happened?"

He stiffened for a moment, then relaxed, kissing her quickly on the lips. He slipped out of bed, and before she could react, he was on the balcony. A moment later he was gone.

"Cornelius?" she whispered.

There was only the promise of two nights hence. Longing filled her heart. What was he waiting for?

* * *

Armitage Manor, England, July 7th, 1856, 23:34

Crane's vampire attack had weakened Chloe past the point of being able to take action. She was powerless to resist.

Chloe had first met Crane three weeks before. It was a warm summer night, she was practicing with her weapons in the moonlight, pistol, longsword, and rapier. Crane emerged from the shadows and offered himself as a training partner. Intrigued, Chloe accepted, and they fenced throughout the night. He was clearly a champion of the blade, and a seasoned Ramp master. Time flew, and before long the first glimmerings of dawn appeared in the east. Crane frowned and begged her leave to depart. She allowed it, on the promise that he return the following night.

Crane was true to his word, returning the next night and every night after that until two nights past.

At first, she believed he was a Ramp master, an unknown member of the Order of Thoth, but quickly, she understood precisely who and what he was – one of the most powerful vampires alive. By rights, she should have followed her allegiances to the Order and fought him to the death.

But her loyalty to the Order had died along with all hope for the Order's eventual victory. Confirmed as a full member of the Order of Thoth at sixteen, the youngest confirmation on record. She'd taken little more than a year to come to the conclusion the Order would lose the war. The Red Empire was larger and more ruthless, and the vampires had the unbeatable strategic advantage of rapid recruitment. It took years to grow and develop new Ramp masters. One vampire could create another in minutes. No matter how many vampires the individual heroics of the Order killed, vampire numbers could always swell faster than the Ramp masters could destroy them.

Chloe couldn't see her life spent to an empty purpose, to someone else's broken dream. She set her sights on becoming a vampire and using her gifts to master the vampire world. To rule vampires and men – for she would never submit to the rule of another. Only one question had remained, when would her transformation occur?

The appearance of Crane answered that question, but then he'd delayed, and delayed again. He was waiting for something, something he needed before he could proceed to the next step; the arrival of Jean Philippe Allemande.

Chloe lay dying of blood loss on a divan in her library.

Crane stood over her, his generals a respectful distance beyond him. He pulled a glass vial filled with a dark red fluid from his vest pocket. He uncorked it, upending it over the twin bite wounds on her throat. The 'blood,' crawled over her skin. Running in tiny rivers, the animated fluid seeking the holes in her neck. In moments, the blood had vanished, dark lines tracking beneath her skin in its wake as it flooded through her diminished bloodstream.

"What is this? What have you given her?" the blond general asked, his face rigid with suspicion.

Crane held up his hand in abrupt dismissal.

The chamber flickered around her. Shadows stretched across her vision before a searing white light washed them away. Shrill screams and gasping silence competed with each other while every bone in her body splintered and renewed itself. Fire surged along every nerve, muscle fibers tore and then knitted anew. Time fled and eternity reigned a world of suffering. A rapid trembling rippled over her limbs. Her eyelids fluttered. She sighed once. The transformation was complete.

All new things are born in agony.

Chloe opened her eyes to a wondrous world of superb clarity, every sense perfectly attuned to the world around her. Someone was speaking in a strange language, each word cutting her mind like a razor.

"Who's speaking," she whispered. "I didn't—"

Allemande's face leered above her, his voice a dreadful whisper as he pronounced the final words of the binding curse. Faint rainbows flickered, the light of the room faded, shadows blooming before her eyes. A veil wrapped itself around her mind, extinguishing any ability to directly harm the man who stood beside the Haitian sorcerer, staring at her with obsessive interest.

Crane had been hunting her for some time – her transformation was not a whim, but the result of a carefully laid plan. It galled her to realize he'd duped her. He'd promised her so much more, but had instead delivered her into slavery to his will.

Pure rage flooded her; she conceived her attack in a moment – Allemande's curse be damned. Her nostrils flared, a vast lust for violence throwing down her mind. She stared at Crane, her eyes flashing with hatred, but before she could move another need overwhelmed everything else.

Cowering in the corner of her library, his hands and feet bound, his mouth gagged, crouched a brigand. Recently captured and brought to her manor. A man no one would miss, and certainly not missed by anyone who could do anything about it.

Chloe rose from the divan, rushing over to where the brigand cringed, his face white with terror. She grabbed his lank hair with one hand, drew his head back, exposing his throat. She arched back, her nostrils flaring with the scent of prey. Her mouth gaped open, brand-new fangs flashing in the lantern light. Filled with an overwhelming, hideous need, she crunched forward, sinking her fangs into his neck. His hot blood flooded into her mouth. She swallowed desperately, instinctively smacking his chest to keep the heart flow coming until she drained the last available drop.

She found herself on the floor, the brigand's body limp and pale beneath her. She bounded to her feet, the others in the room staring at her with curious interest. A new power coursed through her being. She screamed in exultation. Opposite her stood Crane and his minions. Her gaze flicked over them. There was Allemande, the voodoo priest, a smug smile on his face. She silently promised herself, *you will pay for your curse, this I swear.* Beside the Haitian stood a powerfully built African, a slimly built east Asian, an athletic Persian, and a tall, strong northern European. All were Crane's generals, and he'd cursed them all as he'd cursed her.

Crane and his servants. She despised them all. Crane had tricked her. The binding lay like a hot net around her soul. She locked gazes with Crane, his eyes narrowing slightly – waiting for her response.

She drew upon her Order training, now enhanced with extraordinary vampire strength. Reaching up and sweeping an ancestral sword from the wall, she whirled toward Crane. His generals, immediately drew weapons, reflexively blurring forward to defend their master. She evaded them, faster than the eye could see. Her thrust carved through open space toward Crane's heart. Lightning crackled; rainbow flecked shadows danced through the room. The air shuddered, blowing her backward against the wall. The sword, livid with flame, fell from her nerveless fingers and crashed to the floor.

She staggered back to her feet, the stench of burning metal ripe in her nostrils.

Crane's voice cut through the silence in the room, "Such perfect ferocity."

"What have you done?" the blond general asked. "What was that blood? I've never smelled its like."

Crane blurred forward, grasping Chloe's shoulders possessively. He stared hard into her eyes and declared, "You will enforce my laws, even unto my generals. I have given you the strength to carry out my edicts."

They stared at each other for a long moment.

A hot vow sprang from the depths of her soul. *Never, never, never will I serve you. I will have my freedom, and you will regret this night before you die.*

She paused for a moment, her mind spinning – she would have to deceive Crane, now and until she'd broken the curse, and restored her liberty. She stood tall, stepped back from his grip and relaxed; a slight smile caressing her lips. Bowing respectfully, she said firmly, "My Lord, I will serve you."

Crane smiled triumphantly.

Rising from her bow, she glanced up at him, her face calm.

Beware my fury – for I will never rest until I am free to live my own purpose and not yours.

Chapter Seventeen

Customer Name: R.I.S.C Enterprises Pty Ltd
Job: Transport
Priority: Urgent
Security: Secured/Armed
Pick Up Address: Hangar [REDACTED], Logan International Airport, Boston
Destination Address: [REDACTED], Chicago, IL
Pick Up Time: 09:00, Wednesday 23rd August
Description of Goods: 16x palletized crates of machine parts.
Mass: Not more than 20,000 lbs. (est. 18,000 lbs.)
Insurance Value: $40M
Vehicle Type: Semi-Trailer
Container Type: Large
Quoted Price: $79,900.00
Customer Contact: James Halifax.
Customer Contact details: [REDACTED]

– Quote metadata for contracted secured transport of 'machine parts,' from Boston to Chicago

* * *

South of White Hill, Maine, August 21st, 21:20

The engines of the two SUVs idled quietly.

Anton Slayne lugged a strong box filled with FN P90 submachine guns and magazines with a mix of high-performance armor piercing and silver ammunition into the back of the rear SUV. Every fifth bullet was silver, a general-purpose magazine load for when you could not be sure what you might be facing.

Peter threw a dark brown, leather battle vest on top of the box. He'd loaded his vest with his favorite weapons, a pair of razor-sharp battle-axes and four tri-bladed throwing axes.

Anton closed the tailgate, and they walked around the big vehicle to join the other members of the Mirovar force team.

Francis Mirovar stood on the doorstep of the log cabin. Gripping Justin Blake's arm, he asked, "Can I convince you to come with us? You could make a real difference to our chances."

Justin frowned, shaking his head. "Not this time my friend. I have to see to my team and organize the next Order conclave."

"When will it be?"

"Two," Justin shrugged his heavy shoulders, "perhaps two and a half weeks. You'll all be back by then." He leaned in close to Francis and requested with a wry grin. "Make sure you bring Ramin Kain back in one piece, I would like to see him squirm during an impeachment."

Francis nodded; his eyes flat. Necessity drove the rescue of Kain, not concern for the man himself.

Anton halted a couple of feet back from the two force leaders. Li Wu appeared at his shoulder. She carried the Blue and Green Dragon swords and thumped him hard on the side with the Blue Dragon as she thrust it into his hands. She stared at him for a moment, before flicking her head back at the log cabin. The message was clear – were you going to leave this behind?

"No," Anton whispered. "Of course not."

Li lifted both eyebrows skeptically. Coldly pushing past him, she hugged Justin.

"Bye, Uncle. Keep safe and kick ass."

Anton shook his head in bewilderment. Why was Li upset with him? She wasn't even talking to him.

Justin hugged her back. They broke apart. Putting a big hand under Li's chin, his face became serious, and he said quietly, "Take care Li, it's one big trap over there, and we don't know what Armitage's real target is."

"What about the inquisition?" Li asked. "Is that still hanging over my head?"

Justin sighed. "Unfortunately, yes. However, we must put it aside until we either get Ramin Kain back in one piece or we hold the next conclave where the Head of the Order will resolve all these matters."

Li's face fell, she backed away from Justin, joining the rest of the team standing near the two SUVs.

Juliette stood next to Francis, one hand resting gently on his arm. A far-away look flitted across her eyes, and she reported, "Joan is aware of the situation. The Walker force team have pledged their assistance."

Francis smiled grimly. "A second force team will even the odds. Are all the other loremasters aware?"

"Yes. The news will filter through the rest of the Order over the next few days."

"See – you don't need me," Justin remarked, striding away from the porch and onto the track. He stood in the headlights of the front SUV, shouldered a backpack, put on a pair of Order nightglasses and called out, "Godspeed to you all." He jogged off down the track, quickly vanishing into the dark.

Anton stepped up next to Francis and inquired, "The Walker force team?"

"The English team. Just like us," Juliette answered. "Joan Lewis is their loremaster, and Richard Walker is their force leader."

Luther pushed himself off the wall of the log cabin and stated derisively, "A real force team, one the Order can count on."

Anton's lip curled. He was about to respond, but pulled himself up short, thinking, *I can't let this guy get under my skin.*

Francis stepped toward Luther. His hand flashed out, hitting Luther hard across the face. Luther's head rocked to the side, and he staggered back. Francis snarled. "I've had enough of your disrespect."

"What the hell," Luther snapped, blood dribbling past his lips. He blurred forward to tackle Francis. Francis met his attack, flowing around Luther and bringing him to the ground with a thud.

Kneeling on top of him, Francis pressed down hard on Luther's right arm, twisted up high behind his back. "Shut up, or I'm leaving you here."

Luther grunted, and gritted his teeth. "You can't do that."

"I damn well can."

There was a long moment of silence.

"Are we clear," Francis added.

Luther nodded and grunted again.

Francis released his hold, allowing Luther to regain his feet.

"Ramin Kain is not a traitor," Luther asserted hotly, glaring at the others. "I will keep this mission honest."

"Yes, you do that," Juliette remarked, sweeping past him and taking a position in the front passenger seat of the lead SUV. "Peter, come up here with me and drive."

"Sure," Peter agreed.

Francis stared at Luther for a second and shook his head. "We can't waste more time. We're leaving now, everyone on board."

Anton got into the back seat of the front SUV and sat next to Li. Chiara jumped in beside him in the last remaining seat. Peter put the SUV into gear rolling forward along the track to the main road. Li turned her head away, looking out the window. Anton decided not to press the issue, it was clear she was upset with him about something. He thought back over the night's events. *I protected her when she couldn't fight, what is she so upset about? ... Oh, I ran off after Drake.*

The pieces finally dropped into place.

"Damn," Anton whispered.

He'd abandoned her in the middle of a battle.

"Li," he whispered. "I'm so sorry."

Li stiffened for a moment and then sighed. She turned her head forward, not looking at him. Her eyelids half-closed, she declared in cutting tones, "You will be if you do it again. What would have happened if they'd turned on Peter and me in numbers too high for him to handle? I couldn't fight, not properly. The Red Empire could've killed us and just because you'd run off to satisfy 'what?' ... I don't know. How often do I have to ask myself, 'what were you thinking?' You're too smart to be losing it like this. Get a handle on your emotions before they cause damage to the team you can't repair."

Anton frowned for a moment, and promised, "I will. I understand what you're saying. It won't happen again."

Li tilted her head and looked at him askance. "Don't make promises you don't know how to keep."

"I'll keep it," Anton vowed, looking forward through the car's windscreen.

The SUV turned onto the main road and accelerated away, the second SUV following tightly behind it.

* * *

The Spike 512 supersonic business jet flashed through the night sky over the Atlantic.

Chloe Armitage glanced at the monitor seamlessly merged with the front wall of the cabin. It was 22:30 on Monday night in Boston and 03:30 on Tuesday morning in the United Kingdom. Stats streamed along the bottom of the screen. Altitude 51,034 feet, Speed 1253 miles per hour. In another two hours, she would be landing at her private airfield outside the town of Goathland, ten miles from her ancestral home near the town of Whitby – Armitage Manor.

It had been more than a century since the property had been known by that name. She'd begun obfuscating her personal history back in the 1890's but still owned the manor house. It was the home of her human retainers, including the pilots who flew her plane. She'd made it almost impossible to discover who really owned 'Armitage Manor.'

She didn't need Shadowstone to hide her own tracks, she'd been doing that for most of her life.

Her smartphone pinged, there was a message from James Haley that read, 'Tech crew dismantling the 3rd blackwidow. All deaths attributed to Order actions. Remaining Red Empire personnel en route to a Shadowstone safe house in Boston.'

She responded with, 'Noted.'

The four Red Empire assassins in Boston, a fist team led by Nasr al Dam, aka Blood Eagle, would no doubt prove useful. Having a secret force in reserve in North America was an edge over her opponents. Chloe hungered for every advantage she could establish. Regime change was no easy task, and while she believed in her eventual victory, she had no illusions about the difficulties, risks, and challenges that lay before her. If Crane ever discovered what she was doing, he would surely kill her. Events had gone too far. There was no going back now. There would be no opportunity for forgiveness and redemption. He would cut her in half with his blade and rip her living heart from her chest – and there was nothing she could do to stop him. Jean Philippe Allemande's curse ensured Crane was the one man she could never defeat in open combat, the one man she couldn't fight against and win.

Everything was at stake. The game was live, and there would be only one winner.

At the back of the cabin under the watchful gaze of Marcus Drake sat Ramin Kain, head of the Order of Thoth. Kain was awake, bound and gagged. She could've drugged him, but she wanted him conscious, aware and frightened. She needed to break him before the Mirovar force team arrived at her manor house.

There were many questions to answer. After the battle at the Boston docks where she'd killed the Order grandmaster, Gang Wu, it had become clear the Order had managed to partially corrupt the feeds to the Panopticon. They'd demonstrated their capacity to shield operations from Panopticon surveillance on the night of the second battle in Boston where she'd killed Crane's praetorians. Just how the Order had accomplished this feat was a question at the top of her list. A list which included, where were all the Order safe houses? What was the disposition of Order forces? Who were the Order loremasters? Where and when would the Order hold their next conclave? These and many other questions she expected to answer today.

Chloe would have to wait until she got Kain into the dungeon beneath her manor house before she could begin the interrogation. The supersonic Spike 512 had bought her another three hours of lead time. She was six hours ahead of her pursuers.

Chloe tapped her fingers on the arm of her seat. There would be some necessary preliminaries before she could properly put Kain to the question. Then there were the inevitable preparations and final checks on the trap for the Mirovar force team she'd ordered built by the Red Empire assassins currently occupying the manor house. James Haley and the Spike 512 had delivered a four-man Red Empire fist team and a host of specialized equipment to the manor before completing his flight to Boston with the rest of the Red Empire assassins. She needed to be sure the trap was ready and fully functional – she'd explicitly designed it to condition Anton Slayne into a living weapon against Crane.

Li Wu's death at the hands of vampires would be the final straw that would break Anton's restraints, making him completely vulnerable to Chloe's will.

She paused, frowning. With all the checks and preparations, her six-hour lead could easily become four, would it be enough time to learn everything she needed to know. Interrogating the Head of the Order of Thoth was a once in a lifetime opportunity, well … once in a human lifetime. Still, she should not waste the opportunity, and four hours would pass quickly and may prove to be insufficient.

She needed more time.

Her fingers froze, her eyes widened. She'd made a mistake. She was not six hours ahead of her pursuers, she was at best two hours ahead. Once the Order realized that the Embraer jet carrying the decoy GPS signal was not heading toward London as per its flight plan, they would look for another landing site. Once the pilots in the Embraer posted their changed flight plan to land in Goathland, the information would be accessible to anyone with Internet access.

The United Kingdom had its own members of the Order of Thoth. She was well aware of the existence of the Walker force team. Their center of operations remained hidden in the sprawling metropolis of London. The initial flight plan of the decoy Embraer should keep them there. They would only begin to move once they became aware of the new flight plan to Goathland in Yorkshire, and London was hours away from Yorkshire.

How much time she had to question Kain rested on the capacity of the Order to realize the decoy Embraer had changed flight plans and transport the UK force team to Yorkshire. It was a capability of the Order that was currently unknown.

Chloe didn't like unknowns in her plans, and she hated relying on the inefficiency of either the Mirovar or the Walker force teams.

It was safest to assume the worst and plan for it. The Mirovar force team would already be in communication with the Walker force team. They would pass on the decoy GPS signal, and the UK team would track it to Goathland and from there to the town of Whitby and her manor house. They could move into position to attack the manor house and rescue Kain. But would they attack immediately, or would they wait until the arrival of the Mirovar force team to ensure they had an overwhelming force?

Unless Walker was stupid, or desperate, he would wait. Whether the Order attacked or waited for reinforcements, she needed to consider and plan for either possibility.

The four Red Empire assassins she'd stationed at her manor house would help. They were a second, elite fist team. Like the team led by Nasr al Dam who had all bar one survived the battle at the Maine safe house, they were an elite squad, a notch above the regular fighters of the Red

Empire. As effective as they were, they were too few to prevail against a full-sized Order force team, especially one that was prepared for combat.

She needed to keep the UK team, and the Mirovar force team separated for as long as possible, and she would need to deter an early attack by the UK force team.

Chloe frowned. She would have to deliberately delay the pursuit by the Mirovar force team. What were her options? The Spike had long overtaken the decoy Embraer business jet transporting Kain's phone. The decoy plane would arrive at Goathland at 08:00 UK time. The GPS signal of the phone drawing the Order to the airfield. She could divert the decoy to another site, but then how to reacquire the Mirovar force team and draw them back to Armitage manor and the trap that waited there? She could get her staff to transport the phone, but what if the UK Order caught up with them before they arrived at the Manor. No, the decoy plane had to complete its mission, delivering the GPS/phone to her private airfield and from there to her manor house.

She had to throw something in Mirovar's way, something that would give her enough time to drain Kain's mind, but not so strong they would never arrive. Her fingers drummed the armrests of her seat. Focusing her gaze beyond the cabin, her mind raced through a dozen options before she settled on a new plan.

She commanded her phone, "Call James Haley."

The phone rang three times before James answered, "Yes, Ma'am?"

"Where are you?"

"Logan airport overseeing the teardown of the last blackwidow. What do you need?"

"Good. Delegate it. I need you to keep an eye open for the arrival of the Mirovar force team."

"Yes, Ma'am. If they have a helicopter—"

"They don't have one. They will come by car ... expect them after midnight, one a.m. at the latest."

"And when they arrive?"

"I need a photograph of 'Anton Smith,' getting on whichever plane they're using to follow the decoy. Once you have that, bypass the Panopticon and alert Shadowstone UK to arrange a welcoming committee for Anton's arrival in UK airspace."

"Yes, Ma'am, will do. Anything else?"

"Yes. Don't send the photo too soon; make Shadowstone in the UK wait. I want them rushed and under pressure."

"Copy that. Anything else Ma'am?"

"I need you to intercept any communications traffic from UK Shadowstone to Crane's personal line for the next twenty-four hours. I need Crane isolated from the UK, and I need a very plausible excuse for it."

James' breathing whispered hesitantly over the line. "… When do you need the intercepts to start?"

"As soon as possible, but not later than your notification to the UK of the imminent arrival of an Order of Thoth operative."

"Yes Ma'am, there is a way this can be done."

"Thank you, James, that will be all," she said, disconnecting the call.

Now it's time to focus on extracting everything I can from Kain.

Chloe smiled, her eyes shining with anticipation.

Her phone vibrated in her hand; the screen indicated a call from Crane. She tapped the answer icon and put the phone on speaker – there was nothing here she wanted to hide from Marcus or Kain.

"Yes, Sir. What can I do for you?" she asked.

"Where are you?" Crane responded.

"Over the Atlantic."

"Are you in a drone?"

"Personal jet. I wasn't anywhere near Fort Dix when Kain decided to fly to the UK."

"What the hell is he doing?" Crane demanded.

"I don't know. I'm following him now. I'm sure to find out soon."

"What happened in Maine? It's a mess over there."

"Shadowstone hit a live Order safe house. The first in years. There have been Order casualties."

"Was it Mirovar?"

"Yes," Chloe replied, rising lithely out of her chair. Walking casually down the aisle toward Kain, she held her phone in front of her. "But at least some of the Mirovar force team survived, perhaps the majority of them. I will know more soon; it appears they're also following Kain."

"Remember what I told you – keep Kain safe. We need the stability of the secret detente for another year. It is essential you keep Kain alive until the Day Guard is ready. Of course, afterward, he will be of no further use."

Kain's eyes bulged above his gag, his face flushing red.

Chloe tilted her head slightly, staring at Kain and said affirmatively, "I can guarantee he's perfectly safe right now."

"Excellent. Keep it that way."

Chloe smiled slightly. "Yes, Sir. I will do my best."

"See that you do," Crane said and hung up.

Chloe arched an eyebrow at Kain. Turning on her heel, she strolled back to her seat. Crane's call had been unexpected but useful. Events were tracking well toward her goals. She would remain vigilant to ensure that remained the case.

* * *

Electric motors hummed; the hangar doors grinding along their tracks with a low rasp.

The Order owned Embraer Legacy 500 business jet, taxied through the opening and out onto the tarmac. Everyone in the Mirovar force team was on the plane. Peter and Anton were in the cockpit. Behind them in the main cabin sitting in pairs along the aisle were Francis and Juliette Mirovar, Jay Creeley and Yvette Mirovar, and Li Wu and Chiara Romano. Sitting by himself at the back, Samuel Luther stared out the window.

Juliette leaned back in her chair and engaged her mind palace. The external world vanished, an internal landscape blooming into view. Recent events since the arrival of the Order traveler Deon Lamar, at the destroyed safe house in Maine, flashed before her.

She 'reached,' for what she needed. The abduction of Ramin Kain by the Red Empire and their escape in a nightfalcon helicopter arrested before her. She leaped up into the nightfalcon's cabin, the helicopter behaving as a solid object in her vision. The surviving Red Empire assassins stood around Kain's body, slumped on the floor. One of the assassins quickly bound him. The tallest of the assassins let his cowl fall back to reveal a head of close-cropped blond hair. It was Marcus Drake; he went forward to the helicopter's cockpit. Chloe Armitage emerged from the cockpit and stood near Kain. Kain moaned, beginning to wake up.

Her mind flashed forward to Logan airport. She was standing alone on a runway. Racing toward her was an Embraer business jet, it lifted off, zooming overhead. Turning around she tracked its ascent into the night sky. A sheath of light glimmered around it, before streaking over the horizon. The plane was bound for England. She followed the light, her mind palace providing an intuitive leap. The light split in two, one strand heading to London, the second, brighter strand, heading toward the northeast coast.

Yorkshire? The manifest for this flight indicated London as the destination, but Yorkshire is more likely.

Juliette briefly dropped out of her mind palace. Francis reached across to touch her forearm and asked, "Are you okay?"

"Working," she replied.

She flipped open her laptop and logged in. The implant in her right forearm completed the routing, giving her access to everything on the Internet. Less than two minutes later she identified a private airfield near the village of Goathland in northern Yorkshire as the most likely destination of the Embraer jet.

Is Kain, Armitage, and Marcus on that plane?

Numbers flashed through her mind. The projected arrival time approximated 08:00 am in England, more than two hours after sunrise.

Is Armitage planning to transport herself off the plane in a box? She was in control of the schedule for the attack on the safe house. What was her exfiltration plan? Surely, she would have planned better than this.

A second plane?

Only a supersonic plane could deliver Armitage and Drake to England in time to beat the sun. That restricted the options. Juliette used her implant, laptop, and the Internet to directly feed her mind palace vision. She remained at the end of the runway, the airport around her now inactive and silent, shrouded in shadows, the dark of night closing in. A half dozen aircraft appeared arrayed around her in a broad semi-circle. The Spike 512 stood out. Designed in Boston and locally produced in England, possibly favored by someone with an English heritage. It could take Armitage to Yorkshire before sunrise. She checked departures from Logan airport. A Spike 512 had left at 21:35. A time that conveniently matched the flight time of a nightfalcon from the Maine safe house to Logan International Airport with a few minutes to spare.

Juliette took a step, the runway vanished, and she was back in a hangar similar to the one she'd just left. There were two planes, a Spike 512 and an Embraer business jet before her. Marcus Drake was carrying an unconscious Ramin Kain onto the Spike 512. A tall, dark-haired woman turned at the top of the stairs into the supersonic jet. It was Armitage, leading Drake and Kain onto the plane.

Armitage had the Spike 512 waiting at Logan International airport and had used it to beat the sunrise in England.

She's further ahead than we thought. More like six hours, we are far behind her.

Juliette paused for a moment, using the implant in her forearm to send a private message to Joan Lewis, the loremaster in the English force team. 'Armitage arrived in a supersonic jet before sunrise. The Embraer is a decoy carrying a GPS beacon only.'

She dropped out of her mind palace and declared, "Francis, we need to go to Goathland in England."

Francis nodded. "Peter, set course for Goathland, UK."

"Sure, Boss," Peter replied. "I'll file a new flight plan once we take off."

"Good work."

Juliette sat back, she had two main questions to answer. What was Armitage's plan, and who was the Red Empire spy? It was clear that Peter, Yvette or Chiara was an opposing agent, but she couldn't identify who. The team couldn't afford to drop all three due to the risk of one. It was clear that whoever was the spy had provided Armitage with the information to compromise the safe house sensor array – it could have got them all killed – and yet it hadn't.

Armitage had been in the perfect position to wipe the team out but had failed to do so. She'd achieved a stunning victory against the Mirovar force team and had kidnapped Ramin Kain from under their noses. The obvious part of her plan was that she could torture Kain to reveal a host of sensitive information about the Order.

The obscure part of her plan was using Kain as a lure and providing a trackable GPS signal to follow. If she wanted to kill the team, she could have done so already – it had to be something else – but what? What were the implications of Armitage keeping the Mirovar force team alive, and how much longer would she stay her hand?

Juliette re-entered her mind palace and began searching for answers. What were the patterns in everything she knew? What were the gaps in her knowledge? She found herself in the midst of a large, well-lit hall. The rest of the Mirovar force team appeared in a circle around her, their faces impassive. A door opened on the far wall of the room. The light in the room retreated, casting everything into gloom. Armitage walked into the room, striding purposefully toward the team. The shadows deepened until only Armitage, and the members of the team were visible before the surrounding darkness.

Armitage slowed as she approached the edge of the team. She slipped through the ring. Walking past Juliette, she approached someone behind her.

Juliette whirled around.

The world shifted violently.

The shadows vanished. Juliette stood before a massive warehouse. Bright lights seared between the weathered gantries overhead. Dead men in matt-black body armor littered the Boston docks. Armitage stepped forward, putting her hands on the shoulders of two young people standing casually together, dragon swords in their hands.

Anton and Li! Her plan is about Anton and Li. But what does she want with them?

Juliette dropped out of her mind palace, turned toward Francis and whispered urgently, "Her plan is focused on Anton and Li!"

"… We still have to rescue Kain."

"We have to block her plan."

Francis nodded, his lips pressed firmly together, he whispered, "Strategy my love, we need to vary our strategy." He stood up, turned around and addressed the rest of the team, "Everyone, you have three hours to get some sleep. That will leave us with two and a half hours to prepare before we land in England. So, get some rest while you can."

The team responded by reaching for pillows and blankets. The lights in the cabin dimmed, someone flicking a switch for the team.

Juliette reached across the aisle and found Francis' hand heading toward her own. They squeezed each other's hands, and she caught his gaze in the shadows. His eyes lay shrouded with serious thought. He wouldn't get much sleep tonight. She closed her eyes, knowing she wouldn't get much sleep either, her mind bedeviled by a single question. What does Armitage want with Anton and Li? She didn't know, and she felt in her heart that this was the most important question to answer.

She sighed and drifted off into a restless sleep. Sleep disturbed by a dream where Chloe Armitage wore a delicate golden crown, and to her left and right stood Anton and Li. Both wore black armor emblazoned with a red dragon on their chests, their dragon swords sheathed at their waists, and long vampire fangs resting over their bottom lips.

She woke with a start, whispering hoarsely, "No. Never."

No one else heard her.

* * *

The Embraer business jet sat on the tarmac waiting for permission to take off. Peter and Anton sat in the cockpit. Peter began preparing a new flight plan – they were going to a private airfield outside a village named Goathland in Yorkshire, England.

Anton slapped his knee, and declared, "We have to take the initiative, we're always on the back foot."

Peter flicked a button on the console, setting the communications with the air traffic control tower to receive only. They would tell him soon enough when it was time to leave.

"You're right. The last few months have been crap," Peter agreed, raising an eyebrow and looking at Anton wryly. "Ever since we met you on the Boston docks. It's probably all your fault."

"Peter – I'm serious."

"Yeah, I know," Peter sighed. "We just got our asses kicked. We should be dead. They cut through our sensor array like it wasn't there and took us by complete surprise."

"How did they do that?"

"I hate to think, but seriously, someone had to have told them how to do it."

They sat back in silence for a moment.

Anton's heart sank and he whispered, "Who would've done that? Everyone's loyal, aren't they? Look how we fought together against those gangster vamps a couple of weeks ago, and tonight – everyone fought against the Red Empire and Shadowstone. Who could do that? Who could put their lives on the line in battle and then turn around and betray us?" he shook his head. "It doesn't make any sense."

Peter paused for a long moment, staring out through the aircraft's windscreen before replying, "There's only one conclusion I can draw. I'm sure I'm not the only one in this team to put two and two together and come up with four. There must be a spy in the team. Someone is working for the Red Empire or the Vampire Dominion, or both – whoever they are – they're buried deep."

Anton looked hard at Peter. "How deep?"

Peter grinned. "Well, of course, it wasn't me."

"You wouldn't admit it anyway."

Peter's grin evaporated. "Well, that's true enough. You'll have to make a decision about who you really trust."

Anton paused for a long moment, frowning.

"I'm cut – we share a room. While I haven't exactly saved your life, I did clean up after you with a vamp who was escaping that apartment building a couple of weeks ago."

Anton remembered Peter's battle axe flying past his shoulder, tumbling end over end before it sheared through a vampire's skull in the midst of a battle in Boston. He hit Peter on the shoulder. "Yeah," he shrugged his shoulders, "it couldn't be you. I would be dead by now if it were you. You could've killed me a hundred times by now."

"What makes you think that I would reveal my hand by killing a novice. C'mon, if I was a spy, why would I reveal myself over a small fish like you?"

Anton smiled briefly, then frowned.

"Hey, you opened this can of worms," Peter noted.

"Yeah, it's a problem I can't solve at the moment, but getting back to what I really wanted to say. I'm never going to defeat Armitage unless I can seize the initiative."

"That would be 'we.'"

"Yes ... unless we seize the initiative."

"What are you proposing?"

"We need better weapons. I mean, you're an armorer, can't we be doing something more? What about using a lot more silver?"

"Silver?"

"Yeah silver. Why aren't we using silver weapons across the board?"

"We used to decades ago."

"Huh! What's the problem?"

"Well think about it. Imagine a force team carrying a lot of silver and then match that up to a vampire's sensory ability. Their sense of smell is far more powerful than a human, and they have a massive aversion to silver. They would typically detect the Order team well before we found them. Add in modern air combat systems like helicopters and drones, and they simply stand off and vector in air attacks on us. That's when we really dropped the use of silver, the advent of aerial weapon systems killed its usefulness. The Order had to give up using a lot of silver as it kept giving our position away and getting us killed. It was more trouble than it was worth. We can get away with using a small amount of silver in bullets and in specialized traps where the silver is well hidden. Otherwise, it's more of a problem for us than it is for them. The Order has been well and truly down this path time and time again. We've already optimized our combat systems. There are no special weapons modifications that are going to give us a decisive edge."

"Oh," Anton noted. "At best, we can get away with a carefully concealed silver weapon."

Peter nodded.

Anton sat back in his co-pilot's chair. There were no easy fixes for seizing the initiative away from Armitage. He shook his head and asked incredulously, "Why didn't she take the opportunity to destroy us in Maine? She could have done both. She could have abducted Kain and killed the Mirovar force team. This is a critical point. The Mirovar force team being alive suits her goals."

"Clearly, but what's her plan?" Peter asked.

"Precisely, if we knew that, we would know what to do to counter it."

"And there you have it."

Anton stared at Peter for a long moment. "But how do we find that out?"

"It's an age-old question in any war. How do you find out your opponent's plans?"

Anton looked out the windscreen at the runway stretching in front of them. "There has to be a way. I don't accept that she's always going to be ahead of us."

"You and me both."

"Juliette said it's a trap. We can anticipate that and plan for it. How's she going to maximize her advantages?"

"She'll want to shut down our situational awareness and divide us up into smaller groups. Then pick us off one by one." Peter paused. "But, in her case, splitting us up into pairs would be enough."

"She's that good?" Anton asked, "Gang almost killed her."

Peter sighed. "Her skills are legendary. Gang was a rare talent with the sword."

The two young men fell silent for a long moment.

"We used fireworks in the warehouse at the Boston docks to haze the vampires," Anton reminded Peter, his gaze intense. "She'll use darkness."

Peter nodded. "Our nightglasses won't be enough. We'll need portable lights."

"Small ones we can keep hidden, so she doesn't realize we've got them until it's too late."

"We've got flashlights on board, but they will be a little too obvious."

"Do we have time to pick up some portable LEDs?"

"We'll see."

The voice of an air traffic controller came across the comms link. It was time to take off. Peter switched the comms link back to bi-directional, acknowledged the command and pushed the throttle forward.

The pursuit was underway.

"Once I take off and get this ship on auto-pilot, I'll get you to take the first watch, wake me up if anything seems off. I'll grab the spare seat in the cabin. I've got to get some sleep; I'll relieve you in a couple of hours."

"Sure," Anton agreed.

"Hey – don't crash the plane while I'm sleeping."

Anton rolled his eyes. Peter grinned at him and said, "Oh yeah, one last thing." He reached into a document holder and pulled out a booklet. "Read this, its got public data on the details of the latest tech deployed with the UK military. Shadowstone typically uses the same gear as part of blending in with the locals."

Anton took the book. On the cover was a menacing twin-barreled main battle tank called the 'commander.' He put it aside to read later. He focused his attention on assisting Peter with taking off. A minute later the aircraft was off the ground and winging its way toward England.

* * *

Chloe Armitage still trusts my loyalty.

The Raven fitted a U-shaped pillow around their neck and curled up underneath their blanket. Doing their best to get comfortable in the reclined chair. Their mind was on fire, their emotions roiling in fits and starts. Less than six hours before, they'd discovered the Red Empire had allied with Chloe Armitage and Marcus Drake. Shabbah al Ahmar's second agent in North America was Armitage, the right hand of Cornelius Crane, king of the Vampire Dominion. The Raven had flip-flopped between belief, denial, elation, and despair a dozen times since the battle in Maine had revealed the truth. They didn't want to believe it. Surely their father, the Red Ghost, could not have betrayed everything the Red Empire stood for. An alliance with a vampire was anathema and no true follower of the Way could allow such an arrangement to persist. It would have to end and soon, and even then, they could only expiate the stain on their father's honor in one way – through his death.

What had happened to the Red Empire in their absence? Could things have changed so much in a little less than ten years? What of the elite warriors of the 'fist' teams, why hadn't they done something to stay the Red Ghost's hand? Were they all so swayed by his aura of command, to lose sight of the essence of their faith?

The Raven had been little more than a child when they'd left the Red Empire. The question loomed before them. Had they misunderstood the true nature of the Red Empire? Only understanding what a child could understand. Albeit, a clever, talented child, but a child nonetheless. Had they only seen what their instructors allowed them to see?

The Raven shivered beneath their blanket. Finding precious little comfort as they pulled it tighter around themselves. Slowing their breathing, turbulent emotions steadied, ebbing away, evolving into profound loneliness. Wherever they stood, they now stood alone.

They glanced around the dimly lit cabin. The Mirovar force team was now the only real family they knew, but the relationship was one-sided. The Raven knew them, they didn't know the Raven, only the mask the Raven wore. The Raven shuddered beneath their blanket. Their heart sank – there was no hope of acceptance if they revealed who they really were. They'd done too much damage, revealing how to bypass the sensor array to Armitage, and inviting the devastating attack that had destroyed the safe house and taken so many lives.

The Raven resolved to earn their forgiveness, to redeem themselves. They could do it, especially if they managed to thwart Armitage's current plans.

Her trust is the one lever I have that could change everything. I must be watchful; a critical moment will come where she will rely on what I know. It will be at that moment I will be able to betray her to her doom.

The Raven sighed, everything would rest on a single decision, they would have to make it count. With that in mind, they closed their eyes and drifted off to sleep.

Chapter Eighteen

"The mind palace relies on two interlocking factors. The fundamental mind palace discipline, and the use of the implant-laptop-Internet cloud to access massive data. The first is personal training and discipline, and the second is technology. The human-machine interface has a quirk. There is no way you can physically access the raw data and comprehend it as a totality. The technology creates a gestalt experience, essentially a vivid, lucid dream, where the information is presented in metaphorical imagery. A skilled loremaster can guide and interpret the dream to establish an augmented view of reality that approaches precognition." – Juliette Mirovar, loremaster of the Order of Thoth.

"One caveat – without due care, lucid dreams can easily become nightmares beyond your control." – Juliette Mirovar.

* * *

Private airfield, Goathland, Yorkshire, August 22nd, 05:31

Overhead lights gleamed off the sleek body of the Spike 512 supersonic business jet as it rolled to a stop in the middle of the hangar. Within moments, an upright rectangular seam appeared in the white skin behind the cockpit. A door emerged from the body of the aircraft and swung down to the ground with a faint hum. Stairs pushed up from the inner surface of the door.

Chloe Armitage walked through the Spike's open doorway and descended the stairs. She wore her dark-gray combat fatigues from the night before. Before her stood five men. A loose knot of Red Empire assassins, wearing their traditional garb and weapons. A four man 'fist' team led by Tamsah al Ramil, aka the Sand Crocodile. The fifth man, was tall, lean, much older than the others, with sandy-gray hair and dressed in a well-made black suit. He stood at attention next to a dark-blue Rolls Royce.

Behind Chloe, Marcus Drake hustled the struggling form of Ramin Kain from the plane. Kain's head twisted this way and that, hidden beneath a tight-fitting black hood with a single opening over his nose.

Chloe came to a halt before one of the Red Empire assassins. He was the shortest of the four, barely five feet six inches tall, but thick-set, a veritable barrel of muscle and grit.

He looked up at Chloe with a pair of dark brown eyes like flat river stones, and introduced himself, "Ms. Armitage. I am Tamsah al Ramil, you may call me by that name or by Sand Crocodile. My men and I are at your service."

"Please, Mr. Tamsah. Call me, Ma'am."

"Yes, Ma'am."

"Your master's instructions are clear? You are fully aware of our rules of engagement?"

"Yes, Ma'am. We are to serve you unto death, or if you order us to attack each other or the Red Empire – whichever comes first."

"… Indeed," Chloe observed, a slight smile caressing her lips. She looked intently into his eyes. "Are all the preparations made?"

"Yes. We have built the trap you requested."

"And tested?"

"Yes, of course. The Red Empire does not lack advanced engineering skills."

Chloe's left eyebrow arched quizzically. "Of that, I'm sure." She glanced briefly at Kain. "But you will show me while Marcus ensures our guest is properly attended to."

Tamsah al Ramil nodded. "Yes, Ma'am."

"Then let's proceed. Time is short."

Chloe strode to the Rolls. Her driver bowed low and declared, "Ma'am. It is good to see you home again."

"Yes, David, it is good to be home. Now please make haste for there is much to do, and little time to do it."

"As you wish, Ma'am."

Chloe slipped into the rear of the Rolls Royce saloon. Marcus, Kain and the Red Empire assassins went to a pair of Land Rovers. In less than thirty seconds, all three vehicles left the hangar in convoy heading east to Armitage Manor.

* * *

Ramin Kain's heels dragged down a set of stone steps, clunking one after the other all the way to the bottom. He counted twenty steps curving to the right as they descended, clearly a spiral staircase. He sucked in air, there was a faint aroma of sea salt, the ocean must be nearby.

In a moment of clarity, he was thankful Marcus Drake wasn't dragging him feet first into whatever hellhole the vampire was taking him to. The stairs ended, Drake pulled him to his feet, a grip like iron on the back of his neck.

"I'm sick of hauling your carcass around. You can walk from here," Drake declared, his voice heavy with irritation.

Ramin obeyed. Drake could rip his head off faster than he could think about it. The only thing stopping him from doing so was the will of Chloe

Armitage. Ramin had no illusions about bargaining his way out of this mess. His only hope was to stay alive long enough for the Order of Thoth to rescue him. The Walker and Mirovar force teams would try to find him. Within a day or two, the other force teams would mobilize resources. He hadn't lost yet, he still had options. Armitage would question him, that was obvious – he would have to spin it out as much as possible. Keep her thinking there was more to learn, keep giving her a reason to keep him alive.

He stumbled on a bit of rough, ancient flooring. "What the hell!"

"Shut up, and keep moving."

"Do you think someone could build a level floor?"

A fist slammed into his gut, he jack-knifed forward, gasping for breath. Drake dragged him back upright, his heels coming off the floor. "Shut up, I said. Was that not clear enough for you?"

"Uh huh," Ramin grunted.

He staggered forward. Drake helping him along with a ruthless slap here and there to guide him around corners and along corridors. A barely detectable breeze whispered past him – somewhere there was an opening to the outside – and a possible escape path. As bleak as things looked, Ramin had not given up on the idea of escape.

Drake twisted him around and pushed him hard up against a cold stone wall. Something swished through the air and the bonds on his wrists fell away. Drake instantly pushed his right hand up high. A new manacle snapped around his wrist, a chain clinking against the stone. Drake lifted his left hand up and manacled it too. Then Drake locked a third brace tight around his throat with a loud click. The big vampire kicked his right foot back, a fourth manacle snapping tight around his right ankle. A second later, his left ankle was bound with a fifth manacle.

Ramin leaned forward. The chains attached to his throat rattling with him over the rock, jerking his hands back hard. The chains were all attached to each other behind him. If he pushed his face forward, his hands would pull backward, and vice versa.

He ramped hard, testing the strength of the chains, but without success. No matter how hard he struggled, there were no obvious means of escape. The black hood became wet with perspiration, clinging to his face like a mask alive with his growing fear. He took a deep breath, exhaled, sinking back against the cold stone of the wall.

A hand gripped the top of the hood, ripping it off Ramin's head. He blinked owlishly, his eyes adjusting to the bright lights strung along the ceiling. He stood chained to a solid stone wall. The chamber was four yards across and six long. There were two open entrances, one to his left and the other to his right. Drake and Armitage stood behind a waist-high wooden table in the middle of the room. A brown leather satchel and a large white bucket sat on the table.

Armitage reached into the satchel and withdrew a large carving knife. She regarded it skeptically for a moment and remarked to Drake, "This looks a little blunt." She sniffed with disdain. "But I suppose it will have to do."

Ramin's eyes widened; he pushed back hard against the cold stone of the wall. All thoughts of 'toughing it out,' evaporating like snowflakes in the summer sun.

Armitage fished around inside the satchel for a moment, then withdrew a large hypodermic needle and lifted it up to the light, studying it closely. She asked Drake, "Has this been cleaned since we last used it?"

Frowning and shaking his head, Drake sucked air through his teeth. "No, Chloe. I'm pretty sure it hasn't."

Ramin shivered.

Armitage sighed, raising an eyebrow. "Do we have any tourniquets?"

"Sorry – it's another mess."

"Really Marcus?"

"I've been rushed," Drake offered, shaking his head. "It's been the very devil lately to keep up with events."

Armitage stroked his cheek lovingly. Leaning up, she kissed him. "It's alright my dear. We'll make do with what we have."

Armitage and Drake dropped their embrace, turning to stare at Ramin, their eyes flashing, their grins sporting long fangs.

Ramin wondered what had gone wrong. The last twenty years had proceeded smoothly, beginning with the assassination of George Madison, the previous Head of the Order of Thoth, and his lover Mary Creeley. The framing and exiling of his chief rival, Arthur Slayne, had ensured his rise to the Head of the Order. For nearly twenty years, he'd subverted the leadership of the traditionalists and promoted men loyal to his cause. Establishing a secret detente with Cornelius Crane had been the last step in his master plan.

The goal was the transformation of the Order of Thoth into an efficient fighting force under his unquestioned rule. With most of the old traditions thrown into the bin of history where they belonged, he could wield the force teams as their sole commander-in-chief. The force leaders would be his trusted lieutenants. Then he could use the detente with the vampires to draw their forces into a deadly trap and victory would be his.

His plan was the fruit of genius and deserved to succeed. It would have succeeded if it hadn't been for the insane arrival of Anton Slayne. A plague on his damned family. He had to see the Slayne family line stopped, and extinguished to the last leaf on the last branch. If he ever managed to get out of this mess, he would see to it personally.

Anton Slayne gripped his imagination. An insolent, head-strong boy; no match for a man of his genius, and yet, Slayne was walking free somewhere while Ramin languished in a vampire's dungeon.

A deep sense of injustice boiled within his soul. Incredulous rage ripped through him, making him bold. Ramin stood tall and called out, "Do your worst Armitage. Once Crane finds out that you haven't kept me safe, you're done for."

Armitage laughed briefly. Blurring forward, she halted six inches in front of his face.

There was a slight pressure in his groin. He glanced down, the carving knife was in the crease of his thigh, pressing his trousers against his skin.

Armitage arched a quizzical eyebrow and asked, "Shall I cut left, or right? Shall it be a quick death, or shall I make you into a … what was the word you used?" her eyes sparkled with delight. "A girly."

Oh my God! She remembered that.

Ramin's testicles attempted to retreat into his body cavity. His anger vanishing, replaced with frigid tentacles of terror writhing in his gut. He pushed back hard against the stone wall and gasped out, "You will pay for this."

Armitage stepped back for a moment, twirling the knife in a circle with her right hand. "I don't know what it is, everyone keeps saying 'you will pay,' and yet, it never happens."

The knifed flashed in the overhead lights; the blade slicing through the skin and muscle an inch below the inner crease of his right thigh. Ramin gasped in shock, it all seemed so unreal. A part of his mind had never admitted this could actually be happening; not to him, not to Ramin Kain, not to the smartest man in the room. Not to the one who always managed to get away with everything. The sight of his own blood spraying onto the flagstones of the floor and the ravenous fingers of pain radiating up from his groin destroyed any remaining doubts.

Armitage flashed away. Drake rushed forward with the white bucket. He placed it underneath the wound, catching Ramin's blood as it rushed through his severed femoral artery.

Perspiration slicked Ramin's forehead, a bead of sweat rolling into his left eye. His heart raced. He gasped for air, his life draining away with every beat of his heart.

Armitage scrunched back the left sleeve of her dark-gray combat fatigues, exposing the fair skin of her arm. She picked up the syringe, pressing the needle against the vein in the crook of her elbow. She applied more pressure and broke the skin. Drawing back on the plunger, the syringe filled with her blood.

She stared at Ramin; her eyes filled with intent. She was not playing with him anymore – the real game was about to begin.

476

Ramin's skin paled with blood loss. His heart began to struggle to find blood to move through his veins. His breathing was almost useless. Armitage appeared in front of him, the needle of the syringe plunging between his ribs into the left ventricle of his heart.

It was like pouring nitrous oxide into a hard-revving V-8 engine. His heart surged. Armitage's blood began spreading throughout his body. A ravishing fire sweeping through him, burning away all vestiges of his humanity. Transforming him into an apex predator, a creature of the night, a vampire.

Reality strobed, flashing in and out, bounded with utter darkness and searing light. The agony of the transformation went beyond sensation – becoming unutterable – beyond words and forms, shattering all distinctions, and rendering Ramin mute. Time disappeared, his mind fled, but there was nowhere to run to. There was only the experience of boundless suffering. A thing unto itself, overwhelming his reality and throwing down the walls of his sanity.

Ramin drooled, his lips trembling, mouthing words he couldn't utter. His body vibrated. The chains binding him rattled and scraped across the cold stone.

The agony peaked, then evaporated away. Ramin sucked in a great breath and released it all at once. The transformation was complete.

Hard light lit the room, the angles sharp and clear. Down a corridor to the right, a noisy mouse scurried along the base of a wall. Its musky scent indicating it was moving into a fertile cycle. Waves were slowing breaking against the stony beach far to his left. The salty aroma of the sea was everywhere. Above him human voices talked in the Manor house – every word was crystal clear. Armitage stood in front of him, poised, immaculate, filled with dreadful purpose. Drake loomed beside her, relaxed, alert, and deadly.

The smell assaulted him like a hard slap in the face. His own blood, in a bucket near his feet. He lunged for it, blurring forward, the chains snapping taut dragging his hands back. Drool splashed from his mouth; he grinned a harsh joyless grin of ultimate effort. His tongue flicked desperately over his lips, his gaze focusing hard on the bucket. His nostrils flared, the need flooding through him was equally exquisite and horrible. A cavernous desire, an overwhelming force demanding immediate action.

"I must feed!" he shouted, staring ravenously at the bucket of blood. "Feed me. Give it to me. I must have it."

Armitage dipped a handkerchief into the blood, wetting one corner. She placed it an inch in front of Ramin's face. He strained to reach it. She moved it closer, a drop trembling on the corner of the cloth.

Ramin strained, the drop of blood fell onto his outstretched tongue.

Ambrosia! Nectar of the gods! His eyes fell shut for a brief moment as he savored his first taste of blood as a vampire.

Ramin swallowed, but there was almost nothing there. The thirst for blood, the ravenous hunger returned, now doubled in strength for he'd tasted its release. He wanted to tear at his face with frustration, but his manacled hands couldn't reach. He stared at the still damp cloth in Armitage's right hand, and at the bucket of blood behind her.

He panted, reflexively straining against the manacles and chains, but to no avail – they were beyond his new vampire strength to break.

Armitage leaned forward slightly and declared with avid interest, "Now we're ready to begin the interrogation. Tell me, how does the Order haze the Panopticon feeds when conducting operations?"

Ramin stared at her in helpless desperation.

She waved the bloody cloth before his nose.

He started talking.

* * *

Richard Walker, the force leader for the United Kingdom arm of the Order of Thoth, scanned the private-airfield hangars with high-powered binoculars. He descended into silence, activating a partial ramp to become perfectly still.

Joan Lewis, the Walker force team loremaster sat on a fold-away stool next to her commander. Her laptop was open, and her implant lay warm in her forearm. She studied the private airfield and waited for Walker's directions.

There were two hangars. A larger one, its doors shut, and a smaller one that had recently accepted an Embraer Legacy 500 business jet. A jet chartered out of Logan International airport by one Ramin Kain, a New York City businessman, or so stated its public flight plan.

A single, dark-blue Rolls Royce left the open hangar. Driving sedately through the private airfield's main gate, it turned onto the main road heading toward the town of Whitby. The driver, dressed in a dapper black suit with sandy-gray hair was the only occupant.

"No sign of Ramin. Where's the GPS signal?" Walker asked in a gravelly voice.

"Within the Rolls," Joan replied. "Just as Juliette said, the Embraer is a decoy. Armitage's jet will be in the other hangar."

Walker lowered the binoculars, put his hands on the well-maintained wire fence surrounding the airfield and asserted confidently, "We can't trust everything the Mirovar force team says. They've been compromised."

"My own analysis concurs with Juliette's."

Walker scowled. "You're both coming from the same information. You have the same blind spots."

"I know the mind palace is not perfect. I take that into account."

"Still," he remarked, "we'll send in Wilkinson and check the hangars before we follow the car."

Joan glanced down at her laptop. The Rolls Royce was continuing to Whitby. The small town on the coast of Yorkshire was its most likely destination.

"Don't worry," Walker directed. "You can haze the cameras along our route. Wilkinson will be in and out in five minutes, and then we'll follow the car." He turned away from the fence and strode purposefully toward a pair of dark-gray, late model Range Rovers occupied by the rest of his team.

Joan snapped her laptop shut, flicked a stray strand of dark-red hair out of her eyes and followed after him. Her lips thinned, frowning, she tried to reconcile her force leader's words with the honesty and trust she'd felt in Juliette's mind over the implant link.

There was no betrayal or falsehood in Juliette Mirovar. Whatever Walker believed about the Mirovar force team, it didn't extend to their loremaster.

Reaching the front Range Rover, she paused at the door, glancing down the road to Whitby. The second most famous vampire alive was somewhere down there waiting for the Order to arrive. They would be following a GPS signal provided by Armitage in an attempt to rescue Ramin Kain. At twenty-three years old, Joan was the youngest of the loremasters and had only recently joined the Walker force team after their previous loremaster committed suicide.

She hesitated at the car door, her every sense taut. The gray sky lowered oppressively, shadowing the road with threat. Her mind palace hung like a web behind her eyes, ready to activate at a moment's notice. But no awareness, examination, or predictive foreknowledge could shift the dread pooling within her. At the end of the road waited the most dangerous foe she'd ever encountered.

She shivered, blinked and got into the car.

Walker rubbed a hand over his close-cropped gray hair and asked, "Are you okay?"

"Yes," Joan lied; she knew her force leader was in no mood to hear anything else. *I'm not okay. Not okay at all. We don't know enough to be sure of what is going on here. There are too many unknowns. Too many open questions and the answers could kill us all.*

"Good," Walker noted. "The last thing I need is another loremaster cracking up on me."

Joan looked out the car window, cold fingers of fear working their way around her soul. She clenched her fists and hoped she would be strong enough to deal with whatever may come.

* * *

Tamsah al Ramil and his fist team had been at Armitage manor for just on six days.

It was a very short timeframe for implementing the trap in the dungeon underneath the manor and running an isolated network of cameras along the road from the airfield. They'd worked feverishly, like men possessed, in accordance with the plans and requirements provided by James Haley. The camera network was brand new and disconnected from the Panopticon. Whatever technique the Order was using to haze the feeds to the Panopticon would be unable to impact his dedicated camera network.

He sat alone in a pleasantly appointed drawing room near the main entrance of the manor, a small water-cooled server rack whirring softly away in the corner. His laptop fed a pair of twenty-four-inch screens sitting on a table in front of him. A window on the right screen switched from camera to camera, tracking two dark-gray Range Rovers heading from the airfield to the Manor house. If they kept coming, they would arrive in about fifteen minutes. Order operatives packed the vehicles. He counted nine of them and suspected the eldest was Richard Walker, the elusive head of the UK force team.

He stroked the closely-cropped dark beard on his chin, his gaze flicking over the other windows on his screens. There was a multitude of camera feeds including an aerial view from a small drone shaped like a peregrine falcon flying a thousand yards above the manor. A map of the immediate vicinity of the manor showed where his men were. Three small red circles indicating the locations of his own team members. They were all men who had grown up in the Red Empire, their loyalty beyond question.

All the members of his team had passed the first level of the test of the Olgoi Khorkhoi. An initiation that demonstrated survival capabilities and raised them above the common ranks of the Red Empire. A second fist team, accompanied by a group of young recruits and led by Nasr al Dam had deployed on a mission to the United States. He shook his head slowly, the recruits had barely completed their ramp mastery training, to send an inexperienced force suggested they were expendable and expected not to survive.

His team was the more capable of the two fist teams sent by the Red Ghost, more experienced, more highly trained, more exposed to combat. He trusted that whatever happened to Nasr al Dam's mission, his own team would fare far better.

Tamsah al Ramil had earned his name, 'the Sand Crocodile,' from the Red Ghost himself after passing the second level test of the Olgoi Khorkhoi. His reward had been leadership of an elite fist team. If he survived, and the Red Ghost released him from this mission he would commit to the training necessary to submit for the third and final level test of the Olgoi Khorkhoi. Surviving the final test would raise him to the level of a prince of the Red Empire, second only to the Red Ghost, and equal to the likes of Taipan.

Shabbah al Ahmar had personally selected him for this mission. It was a great honor, and of course, he'd accepted. The orders of the Red Ghost were as law. There was no option to decline, and success would bring great honor to his name. Shabbah al Ahmar had instructed the Blood Eagle and himself on what to expect. The arrangement with the vampire general Chloe Armitage was an elaborate ruse. A game of advantage that would see the Order of Thoth and the Vampire Dominion both diminished and the vampire king, Cornelius Crane destroyed.

The Red Ghost valued the mission highly enough to release for use the most advanced and secret technology the Red Empire possessed. Tamsah frowned, he was uncomfortable with exposing the capabilities of *Gossamer*, especially to the vampires.

Such thoughts bordered on insubordination and were inappropriate for a Red Empire assassin, especially one who had passed into the second rank.

Questioning your superiors was not a normal practice for a loyal warrior of the Red Empire. The Sand Crocodile considered himself to be exemplary in his loyalty, and yet, he found himself harboring doubts. He'd assessed Chloe Armitage on meeting her. She was clearly the most capable and deadly vampire he'd ever encountered, and he wondered if the Red Ghost may have underestimated her.

Underestimating your opponent was not something the Sand Crocodile was vulnerable to. Growing up shorter than most had led others to underestimate him, he understood it as a weakness that others could easily fall into. He vowed to himself to be wary of Ms. Chloe Armitage, general of the Vampire Dominion. She was a dangerous force beyond all reckoning, and he would maintain an escape path for his team in case she betrayed the terms of their engagement.

The two Range Rovers took a critical turn-off, there could be no mistake as to their objective. Tamsah al Ramil tapped his in-ear communicator and reported, "Ma'am. The UK Order team is heading toward the manor."

There was a lengthy pause, then Chloe Armitage commanded, "Hold your positions and observe. Expect them to stage their main force nearby and send in a two-man team to scout the manor house and the dungeons underneath. Guide the local staff to the upper floor and allow the Order scouts to come into the lower levels. I will deal with them there. If they do anything else, then call me immediately."

"Yes, Ma'am, it will be done."

"Excellent," she finished with, the line muting automatically.

Tamsah al Ramil sighed and went to work, issuing orders to his men. He put doubts about the mission aside, there was work to do and honor to win.

What more could a man ask for than that?

* * *

Frowning, Chloe Armitage muted her ear-piece and stepped back from Ramin Kain.

The UK force team were proving to be overly efficient. She glanced at a clock she'd positioned on the table, it was 08:35. She stared into empty space for a long moment. How best to deal with a second Order force team? If she played today to the best of her ability, she could deliver a victory over the Order to Crane, hide what she was doing with Kain and drive Anton Slayne into a fury of vengeance aimed at her king.

Outcomes, she considered well worth taking calculated risks for.

Kain struggled fruitlessly against his chains. They rattled and scraped, he leered at the bucket of congealing blood on the floor a yard in front of him. His left eye twitched, his tongue darting between his lips, his new fangs gleaming in the lamplight.

Chloe stood still, silently contemplating her options. She relaxed, a smile growing on her face. Picking up a blood-stained mug from the table, she dipped it into the bucket and lifted it to Kain's open mouth. The half-congealed blood slid thickly out of the mug. Slurping loudly, Kain tried to drink it all at once.

"Marcus, could you please call the staff upstairs and get them to deliver a couple of good-sized towels and a large bucket of fresh water to the first level."

Marcus nodded and vanished.

Chloe dipped the mug back into the bucket. Filling it to the brim, she fed it all to Kain.

"More," Kain whispered.

"No."

"More," Kain pleaded.

"No."

"More!" Kain shouted.

Chloe's open hand flashed out, a resounding crack echoing off the walls. Kain's left cheekbone shattered, his head almost spinning off his shoulders. "Enough!" she commanded, leaning in close to Kain's face.

Kain panted, blood dribbling from his open mouth. His cheek swelled into a deep purple bruise, which immediately began to fade as it healed.

"I have a deal for you," Chloe offered, arching an eyebrow.

Kain stared at her for a moment, his mouth still healing and said thickly past swollen lips, "You won't keep me alive. Crane would punish you for turning me."

"There are lots of things Crane doesn't know. You can be one of them."

"How could you hide me?"

"Oh – I can hide you. Have no doubts about that."

"I can't trust you."

Chloe sniffed disdainfully. "Are you still deluding yourself that the Order will save you."

Kain stared at her.

Chloe moved in close and whispered harshly into his face, "What hope do you have? The Order will kill you without hesitation. Your only hope of survival lies with me."

Kain hesitated. His eyes flicking down to the blood-filled bucket and back up to Chloe's face. Pride warred with fear on his face. Then something snapped within, his face fell, resignation filling his voice as he asked, "What do you want?"

"It's very simple. When the UK Order team come into the manor, start calling for help."

Kain's gaze lifted from the bucket. "Is that all?"

"Yes," Chloe smiled, her eyes dancing.

Kain murmured defeatedly, "Right. Got it."

Marcus blurred into the room, coming to a halt next to Chloe. He had a pair of soft, white bath towels and a bucket of fresh water.

"Clean him up," Chloe directed, picking up the bucket of Kain's blood and moving to stand next to the exit back to the manor house.

Marcus set to work, Kain looked longingly at the bucket as Chloe carried it away. In moments, he was clean of blood. Marcus turned and sloshed the remaining water across the floor, disappearing any blood splashes.

"Now remember," Chloe said, "the Order are trained killers who will cut your heart out as soon as they understand what you are. Marcus and I will be nearby, we will make sure they don't hurt you, but you must first call out for help and draw them to you."

"I'm bait?" Kain asked.

Chloe's face crinkled into a smirk, her answer hanging in the silence between them.

Kain nodded once, water dripping from his soaking clothes to the floor. "Yes, yes, I'll do it."

Chloe and Marcus turned away, walking into the corridor. Chloe put a finger to her lips and mouthed, *quiet.* She grabbed Marcus' arm, taking him down a side corridor away from the spiral staircase to the upper level of the dungeon.

We have to hide, she mouthed silently, pointing to the solid wall at the end of the corridor. She took a remote control from a thigh pocket on her dark-gray combat fatigues and pressed a stud. The lights in the side corridors dimmed to almost nothing, except for Kain's prison chamber and the main corridors.

They vanished into the shadows.

* * *

Someone was shaking Anton's shoulder.

He woke up, opening his eyes wide. Chiara was leaning over him, her brown eyes luminous in the half-light of the Embraer's cabin.

"Time to get up big guy. We have to do strategy," she said. "C'mon you need to be involved."

"Sure," Anton replied, throwing back his blanket. "How long before we land?"

"Ninety minutes. 11:30 local time."

Anton sat up, facing forward from the back of the cabin. Francis Mirovar stood in the middle of the aisle facing most of the team. Peter sat alone in the cockpit, leaning to the side, listening in – the plane flying itself on auto-pilot.

Juliette sat next to Francis, having swiveled her chair one hundred and eighty degrees. She faced the team with her hands in her lap and a serene expression on her face.

Francis declared, "We have made contact with the Walker force team. They have stationed off a manor house just outside the town of Whitby in Yorkshire. We will be landing at," he lifted his eyebrows to emphasize the next words, "a private airfield about ten miles west of Whitby." He paused, looking at the team. "Walker confirmed there was a supersonic Spike 512 business jet at the airfield. It looks like Armitage owns or at least operates this specific 'private airfield.'"

A low murmur swept through the cabin.

"The Order will provide local transport. We will join the Walker force team and prepare for a joint assault on the manor house."

"What's the disposition of opposing forces?" Jay inquired.

"How can we be sure Kain is even in there?" Anton asked, frowning.

Luther snapped, "The GPS signal."

"C'mon," Anton asserted, "The GPS signal could be faked."

Francis declared, "The GPS signal is real, and Richard Walker is verifying the status of Ramin Kain, we'll soon know if he is alive or dead … or worse." He glanced at Jay. "They haven't encountered any hostile forces yet. They're sending in drones to scout the site."

"Drones. That's good," Jay observed.

"We will soon have confirmation that the GPS signal is associated or not with Ramin Kain, and who or what guards the manor house."

"We'll know if Ramin is alive and what we're facing," Juliette stated. "We're not going into this blind." She stared down the aisle at Luther. "We know this is a trap. The trick will be to steal the cheese without springing it."

Luther grimaced sourly.

Anton spread his hands wide and asked, "What if Chloe Armitage is just waiting for two Order force teams to show up, and simply blows up the place with a fuel-air explosive?"

Juliette locked eyes with him. "That's not her plan. She's playing a subtler game."

The knowledge implicit in Juliette's gaze sent a cold shiver up Anton's spine. He gasped out, "How do you know?"

Juliette stared at him for a moment, a glimmer of fear passing behind her eyes. She shook her head once and remained silent.

Juliette's concern washed off Anton. The lash of fear fled before a thrill of anticipation. He wondered if today would be the day he would confront Chloe Armitage with her villainy and extract vengeance for her crimes against his family.

It was about time; he was sick of waiting.

* * *

The shotgun blast rang out, the aerial drone fragmenting into a haze of metal and plastic.

"Damn! They took out our last drone," Mary Turner swore, adjusting her Order nightglasses. She sat with her back against a tree, across from the manor house resting atop a cliff on the Yorkshire coast. The nightglasses networked with mini-cameras on the drones, providing her with first-hand visuals of whatever they encountered – while they'd lasted.

"Maps? How far in did you get?" Richard Walker demanded. He glared in annoyance as his second netmaster worked feverishly over her laptop.

"Not far enough. Our second flier got about forty yards into a large open space leading from the cliff face over the ocean. Add that to the ground drones we got to the front door, and we still have a lot of unexplored territory under the building. There's a couple of levels of cellars, dungeons or something else down there."

"How many humans did you count in the floors above ground before we lost our first flier?"

"Ten. Four on the ground floor, and six on the upper floor."

"Anyone running cold? Any sub-37? Any vampires?"

"None. But they could be far enough below ground to be out of reach of our drone's sensors."

There had been rumors the Red Empire had allied with the Vampire Dominion to wipe out the safe house in Maine. Calvin Woodstock had phoned him in the middle of the night to tell him the dreadful news of Ramin Kain's abduction and the Mirovar force team's inability to prevent it.

"Joan," Richard called out to his loremaster. "Analysis?"

Joan Lewis blinked, her eyelids fluttering for a handful of seconds. Dropping out of her mind palace, she said, "Any skilled shooters could be destroying our drones. There is no direct evidence of Red Empire presence here, but—"

"Good," Richard interrupted her, putting his hand up.

With all the drones destroyed, the only option remaining was to send in a squad, he called out to his best pair of warriors, "Frannie, Mikey, load up on silver, it's time to go in and verify the target."

"Yes, Sir," they chorused together. They donned Order nightglasses, picked up their weapons and blurred away. They would be going in hot and fast, relying on the Ramp's heightened senses and reflexes to keep themselves safe. Their nightglasses were equally effective in daylight or darkness and would transmit what they saw or heard back to the Order force team.

Richard stepped away from his loremaster and stared at the imposing manor house. He was confident he would soon know precisely where Ramin Kain was, and whether he was alive or dead. His lead combat team may even be able to extract Kain without risking the rest of the team.

He smiled broadly; it was a good day to fight vampires.

* * *

Joan Lewis moved over and sat down next to Mary Turner.

She fitted her nightglasses. The feeds from Francine and Michael would form images in front of her eyes. She stilled her mind and prepared to enter her mind palace with her eyes open. It was a difficult state to be in, drawing information from the external world and feeding it directly into her mind palace to generate inferences about what was happening. It was the best way she could help her teammates survive whatever was beneath the manor.

She wanted to do her best; especially if there was a weird alliance of the Red Empire with the vampires.

* * *

Francine Parker, Frannie to her friends, paused for a moment at the bottom of the spiral staircase. Her Order nightglasses, adjusting automatically to the improved light in the corridor of the second level of the dungeon beneath the manor.

She half crouched, sighting along the barrel of her FN P90. Fluorescent lamps bolted onto the stone ceiling a dozen feet overhead lit the corridor in front of her. Twenty feet in front of her the corridor branched to the left and right. Another thirty feet past the intersection, the corridor opened up into a well-lit room.

"Help! Help!" Ramin called from within the room.

He was somewhere in there, out of sight from where Frannie stood. She recognized his voice, it sounded real, like he was alive, but it could be a clever, high-quality recording. She needed to be sure before Michael Wilson, and she could take further action.

Frannie took a step forward, Mikey moving silently into the space behind her. His head swiveled, taking in everything else around them. Frannie would cover their front, and he would cover her back. They'd worked together as a team within a team for years; their combat awareness with each other honed to a fine edge.

She held up her right fist, Mikey halted. With two fingers, she indicated left and right. They would clear the corridors before they advanced into the room. Ramin called out again, his voice filled with desperation. Frannie ignored him for now. There was no way she was going to lead them blindly into a room, not for anyone, she was too experienced an operator for that.

Frannie sank into silence, accelerating her perception of time, and heightening every sense. Dust motes floated lazily in the pale light. The edges of the flagstones stood out in razor sharp relief. Waves crashed against distant rocks, and nearby chains rattled and scraped across stone. She scanned the floor, looking for tripwires, or a sensor lattice. The floor was clean, her nightglasses and enhanced vision picking up nothing but worked stone and ancient ant trails.

She blurred forward to the edge of the intersection, Mikey a step behind. The two side corridors were unlit. The whole site stank of 'trap,' the hairs on the back of her neck quivering in response. They'd almost reached Ramin, whatever was going to happen would happen soon.

There had been no sign of the shooters who had taken out the drones. All the people in the house had fled upstairs as they came in through a side door into a ground floor kitchen. The way into the basement level had been open, and Ramin's calls for help had been easy to follow. They'd cut through the first underground level in a couple of minutes, mapping the pathway through a maze of intersecting corridors and rooms for anyone else to follow. Their nightglasses recorded their steps, transmitting the information back to the team's netmasters.

Joan's voice whispered in their ears, sounding ghost-like through their ear-bud communication links, as she muttered from within her mind palace, "They're hiding, they're hiding in the walls."

Despite years of combat experience, the words sent shivers rippling over Frannie's skin. Her fingers found a stud on her FN P90. A flashlight slung underneath the barrel switched on, sending a beam of focused light down the left corridor. Mikey, facing in the opposite direction, immediately followed suit, illuminating the opposite corridor.

They moved their beams of light carefully over the nooks and crannies of the corridors – nobody was there. The corridor on her side ended in a stone wall forty feet away. There was nothing but featureless walls carved into the rock and a flagstone floor.

She glanced at her partner.

He shook his head.

Well, Frannie thought, *loremasters aren't perfect, sometimes they get it wrong.*

She signaled 'forward' with her right hand, moving across the intersection into the corridor heading toward Ramin's prison. Mikey followed, his eyes tracking left, right and behind them. Frannie reached the threshold, crouching down next to the right side of the entrance. Ramin Kain, his eye's wild, stood chained to the far-left wall. He was dripping wet, water pooling in the gaps between the flagstones at his feet. Opposite him stood a table on which sat a brown leather satchel bag, a clock, and a blood-slicked knife.

Ramin's face twisted with rage and desire, he screamed, "You took too long!"

At the corner of her left eye, a shadow moved across the floor. Twisting around, she darted to the left toward her target. Mikey was already blurring in the opposite direction, his own FN P90 coming up. Frannie hit her trigger, her FN P90 exploded into life, a stream of silver rounds raking the ceiling.

The lights went out, pitching the dungeon into utter darkness.

Afterimages faded in her nightglasses. The crimson outlines of two vampires scrambling like flying shadows along the ceiling. Diverging violently to the left and right as the silver rounds ricocheted off the stone between them. Her left hand ripped the submachine gun toward the nearest target, her right flashing to her shoulder where the handle of her katana jutted up.

She drew her sword free, her gun barking, the shots cracking along the corridor. She fell deeply into silence, the Ramp flowering within her.

It was time to fight.

* * *

Nothing beats vampire vision in the depths of the dark.

The Ramp masters blurred to the left and right, streams of submachine gun fire lancing up at Chloe and Marcus.

Chloe twisted hard right, letting go of the ceiling, dropping to the floor in front of the male.

He drew his katana from over his left shoulder in a sweeping vertical arc. His FN P90 flamed as he sprayed a second burst of 9mm silver bullets at Chloe's chest. The flash of each round leaving the barrel strobing along the corridor, the stone walls stuttering in the fragmented light.

Chloe leaned backward, almost becoming an upside down 'U' as her head dipped back toward the floor. Her left hand brushed the flagstones, her right hand bringing her sword over her in an arc. The bullets streamed above her, a stray one ricocheting off the immaculate blade of the Red Dragon, instantly fragmenting into a cloud of burning silvery dust.

There was no time to evade. Chloe shut her eyes and held her breath. Rebounding off the floor, she passed through the thin edges of the silver mist. The Red Dragon's arc completed, lancing forward toward her opponent.

Numbness bloomed across her skin.

Her blade beat past the Ramp master's katana, slashing through the center of his face, its blood-soaked tip emerging from the back of his head. His eyes bulged, his mouth gaped, he quivered for a moment. She drew her sword back with a wet swish, and he dropped to the floor like a stringless puppet.

Chloe staggered back to the nearest wall.

The woman blurred backward into the room letting rip again with her FN P90, the silver bullets spraying down the corridor in a disciplined 'S' pattern, while her katana lifted into guard position.

Chloe dropped to the floor, the bullets skittering off the stone wall above her head.

Marcus launched himself from the top of the wall, flying through the shadows above the stream of bullets. Landing beside the woman, his big hands grasped her head.

She started to scream, her katana blurring around in her hand.

His hands flicked left and right.

There was a sickening crack, she went limp, her submachine gun clattering to the floor. Marcus dropped her, and she fell in a heap over her smoking gun.

Marcus grunted, staggering backward. The woman's katana jutted from his right side where it pierced his body beneath his ribs. He dragged the blade clear, dropping it onto the floor. Blurring back to Chloe's side, he ignored his wound and bent to lift her from the floor. She leaned on his arm as he helped her back to her feet.

"Nu-u-mb," she muttered, shaking her head slowly.

"You, OK?" Marcus asked, his voice filled with concern.

"Ge-ar, kill … the … gear."

Marcus left her propped against the wall, where she wobbled on unsteady legs. The touch of silver had been fleeting, a minimal dose, but made worse by the bullet transforming into a hot aerosol after colliding with the much harder meteoric iron of the Red Dragon.

Marcus reached down, picked up the man's nightglasses and ear-buds, crushing them into powder with his hands. He did the same with the equipment worn by the woman.

Chloe touched a remote at her waist, and the fluorescent lamps flickered back on.

She took a step, standing straighter, the effect of the silver ebbing away. "Now … they've … proof of life."

Kain wrinkled his nose and stated with utter disgust, "God that stinks."

Marcus glanced at him, snarled and said, "Silver! Welcome to our world."

Chloe shook herself, took a couple of deep breaths and flicked the Red Dragon clean with a flourish. She strode forward, stood in front of Kain and declared, "Now that little interruption is over, let's continue. Please tell me more about the network of Order safe houses."

Kain grinned lopsidedly and said, "Sure, sure, I'll tell you everything."

"Marcus," Chloe directed, "fetch the blood bucket." She indicated the two dead Order operatives with a casual wave. "Refresh it with one of these two bodies; we have work to do."

Marcus blurred away.

Kain continued explaining everything he knew about the Order safe houses.

* * *

Everyone in the cabin of the Embraer jet watched Juliette Mirovar as she communed with the other loremasters. The implant on the inside of her right forearm linked wirelessly through the laptop on her thighs. A network of satellites transmitted the signal via an encrypted quantum cloud, enabling direct mind to mind communication with her peers.

Juliette started suddenly, then blurted out, "Two of our people just died."

Francis frowned, shocked. "Who?"

"Wait. Joan is sharing now," Juliette advised, her eyelids closing, her eyes vibrating beneath them as if she was dreaming. She sat still for a few seconds, then abruptly stood up. "Michael Wilson and Francine Parker are dead. Vampires, most likely Chloe Armitage and Marcus Drake killed them."

Anton's eyes tightened with sharp intent, he asked, "The manor house is hers?"

"Is Ramin Kain alive? Is he safe?" Samuel Luther asked urgently.

Juliette glanced at Luther first and answered, "He's alive, chained in a dungeon." She turned to Anton. "Yes, most likely the manor house is something to do with Armitage. Perhaps her original home. It's a place she knows well."

"Home territory," Li said grimly. "A powerful advantage for her."

Juliette shook her head. "Richard Walker is enraged; he wasn't expecting this."

"He should have been," Anton chimed in. "He's a force leader, he should know better."

"Who are you to judge?" Luther snapped. "You're a novice, you know nothing of the world."

Anton took a breath, reminding himself not to rise to the bait. Li's response after the battle at the safe house had cut him deeply. He vowed to himself to remain mindful and focused on the mission. Ignoring Luther, Anton asserted, "Li is right. Armitage has the home ground advantage. She probably expected the Walker team to send in two people and just waited for them to show up. Now we know precisely what she wants us to know and nothing more than that."

Luther snapped incredulously, "You can't know—"

"Enough Luther," Francis declared. "Anton has made a good point."

Juliette nodded. "We know it's a trap and so far, nothing has happened to change our evaluation of the situation."

"It's hers. I'm right on this." Anton asserted, a grim smile crossing his face.

"All I've got on the manor house is that it's important to her," Juliette answered. "There is nothing tying it to her."

"All her tracks have been wiped clean," Anton declared. "She's been playing this game for decades."

"How do you know?" Jay asked.

Anton looked directly at Jay and replied, "We've been underestimating her every step of the way."

"You're just speculating Slayne, you know nothing," Luther declared, frowning, his voice rough with emotion.

Francis stood up from his seat, taking a position at the end of the aisle facing everyone in the cabin. "A high price has been paid," he declared to the team. "But the Walker force team has mapped the target environment, and we have absolute confidence Chloe Armitage, and Marcus Drake are in the manor. We may be able to rescue Ramin Kain and deliver a defeat to the Vampire Dominion at the same time."

"About time," Luther snapped bitterly.

Francis stared at Luther until Luther looked away. He looked approvingly at Anton and said, "Well done Anton, you've made an astute observation. While we don't know how long Armitage has been working on her current plans, it is clear she is prepared for our arrival." He glanced knowingly back at Luther. "Only a fool would think otherwise."

Luther sucked air through his teeth.

"Despite these losses, our plans stand. We will land at Goathland, join forces with the Walker force team and make a combined assault. Any questions?"

There was a long moment of silence.

"Very good. Do what you can to prepare, today we go to battle against a general of the Vampire Dominion."

Anton glanced at Li. She lifted an eyebrow, a slight smile curving the edges of her mouth, her eyes alight with anticipation. With the combined might of two Order of Thoth force teams behind them, trap or not, now was the opportunity to deliver justice for their lost loved ones.

Anton looked away from Li, his gaze going up to the ceiling. His fists clenched, a wild emotion surging through him. His soul flowed with it, a boat on a heaving sea of wrath.

He took a deep breath, letting it out with a sigh. The rage ebbed but did not go away.

He wondered if he would ever be truly free of it.

* * *

Gordon Heathmont's laptop gave a specific ping. He'd received an email from James Haley, the head of the US arm of Shadowstone.

While nominally at the same level within the worldwide Shadowstone organization, as the head of the founding United Kingdom arm of the service, Gordon saw himself as the more senior of the two men. Crane had created the UK arm of Shadowstone in the late 1880s, almost a full forty years before the establishment of the more junior service in the United

States. If Gordon were able to have his way, the UK arm would subordinate the US arm. Certainly, he would not have led sixty plus men to their deaths in an Order of Thoth slaughterhouse.

The UK organization was too experienced and too careful to fall into such a trap. The gung-ho mentality the yanks had been born with had never infected the UK organization. The UK arm was old school, there was no way such a disaster would occur on his watch.

He clicked the email, a counter in the upper right-hand corner of the email started counting down from sixty to fifty-nine to fifty-eight. The email was self-obliterating with a sixty-second time limit once opened. In sixty seconds, the email and every track it had made from its origin point to Gordon's laptop would vanish. It would be as if the email had never existed. Haley was ensuring no one else, not even the Panopticon, would be aware he'd sent the email and that Gordon had opened it.

Gordon read the email, his eyes widening. He studied the attached photograph, committing it to memory. A young man, hooded, medium-tall, athletic, getting onto an Embraer Legacy 500 business jet. Anton Smith, a member of the Order of Thoth directly implicated in the battle on the Boston docks. He jotted down the aircraft's identification numbers, noting the flight plan had changed from London to a private airfield in Goathland.

The counter hit zero, and the email disappeared from his screen.

There was no way the Embraer was landing anywhere near Goathland. He lifted the phone and dialed RAF Command. Interceptors would be taking off in another five minutes.

There was no time to waste, he must organize a suitable welcome for Anton Smith. He would be waiting to see a member of the Order of Thoth taken into custody. He flipped his laptop closed, packing it into a protective travel case. He stood up from his desk, stepping around it to a nearby coat rack. Picking a long dark-gray coat, he put it over the beautifully crafted bespoke dark-blue suit gracing his slim frame.

Grabbing his laptop case, he strode from his office, calling to his men in the main room. In minutes, they would be on the road north to the RAF airbase at Coningsby.

The Order and Red Empire operatives possessed special skills and abilities. His men and the troops under his immediate command had graduated from the ultra-secret, Phase IV, Day Guard program. It was time to test them on Anton Smith.

Leading half a dozen suits from his office, he whispered to himself, "We'll soon see who's stronger."

Gordon was confident in his men, they could perform amazing acts of speed, strength, endurance, and healing. They would be a match for a single Order of Thoth operative, of that, he was certain.

493

* * *

Peter stared through the windscreen at the bright blue sky, rubbed his hands together and flexed his fingers. He enjoyed flying, but piloting a plane in a straight line, mostly on auto-pilot, was a recipe for boredom.

The comms-link to air traffic control squawked, "Flight N971AZ, acknowledge communications."

"Control, flight N971AZ acknowledges communications," Peter replied,

"You have a new flight plan. The destination is now RAF airbase Coningsby. Begin descent in ten minutes. Acknowledge."

Peter paused for a moment, somewhere, shit was hitting the fan. "Flight N971AZ acknowledges new flight plan."

"Control out."

Peter twisted around in his seat until he could see into the cabin. He saw Francis look up and caught his gaze.

"Hey boss, we've got a problem."

"What's that?" Francis asked.

"We've been redirected to the RAF airbase at Coningsby."

Juliette said, "They know who we are or at the very least suspect it."

The other members of the team leaped up from their seats, crowding the aisle just behind the cockpit.

"UK Shadowstone in action?" Jay asked.

"For sure," Yvette asserted, leaning past Jay's shoulder.

"Okay Peter," Francis directed, "do as they ask. We'll have to adapt our plans."

"Sure Boss," Peter agreed and began setting the plane up for the new flight plan. In another forty-five minutes, they would be landing at a major RAF airbase, surrounded by Shadowstone and regular UK military forces.

Peter sighed; this could get messy in a hurry.

* * *

Bright sunlight gleamed off an ocean of fluffy white clouds beneath an azure sky.

Flight Lieutenant, Gracie Williams' F-35 Lightning II interceptor did a slow looping roll over the Embraer Legacy 500 business jet. The maneuver allowed her to closely examine the plane. She was close enough to see the pilot, a big red-headed fellow. He nodded politely at her as she passed overhead.

She took a position to the left of the Embraer, her wingman mirroring her position on the right. She flicked a switch, opening the doors to her missile bays and tilted her F-35 slightly to show what she was carrying. Having bared her teeth, she righted her aircraft and looked at the red-headed pilot.

He was smiling at her with a dopey 'love at first sight' grin and gave her a thumbs up.

"What the hell," she whispered. It wasn't the sort of reaction she expected to see when showing off four MBDA Meteor ramjet air-to-air missiles. Just one of which could turn the Embraer into a smoking ruin on the ground.

The pilot grinned again, nodded and waved. He pointed down to the ground and then gave her a double thumbs up.

Gracie waggled her wings left and right. Message understood, there would be no trouble. The red-haired pilot of flight N971AZ would comply. She waited another handful of minutes, and the Embraer started its descent toward RAF Coningsby airbase.

She wondered who these fools were. The intercept orders had come from the highest operational ranks of the Royal Air Force. She and her wingman had been on duty and had scrambled their aircraft. She'd expected to see a Russian Tupolev bomber or a pair of Sukhoi fighters testing UK air defenses. She'd been surprised to discover they would be escorting a business jet down to her home base.

Whoever was on board the jet had clearly pissed off someone important. Gracie didn't know who that could be, it was a question well above her pay grade. She shrugged, getting down to business, the fine art of shepherding the Embraer all the way down to the ground. They wouldn't be able to do anything without her wingman or herself knowing about it.

* * *

The two RAF F-35s descended in close formation with the Embraer business jet just under two thousand yards above the ground. There would be no arguing with the escorts, they were all heading to RAF Coningsby and would be landing in less than ten minutes.

Organized chaos filled the cabin of the business jet. The Mirovar force team had opened a locker built into the floor and extracted eight stealthy wingsuit gliders. A set of parachutes remained in the locker, unusable in a situation requiring daylight capable stealth. The team members were variously checking weapons, clambering into their wingsuits, and checking each other's webbing and attached gear.

"Okay everyone," Francis called out. "Peter will set the autopilot to land the plane, and we will escape with our stealth wingsuits. They have the radar cross-section of a marble and are the next thing to invisible to the human eye." He looked at Anton and Li. "Don't worry about your lack of wingsuit training, just follow your guide closely all the way down. Anton pair up with Chiara, Li, your guide is Juliette, is that clear?"

Anton and Li both nodded, moving with their wingsuits to pair up with their guides.

"Furthermore, we will be landing in farmland to the southwest of the airbase. Once you hit the ground, evaporate the wingsuits, grab your gear and form up on Jay. Is that clear?"

"Yes, Sir," resounded through the cabin.

Chiara helped Anton with the final touches of his wingsuit. Checking the fit, adjusting the armored hood over his head and zipping him up at the front.

Anton said, "I've seen this on video, shouldn't we have parachutes? How do we actually land these things?"

Chiara smiled. "Don't worry, we just ramp all the way down. These wingsuits are super cool. They allow for a rapid brake just above the ground. Don't worry, you'll love it. Follow directly after me, mirror what I do, and be ready to brake when I do. Whatever you do, don't drop out of the Ramp, if your reflexes aren't in a heightened state – you won't brake in time, and you'll hit the ground."

"Hit the ground? How hard?"

"Hard."

Chiara and Anton looked at each other, Chiara raised a quizzical eyebrow, a slight smile curving her generous lips.

"Everyone ready?" Francis called out.

"We have a problem," Jay said with a frown.

"What?" Francis asked.

"We're one glider short."

"C'est un foutu bordel!" Francis swore. "What a mess." His eyes flicked over Luther, and he said, "Of course – we have an extra man."

Francis rubbed his chin. "We need a volunteer. Someone must stay on board, land the aircraft, breakout of the airbase and meet us at rendezvous site number two by 12:00 at the latest." He looked around the cabin. "You will have to make it on time. Our mission is time-critical. We cannot afford to leave Ramin Kain in the hands of our enemies – he knows too much about the operations of the Order."

Peter called out from the cockpit, "Hey Boss, I'll take the job."

Francis nodded. "Good man."

"Trust me," Peter asserted, loud enough for everyone to hear. "I'll see you all at twelve, don't be late – I don't like waiting."

"Francis," Anton said, "I could stay with Peter, with the two of us it would double the chances of escaping the airbase."

Francis shook his head. "No, it would double the chance of losing both of you." He reached out, grasping Anton's shoulder firmly. "You come with us. We put one man at risk and make sure the rest of the team escapes."

Peter called out from the cockpit, "Anton, take my battle vest with you, I doubt I'll be fighting vampires this morning, and I'll get it back off you later."

Anton snatched up the battle vest, tucking it inside his wingsuit. Chiara rechecked his fittings and nodded once; he was good to go.

"Ten minutes to landing," Peter advised. "I'll yaw the plane and make it look like I'm about to crash. It'll focus all eyes on me and make your escape easier."

"Good work, Peter. Okay team, get ready. Form up in a line behind Jay. We need to land outside the airbase. We have to go now. Peter – open the escape hatch!"

The team moved, in moments, they formed a line behind Jay. Yvette put her hand on Jay's shoulder. Behind her Luther put a hand on her shoulder, followed by Juliette, Li, Chiara, Anton and Francis at the end. An electrical whirr emanated from the floor just behind the cockpit. A six-foot seam opened up, exposing the cabin to the exterior, the air rushing past howled like a banshee. The seam widened to a three foot by six-foot hole in the floor. Jay leaped through it, immediately followed by Yvette. The plane began to yaw left and right. The line began disappearing through the hole. Chiara leaped through it, Anton didn't hesitate, he followed her, ramping hard as he did so. Time slowed, the world snapping into sharp clarity, the plane drifting away above him. A dozen feet below him, Chiara was already in position, her arms out in a 'T' and her legs spread in a 'V.'

Anton copied her, she was just visible, an outline against the verdant landscape beneath them. The stealth effects of the wingsuits were excellent, almost too good, Anton sharpened his focus, vowing to copy her movements all the way down.

They'd come out of the plane about fifteen hundred yards above the ground. The coating on the gliders would make them essentially invisible to radar. The color schemes would defeat human observers. Still, there was a window of risk where the RAF or Shadowstone could spot them. There was nothing else they could do, every other option led to the immediate capture of the entire team.

Anton had no time for thought as he dropped toward the ground. He watched Chiara closely, waiting for her signal to brake. The ground rose toward them, the Ramp reducing the sense of onrushing speed.

Anton eased off the Ramp slightly, it was fun, exhilarating. Then a thought struck him, *how the hell did they find us?*

He almost missed Chiara's brake. He sharpened his ramp, twisting in the air, his arms flinging out hard.

The wingsuit filled with air as Anton braked hard, a grassy paddock rushed toward him in slow motion.

"Damn—"

* * *

The F-35s roared overhead.

The Embraer business jet had already landed and was taxiing over toward a large hangar. Gordon Heathmont had ordered his men to direct the plane nose first into the broad cream-colored building. It was never going to fly again. They would impound it and strip it to reveal every last shred of information about the Order of Thoth. Men with flags indicated where the jet was to go, and it obediently moved into position within the hangar. The engines slowed to a stop. A big red-headed pilot clambered out of the cockpit, disappearing into the cabin of the aircraft.

Gordon studied the aircraft; it was the expected flight. In addition to the pilot, the Order of Thoth agent, Anton Smith, should be on board. He ordered his men forward. Six suited operatives armed with H&K MP5 submachine guns stepped forward and flanked him. Four squads of four Shadowstone operatives, wearing full tactical combat armor, and armed with H&K assault rifles, took up positions on the corners of a rectangle surrounding the aircraft. Beyond them, were another four squads of Shadowstone operatives armed with rifles with net throwers instead of grenade launchers. Outside the two rings of Shadowstone operatives were another thirty members of RAF regiment regular soldiers. At the hangar's main entrance, a pair of light armored RAF Regiment vehicles, armed with 7.62mm machine guns on their roofs, rolled in from Gordon's right. They faced the rear of the aircraft, blocking any escape in that direction.

All of his Shadowstone men, the suits, and the armored warriors were all participants in the Phase IV Day Guard program. His commander, Cornelius Crane, the head of Shadowstone, had provided the serums for the program a year earlier. Crane had hinted of a new program in the works. The Phase V program which would provide another leap forward in the capability of his operatives.

Gordon lifted a loud-hailer to his mouth and called out, "All personnel on board the aircraft. We have surrounded you. There is no chance of escape. Come out with your hands up, and you will receive fair treatment."

The plane's cabin door swung open with a soft hum, revealing a set of steps and part of the interior of the cabin.

The Shadowstone operatives tightened their stances. Their guns lined up on the open doorway. Silence fell over the hangar.

Gordon wondered if Anton Smith and the red-headed pilot were foolish enough to resist capture.

He smiled grimly and hoped they were.

* * *

Peter lined the Milkor MGL up on the tail of the Embraer and pulled the trigger.

A 40mm grenade 'chuffed' from the barrel of the launcher. It sailed along the aisle toward the back of the aircraft, trailing a plume of gray smoke. Keeping his finger on the trigger, Peter pulled the weapon slightly to the right. The first grenade passed through the left side of the luggage compartment at the rear of the plane, detonating immediately. The backwash of the first blast lit Peter's face with a fiery light. The next grenade launched as the explosion of the first was dying away. The shaped charge of each grenade directed the vast majority of its energy in a narrow cone, slicing through the aircraft's bulkhead. The second grenade flashed and boomed in the narrow space of the cabin.

Peter lifted his launcher, the third grenade chambered into the barrel and shot toward where the ceiling met the rear bulkhead. It struck the target like a God-driven hammer, slicing through the plane's spine with ease.

Peter ramped hard, blurring down the aisle toward the back of the plane. Smoke filled the cabin. Electrical cables hung sputtering from the ceiling. Light from the hangar cut through ragged tears in the walls and ceiling, gleaming off the smoke. The floor shook as he ran along it, the wounded plane trembling with each step. He hit the back wall with his hip and shoulder at full speed – and the fractured rear of the Embraer came apart like torn paper.

Around him, the tail of the Embraer fell away in pieces from the body of the main plane. Peter rolled out onto the concrete of the hangar floor, his eyes taking in everything around him. The Shadowstone operatives in close-fitting matte black body armor were already on the move, as were the suits armed with H&K MP5s. Beyond them, regular RAF soldiers were just beginning to react, their faces marked with shock, amazement and grim fear. The Shadowstone operatives were rushing toward him at faster than normal pace. The bastards had found a way to enhance their men. It was the sort of situation he would normally call 'target rich,' but today he'd no time for quips.

The main gates of the hangar were in front of him. A pair of uprated RAF Regiment Land Rovers stood in his way. He dodged to the right, sending his fourth and fifth grenades through the front radiator grills of each vehicle. The two grenades ripped through metal and piping, shattering the engine blocks. Smoke and flame exploded from the front of each vehicle. RAF soldiers shouted with alarm, spilling out of the cabins.

A slim gray-haired suit with a loud hailer shouted, "Take him alive."

Some of the RAF soldiers weren't listening, letting rip with automatic weapon fire, bullets whizzing through the air behind him. They lacked experience with shooting at a fast-moving target, their bullets slashing through a helicopter parked on the far side of the hangar.

Peter bounded to the top of the nearest vehicle, twisting, his right arm outstretched, firing the last of his grenades into the left wing of the Embraer. Ninety pounds of reserve jet fuel exploded, most of the wing and half the body of the plane disappearing in a fiery cloud of fragments. A moment later, the reserve fuel in the right wing evaporated in a secondary explosion. The detonations blew through the hangar, men falling away with the wash of the explosions.

Peter launched himself forward, leaping off the top of the vehicle and out of the hangar. Bullets zipped past him, RAF Regiment soldiers firing wildly in the chaos within the hangar.

To his left and right, four Shadowstone operatives armed with net throwers ran to where he was landing. Peter landed on his feet, dug in and began blurring forward. The men fired their net throwers. Black, weighted nets flew through the air, spreading out as they approached him. Peter turned hard right, the first net missing. He twisted to the left; the second net flew past him. He leaped, the third one caught his ankles, flipping him mid-air. He started falling, the fourth net reached out, wrapping around him like a giant's hand.

Peter hit the ground hard. The four men rushed forward, firing tasers. He shivered and trembled as the electric shocks froze his nervous system. They rolled him in the nets like spiders trapping a fly.

In moments, he could barely move, Shadowstone had caught him.

* * *

Gordon Heathmont strode over to the red-headed man wrapped up in weighted nano-fiber cables. He reached down, plucking a pair of earbud communications devices from the man's ears. He wrapped them in a gel-impregnated cloth and put them in his pocket.

Gordon stared down at the man and demanded sharply, "Who the bloody hell are you?"

The man attempted to shrug, failed, and then replied, "Why would I tell you?"

"Where's Anton Smith."

The man's eyes widened, nonplussed. "Who?"

Gordon frowned. "Are you going to keep answering everything with a question?"

"Are you going to keep asking them?" he answered, one eyebrow raised.

Gordon glared at the bound man coldly, he indicated with his forefinger left and right to two of his suits. "Pick him up." He turned to a third man and commanded, "Call your van around, we'll take him to the Facility. We can question him properly there."

The first two suits dragged the Order operative to his feet. He was about the same height as his men, around six feet two or three, but appeared to be twice as wide. *Gods*, thought Gordon, *he's a big fellow, he must weigh two sixty, two seventy pounds, and there's no fat on him.*

He was obviously enhanced, faster and stronger than anyone Gordon had seen before. He'd almost got away. Only the closest of the Phase IV day guards had been in a position to stop him, and they'd almost failed.

Gordon stepped forward, stood as tall as his slim five feet, seven-inch frame allowed and stared into the man's eyes. They were blue, serious and filled with secret depths. A slight dusting of freckles ran across the skin of the man's cheeks, and a shock of thick, red hair framed his face. There was a reservoir of bold confidence in his manner at odds with his current helplessness. The young man stared back at him with a look that Gordon would have called insolence in anyone else, but there was something else about this fellow, an unwavering sense of purpose that was larger than both of them.

An uncharacteristic shiver ran up Gordon's spine. He held the man's gaze, but took a step back and said, "You won't be such an arse later today, not once we're done with you."

He looked away, a nondescript dark-gray Shadowstone van rolled to a stop next to them. In moments, his men hooded the Order operative and threw him into the back of the van, four of the enhanced Shadowstone agents leaping in after him. A second car, a late model dark-blue Jaguar sedan pulled to a stop behind the van. Gordon walked over and got into the luxurious rear of the car. The last two of his suits joined him, and the Jaguar rolled forward after the van.

He leaned forward, tapping the driver on the shoulder. "Make all speed to the Facility. There is no time to waste."

The operative, tapped his earbud, giving quick commands to the driver of the van. Both vehicles accelerated away toward the main entrance of the airbase.

As they approached the gates, Gordon stared out the window, silently vowing to break this Order of Thoth operative if it was the last thing he ever did. There could be no mercy shown to those who would oppose the agents of stability and control. They had to maintain a stable world order for the good of all. The only alternative was chaos and destruction, and Gordon Heathmont was willing to do anything that was necessary to defeat Shadowstone's enemies.

Chapter Nineteen

"I can categorically affirm there are no military or paramilitary forces operating in this country without the express permission and knowledge of his Majesty's government." – The Prime Minister of the United Kingdom on the floor of Parliament.

* * *

Near Coningsby, Lincolnshire, August 22nd, 11:16

Anton awoke upside down, his cheek brushing against the warm fatigues of one of his teammates. He blinked, there was a break in the cloud cover, and the sun was shining.

Jay was carrying him over his shoulder on the edge of a slim bitumen road. On one side was a caravan park, on the other side, a river shone with a silvery light.

His head bounced painfully as Jay jumped over a pothole in the path.

"What the hell!" Anton said, squirming in Jay's grip.

Jay grunted, leaned over and stood Anton up. "About time, you've been gaining weight."

Anton glanced around, rubbing his head. The team was moving along a paved bike path toward a newly constructed industrial estate on the left past the caravan park. F-35s thundered to the far right, about a mile away from the Mirovar force team. Suburban housing and rows of low trees partially obscured the airbase.

Chiara handed him his slim backpack, Peter's battle vest, and the Blue Dragon, and stated matter-of-factly, "Here's your gear."

"Thanks," Anton replied, putting on Peter's vest and cinching it tight as it was easier to wear than carry. He shrugged on his backpack, carrying the Blue Dragon in its scabbard with his left hand. He glanced at Chiara and asked, "What happened to our wingsuits?"

"They self-immolate: smokeless, very little heat, a little bit of ash. How's your—"

"Keep moving," Francis ordered from the rear of the line, "and pick up the pace, we have to reach our first rendezvous point with the Order helper."

"Order helper?" Anton asked rhetorically, looking back over his shoulder. "That was quick. The RAF intercepted us less than an hour ago."

Francis shook his head slightly, and said, "Juliette and I switched everyone in the UK to active hours ago. There's a helper nearby."

Anton's eyes widened. The Order was more pervasive than he'd thought.

Three explosions cracked in a tight sequence from the RAF airbase on their right-forward flank.

"That'll be Peter," Anton said. "Damn, we shouldn't have let him go in there by himself."

Juliette brushed past him; studying the distant airbase. "He's still online. Check your earbud communications."

Two whip-like cracks ripped through the air. Another pair of grenades going off. A second later a powerful explosion echoed in the distance, and gray smoke billowed out of a hangar on the northern side of the airbase.

"Give 'em hell Peter," Anton whispered. He tapped his right ear. The earbud was still in place and activated with his touch. He picked up what was happening with his friend.

There was a sharp crackle of gunfire through the link, Peter had to fight his way clear. The noise abruptly stopped; they'd lost the communications link with Peter.

"What the hell," Anton snapped angrily. He shook his head, his face flushed. "This is a disaster."

Francis jogged past everyone to reach the front of the line, he put his hand out to signal 'stop.' He signaled 'silence,' by placing his hand over his mouth for a moment and then pulled his earbuds out, and indicated everyone do the same. In moments, all the team members removed their earbuds. Once out of contact with a warm human they shut down. He addressed the team, "They are attempting to compromise our comms. Everyone, put your earbuds back in and shift to our backup channel now."

Anton popped his earbuds back in and tapped his right earbud three times. The earbud gave a chirp as it switched to the backup channel. "But, what about Peter, he won't be able to hear us."

Francis looked at Anton and said, "His earbuds will have been taken."

Juliette brushed past Anton to speak with Francis, she said softly, "There is an opportunity here to deceive Shadowstone."

"Precisely."

Juliette nodded and put a hand on Anton's arm. "Don't assume the worst, it's not over yet, Peter is very resourceful. We'll go to the second rendezvous point and wait for him there."

Anton looked at her, his eyes questioning. "I really hope he makes it."

He wasn't comfortable with hope. Hope was one of the most useless and unreliable things in the world. He gripped the scabbard of the Blue Dragon, his eyes narrowing. There was no way he was leaving his friend to languish in captivity, facing torture or worse – not if he could do anything about it.

God only knows what's happening to Peter.

Anton vowed to find a way to rescue his friend. After all, his friends were far more important to him than Ramin Kain.

* * *

The Jaguar sedan passed through the northern gates of the RAF airbase and raced along the street behind the dark-gray Shadowstone van. They needed to get through the suburbs of Coningsby before they could hit the main roads heading south toward the Facility.

Gordon Heathmont dialed Cornelius Crane on his secured, private line. It was time to report the capture of a member of the Order of Thoth. His call rang out unanswered, it didn't even go to voicemail. Nor was the call picked up by Crane's executive secretary Ursula Zielinkski, or another functionary. In his thirty-two years with Shadowstone, the last nineteen heading the UK arm, Gordon had always been able to contact his commanding officer or a designated functionary.

He frowned and tried again. The call rang three times, and then blipped as it transferred to another Shadowstone phone. The familiar voice of James Haley, the head of US Shadowstone answered the call, "Hello Gordon, what can we do for you?"

An undercurrent of false conviviality flowed beneath the American's words. Gordon glowered with distaste, Haley had pitched the words perfectly to skate a thin line between insult and parody, leaving Gordon with no room to call the uncouth man out for his lack of manners. As to why the man had not resigned after his utter failure with the Boston incident on June the 11th was beyond his comprehension. The man had no breeding and was clearly little more than a trumped-up barbarian who had risen far above his natural station.

Unfortunately, and to his great dismay, Gordon still had to deal with him as an equal. It was an appalling situation and a sad indictment of the world that it tolerated the likes of Haley in positions of real authority. Gordon vowed to himself to do his utmost to see Haley removed and replaced with someone better suited to administrate a transnational security service. A man with the right background. A man with an Eton education and a doctorate in law from Cambridge University. A man who had come from a long line of serious men who had done great deeds of service.

A man like himself.

This will jam it right up him, the upstart bastard. Gordon's thin lips curled into a smug grin, and he declared, "I've caught an Order of Thoth operative, and it is imperative Cornelius Crane is notified."

There was a momentary pause before Haley replied, "Have you identified the operative?"

"Not yet, but we will. Where is Crane?"

"Cornelius Crane is unavailable at this time. Can you describe the operative?"

"Why is Crane unavailable?"

"There is a glitch in the communications system. No one can reach Crane."

Gordon paused, why should communications be down on the very day Order of Thoth operatives were landing in England? Had the Order managed to compromise the system? It beggared belief. He frowned; it was infuriating to have to deal with Haley instead of Crane. He sighed, submitting to answer the American. "Male, about six feet two inches tall, heavy, muscular build. Thick red hair, blue eyes, and an insolent, over-confident manner."

"His name is Peter Lamb," Haley advised. "He is a known member of the Mirovar force team."

Gordon's mouth turned down in a disappointed sneer. How did Haley know so much about the operative? He'd already checked the Panopticon, it was the first thing he'd done as his car crossed the RAF airbase from the hangar to the front gates – there was nothing on 'Peter Lamb,' in the system. Why hadn't Haley shared this information earlier? Was Haley deliberately withholding information from his peers in Europe? Gordon shook his head, he wouldn't be surprised to discover Haley had done precisely that, most likely motivated by personal ambitions to bring the US arm of Shadowstone to a position of global primacy with himself at its head.

Just another example of the hubristic over-reach of a small-minded man given too much power.

Gordon demanded, "Why isn't this information in the Panopticon?"

Haley ignored the question and asked, "Where are the rest of the Mirovar force team?"

Gordon glared at his phone. "What do you mean? The plane landed. Only one man came off it, and he is in custody. Anyone else on the aircraft would be dead. It's a smoking ruin in a hangar at RAF Coningsby."

Haley snorted.

Gordon seethed; *how dare he laugh at me.* "Answer me, man! What do you mean?"

"The Mirovar team are in England. They're on an operation right now. You have one of their number. There are at least another six to nine members in your vicinity. I don't know how they did it, but they evacuated the plane before it landed."

"Not possible. We intercepted the plane before it flew over England and then escorted it all the way down. No one left the plane."

"Well, it happened."

Gordon sniffed disdainfully. "If they're here we will soon find them."

"Or they will find you."

"I hope they do. They will discover we're able to defend ourselves."

The line was quiet for a long moment. "Don't underestimate them."

Gordon shook his head. "Not a chance. Now please ensure Crane receives this good news at the earliest opportunity."

"I guarantee it, I will pass it on as soon as communications have been restored."

Gordon stared at his phone as if the sheer intensity of his will could reach through the network and pin Haley down. "I'll hold you to your word."

"Of course."

The line disconnected as Haley hung up.

Gordon took a deep breath and let it out slowly. Calming himself; he considered a list of options in his mind. It was better to be safe than sorry. He would mobilize Shadowstone, and UK government agencies and military forces. He would set a net so tight that not even a mouse could fart without him knowing about it. If the Mirovar force team were operating in the UK, he would discover them, and then he would direct the full force of his Phase IV day guards upon their heads.

Gordon smiled avidly; he'd more than one ace up his sleeve. He pulled the captured earbuds from his pocket and fitted them into his ears. Before he marshaled his forces, he would see what he could hear from the mouths of his opponents. Of course, his enemies could have realized that their operative's earbuds had fallen into the hands of Shadowstone. Whatever he heard could be false information.

He was confident he would be able to tell the difference. His smile broadened as the communications link became live in his ear.

Today would be a special day.

* * *

The industrial park loomed before them.

Francis held up his hand, signaling the team to stop, he turned and directed, "It's time to start a ruse. Juliette and I will be the only ones involved. We'll be on our normal communications channel until further notice. It's important that everyone stays quiet."

Anton nodded with the rest of the team.

He half listened as Juliette and Francis discussed their plans to abort the mission and head to the west coast of England for a boat pickup with the remainder of the team. Their conversation touched on the loss of a single man, Peter, and their belief that he would have to be 'left behind,' for the good of the Order. They finished by declaring future communications silence to minimize risk.

Anton imagined catching up to Peter's captors and freeing his friend. He couldn't imagine doing anything else.

* * *

Jay took point as they trooped in a loose line along a street filled with various small factories and workshops.

Anton turned left with the rest of the team, following Jay into a laneway. A neatly painted white roller door began to rise up on the third building on the right. The building sported a bright red sign on a white background that read, 'Dogdyke Motor Repairs.'

The roller door pulled to a halt at the top with a clatter of chains. A young woman stood in the shadows inside the door. She'd pulled her dark hair back beneath a red scarf and wore dark, oil-stained coveralls, and black work boots. She nodded, gesturing for them to come into the automotive workshop. They all filed in, spreading around the workshop, wary eyes watching everything. The young woman punched a black button on the wall, and the roller door descended smoothly. In moments, they were alone with her and a pair of late model Range Rover SUVs resting on the cold concrete of the workshop's floor.

Francis approached the young woman and asked, "You already have our message?"

"Yes. Everything is prepared."

"Good work, show us."

The woman moved behind the charcoal-colored Range Rovers, lifted their rear doors and said confidently, "The fit out is the same for both cars. Full tank of fuel. Supercharged engines. Reinforced stealth body armor good against 5.56mm or 9mm ball, not so good for anything more potent than that. Top speed of a hundred and thirty miles per hour and zero to sixty in six and a half seconds. On board each vehicle, you'll find four H&K MP5s, each with two mags strapped together, and four extra mags of high-velocity rounds each. A .50 cal sniper rifle with thirty rounds. A Milkor MGL with six HEAP rounds, and one spare load of another six HEAP rounds. There's a satchel with a dozen AP hand grenades."

Francis frowned. "Define, 'not so good.'"

"Right," The young woman nodded. "Sustained 7.62mm fire will break through the windscreens and the armored panels. Don't go anywhere near depleted uranium rounds – they'll tear these babies apart."

"Any silver?"

"Only what you brought with you."

Francis nodded. "Thanks, you've done well."

The young woman nodded once without smiling, her brown eyes serious. She turned, striding back to the roller doors, she said over her shoulder, "Follow the street north along the river for about a mile. You'll hit a 'T' intersection, that's the A153, Sleaford road. Turn to the north and cross the Witham River, from there on, head for Whitby."

The team split into two groups, loading their packs, edged weapons, FN P90s and magazines into the two cars. Francis climbed into one of the Range Rovers, Juliette took the other side and opened her laptop on her knees. Anton clambered into the back seat behind Juliette, and Li took the other side, the Green Dragon joining the Blue Dragon resting between them. Anton looked to his left across the workshop, Jay had taken the driver's position in the second Range Rover with Yvette at his side, and Luther and Chiara were behind them. In moments, the engines were idling smoothly. The young woman, her dark eyes flashing beneath the fluorescents hit a black button next to the roller doors. They ascended in a handful of seconds. Francis gunned the SUV's engine. The Range Rover accelerated forward and into the street, the second car joining it a moment later.

It was sinking in. They were leaving Peter to his fate. His absence cut through Anton like a cold blade. "We need to find Peter. We can't leave him behind."

Francis replied firmly, "Peter accepted the mission. He knew the risks, and we haven't lost him yet. He may still escape his captors. We'll go to the second rendezvous point and wait for him there." He paused for a moment, his face still, but his eyes were alive with emotion. "We must forge ahead, speed is of the essence, Ramin may still be human, we must recover him as soon as possible."

Juliette twisted around in her seat to look Anton in the face. "We have a dilemma, no one wants to leave Peter. But, where is he? He could be anywhere. We have no way of knowing where they will take him or how soon he might escape."

"What of your mind palace? Surely you can do something."

"It's not magic Anton. I need something more to work with. There are too many options, but I'll see what I can see." Juliette turned back to her laptop and closed her eyes. Her eyelids fluttered like she was dreaming for about ten seconds. She opened her eyes, and her eyebrows lifted slightly. "Peter could still be on the airbase, but it is more likely he will be in transit right now. The only thing I can rule out is that he's not in the air. Clearly, no planes have taken off. There's not enough information to be more conclusive than that." She reached around and patted Anton's knee. "For now, we can do nothing to help Peter. He will have to help himself." She paused for a moment. "Do not doubt him. I would not want to try to hold Peter captive."

Francis declared, "We will go to the rendezvous point and see if he turns up. He's got another thirty-five minutes to get there."

Anton sank back in his seat. But what if they'd tied Peter up, or drugged him, or worse, and he was unable to do anything to get free? What then? He glanced knowingly at Li, she raised a quizzical eyebrow and then frowned, appearing torn between the mission and the option of rescuing Peter.

Whatever he was going to do, it was clear that he would be doing it on his own.

He could live with that. After all, he wouldn't be abandoning Li in the middle of a battle – he would be saving Peter.

* * *

The lead Range Rover pulled to a stop at a 'T' intersection. A weathered sign on the far side of the road pointed to 'Horncastle' on the right and 'Sleaford' on the left. Francis waited for the traffic to clear from the road on the right so that he could turn to the north.

Anton rubbed his forehead; he still had a headache from knocking himself out with a clumsy landing in the wingsuit. Gray clouds arched overhead from horizon to horizon. The sun rested; a dim orb vaguely present somewhere above them. The daylight dimmed like a sudden onrush of twilight. Anton wiped his brow; his hand came away slick with perspiration. A queasy feeling overtook him, and he rocked forward in his seat.

Li's left hand grasped his shoulder, and she inquired, "Anton, are you—"

Her voice trailed off as Anton's perception suddenly accelerated, time slowing down in a deep spontaneous Ramp. Anton shivered, his breath misting before his face. A nondescript dark-gray van was passing in front of the Range Rover.

The world faded, the van coming into sharp relief. It dragged his eyes with it as it rolled through the intersection in slow motion. Faint scratches were crystal clear on the almost immaculate paintwork. The rubber tires thrummed hard on the bitumen. Air rushed over the blocky vehicle. Near invisible smoke puffed from its exhaust. The two men in the front seats were both young, wearing suits and high-end sunglasses, the nearest was touching an in-ear communications bud with a well-manicured finger.

Conviction flooded through him; they were Shadowstone operatives.

Anton tried to drop out of the Ramp, he needed to tell everyone the van passing them right now was Shadowstone, most likely it had Peter in it. He couldn't do it, the Ramp had him in its grip and wasn't letting go.

Time almost stopped. Anton could no longer feel his heart beating – he could barely move; it seemed the slightest movement would require maximum effort. He stared, the men inside the van withered inside their suits, their skin shrinking back over their bones, their eyes darkening to gleaming black orbs. Black streaks stretched across the gray sky like the ill-formed fingers of a malevolent god's dark desire.

Thunder rumbled, lightning flashed, the side of the van corroded away. Inside was Peter, hooded in black, bound in cables and chains. The sky became flame, great gouts of fire storming over the world.

A dreadful terror filled Anton to the brim. Peter writhed on the floor of the van, screaming once in utter agony before collapsing into dust. Above, flames roared and lightning sheeted over the sky. A gust of wind picked up Peter's ashes, flinging them at Anton in a dark storm.

He tried to lean back out of the way but remained frozen in place. The ashes washed around him, ripe with the charnel house stench of death.

Peter was dead.

The Ramp collapsed. The vision vanished. Li's hand clenched tight on his shoulder. "—Okay?"

For an instant, the world felt less real than the vision it replaced.

Anton's head snapped around to face Li. "Peter's dead!" he shook his head. "No, he's not, he's," his left hand shot forward between Juliette and Francis' heads to point toward the van, but the van was no longer there. He twisted left. The van was disappearing southward down the road, closely followed by a dark-blue Jaguar sedan. "There, in that van!"

The Range Rover slammed to a halt. Francis and Juliette both twisted around to stare at Anton.

"What the hell are you talking about?" Francis demanded.

Juliette reached around, putting her hand on Anton's knee and asked, "Anton what happened?"

Anton shook his head, his voice rising, he declared urgently, "There's no time to explain." He glanced out the window. The van and the Jaguar sedan had disappeared around a bend. "They're getting away. We have to follow them."

Francis stared at Juliette intently. "Is there anything to this? Did you see enough of the van?"

Juliette's eyelids closed; her eyes vibrated behind them briefly as she accessed a tightly focused mind palace. She gasped and said, "Yes, mon amour." Turning to stare at Anton, she said insistently, "After this is done, you must tell me exactly what you saw."

Francis declared, "We need to be quick." He floored the accelerator. The supercharged engine roared, the SUV's big wheels smoking as the car shot forward through the intersection and raced away to the south. The second Range Rover with the rest of the team racing after them.

Luther's voice screamed over the communication links, "What are you doing? We have to go north."

Anton said, "We're getting Peter."

"Where is he?" Luther asked.

"In a van," Anton asserted with absolute confidence. "It just passed us heading south."

"A van? What? Are you claiming x-ray vision now? Hell, this is madness. Francis, what of the mission?"

Francis glanced at the clock. "We still have thirty minutes before we need to be at Peter's designated rendezvous point. Even if Peter is not in the van, we can still get back there in time without affecting our overall schedule because we would have waited there until noon anyway." He glanced knowingly at Juliette. "We have the information he is in the van on good authority."

"Mind palaces," Luther uttered in disgust. "They're unreliable. This is a wild goose chase when Ramin Kain needs our help."

Li chimed in. "Peter would never leave any of us behind."

"He's expend—" Luther hesitated for a split second. "Going to have to make a noble sacrifice for the good of the Order."

A chill silence fell over the comm links.

Juliette said clearly, "It's an unnecessary sacrifice when he is within reach."

"The mission has to take priority," Luther said, but the force had drained from his voice.

"Who are we?" Juliette asked as if instructing a wayward child. "What do we stand for if we can't even look after each other?"

Luther fell into silence.

A wave of relief rolled over Anton. They were going to save Peter. He sucked in a deep breath and sighed, left with the mystery of what had just happened. This had been the third vision he'd experienced in his life. The first one was an uncanny sexual encounter with Chloe Armitage at the homeless shelter. It had left him feeling violated, even though he'd given in to it in the end. The second vision occurred during the battle on the Boston docks, where Armitage had beckoned to him. What was going on? Where were the visions coming from? What did the first vision mean? Was Armitage inside his head? Was she figuratively screwing with him? Why did he give in to her at the end, did some part of him want her to win? What the hell was going on? One time he could dismiss as something freakish, twice as coincidence, but three times?

And what was the extreme Ramp experience where time external to the vision seemed to freeze? His mind must be racing through each event, and if the Ramp was involved, how on Earth had he had the first vision *before* Gang had initiated him?

He had no answers. The only thing he was sure of was he had to rescue Peter or something terrible was going to happen. Something terrible like the end of the world terrible. The shadows and flames in the sky had felt malignant as if driven by a horrific and malevolent intelligence.

Li was looking at him with a 'what the hell is going on?' expression on her face. His face froze, he would like to be able to tell her, and he would if only he knew what the answer was. He decided to talk with her later, and explain all three visions. No doubt, Juliette would want to know too.

He hoped they wouldn't think he was going mad.

He prayed he wasn't going mad.

He craned his neck, looking through the windscreen. There was no sign of either the dark-gray van or the dark-blue Jaguar sedan.

He whispered harshly, "Damn it."

* * *

"Where the fuck are we?" Luther asked, his voice dripping with contempt.

The pair of Range Rovers were flying along the road at well above the legal speed limit. There was no sign of the Shadowstone van or its trailing Jaguar sedan. Unless the Shadowstone operatives were hammering their vehicles or had pulled down another road, they should have caught up with them by now.

Juliette glanced up from her laptop and said, "No police radars on this road, … which in itself is an oddity. The UK is one of the most surveilled societies in the world. Why are there no cameras here, especially this close to a major RAF airbase?"

"Juliette," Francis stated, without taking his eyes off the road, trees, and farms whipping past like ghosts of the daylight beneath a gray sky. "We have a fork in the road coming up. Which one did they go down?"

Juliette touched a key on her laptop's keyboard, a GPS map swapped to front and center on her screen. Two miles ahead, the road forked. What would she give for a drone right now? She stared into the distance, dropping into silence and bringing her mind palace into being. Her mind integrating everything she had to hand.

Her mind palace bloomed into being, the external world dropping away. She found herself standing at an empty crossroad, the world was silent, a zephyr of a breeze tickled her nose. The sky hung low overhead, an oppressive grayness smothering the light.

She spun around, four roads, all seemingly identical. But it was a fork they were heading to in the real world, how could there be four choices? Was there another dimension to this problem? Something else, in the air, or underground? Alternate pathways in a mind palace vision could also mean something from the past or future intervening deeply in the present.

Shadows pressed in from each direction.

Despite her stillness, silence, and depth of concentration, Juliette shivered. There was something else here, something very dangerous was moving through her vision. Her skin crawled, loneliness bordering on terror sweeping through her. The real world receded further away.

Her mind palace deepened, the roads and shadows falling into sharp relief. She breathed deeply, sighed softly, and reached along the roads.

The implant in her arm burned like a hot coal, hooking through to her laptop, accessing all the available information. The nearest police camera was on one of the roads, the rest fell into deep shadows. It was the clue she needed, the road with the police camera was the wrong road.

The lurking presence receded into the darkness; the gray clouds lifted. She ascended out of her mind palace, the world snapping back around her. The fork in the road was upon them. "Left," she advised urgently. "Left, now!"

Francis turned the steering wheel slightly, the car careered forward along the left road.

The sense of threat hung around Juliette for a long moment after the mind palace had closed down. A rare frown hung over her forehead. She'd never experienced a mind palace so filled with portentous evil. Something dark and deadly was waiting in the near future – she was sure of it.

She stared through the windscreen. The Range Rover was eating up the miles. There was still no sign of the van or the sedan, but they were out there, somewhere in front of them. Driving at their limits to whatever destination they sought.

Wherever they were going, both Shadowstone and the Mirovar force team would be there soon.

* * *

A thick cloth hood clung to Peter's face, blocking all sight and dulling sound.

The four Shadowstone agents who shared the back of the van with Peter had barely said a word, giving nothing away. One had kicked him hard in the guts. Still immobilized by the nano-fiber nets, Peter had been unable to respond in kind. He filed the position of that agent away. If he got the chance, he would extract a little payback. Kicking a bound captive was beyond the pale, an unforgivable cowardly act.

When the fourth net had begun to wrap around his body outside the hangar, he'd flexed every muscle he could to maximize his size and give himself room to maneuver within the net. But the smart materials comprising the net tightened as he inevitably relaxed, eliminating the use of an old Houdini trick to deal with being bound.

As soon as the van started moving, he'd begun a one count per second count. He was already at one thousand and seventy-two, nearly eighteen minutes had passed since his capture. Lying on the floor of the van allowed Peter to feel the vibrations of the motor, driveline, and the tires rolling over the road. He could sense acceleration and changes in direction. The engine was working hard, and the driver had barely touched the brakes. He was pretty sure they were heading south, and fast, at an average speed well over the speed limit. He estimated they were already at least twenty miles south of Coningsby. He would need to steal a vehicle once he escaped, otherwise he would miss the rendezvous with the Mirovar force team at 12:00.

In any event, he only had a little less than half an hour to affect an escape from the van and break contact with Shadowstone.

His hand reflexively went to rub his chin thoughtfully as he planned an escape but got nowhere. The inability to perform simple gestures almost irked him more than lying hooded and bound in the back of a Shadowstone van. He grinned at himself beneath the hood and chuckled softly.

One of the agents kicked him in the stomach again. "What are you laughing at asshole."

Pain shot through him; this could get ugly. He needed it to get uglier, and said derisively, "I was just thinking of your mother pleasuring the village idiot on the night you were conceived."

"Are you asking for it?"

"Of course," Peter snarked, "it wasn't the first time for her."

"Fuck you!"

The four agents started in on Peter with hard, booted feet and fists like steel. The kicks were relentless, they must have been crouching over him, giving him everything they could in the cramped space. Fists pummeled him remorselessly, the punches snapping in whip-fast.

Peter grimaced, waiting for his chance.

He crunched, lifting his head half a dozen inches off the floor. One of the agents smashed him hard on the right cheek. He went with the blow, hitting his head against the floor of the van. Stars shot before his eyes, and he went limp.

"Check him," one of the agents growled.

A pair of fingers pressed against his throat, finding his carotid artery. "He's still got a pulse, damn slow but strong."

"He's out cold, you might have thumped him a bit too hard."

"Heathmont won't be happy if you've damaged him too much."

"Fuck Heathmont."

"Stow that shite, Collins."

"Yes, Sir."

The agents fell silent.

Peter continued breathing slowly. Let them think he was unconscious. It was a lever he could use to escape. All he needed was the slimmest of openings, the slightest mistake and he would be gone. He'd already shifted the situation in his favor. They were unaware he was awake and waiting for the first opportunity to take action.

They would regret underestimating him.

He continued his silent counting.

* * *

A flash of dark-blue disappeared around a broad-left curve in front of them.

"It's the Jag!" Anton asserted, pointing forward with his right hand between Juliette and Francis.

"We've caught them," Francis declared.

The two Range Rovers barreled around the corner, ten or eleven seconds behind the Shadowstone vehicles. The road stretched straight for half a mile before curving to the right. Halfway along was a turn off to the left. The dark-gray van slowed down, the Jaguar sedan with it. Francis tapped on the brakes, bringing the Range Rover back under the speed limit. The Shadowstone vehicles took the left turn, keeping their speed low as they moved along the side road.

There were thick screens of trees along both sides of the main road. Anton's SUV approached the intersection, a gatehouse and boom gate nestled down the side road emerged from the tree line. Camouflaged painted metal dominated on the far side of the boom gate, a pair of long gun barrels jutted out to the left and right of a bulbous turret, pointing down the side road toward the main road.

"A tank," Anton said, a nebulous idea sparking into being on the edge of his mind. He stared intently at the massive vehicle as the SUV approached the intersection. Details of the military manual Peter had given him to read on the flight over flashing through his mind. It was one of the newly deployed 'commander,' tanks, named for their ability to dominate and take command of a battlefield. It was the first tank deployed with a viable rail gun able to deliver a kinetic spike made of tungsten at nine times the speed of sound. It had a more conventional 105mm gun with high-explosive rounds, a 7.62mm minigun, and a belt-fed grenade launcher. Its weapon systems were largely automated, simplifying operations down to two people, a driver/gunner, and a commander. If necessary, the driver/gunner could operate the tank on their own. He crinkled his nose with thought. The commanding officer was probably just there to make sure the driver/gunner didn't get up to no good. A grin flashed across Anton's face and then vanished.

Francis took the SUVs past the intersection, as if they were just simple, law-abiding traffic with no interest in what lay down the side road.

Anton stared out the window as they passed by. The boom gate was up, the van and the Jaguar were passing beneath an arching sign that proclaimed 'Squadron F,' in large black letters. The gate guards obviously expected the two vehicles, waving them through without checks.

The commander tank sat on the right side of the gate, opposite the main gatehouse. One of the crew was climbing down the side of the tank, heading toward the gatehouse, leaving the turret hatch open. Fifty yards behind it, a pair of wheeled armored personnel carriers bristled with firepower and menace. Beyond them, the side road ran another fifty yards before turning to the right and disappearing behind a stand of trees stretching parallel to the perimeter fence. Anton counted heads as the Range Rover sped past at sixty miles per hour. There were four men in standard dark-gray combat fatigues manning the gate. Another eight men, wearing the standard matte black Shadowstone body armor stood on the far side of the gate. All of the men carried automatic rifles.

"It's a secret Shadowstone base," Li suggested beside him. "Hiding in plain sight."

Juliette nodded. "Most people would just see another UK military special forces base."

"Squadron F?" Francis asked.

"The Stateless Warfare Wing," Juliette answered, glancing down at her laptop. "Apparently a recently formed branch of the SAS, less than six years old."

"A great place for Shadowstone to hide," Francis said confidently.

Anton slammed his right fist into his left palm and declared, "Well we need to find a way in, and soon – anything could be happening to Peter in there."

"Yes, of course. But easier said than done." Francis said, keeping the Range Rover moving at speed. Soon they were traveling around the right-hand curve in the road and out of sight of the gatehouse.

Francis slowed the SUV, pulling it over and stopping on the loose gravel beside the road. Jay brought the second Range Rover tight in behind the first.

Francis twisted in his seat, glancing left and right at Li and Anton. He tapped his in-ear communicator to broadcast to the others in the second car and directed, "Okay everyone, we need to establish a good and careful plan to get Peter out of this base."

* * *

"Don't take any chances with him. He's enhanced somehow," The lead agent declared in the back of the van.

Tasers crackled in the dark.

Three sets of prongs lanced into Peter's flesh, sending hot electric current raving through his nerves. His muscles spasmed and drool wet the mask over his face. The tasers stopped, the rear door to the van burst open with a click and a pair of clangs. Strong hands gripped the nets wrapped around him, and dragged him from the back of the van. More hands grabbed his feet, lifting his legs, and together, the agents carried him bodily over the concrete floor. The faint echoes of their boots resounding within a large enclosed space.

"Drop him and stand clear," the lead agent shouted.

Peter thudded to the concrete. Tasers lanced forward again, the charges almost knocking him out. Lights and shadows flashed before his eyes. When his vision began to clear, he was free of the nets and hood.

A large tan vehicle loomed before him. A purpose-built semi-trailer rig attached to a v-hulled container. A pair of thick doors were open at the back of the container, bright lights illuminating a white and chrome interior with a striking resemblance to a dental clinic.

The agents dragged him up a set of portable stairs and into the rear of the container. He tried to ramp, but the half-dozen taser shots left his nerves too jangled to cooperate. They lifted him bodily, carried him forward, and strapped him into an oversized dentist's chair at the front of the container. Quickly wrapping heavy metal cuffs around his ankles and wrists, and strapping thick belts over his shins, thighs, chest and forehead.

A port into a vein on his left hand seemed to magically appear as the agents stepped back. A slim, plastic tube ran from the port to a drip feed of clear fluid in a bag hung from the top of a thick, chrome pole jutting up behind his left shoulder.

The agents left the chamber. Peter's mind cleared, and his nerves settled back to their normal functioning. He assessed the space around him. There were two men, one tall and lean, one short and round, dressed in white fatigues. *Med techs!* He nicknamed them Bud and Lou. The ceiling was about eight feet above the floor. The room was a narrow rectangle, about ten feet wide and thirty feet long. The chair he sat in was hard up against the front bulkhead. A pair of double doors with a spinlock dominated the rear end of the chamber. Halfway along the ceiling, there was a hatch a man could fit through; shut tight with a heavy spinlock. Along the walls were racks of equipment, much of it medical in appearance, the rest were mostly computers, recording, and communications equipment.

A pair of chairs sat either side of the rear doors with air-transport style harness seat belts.

Someone had designed the vehicle to keep its operators safe under acceleration and flying conditions. His mind ticked over; it was the right size to fit inside a large military transport aircraft. He shook his head once, and pressed his lips into a thin line of grim recognition. It was a mobile rendition unit, an MRU. A system designed to transport a prisoner anywhere in the world, to facilitate torture away from jurisdictions that would frown upon such activities.

The plummy voice of the lead Shadowstone operative who had spoken outside the hangar came over an intercom in the ceiling, "Prepare the prisoner with the truth serum."

Bud, the tall, slim technician said, "We have already started Sir, he'll be ready to question in five minutes."

"And the enhancers?" asked the voice over the intercom.

"About to start, Sir."

"Good work."

"Enhancers?" Peter asked. Whatever they were pumping into him wasn't anything like Truther, that took about two hours to reach full effect. A clock on the wall read 11:46. He had fourteen minutes to reach the rendezvous point to catch up with the rest of the Mirovar team. That was starting to look impossible unless he was able to escape immediately and capture a helicopter.

Lou, the shorter, rounder technician approached, and said with avid interest, "Pain enhancers." His eyes crinkled and he grinned. "This should be fascinating. I've never tried this on an Order of Thoth operative before."

"Cool," Peter observed drily, "I always like being first to try something new."

Lou snorted. "Well, aren't you a confident one."

Peter could just move his head and tilted it a little to the side. There was a lock unit, a small chrome lever on the arm of the interrogation chair, just below the manacle. Hopelessly out of reach for anyone strapped in the chair.

He ramped hard, his muscles bunching and straining. A drop of perspiration appeared on his hairline above his left eye and started to roll down his face. Did the right manacle budge? Possibly, but maybe it hadn't moved at all.

Lou watched him curiously. "What are you doing? There's no hope of escape here." He approached with a large syringe filled with a pink fluid and pumped it into the port on Peter's left hand. A cold fire ripped along his arm and just as quickly faded away. He followed it with another syringe of saline fluid to flush the port. The tech stepped back and reported to the overhead cameras and intercom, "Sir, the enhancers have been applied."

Bud stepped forward to Peter's right, grasping a device that looked a lot like a cross between a cattle prod and a stun gun in his right hand. He frowned dispassionately at Peter and pressed a stud on the top of the baton like device. A pair of blue arcs crackled between the prongs on its forward end.

Lou moved up on Peter's left and said matter-of-factly, "Don't worry, this won't knock you out like a taser would ... even though you might wish it would do so."

The lead Shadowstone operative's voice came over the intercom and commanded, "Begin the interrogation process."

Bud lifted the baton toward Peter, the sparking end of it looming before his face.

Peter involuntarily winced in anticipation.

Bud pressed the baton forward.

* * *

"Whatever we do – we have to do it quickly, and we have to do it quietly," Francis instructed. He stabbed down toward the floor of the car with his finger. "No one knows we're here. We need to preserve stealth while we can."

He glanced at his wife. "Juliette, is there any way through the perimeter fence."

Juliette consulted her laptop. "There are public warnings about approaching the site, the fence is heavily electrified. There will be a control center on the base where they'll monitor the perimeter alarms. A site like this will also have active perimeter defenses."

"Such as?" Francis asked.

"Flechette guns are a popular choice for perimeter defense in the UK," Jay said, his voice crystal clear over the tactical comms link. "Imagine thirty or forty razor-sharp slivers of metal hitting you. They'll cut you in half."

"What about drones?" Chiara asked from the other car. "Has anyone seen one yet?"

"No. But we should assume they're there even if we can't see them," Juliette advised.

Anton squeezed his eyes shut for a moment and then pleaded with the team, "We're wasting time."

"Anton," Francis cautioned, "We can't rush in all guns blazing, we'll have these Shadowstone operatives all over us. We're not invulnerable, and a big enough force can easily swamp us."

Anton's eyes widened with barely contained anger. A ball of frustration burning in his gut. He had to save Peter, and soon. Anton didn't need the threat of terrible things happening to the world if they lost Peter today to motivate him. It was enough that his friend was in danger and he was able to do something about it.

The other's continued discussing the tactical parameters of the site.

Anton fingered the lace ends on Peter's battle vest. Even with the muscle he'd grown over the last three and a half months, the vest sat large on him. Peter would need his weapons and Anton would get them to him.

He quietly unlatched the SUV's door.

Fortune favors the brave.

Grasping the Blue Dragon in his right hand and one of the H&K MP5 submachine guns in his left, Anton pushed open the car door with his shoulder. Blurring away to the tree line, he disappeared between the trees, with the voices of his teammates shouting over the comms link.

It was time to kick in the front door.

Chapter Twenty

"Damn it – I'm just going to have a go. No one ever won a game without attacking the goal." – Anton Slayne

"The new commander tank comes equipped with the latest nano-ceramic, reactive-ablative armor matrix. This armored shell integrates with the command-and-control system, ensuring heightened crew awareness of protection levels in the face of the most lethal threats on the modern battlefield." – Commander Tank Sales Brochure.

* * *

The Facility, South Lincolnshire, August 22nd, 11:46

Peter screamed in agony.

His nerves were on fire, whatever the 'pain enhancer,' drug was, it was certainly effective.

Bud, the taller of the techs stepped back, and the Etonian tones of the lead Shadowstone operative came through the intercom in the ceiling above the chair. "I see you have begun to understand the nature of your confinement … Mr. Lamb. Are you feeling more relaxed now, more willing to tell the truth, more compliant?"

Peter grimaced, somehow, they knew his name. He gritted his teeth, admitting to himself that beneath the pain, he was feeling like a neighborhood gossip with a juicy bit of news. A strange urgency to say something was building within him. He bit back the first words that came to mind and said, "You know what? I really want some ice-cream … preferably chocolate."

Peter stared at a camera mounted next to the intercom. Presumably, he was staring at the man who was asking the questions. He grinned broadly.

"Very well, Mr. Lamb. I see there is still work to do," the disembodied voice said coldly. "Increase the pain enhancer dose."

"Sir," the taller tech said, "we've already given him the maximum recommended amount."

"Double it."

The tall tech frowned and nodded at his shorter assistant. Lou picked up a fresh syringe, loaded it with the pink fluid and pumped it into Peter's veins.

The cold fire assaulted Peter again and then faded away.

"Repeat the process," the voice commanded over the intercom.

Bud, the taller tech stepped forward once again. He surveyed Peter's face, looking for fresh skin. He adjusted his aim, caressing Peter's right ear with the coruscating tip of the baton.

Peter's world disappeared as white lightning surged through him.

* * *

Anton kept the perimeter fence to his right, blurring from tree to tree.

Francis and Juliette's voices were in his ears, urgently ordering him to return to the car. He ignored them, he was already committed to a course of action, and there would be no turning back.

He was going to get his friend Peter out of this place alive or die trying. He wasn't going to lose anyone else – not if he could help it. He came to the last tree and pressed his back hard up against it. Its trunk was thick enough to shield him from the guards at the gatehouse another forty yards away.

He scanned the woods in front of him. No one had followed him, not even Li. She had too much good sense, but damn it all to hell, he had to do something. All the talk in the car had got to him. A part of him acknowledged that it probably made very good sense to sit back and plan, but Peter could die while they talked. He couldn't stand it anymore, the waiting, the inaction – he had to go in and save his friend.

Francis' voice cut through his earbuds, and he ordered, "Anton, hold there. We'll come to you."

Anton checked his H&K MP5, it was ready to go, thirty high-velocity, armor-piercing rounds in the magazine. A second magazine was strapped upside down to the first with black duct tape to allow a quick reload. He held it in his right hand. The scabbard of the Blue Dragon lay strapped over his shoulder, the handle jutting up for a quick draw. He tapped his earbud and declared, "No, Francis. I'm gonna blow the power. The fence and the perimeter defenses will be down, and you can cut through it."

"Non, Anton—"

He centered himself, fell into silence, the Ramp flowering within. A brief break in the cloud cover let sunlight cut through the trees, spearing in bright shafts to the grass covered ground. He turned, rushing around the tree and forward to the commander tank.

He was beside it before anyone could react. He leaped over the 105mm gun mount to the top of the turret. The Shadowstone guards in their body armor started to move, lifting their assault rifles. His H&K was the first to fire, rounds cutting a line through the black-armored troopers. Two fell back, the rest ducked for cover, firing back at him with short, controlled bursts.

Bullets whistled past him, ricocheting off the armor of the commander tank. In one quick motion, he was inside. His feet dropping to the floor. The commander's position was empty.

The driver twisted around beneath him, shouting, "What the—"

Anton's left fist lashed forward, striking the man on the top of his head. He jerked down, unconscious. Anton grabbed hold of the man's uniform, dragging him out of the lower position and pushing him up and out of the tank. More rifle file struck the man's body with wet thuds before Anton pushed him out of the tank, and he disappeared limply over the side.

Something struck the tank, pinging off the armor. The slow stutter of a heavy machine gun firing resounded nearby. Someone was firing a .50 cal at the tank. The standard ball rounds making a lot of noise but not doing any significant damage.

Anton pulled off the Blue Dragon, and dropped into the driver's position, placing his sword next to him in the cramped cabin. The tank sat in hot standby mode. He picked up the controls which the tank's manual had declared, 'were specifically matched with those of a popular games console to minimize the cost of training operators.' A heads-up display appeared, painting a three-dimensional picture of the surrounding battlespace in a holographic bubble around his head. He turned his head, he could see whatever the tank's sensors could access, including feeds from the tactical links to the Shadowstone base.

He floored the accelerator, the tank responded, it's engine roaring as it surged forward. He swung the tank around in a tight circle to the right, taking out the gatehouse, Shadowstone troopers running to escape the collapsing building. The two armored personnel carriers began firing their main weapons, 25mm Bushmaster cannons, rapid fire rounds smashing off the commander's nano-ceramic armor. They were unlikely to destroy the tank, but they could blow off a track, bringing the tank to a halt, or damage the external weapons, or sensor arrays if they got lucky.

They were less than forty yards away, point blank range.

Anton used the console to select his first target and pulled the trigger.

Nothing happened. A flashing red line appeared and outlined the APC in the heads-up display. The word 'FRIENDLY,' flashed above it in bright yellow letters. A set of icons along the bottom border of the HUD caught his eye. One was marked IFF, 'Identify Friend or Foe,' he selected it. A disable option appeared. He punched it – the red line around the APC and the bright yellow warning message disappeared.

Anton pulled the trigger again.

There was a slight momentary hum to his right, then a whip-like crack as the rail gun fired.

Heat fins glowed hot behind his right shoulder, the rail gun system jettisoning waste heat. The eleven-pound tungsten kinetic spike traveling at two miles per second rammed into the middle of the turret of the APC on the right, which promptly evaporated in a fireball. The backwash of the explosion vibrated through the commander tank's hull. An ammo counter on Anton's heads-up display dropped from fifty to forty-nine. Another dial marking the heat dissipation spiked into the red for half a second before returning to green.

Anton didn't waste any time wondering how many rounds the rail gun could fire before heat became an issue. If he needed to break the tank using it, he would. He pivoted the tank's turret slightly to the left, bringing the rail gun to bear on the second APC. Its main gun continued to fire bravely, taking out the grenade launchers on the left-hand side of the commander's turret. The launchers exploded, a ball of flame enveloping the tank, obscuring Anton's vision for half a second.

The flames blew away, the APC resolved into view. The HUD indicated the target with red crosshairs painting the middle of the APC's turret.

Anton pulled the rail gun trigger, there was a slight recoil, the commander tank rocking back momentarily as the rail gun cracked again. The top of the APC disappeared, the wall of a building two hundred yards behind it imploding as the remnants of the kinetic spike tore it apart.

Anton floored the accelerator, the tank rolling forward between the burning wrecks of the APCs.

"I'm in," he broadcast over his in-ear tactical link to the rest of the Mirovar force team.

Anton fired up the full power of the tank's sensor arrays. The sensors connected to a high-flying drone and the base's tactical links. The main power substation for the site was clearly visible on an online map, less than four hundred yards from where he was now. There were at least two buildings in the way and no clear shot. Anton kept the accelerator hard to the floor, the tank surging forward along the road.

There was no time to waste.

* * *

Fire and lightning rushed along Peter's drugged nerves.

The physical transformation of the Ramp increased pain tolerance. A Ramp master still felt pain, but the Ramp transformation greatly enhanced the ability to act through the pain. Shadowstone had developed the drug administered to Peter using regular people as test subjects. As 'Lou,' the short and chubby technician had remarked, they'd never used the drug on an Order of Thoth operative. This was the first time they'd used it against a Ramp master. The results were unpredictable as Shadowstone science encountered ancient genetics honed in a far more hostile environment than the modern world.

The stench of his own burning flesh assaulted Peter. He'd been attempting to fall into silence, to find a secret center where he could master the pain, but the enhanced agony coruscating through his body destroyed every pathway to stillness.

The pain blew through all his barriers, wiping the emotional slate clean. A primal fighting rage exploded through Peter's consciousness, the pain evaporating like damp mist before hell's own furnaces. A dark lightning flashed unseen through nerves and muscles born to war. Something cracked like a whip, Peter's right arm blurring up and right.

Blood, bone, and brains splashed in a broad swathe across the clinical whiteness of the right wall. An instant later, Peter drove a stainless-steel spike through the head of the smiling, chubby faced, second tech on the left. He pulled back his right hand. It was still dripping blood and gobbets of flesh from the thick manacle and half its housing. Descending from the manacle was the lock unit and a half-foot-long steel spike covered in gore ending in a twisted, fractured finger of metal.

Peter glanced right and left. The taller tech's body, now headless, lay crumpled on the floor gushing blood in a spreading pool from the open remains of his neck. Of his head, there was no sign, except the lumpy dripping residue over one corner of the room. The shorter tech had slumped to the floor, blood spouting from two one-inch-wide wounds in his skull to mingle in a spreading pool emanating from the headless body of the other tech.

Peter reached around, pulling the small chrome lever underneath the manacle on his left hand. The manacle opened with a satisfying mechanical click. With his left hand, he freed his right, dropping the gore-slick manacle to the floor. Loosening the belts from his chest, thighs, and shins, he opened the manacles around his ankles and stepped out of the chair.

He rubbed his face with his left hand, and it came away bloody. His left eye was a little hazy, and the top of his right ear was missing. The rage had subsided from a tidal wave to a swollen river. His chest heaved, his eyes narrowing with deeply felt purpose. Explosions resounded dully, the sound struggling to penetrate the armored walls of the mobile rendition unit. Somewhere a siren began wailing in the distance.

"Hey, you pommy bastard, are you still listening?"

The intercom remained silent.

He smiled grimly, the Order had come to rescue him, and the local Shadowstone boss now had bigger problems to deal with.

Peter approached the back door. Its spinlock had four chrome handles jutting out of it. He grabbed them, his rage bubbling away in the background. He ramped hard, twisting the device counter-clockwise. Metal groaned, his face flushed with blood, but the wheel wouldn't budge. Above the spinlock was a retinal scanner. A small light above the scanner glowed a solid red.

"Damn." He had a sneaking suspicion luck wasn't on his side today. He dashed back to the chubby tech, picking his body up by the scruff of his neck, he carried him back to the rear door. In moments, he'd tested the dead tech's eyes with the scanner – the light remained red. He dropped the body, looking back at the wet, congealing splash across the front left corner of the chamber. Somewhere in that mess was a retina that could open this door.

"So much for plan A," Peter said, frowning.

He needed a plan B, and quick, before Shadowstone responded with knockout gas or something else to immobilize him.

Peter shook his head; he wanted his earbuds back. They were a loose end he needed to tie off, and catching up with the upper-crust Shadowstone vampire flunky who had stolen them was high on his to-do list.

But that would have to wait.

He needed to get out of this damned vehicle first.

* * *

All hell was breaking loose.

A wall full of screens told a tale of mayhem and chaos. Three screens, one fed by a high-flying drone, showed various angles on a commander tank accelerating away from the smashed remains of the gatehouse and the burning wrecks of a pair of armored personnel carriers. A dedicated screen revealed the butcher's abattoir the interior of the MRU had become. Somehow the red-headed Order of Thoth operative, 'Peter,' – if that was his real name – had broken free of the interrogation chair. A feat that was supposed to be impossible, but it had happened.

Gordon Heathmont's pale lips thinned into a grim slash, he thumped the desk in front of him and screamed, "Scramble the blackwidows. We have to kill that damned tank before it destroys the Facility."

One of his aides looked up from his command station and asked, "Sir, which wings should I scramble?"

"All of them!" Gordon shouted, staring at the man. He quailed before Gordon's gaze and issued the orders.

"Williams, get me a direct line to Major Quiver."

"Yes, sir," another young aide replied, establishing a secured communications link with the Head of Squadron F, the Phase IV Day Guard contingent in the UK.

The Major's voice came over the line, "Sir, what are your orders."

"We need to stop this bloody tank and secure the Order operative in the MRU."

"Yes, Sir. Consider it done."

"You have tactical command of our assets and full release of weapons. The defense of the Facility is in your hands."

"Understood sir, they won't get past us."

Gordon began to calm down. The defense of the base was in the care of the best men that Shadowstone could find.

He stared at the screens showing the tank. It was accelerating along a road toward a pair of logistics storehouses. That didn't make any sense, there was nothing of great importance in those buildings. The view in the screen shifted as the tank approached the storehouses, bringing into view what was beyond the buildings – the electrical power substation.

"Oh my God," Gordon whispered.

The blackwidows would be too late.

His guts tightened as he watched the screens, powerless to affect what was about to happen.

Gordon slammed both fists on the desk. "Damn! Damn! Damn!"

The Order of Thoth earbuds lay on the desk in front of him. He snarled and crushed them with his fists. They hadn't been aborting the mission and heading for the west of England for a boat pickup, and there was no doubt more than three members in the team. He'd sent half his forces in the wrong direction and would now have to recall them.

They've tricked me!

It was galling.

* * *

Anton didn't believe in doing things by halves.

The commander tank raced along the road belying its massive body. The HUD automatically and seamlessly updating what he could see. Shadowstone hadn't yet shutdown the data feeds, allowing the tank to automatically pull-down data about the base. The manual he'd read on the plane said he could give the tank verbal commands and limited instructions. Anton had no real idea how that would work, but he was determined to give it a try.

"Prisoners. Where are prisoners held?" Anton asked the tank.

In the electronic circuits of the tank a dedicated, natural-language-processing artificial intelligence responded, drawing a map overlay on the HUD. The prison section of the base was located on the southeast corner, almost directly opposite from the side of the base Anton was on. The AI drew two lines that zigzagged around the buildings to the prison section. It labeled one 4:46 and the other 4:58, clearly the amount of time in minutes and seconds it would take the tank to get there by following the roads.

"I've found Peter," Anton called out over the earbud link back to the rest of the Mirovar force team.

"We can't get past the automatic flechette guns, they're tracking too fast," Francis stated. "We're still outside the base."

Anton glanced at the location of the power substation and said, "I'll deal with that now."

He slammed the accelerator, the tank racing forward along the road. The speedometer running up to fifty miles per hour as the two logistics buildings passed to his right. The power substation came into view. He designated three of the biggest structures he could see as targets and set the rail gun to autofire. There was a hum, it fired the first kinetic spike which slammed through the center of a transformer the size of an SUV. The tank rocked slightly with the recoil of the rail gun. The transformer exploded in a shower of sparks. The second and third spikes followed the first at one-second intervals. The substation caught fire as more transformers blew up, streamers of sparks snaking along cables in all directions. The kinetic spikes cut through everything in their way, disappearing through the woods surrounding the base.

"Anton," Francis called angrily over the comms link, "those spikes just went over our heads."

Anton frowned. The heads-up display stuttered for half a second as the data feeds from the Facility failed for a second, then came back online. Batteries, backup diesel generators, whatever – taking out the power substation wasn't the knockout blow he'd expected.

"Get your heads down," Anton broadcast to the team. "I know exactly where you are now." He then asked the onboard AI, "Where are the backup power units? Show me a power grid."

Red lines snaked across the map on the HUD. There were three nodes spread across the base. The backup power in a redundant, distributed array. A slick solution, but not good enough today. Anton targeted all of the nodes, specifying the 105mm gun which began raising its barrel until it was pointing nearly vertical. It fired three times, the shells disappearing through the clouds, leaving smoke-ring indentions in the sky. They would be back in seconds. Anton floored the accelerator again to get the burning power substation out of his line of fire. He targeted the perimeter fence. The 105mm gun lowering, and firing another three rounds on a flat trajectory. The high-explosive rounds destroyed the fence and the flechette guns mounted along that section of the perimeter.

"Fixed?" he asked over the comms link.

Three explosions erupted in the base behind him as the initial three 105mm rounds returned from their highly parabolic flights and struck the backup power generators. Buildings crashed to the ground, debris blowing high into the air, thick plumes of dark gray smoke streaming into the sky. The data feeds from the Facility dropped out and didn't come back on.

There was a pause, then Francis said, "Jay is leading an exfil team to help you and Peter get out. Mon Dieu, Anton – try not to kill them."

Jay's voice came over the comms link, "We'll keep you appraised of where we are by voice. Where's Peter?"

"On the other side, I'm going to get him now."

The tank pivoted on its tracks. There was one functioning asset still feeding data, a Shadowstone drone flying high overhead. Four helicopter icons took off from a flat area on the southwest corner of the base map. The icons, now labeled Widow-1, through to Widow-4, began to accelerate toward him. The last thing Anton needed was four tank-killing gunships catching him out in the open.

"Give me a straight-line path to the prison."

The AI responded with a green line labeled 2:02, cutting from where Anton was through to the southeast corner of the base. A straight-line approach would cut two and a half minutes off the time to reach Peter.

The helicopter gunships were coming up on Anton's right forward flank. He punched the accelerator, the tank surging forward along the green line. A quarter mile away, the first building stood in his way, a long two-story office block.

"Identify structural targets."

A green rectangle marked the office block. Critical support structures popped out in red glows on the HUD. Anton pulled the triggers for the 105mm and the rail gun. The tank slowed momentarily as both guns fired. The kinetic spike hitting first, tearing through the main structural beam of the building before disappearing further into the base. The 105mm high-explosive shell hit next, the middle of the building evaporating in a fiery blast, collapsing to the ground, dust, fire, and smoke billowing into the air.

Anton drove the tank straight at the breach, hoping this new tactic would hold off the blackwidows. He whispered to himself, "Let's see if they'll fire on their own people."

The HUD flickered slightly; the drone data feed had dropped out. The gunship pilots had cut him off from his one remaining external source of data. He was down to what was directly visible from the tank. In seconds, the blackwidows would rise over the base, drawing line of sight on the commander tank. Anton expected they would begin by attacking him with their purpose-built anti-tank Hellfire III missiles. He selected another icon on the HUD, setting the 7.62mm minigun sitting on top of the turret to defensive fire vs missile threats. It might buy him some time against the blackwidows.

Time, he suspected he was rapidly running out of.

* * *

Li took a position on the fence line opposite the ruined gatehouse.

Shadowstone had abandoned the entrance to the Facility as they concentrated their forces on defeating the commander tank running amok through their base.

Li, Jay, and Yvette had left the breach in the perimeter fence alone, moving straight to the destroyed gatehouse. It was the best location to organize a quick exfil from. They only needed Anton and Peter to arrive, and they could all escape the base together.

She sighted along the top of the buildings with her .50 caliber sniper rifle. The handle of the Green Dragon jutted up over her right shoulder where it lay strapped to her combat webbing. Nearby, Jay and Yvette took up positions, armed with their katanas and a pair of H&K MP5 9mm submachine guns, and a Milkor MGL respectively.

Almost half a mile away, a ragged scar cut into the base. Judging from the smoke, explosions and the rapid-fire cracks of a 105mm cannon set to autofire, Anton, and the commander tank were almost a third of the way through the base heading directly for the southeast corner.

Four blackwidow helicopters were in the air, zeroing in on Anton's location, they fanned out in a loose semi-circle. Two new armored personnel carriers rushed along the road toward the smoking rip in the buildings.

Jay said, "Anton, we're at the gatehouse, and you've got another two APCs on your six."

Four Humvee-sized vehicles, with 7.62mm M240 machine guns on their roofs, and packed with fully-armored Shadowstone troopers followed after the APCs.

Li stared at the Shadowstone base and the forces beginning to swarm against Anton. *How are we going to get out of this? My God Anton, what have you done? At least they don't know the rest of us are here yet and their power is knocked out.* She called out over the tactical link, "Anton, Shadowstone are coming in numbers, move faster, there is no more time."

"Yeah, I got that," he replied, his voice calm.

He's becoming reckless and fatalistic.

She watched, powerless to help as gunships, APCs and Shadowstone troops converged on Anton's position.

What would happen now?

She had no idea.

* * *

Gordon ran through the open front doors of the command center, surrounded by his aides and Phase IV Day Guard security detail. The building next to the command center blew up in a tower of flame as successive high-explosive 105mm shells ripped it apart. Cutting through the noise of the explosions was the whip-crack of the commander tank's rail gun.

His jaw gaped open in horror as the rogue commander tank emerged into view. The heat dispersal fins at the back of the tank glowed a dull red, the air shimmering thickly above them. Beyond the tank, four blackwidows hovered in a fan formation about five hundred yards above the base. The formation allowed them to concentrate their attacks on a single target.

He could see them hesitating to fire. His previous order releasing all weapons for use against the commander tank had not been clear enough. They'd standing orders not to fire on the Facility itself lest they kill other Shadowstone personnel remained in place. They hadn't fired as they didn't have a clear shot that avoided friendly casualties. Gordon glowered; friendly casualties were a given at this point, there was no time to be overly cautious.

The commander tank disappeared into the wreckage, in less than a minute it would be breaching the prison section where the mobile rendition unit and the most high-value prisoner he'd ever captured waited.

Gordon fingered his smartphone as he ran away from the defunct command center, setting up broadcast links with Major Quiver and the pilots of the blackwidows. "Fire on that damned tank," he shouted. "Fire now men, be about it."

"Yes, Sir," Major Quiver replied. "Widows one through four, fire at will."

"Roger," chorused the pilots.

Gordon remembered James Haley's warnings. "Major Quiver, there's no doubt an Order of Thoth team is waiting nearby to exfiltrate their own operatives. Find them and deal with them."

"Yes, Sir."

Gordon glanced up; thin trails of white smoke were lancing across the sky. All four of the blackwidows had fired a volley of Hellfire missiles at the rogue commander tank.

The eight missiles darted forward. He stared at them, willing them to destroy the tank with every fiber of his being.

* * *

The 7.62mm minigun whirred above Anton's head, its six barrels rotating in a blur, spent shell casings spraying in a wide swathe to its left.

A long tongue of fire gushed from the minigun's throat as four-thousand rounds per minute of depleted uranium penetrators speared up at the incoming Hellfire missiles. The commander tank's onboard AI integrated the available missile tracks, calculating their future paths relative to everything else within reach of its onboard sensor arrays. It discarded two missiles as threats, their paths destined to intercept falling masonry, and other debris. The remaining six it methodically picked off from right to left. The last exploded half a dozen yards from the tank, the thermobaric blast momentarily engulfing the vehicle in bright fire.

Anton rocked in his seat as the ear-splitting explosion of the last Hellfire missile washed over the turret. An armor-integrity counter on the HUD dropped from ninety-eight to seventy-six and shifted from green to yellow.

The commander tank emerged from the flames, both main guns leveled at the last remaining barrier to the prison – a stone wall. Anton drove forward, the tank crunching over the smoking remains of a fallen building. The 105mm fired, the rail gun cracked, the last barrier fell before the barrage. The way was clear, Anton drove the tank through the last of the wreckage and into an open area before the warehouse that was doubling as a prison.

In moments, he would be through the prison wall.

Alarms beeped, the rail gun was down to five shots, the same with the 105mm. The minigun was at thirty percent and falling as it dealt with the last of a second volley of Hellfire missiles.

The final Hellfire missile in the second volley exploded a yard short of the hull. Anton lurched against his restraints, the tank rocking on its tracks as a wall of flame washed over it. Multiple alarms resounded through the cabin, half the indicators on the heads-up display were solidly in the red, the rest were a sea of yellow warnings with the occasional island of green.

In the ascending chaos, Anton gritted his teeth and pushed forward. The tank's tracks ripped through grass, soil, and concrete as he lined up on the wall of the prison.

He wasn't going to survive the next volley. The blackwidows were re-arranging their positions, taking up the points of a square and coming closer to minimize the vulnerable flight time of their missiles.

With the armor-integrity counter dropping to thirty-six percent and solidly red – time had run out.

* * *

Juliette's eyelids fluttered.

She sat next to Francis in the front Range Rover. Francis brought the vehicle into position to run hard past the Shadowstone base and pick up his team to head north. The second Range Rover with Luther and Chiara in it was a dozen yards behind them.

At least that was the plan they'd cobbled together after Anton had rushed into the Shadowstone base. In her mind palace, everyone was in terrible danger. Anton's precipitous actions had risked the whole team, and the probability of his own survival was close to zero. They'd lose Peter and Anton with him. She dropped out of her mind palace, cut deeply by what she'd seen.

"Mon, Dieu," she whispered, her eyes wide.

"Juliette?" Francis asked in worried tones.

"Soon my love, soon we must flee."

Francis' face was grim beside her, and he whispered harshly, "I had my doubts about Anton back at the safe house. We can't manage him – he's too much like his grandfather."

"Don't give up on Anton yet, there is something powerful working through him."

Francis stared at her. "What have you seen?"

"Not enough, but give him time. He could save us all."

"Or destroy us."

Juliette's eyelids dropped for a second. "That remains to be seen."

The future remained deeply hidden in shadows, unknowable, wreathed in darkness. Was there any room left for hope? Juliette knew where she would always stand – come what may. She grasped Francis' hands with her own, squeezed and declared passionately, "We will win through in the end."

"Will we be alive to see it?" Francis asked, his face betraying sudden doubt.

She looked in his eyes for a long moment, her heart filled with faith and promised, "Yes, we will."

* * *

Anton scanned the heads-up display, his eyes intense, his mouth grim.

He used the controller to direct the rail gun, and the 105mm gun at the two blackwidows moving into position in front of him and pulled the triggers.

His guts clenched tight as the third volley of missiles leaped from the hovering gunships at his tank. The minigun above his head whirred into life, its ammo counter descending through the low twenties toward zero percent. The 105mm gun fired first, a great tongue of flame leaping from its barrel as the round speared upward at the first helicopter gunship on the left. The rail gun was next, the kinetic spike flashing faster than an eye could follow at the second blackwidow on the right. Behind Anton, the tank's heat fins failed catastrophically, overloaded by the nearly continuous firing they blew apart in a brilliant shower of burning fragments.

The rail gun would never fire again.

Incoming Hellfire missiles, the 105mm high-explosive round, and the eleven-pound tungsten kinetic spike all passed each other in mid-air halfway between the commander tank and the blackwidow gunships.

Above the jagged remains of the heat fins, the minigun spewed fire, ejecting spent shell casings in a wide swathe as it rotated around to cover the incoming missiles. Its barrels were a blur of motion, the onboard AI dedicating every resource to defending the tank. Missile after missile blew apart mid-air as the minigun's depleted uranium rounds sliced through them.

The blackwidow on the right took the eleven-pound kinetic spike, through its nose. The tungsten slug shot through the cabin, instantly turning the crew into a pink mist. Without any visible loss of momentum, the slug sliced through the right-side engine, clipped the main rotor on the way through and disappeared somewhere into the next county.

The second last Hellfire missile speared through the minigun's defensive fire. The exploding warhead evaporated the minigun in a nightmarish thermobaric glare. The rail gun cracked along its spine, and all the tracks on the right side of the tank blew off. Ablative, ceramic armor around the main cabin disintegrated; partially dissipating the force of the Hellfire missile blast away from the crew.

Anton rocked in his seat, a wave of heat washing over him. Sparks flew from shorting equipment. The heads-up display failed. The stench of singed hair filled his nostrils.

The blackwidow on the left took the high-explosive 105mm round in the middle of the cabin, the resultant explosion scattered the gunship across the roof of the prison facility in a cloud of burning fragments.

The last of the Hellfire missiles struck the front of the commander tank. The thermobaric explosion dislodged the 105mm gun, cracked open the hull and ripped apart the front half of the tank. The turret canted backward at a twenty-degree angle, its ablative ceramic armor stripped away, exposing the bare metal of the cabin shell.

The stricken gunship on the right, its crew vaporized by the kinetic spike, its right engine shooting flames like a giant's toy firework, fell like a stone. Diving nose first onto the edge of the prison building, it promptly flipped over toward the ground. It never reached the concrete pathway beneath it, exploding in a huge fireball as the rest of its munitions and fuel detonated in a blinding glare.

The commander tank stood silently, canted to the right on its shredded tracks. Its 105mm gun barrel sloped crazily away to the left, the rail gun was a useless tangle of steaming metal on the right. Heat waves shimmered off the rear of the tank. Smoke and steam issued in plumes from ragged holes over the engine bay.

A gaping hole in the prison wall, next to the burning wreck of the second gunship, stood directly in front of the tank. Behind the tank lay a long, thick trail of smoking ruins.

The last two blackwidows peeled away, racing toward the front gate and their next engagement with the forces attacking the Shadowstone base.

* * *

Gordon Heathmont watched in horror as two of the blackwidows fell from the sky in flaming ruins.

There was a bright glare next to the prison section as one of the helicopters blew up, a plume of greasy smoke rising high in the air. Scattered fires and burning debris lit the prison section's roof. The surviving blackwidows veered away from the battle and raced toward the front gate.

They must have destroyed the rogue commander tank, or else the blackwidows would have stayed there to continue the fight.

Gordon fitted a pair of Shadowstone earbud communicators slaved to his smartphone, all his comm links became live.

Major Quiver's voice came over the tactical link, "Sir, our overhead drone has identified three intruders near the main gate, I am vectoring the remaining blackwidows onto their position."

"Get the MRU in motion. The base is without power. It's indefensible. Get the prisoner to Coningsby airbase. We have an A400 transport inbound, I will re-purpose it to this mission. We can airlift the prisoner out of the country and out of range of this Order of Thoth team. It's imperative the prisoner gets to the airbase alive. Ensure the blackwidows guard the MRU."

"What of the three Order operatives at the gate."

"Kill them if the opportunity presents itself, otherwise ignore them – three can't make a difference. The MRU and the prisoner are your sole concern now."

"Yes, Sir," Major Quiver growled. "… I've given the order. The MRU is in motion."

"Keep me in the loop. I'm evacuating this base with my security detail."

"Roger, that."

"Good man – now protect the prisoner."

"Yes, Sir."

The line muted. Gordon climbed into the back of his dark-blue Jaguar sedan. Three members of his security detail came with him. The rest boarded a pair of four-wheeled, armored Humvee-sized MRAP vehicles armed with 7.62mm M240 machine guns on their roofs. He would follow the MRU and ensure it made it onboard the A400 transport aircraft. He would fly out with the prisoner. Where would they go? Saudi Arabia was always helpful, but shockingly hot in the middle of August. He frowned, unfortunately, the kingdom would have to do; the Saudis had one key advantage, he could trust them to turn a blind eye and see the bigger picture.

Once on the plane and safely in the air, he would phone ahead, making sure the local Shadowstone cells were active and positioned to deal with the prisoner. He was sure Peter Lamb would eventually break and would be a treasure trove of information on Shadowstone's enemies.

The information inside the Order of Thoth agent's head was of primary value. He'd just about sacrifice anything to keep it within his reach.

Gordon stared through the car window and ignored what was outside the vehicle. The next hour would be the most important in his life. It would be pivotal in determining the future of the secret war between Shadowstone and the Order of Thoth.

Of that, he was sure.

* * *

Anton surfaced into agony, the darkness ebbing away.

A terrible ringing was clawing at his ears. Half-dazed, Anton shook his head and then swore mightily, his hands rising to cover his face. Moving his head had been a mistake.

He wriggled his fingers and toes – everything hurt like hell, but everything also moved.

The interior of the tank felt like a sauna on overdrive. A dull red light, running off emergency battery power filled the cabin. The air was thick with smoke, Anton wheezed and coughed, tasting blood in his mouth.

He reached up, punching a button next to the top hatch. Explosive bolts fired, the top door of the commander tank promptly blowing off. Grabbing the Blue Dragon and his H&K MP5, he jumped up onto the top edge of the tank. His boots sizzled on the hot metal, and he immediately leaped onto the ground.

He fell to his knees, coughing hard again, spots of blood appearing on the torn-up ground in front of him.

"That's not a good sign," he observed, pushing himself up onto one knee.

Juliette's voice sounded in his ears – a precognitive whisper, "Peter's being moved." Her voice firmed. "Everyone, head for the main gate; they're taking him from the site. We'll pick you up, exfil now!"

Anton had fought his way to a standstill to reach the prison, and now he had to go all the way back. He stood up, blinking his eyes, gritting his teeth and sucking air in through his nose. He started jogging back along the trail of devastation left by the tank. His ribs hurt abominably with every breath. He grimaced in pain, whatever was necessary – he'd get the job done.

Peter wasn't free yet.

The ringing in his ears was dropping away, and his lungs started to clear. He fell into silence and managed to Ramp. In moments, he was blurring over the rubble of the base back toward the entrance.

* * *

A turbine ignited and began spooling up with a steadily increasing whine.

"This thing's jet-powered?" Peter asked incredulously. He put his hands on his face, then jerked them away. His face was still painfully tender after the ministrations of Shadowstone's torture techs.

The truck started moving, rolling smoothly forward over the concrete floor of the prison section. The engine gave a low throaty rumble. His enemies had built the mobile rendition unit for speed and protection, it would be hard to stop.

He needed to get out of this mobile prison, the longer he stayed in, the worse his chances of survival were. He reached up to the wheel lock on the overhead hatch. With the ceiling only about eight feet off the floor, he could reach the arms of the spinlock. But with his arms extended over his head, he had virtually zero leverage.

The spinlock on the overhead latch was half the size of the one on the rear door. Peter grinned; it might be within his ability to literally tear it apart. He needed to solve his lack of leverage. He crunched hard, pivoting upward, planting his big boots to either side of the hatch in the ceiling. Crouched upside down from the ceiling, his big hands wrapped around the chrome handles of the spinlock, he plunged deep into silence. The Ramp flowered within, power flowed along muscles and nerves already configured for extraordinary strength. His muscles bulged; his veins popped – the wheel didn't budge.

He strained for another ten seconds, then dropped back down to the floor.

Wiping perspiration from his brow with his forearm, he declared with a measure of respect, "Damn, they built that tough."

The truck turned hard to the right, the wheels began running over a rougher surface and started to pick up speed. There were no windows but it was clear the MRU was outside the building, and on a road, before long it would be off the base.

"I need a lever."

Peter started looking for something within the chamber he could use to break the spinlock on the top hatch. Then an idea struck him, and he smiled broadly.

He dashed to the back of the chamber to check the larger spinlock. If the spinlocks had the same basic construction, he might have a way out.

* * *

The two MRAPs burned on the right side of the road, seventy yards inside the base. Half a dozen black-armored troopers lay scattered around them.

Yvette hunkered down under cover of the smoking hulk of one of the armored personnel carriers. She pushed the last of her reloads into the Milkor MGL and glanced over to Jay and Li sheltering next to the second APC on the other side of the road. They'd completed their ammunition reloads and were ready for the next attack. A pair of Shadowstone troopers – the faster than normal ones – were hiding behind their wrecked vehicles waiting for reinforcements.

Jay, Li and Yvette's position was indefensible. They had to break contact with the enemy and make an escape as soon as possible. The sound of approaching gunship helicopters screamed it might be too late. A single hellfire missile fired at their position would wipe them all out.

Juliette's voice came over the comms link, "I've hacked their drone. Two blackwidows are inbound. They're providing top cover for a convoy approaching your position. There is a lead vehicle, looks like an armored version of a semi-trailer rig with an armored trailer – it's a mobile rendition unit. There are two APCs and four MRAPs following it. Prepare for immediate exfil."

Yvette risked a quick glance around the edge of the APC. The convoy was passing the destroyed buildings on the edge of the main base, where Anton had driven the commander tank on his quest to rescue Peter. She pulled herself back, a three-round burst from an assault rifle pinging off the armor of the APC. The two surviving troopers near the burning MRAPs had her position under their crosshairs.

"I'm on, I'm on," Anton shouted across the comms link.

"Where are you?" Francis growled.

"I'm on top of the MRU. Peter's inside, this is what they're using to transport him."

"… Agreed," Juliette observed. "It's the most likely way they would move him."

"You're mad!" Luther declared. "… Not you Juliette, I mean Slayne."

Francis demanded, "Anton, what do you hope to achieve?"

"This truck has to stop sometime, and I'll be waiting to get Peter out."

"Don't try and do this by yourself," Li warned.

Yvette looked across the road at Li. The novice loremaster's face creased with growing desperation. Too many of her friends were at risk. Yvette glanced knowingly back at Jay, a decision passing between them in an instant. They would not leave Anton to fight this battle alone.

The specially designed armored truck slowed to turn the corner facing onto the road beside the destroyed gatehouse.

"The truck! Get on the truck!" Jay shouted urgently.

Li nodded; her face filled with intent.

Yvette readied herself, as soon as she moved from cover the troopers would start shooting at her, she would have to be faster than they were. Slinging her Milkor MGL over her shoulder, she adjusted her katana shoulder straps and silenced her mind. The Ramp overtook her, time slowed down, and she waited, still as stone for the right opportunity to move.

The MRU was the first vehicle in the convoy. It drove between the two APC wrecks, its powerful bulk moving between them like a great white shark indifferent to anything else in its domain. The rig's turbine engine rumbled, its metal flanks armored and curved, an indomitable steel beast seemingly from another world, it passed her, towing the armored trailer behind it.

Yvette wasn't sure if what Anton had just done was bold or crazy – perhaps it was a bit of both. She accelerated forward along the road, leaping onto the side of the armored MRU trailer. There were multiple service handholds for maintenance staff, she grabbed hold of them. Bullets whined past her, striking sparks off the trailer. She scrambled to the flat top of the trailer as it accelerated past the ruins of the gatehouse.

Anton was already there, hugging the top of the vehicle and looking like he'd passed through a furnace. The left side of his face lay raw and bloody. What remained of his hair clung half-burned to his scalp. Lines of dried blood ran from his nostrils and the corners of his mouth over his chin. His eyes burned wild and hot with a fearsome resolve.

Jay and Li both appeared on the other side of the roof at the same time, a fraction of a second behind her, bullets and tracers flying overhead. The height of the trailer created a sheltered area on the roof above the trooper's angle of fire.

The MRU approached the main road, its great horn blaring. It barely slowed to take the corner to the right. They straightened up; they were on the road heading north. A pair of blackwidows angled in to pace the convoy.

They were heading back to the RAF airbase at Coningsby.

Yvette looked around herself, her lips thinned. *Frying pan, meet fire.*

Chapter Twenty One

BREAKING: Explosions reported at UK MOD site

There are reports of multiple explosions at a Ministry of Defense site in South Lincolnshire.

Published 08/22 11:52

Witnesses report a massive pall of smoke rising over the base of the recently formed Squadron F.

– Breaking News article on the Internet.

* * *

North of the Facility, South Lincolnshire, August 22nd, 11:52

The two charcoal-colored Range Rovers motored along at sixty miles an hour.

Francis had positioned the remainder of his team ahead of the approaching convoy. There was no point being behind the convoy with half of Shadowstone UK between the rest of the team and himself. All he needed to do was stay in front and identify an opportunity to help the team escape.

Scanning her laptop, Juliette stated, "Panopticon hazing has begun. That will hide our SUVs from their drones and any other cameras and sensors. We've got about fifteen minutes, twenty at best." She nodded; her lips pursed. "Shadowstone cyberwarfare units out of Beijing, Saint Petersburg and Seattle have already begun counter attacks."

"Fifteen minutes will have to do," Francis observed.

Chiara spoke up from the second SUV, where Luther was driving, and she was keeping watch, "I don't know if we'll have fifteen minutes. They're coming fast, eighty, ninety miles per hour, and the APCs and MRAPs are keeping pace."

Francis pushed down on the accelerator; the Range Rover's supercharged engine responded with effortless power. The SUV surged forward, the speedometer climbing to eighty-five miles per hour.

"The two blackwidows are flying top cover," Chiara added.

"How far back are they?" Francis asked.

"About half a mile … and closing slowly."

Francis accelerated to ninety miles per hour, the SUV racing along the road. There was no traffic heading in either direction, had Shadowstone blocked the roads? He asked Juliette, "Sitrep, any police roadblocks activated in front of us?"

"Got it," Juliette said, her fingers flashing over her laptop. "Yes. Connecting roads between the Shadowstone base and the RAF airbase at Coningsby have roadblocks. That's the confirmation we've been looking for, they're taking Peter back to the airbase."

"They'll fly him out of the country."

"And half our team is on that truck."

"C'est un foutu bordel!" Francis swore. He didn't need to wonder how the team had ended up in their current position – Anton Slayne. Despite Anton's disobedience, the objectives remained clear. Get Peter back, break contact with Shadowstone and disappear back beneath the Panopticon's radar – and do it all in the next fifteen to twenty minutes – while Juliette's cyberwarfare attacks hazed the Panopticon.

Then they could get back to the main mission, rescuing Ramin Kain, or more correctly, stopping him from leaking all the secret knowledge of the Order of Thoth to the Vampire Dominion.

He broadcast to the team, "Anton, Jay, Yvette, Li. Report in."

Howling wind came over the earbuds, then the voices of the team members clinging to the MRU cutting through, enhanced by technology to pick out their words against any background noise. Jay shouted, "We're on top of the truck."

Yvette and Li reported in, then Anton yelled urgently, "Guys, we've got to move!"

What else was about to go wrong? Francis glanced into the rear-view mirror. A futile gesture, everyone was too far away for him to see what was happening.

Chiara said calmly, "The blackwidows are descending to flank the MRU on both sides."

They're sitting ducks up there.

Francis' heart leaped. There was nothing he could do.

* * *

The mobile rendition unit raced along the road, a pair of armored personnel carriers and four MRAPs hot on its heels.

Victoria Hansen, a flight officer for the aerial wing of Squadron F, lowered her blackwidow helicopter gunship to three hundred yards above the ground and about two hundred yards to the left of the MRU. Her wingman mirrored her position in the second blackwidow on the opposite side of the road. Four Order operatives clung to the roof of the trailer section, barely holding on as ninety-mile-per-hour winds lashed them. Their weapons included a sniper rifle, some submachine guns, and a Milkor MGL. It was primarily the MGL she was concerned about. Without specialized ammunition, the other weapons wouldn't be able to penetrate her gunship's armor. She was at least three hundred and fifty yards away from the MGL; on the practical limits of its range.

"Select your targets," She ordered her gunner. The man was already staring at the four enemy operatives, the right-side minigun pointing directly at the roof of the MRU. With a squeeze of his trigger finger, he would scrape those vermin off the top of the trailer with an irresistible stream of 7.62mm depleted uranium penetrators.

All she needed now was permission to fire. The fight had passed beyond the Facility and was now in open civilian territory, the rules of engagement had changed. She opened her comms link to Major Quiver and Director Heathmont, and reported, "Sir, we have the targets lit up. Ready to take the shot."

Major Quiver ordered, "Weapons are cleared for—"

"Belay that order," Director Heathmont interrupted, cutting across his subordinate. "Widow dash Three, what munitions are loaded in your miniguns?"

"Standard 7.62mm penetrators, Sir," Victoria answered.

"Major Quiver, what is the hull rating on the MRU trailer?"

"Protection up to and including .50 caliber ball, Sir," Major Quiver said.

"The MRU is not rated against 7.62mm depleted uranium rounds, is it?"

"No, Sir."

"A minigun with penetrators could cut that trailer in half, couldn't it?"

"Sir? Yes, Sir."

"You could kill my prisoner, couldn't you?"

"Sir?"

"Widow dash Three, you and your wingman are cleared to fire warning shots only. I want that rig at Coningsby airbase as soon as possible with the prisoner alive. Make sure they stay on the road. Major Quiver, the .50 cal machine guns on the APCs, the M240s on the MRAPs and your trooper's small arms are released for immediate use between here and the RAF airbase. Is that clear?"

"Yes, Sir."

"Then be about it. Clear those Order of Thoth scum off my truck."

"Roger that, Sir," Major Quiver replied enthusiastically.

The line muted. Victoria had her orders. She stared, steely-eyed, at the Order of Thoth operatives riding bold as brass on the MRU's trailer. She tilted her helmeted head to the right, and then to the left. There was a soft cartilage click somewhere near the place her neck connected with her body.

She would just have to wait and play nursemaid for the troops on the ground.

She barked a short, dismissive laugh. A nursemaid! It wasn't what she had signed up with the 'Stateless Warfare Wing,' more commonly known as Squadron F for. 'F' was another one of the squadrons comprising the Special Airborne Service, the famous SAS of the British army. The same, but different; more cutting edge, always outfitted with the very latest technology, and never short of funds. There was a deeper mystery as well, sometimes late at night after she'd shared a bottle of scotch or two with the other pilots, someone would mutter a single word – Shadowstone.

Shadowstone, a nebulous, super-secret outfit that seemed to be operating just out of sight at the highest echelons of government and the corporate world. That was her goal, she wanted into the game, and she wanted in bad.

Being a gunship jockey was just a stepping stone to bigger things.

* * *

The pair of blackwidow gunships paced to either side of the mobile rendition unit. The thunder of their engines muted by the howling ninety-mile-per-hour winds rushing over the heavy vehicle.

Anton crabbed his way along the top of the MRU's trailer, moving from maintenance hand hold to hand hold to avoid the hurricane-like slipstream tearing him off the top of the trailer. He hugged the top of the vehicle, chancing a quick glance over the rear lip of the trailer to see what was chasing them.

A bullet went straight through his hair above his right ear.

He ducked back behind the lip, his earbud communicator broadcasting his voice despite the wind as he swore, "What the hell!"

"Anton?" Li asked.

"There are two armored personnel carriers, and four of those armored Humvee-style vehicles right behind us."

MRAPs, he remembered Peter saying, Mine Resistant Ambush Protected vehicles, he'd talked about them back at the safe house in Maine. Modern, tough, and fast, typically armed with a machine gun or other weapons, and the natural successor to the 'coffin on four wheels,' Peter had called the Humvee.

Yvette said, "The helicopters haven't tried shooting at us."

"Probably don't want to hurt their prize," Jay suggested, tapping the top of the trailer.

Anton stared at his team mates. He was the only one facing forward. Li, Jay, and Yvette, all faced him, more or less in a line across the top of the trailer on the other side of a hatch in the roof. The hatch had no visible means of opening from the outside. Damn it, they needed to get Peter out of the trailer as soon as possible. The top hatch was useless as a means to enter the trailer.

Anton said, "We have no strategy."

"Yeah, no kidding," Jay remarked, staring accusingly at Anton.

Yvette smacked Jay on the shoulder.

"Hey," Jay objected. "Just being honest."

"It doesn't matter how we got here – we're here for Peter," Li declared.

They all looked at each other.

"The rest of the team are in front of us," Li explained. "We need to stay with this vehicle until we can get Peter out of it. Anything else leaves Peter trapped by Shadowstone."

The rest of the team nodded.

Francis called out over the comms link, "We're heading for Coningsby airbase. They're planning to fly Peter out of the country."

Anton shook his head, that was never going to happen, not if he could do anything about it.

Machine gun fire erupted simultaneously from both sides of the MRU, striking sparks off the top edges of the trailer. A moment later, a pair of fragmentation grenades looped into the air from either side, over the edge of the trailer, and began falling toward them.

Anton ramped hard, one of the grenades was heading toward his head. Anchored with his left hand, he drew the Blue Dragon from the scabbard strapped behind his shoulders in a blur. His hand flashed up, the blade arcing around. He twisted his wrist at the very last moment, striking the grenade with the flat of his blade, sending it flying backward.

It dropped out of sight, exploding with a loud crack, a hail of shrapnel rattling against the side of the MRU. The forward rush of the vehicle immediately left the gray smoke of the explosion behind. Jay dealt with the second grenade with the same result on the other side of the trailer.

Machine guns fired again, coordinated bursts from left and right, and from behind the MRU. The only advantage they had, was the height of the MRU's roof forced the Shadowstone troopers to fire up at them, leaving a strip down the middle of the roof that they couldn't hit with their bullets.

The very location they were throwing their grenades into.

Chiara said through the comms link, "Right hand curve coming up in three, two, one—"

Four grenades flew overhead as the MRU shifted to the right.

Jay and Yvette both batted grenades away with their swords. Two of the grenades flew toward Anton, one from the left, and the other from the right. If he allowed himself to rise up too high, he would become an easy target for the gunners. He flipped over, his sword flashing left and right.

The grenades flew away exploding mid-air but out of range to do any damage.

Li scuttled over to take a position next to him.

Chiara directed again, "Left-hand curve coming up in three, two, one, now."

The truck turned back to the left.

Anton glanced at Li.

She caught his gaze and frowned, her large, brown eyes flashing fiercely. "You broke your promise."

"No, I didn't," Anton objected, indignation rising in his voice.

Li shook her head once, her eyes wide. "Don't try and justify what you did … Oh, why do I bother?"

A grenade sailed over the side of the MRU trailer. Anton blurred over Li, striking it away with the flat of his blade. It exploded harmlessly, well behind the trailer. He came back down as fresh machine gun fire flashed overhead. Li had moved to the other side of the trailer, a grenade falling toward her.

Anton yelled, "Watch—"

Li blurred, the Green Dragon flashing above her. The grenade vanished back the way it came. A thin scream of horrified despair wailed on the air as the grenade exploded over the MRAP it had come from.

"—out," Anton said, his voice tailing off.

Li glared at him. "I haven't finished with you yet."

Anton shook his head. Li was disappointed with him. It was happening a lot lately. What did she really want from him? He made himself busy looking for fresh threats. What would happen next? Would the Shadowstone troopers run out of grenades, or would they get lucky?

Bullets whizzed overhead, forcing the team to keep their heads down.

Anton looked past Li, scanning the edges of the trailer.

What attack would Shadowstone try next?

* * *

Peter cocked his head, a hail of metal fragments smashing against the MRU's flank. Their sharp, sudden rattle adding to the muted cacophony of explosions, and almost constant ricochets of bullets hitting the trailer's armored hull.

"L109A2 high explosive grenade," he whispered to himself distractedly, "Standard issue for British special forces."

He returned his attention to the task at hand. Unscrewing one of the handles of the ceiling hatch spinlock. It fell free in his hand. He stepped back from the hatch, comparing the threads of the short handle with another larger one he'd taken from the spinlock on the back door.

The two threads matched, they were the same length and width. They were interchangeable. Peter started working as fast as he could to remove a second of the short handles opposite the first one on the ceiling spinlock and replace them with two of the longer, heavier handles from the lock on the main door.

Soon he would have a second chance with the ceiling hatch, this time with double the leverage.

The second short handle dropped to the floor with a sharp clank, before rolling away beneath a white enameled cabinet. Peter rushed back to the rear door for the replacement handle.

He worked fast – tight and focused.

In a couple of minutes, he would be ready to open the ceiling hatch.

At least, that was the plan.

* * *

The Squadron F trooper tightened his white-knuckle grip on the steering wheel of the MRU.

A bead of perspiration slowly tracked its way from his short, salt and pepper hair down his left temple. He was beginning to wonder if being an MRU driver was such a great career choice, what with the constant shooting, explosions and navigating bends at ninety miles per hour when the speed limit was sixty. He glanced across at his colleague who was riding shotgun, armed to the teeth and grinning like a lunatic.

His thin lips pressed tightly together.

The new blokes were all adrenaline junkies; completely hyped up on 'the juice.' As a driver, participation in the Day Guard program had been optional, and he'd opted out. In another two months, his twenty years of service with the squadron would be up, and he would be taking the package. He'd seen things to give a man nightmares, and enough was enough; it was time to get out.

Director Heathmont's voice came over the comms link, "MRU Driver?"

"Yes, Sir."

"Drive faster," Director Heathmont ordered. "The wind will blow those scoundrels off the top of the truck."

Why on Earth would I want to go any faster?

"How much faster, Sir?"

"Isn't it obvious man? As fast as possible."

"Yes, Sir."

"Do it, man, knock those bastards off my truck."

"Yes, Sir."

The line muted.

The driver blinked. He sucked air in through his nose and let it out in a long sigh, it didn't help. He pushed forward on the accelerator. The turbine behind the cabin roared, and the truck surged forward to one hundred and ten miles per hour.

He wondered what would happen to the poor fools on top of the MRU's trailer. No one could hold on in such winds.

Surely, they're doomed.

* * *

The howling wind threatened to tear the clothes from Anton's body.

Anton tightened his grip on a hand hold, silently thanking the safety conscious engineer who had put maintenance handholds over the top and sides of the truck. He squinted his eyes to look into the wind. Every five or ten seconds, a burst of gunfire would go over their heads, or strike sparks off the side edges of the trailer roof.

Sometimes, grenades would fly up, and they would beat them away. The Shadowstone troopers were mixing things up, holding onto their grenades until the last second so they would explode before Anton and his friends could deflect them away. The team had anticipated the tactic, getting as close to the edge of the roof as possible. The last grenade had exploded a split second after Jay had smacked it back the way it had come. The bulk of the blast had occurred over the head of whoever had thrown it, but Jay sported nasty lacerations along his left arm for his trouble. Blood dripped down his arm in a red streak and pain gripped his face, leaving him scowling and gritting his teeth.

"Yvette?" Anton shouted. "How many rounds have you got left in the MGL?"

"A full load, but we can't use it from here. Their fire is too concentrated."

Anton nodded. "Right." He sheathed the Blue Dragon and scrambled forward along the top of the truck. Yvette gave him the MGL as he passed by, a nonplussed look on her face. He dropped into silence, ramped hard and blurred over the forward lip of the trailer's roof. Dropping down, his boots landed on a triangular articulated frame attaching the trailer to the rig.

He backed up to the rear of the rig's cabin. Sheltering from the wind, he checked the MGL, it was ready to fire. Where he stood, he could see the outside front corner of an MRAP less than six yards away. If he leaned out a bit more, he'd be able to get a clean shot straight into it.

Of course, they would be able to see him too.

Without hesitation, Anton crouched down low on the frame, anchored himself with his left hand and leaned out as far as he could. The dark-gray bitumen of the road whipped past beneath him. The leading wheels of the MRU trailer thrummed against it. The hurricane force winds tore at his shoulder and arm, threatening to rip the MGL from his grip.

In front of him, a black-clad Shadowstone trooper stood up through the MRAP's hatch. With a grenade in each hand, he drew his arms back to throw them up at the rest of the team.

Anton pulled the trigger, the MGL fired, the grenade lancing forward through the base of the windscreen of the MRAP. Its shaped charge warhead sent a molten copper whip slashing through the cabin, obliterating the crew. The trooper collapsed back into the MRAP as smoke billowed out of the hatch, and the MRAP veered away from the MRU.

The dead trooper's live grenades bounced off the road, promptly exploding next to the rear wheels of the MRU, shredding the rubber on the nearest wheel. The next two wheels behind it took up the load, while a subtle vibration settled into the trailer.

Anton pulled back behind the rig, clambered to the other side, chancing a quick glance to see what was happening. The second MRAP, its roof splashed with blood, was pulling back. A small turret on top of it swiveled slightly, machine gun fire lashed toward him, striking the side of the rig behind him as he pulled his head back.

After the loss of one MRAP, and losing at least one man from the retreating MRAP, sure as hell, Shadowstone were going to change tactics.

Anton ramped again, blurring back up to the roof of the trailer to join his teammates.

* * *

The roadblock consisted of a police car parked at right angles in the middle of the side road, its police lights strobing red and blue, and a set of bright orange witches' hats crossing the intersection with the main road between the Squadron F base and Coningsby.

A loud crack, resounded from the south, a plume of dark-gray smoke erupting into the air. The crunch of a heavy vehicle hitting a tree line followed a second or two later.

A young policeman, fresh out of cadet school and on his first posting placed the last of a row of orange witches' hats. He jogged back to the police car; his face filled with concern. A pair of military helicopters flew about six hundred yards apart, flying parallel with the road and heading straight for them. The roar of their engines grew with every second, becoming a howling thunder, driving the young man to stuff his fingers in his ears.

His partner stood next to the car, lighting a cigarette. Smoking on duty was a reportable offense, but the younger man turned a blind eye to his partner's habit. He may be the youngest officer at his station, but he knew well enough, you didn't rat on your fellow officers for something as minor as smoking a cigarette.

The older man blew a gray cloud of smoke and shouted, "Damn crazy MI5 horse shit. That's what this is."

"MI5?" the young man asked nonplussed, staring down the road. Whatever had crashed was now burning about half a mile away behind a long stand of trees on the side of the road.

The older man nodded knowingly. "Yeah, sure."

A pair of charcoal Range Rovers sped around a shallow bend, racing past the roadblock at more than a hundred miles per hour.

"What tha' hell!" the young man shouted, clutching his police cap tight to his head to stop the wash from the two vehicles blowing it off. "What about them? They're speeding."

The older man shook his head disdainfully, taking another long drag on the cigarette. "MI6, just part of the exercise."

"What about that explosion?" the young man said, pointing down the road at the dispersing plume of gray smoke.

The older man stared at his young partner, with a 'prepare to be schooled,' look and said, "They make it all look realistic for the exercise, they have to. The Stateless Warfare Wing that would be Squadron F for newbies like you, is a force apart. They can go anywhere in the world, fight anyone, and answer to the highest echelons of the government via MI5 and MI6." He waved his hand at the witches' hats. "We're just here to keep the public out of the way."

Something big and fast came around the bend. A snub-nosed semi-trailer rig, its turbine engine roaring, flames shooting from its exhausts, flashed past them. It towed a long trailer, with sloping sides, about the size of a shipping container. The backwash blew over all the witches' hats and sent the young man's cap fluttering away.

Following it were three MRAPs and a pair of armored personnel carriers. The young policeman could've sworn blood splattered the roof of the lead MRAP's roof and numerous dents scored the vehicles armor as if someone had dumped stones all over it.

The helicopters flew overhead, the hard points for missiles on both sides had space for four missiles each, but only carried one.

Where were the rest of the missiles? Had they been firing them already?

The young policeman stood open-mouthed as the convoy of vehicles raced away to the north. His partner took another drag on his cigarette and began casually picking up the witches' hats and putting them back into a neat line.

"C'mon mate, quit gawking and give us a hand."

The young policeman frowned for a brief moment, and then shrugged his shoulders. What did he know, he was a newbie? He joined his partner in making the roadblock whole again.

They had a job to do, and they were doing it.

What more could anyone ask of them?

* * *

The charcoal Range Rovers shot past the police roadblock at close to one hundred and ten miles per hour.

Francis glanced at Juliette, and she said, "They think we're part of the convoy."

Juliette's fingers flashed over her laptop. She used prepositioned Order software to hack into the local police networks. A moment later, her eyes scanned down the list of the day's police reports. "... They think that 'Squadron F,' is conducting an impromptu training exercise between their military base and RAF Coningsby. Shadowstone have ordered them to clear all civilians out of the way."

"That's a small mercy. Any information on how they might be planning to take Peter out of the country?"

"I've checked the available air traffic reports, but there is nothing there."

"Wait," Francis said, ducking his head to look up high in the air. There was a large, gray, four-engine transport aircraft flying a couple of thousand yards above the ground. "That's a transport. It's heading straight for the RAF airbase."

Juliette followed his gaze. "Yes, that is the one. There is no mention of that flight anywhere."

Francis studied the aircraft, relying on his reflexes to keep the SUV tracking along the road. He had to ensure the truck never got onto that plane. With the speed they were traveling at, they were eating up the miles, in minutes they would be at the airbase.

He had to get Peter out of the truck, every other option led to failure and potentially the destruction of the team. The only question was how. Francis didn't have an answer, he would have to trust Jay, Yvette, Li, and Anton to get Peter out before the truck reached the airbase.

With time running out, he didn't like their odds.

* * *

The MRU driver's eyes flicked down to the speedometer. Nothing had changed, it still read one hundred and ten miles per hour. The turbine roared at full power beneath and behind the cabin. Its scream muted by thick armor and noise suppression insulation surrounding the rig.

There was something 'not quite right.' There was a little vibration in the trailer. He dearly wished to be able to slow down. Anything going wrong at this speed could easily create a total catastrophe.

The driver wanted nothing to do with anything remotely approaching such a disaster, not with two months left before retirement.

The comms link, opened up, and Director Heathmont's voice came over the line, "MRU Driver, I have new orders for you."

Oh hell, what now?

"Yes, Sir."

Drop your speed back to sixty miles per hour until further notice."

There really is a God.

"Yes, Sir."

The line muted. The driver pulled his foot off the accelerator and started braking. The big rig began sloughing off speed. He sighed with relief as the speedometer dropped to sixty miles per hour and stabilized there.

Now, maybe the shooting will stop too.

* * *

The MRU slowed down.

The hurricane force winds dropped back to a gale.

"What now?" Yvette asked in exasperation, applying a hurried strip bandage to Jay's upper arm.

Anton stared at Jay, a common realization flashing across their faces as they chorused together, "Boarders!"

Li readied the Green Dragon, crawling toward the back of the trailer. Anton tied the MGLs straps to a hand hold. Gripping the Blue Dragon, he followed Li, taking up a position beside her. Yvette took one of the H&K MP5s in her left hand and her katana in her right, using her feet to hook onto a pair of handholds. Jay flexed his bandaged arm and did the same. Between them all, the team covered the four corners of the trailer.

Fiery tracers from the APC's .50 caliber machine guns flashed overhead. The M240's on the roofs of the MRAPs joined in, their bullets sparking off the lip surrounding the roof of the MRU's trailer.

The firing all stopped at once.

"Now," Anton whispered, ramping hard, along with his teammates.

Black shadows rose up in the air, resolving into the shapes of men. H&K MP5 submachine guns erupted in their hands, short, bright tongues of fire leaping from their barrels.

Anton leaped to his feet, twisting violently, bullets whipping past him. He drove the Blue Dragon up through the torso of the nearest trooper, then pulled the sword out in a wide slash. The man's agonized grunt fled with the wind as he toppled backward off the trailer.

Anton dashed toward the middle of the trailer roof, another two troopers landing to his left and right. Both troopers aimed their MP5s directly at his chest. His left hand blurred, grabbing the first man by his leading wrist, pushing upward against heavy resistance. These troopers were strong. Anton's right foot lashed out, catching the second trooper in the gut. He staggered backward toward the edge of the trailer's roof.

The first trooper's submachine gun started firing, the bullets ripping above his shoulder.

Too close for comfort.

Anton's right hand lashed forward, the Blue Dragon now reversed, the end of the handle breaking the man's jaw. The trooper fell backward, toppling over the edge of the trailer.

The second trooper recovered his balance. Stepping forward he leveled a gun at Anton's ear, snarled and said, "Dodge this, mother—"

Anton blurred aside, the bullets blasting past his head with whip-like cracks. He moved back in close, his hands pushing out on the man's shoulder and hip. A quick thrust with his hip and the man flew screaming through the air off the MRU. The rest of his words lost in the howling wind as he disappeared amongst the trees lining the road.

Anton spun around, all the other Shadowstone troopers were off the MRU, or lying still on the blood-splattered roof.

The team returned to their positions, guarding the corners of the MRU's trailer.

Li grimaced, stretching her right foot out. Anton's heart jumped, and he asked, "You, okay?"

She shook her head, a look of uncomprehending dismay crossing her face. "I don't know how it happened, one of them fell across my ankle, and it got twisted."

"Tell me if it gets worse."

Li paused for a second as if remembering that she didn't like him. "Yes, kemosabe."

A grimly ironic half-grin spread slowly over Anton's face. "Riiight!"

He looked away. The fight had left Jay and Li injured, the team was slowly getting beat up. Sooner or later, they would have to slow down. No one could ramp forever, and then they would be in real trouble.

They had to get Peter out and get away soon.

As soon as possible.

* * *

Peter twisted the last of the large handles into the spinlock on the ceiling of the MRU.

It was good and tight, he grabbed hold of the extended handles of the spinlock, and crunched upward. Planting his big boots to the left and right on the ceiling, he crouched upside down over the spinlock. He focused his mind, descended deeply into silence. The Ramp flowered within, power rippling through him in increasing waves.

He started to push, and push, and push.

Heat washed off him. His face flushed, perspiration running up his forehead and into the dangling shock of thick red hair falling down from the top of his head.

He grunted, and moaned, veins popping on his wrists and hands.

The metal heart of the spinlock resisted his efforts with mute indifference.

He descended deeper into the silence.

The world darkened around him.

He pushed harder than he'd ever pushed anything before.

Nothing happened.

Peter dropped out of the Ramp. Sucking in great lungfuls of air while holding on upside down, he adjusted his position to get his thighs and hips involved in the effort. A second later, he dropped back into the Ramp. His focus on the present moment sharpened to a laser-like point. Silence overwhelmed him. Lightning coruscated from the base of his spine, flashing along his nerves and sinews. His muscles bunched, his knuckles whitened, his fingers almost penetrating the steel of the spinlock handles.

His mouth gaped, a scream from deep within filled the chamber. A noise of suffering, unlike anything heard in that dreadful, antiseptic room before.

Something screeched, as it went beyond all-natural limits of endurance.

Something tore, and something else snapped like a whip.

Peter fell down to the floor.

* * *

A pair of charcoal Range Rovers paced in front of the convoy.

Victoria Hansen double checked her scopes. What she was seeing didn't make any sense. Squadron F, or was it Shadowstone, had optimized blackwidow gunships for ground assault. Nothing the size of a car could move anywhere within five miles of a blackwidow without the helicopter's sensor arrays spotting it. But as far as her ultra-high-tech sensors were concerned, the two SUVs half a mile in front of the MRU didn't exist.

Cyberwarfare. They must be Order of Thoth. I'd better call this in.

"The prisoner's out!" her gunner shouted.

Victoria stared in amazement at the hatch door on top of the MRU trailer. It was standing hard upright, the wind holding it in place like a lonely tombstone. In front of the hatch door, a thick-bodied, red-haired man leaped onto the roof of the trailer.

He blurred left and right, impossibly fast for a human, .50 caliber tracers from one of the trailing APCs flashing past him.

"Madness," she whispered. It was time for a warning shot, she tilted her gunship, swinging it in toward the MRU. All she needed to do was scare him back into the trailer and give him second thoughts about escaping – her 20mm cannon would do the trick.

The red-haired man bent down, grabbing the hatch door, ripping it left and right, an instant later it was in his hands. He twisted and twirled around on the spot like an Olympic level discus thrower before launching the hatch door directly at her.

She shouted, "What the—" Instinctively veering left, the gunship roared, responding like a hawk in flight. The hatch door, spinning perfectly on its axis, flashed four feet to the right of her cockpit.

"Fuck!" she yelled, as something crashed behind her.

Alarms screamed, and red lights flashed, the helicopter twisted around her, diving back to the right, moving with her original momentum back toward the MRU. She pulled on her controls, nothing happened, they were dead in her hands. The Helicopter continued the slow descending turn, starting to twist around its central axis.

She turned around in her chair. The tail rotor hung stationary on a thread of metal; the MRU's top hatch door embedded in its main housing.

Her heart froze. There was no escape, they were stuck in a dead helicopter that was gathering speed as it sailed over the top of the MRU toward the road directly behind it.

The dark bitumen rose up toward her.

Victoria pushed back against the windscreen and screamed, "Fuck! Fuck! Fu—"

In a single crushing instant, her world went black.

* * *

Eighteen tons of blackwidow gunship hit the bitumen of the road at over one hundred miles per hour.

The helicopter disintegrated upon contact with the hard tarmac. The turbines separated from each other, spearing forward with several tons of 'inevitability' each, straight into the paths of the armored personnel carriers.

The APC on the right took one of the turbines just inside the right front wheel and the chassis. The impact flipped the APC over onto its left side. It screeched along the road in a shower of sparks for another twenty yards before it encountered the miraculously intact fuel tank of the blackwidow. The fuel tank promptly exploded in a blinding glare, greasy black smoke fountaining upward in a tall plume. The APC, burning furiously, ground its way into the nearest ditch.

The second APC was not as lucky as the first. The second turbine struck it end on like a giant's fist punching through the front of the APC's hull, obliterating the driver and half the crew as it disappeared somewhere into the belly of the vehicle. The APC careered blindly through the front half of the blackwidow's tumbling cabin, a canister of 70mm Hydra rockets flew through the gaping hole into the APC's interior. The rockets instantly detonated in a colossal explosion, converting the APC into a cloud of burning metal confetti.

While the APCs were taking the brunt of the impact of the crashing blackwidow, the crews of the three remaining MRAPs shadowing the MRU were attempting to evade as best they could. Shadowstone enhanced reflexes dragged on steering wheels, floored accelerators or slammed on brakes.

One of the trailing MRAPs, attempting to avoid flying helicopter debris, ran through the exploding second APC, evaporating itself in a gray-black cloud of burning metal. The second trailing MRAP pulled wide, accelerating snake-like between the two APC wrecks, directly into half the armored hull of the blackwidow. The MRAP flipped vertically into the air, looping over itself before landing on its roof in the middle of the road, its wheels spinning wildly in the air.

The leading MRAP accelerated up to the MRU, a stray section of rotor blade shearing through the M240 mount on its roof. The machine gun fell away, joining the wave of destruction taking out everyone else behind them.

Streaming forward at sixty-five miles per hour, the MRU, trailed by the single surviving MRAP, left the burning wreckage in its wake.

Peter dropped to a prone position, his eyes flashing with excitement. He said brightly, "I told you I'd be on time."

Grinning with a mixture of relief and joy, Anton slapped Peter's shoulder. He shrugged out of the over-sized battle vest and handed it to Peter.

Peter pursed his lips, his eyes shining. "Beautiful."

The team was back together again.

Chapter Twenty Two

"The oppression we all face is guarded by what we are unwilling to question." – Juliette Mirovar

* * *

South of Coningsby, Lincolnshire, August 22nd, 12:01

At breakfast, there had been four blackwidow pilots in the mess hall at the Facility, now there was only one left alive.

He put a gauntleted hand over his chin mike, and addressed his gunner, sitting half a dozen feet behind him, "Fuck this. Fucking Director Heathmont can climb up my fucking asshole as far as he wants. I'm not going anywhere near those fuckers on that truck."

"Fucking amen to that, Sir," the gunner swore.

"Well ... unless I've got full weapons clearance."

The comms link activated, the director's voice resounding in his ears, "Widow dash Four, report in."

What the hell am I supposed to say, we just got our asses kicked by one man with a fucking flying frisbee.

"On station, Sir. Three hundred and fifty yards to the right of the MRU."

"Your miniguns are cleared for use," Director Heathmont declared, in tightly clipped tones, like he was reluctant to admit the necessity. "However—"

Of course, what now?

"—we need to recapture the prisoner alive."

The pilot wanted to rub his eyes, but his helmet's visor and gauntlets got in the way. His hands stayed resolutely on the controls of the blackwidow, and his lips pressed into a thin gash.

"Sir, in all honesty, how are we supposed to do that with a blackwidow? We're designed to kill things, not capture them."

There was a short pause over the comms link, while the pilot considered that his career may have just nosedived into the toilet.

"Just to be clear Widow dash Four, I want you to ensure the terrorists on top of our mobile rendition unit do not access the cabin or interfere with the progress of the unit to the Coningsby airbase. I have a ... reception, waiting for them." The director's voice dropped into the freezing range as he inquired, "Are you able to comply Widow dash Four? Or, do I need to find another pilot who can do the job."

The pilot glowered at the targets. His gunner could avoid the body of the truck – if he got closer, but the terrorists were carrying an MGL, and one of those placed in the right spot could kill his bird.

He replied, "Wilco, Sir."

The director's voice warmed from frigid to merely icy, and he ordered, "Carry on, then."

The line muted. The pilot closed the distance between the MRU and his gunship to two hundred yards. He kept a close eye on his targets. They were hugging the roof of the MRU as it accelerated back up to maximum speed.

The pilot covered his chin mike and directed his gunner, "You see any of them point an MGL at us, you shoot those grenades in flight. Right?"

"Roger that, Sir," the gunner replied with quiet conviction.

Within minutes they would be at Coningsby airbase and whatever 'reception,' the director had planned for the terrorists would come into play. In the meantime, the pilot had decided discretion was the better part of valor.

At least it was against these Order of Thoth operatives.

* * *

The hurricane force winds rolling over the top of the MRU stretched the earbud communicators to their limits.

"We have to get into the cabin," Anton yelled.

Li looked doubtful, and shouted, "The last blackwidow has us targeted. You can bet they've orders to stop us doing that."

"Anton," Francis said, his voice was faint but clear over the comms link. "We need to create a distraction to allow us to break contact with Shadowstone."

Juliette said, "Panopticon hazing will start to run out in seven minutes, and not later than twelve minutes."

"We have to break contact in under seven minutes," Francis declared, "and by then, the truck will be at the airbase."

Anton looked around at the rest of the team, they were all facing in, while hugging the roof of the MRU. "This truck is fast, if we have control of it, we can use it as a weapon." He grinned. "We just need to run it into something important."

"And who would be driving it?" Jay asked.

Anton lifted his eyebrows in answer, he wasn't going to ask anyone else to take the risk. He reached over, undoing the straps on the MGL, it still had five high-explosive armor piercing rounds in it. "In the meantime, we've gotta keep pushing at Shadowstone and keep them off balance."

"Anton, wait!" Li yelled.

Anton blurred forward against the wind. He appeared, crouched on the front right corner of the MRU trailer. He anchored himself with his left hand. Raising the MGL with his right hand, he aimed it at the armored door next to the driver. He pulled the trigger, the MGL fired, the noise lost in the howl of the wind. The grenade traveled the three yards to the door in a tiny fraction of a second, exploding in a bright glare. The molten copper of the shaped charge carved a shallow rent all the way along the front right-hand side of the rig.

The door stayed solidly attached.

A burst of 7.62mm rounds speared between the rig and the MRU, barely a yard in front of Anton. He jerked backward, the blackwidow was closing to one hundred and fifty yards. The port side minigun was pointing straight at him.

"Over the side," Peter yelled. The team blurred behind Anton, disappearing over the far lip of the trailer away from the blackwidow. The only thing left trailing the MRU was a beat-up MRAP about fifty yards back, it's M240 machine gun lost miles behind them in the gunship wreck. It was the lesser of two evils.

His friends were in immediate danger from the blackwidow, a red mist descended over Anton's mind. He had to do something. He blurred along the trailer, his finger hard on the trigger of the MGL. The grenade launcher fired three times in the next second, the grenades looping toward the blackwidow.

The port side minigun's barrels whirred, a line of tracers spearing through the air, connecting with each of the grenades in turn. They all exploded in a row halfway between the trailer and the helicopter gunship.

Anton grabbed a hand hold, swinging over the far side of the trailer. He landed next to Peter, who was precariously hanging onto handholds on the trailer's side.

Peter dropped back from the top edge of the trailer and said drily, "That was pure ass on their part—"

The last MRAP pulled into view behind them, a trooper standing up through its top hatch, his assault rifle coming to bear on them. Bullets flew in both directions, Jay firing back with his submachine gun.

"On top!" Peter called out, the team blurring back onto the top of the trailer.

Out of the line of fire from the MRAP, but exposed to the blackwidow pacing the MRU at one hundred and fifty yards on the right-hand side.

Anton stared up at the gunship, the barrels of the minigun were pointing right at him.

They could've taken the shot, but hadn't. They wanted them all alive.

Anton's eyes widened, Shadowstone expected to capture them all.

* * *

The charcoal-colored Range Rover slowed as it entered Coningsby, passing another pair of police roadblocks keeping local traffic off the main approach to the airbase. The SUV peeled to the left, past the entrance to the airbase. The second Range Rover running tight in behind it.

Juliette glanced up from her laptop and stated, "Panopticon cover will begin to run out in two minutes."

Francis glanced back at her, broadcasting to the team, "Thirty plus Shadowstone troopers at the airbase entrance. One commander tank, two APCs and four MRAPs. Sixty plus RAF regiment soldiers with their vehicles."

"C'mon Boss," Peter replied. "That's hardly fair against us. The poor bastards won't stand a chance."

"Can you get off the truck before it hits the airfield?" Juliette asked.

"Sure, we can," Jay confirmed in a clear voice, "but Shadowstone will be all over us. The blackwidow will be able to track us, and we'll never break contact."

"It's too late," Li declared. "We're a minute behind you – we're almost there."

"Get ready to fight," Anton said. "We're hitting this gate hard."

"Don't get caught at the gate," Francis directed. "Breakthrough, we'll reposition to pick you up on the other side of the airbase."

"The MRU is starting to slow," Yvette said.

Anton said with hard enthusiasm, "It's game time."

Juliette and Francis' Range Rover sped along the street parallel to the RAF airbase perimeter fence. The team needed to do something terrible to create a distraction big enough to break contact with Shadowstone.

Innocent people, such as the RAF Regiment soldiers, would die. Juliette shook her head, a sudden sadness lashing through her. The innocent would die and the Mirovar team would pay a price for breaking their own rules.

She was sure of it.

* * *

Francis pulled the Range Rover to a halt on the side of the road. Samuel Luther pulled the second SUV in hard behind the first car.

Francis commanded, "Chiara, MGL, and the spare ammo. You're with me. Luther, follow Juliette. We rendezvous in five minutes on the other side of the base."

"Copy that," Luther said dryly.

Francis frowned, glanced at Juliette who nodded at him. She would be okay. He opened the door, grabbed the White Dragon, and an H&K MP5 with a couple of spare magazines of high-performance rounds. He paused at the edge of getting out, leaned back in and kissed her once on the lips.

"See you soon, mon amour," he promised.

"Yes, mon amour."

He leaped out, shutting the door behind him. Chiara was already crouching near the perimeter fence watching him calmly, her long dark hair snaking down her back in a long plait. Her katana lay strapped across her shoulders, an H&K MP5 dangled from straps at her side, and she carried the Milkor MGL with her hands.

Francis dashed over to her, drawing the White Dragon clear of its scabbard with a smooth flick of his wrist. Barely slowing down, he went through the perimeter fence as if it wasn't there. Leaving a two-and-a-half-yard high triangle gap in the wire mesh, the edges of the metal wire smoking lightly from the impact of the White Dragon.

Chiara followed closely behind him.

There was a fifty-yard stretch to the nearest building, a large gray-metal hangar. They blurred across the open space in under three seconds, coming to a halt, hard up against the wall of the building. They dashed to the right corner and Francis peeked around it.

He pulled back and directed, "Go to the right, I'll go left and watch your back. The name of the game is thunder and smoke. We need as much damage as possible to pull everyone we can away from the main gate."

"Got it, Francis."

"Go."

Chiara blurred around the corner, disappearing into the RAF airbase.

Francis followed after her, his eyes everywhere. Soon, everyone was going to be trying to kill Chiara, and he was the only person there to watch her back.

* * *

The RAF airbase at Coningsby was a model of a modern airbase, large open areas, fresh, clean buildings, and rows of brand-new F-35 Lightning II fighter jets.

Chiara lined the MGL up on an F-35 sitting three hundred yards away and pulled the trigger. The grenade chuffed away, trailing a thin line of smoke that vanished against the leaden sky. A second later, the grenade punched into the body of the fighter aircraft. The plane instantly exploded, sending a plume of black smoke rushing into the sky. Secondary explosions ripped the aircraft apart sending glittering streamers of bright fire in a dozen directions.

"Certainly, burns pretty," Chiara whispered to herself.

With a smile curling the edges of her full lips, she set her eyes on a fuel bowser four hundred yards away.

She blurred deeper into the airbase. No one had seen her yet, there were no alarms, no shouts – nothing. It was her job to make sure that changed. The row of twelve F-35 jets lined up in the open air represented the best opportunity to attract attention.

There were no pilots, no ground crew, or anyone near the aircraft. It was just another Tuesday at lunchtime, they were probably in the mess hall stuffing their faces with 'bangers and mash,' or something else typically English.

The bowser came into range, she pulled the trigger, her second grenade looping away. She didn't wait for it to land. There was too much to do. She blurred along the tarmac for another three seconds, firing another four rounds.

She pulled to a halt.

The bowser was gone, a smoking pit fountaining thick, black, oily smoke had replaced it. Five of the fancy new F-35s lay in tangled fiery wrecks, each attended by a rampant plume of dark smoke. It was as if fire djinns from some ancient fable had come to life, and hovered malevolently over the ruins of each aircraft.

Chiara paused and began reloading the MGL.

Her head flicked left and right, was anyone going to notice what was happening?

* * *

"Oh my God!" the RAF regimental officer uttered under his breath as half a dozen explosions echoed across the base in as many seconds.

"Sound the alarm, we're under attack."

One of his men punched a button, a series of klaxons began wailing across the length and breadth of the base.

A dozen screens occupied a wall in his command center. Four of them remained focused on events at the front gate. A specialized rig was slowing as it approached the gate. Most of his available force was there, along with a contingent of Squadron F troopers. He hadn't been comfortable with shifting most of his resources to one part of the base, but the orders had come from the top. Squadron F command had seconded his RAF regiment soldiers, and that was that – there was nothing he could do about it.

"There," he said, pointing at one of the other screens, a tiny figure crouching in the middle of it. "Who the hell is that?"

One of his men zoomed in the camera. The screen pixelated for half a second and then resolved. It was a girl, with a sword across her back and a grenade launcher. She threw away an empty bandolier. She'd just reloaded her weapon.

Beyond her, other screens showed half a billion pounds worth of ultra-modern jet fighters burning into scrap. Next to the wrecks were another half dozen F-35s; a brief break in the cloud cover opened up, the jets gleamed in the summer sunlight.

The girl lifted her MGL, her long dark plait of hair swinging across her shoulders. Grenades started launching from her weapon.

A horribly sick feeling settled in the regimental officer's guts, this was his worst nightmare come true. Squadron F be damned, the purpose of the RAF regiment was to protect the base, he had to act.

He shouted, "Get our troops away from the gate, secure the base."

"Yes, Sir," chorused a handful of subordinates in the command center.

Rapid commands were issued. The screens displayed the RAF Regiment soldiers leaving the front gate, their armored Land Rovers heading out across the base. Two of the bulky sand-colored vehicles were heading directly for the girl on the runway.

Then she started running, sprinting, blurring toward a hangar. She disappeared off the screen, the camera couldn't pan fast enough to follow her.

Who is she?

What is she?

* * *

The commander tank's main weapons tracked the mobile rendition unit as it approached the gate.

The MRU driver stared at the bore of the 105mm gun. It looked awfully big when it was pointing straight at him. The commander tank sat outside the gate on the left. In front of the driver was an array of Squadron F troopers and their equipment. A pair of armored personnel carriers, their .50 caliber machine guns and 25mm Bushmaster cannons pointing straight at him, sat like iron guardians on each side of the entrance. Another four MRAPs sat in a loose semi-circle in front of them, their M240 machine guns all manned and pointing at him. Most of the Squadron F troopers stood next to their vehicles, armed with net throwers, their intent to capture clear in their choice of equipment.

The RAF regiment soldiers were all leaving the gate, their vehicles streaming into the airbase. In the distance, explosions cracked, and nearly a dozen plumes of dark smoke rose into the gray sky.

An A400 transport descended to land, despite the chaos on the main runway.

"Gods," the driver whispered, what was going on? He hit the release on his seatbelt. He needed to evacuate in a hurry. He reached for the door.

A bright blade appeared through the side door next to him. It jerked downward, slicing through the locking mechanism. Beside him, the Squadron F trooper riding shotgun slammed his H&K 416 rifle against the driver's face, breaking his nose. Collateral damage as the trooper lined up on whoever was about to open the door.

The driver flattened himself back into his seat, blood pouring from his nose.

The door ripped open with a scream of tortured hinges.

The H&K rifle burst into life, flames shooting from its barrel mere inches from the driver's face.

Something shiny flashed past him.

Someone grabbed his arm, jerking him out of his seat. He flew through the air, feeling quite helpless and foolish. He crunched himself up as much as he could, the bitumen of the road rising to meet him. He landed hard, rolled and came to a stop on his back.

Everything hurt, his nose was bleeding, his shoulder felt dislocated, but he was alive.

The troopers at the gate shouted, "Halt! Halt! Halt!"

The rig's engine roared. The vehicle surging forward between the MRAPs and the APCs. Machine gun fire erupted all around, bright tracers lancing toward the rig from half a dozen machine guns at once. A blackwidow helicopter cruised overhead, its guns silent, a lazy bystander given the fury spearing toward the MRU.

The driver lay back.

All the fire was flying above him.

Two months to retirement, it was so close he could taste it.

* * *

Anton floored the accelerator.

Peter squirmed over him, pushing the dead trooper hard up against the far door, then pulled one of his throwing axes out of the man's forehead.

Anton slammed the side door shut, but it hung loose – the locking mechanism cut to ribbons by the Blue Dragon. All around, .50 caliber and 7.62mm machine guns fired at them. The bullets ricocheting off the sides of the rig in a deafening racket.

"What are they trying to do – scare us to death?" Peter asked, more bullets bouncing off the transparent armor of the windshield in front of his face.

"They still want to capture you … us."

Shadowstone troopers lowered their guns, aiming for the tires. The rig continued to accelerate, the turbine roaring as the MRU passed between the APCs and into the base. Fusillades of machine gun fire opened up from behind the MRU. It rocked left and right, its tires shredding on both sides of the rig and the trailer. It kept on rolling, the tires designed to run flat, but for how much longer Anton didn't know. He hoped it would hold together long enough to matter.

"Everyone okay?" Anton yelled.

"We're still holding on up here," Li called back.

Peter pointed forward. "That transport aircraft is heading toward us."

Anton nodded. "Perfect."

"Anton?"

"Distraction — a big fat one."

No doubt, the plane was made of light materials, certainly a lot lighter than the armored mobile rendition unit. The rig reached a quarter mile into the base, accelerating past fifty miles per hour. Behind it the four MRAPs gave chase. The APCs were backing and turning, blocking the commander tank at the base entrance. The shadow of the blackwidow passed over the top of the rig as a brief shaft of sunlight penetrated the cloud cover.

The A400 transport plane rolled to a stop two hundred yards in front of the rig. The pilots stared at the MRU rushing toward them. A pair of RAF Regiment MRAPs, little more than uprated land rovers pulled to a halt near the plane's nose. Soldiers spilled from them, raising their rifles to their shoulders and began shooting at the onrushing rig.

"Get off the trailer. Get up close to the rig," Anton shouted.

Jay, Yvette, and Li blurred over the edge of the trailer and hugged each other directly behind the rig cabin.

Anton stared hard at the transport. The pilot's faces blanched with fear, they pulled on their controls. The aircraft's engines roared, it started to pull forward and turn.

Too late.

It was all too late.

* * *

Francis' hand flashed out, catching the RAF regiment soldier on the side of his chin. The man's head whipped back; he fell stunned to the pavement. Francis scooped up his H&K 416 rifle before it struck the ground.

"You've seen one of these before?" Francis asked Chiara, pointing to a tracked, anti-air gun system next to them.

"Got it," Chiara affirmed, leaping in front of the control console of the weapons system, while Francis scanned the airfield, the captured H&K 416 rifle in his hands. The short range MP5 submachine gun slung for the moment.

Chiara flipped a pair of switches, the massive twenty-foot gun swinging left and right on its base in front of her. "We're hot."

"The gunship first, and then the MRAPs."

Chiara deactivated the identify friend or foe system and selected the lone blackwidow as a target. A fraction of a second later, the gun opened up. It was a short-range anti-air weapon built around a 30mm multi-barreled chain gun. Originally designed for use on A-10 Fairchild ground attack aircraft as an anti-tank weapon, some bright spark had decided it could double as a ground-based air-defense system.

The weapon roared. A tongue of fire leaping another ten feet past the end of the barrels. Empty shells the size of coke bottles flew to the left in a spray as fifty rounds a second of armor penetrating high explosive rounds zeroed in on the blackwidow.

The helicopter gunship evaporated in a mid-air explosion, raining glittering fragments of burning metal onto the runway.

The four MRAPs ran through the descending cloud of debris, and then began diverging away from each other. Still chasing the MRU, but avoiding being easy targets.

Francis frowned. During the whole engagement, the Shadowstone forces had been adapting their tactics at every step of the way. Sooner or later the Ramp wouldn't prove to be enough of an advantage, and his force team's luck would run out.

The MRU was racing toward the gray bulk of the transport aircraft, impact was seconds away.

"Kill the MRAPs," Francis commanded.

Chiara swung the weapon down toward the new targets.

* * *

The speedometer of the MRU ran past seventy miles per hour. Its shredded tires thundering over the runway's dark-gray tarmac. RAF regiment soldiers ran desperately to the left and right. The A400 transport aircraft lurched forward, its four turbines roaring, its propellers ripping at the air.

"Brace!" Anton yelled.

Everyone on the rig ramped hard, holding on with grips of steel. Jay, Yvette, and Li crouched together just behind the rig cabin, the body of the trailer three yards behind them. Peter braced himself against the dashboard.

Anton held the steering wheel with arms hard as iron. Time slowed down, the side of the aircraft looming to fill his vision. He jigged the MRU rig slightly to the left, catching the A400 at the point where the rear of the wing attached to the body of the transport aircraft. The impact rippled through his bones. The skin of the aircraft stretched, and then split, falling inwards as it broke apart. Aluminum struts crumpled and tore. The rig dropped ten miles per hour in a fraction of a second as it carved through the body of the transport, ripping a huge hole through the aircraft. Debris filled the air as the rig punched out the other side.

The trailer kept the aircraft upright as it passed through it, leaving a thin spine running along the top of the plane's body, connecting the front half of the aircraft with the back half.

The MRU completed its passage. The transport aircraft teetering like a wounded dinosaur almost ripped in half by the massive bite of a carnivore. The front and back collapsed inward, the nose and tail rising in the air to make a tragic 'V' shape. Fuel gushed from half-empty wing tanks, pooling beneath the gaping belly wound in the aircraft.

They were through, Anton glanced into the rear-view mirrors, he needed the aircraft to explode. The Shadowstone MRAPs were hot on their tail. He could catch them within an explosion.

He looked forward. A fuel truck sat parked on the tarmac. The rig would pass safely to the right of the truck.

Anton glanced sideways at Peter, pointed at the fuel truck, and said with relief, "Good thing we saw that; we could've hit—"

The left rear axle coupling gave way, the damage done by the grenades on the road approaching the airbase finally reached a tipping point. The rear wheels on the left side of the trailer wobbled for half a second before coming loose and flying off. The trailer lurched to the left, a storm of sparks erupting along the edge of the trailer as it dragged along the tarmac.

The MRU's failsafe systems locked up the steering wheel and switched off the engine.

The MRU was a rolling hulk, pulling to the left and heading straight toward the fuel truck.

"Out! Out! Out!" Anton screamed.

The team blurred away from the rig. Jay, Yvette, Li and Peter all went left; Anton being on the right-hand side of the rig, dived out of the cabin to the right. He rolled, picked himself up and began blurring back toward the space between the transport aircraft and the MRU trailer.

Anton had taken a dozen steps when the nose of the MRU ran into the fuel truck. The bowser detonated with a thunderous roar, a wave of superheated air picking him up and throwing him thirty feet through the air.

His reflexes kept him alive, moving as fast as he was, he was able to land and roll with the blast, diminishing its effect. Burning debris was falling through the air. He was dangerously close to the leaking fuel of the transport aircraft.

He focused hard, launching himself forward, running faster than he'd ever run before. He shot forward, the rest of the team were streaking away, lines of burning fighter aircraft in front of them. Clouds of smoke drifted across the runway, providing cover. They just had to run through it.

The fuel around the transport aircraft ignited, flames leaping and flashing toward the main body of the plane. Explosions ripped the wings off the body. The aircraft exploded in a fireball as reserve fuel tanks detonated with thunderous cracks that echoed across the runway.

Anton blurred forward, the heat of the explosion washing over him, but now too far away to cause real damage.

Thirty to forty yards in front of him, Yvette, Jay, Li, and Peter sprinted in a line through the smoke. Anton blurred, gaining on them. Eighty yards to his left, three Shadowstone MRAPs cleared the smoke, accelerating toward the rest of the team.

Their top-mounted M240 machine guns swung around to target his friends.

All Anton had left on him was the Blue Dragon. He pivoted, drawing his sword, and blurred toward the nearest vehicle.

* * *

The MRAPs were streaming toward the team.

Chiara manipulated the big gun's controls. Its integrated sensor array could pick up a vehicle shrouded in smoke with ease. There were three targets. One of the four MRAPs had been too close when the A400 transport aircraft exploded, and hungry fire had leaped out, claiming the MRAP and its crew as a prize.

She depressed the trigger. The gun shivered, the barrels whirring. Fire leaped as round after round of 30mm armor-piercing high explosive warheads speared down range toward the speeding MRAPs.

It was no contest. The three vehicles evaporated in wild explosions, their crews disappearing in pink mists. A lone Order warrior ducked away from the explosions, blurring toward the rest of the team. Chiara's lips curled into a half smile – only Anton would be crazy enough to attack when everyone else was evading.

The two armored personnel carriers and the commander tank were through the main gate and heading into the base. She selected them all as targets and set the system to auto mode. As soon as there was a clear shot, the gun would take it and keep firing until it destroyed all three targets. While the gun would carve the APCs into pieces, the commander tank was another proposition entirely, and the gun was no place to be when the commander tank inevitably targeted it.

Chiara glanced at the far end of the base. A pair of charcoal Range Rovers sat parked on a side road, just beyond the perimeter fence. The rest of the team were blurring through the wrecks of the F-35s.

It was time to go, she looked at Francis and said, "All set."

"Let's move," Francis commanded.

They ramped hard, blurring away from the big gun. Behind them the big gun ripped into life, roaring like a grounded dragon spewing angry flames. One of the APCs exploding about nine hundred yards away. A second later the other APC lit up with flames shooting out of its top hatch. Then the big gun exploded, torn in half by a tungsten kinetic spike fired from the commander tank.

Chiara kept running, Francis beside her, smoke from the burning aircraft and fuel bowsers, cloaking their escape.

There was only the commander tank left to pursue them.

* * *

Tom Wilkes, 'Tommy,' to his friends picked himself up off the tarmac.

His RAF regiment issued H&K 416 rifle lay in front of him. He'd emptied the magazine firing at the MRU before it ran into the transport aircraft. He fumbled for a moment, pulling a fresh magazine from his combat webbing. The other members of his squad lay around on the tarmac, alive or dead, he didn't know. He dumped the empty magazine and slammed the fresh one home. Cocking the rifle, he took a professional firing stance on one knee.

In the distance, shadows blurred through the smoke – faster than he could believe anyone could move – but it was happening.

He sighted along the barrel; the targets were already near maximum effective range. He pulled the trigger. The gun thrummed in his hands; in full auto mode it sent thirty rounds of high-performance ammunition into the smoke before clicking on empty.

The dark-gray pall thickened and swirled like hostile fog, had he hit anyone?

A bitter hope filled his heart.

* * *

Yvette stumbled, her hands flying out to either side, her hair an auburn halo around her head. She started to fall.

She didn't hit the ground. Jay swooped in from the side, scooping her up in his arms without missing a stride. With no visible loss of speed, he blurred forward to the perimeter fence.

Peter was there first, using his double-bladed battle-axe to carve a hole in the wire. He stepped forward, using his axe to hold the wire back so that Jay could easily carry Yvette through.

Li ran up and put her hand on the exit wound in the upper left corner of Yvette's chest. Blood sluiced between her fingers; Yvette was bleeding badly.

"The cars, we've got to get her away from here," Jay shouted, his eyes alive with fear.

Somewhere in the distance, a commander tank was hunting for them. Smoke shrouded the air between them and the tank. Klaxons wailed all over the stricken base.

Juliette appeared in front of Jay and ordered, "Put her on the back seat of my car, and drive to the rendezvous point."

The team rushed into action. A handful of seconds later, everyone was in the Range Rovers, the SUV's wheels spinning in the loose gravel on the side of the road before finding traction on the bitumen and launching the cars away from the airbase.

They broke contact with Shadowstone. The fading seconds of Panopticon cover as effective at hiding the SUVs from the commander tank's sensor arrays as it had been for the blackwidow's sensor arrays minutes earlier.

In the back of the leading Range Rover Juliette applied pressure to Yvette's wound and said urgently, "Jay, we need to be there as fast as possible."

"I'm on it," Jay snapped, the SUVs supercharged engine snarling in response as he floored the accelerator.

"She needs surgery – now!"

"Damn it," Jay swore.

The Range Rover hurtled along the streets. There was no one to dodge or pass. The streets were clear of traffic. The klaxons continued to wail in the distance. No one was on the streets, with the airbase under attack, the local population had fled to the safety of their homes.

Jay prayed that he would be in time, and Juliette could work her surgical 'magic.'

His heart wrenched. His eye's moistened. He could lose Yvette.

He loved her.

He drove like a man possessed.

His heart felt like it had expanded to fill his throat, robbing him of the ability to speak.

The rendezvous point was clear on the SUV's GPS. The device reported he had two more minutes to get there at the regulation speed limits.

He vowed to arrive in under sixty seconds.

The Range Rovers sped along the streets.

Chapter Twenty Three

Section 2.2.9 False Narratives in Common Media

Summary: Operation of False Narratives

[1] The purpose of this method is to satisfy and exhaust the target populations ability to inquire, with false narratives. Begin by establishing at least two opposed, mutually exclusive, false narratives aligned with the belief systems of separate opposed social cohorts.

[2] Leverage social division between the social cohorts to entrench the narratives as intrinsic to the tribal identity of the targets. Once established as intrinsic to the identity formation of the target population, the narrative will be beyond question and disbelief in the narrative will signify lack of social belonging.

[3] Publish media reports that support the adopted narratives from authoritative members of the social cohorts.

[4] Publish media reports that deny the opposing narrative from authoritative members of the social cohorts.

[5] Provide 'neither confirm nor deny,' statements from senior Government sources.

[6] Provide separate anonymously leaked statements from Government sources that support all false narratives in play.

Detail: Definitions and worked examples

The details of this tactic with worked examples is described below.

[REDACTED]

– Excerpt of Section 2, Methods of Obfuscation, Shadowstone Covert PSYOPS Manual

* * *

Coningsby, Lincolnshire, August 22nd, 12:14

The dark-blue Jaguar sedan pulled to a stop forty yards short of the entrance to the RAF airbase at Coningsby. Two MRAPs filled with Shadowstone troopers in full body armor halted behind it.

Gordon Heathmont looked through his car's front windscreen and surveyed the airbase. Dark-gray smoke sat in a thick pall over the whole site. Sirens wailed, cutting through the base's klaxons as emergency workers strove to contain the fires. The wreckage of a pair of armored personnel carriers burned a hundred yards beyond the gate. They'd been torn open like cans of tuna given to a chainsaw. Someone had used one of the new anti-air guns on them. Nothing was flying, all the blackwidow's were gone. The one major asset left was a fully armed commander tank patrolling the middle of the base.

Gordon consulted his laptop. The commander tank's sensor arrays were clear of threats. The Order of Thoth had vanished like ghosts. The temporary hazing of the Panopticon had passed. Shadowstone cyberwarfare units operating out of Beijing, Saint Petersburg and Seattle, had finally neutralized the Order's attack on the Panopticon.

The Order of Thoth team had successfully broken contact. It was a temporary setback; he consulted his laptop again, the latest flight path for the Order's Embraer jet had been to a private airfield near Goathland in the Yorkshire Moors, about ten miles from Whitby. The location had to be critical to the Order team's mission; they would return to Yorkshire.

There were two angles of attack to reacquire the Mirovar force team. He would lock up the approaches to their target in Yorkshire, and pursue them from Coningsby. The first was a straightforward objective, the second would require detective work. The force team must have used vehicles to escape the airbase. Staying on foot, or nearby would be grossly stupid, and they were clearly not stupid, possibly mad, but not stupid.

They would have vehicles, something that would blend in, but with the streets cleared under standard protocols for an airbase disaster. People would respond to the sirens by retreating into their homes. People who could be curious enough to stare out their windows at what was happening. Perhaps someone had seen something, like a vehicle speeding away from the airbase.

Half of Squadron F had deployed west on a wild goose chase. The Mirovar force team had tricked him with false information provided over the Order earbuds taken from the red-headed Order operative. Those Shadowstone forces were already flying back to the ruins of the Facility. Fortunately, the hangars at the Facility were still operational. His forces would have to refuel before they could head north. It was a terrible delay, but he couldn't avoid it.

A single Order of Thoth team member had captured a commander tank, nearly destroying the Facility. The casualty list at the Facility remained to be tallied, but ten to fifteen percent of the base's working population were in the path of the rogue commander tank. Casualties in the affected buildings would be high. He had also lost four blackwidow gunships and more than sixty Day Guard phase IV troopers. Add in the destruction at the RAF airbase and there were a couple of billion pounds worth of damage that would take more than a year to rebuild and replace. The highest levels of Shadowstone would demand an accounting for these losses. He was on the hook to explain them.

Gordon consigned the original plan to capture and question an Order of Thoth operative to the dustbin. The mission had evolved – he would have to kill every last member of the Mirovar force team before the day was out.

It was the only result that could justify his losses. He would use any and all forces to fulfill this new plan. Any losses or collateral damage was acceptable to reach the new objective.

Gordon briefly considered redirecting the local police force to lock up the northern roads out of Coningsby, but without the rest of Squadron F to back them up, the Order would cut them to pieces. James Haley's words regarding the Mirovar force team, 'don't underestimate them,' came back to haunt him. As much as he didn't want to admit it, recent events forced an obvious conclusion – he'd thoroughly underestimated the Order of Thoth operatives in every possible way.

That would stop now. He would change his tactics. He would position his forces for rapid deployment in Yorkshire and await his enemy to come to him. He would rely on what he had that the Mirovar force team did not – massive firepower.

He reached for his quantum encrypted smartphone. He needed to inform Major Quiver of the change of priorities and the need to tightly monitor the approaches to Yorkshire. He would also send his personal security detail to investigate any breaches in the RAF airbase's perimeter fence and to question the locals living nearby. By the time his remaining Day Guard forces were in place, a mouse couldn't cross into Yorkshire without him knowing about it, and there was a good chance he would know what vehicles he should be looking for.

The net was tightening, and soon the Mirovar force team would have nowhere to run to.

* * *

The rendezvous point was a rundown house on the northern outskirts of Coningsby. Its one redeeming feature was a large four car garage.

A gray and black striped blanket covered part of the garage floor. Yvette lay face up in the center of the blanket, a rag between her teeth. Chiara had cut away her blood-drenched shirt and bra to expose the ragged exit wound above her left breast.

Yvette remained fully awake while Juliette's hands blurred over her chest. Tears squeezed from her eyes as she clenched her teeth on the rag, a soft moan escaping from deep within her body.

Juliette had begun work without the administration of anesthetic. Yvette was doing it 'raw,' relying on her system zero genetics to allow her to cope with the agony of emergency thoracic surgery while awake.

Yvette resisted stilling her mind to escape the pain, ramping would only make the experience seem like it was lasting forever. Her mind kept going to what was happening to her, it was impossible to step away from reality.

Juliette knelt to Yvette's left, her medical satchel resting next to her right leg. Her usual combat surgical equipment and supplies filling it to the brim.

Chiara hovered on the opposite side, a towel spread before her, covered with surgical equipment.

Juliette had already clamped the severed artery running up into Yvette's shoulder. She requested in crisp efficient tones, "Needle."

Chiara passed a stainless-steel needle above Yvette's face.

"Thread."

That also passed over her face.

Juliette's face stilled as she dropped into silence, ramping hard. Metal flashed beneath the overhead fluorescent lights. Her hands blurred, needle and thread moving with machine-like speed and precision. Forty-eight seconds later, she'd stitched the loose ends of the artery back together.

Juliette asked for supplies and Chiara passed them to her. She quickly applied an adhesive, biodegradable gauze netting to reinforce the blood vessel. Then she took up a preloaded syringe and applied anesthetic to the wound sites, front and back. She then stitched up the entry and exit wounds, applied dressings, strappings, a broad-spectrum antibiotic, and then rocked back on her heels and stood up.

"I need some blood donors, any volunteers?" Juliette asked the room in a calm voice.

Everyone volunteered.

"Not you Jay, you've already lost some with your arm. I'll stitch you up next. Okay, Anton and Li," she indicated spots to the left and right of Yvette, "take a seat. Chiara will hook you up. Peter, find the jar of herbal balm. Both Anton and you need it on your faces, and Anton – you're a mess. But given your recent actions, you can't be too badly hurt, I'll tend to you last."

Anton nodded, and moved with Li to kneel on either side of Yvette. Chiara inserted clear lines between Li and Anton's arms, and Yvette's left and right arms. Blood filled the lines flowing into Yvette's depleted veins.

Yvette turned her head to the right, her gaze locking with Jay's. Juliette was stitching up a number of rips in Jay's arm received when a grenade exploded too close to the top of the MRU trailer. The grenade would have shredded a normal man's arm down to the bone or taken it off entirely. Yvette thanked God for the Ramp, and for the genetics that underpinned it. Without it, the Order would not have been possible, and the vampires would rule unopposed.

Jay remained whole because his skin was hard to tear, his bones resisted breaking, his nerves operated multiples faster than normal, and his muscles could exert forces five times more powerful than normal on a pound for pound basis.

She clenched her left fist, power still flowed through her damaged shoulder and arm. Her wounds compromised her, but she remained undefeated. She would heal in the next hour what would take ten hours for a normal human being. By nightfall, she would have experienced the equivalent of nearly four days of healing.

Yvette clenched her left fist again. Anton's and Li's blood was flowing through her veins. Another gift of system zero genetics – every Ramp master was a universal donor/receiver. She was feeling stronger already.

Soon she would be ready to fight again.

* * *

The Range Rovers were leaving the town of Coningsby behind. Anton sat behind Juliette in the lead SUV, with Li next to him, Peter on the far side of Li, while Francis drove. Luther followed in the second Range Rover, with Jay, Yvette, and Chiara.

"Where are the local police?" Anton asked. "A major RAF airbase is in ruins, and there are no roadblocks."

"It's a good question Anton," Juliette said.

"Did they run out of resources?" Li asked. "First, they're blocking side roads on the other side of town, and now perhaps, they're helping out with the airbase disaster."

Peter's lip curled. "C'mon, surely, they'd want to lock the town down and prevent anyone escaping. We just spent an hour in a safe house patching everyone up. They could have brought in resources from neighboring towns."

Francis frowned and remarked, "And yet they didn't."

Juliette sighed. "They're letting us go for now."

Anton gazed into the distance and said, "They don't have the forces to follow us – we gutted their main strength."

"If they fell for our ruse," Francis said, "they would have divided their forces. That other force, it will be returning by now from the west country. Perhaps it is even refueling back at the Squadron F base as we speak."

"We should assume that Shadowstone will send a second force against us," Juliette recommended.

"Yes," Francis agreed, "and they will update their tactics. They've been adapting the whole time we've been fighting them."

"They're stronger and faster than normal," Peter said.

"Yeah, noticed that," Anton agreed.

Li spread her hands apart and said, "It's like they can do a partial Ramp."

Juliette said, "Ramped or not. We can expect them to hit us hard if they get another chance at us."

The cabin of the car became silent for a long moment.

"Stealth to avoid Shadowstone or speed to reach Armitage? We can't have both," Francis observed with a frown, "but we need to make haste. It's already quarter past one. We've lost an hour. I know we had wounded to attend to, but we could ill afford the time."

He looked across at Juliette. "What have you got left to shield us with?"

"It appears Shadowstone do not know we have these Range Rovers. I can run a signal from my laptop with a one-mile radius of effect that will airbrush our cars out of any cameras we pass."

"Cool," Li enthused from the back seat.

"Can't trick eyeballs," Peter remarked, arching an eyebrow.

"You're right Peter," Juliette conceded. "If Shadowstone knows what we are driving, then we're exposed to anyone physically watching for us, or by high flying drones and satellites."

Francis said patiently. "We don't want to assault the dungeon holding Kain after nightfall. We don't know what reinforcements Armitage may have access to. The longer we take, the stronger her position grows and the more information she will take from Kain."

"Are we assuming that Kain will talk?" Li asked.

"He'll squeal like a pig," Anton remarked.

"Anton!" Juliette said. "Manners – he is still the Head of the Order."

"And demonstrably corrupt," Li said.

"Li has a point," Francis conceded with a frown. "The issue is not the man, but the information he holds. We have to assume he has broken and is talking. The longer we delay his rescue, the more damage he does."

Juliette nodded. "Of course, it must be so. If we stay on the main roads, we can reach the manor house by quarter past four. That gives us four hours before sunset."

Francis and Juliette looked at each other. They resolved the arbitrage between speed and stealth with a single glance. The decision made, Francis focused forward, the Range Rover smoothly eating up the miles on the northbound road.

Anton glanced out the window. A sign whipped past. It read, 'Welcome to Horncastle.' In another three hours, they would be on the threshold of confronting Chloe Armitage in her own home. She'd come into Anton's home and taken his parents away from him. She'd ripped his life apart, and now he would be able to extract payment for the debt she owed his family.

Anton took a deep breath and let it out slowly. All the months of training, the blood and the pain, had led to this day. To this opportunity to finally confront Armitage with the consequences of her actions. The need burned deep within him. To see the Blue Dragon flashing in the light. To beat past Armitage's blade. To separate her head from her body and lift it aloft in vengeful triumph.

How his heart would sing.

And then, with the instrument destroyed, he would turn his attention to her master – Cornelius Crane.

The need was so strong he could taste it.

* * *

The humble residents of the town of Coningsby had been fruitful with information.

Gordon Heathmont's men had discovered a pair of coal or dark-gray colored, late-model Range Rovers had sped north out of town. The prize had been an elderly woman who had witnessed them come and go from a house nearly opposite her own. A house without inhabitants and possessed of a large garage. She'd noticed the SUVs because normally no one, apart from a monthly gardener, ever visited the place.

Gordon's sedan rested in the driveway of the abandoned house while his men forced up a pair of roller doors on the garage. He stepped out of his car, he wanted to see for himself what signs the Mirovar force team had left for him.

The faint smell of exhaust fumes laced the air inside the garage. They'd left recently, less than fifteen or twenty minutes before Gordon had arrived. He shivered with delight; he was close behind them. They were fleeing before him, and he would pursue them all the way to hell.

"Sir, you'll want to see this," one of his men remarked, holding up a darkly splattered, gray and black striped blanket.

Gordon peered at the stains. It was blood, mostly dry, but there was a lot of it. At least one of the Mirovar force team had bled badly. They hadn't got off Scott free during the recent engagements, but there was no body.

He scowled, his mood turning dark. The enhancements of the Phase IV Day Guard program hadn't made any difference so far. He silently hoped the new Phase V Day Guard program would deliver a better result. Cornelius Crane had hinted much without offering confirmation of how effective the new program would be.

For the fifth time today, he attempted to contact Crane's personal line. The signal came back null, empty, void – communications with the head of Shadowstone remained down.

Gordon's laptop started pinging, multiple messages arriving at the same time. He returned to his sedan and sat in the back. He opened his laptop; scanning the new messages. His men had not recovered any bodies from the wreckage of the Mirovar force team's Embraer jet. He'd been skeptical that the Order operatives had evacuated the aircraft before it landed. He shook his head once, the evidence was compelling, they'd done precisely that.

How they evaded detection was a mystery that would have to wait for a quiet moment to solve. It was another riddle to add to the growing list of questions he had about the Mirovar force team.

Just how many Order operatives were active in the UK right now? How many were members of the Mirovar force team? Where the bloody hell were they and what was their objective? He had too many questions and too few answers.

One message stood out, the results of the Panopticon searches for cars matching the descriptions provided by the local Coningsby villagers. There were two hundred and forty-eight hits within a sixty-mile radius of the town. all the matching cars remained actively tracked. He filtered the results for pairs of cars traveling together, and the number of hits went to zero.

Had the two SUVs split up outside of Coningsby? Had they swapped vehicles and were now using something else? Were the Order operatives hazing the Panopticon without tripping countermeasures?

If they'd doubled back and were now heading south, east, or west, he had no idea where they might be or what their objective was. It was only to the north that he had any hope of finding them. He put his hands over his face, then dragged them down over his cheeks and jaw. The next decision was critical, he had to make the right move or lose everything.

The one piece of information he could rely on was the flight plan to Goathland – it was the key. There would be no more wild goose chases after phantoms or will-o-wisps. He would not waste time and resources searching anywhere but the north. He needed to adapt. The Order operatives were faster and stronger than he'd anticipated. He needed to apply area of effect weapons to defeat their ability to evade fire. Hellfire III missiles would be the weapon of choice, and that meant nightfalcon and blackwidow helicopter gunships.

Gordon closed his eyes; his thoughts intensifying. He needed to find the Mirovar operatives before he could kill them. With two hundred and forty-eight hits from the Panopticon, it was like looking for a needle in a haystack. His gut instinct was the Order team was somehow still hazing the Panopticon. They would still be in their original cars, running hard to the north and whatever objective they had there.

He broadcast the details of the cars, and photos of Peter Lamb and Anton Smith, to the remaining operational Shadowstone forces in the UK. He issued clear orders; report all contact, track, and do not engage unless fired upon. He then placed a call to his agent on the Privy Council, it was time to get the king to declare a state of emergency and get everyone in the north of England off the roads.

Gordon's phone started dialing. He frowned, glancing at the face of his smartphone, it read 13:32. The wheels of government were slow to move but move they would. In another ninety minutes, perhaps two hours, the traffic would start disappearing from the roads.

Gordon's eyes sparkled, if you can't find the needle, then remove the haystack.

* * *

The road sign flicked past on the left. In another five minutes, they would be entering Scarborough. From there it was twenty miles to Whitby and the manor house holding Kain.

"With a little luck," Francis said, "we'll be there by four o'clock this afternoon."

Peter said, "Is it just me, or is the traffic thinning out."

Juliette looked up from her laptop and frowned. "Camera counts are dropping." She shook her head. "Cars are disappearing from the roads, and hijackable phone cameras are disappearing with them."

Her fingers flew over the keyboard. "Oh no. There is a state of emergency in play. The government have issued orders for everyone to avoid travel and return to their homes until further notice."

"Why didn't we hear about this earlier?" Anton asked.

"The UK government doesn't have your phone number Anton," Li said sarcastically.

Juliette shook her head. "Don't fight. Unfortunately, the technique I'm using to haze cameras as we pass them requires my full attention."

"You're being squeezed," Li said. "Can I help?"

"Not without an implant."

"Lights ahead," Peter noted.

There were a pair of local police cars parked in the distance, their lights strobing blue and red in the universal police pattern. Before them, there was a turn off to the left and a sign above it that read, 'A170.'

Anton asked, "Are the police looking for us too?"

"They could be," Francis answered. "We have to assume they are. We need a new route, is the A170 any good?" Francis slowed the Range Rover, giving Juliette more time to check options. The intersection was approaching rapidly, and beyond it, the police cars were waiting.

Juliette paused for a handful of seconds, her face still, her eyelids closed as if she was dreaming. "Yes, take it. It's the next best route."

"Are they funneling us?" Li asked.

Francis took the off-ramp to the new road. Juliette twisted around in her seat to face Li and replied, "No evidence of that, but cutting traffic is clearly a strategy directed at us."

"With no other traffic," Anton observed, looking at Li. "We'll be easy to find."

"I kinda worked that out, Anton," Li said drily.

Francis directed, "We'll keep the cars as long as we can. Then, we'll leave them, and disappear."

He looked along the road in front of him, there were only a handful of cars and a lone truck visible heading in both directions. He accelerated back up to the speed limit. "No one promised this was going to be easy," he broadcast to the team. "Of course, Shadowstone will do everything they can to find us and kill us. We've got to stay one step ahead of them. Keep your eyes open and your weapons handy. We may need to fight at a moment's notice."

Francis kept his concerns to himself. It would be a miracle if they could get to Whitby without Shadowstone discovering them. They'd been lucky not to lose anyone so far, and he felt in the depths of his soul, that sooner or later their luck would run out.

The team had never been this exposed on a mission.

* * *

The Shadowstone agent put the freshly made cafe latte next to his briefcase.

He'd taken a position in a cafe booth overlooking the main road through Thornton Dale, about four hundred yards before the intersection of the A170 with the Whitby Gate road. The second road was a much-used route north into the Yorkshire Moors, and his superiors had assigned the agent to the task of monitoring it. He'd positioned himself a little to the east of the intersection as he'd liked the look of the cafe he was sitting in.

The agent's case was on the large side for a briefcase, more like a small suitcase. It rested on the table, its lid up, revealing a twenty-four-inch high definition screen and a server sized computer in the body of the case. Four gray spheres rested on the edge of the table. Shadowstone sensor arrays wirelessly connected to the main server in the case. The system was fully operational, covering a hemisphere of territory one mile in radius centered on the case.

The agent sipped his latte; he'd made it himself. The owner of the cafe was sleeping on the floor of the kitchen, struck down by a Shadowstone sleeper dart. He'd be stiff, cold and sore when he woke up tomorrow, but he would still be alive and the previous twenty-four hours would be a black hole, his memory wiped clean.

The agent silently lamented the need to be working. He was on annual leave, holidaying in the north with his girlfriend. Summoned into work by the boss, he had reluctantly left her watching videos in a hotel room while he sat out here in the middle of nowhere watching an empty road. He'd taken a first in psychology from Oxford University and completed a masters in public relations at Bristol University. Acquiring a senior operator role in the PSYOPS directorate of the Shadowstone organization had taken hard work and commitment. But it was days like today, boring days that impinged on his personal time that made him wonder if he'd made the right choices in life.

He stared at the screen, there was not a single hit within a mile of the cafe. The roads remained deserted, everyone had fled to their homes under the state of emergency. A sudden movement caught his eye. He glanced up from the screen, peering out at the main road running past the cafe. A pair of charcoal Range Rovers drove past at speed.

"What the hell!" he said. "Not a bloody sign of them on my scopes."

He grinned triumphantly and dialed Gordon Heathmont's direct line. The director would want to know about this straight away.

* * *

Juliette's laptop pinged.

"Damn," she swore. "Shadowstone just found us again."

"How do you know?" Anton asked.

"There's a big difference between a Samsung, Amazon, or Huawei-Apple camera and what I just hazed. I'm certain it was a Shadowstone sensor array."

"If we hazed it, maybe we're still okay?"

"No chance Anton. A sensor array takes my system about ten seconds to fully resolve. It put the center of the array back up the street. The array's operator was watching the main road through this town, we literally passed them at a range of less than forty yards – they would have noticed we didn't 'show up,' on their scopes."

Francis spotted a side street and cut down it to the left. "Let them think we're heading south. He circled around to the right and a minute later was heading north out of sight of the location where they'd passed the sensor array.

He floored the accelerator, the car barreling along the street. "Now it's speed that matters – we've got to put some distance between us and this town. We'll ditch the cars where they won't be noticed before Shadowstone can re-establish visual contact, and proceed on foot. Where is the nearest main town?"

Juliette consulted her laptop. "Goathland. It's about eleven miles north of here, and ten miles from the manor house at Whitby."

"Goathland – where we were heading to at the start," Peter noted.

"Small world," Anton remarked.

Francis flicked the steering wheel to the right, then left. The car raced through a dogleg corner onto the main road heading north. "Ten miles is close enough. We'll be in Whitby by five thirty, an easy two and a half hours before sunset. Jay, all speed."

The supercharged engines roared as the Range Rovers surged along the road in a tight convoy. There was no other traffic, not even a police presence to slow their progress.

The eleven miles to Goathland would disappear in minutes. Juliette took a deep breath and sighed. Normally serene, the day was beginning to wear on her. How many more things could go wrong?

It was a question she feared to ask.

* * *

The semi-trailer rig spouted steam from its punctured radiator. It lay on its side, its white trailer, emblazoned with the livery of a local supermarket chain, blocking both lanes of the A169 road.

A pair of Squadron F MRAPs were parked tail to tail behind it, carefully hidden from any traffic coming up from Thornton Dale to the south. Eight Squadron F troopers were guarding the main road leading to Goathland or Whitby. Thirty yards in front of the 'crashed,' truck was an intersection with a road leading off the A169 directly to Goathland. The roads had become deserted in the last half an hour, the locals retreating into their homes under the declared state of emergency.

The Shadowstone trooper glanced up at the western sky. The clouds were rapidly darkening, a storm was on its way. There had been an operational weather report fifteen minutes before, warning of strong winds and heavy rain throughout the late afternoon pushing eastward overnight.

Lovely, he thought sarcastically. He hated bad weather and the cold. Work assignments anywhere in the north of England set his mood midway between sour and homicidal.

His mouth was a grim slash, he whispered to himself, "Suck it up, princess." There was work to do, bloody work. They'd lost almost half the strength of Squadron F that morning. The enemy were still at large and had to be found. His orders were clear – report all contacts, track them, and do not engage unless fired upon.

Of course, following orders was a matter of interpretation, and 'fired upon,' – well, sometimes it can be difficult to determine who fired first. He had command of the two squads manning this post, and he'd lost close friends that morning. If the enemy showed up, he would make sure they were not going anywhere else – except, in a body bag.

He checked his squads. Four of his men were inside the MRAPs, the drivers, and the gunners operating the M240 machine guns mounted on top of the armored vehicles. The other three troopers were with him, outside the vehicles and armed with large caliber H&K 417 assault rifles fitted with under-barrel grenade launchers and red dot laser sights. Shadowstone command had provided descriptions of the vehicles the enemy would be driving and photos of two of their operatives. If they came along this road, he and his men were sure to find them.

The trooper took a position just to the left of the tail end of the overturned trailer. He lifted his binoculars and scanned the road to the south. The landscape of the Yorkshire Moors stretched in all directions, the roads gently curving around low hills. Unkempt grass and low mauve bushes covered the land. The sky hung low, a dark-gray sheet tending to black in the west, dimming the sun to a dusk-like shadow.

His binoculars were fully digital, linking seamlessly back to the Panopticon. In the distance a pair of SUVs came over the crest of a low hill, racing along the road toward his position. The Panopticon marked them as matching the description given for the target vehicles. Metadata streamed through the viewfinder; a Shadowstone operative had marked the vehicles as targets nine minutes earlier.

The Range Rovers began to slow, their speed dropping below one hundred miles per hour, down through ninety, eighty, seventy, back to the speed limit of sixty miles per hour. The trailing SUV pulled out to shadow the shoulder of the leading car, and then moved further apart, making full use of both lanes.

They're suspicious. They should be.

The trooper twisted around to face his men. Pulling his sidearm from its holster, he swung the 9mm pistol toward the MRAPs. He pulled the trigger, blowing out the nearest MRAP's headlight with a single round.

"Right men, we've been fired on," the trooper snarled, holstering his pistol. He shouldered his H&K 417 assault rifle and shouted, "Now open up on those bastards!"

The MRAPS surged left and right, racing clear of the semi-trailer, allowing their M240 machine guns to bear on the approaching Range Rovers. A second later both machine guns erupted into life, streams of bright tracers and 7.62mm ball heading down range toward the onrushing SUVs.

All hell broke loose.

* * *

Francis stared through the front windscreen; his heart filled with dread.

Two MRAPs appeared to the left and right of the overturned semi-trailer. The M240 machine guns on their roofs spurted orange tongues of flame, stark against the darkening sky. Black-clad Shadowstone troopers raced on foot behind them, firing large-bore assault rifles straight at the Range Rovers.

A storm of bullets hammered the Range Rovers. The SUVs had been subtly armored, their defenses hidden beneath their ceramic toughened skins. Their windscreens and windows were bulletproof transparent armor designed to mimic glass in appearance. Their tires could run flat with minimal loss of performance. But everything has its limits and enough firepower would overwhelm the vehicles' defenses.

The Range Rover slammed to a halt. Francis shouted, "Weapons, out!"

The second Range Rover ran another twenty yards before the wheels twisted hard left. The SUV bucked like a wild animal, taking off and twisting in a sideways roll through the air. The doors flew wide. Jay, Yvette, Luther and Chiara, all ramped to the max, leaped from the SUV as it spun in a flat arc into the right-side MRAP.

The SUV smashed into the MRAP, coming apart with an earsplitting bang. Metal tearing itself to pieces as two tons of SUV encountered seven tons of MRAP at sixty miles per hour. The Range Rover evaporated to pieces, taking out the crew of the MRAP with it. The front half of the MRAP caved in, the impact shoving the heavy vehicle back a couple of yards, leaving the crew unconscious or dead.

The left-side MRAP continued firing its M240 machine gun at the lead SUV. All the doors of the Range Rover opened at once. The SUV's windscreen starred and cracked, sparks flying from the front panels as 7.62mm rounds ripped into the ceramic armor. Francis, Anton, Peter, and Li blurred from the wreck, rounds from Shadowstone troopers whizzing through the spaces behind them.

Francis ramped hard, blurring away from the deadly trap the SUV had become. He lifted his H&K MP5, firing at the Shadowstone troopers near the MRAP. From his peripheral vision, he could account for everyone else in his team. Jay, Yvette, Luther, and Chiara were looping through the air to land behind the troopers. In moments, they would catch the troopers in a fatal crossfire. Anton and Li had gone left, their guns blazing as they cut the distance to the surviving MRAP. Peter appeared near Francis' shoulder, his submachine gun hammering as he drew a battle-axe from his belt.

His heart leaped into his throat.

Where's Juliette?

He turned in horror toward the SUV, the windscreen shattering as round after round pummeled it.

"No!" he shouted, blurring over the SUV in a mighty leap to the other side.

Francis landed, twisting around behind the armored car door. Bullets streamed a foot over his head or slammed into the open car door.

Juliette lay still in her seat, still strapped in, the left side of her face covered in blood.

"No, no, no," Francis moaned.

* * *

Time slowed to a crawl.

Anton blurred forward, Li at his shoulder, his H&K MP5 vibrating in his left hand as it sent high-performance 9mm rounds at the troopers thirty yards away. He carried the Blue Dragon in his right hand, its naked blade dull beneath the leaden sky. Grenades were looping in toward the surviving MRAP from Jay and Yvette, while Chiara and Luther cut down the two remaining Shadowstone troopers near the smashed MRAP and the ruined Range Rover.

Anton locked gazes with one of the Shadowstone troopers for a fraction of a second, long enough for each man to bring their weapon to bear on the other. The trooper glared at him, moving faster than normal, his H&K 417 assault rifle swung around.

Anton found himself staring down the barrel.

The under-barrel grenade launcher fired, smoke burst from the barrel; 7.62mm rounds and a 40mm grenade flying toward him.

Anton leaned over backward, the bullets flying over him.

Li fired back, her rounds taking the trooper in the face. His head rocked back, blood and bone spraying over the underside of the overturned trailer. He slumped forward, explosions rattling the MRAP before his body hit the ground.

Anton stood upright, the trooper's grenade exploding harmlessly behind him in the scrub. Twisting around he scanned the team, everyone was okay, but there was no sign of Juliette. He sucked air through his teeth, turning back to the Range Rover. Francis was reaching into the front left cabin of the SUV. There was a flash of dark-brown hair, there were flecks of blood on the smashed windscreen.

"What the hell?" Anton whispered.

He dashed back to the Range Rover.

* * *

Francis stepped back from the Range Rover. The look of horror on his face disappearing, replaced by one of utter desperation.

"Chiara, quickly, the—"

Chiara appeared at his shoulder, Juliette's medical bag in her hands.

"—medical kit."

Chiara crouched down next to Juliette, putting her fingers on the right side of Juliette's throat. A handful of seconds later she declared, "She's got a pulse." She started checking her for other wounds. Blood covered Juliette's left thigh in a dark sheen. She reached into the bag and took out a tourniquet, which she placed high on Juliette's thigh. "Two bullets through the left thigh. This'll stop the bleeding – for now."

Francis stepped back, scanning the horizon. "Team, collect what you can from the SUVs and form a perimeter. The only people on the move now are Shadowstone."

He left his command at that, the team members all knew what they needed to do.

The team had to move. Shadowstone would know they'd destroyed this site within minutes. For all Francis knew, Shadowstone routinely wired and monitored the vital signs of all their troopers. Some command center somewhere could be registering a set of flat-lined readouts. At the very least, they would make regular reports, and their command would miss the next report and work out something was wrong.

The perimeter line in place, Francis ducked his head in over Chiara. She was probing Juliette's head wound with her fingers.

Chiara turned her head to look up at Francis, her face filled with concern and said, "The bullet scored her scalp, hence all the blood, but she may have a fractured skull. We need to find a medical clinic with a modern med-sensor."

"Patch her head first," he directed. He stood back, looking at his team. "Li, check the net and see if there is a medical clinic nearby with state-of-the-art sensor equipment."

"Yes, Francis," Li said, pulling her smartphone from a chest pocket.

Francis stepped away from the SUV, hovering over Chiara wasn't helping her focus on her work. He scanned the horizon and his team. Everyone was where they should be, and there was no sign of Shadowstone. He opened up his smartphone and dialed Walker. The phone rang six times before Walker answered it.

"What do you want?" Walker said brusquely.

"Juliette's been shot. I need your help."

"And what do you think I can do?"

"Send two cars, we have no transport."

Walker laughed bitterly. "Surely you could not have missed the state of emergency."

"Yes, I know. We still need cars. We have to get Juliette to a medical surgery."

"Mirovar, it's not possible. Right now, Shadowstone has no idea we're here. I'm not compromising my team or the mission to rescue you from your own incompetence."

Francis seethed, pulling the phone away from his ear and swearing under his breath. He brought the phone back to his ear. Walker was still talking.

"—have to get yourself out of your own mess and get over here with your surviving fighters. We'll need them to assault the manor house."

"I'm taking Juliette to a medical center – you'll have to wait."

"Fuck you Mirovar – the mission comes first."

Francis' eyes became dark hard stones. "We'll be there. Sit tight Walker."

"I'd heard the Mirovar force team was incompetent, now I know it's true."

Francis shook his head, what was the source of Walker's enmity?

"Do us all a favor and put a mercy bullet in her brain," Walker proposed in tight cold tones. "Then move everyone to Whitby now."

Francis snapped, "Vas te faire encule, fils de pute." He hung up. There would be no help from the Walker force team. They were on their own.

"Francis," Li called out. "There is a medical center in Goathland. According to their advertisement, they offer advanced medical facilities. With the state of emergency, the place is probably empty, all I'm getting is voicemail."

He poked his head back into the SUV, Chiara was completing the bandaging of Juliette's head. "Can you operate their medical equipment?"

"Absolutely."

"Excellent," Francis said, a flicker of hope igniting in his chest. "We'll go on foot. Help me with her. Strap her to me, I don't want her head moving around when I carry her."

Chiara stepped back, and Francis scooped up Juliette's limp form, cradling her in his arms. A minute later, Chiara completed strapping Juliette to Francis, ensuring she would be as stable as possible when Francis ran.

Chiara put a hand on Francis' shoulder looking into his eyes. "Watch her breathing, we haven't been able to intubate her, she could stop breathing at any time."

Francis nodded, and then stepped away. "Team, form up on me," he commanded. "Keep your eyes open. We're running hard for Goathland. Li, you're navigating, take us to the medical center."

Li blurred away, Francis a yard behind her, racing down the road. The team paced with them, they had three miles to cover to get to the heart of the town of Goathland.

They would be there in ten minutes.

* * *

The medical center was a two-story white block with a flat roof.

The team left Jay guarding the front door, while Luther ascended to the roof with a set of digital binoculars to guard the approaches. The medical center had been locked up before they arrived, shut down during the state of emergency while the staff evacuated back to their homes. Breaking in had been a trivial task, and the team had followed Francis as he blurred into the empty doctor's surgery.

Chiara released the bindings holding Juliette close to Francis, and he laid Juliette carefully onto the examination table.

Juliette moaned. The first noise she'd made since getting shot. Chiara glanced at the wall clock, it read 16:21, nearly twenty minutes had passed since the last battle with Shadowstone. It was a long time to be unconscious, concussion was a certainty. Now she'd to find out the true extent of her injuries.

Juliette had taken a bullet along the left side of her skull, scoring a long, deep cut along her scalp an inch above her ear. If the bullet had been an inch to the right, it would have taken the top of Juliette's head off. She was lucky to be alive.

Chiara checked the leg wounds. Two bullets had ripped along Juliette's left thigh. There was a lot of blood, but both bullets had gone through muscle on the outside of the thigh, the inner thigh leading to the vulnerable femoral artery was untouched. It was a small blessing.

Li stood on the opposite side of the table and asked, "Can I help?"

"Sure," Chiara said, grateful for any assistance. Having Juliette's life in her hands was a responsibility she didn't want. Normally Juliette would be in charge, and Chiara would take her guidance. Taking responsibility for killing someone was easy. Taking responsibility for saving someone's life, especially when you loved them like a mother was something entirely different.

Juliette moaned again. Was she about to wake up? Her eyelids fluttered and then stilled. Chiara checked her vitals, she was still breathing, and her pulse was a steady thirty-five beats per minute.

Francis stepped closer, frowned and said firmly, "Time is wasting."

"Yes, yes," Chiara said, a touch of exasperation leaking into her voice. She rolled a trolley loaded with high-tech equipment next to the examination table. She fitted a brace around Juliette's head and attached it to the table to keep her still. Taking a long silvery wand, attached to a monitor on the trolley by a slim black cable, she approached Juliette's head. She flicked a switch, a pale light emanated from the tip of the wand. She stroked the tip over Juliette's head, first vertically, and then horizontally. Each stroke about half an inch to the side of the previous stroke. An image of Juliette's skull appeared on the monitor and began to fill in with heat mapped detail.

Chiara concentrated on her work.

Behind her, Francis clicked his fingers and ordered, "Anton, Peter, we need supplies. Find us some food and anything else useful. Be back here in twenty minutes."

"Yes, Boss," Peter agreed, and Anton nodded. The two young men picked up their weapons and backpacks, departing the room moments later.

Chiara sat back and turned to Francis. "Juliette's got a fractured skull."

"C'est un foutu bordel!" Francis swore, pacing the room. "How long before she wakes up?"

"I don't know. We have to wait."

"Deal with her other injuries while we wait."

"Will do," Chiara said, glancing across at Li. "How's your suturing coming along?"

"One of the first things Juliette taught me."

"Excellent, let's get started then."

Chiara and Li set to work to repair the two bullet wounds in Juliette's thigh and save her leg.

Chiara breathed a sigh of relief to be working on comparatively simple bullet wounds. Looking after a brain injury was beyond her skills. She hoped there would be no complications and Juliette would wake up soon with nothing more to complain about then a splitting headache.

Chiara bit back a sob, focusing hard on the tasks at hand. Juliette couldn't die, she'd been a mother to her for half her life.

No, it couldn't happen. She would do everything in her power to save Juliette's life.

"Francis, we'll need blood. You haven't donated yet."

Francis began rolling up his sleeve.

A minute later Chiara returned to her work. Li had neatly cut away Juliette's pants leg revealing the full extent of the injuries. There were four wounds, two entry points a few inches above the knee and two exit holes high up on the thigh. The bullets had carved through the muscles, long but shallow wounds. Much like long stab wounds. Chiara settled in with Li and got to work. Checking to make sure the wounds were clear of foreign material and then suturing them up.

As Juliette's surgical apprentice, it was work she had plenty of practice with.

* * *

Peter looked at the lock on the front door of the home-mart store for a second. His hand blurred forward. The wood and thin metal around the lock tore away, the door swinging free.

"We're in," he whispered to Anton.

"Right," Anton said sardonically, heading along the aisles, filling his backpack with high-protein fitness bars, and anything else that was high calories in a small package.

Peter did the same. Half a minute later he exclaimed, "Bonus!"

Anton jogged over to where Peter was collecting battery powered LEDs. They were general purpose headlamps, small, powerful, and easily hidden.

"Stick these in your pockets," Peter advised. "Just like we said, if Armitage switches off the lights, we'll have a backup plan. Anton smiled; he liked the idea of confounding Armitage if she plunged the team into darkness as part of her 'trap.'

On the wall opposite the LEDs was a rack of climbing equipment. A pair of product signs and a corkboard of photos indicated that someone associated with the store was a climbing enthusiast, perhaps the store's owner. Anton picked up a coil of rope and put it over his shoulder, there was a multi-pronged hook attached to the end.

"Thinking of climbing something?"

"Armitage's house is on a cliff face, isn't it? We might need to come in from that angle."

"Good idea, gives us another option."

"Time to go," Anton observed, patting his full backpack. "Francis wanted us back in twenty minutes."

"Hang on a second," Peter said, rummaging around in the bottom of his backpack. He withdrew a fat wallet stuffed with cash. He pulled out half a dozen fifty-pound notes and placed them on the counter next to the till. "That should just about cover it."

Peter's actions were a relief, Anton was uncomfortable with the idea of 'just stealing stuff,' even if it was a life or death situation, it didn't sit right with him.

Peter grinned at him. "Hey, I came prepared. We're not thieves you know."

Anton smiled; Peter's irrepressible good humor always lifted him. He was lucky to know him; his life could have gone a far different path after the death of his mother and the abduction of his father. It could have easily spiraled into a short-lived hell of wrath and violence.

The friends he had in the Mirovar force team had become more important to him than anything else. A voice nagged him at the back of his mind, it whispered, *'Liar, vengeance is your god now.'*

"No," he whispered to himself, following Peter from the shop but he lacked conviction in his denial.

* * *

Eight turbines roared as the helicopters circled to land.

The four fully-armed nightfalcons descended to a private airfield outside Goathland. It provided a perfect staging point for the remaining elements of Squadron F to cover Yorkshire. A pair of hangars stood mutely in the distance, silent witnesses to the paramilitary force landing in the middle of the airstrip.

An extra Mk-19 grenade launcher sat opposite the 7.62mm minigun on each of the heavily armed gunships. The waist-mounted MK-19 could fire six grenades per second, the perfect anti-personnel weapon to provide an area-of-effect attack on fast moving targets. They also carried their main armament of eight Hellfire III and eight Stinger II missiles for air-to-ground and air-to-air combat respectively. The final element was a pair of tri-barreled .50 caliber machine guns equipped with two thousand rounds of depleted uranium ammunition mounted in the hull beneath the nose of the helicopters.

Each helicopter carried a crew of two pilots, and two gunners, and sixteen fully armed and armored Day Guard phase IV Shadowstone troopers.

The lead craft landed first. Sixteen troopers streamed from both sides of the nightfalcon to create a defensive perimeter fifty yards from it. Major Frank Quiver, tall, slim, and sandy-haired, with a distinctive wing commander mustache was the last to exit.

Major Quiver was the commanding officer of Squadron F and immediate subordinate to Director Heathmont. He strode away from the nightfalcon along the runway tarmac. He glanced at his watch, it read

16:40. It had taken nearly four and a half hours to bring his forces back to the Facility, refuel, rearm and reposition to this airfield.

His wing commander mustache twitched with annoyance. He didn't like a civilian ordering him around like some navvy. Director Heathmont was adamant that the Order of Thoth team had an objective in or around Goathland. Major Quiver had ordered the fitting of the MK-19 multi-grenade launchers to the port side mounts of the nightfalcons. The extra weaponry would be an asset versus the incredible speed of the Order operatives. If Heathmont was right, his men were as prepared and as well-equipped as they could be.

The other helicopters landed, the men moving out from them to take up defensive positions and stretch their legs. The whole force remained on hot standby, the helicopters idling their turbines, ready to take off at a moment's notice. With a two-hundred miles per hour top speed, his force could be anywhere in the north of England in short order.

He stroked his mustache, an unconscious gesture performed out of habit, it soothed his mind and helped him think.

There had been contact with Order of Thoth forces three miles out of Goathland on the A169 forty minutes ago, presumably the Mirovar force team. The enemy had wiped out two squads of his men in the engagement. So far, he'd expended half of Squadron F without claiming a single casualty on the opposing force, it was an unprecedented result.

Major Quiver vowed to concentrate on using his Hellfire missiles, and the Mk-19 grenade launchers to even the odds. His forces would stand off with the nightfalcons and pound the ground wherever the Order of Thoth operatives chose to stand.

They would not catch him out twice. The next time he came into contact with the enemy, he would blow them all to hell.

* * *

Juliette's eyelids fluttered, sharp light edging around them.

She had a splitting headache, and her left leg was on fire from the hip down. The good news was, she was still alive. There was a hard surface beneath her; she had enough medical experience to place it as an examination table without thinking about it.

She whispered, "What damage?" it sounded more like, 'Whaf damf?'

Juliette took a deep breath, her head hurt like hell, but her lungs were working fine.

"Juliette, you're waking up," Chiara said softly. "You've been shot, you took a head wound."

"The others?" Juliette squeezed out; her voice raspy.

"Sip this," Chiara said, offering Juliette a straw in a glass of water.

"Juliette sipped, the water soothing her throat.

Chiara explained, "Everyone is safe, we're holed up here in a small town called Goathland, about ten miles away from Whitby."

A shadow loomed over her; Francis leaned down to kiss her forehead. "Mon amour, you have come back."

Juliette looked up at Francis' face, his concern writ large on his features. His eyes were liquid with unshed tears. She lifted her hand up to stroke his face but never made it.

The last thing she experienced was Chiara shouting, "There's something wrong."

* * *

"She's bleeding on the brain," Chiara shouted. "She needs immediate surgery."

Chiara looked around at everyone in the room – they stared back at her. Her heart sank. There was no one else; she was the best qualified to do the surgery. She just didn't trust that she could do it.

She looked hard at Li. "Okay, let's prep."

The two young women blurred into action.

"Yvette," Chiara half-shouted, pointing to a second trolley on the other side of the surgical theater. "Bring that one over here."

Yvette blurred, the trolley appearing next to the table. Chiara reached over and grabbed the equipment she needed. Yvette started to back away, a shocked look on her face.

"Wait, I need your help," Chiara pleaded, catching Yvette's gaze with her eyes. "Here take this," she requested, handing Yvette an oval balloon the size of a football, with a nozzle at one end. She concentrated on Juliette's mouth, opening it, and inserting a firm tube down her throat. She attached the end of the tube to the nozzle of the balloon.

"Yvette, press on the balloon in a steady rhythm and keep her breathing."

Yvette swallowed, stared at Juliette's chest and kept her breathing with the balloon.

Chiara picked up the silvery wand, activated it, and ran a set of short sweeps over the wound site. The bleed showed up on the monitor as an angry red welt on the screen. It was just beneath the skull. An acute epidural hematoma.

Using the wand, Chiara located the exact center of the bleed, took a black pen and marked a line to the edge of the wound and a second line to make an 'X,' on Juliette's scalp.

There was an electric razor on the trolley. Twenty seconds later, Chiara had cleared a strip of hair away from the 'X.' Disinfectant was next, then she scanned the room, rushed to a cabinet and came back with a drill with a shiny stainless-steel bit.

Chiara paused for a second, staring at Francis. "You may want to look away for this bit."

Francis lifted his gaze away from Juliette for a moment. He looked at Chiara with eyes wide with dread and pleaded, "Do what you have to do, just … please … save her life."

"We will," Chiara replied, more confidence in her voice than she felt. She moved the trolley aside to give herself room, there was no time for hesitation.

She ramped, her hands becoming stonelike in their stillness. Time slowed, she activated the drill and placed it precisely on the center of the 'X.' It was essential that she reach into Juliette's skull far enough to allow the collected blood to drain but no further.

Chiara pushed the drill forward. It cut through Juliette's scalp with ease, then struck the bone. She lifted the pressure slightly and the steel bit ground into Juliette's skull.

The whine of the drill cut through the air like a knife. Chiara ripped it back, dark blood spurting from the hole. The flow slowed to a steady trickle. Chiara placed an absorbent pad against the hole and strapped it in place.

"Normally," she noted. "A surgeon would repair the blood vessels and possibly put in a drainage tube. Here, we have to rely on Juliette's system zero genetics to stem the bleeding. We'll need to keep an eye on her now and monitor her progress."

Francis looked at his wife, his face clouded with worry. "When will she wake up?"

"She has to stay still, or she will most likely die. The longer the better, certainly, at least an hour."

Francis looked up at the wall clock, Chiara tracked his gaze. The clock read, '17:12.'

"We're here at least until after six pm," he promised, gently stroking Juliette's hand.

Chiara nodded and prayed silently for Juliette to wake up.

* * *

Thunder cracked overhead, and rain hammered the front windows of the medical center. The street lights had come on, responding automatically to the darkness of the storm.

The clock on the wall read, '18:30,' a little less than two hours to sunset. The team had congregated in the main reception area as they prepared to leave. Everyone had picked up a large black plastic garbage bag from the cleaning cupboard, cutting holes in them for their head and arms, to make impromptu raincoats.

Juliette had woken up twenty minutes earlier. She was sitting in a chair in the waiting area, dressed in a fresh pair of pants. The only visible hints of her recent injuries, the heavy bandaging of her skull, and thick wrapping that tightened the fabric over her left thigh. Her eyes were alert, and she carried her head high.

Anton walked into the room carrying a pair of crutches, went over to Juliette, and said, "I found these, I've already adjusted them for your height."

Juliette smiled. "Thanks."

"Good work Anton," Francis said. His lips tightened, he frowned, catching Anton, Peter and Li's gazes. "I have a very difficult mission for the three of you."

"The best sort," Peter observed, crossing and flexing his fingers, his knuckles cracking loudly.

Anton nodded resolutely and said, "Whatever you need Francis."

Li glanced at Anton and sighed softly. "I will do my best."

"Good," Francis noted. "Juliette's going to conduct another full Panopticon hazing operation. She will center it on her laptop. It will create an information black hole three miles wide for fifteen minutes ... However, Shadowstone is on full alert, they will notice the hazing as soon as it starts and they will send all their available forces toward the center of the hazing."

"So, we leave the laptop here and escape?" Anton asked.

"No. We'll send it with you. The hazing begins at 18:45 and will run to 19:00. Between now and then, you will take the laptop as far north as you can go."

Luther looked up from his seat, smiling grimly at Anton. "With all this talk, you've got less than thirteen minutes before the hazing starts. We don't want you starting from here and giving away our position."

Francis threw Luther an irritated glance. "One last thing, the laptop has a thermite charge in its base, it will self-destruct when the hazing ends."

Anton asked, "Why destroy the laptop?"

"A normal hazing is defined on a single geographical location," Juliette explained. "The laptop governing the hazing doesn't even have to be there. This hazing is located on the laptop itself. When the hazing stops, the laptop is going to be in the middle of it. We have to destroy it to ensure it doesn't fall into Shadowstone's hands."

"You don't trust us to be able to escape with it."

Luther stepped forward. "It's standard operating procedure. The Order can't take the risk. When we perform a hazing this way, we always destroy the laptop. It's known as a 'sacrifice play.'" He stared at Anton. "Like when a lizard drops its tail to escape a predator."

Anton fell silent. He became preternaturally still, on the borderline of ramping. Luther's presence always filled him with a sense of veiled threat. The situation could only last so long before it blew up. He believed the time was coming soon when either Luther or himself would be dead.

"Very encouraging," Juliette said sarcastically, her eyes flashing at Luther.

Luther snapped. "I told you before we left. I would keep this team honest."

Anton shrugged off the incipient Ramp, and stepped forward, crouching before Juliette. "It's okay. Let's get you safe."

Juliette reached out, taking his hands in hers and said softly. "You're just like your grandfather you know, and in the best possible way."

Anton stood up, turning to the rest of the team. "Don't worry about us."

Francis directed, "You must go now, time is short. We will be at the manor house at Whitby in two hours."

Peter nodded, grabbing the laptop in its protective satchel, he made for the door. Anton and Li, shouldering their weapons and gear, following behind him. A moment later, they were out on the street.

"North then," Anton offered, shielding his eyes from the rain with his left hand.

"North it is," Peter replied.

They ran off down the street. In ten minutes' time, the hazing would begin, and Shadowstone would throw everything they could muster at them.

"We're bait," Anton said wryly, his face caught halfway between a grin and a grimace.

"Better get used to it princess," Peter remarked. "It won't be the last time."

"You hope," Li said, running next to them.

Peter didn't have anything else to say.

They ran on in silence, putting a mile every four minutes between themselves and the rest of the team.

Chapter Twenty Four

"Low to medium level wars, proxy wars, and wars by non-state actors all provide excellent cover for the secret war between the Vampire Dominion and the Ramp masters. War within the human community is to be maintained at a level aligned with the goal of providing ready, and believable scapegoats to blame for those occasions when the operations of the Vampire Dominion become visible to humans. Note well, that one of our number is missing from this conference because his reckless ambitions plunged the world into six years of wasteful conflict. Let Dieter Franz's punishment be a lesson to you all – world-wide conflagrations will not be tolerated. I trust I have made myself clear." – Cornelius Crane, King of the Vampire Dominion at the Conference of Generals, New York, 1946.

* * *

Outside Ogton, Yorkshire, August 22nd, 18:58

The storm winds whipped past the open doors of the nightfalcon helicopter.

The gunship was hugging the ground, flying at one hundred and eighty miles per hour at one-hundred yards altitude over the Yorkshire Moors. Four four-man squads of fully armed and armored Shadowstone troopers crowded the main cabin of the craft. Corporal Brian Jenkins strode up and down the aisle, slapping shoulders and checking equipment.

"Well fuck a doodle doo boys, it's showtime," he shouted over the roar of the helicopter, clasping the broad shoulders of one of his men.

The man grinned back, a wild light behind his eyes. They were all participants in the Phase IV Day Guard program. They'd been told it was a UK government program to create a superior fighting force to fight terrorists anywhere in the world. For the last two years, he'd been on a steady program of injected serums, steroids, and stimulants. The effects had been dramatic, Corporal Jenkins could bench press four hundred and eighty pounds and run a marathon with full kit in two hours. He could easily win gold in a host of Olympic events, but of course, he couldn't compete. He was disappointed about that, he was sure there was no 'official,' drug testing regime that could detect the exotic cocktail flowing through his bloodstream.

Jenkin's eyes tightened, he snarled and declared, "Time for some payback."

"Hell, yeah," came back from the men surrounding him.

He thumped an armored shoulder with his gauntleted fist. For a normal man, the blow would have cracked the joint. The trooper grinned back at him, eager, and ready to fight.

"ETA, one minute," came over his tactical helmet comms link.

The major was on this bird, personally commanding Squadron F for this battle. An unknown number of hostiles faced them. They anticipated more than twenty, and perhaps as many as thirty individuals had been warring with the 'F,' all day. The results had been horrific, with nearly half the squadron lost. The four nightfalcons in this flight and the attached eighty troopers were the bulk of the remaining force.

Now they'd found the enemy. They were on the move, heading toward the village of Ogton. Luckily, the squadron had staged at a private airfield east of Goathland, mere minutes away from their targets.

It was a God sent opportunity. The enemy had appeared in their laps, and Jenkins would happily assist in hammering them into dust.

Jenkins looked out through the open cabin doorway; the trooper next to him was manning a Mk-19 grenade launcher. They'd fitted the weapon to the helicopter earlier that day – an equalizer – there had been rumors that the enemy was enhanced with extreme speed; and the capability to fire half a dozen 40mm grenades a second was deemed necessary.

Were the enemy that dangerous? Jenkins stared into the stormy darkness outside the nightfalcon. The street lights of Ogton were just visible in the distance. He was keen to answer that question for himself.

Thunder cracked overhead, lightning flashing nearby, rain fell in sheets. The nightfalcons flew on in the dusk-like darkness without running lights. The whole of the remaining force of Squadron F converging on the hamlet of Ogton.

* * *

The trio ran through the lamp-lit streets of Ogton at Olympic level marathon pace.

Li pulled to a halt, Anton and Peter stopping a couple of yards later, turning back to her.

Thunder cracked overhead, lightning dazzling across the sky, gleaming off the wet black plastic of their impromptu raincoats. Li declared, "They're here, or will be in seconds."

The roar of jet turbines cut through the air, four nightfalcons emerging from the gloom beneath the storm clouds. The wedge formation separated, two helicopters veering to the left and the other two peeling off to the right. In moments, they were flying in concentric circles around the hamlet of Ogton.

Peter twisted around, watching the gunships circle and said sardonically. "Geez, if brute force doesn't work, we might need to use finesse."

The nightfalcons slowed, hovering thirty yards off the ground beyond the edge of the village. Dark lines dropped from the helicopters, Shadowstone troopers followed, rappelling down the lines. They completed the operation in less than ten seconds. The troopers immediately dashing off in the gloom to take up positions in a cordon around the village.

There was a gas station, forty yards away, on the main road leading out of town. Given the state of emergency curfew and the storm, it lay empty. Peter glanced inside the laptop satchel; his face momentarily lit by a faint red glow. "Thirteen seconds to go." He blurred to the station, pulling the laptop from the satchel as he ran.

Anton and Li ran along the other side of the street.

The nightfalcons veered upward, making a single evenly spaced circle around the village. They were flying in a broad circle from right to left, their waist mounted Mk-19 grenade launchers swinging toward the village.

Peter blurred back to their side, guiding them further back from the gas station. A second later the laptop's thermite charge detonated. A bright glare appeared next to one of the fuel bowsers. Half a second later, the bowser erupted in a towering fountain of flame.

"The hazing is over," Peter declared. "That's the distraction, now we break through their lines and escape."

"It's still too light to avoid being seen," Li observed.

Li was right. Shadowstone would have them in their sights and were only positioning to take the final shot. Anton's face became still, his eyes deadly serious in the gloom. "Then we will have to kill them all."

He turned and blurred down the street. He didn't know what he would do yet, but he was sure he didn't want to leave an operational Shadowstone unit hunting them, or the rest of the Mirovar team, alive and on their tail.

The forces circling overhead, and setting up a perimeter around the village, would have to die. It was the only way he could be sure to keep his friends safe.

A dreadful fury boiled within him, his eyes glistening beneath the storm clouds and pelting rain. Ripping away the plastic sheet around his shoulders, he lifted his FN P90 submachine gun from a holster at his side. The Blue Dragon's handle jutted over his right shoulder, ready to swing into action at a moment's notice.

He headed back into town, looking for a high spot to get to, he needed to see all of his enemies so he could see who needed to die.

"Violence will be my friend," Anton uttered, a ferocious light behind his eyes.

He blurred into the shadows, Li and Peter following closely behind him.

* * *

Major Frank Quiver rolled along in his railed chair, scanning the wall of screens in his command nightfalcon. The vital signs of his ground troops were all displayed underneath feeds from their individual helmet cams. Everything was in the green and proceeding according to plan.

The Order of Thoth's hazing operation had just ended, defeated by cyberwarfare counter attacks from Shadowstone units across the world. With the storm and the curfew, the streets were empty; except for three newly identified forms running hot in the infra-red and super-fast toward the center of town.

He ignored the flaring gasoline fire on the edge of town. It was an obvious distraction; he wasn't about to be tricked by something so simple.

With the Panopticon linked into the networked sensors on the four nightfalcons, he had a clear three-dimensional view of the village and everyone in it. This was going to be easier than he'd expected. The enemy had divided their forces. The three operatives discovered in the village at the center of the Panopticon haze lay exposed to every weapon he had at his disposal. But he had to be wary, the Shadowstone mandate was to operate in secret. There was only so much he could do out in the open. He couldn't simply blow away a whole village to get to three operatives. It would be next to impossible to explain, especially on top of the disasters at the Squadron F base, and the RAF airbase at Coningsby.

The Shadowstone PSYOPS directorate was shitting kittens, secrecy was not something he could throw away on a whim. He would have to send in his men and flush the enemy out into the open where his heavy weapons would prove decisive.

He opened his tactical comms link to his squad commanders. They were all on the ground, manning a cordon around the village. He gave the order to flush the enemy to the south. The hostiles were moving toward the center of the hamlet at frightening speed, but it only took him a moment to vector his squads after them. He pulled two of his squads away from the south entrance of town to give the Order operatives a path of 'escape.'

His men would push the Order operatives back to the south, once clear of the village, his nightfalcons would take them out with Hellfire missiles.

They would not be able to escape him this time.

* * *

Thick, dark clouds glowered overhead.

Corporal Brian Jenkins peered through the sheeting rain, looking for the hostiles he was supposed to push south. To his right, a wall of flames consumed a gasoline station. A heads-up-display filled his tactical helmet visor, overlaying everything he saw with metadata provided by the Shadowstone Panopticon. It was too much to take in at the same time, the flames, the storm, and all the high-tech crap clouding his vision.

He lifted his visor.

"There's no one here," he muttered.

Four men emerged from the gloom, running across the street toward the gas station. Each one carried something in their arms. Weapons, bombs, he didn't know, but they weren't Shadowstone. He lifted his H&K 416 assault rifle, letting rip with a long burst. The bullets flashed through the men, cutting them down. The nearest one fell forward, the object he was carrying rolling across the ground.

It was a red fire extinguisher, wet and gleaming in the firelight.

"Stupid bastards."

They were locals.

He signaled his men with a raised fist to advance. He walked past the fallen men, dark pools spreading from their bodies. Shaking his head, his mouth set in a grim slash, he thought, *This is going to get ugly.*

* * *

The command screens reflected the carnage on the ground.

Major Quiver glared at his displays. He didn't need collateral damage. The Phase IV stimulants made his men faster, but they could lead to careless risk-taking. The four bodies cooling in the rain were a testament to that.

A green light flashed in the corner of his set of screens. A call from Director Heathmont was coming in.

He answered, "Sir?"

"What the hell is happening?" Heathmont asked. "Have you killed them yet?"

"No, Sir. We have three hostiles in Ogton."

"They must've split their forces. It will be their undoing."

"Sir, I've sent in my men. I'll flush them into the open and destroy them."

"No," Heathmont snapped. "Don't risk your men. Pull them back now."

"Sir?"

"Take out the town, it's the only way to be sure. It's sitting over a major gas line. We'll explain everything away with a gas explosion. Erase everyone, there can be no survivors."

Major Quiver took a deep breath, and replied, "Yes, Sir."

"Make sure it's done. No survivors."

Without blinking, Major Quiver said, "Roger, Sir."

The line went dead.

Major Quiver didn't hesitate, issuing orders over his tactical comms link to his squad commanders to pull back beyond the edge of town. He followed with orders to his pilots to fire at will at the three hostiles in the center of the village.

The helicopters started to pivot as one, bringing their main weapons to bear on the three operatives highlighted on his screens.

"This will be over soon," Major Quiver whispered to himself.

* * *

The nightfalcons turned.

"Move!" Peter shouted.

Peter, Anton, and Li blurred away from the center of the village. Hellfire missiles streaked through the rain toward where they'd been standing. The blasts ripped away the dusky gloom beneath the storm clouds. Buildings evaporated, windows shattered, dust, smoke, and flame bursting upward in a hellish tower over the hamlet.

The edge of the blast wave hit them like a giant's fist, hurling them along the street. Anton scrambled off the slick cobblestones. Li bounced to her feet a couple of yards in front of him, shaking her left hand. Peter rolled to his feet and shook himself.

"They're destroying the village," Li shouted, glancing down at her bloody hand.

The nightfalcons roared overhead, circling for their next attack.

"We have to stop them," Anton declared. He twisted around and pointed at the tallest structure in the town. "The water tower."

Peter and Li looked at Anton, nonplussed for half a second. Anton threw his FN P90 submachine gun to Peter, and said, "I won't be needing this."

Peter grinned, hefting an FN P90 with each hand and shouted, "Yes! Go! I'll keep 'em occupied down here." He blurred back through the smoke and falling debris, firing short bursts of 9mm rounds from his submachine guns at the circling helicopters.

Anton ramped hard, blurring away to the base of the water tower, loosening the climbing rope he'd picked up in Goathland. He leaped ten feet up to a steel stairway, snaking up and around to the top of the tower.

Li followed a step behind him. Blurring up nearly fifty yards of rusting steel stairs, they burst out onto the brick and cement platform at the top of the tower.

One of the nightfalcons was approaching at about forty miles per hour. Its port side gunner firing his Mk-19 grenade launcher down at the village. He was chasing Peter with his weapon, patterns of two and four grenades exploding along the main street. The helicopter was going to pass the water tower in seconds. It was flying about thirty yards higher and another twenty yards away from the top of the tower.

Anton unbound his climbing rope, swinging its hook in a circle. He figured he had one chance, any second now, Shadowstone would notice their presence on top of the tower. He dropped into silence and time slowed down. The steady beat of the nightfalcon's rotors separated out into individual thumps, reverberating through the air. The fires below lit the gunner's helmet, a faint reflection of Anton and Li appearing on his visor. In the distance, the lightning seemed to crackle forever as it reached hungry fingers down to the Yorkshire Moors.

The Mk-19 fell silent. The gunner's stare fixing on Anton.

Anton released the hook, throwing it with all his might. It flew like an arrow into the nightfalcon's main cabin, missing the gunner by a couple of feet.

The gunner swung the Mk-19 up toward the top of the water tower.

Anton whipped the rope, the tri-bladed hook swinging back through the cabin, embedding itself in the gunner's back. He arched backward, his arms swinging wide. The barrel of the Mk-19 dropped as he lurched forward against his restraints.

"Now!" Anton shouted, wrapping the rope tight around his wrist. Li leaped onto his back, her arms wrapping around his neck and her thighs locking around his hips. The rope snapped taut, Anton moved with it, blurring forward, and leaping into the darkness beneath the nightfalcon. The rope snapped tight again, Li and Anton swinging underneath the helicopter. His hands blurred, ascending the rope, shortening their loop as they came up the other side of the helicopter.

They landed in the main cabin. The Mk-19 gunner writhed within his harness, trying to extract the hook from his shoulder. The trooper manning the starboard side minigun reached for his 9mm sidearm.

Li's foot lashed out, taking the nearest trooper beneath his helmet. He slammed backward within his safety harness, then fell forward, dangling in his restraints with his head at an unnatural angle.

Anton drew the Blue Dragon in a horizontal slash, beheading the hooked trooper struggling in his harness. The man's helmeted head fell forward, disappearing into the gloom, his blood painting the ceiling in a dark crimson streak.

Shadows stretching from the cockpit fell across the floor. A hidden submachine gun erupted, 9mm bullets wildly spraying the back of the cabin. Anton and Li sprang forward, taking up positions to the left and right of the entrance to the cockpit.

The co-pilot darted forward, attempting to rush through into the cabin while shooting to his left. He came to a sudden halt, held upright by the Blue and Green Dragon swords piercing his torso from both sides. The blades swished out; a look of helpless despair flitted momentarily over his face before he slid bonelessly to the floor.

Anton didn't wait for the co-pilot to land, leaping high over his dying body, and blurring forward into the cockpit. The pilot's left arm swung left, a 9mm automatic in his grip. The gun barked, the bullet going beneath Anton as he flew off the opposite wall. The Blue Dragon arced downward, entering the pilot's chest just above the collarbone and diving deep down through his body. He coughed once, blood splattering the console.

Anton drew the Blue Dragon clear of the pilot's body. He leaned forward, snapped the pilot's harness clips, dragging him clear of the cockpit and dropping him next to the co-pilot on the floor of the nightfalcon's main cabin.

He glanced at Li, and then at the 7.62mm minigun. "Can you fire one of those?"

Li ripped the body of the trooper from the harness next to the gun and cast it aside. She arched an eyebrow, glancing at the cockpit. "Can you fly one of these?"

Anton grinned, dashing back into the cockpit, leaping into the pilot's seat. His hands flew over the controls with practiced ease, all the long hours spent in training simulations with Peter back at the safe house in Maine were now paying off.

The nightfalcon had been circling on automatic pilot for the last dozen seconds, and it looked like no one had noticed Anton and Li's capture of the craft. Digital displays showed his weapons inventory. Only four of the Hellfire missiles remained. The tri-barreled .50 caliber machine guns under the nose had full magazines. The prize was the eight Stinger II air-to-air missiles sitting on hard mounts to the left and right of the cockpit.

He flicked off the identify friend or foe system. Reset the combat system for sole pilot control and armed all weapons. A heads-up display painted the windscreen in front of him. It wasn't as advanced as the system deployed in the commander tank, but it was good enough for what he needed tonight. The HUD lay a color-coded ninety-degree wide map centered on the mid-line of the nightfalcon on the front windscreen – the off-boresight field of fire for the Stinger II missiles. He could reliably target any opponent in the front quarter of the gunship with the Stinger missiles.

Anton broke left out of the circle formation, flying hard toward the next two nightfalcon's in front of him. Their port side gunners equipped with Mk-19 grenade launchers, their attention fixed on pummeling the village below.

The sustained use of massive numbers of 40mm high explosive grenades was ripping the village apart. The HUD display showed dozens of warm bodies sprawled in the street. It was a massacre. Anton swallowed hard, pushing the throttle forward. The nightfalcon surged, he targeted the two helicopters flying from right to left before him. They were about three hundred yards away, and he was closing rapidly. He selected the Stingers, firing two at each craft. The missiles launched from the hard points on either side of his cockpit, jagging hard to the left and right, matching up on their designated targets. They speared away, crossing the distance to the nightfalcons in less than a second.

The targeted nightfalcon's defensive systems recognized the threats immediately. Bright flares automatically ejecting to the left and right of each helicopter. Chaff bloomed and glittered above the village fires. The defenses defeated two of the missiles, sending them past their targets to fly harmlessly off into the stormy darkness.

The other two rammed into their marks, detonating with thunderous explosions, the helicopters transforming into furious balls of light and flame. Anton pulled back on the controls, his nightfalcon flying above the falling debris.

He banked his helicopter hard to the left, curving around in a tight circle. It was time to hunt the last surviving nightfalcon.

* * *

Major Quiver's pilot shouted through the tactical comms link, "Falcon dash Seven's gone rogue!"

Quiver leaped from his command chair, rushing forward to the cockpit. The rogue nightfalcon fired two pairs of Stinger missiles. They speared into two of his remaining birds, the gunships exploding in great balls of fire, filling the left half of the nightfalcon's canopy with light, stark against the storm clouds covering the sky. The rogue gunship banked hard left, soaring above the flaming wreckage as it fell toward the ground.

"Take evasive actions. Bring our weapons to bear and take them down!" Quiver shouted.

The rogue gunship wheeled about; in seconds it would be heading straight toward them.

Quiver's pilot slammed the throttles to maximum power, the engines roaring like colossal demons. The nightfalcon veered upward, banking in toward the rogue bird. Whoever reached a firing solution first would have the advantage.

The rogue gunship straightened up, accelerating to pass his gunship on the right. Both pilots fired simultaneously, a pair of Stinger missiles leaping away from each nightfalcon toward the other. Missile warners rang shrill alarms. Dazzling flares shot out to the left and right. Clouds of silvery chaff bloomed, swirling in the backwash from the rotors.

Quiver's Helicopter jigged hard left, running through the chaff of the other bird.

Minigun fire rippled through the chaos, his two gunners screamed in the main cabin. He twisted back, searching for his men. They'd disappeared, carried away by the depleted uranium rounds, their empty harnesses dripping blood. A line of golden fire ripped through the rear section of the helicopter. His nightfalcon shuddered, rising higher under full power. The opposing minigun fell silent, no longer able to bear on his bird.

Engines roaring, Quiver's nightfalcon wheeled hard through the air. The other gunship was also banking hard, the pair of nightfalcons describing a long figure eight over the burning village.

They were going to make another pass at each other. The rogue gunship only had two Stinger missiles left, his bird had six. Quiver shouted to his pilot, "Fire all the missiles."

"Roger, Sir."

This attack would overwhelm his opponent's defenses.

It was an all or nothing play.

One he had to win.

* * *

A hellish version of the fourth of July was erupting over the village.

"Anton," Li shouted. "They'll fire more missiles, open the angle so I can use the minigun."

"On it," Anton shouted back.

Anton pushed the nightfalcon to it limits. The frame of the craft shuddered as it veered left, positioning the opposing bird on the right forward flank.

Li swung the starboard mounted minigun as far forward as she could. She ramped to her maximum extent. Her mind stilled, a supreme calm descending through her, met by surging power from within her depths. Time slowed down. The rotor blades above her entered a lazy rhythm. Individual raindrops resolved as they fell past the open doorway next to the main cabin. The opposing nightfalcon loomed in her vision. The pylons jutting left and right from the cockpit hosted hard points holding four Hellfire and six Stinger missiles.

Anton fired his last two missiles, the Stingers streaking away into clouds of gleaming chaff and spinning flares.

All the opposing Stinger missiles fired at once, spearing toward her like hot silvery talons. Defensive flares sailed lazily to her right, their actinic glare reflecting off the noses of the incoming missiles. She depressed the minigun's trigger. Time dragged as the minigun's electric motor hesitated before spinning the barrels. Flame gouted from the mouth of her weapon, bright tracers lancing in a hotline toward the nearest Stinger. The depleted uranium rounds connected with the missile, smashing it in a bright ball of flame.

Li's eyes narrowed, her face a mask of intensity as she swung her minigun to the right. The missiles were closing fast, accelerating to more than twice the speed of sound. The tracers followed her gaze to the second Stinger, her fire consuming it halfway along its path. There were four missiles left. She reached deeper into the silence, the individual barrels of the minigun snapping past in front of her, long tongues of flame flickering after each shot. Spent shell casings floated to her left like gravity-defying confetti, every fifth round a bright tracer lancing away, the ripping whirr of the gun lost in a wave of rolling thunder.

The third missile evaporated in a bright puff of brilliantly burning debris at sixty yards.

Li's heart paused, waiting for the next beat.

She moved the gun slightly to the right, machine-like in her precision, the fourth missile splitting into a cloud of flaming fragments at forty yards. The fifth missile streaked in, piercing the defensive flares and chaff clouds, before detonating at fifteen yards, a mist of razor-sharp fragments carried forward by momentum reaching out at her with a thousand glittering fingers.

The last missile had been accelerating the longest, hitting its top speed as it reached the cabin doorway eight feet to Li's right.

She blurred left, away from the minigun, pushing herself hard up against the cabin bulkhead. Her arms flew up to shield her face, the lip of the doorway providing extra protection.

The last missile shot through the open cabin without connecting with anything. The debris of the fifth missile close behind it, ripping away equipment and scouring the back half of the main cabin.

Her heart beat again.

She dropped out of the ramp, the opposing nightfalcon disappearing past her behind the shield of its failed missile attack, flares, and chaff. It was already past the field of fire of her minigun.

The captured nightfalcon started banking hard to the left. Anton was going to make another run at the other helicopter.

All the air-to-air missiles were gone. The only weapons left they could use for air-to-air combat were the .50 caliber machine guns in fixed mounts under the nose.

To use them in a face-to-face pass against another nightfalcon would be mutual suicide.

* * *

The two nightfalcons lined up on each other at two hundred yards.

In the HUD display, the topography of the burning village lay drawn in ghostly shapes. One building stood out dead ahead – the water tower.

Anton slammed the nightfalcon's throttle to maximum, the turbines roared, the craft leaping forward. He depressed the trigger for the two tri-barreled .50 caliber machine guns, bright fire leaping from beneath his cockpit toward the opposing helicopter.

The other nightfalcon fired back, tracers streaming toward Anton's craft. Both nightfalcons were traveling at above fifty miles per hour, accelerating and closing. Whoever's weapons hit first would win, killing the other crew, destroying their craft, and then allowing the surviving pilot to bank hard, avoiding a mid-air collision.

The heavily armored noses of the nightfalcon's absorbed the fire, metal-ceramic armor ablating away from the raw metal underneath, the protection would last a second or two.

Anton anticipated a left-hand bank from the opposing pilot, he'd been doing it consistently all battle. Anton made a final adjustment to set the nightfalcon's course to automatically bank hard right in three seconds. He ramped hard, blurring from the cockpit, scooping up the Blue Dragon from the floor as he dashed back to the rear of the craft.

Pulling the tri-bladed hook from the headless body of the trooper who'd manned the Mk-19 grenade launcher, he swung the hook once, hard and fast, snagging the parapet at the top of the water tower as it passed thirty yards underneath.

There were two seconds left before the gunship would bank.

"Time to go," he yelled.

Li ran to him, leaping upon his back. They sailed out through the side of the nightfalcon as .50 caliber rounds cut through at ankle height from the front of the helicopter.

The empty gunship banked hard above them.

They fell together, thirty yards down to the height of the tower, Anton's leap taking them past the tower's top. They fell toward the ground fifty yards below. The rope was just over thirty yards long, Anton looked up along it, silently praying the hook would hold. He ramped hard, silence overwhelming his mind, time slowing to a crawl. His left arm became hard as stone, his grip like iron on the rope. It was a combined sixty-yard fall, with Li's and his weight hanging on his arm, the rope, and the hook.

The rope snapped tight, Anton and Li swinging with their momentum through a long arc coming up above the height of the tower. They paused there momentarily, before reversing back down toward the side of the tower. Hitting the bottom of the swing beside the tower, Anton let go, falling the final twenty yards to the ground below. They landed, rolling smoothly forward on the well-maintained lawn around the base of the tower.

Anton sprang to his feet with Li at his side.

They looked up, the nightfalcons were lurching toward each other.

* * *

The exterior of the rogue nightfalcon started to break up under the sustained fire from his gunship's heavy machine guns.

His pilot banked hard left to avoid a mid-air collision the gunfire spearing past the oncoming machine.

The other helicopter banked hard toward them.

Major Frank Quiver, the leading officer of the ultra-secret Phase IV Day Guard program, stared in growing horror at the nightfalcon rushing toward his bird. His pilot dragged on his controls, the airframe shuddering under the load as it banked harder to the left.

His upper lip stiffened, his wing commander mustache twitched, he raised a hand in helpless defiance.

It was all too late.

The canopy of his aircraft caved in, tearing metal and shattering transparent armor silencing his pilot's despairing scream in an instant.

A tiny fraction of a second later, the nose of the rogue nightfalcon pinned Major Quiver against the bulkhead at the back of the cockpit, and his world vanished forever.

* * *

Peter dashed up to the base of the water tower, flaming helicopter debris crashing to the ground behind him.

He grinned, slapping them both on the shoulders. "Awesome guys."

Li turned, grabbing Anton by both shoulders and giving him a hard shake of annoyance. "See what happens when we work as a team."

"Hey," Anton said, "Where did this come from?"

Li snapped, "You've been off the rails all day."

"I've only done what I needed to," Anton asserted, his eyes narrowing.

Peter leaned in between them. "Hey, we need to be on the move."

Li and Anton stared at each other, emotions boiling beneath the surface.

Anton breathed out, shrugged his shoulders and asked, "When are you going to stop treating me like your student?"

Li frowned, stepped in close and stated, "When you start acting like a master." She tapped him on the chest. "And you broke your promise about handling your emotions and not taking off on your own."

"For God's sake Li, I took the initiative in a combat situation."

"And nearly got everyone killed."

Anton glanced at Peter and said, "I saved Peter."

"No," Li declared. "We saved Peter after you got yourself stupidly stuck in the middle of a Shadowstone base."

"That base needed taking down. It's one less place for them to launch against us."

"Oh, c'mon Anton," Li said, exasperatedly. "They'll just rebuild, and next time they'll be stronger."

Peter put his hands between his friends, pushing them gently apart. He leaned in, a shadow of tension at the edges of his eyes, and declared, "We really need to move now. The window of opportunity is closing."

Anton glanced at him. "Sure, I'm okay. Let's do it."

"Of course, Peter," Li agreed with a pointed glance at Anton. "Very sensible."

"Whitby is pretty much due east of here," Peter noted, leading them away from the water tower.

Li and Anton glanced at each other, she frowned, her lips pressed tightly together.

Anton sighed. *Li is … complicated.*

He fell into step next to Peter. In a couple of minutes, they would be through Shadowstone's perimeter. The troops were in disarray, all their air cover was gone, and their command structure lay broken.

Anton's face hardened in avid anticipation, the next stop was Whitby and Chloe Armitage.

They blurred into the gloom beyond the fires.

* * *

Gordon Heathmont slumped back into his seat in the rear of his Jaguar sedan, his fingers absently stroking the fine leather upholstery as he stared out the window into the storm.

He lifted both hands to his face, rubbed the bridge of his nose, and then dragged them down his cheeks.

There would be repercussions, the day had descended into absolute, unmitigated disaster. He shook his head slowly; it was beyond anything he could have imagined. The capture of Peter Lamb had been a gift, a decisive step forward in Shadowstone's secret war against the Order of Thoth and the Red Empire, but whatever advantage that capture represented was lost the moment an Order of Thoth operative stole a commander tank.

From then on, the day had descended into chaos.

What could he report to Cornelius Crane?

He was numb with shock. He would have to rally the survivors and provide a full accounting of events. His only hope was that he could demonstrate he'd made a reasonable decision at every step.

He sucked air through his nose, had he done everything he could have done?

He shook his head again, he didn't know.

Of one thing he remained certain, Cornelius Crane would decide his fate, and he would decide it soon.

Chapter Twenty Five

"I have no interest in inflicting mindless, empty, meaningless suffering. When I cause suffering, it is always for a greater purpose." – General Chloe Armitage

* * *

Armitage Manor, Yorkshire, August 22nd, 19:11

"Chloe, you need to see this," Marcus declared.

Chloe stepped away from Kain. He hung within his chains, pale and drenched in sweat, strung out from the constant interrogation and blood-hunger over the last thirteen hours. She'd almost wrung him dry of useful information. She walked back to the table in the middle of the room where Marcus had opened up a large, military-style, ruggedized laptop. The screen displayed four separate Panopticon feeds of the aftermath of a devastating Shadowstone defeat seven miles from her manor house.

The Mirovar force team would arrive soon, she'd no doubts they'd survived the best efforts of the UK Shadowstone forces. The delaying tactic had worked perfectly, the Order was now unlikely to be able to mount an attack before sunset. With the onset of night, her freedom to move around outside would return, providing her with a powerful tactical advantage.

This was her home territory, and she knew it better than anyone else. She'd successfully brought her opponents to a battlefield of her own choosing, and tonight would see a telling blow delivered against the Order of Thoth, and the advancement of her own secret agenda.

She pulled out her phone and sent James Haley a text, 'Communications status?'

His reply came back in seconds, 'Still down. Order of Thoth operations continue to disrupt direct communications to the head of Shadowstone.'

Chloe smiled; her eye's alight with the game. James was using neutral language, he was most likely with someone, and taking action to keep her secrets. The communications links to Crane's direct lines were all down. Crane was in the dark and would stay that way for a while longer.

She sent another text, 'Where is he?'

'His personal drone, departing Israel for New York.'

Crane was in transit from Jerusalem after supervising the evacuation of his assets in the Middle East. His personal drone was not a quad-pod vehicle like the shadowstar drones, it was single crew craft with vertical take-off and landing capability. He would land in his citadel's main hangar in about ninety minutes time. As soon as he stepped from the drone, his executive secretary Ursula Zielinkski would meet him, and she would tell him precisely what was happening with his Shadowstone forces in the United Kingdom.

His fury would be epic.

Then nothing would happen – for a while. Crane was not one to engage in precipitous action. He would assess what had happened, sit back and strategize a fresh approach to achieve his goals. Chloe frowned slightly, there was no way for her to attack Crane directly, but a succession of rapidly changing events would undermine the foundations of his world until he made a mistake and put himself in a position where she could bring him face to face with her weapon – Anton Slayne.

There was one last critical piece of information she needed from Kain, she moved back to stand in front of him. She leaned in close, her face a handful of inches from his. His blood-hunger was a physical stench, like rotting meat, it had been steadily getting worse for more than half a day. She hid her disgust; she needed the information in his mind.

She inquired, quietly and with perfect diction, like she was asking a polite question in pleasant company, "Where and when will the next Order conclave be held?"

"I don't know," Kain spat, his eyes rolling on the edge of delirium. "Of course, I don't know."

"Come on Ramin, don't be difficult," she encouraged, lifting his chin with her finger, forcing him to meet her gaze. He stared back at her for a second before averting his eyes. She said, "You know I'll find out sooner or later. Here," she moved the bucket of congealing blood closer, "I promise you, this is the last question, and then you can have the rest of this blood."

Kain's pale face twisted into a grimace of thwarted desire, he panted, and stated, "I really don't know, I'm told by my staff."

"Hmmm," Chloe stepped back. "Then tell me how the process works?"

Kain started, and shouted desperately, "That's another question. You promised!"

Chloe sighed. "It's still the same question, describe the process of how a modern conclave is called, and I will have the answer to my last question."

Kain stared at the bucket of blood in silence, a thin line of drool running from the side of his mouth.

"Answer me in full, and not only will you have this bucket, but you will also have fresh, hot blood, as much as you desire, and your freedom before the next dawn."

Kain's eyes stilled and widened, fixing tightly on Chloe's face. He licked his lips and said urgently, the words tumbling from his mouth, "A force leader calls the conclave. Justin Blake will call the next one. The loremasters use their implants and secured cloud access to spread the word. The notice is always short, a matter of days."

"With your 'disappearance,'" Chloe observed, arching an eyebrow. "They will call another one soon. The Order must have a head." She frowned for a second, an idea on the edge of her mind. Something important, resting just beyond her awareness. She just needed to tease it into the light. "What happens if you can't use the loremasters to spread the word?"

Kain looked at her for a long moment. "There is a default protocol. A message defined at the last conclave that provides a once only predefined conclave location, the date and time are variables encoded into the message. The Order broadcasts the message in the general media – it will look like an advertisement. Only the force leaders will know the truth."

"Why not use your quantum encrypted smartphones to simply spread the details?"

Kain glared at her, a semblance of sanity re-establishing itself. "As we both know, after you hacked my phone during breakfast a couple of months ago, if the quantum signature is known, anyone with the skills can compromise the phone. We designed the default protocol to be foolproof."

Chloe stepped in close and whispered, "And the encoded message is?"

Kain whispered the answer, and she remembered every word perfectly. She stepped away from him, turning to stare into space. A handful of seconds passed before a slow smile crept across her face. "We need to adapt our plans. Give him all the blood – we need to move quickly."

Marcus passed the bucket to Kain, and he plunged his face into it. He leaned back, the bucket upturned over his gaping mouth, blood slopping down his throat, the excess spilling in great splashes around his feet.

If she could force the Order to use the default protocol, she would find out the date, time and location of the next conclave. Her smile broadened, filling her face with light. "What an opportunity."

She knew exactly what she needed to do.

* * *

The Raven's smartphone vibrated silently in their hip pocket.

They dropped back to the rear of the group, and brought the phone out, shielding it with their body from the rain pelting down. It was a message from the other Red Empire agent – Chloe Armitage.

Perhaps now was the critical moment where the Raven could deceive Armitage to her doom. They glanced once at the phone, the message filled the screen and read, 'The Red Empire is running a mission with Chloe Armitage and Marcus Drake against the Vampire Dominion. The Red Ghost has tricked the two vampire traitors into capturing Ramin Kain. All the secrets of the Order now belong to the Red Empire – this is our victory, not theirs. Detail the disposition of the Order forces and the exfiltration paths. Armitage and Drake will die. Victory is ours!'

Armitage still believed they were ignorant of the truth – it would be her undoing; the advantage still lay with the Raven.

The Raven lifted their smartphone, their fingers flashing over the phone's surface, they replied with, 'Understood. The Walker team is in place, and the Mirovar team is approaching with an ETA of 20:30. There are injuries, but the fighting capability of the Mirovar force team is nearly at full strength. I will send exfil data once I have it.'

It was not yet the time to deceive. Telling the truth now would maintain the illusion the Raven was still a loyal servant of the Red Empire, and an ally of the 'Red Empire agent.'

Soon, the time would be ripe, where they could cause maximum damage to Armitage's plans, perhaps even kill her. The Raven hoped for such an opportunity but was willing to see how the night evolved before making a decision. Perhaps the exfil data would prove conclusive, if they sent Armitage in the wrong direction at a critical moment, it could make all the difference.

They would wait and see.

* * *

Storm clouds thundered overhead, rain sheeting down upon the town of Whitby.

Richard Walker stared at the manor house on the cliff overlooking the town, his eyes narrow, his body tense. The manor stood alone, wreathed in dismal shadows. The sun had just set, and with the storm raging overhead it might as well have been midnight.

The Mirovar force team had failed miserably. If they'd arrived during daylight, he could have used their fighters to mount a combined daylight assault with a high probability of success. Instead, night had fallen, and they were mostly still absent.

He barked at his loremaster, "Joan, contact Mirovar and find out their latest ETA?"

"Yes, Sir," she responded. Joan Lewis sat in one of the black Range Rovers ten feet away, her laptop out of the rain. She closed her eyes for twenty seconds, attempting to commune with Juliette Mirovar via the quantum encrypted cloud used by the Order of Thoth.

"She's offline."

"What now?" Richard asked, his disdain for all things Mirovar nakedly visible in his voice.

"She's offline," Joan repeated, her mouth opening in a small 'O,' of concern.

"Damn it," Richard swore, pulling his smartphone from a chest pocket beneath his raincoat and voice dialing Francis Mirovar's phone address.

The phone rang three times before Mirovar picked it up and answered his obvious question coldly, "We're coming. We'll be there in fifteen minutes."

Three of the Mirovar team had arrived ten minutes before, wet and weary, with little to offer except their personal needs for food and water. Peter Lamb, Li Wu, and Anton Slayne, with a tale to tell of defeating a Shadowstone force seven miles away. It had been a miracle Shadowstone hadn't followed them. It seemed that Shadowstone in the UK were currently out of action, a small mercy given all the other problems his team faced.

"Nightfall was a minute ago. You have given our enemies the advantage by arriving late."

"We'll be there, and we will be ready to fight."

Richard snorted. "I certainly hope so."

He stared at the manor house and put his phone away. Lights had come on within the ground floor of the main building. The vampires would be active now and not afraid to hide. He cursed loudly, "Damn it all to hell."

Lamb, Wu, and Slayne looked up at him as one from beside one of the Range Rovers. Lamb arched a quizzical eyebrow, Wu wore an impassive expression that masked her feelings, and Slayne frowned, his eyes flashing with sharp emotions.

Well, let them judge him, they would be going in first. They could serve a useful purpose by springing any traps that might be waiting for his team.

* * *

The other three members of the Red Empire fist team followed Tamsah al Ramil into the library.

The ground floor room was one of the larger chambers in the manor house, it held several classic pieces of furniture including a grand piano, several antique reading desks and divans. A host of leather-bound books filled shelves lining all the interior walls from floor to ceiling. Heavy curtains shrouded the windows. His initial site inspection had revealed transparent armor had replaced the original window panes. Electric lamps dialed down slightly from their normal levels lit the library with a soft indirect illumination. A door leading into an armory stood on the right-side wall.

A long table beneath the windows lay draped with a sheet of heavy black fabric, four, vaguely human-like forms, appeared to rest beneath the sheet.

What was she hiding here? The question tore at Tamsah. Perhaps, Ms. Armitage would answer it; she stood in the middle of the library, with her tall, blond henchman behind her left shoulder. She'd changed her clothes since the morning. She wore fresh combat fatigues in a tiger print of dark grays, tans, and blacks. Her combat webbing carried a holster with a 9mm automatic, four hand grenades, and her katana, the Red Dragon, lay strapped to her waist. She stood relaxed and ready in her combat boots, with a black cap crowning her head. Drake wore his praetorian armor, a broadsword and a double-bladed battle-axe belted on the left and right side of his hips.

"Yes, Ma'am?" Tamsah asked.

"To be clear," Armitage stated, her eyes fixed on Tamsah's face, "your orders are to obey me unless I order you to kill each other or attack the Red Empire. I have done none of those things. You must continue to obey your oaths to the Red Ghost, is that correct?"

A sliver of fear threatened to worm its way into Tamsah's guts, but he pushed it aside, he was too experienced to be intimidated by the vampire standing opposite him. But still, why would she ask this particular question? What were her intentions?

"Yes," Tamsah nodded, "it is so."

"Excellent, then you should accept what follows."

Tamsah's mind raced. Her words were laden with threat. To his left, one of his men staggered, but nothing had happened to cause it. He sniffed, a faint, delicate sweetness filled his nostrils.

Gas.

His throat froze, his voice fleeing as his vocal cords constricted painfully.

"It doesn't affect vampires," Armitage remarked, lifting one eyebrow, "but humans – it's almost instantaneous—"

Tamsah crashed face down on the carpet with his men, darkness to rival the storm clouds over the manor house claiming him.

* * *

Chloe stepped forward and prodded the short Red Empire assassin's shoulder with the toe of her boot. He remained senseless to the world, breathing quietly.

"That was the last of our knock-out gas?" she asked.

Marcus replied, "Yes."

Her eyes widened in avid anticipation and she commanded, "Fetch the staff, it is time to bring them all here."

Marcus smiled. "Yes, Chloe."

She caught his gaze and asked, "How is your appetite?"

He grinned broadly, his fangs descending into attack position. "Famished."

Chloe inclined her head slightly. "Excellent."

Marcus left the library.

Chloe turned, walking to the long table at the back of the room. She pulled the black sheet away, and let it drop to the floor. The bundles beneath the sheet stood revealed, their matte-black surfaces dull beneath the dimmed lights. She reached out a finger, tapping the hard surface of one of them. The material absorbed the impact of her tap, muting the sound. The combat armor was up to specification; especially ordered, built and delivered from a manufacturing unit on the east coast of the United States. Brought into the room the day before by her retainer, David.

David had always been a loyal and efficient aide to her cause and had provided decades of service, it was a pity that he would not survive the night. However, she must make such sacrifices when needed, the end goals were too important to allow hesitation, remorse or regret.

She allowed herself a moment to reflect upon her immediate plans. Soon, she would make Anton Slayne's most dreadful fear manifest, and then he would be at his most vulnerable. He would be unable to resist as she drew him deeper into her web of control.

"Time to start," she whispered, kneeling next to Tamsah al Ramil. She tilted his head, exposing his throat. Her fangs descended over her bottom lip. She lunged forward, her fangs tearing into his neck, a trickle of blood rolling past her lips, falling onto the library's carpet.

The sounds of her feeding were the only noises in the library for the next five minutes.

* * *

The rain fell steadily, peacefully, the lightning and thunder had recently moved further east, promising a respite not yet fully delivered.

Juliette ignored the aches in her left thigh and skull, pushing on through the rain and dark on her crutches. Francis, Jay, Yvette, Chiara, and Luther surrounded her, holding phosphorescent glow sticks to light her way. A short distance in front of her were more lights reflecting faintly off a pair of Range Rovers parked on the edge of a stand of trees. Half a mile away on the left, a manor house stood on top of a cliff overlooking the ocean.

Pale light emanated from some of the ground floor rooms, but heavy curtains shrouded the interiors blocking any casual inquiry.

Three figures broke away from the group near the SUVs and came rushing toward her. Anton, Peter, and Li resolved out of the gloom, Li was the first to arrive, hugging her tightly. Peter and Anton surrounded her, their hands on her shoulders and back.

"I'm not surprised to see you here," Juliette said, "I always believed in you."

Li stepped back. "Shadowstone is broken, they will not trouble us tonight."

Juliette nodded once at the manor house and said with a note of apprehension creeping into her voice, "We'll have enough to deal with over there."

Peter leaned in and whispered, "Walker is not happy with us, thinks we're more or less useless."

"It's expected – but, we'll still work with him," Juliette said, limping the rest of the way up to the Range Rovers.

Walker pushed himself off from the trunk of a tree and stepped forward, the rest of his team moving into a semicircle behind him. "It's about time – now we need to get down to business. How are your ammo stocks?"

"Anton, Li and I are out," Peter stated, looking at the assembled team members.

"You were supposed to bring your own," Walker snapped. "You weaken us all showing up without adequate supplies."

Juliette's head throbbed, the incessant politics in the Order was making her headache worse, she leaned against Francis and whispered, "We need to end this tonight if we can. Something terrible is building."

Francis squeezed her arm and whispered back, "I'll see it done."

"There will be enough to go around," Francis declared loudly, flipping his spare FN P90 magazines to Peter, Li, and Anton. "Just be careful with your fire, stay on three round bursts and avoid full auto." He looked back at Walker as his team adroitly caught the magazines and locked them into place on their weapons. "We have wounded. Juliette and Yvette are not able to fight, I will designate two of my team to guard them here."

"No, I need all your fighters in the mix," Walker directed, his eyes intense in the soft light, he indicated three members of his team. "I'll assign Joan, Mary, and David to protect your wounded."

Francis frowned momentarily, nodded and stated, "So be it."

Walker stood tall, glancing around the assembled Ramp masters. "Complete your preps, we move in three minutes. Loremaster operations will be with Joan Lewis, as Juliette Mirovar is out of action. The exfil location is a clearing on top of the cliffs, four hundred yards on the Whitby side of the manor house – is that clear?"

The combined team gave their assent and moved into action: cocking weapons with sharp clicks, lifting and checking swords one last time, and putting the finishing touches on the configuration of the tactical comms link. Everyone adjusted their Order nightglasses and aligned them with the encrypted tactical network. In short order, the teams were ready to assault the manor house together.

It was rare for two Order teams to join forces. It was only the presence of a high-value target that aligned the Mirovar and Walker teams to a common cause. Normally Order teams worked the jurisdiction of their own territories, hence why Walker was in charge of the assault, the United Kingdom was his territory.

If there were any enemies in the manor house, the combined strength of the two teams would slaughter them, and if Ramin Kain were still alive, they would rescue him and bring him back to the United States.

Juliette put her hand gingerly to her aching head.

At least, that's the plan.

* * *

Francis strode over to Anton and tapped him hard on the chest.

"You, come with me now," he ordered, his voice filled with tightly controlled anger.

The two men walked thirty yards away from the rest of the combined team. Francis stopped first, turning to stand a couple of feet in front of Anton. "What the hell do you think you were doing pulling a crazy stunt like that? You nearly got us all killed? The whole of the UK is looking for us now. You can bet they've got photographs of everyone who was on that truck."

Francis paused for a second, his eyes narrowing. "Worse, you put yourself ahead of the team, you acted selfishly, recklessly and without thought for the consequences." He shook his head, and declared in disappointed tones, "I expected better of you Anton."

Anton stood silently for a long moment, frowning slightly.

"Do you have anything to say for yourself?" Francis asked.

"Yes, I do," Anton began, "Firstly, Peter's capture was a time critical scenario. Without quick action, we would have lost any opportunity to save him, and right now, we would be down one man."

Francis' lip curled.

"Secondly, the UK Shadowstone force has been more or less destroyed. Yes, they wounded some of us in the process, but everyone will heal."

Francis' eyes became flint-like black stones, "Juliette nearly died, Yvette could easily have been killed."

Anton said quietly, "Aren't we all at risk?"

Francis' mouth dropped open for a second, then he declared harshly, "This isn't a debate. You are a member of the Order of Thoth, you have to obey your force leader, especially when on operations – that must be crystal clear."

"I'm not a member of the Order of Thoth."

Francis blinked, and then snapped, "And perhaps you never will be." He tapped Anton on the chest again. "We have a mission to do, this isn't over, we'll have 'words,' when this is done."

Anton nodded.

Francis stepped past him and returned to the team.

Anton turned around; the rest of the combined team were busy getting ready for the mission. He walked back toward them and whispered to himself, "Saving Kain or killing Armitage, I know which mission I'm on, does everyone else?"

* * *

As the rest of the Order teams worked, the Raven stepped behind the nearest Range Rover.

They opened their smartphone, composing a short message to Armitage. The vampire had asked for the exfiltration coordinates, now was the perfect opportunity to send her on a wild goose chase. They could send Armitage in the opposite direction, and when the teams left the manor house, Armitage would never find them in time to stop them escaping with Kain. But she would also know that the Raven had betrayed her.

It was a one-shot tactic.

The mission had barely started, there may be a far more useful time to deceive Armitage in the near future, and the Raven didn't want to waste the one opportunity they had. They completed the message and told Armitage the truth.

Armitage would know the exfil point.

The Raven put their phone away, lifted their weapons and rejoined the teams.

* * *

Francis leaned gently against Juliette, pressing something into her right hand. It was a short-handled dagger, sheathed in a forearm holster.

"Take this blade," he whispered.

"Silver?" Juliette asked, raising an eyebrow.

"Yes. If need be, it'll be your last defense."

"Thank you, can you help me put it on?" Juliette balanced on her crutch, extending her right arm.

"Of course," Francis agreed, strapping the dagger in place. A moment later, her sleeve covered it, hiding its presence from all but the most thorough examination.

They hugged each other for a long minute as the teams bustled around them.

"I love you," Francis whispered in her ear, his lips soft against her cheek.

"I love you too," her heart caught in her throat, her eyes welling with sudden tears. She hugged him tightly and implored, "Come back to me mon amour."

His head nodded next to her own. "I will see you at the end of this."

"I will hold you to your word," she promised with every fiber of her being.

Francis leaned back, a smile gracing his lips, his eyes shining in the soft lights carried by the team. "I would expect nothing less."

The combined team began to move. They broke apart and joined the rest.

* * *

Walker lifted his hand, bringing the teams to a halt on a fork in the path halfway to the manor house.

"We split now," he commanded over the tactical link. "The wounded will go along the left path to the exfil point. With the state of emergency still in effect, we can't use the Range Rovers, we will have to abandon them for now. We have an Order helper with a boat down at the Whitby docks. We will go from the exfil point to the docks and then travel up the coast. Any questions?"

The Raven choked on their words, grunting briefly and almost silently.

Juliette reached out, placing her fingers on their arm and inquired softly, "Are you okay?"

The Raven shook their head once. "It's nothing." They jogged over to where Walker was turning toward the right-hand path. "Sir?" they asked. "I should join the group defending the wounded."

Walker stopped, whirling back toward them. "Are you joking? ... No, you're serious aren't you." He turned back to the path and declared loudly over his shoulder, "Request denied."

The Raven followed him, catching up and pulling on his left arm. "Sir?"

Walker blurred around, his arm slipping free of the Raven's grasp. "Are you a coward? We're in the midst of a combat mission, you will follow orders, or else. Is that clear?"

The Raven, stood for a second, blinking in the rain. "Yes, Sir."

"Fall back, and take up your assigned position."

The Raven stepped aside, letting the other team members walk past until they could re-enter the line. They slipped back into position, their heart in their throat. They'd assumed the wounded and their guards would stay with the Range Rovers, and were nonplussed when they had joined in on the march toward the manor house. Now they were heading away toward the exfil point, a location Armitage knew they would all go to. She could be waiting for them there right now. The Raven shivered, they may have just handed Juliette, Yvette, and the three UK Order team members to Armitage. Walker had sent his own loremaster, Joan Lewis, with the wounded, obviously not wishing to expose her to the risks of assaulting the manor house. There were two loremasters together, defended by three warriors, one of whom was at half strength due to her own wounds.

The Order didn't have loremasters to spare.

They couldn't reveal the risk to Juliette and the rest without exposing who they were.

The Raven's stomach cramped with nausea.

What had they done?

* * *

Manicured gardens and a low stone fence surrounded the manor house.

The gates were wide open, a long driveway lit by low lamps along its sides led up to the main building. External lights lit the manor house, and many of the rooms on the ground floor shone from within. The upper two floors lay shrouded in darkness, the roof of the manor barely discernible against the storm clouds.

The teams halted in the shadows outside the stone wall, about forty yards back from the entrance to the manor grounds.

Anton frowned, the way into the manor was apparently unguarded. Armitage was expecting them. If it were up to him, he would simply blow the site to kingdom come from a distance and be done with it. Kain couldn't reveal any secrets if he were dead, but the Walker team and the Mirovar's were adamant that they must save him.

It was a trap, an obvious trap, and God only knew who would come out alive.

Peter nudged his left shoulder and whispered, "You know … if one of us doesn't make it out of here."

"What?" Anton snapped, glancing across at him.

"I just wanted you to know that it was all worth it," Peter said quietly, grinning in the darkness.

Anton almost laughed out loud, stifling it with a hand over his mouth, but Peter's words broke the tension.

"How do you do that?" Anton whispered. "This looks like madness."

"Were fighting vampires – what do you expect? A walk in the park? We're gonna go in there and mess them up. What did you think – you're gonna survive all this?" Peter rubbed his hands together, then interlaced his fingers, cracking his big knuckles with a sound like stones colliding. "You've gotta love the challenge of it all. You could have a long and boring life, or you could fight vampires, really tough vampires, and on their home territory no less ... could you walk away from that?"

Anton studied the manor house, his gaze intense, his heart thudding in his ears. "No way."

"Then don't worry about it. We'll be together," Peter said, he glanced across at Li, who was listening intently on Anton's right. "That's right Li, we've got each other's back."

Li whispered without taking her gaze off the manor house, "Always."

Walker signaled 'advance,' with a waved fist. The team broke up into smaller combat teams to avoid presenting a single target and to allow each small team to cover the other teams. Anton, Peter, and Li advanced together.

Anton put his game face on – shit was about to get real.

* * *

Anton walked on point, Peter, and Li behind him.

He preferred being in front; point was dangerous, the person occupying the role was most likely the first person to contact the enemy. He preferred it because he didn't want to see his friends hurt, not if he could help it. Too many people he loved had died, he wanted it all to stop – and if he could, he would stop it. There would never be any questions left to ask after a battle. Could he have done more? Had he given his all? Did he do everything he could to save his friends and defeat those who would kill them?

There would be nothing left undone.

He broke into a garden clearing dominated by a stone pool lit by lamps under the water. The lights lay artfully placed to illuminate an elegantly carved statue of a crane. The stonework was impeccable, dragging the eye to the curving neck and majestic head of the bird. An apparently simple subject lifted into a sublime expression of repose and alert watchfulness.

Anton stared at the stone, faintly sparkling in the soft, buttery light.

Crane.

* * *

The front doors of the manor house stood before Anton.

Walker's command whispered over the tactical link, "Lamb, Slayne, Wu, take us inside."

Anton half crouched with Peter and Li on either side of the main door, under cover of the eave. Rain continued to patter softly down onto the graveled driveway. The rest of the team members waited in pairs within the gardens, scanning the approaches and searching for threats. At Richard Walker's direction the combined team was composed of smaller combat teams; Anton, Peter and Li, Jay and Chiara, Francis and Luther, Walker and his youngest team member James Cox, and another pair of experienced warriors, Karen Chapman and David Khan.

Walker had put Anton on point, and the majority of the Mirovar force team at the front of any action. It seemed like people within the Order were still trying to kill him, or was that just paranoia?

Anton didn't give a damn – they could get in line with the Vampires and the Red Empire – he glanced over his shoulder at Peter and Li.

They both nodded, they were ready.

Anton tried the door handle. The unlocked door glided open on well-oiled hinges. The interior light spilled out in a warm glow on the doorstep.

There was no response from anyone inside, the only greeting was silence. Anton lifted his FN P90 submachine gun in both hands. Its magazine loaded with high performance armor piercing rounds; every fifth bullet made of silver. The Blue Dragon lay strapped to his back, its handle reaching up over his right shoulder. He paused for a moment, lifting his nightglasses aside and running a gauntleted hand down his face, wiping away the moisture. The last thing he needed was a stray drop of water dripping into his eye at the wrong moment. Fixing his nightglasses back into position, he dropped into silence. He ramped hard, time slowed, and he blurred over the threshold with Peter and Li behind his left and right shoulders.

The manor's foyer opened up into a large hall, Anton, Peter, and Li blurred to the far corners of the foyer, scanning the hall beyond. The interior of the hall reached up from the ground floor through the first and second floors. Balconies running the lengths of the left and right walls connected with staircases down the walls to the floor.

At the base of the far wall was a large stone fireplace, lit with a roaring fire. Three brilliant chandeliers hung from the ceiling, banishing all shadows from the hall.

A single large painting stood over the fireplace. A portrait of a tall, slim French nobleman dressed for war and carrying an ornate broadsword. His eyes were brown, his hair long and dark. His face rested impassively, as if unconcerned by anything that others may do.

Anton dropped the barrel of his gun slightly, his gaze drawn to the portrait.

"Is that Crane?" he whispered. "Is that what he looks like?"

Peter shrugged his shoulders, and Li whispered, "Could be."

Footsteps padded quietly in the foyer. Jay and Chiara taking up position behind Peter, and Francis, and Luther falling in behind Anton and Li.

Walker commanded over the tactical link, "Clear the upper floors, we don't want any surprises before we go into the dungeons."

Anton glanced behind him; everyone was ready.

He led them into the Manor house.

* * *

Anton, Peter, and Li worked to clear the ground floor, the other teams had moved up the stairs to the left and right to search the first and second floors.

There was one wing left to clear on their current floor. Anton blurred into a room; it was an armory composed of a pair of aisles to either side of a line of cabinets. Unlike the other ground floor rooms, this chamber had no windows. A centuries-old tapestry depicting a French castle covered the outer wall. A baronial shield rested on each corner of the tapestry: a blue crane over a silver field.

In the bottom left-hand corner was a short sentence woven in dark-blue thread, 'Le Baron Cornelius de Grue.'

de Grue, Anton thought, *the Crane.*

A cold fire burned in his heart, he turned to face the opposite wall. A portrait of a young dark-haired woman was the sole display. She stood dressed in silver, red and black, in the classic style of a 19th century Order of Thoth warrior. A training arena surrounded her, the sun above and behind her. She sported a silver rapier in her right hand and a pistol lay holstered at her belt. She wore a relaxed expression, a slight smile playing at the corners of her mouth.

Anton seethed; it was Chloe Armitage – unchanged to the day he'd last seen her. He approached the painting, a metallic gleam catching his eye. He turned in horror, the cabinet beneath her picture held the assassin's rapier she'd used to torture and behead his mother.

Memory flooded back – as clear as if it had happened a second ago.

His stomach clenched with nausea; this nightmare had to be over soon. He pushed the last door open, taking a step into the last room on the ground floor.

It was a library, in the center was an open space where half a dozen human forms lay covered by a black sheet of fabric. Anton, Peter, and Li entered the room ramped, scanning the walls, ready to respond instantly to any threat.

They circled the sheet, Anton dropping out of his ramp. He knelt next to the sheet and lifted it aside from the first form. He was a tall, lean man, perhaps in his late fifties, with sandy-gray hair and dressed in a well-made black suit.

He was dead, his throat bitten through, his flesh pale with blood loss.

Anton tore the sheet away, revealing six dead, still dressed in their household uniforms and all with the marks of vampire attack.

Peter looked on grimly. "They've killed the manor house staff."

"She's not planning on coming back here," Li observed.

Anton nodded. "Let's make sure she doesn't leave – ever."

"Copy that," Peter remarked, his eyes hard and bright.

Li caught Anton's gaze and said, "Time to bring this to a close."

Anton nodded. "Once and for all."

He stood up, glanced around one last time, and led the combat team back out into the hall, he tapped his earbud and reported, "The ground floor is clear."

"Roger," Walker responded.

The rest of the Order team moved into the great hall, joined by the other combat teams descending from the floors above.

It was now time to go below.

Into the dungeons.

* * *

The ill-fated mission of Francine Parker and Michael Wilson had charted the secret stairwell.

Their fatal path captured by their Order nightglasses and recorded by Joan Lewis onto her laptop. Data now reused to chart a path through the dungeons to Kain's last known location. Each team member could see the path as a ghostly green line overlaid on what they could see with their Order nightglasses.

Anton was the first to reach the bottom of the spiral staircase and take a step onto the second level of the dungeon complex. They'd cleared the first level minutes before, and found nothing of interest. The combined team proceeded forward, observing mission silence by using hand gestures for communication. Anton was still on point and tactically leading the advance into the dungeon.

Fluorescent lamps bolted onto the stone ceiling a dozen feet overhead lit the corridor in front of him. Twenty feet in front of him the corridor branched to the left and right. Another thirty feet past the intersection, the corridor opened up into a well-lit room. The green light ran the length of the corridor and ended in the open room – where Francine Parker and Michael Wilson had died.

Somehow Armitage and Drake had surprised them despite their training, and their failure had cost them their lives.

Anton pushed out into the corridor in front of him, hugging the right-hand wall with his shoulder, his FN P90 submachine gun held up high, pointing exactly where he was looking. Peter and Li were on the other side of the corridor and pacing him as he advanced forward.

Anton glanced back, Jay, Chiara, Francis, and Luther were all in the corridor, the rest of the team had reached the bottom of the stairwell. He lifted his left fist to signal a halt, he caught Peter and Li's attention with a flick of his hand, indicating the intersection left and right. They would check it thoroughly before proceeding, he didn't want Armitage and Drake to catch them the same way Parker and Wilson had been.

Anton, Peter, and Li moved into the intersection and then advanced down the left and right corridors. Both were dead ends, running about seventy feet before reaching bare stone. Jay, Chiara, Francis, and Luther took up positions at the intersection, keeping watch while Peter and Li cleared their end, and Anton cleared his.

A secret door would work here, he thought. Was anything disturbed? He found it moments later, a little mortar fragment on the floor. Five feet above the fragment, sat a stone brick in the wall without any trace of mortar around it. He prized the brick free, and put it quietly on the floor, revealing a six-inch deep cavity hiding a black-metal lever.

Anton left the lever alone, backing back to the intersection where Francis watched him with proud eyes, and Luther scowled.

Anton pointed to his eyes and back at the lever – they would need to watch this intersection.

Francis nodded and signaled Anton to advance.

Peter and Li came back, their corridor was empty. Together they moved up to the room where Francine Parker had died, and Ramin Kain was last seen alive.

It was empty, except for a set of chains and manacles attached to the left-hand side wall. The flagstones on the floor in front of the chains were still damp, and water had pooled in the grooves between the stones.

Had someone tried to wash something away?

Anton walked over to the chains, stooping down to examine the water. He dipped his finger in it and lifted it up to the light, there was a faint pinkish tinge – traces of blood. Was it Kain's? It seemed likely it was.

Anton shook his head, traces of blood meant nothing, Kain could still be alive. He stared down the last corridor, it opened up into a much larger space. He flicked his left hand toward it, it was time to go down it. It was the last unexplored space under the manor, it had to be where Kain would be if he were still here.

Anton reached the threshold first. He sidled up to the edge of the opening and looked inside, the well-lit chamber was sixty yards across and twice that deep. The ceiling must have been at least twenty feet high. Two corridors branched off into darkness on both sides, and the chamber narrowed to a final corridor that led to the external cliff face, a cold draught coming from that direction.

It was empty.

"What the hell!" he whispered harshly. How could it come to this? All that effort for nothing, Kain was gone. Armitage and Drake had already left – unless they were hiding in the corridors branching off the chamber – but, why do that? What could possibly be the advantage of doing that?

"Silence Slayne," Walker barked. "Joan just went dark, comms are down."

A figure emerged from the far-left corridor and proceeded to walk into the chamber – it was Ramin Kain.

"RK!" Luther called out, pushing past Anton.

"Sam," Kain declared, smiling, and opening his arms wide. "I knew you would rescue me from this hell hole."

Luther jogged forward, his katana still sheathed, his FN P90 carried before him.

Walker shouted, "Sam, stop."

Luther ignored him.

Francis snapped, "Defensive positions everyone."

Walker whirled on Francis and thundered, "Don't give orders, this is my jurisdiction."

Francis stared incredulously at Walker, pointed at Luther running toward Kain, and shouted, "Mon Dieu?"

Luther's voice rang out, "Ramin! You're safe?"

"Quite so," Ramin said, his smile broadening.

"I knew you would survive."

"And right you are Sam. Loyal Sam, good Sam, I knew I could trust you above all others to find me."

Anton watched in horror as Luther got within touching distance of Kain.

Kain's eyes gleamed with hunger.

Chapter Twenty Six

"You shall not allow a vampire to live." – Quote from The Way of the Faithful, a book of Red Empire lore.

* * *

Armitage Manor, The Dungeons, Yorkshire, August 22nd, 20:46

Li ramped hard, power coruscated through her body, time slowing down to a crawl.

Even ramped, Kain's movement was quick, striking like a snake, his hands snapping forward to grasp Luther's shoulders, his face lunged forward, his mouth agape, his new fangs gleaming in the overhead lights.

He hit Luther's throat hard, blood jetting to the left and right.

Li lifted her FN P90, the barrel lining up on the center of Kain and Luther's bodies. Luther was falling to his knees, Kain following him down – still horrifically attached to his neck. Luther was doomed, there was no way he was going to survive the violence of Kain's hunger. She pulled the trigger, her submachine bursting into life, the bullets flashing down toward the two men.

She never saw them land.

* * *

Li's world turned to mirrors.

A mirrored corridor appeared around her.

The three-round burst she'd just fired disappeared through a mirror a handful of feet short of where Kain and Luther had been standing. The mirror absorbed the rounds, three wave-like ripples emanated out from an inch-wide point four feet off the ground, flexing across the mirror before disappearing along its edge.

"What?" she whispered.

She whirled around; the mirrored walls ran from floor to ceiling. A long-mirrored corridor on all sides stopped at the rear wall of the chamber. The mirrored corridor boxed her in.

She tried to remember in exact detail how the mirrors had come into existence, they'd grown in an instant, congealing, seemingly out of thin air.

Voices started swearing across the chamber. Whatever was happening, it had trapped everyone else too.

Li touched the nearest mirror with the barrel tip of her gun, it was solid with a slightly plastic 'tap,' sound on contact. While perfectly reflective, its behavior when shot indicated it was nothing like a regular mirror.

She put her FN P90 down, allowing it to hang from its straps at her side. The Green Dragon hissed clear of its scabbard, its majestic blade reflecting into infinity within the mirrored hall.

Whatever was about to happen, she would settle it with the blade and nothing else. She advanced forward, approaching her image in the far mirror.

The image of herself distorted. The walls moved, running like fluid as they reshaped to a new configuration. Her teammates shouted warnings to each other. The hall around her shortened, the far wall evaporating to reveal a doorway into a larger chamber.

The maze fell into silence; everyone watched and waited.

A chill clawed at her heart, she blinked, pushing it away – fear would only slow her down.

"Your move Armitage," she whispered. "I'm ready."

* * *

Gossamer!

The quantum field activated smart material had been on the drawing board when the Red Ghost inserted the Raven into the Mirovar force team. As the Red Ghost's child, they'd studied the strategies for technical advancement pursued by the Red Empire. Clearly, their former instructors had perfected the Gossamer technology.

There had to be a control system nearby. A system that would be compatible with the Red Empire software hidden on their smartphone. They held back a couple of steps from the other Order team member trapped with them. They needed to be careful, what they were about to attempt could not be discovered and would have to be done fast. Gossamer was perfect for maze traps, and its deployment here meant that Armitage must need all of its special capabilities. Now was the opportunity to thwart her plans by bringing the maze down.

Armitage may not even realize how her plan had come undone as it would appear as if the system had simply failed.

The Raven smiled slightly, putting their hand into the pocket at their hip. They'd taught themselves long ago how to use their phone by touch and timing alone, able to operate all of its sophisticated functions in silence with minimal risk of detection. But in such close confines, all they needed was for their teammate to turn around at the wrong moment, and they would be exposed.

They activated the phone, quickly delving into the hidden functions that operated the array of Red Empire software at the heart of the machine. Invisible fields washed through the room, probing for the control system. In moments, they would find it, then they would hack it, and once through its defenses, they would command the Gossamer, and the trap would be undone.

The phone vibrated silently; they'd found the master controls.

Now all the Raven had to do was penetrate its defenses, silently, by touch and timing alone, while hiding their actions from their Ramp master teammate standing three feet in front of them.

The Raven had come home.

* * *

They would fall amongst the trapped Order of Thoth operatives as wolves amongst sheep.

Tamsah al Ramil, aka 'Sand Crocodile,' ramped hard. The iris beneath his feet would be open for less than a tenth of a second to maximize the element of surprise. If he weren't careful, the device would cut him in half. He couldn't rely on gravity to complete the passage – he would launch himself downward, a matte-black armored missile, armed with a razor-sharp longsword.

Abomination! Screamed a voice in the back of his mind. Vampire blood ran through his veins, lending strength and speed to his already extraordinary capabilities.

He'd fed upon another human being. He'd become everything he abhorred, and yet he still lived, he was still bound by his oaths of allegiance to the Red Ghost and the Red Empire. Armitage's words haunted him, 'Your orders are to obey me unless I order you to kill each other or attack the Red Empire.'

She'd done none of those things – instead, she'd converted them into monsters, vampires who had all tasted the exquisite elixir of human blood.

Anathema! He and his men deserved nothing but death, but were not free to take their own lives, trapped in the service of Chloe Armitage, General of the Vampire Dominion.

A sworn enemy of the Red Empire.

How had this come to pass, he must have made a severe error of judgment, or committed a grave moral failure – this 'thing,' he'd become exceeded the moral framework of 'The Way of the Faithful,' the revered text at the foundation of the Red Empire.

'Death before dishonor,' was at the core of Red Empire belief. He paused for a second, the future weighing upon him. He could exist in this state for years ... decades ... centuries, before he could end his shame.

The iris opened. Tamsah pushed off from the ceiling of the secret chamber above the Gossamer maze. He shot through the opening and twisted in the air, landing in a crouch, his blade gleaming in the weird Gossamer light. Behind him, one of his fist team landed with the soft scuff of armor composite against stone. He forgave the man his lack of complete silence, neither of them had experience wearing the matte-black armor of one of Crane's praetorians.

A dozen feet away, a tall man with close-cropped gray hair and a callow youth were ramping, their katanas poised in perfect stillness over their shoulders.

Tamsah blurred forward, the youth leaped toward him.

It was time to fight, but not for honor, and if not for honor, then what did he fight for? A vampire can't have honor – not in any way understood by the Red Empire.

His mind clouded with questions, and that would never do – he pushed them aside and allowed his skills to flourish. Now it was time for blood, steel, and death, and that was an arena in which he'd long been a master.

* * *

James Cox leaped forward, engaging the shorter of the two praetorians, their blades clashing in a shower of sparks. Weapons struck each other in the next corridor, Khan and Chapman made contact with the enemy.

The short praetorian's counterstrike ripped through Cox's torso, his heart's blood spraying across Richard Walker's face.

With his eyes shrouded in red gore, Richard spun forward, his sword lashing out at the second vampire. Their blades struck each other, sparks flying, the vampire's sword pushed in toward him. He spun in the reverse direction, allowing the blade to go past him, his spinning kick sending the praetorian flying backward along the corridor.

Richard strode forward, his katana snapping back into a high guard position, his best hope lay in keeping both opponents in front of him, if they surrounded him, survival would be that much harder.

A woman's voice fell to silence mid-scream, Chapman was down. His heart tore, his team was dying. He cursed the day – could it get any worse?

The short praetorian rushed forward, Richard blurred to meet him, his blade slashing down in an overhead strike. The shorter man caught the katana with his longsword, angled his wrist, allowing the blade to slide past him on the right, his blade flicked over, trapping the katana against the gray flagstones.

The vampire appeared inside his guard, looking up at Richard with flat, brown, merciless eyes. His left fist punched through his gut, a gauntleted hand grasped his spine, ripping down and out in a single motion.

There was a sickening crack, the world tilted, all sensation below his chest vanished. He landed on his back, staring upward, gasping for breath.

A longsword flashed above him, descending in a blur.

A sharp fire ignited across his throat, and Richard Walker, Order of Thoth force leader for the United Kingdom, descended into infinite darkness.

* * *

Why do I feel like bait?

Li frowned, her lips pressing together. She edged forward, close to the mirrored wall. Her senses were fully awake, alert to every sound and movement around her. She held the Green Dragon above her, its blade reaching back over her right shoulder, poised to strike.

The noise of combat ebbed away. The tactical links remained jammed, but sound carried well through the mirror maze, and it was clear the Order had just taken losses.

"Walker, Chapman, Cox, Khan?" Francis called out.

No one answered.

Francis called to the team again, "Sound off."

Anton, Peter, Jay, and Chiara all called back. They were somewhere behind her, caught in the maze – she was alone.

"Li," she called out. It was enough to let everyone know where she was.

She passed through the doorway into the large chamber beyond. It was square, about ten yards on a side, she moved carefully toward the middle of the room. There was a faint susurration, her head whipped back, the doorway vanished, the wall congealing behind her.

An opening appeared in the wall to her right, four praetorians blurred into the chamber, forming a line half a dozen feet inside the room. The vampires held their weapons perfectly still, their blades dripping blood onto the flagstones of the dungeon floor.

The wall reformed behind them, the lights brightened overhead, the walls of the chamber became transparent. The walls of the maze beyond the chamber vanished as quickly as they'd appeared. The surviving members of the Order rushed to the wall around her and started pounding on it with their weapons.

Li moved backward to the center of the chamber, shifting the Green Dragon to a horizontal position in front of her face, her eyes tracking the vampires circling around her. The katana's blade gleamed mirror-like in the lights, reflecting the vampires maneuvering behind her.

Four praetorians? The vampire's features beneath their armored helms spoke of Kazakhstan, Mongolia and Tibet, not regions noted as recruitment grounds for Cornelius Crane, but well known to provide recruits for the Red Empire.

"What the hell is this?" Li whispered.

"Your death," the shortest of the four remarked with dreadful certainty. His voice was at odds with his eyes, conflict lay reflected in their dark brown depths, a harsh intensity overlaying a deep well of emotions barely held in check.

She'd be damned if she waited for them to attack.

Li feinted left, the vampire on that side moved to block the attack, her father's voice whispered in her mind, *The four-foe defense.*

Silence overwhelmed her, the vampires blurred toward her, blades arcing in, she leaped over the bright ring of steel. She landed, the Green Dragon sweeping through a broad arc behind her, forcing two of the vampires to leap high over her blade to avoid instant bloody death. She reversed instantly, tumbling forward through the empty space they left behind.

In the silent depths of her mind, she knew one certain fact, no matter how skilled her defenses, the vampires would outlast her.

No one could ramp continuously for more than a handful of minutes.

* * *

The lights in the dungeon dimmed around the walls, leaving a bright spotlight focused on the transparent cage in the middle of the chamber.

Luther's body lay slumped on the floor beyond the cage. Kain stood a dozen feet behind him in the shadows, grinning smugly, a light akin to madness gleaming in his eyes.

Anton had to break Li free of the trap. He brought the Blue Dragon down hard, slashing the katana against the transparent wall.

The meteoric-iron blade scored the wall, leaving a thin white mark floating in mid-air for half a second before it vanished. The material regenerated before his eyes, capable of endless reformation, it could absorb any punishment that didn't instantly destroy it.

"NO!" he screamed in frustration, smacking the wall with his open hand and pressing his face up against it.

Li blurred within the cage, ramping at maximum speed, her face still with concentration, her eyes filled with ferocious intent. She whirled, dodged, leaped and rolled, her blade a gleaming blur amongst the praetorians.

Sparks flew as blades clashed, her defenses were amazing, but unless one of the vampires made a mistake, she had no opportunity to reduce the odds against her.

Anton's heart sank.

Four against one was a death sentence.

* * *

A longsword arced in toward her.

Li snapped the Green Dragon up against it. The angle was perfect, the genius-forged meteoric-iron of the Green Dragon's blade shearing through the lesser sword in a shower of sparks.

The vampire's eyes widened with shock as his sword shattered before his eyes.

Li whirled, her booted foot catching him in the solar plexus. He folded around her strike, flew through the air, crashing against the side of the cage. He slid down the wall into a stunned heap on the flagstones.

Her follow-up attack had left her exposed, all three of her remaining opponent's swords striking down at once.

She swept the Green Dragon over her head, catching all the blades, redirecting them over her while she tumbled forward between their knees.

Li came to her feet, the vampires whirling in pursuit, she ran vertically up the nearest wall. Lifting her FN P90 with her free hand, she launched herself into the air, using the submachine gun to split her opponents, its hammering fire cutting a line and putting one of the vampires to one side of the room.

She landed near the lone vampire. His blade slashed down toward her. The Green Dragon snapped up to meet it, deflecting it aside. She moved in close, firing a three-round burst directly into the vampire's chest.

He staggered back in a cloud of gray smoke, blood streaking the transparent wall behind him.

Li whirled away, and tripped, the vampire she'd stunned with a kick had grasped her ankle. The one she'd shot was slumping to the floor. The other two were leaping in, weapons angled to kill.

She pushed back toward the vampire holding her ankle, the Green Dragon arced down, the blade slamming into his upper back, pinning him to the floor like a bug. She swung the FN P90 underneath her outstretched right arm toward the vampires coming in behind her and pulled the trigger.

The gun fired once before a blade slashed through its barrel silencing it forever. A second blade fell flat on her wrist, knocking her hand away from the Green Dragon.

She spun, her foot lashing out at the nearest vampire, he was short, not much taller than herself, he caught her foot mid-air, twisted backward, spinning her over and onto the floor.

The blow knocked the air from her lungs.

Hands like steel grabbed her arms and pulled them tight.

They'd caught her.

* * *

I am a vampire's puppet.

Revulsion grappled with admiration in the pit of Tamsah's soul. The young woman had fought with exemplary skill, and a rare authority of technique that had left him awed. An awe that had turned his blade at the last minute to knock her hand from her sword rather than cut it off. The only reason she hadn't claimed the lives of at least two of his team was the dark alliance of Red Empire fist team skills with vampire blood.

Two of his men held her arms with vice-like grips, the third stood to the side, his fist jammed into the rent in his chest armor where the young woman had almost killed him. Tamsah marveled again at her swordsmanship, what a pity the Red Empire had never inducted her, and what a loss in the war against the vampires her death would be.

But he'd taken oaths, more than one, and he would not go against his word. It was time to follow Armitage's instructions and begin the theater this strange killing would be.

Tamsah stepped in behind the young woman, forced down to her knees in front of him by his two teammates. He pulled back his long blade and declared sternly, "By order of Cornelius Crane, Li Wu is hereby sentenced to death. Her sentence to be carried out forthwith."

She twisted her head up and back, her gaze caught his with a proud, defiant look, filling him with a dreadful shame.

He hesitated for a brief moment, his teeth clenched, then leaned forward and whispered harshly, "You're a foolish girl, this place was always a trap for you."

She stared back at him, indomitable and without fear, and demanded, "Who are you? You're not a praetorian."

Tamsah's eyes widened with shock. The truth of her words tore at his heart and he whispered without thinking, "I'm someone who has given an oath to obey, and obey I will, but your death serves the vampires, which I abhor with every fiber of my being."

He stood up, lifted his blade, the moment stretching, the sword poised above the young warrior, ready to plunge down and tear out her life.

Something snapped within, breaching a forbidden barrier, Tamsah took a long shuddering breath.

Let Armitage believe what she will, after all, where is the honor in serving a vampire?

He must perform his next action perfectly. The slightest error would foil the plan burgeoning like a wildfire in his soul.

He adjusted the angle of the blade slightly and thrust down, the longsword disappeared into the young woman's body.

She gasped.

He tapped her once on a pressure point just to the left of the C5 vertebrae and her eyes mercifully closed.

He held the blade still for a long second, silence filled the hall, then a young man screamed in anguish less than twenty feet away.

Tamsah pulled the sword clear, the young woman slumping bonelessly forward into a heap at his feet.

It was done.

Armitage had never explained what would happen next.

* * *

Li fell to the flagstones.

I'm too late to save her!

The Raven breached the final defenses of the control system and prepared to issue the command to shut down the Gossamer system. Their fingers raced against the surface of their smartphone.

The transparent walls composing the cage around Li and the four praetorians vanished. The Raven halted what they were doing, someone else had shut down the system.

Anton was the first to move, blurring forward, directly at the short praetorian who had stabbed Li.

The praetorian stepped back, his gore-streaked blade snapping into a high guard position.

The rest of the Mirovar force team raced forward to engage the other vampires.

What just happened? The Raven blurred forward with the rest of their teammates, a chill racing up their spine.

Whatever was happening was nothing like what they'd thought it would be.

* * *

It was real, Li was dead.

Anton's soul exploded with rage, a red fire consuming him from the inside. His vision narrowed upon the short praetorian stepping away from Li's body, his wet longsword slick with her blood.

Power blew through him like a hurricane, he blurred forward, appearing in front of Li's killer. The Blue Dragon arced down toward the vampire's head, a gleaming thunderbolt of retribution.

The praetorian moved, faster than any vampire Anton had ever confronted. His blade angled up, his body flew backward, the swords connected briefly, sparking once – it was enough to deflect Anton's strike.

Anton launched himself after the retreating vampire who was reversing at speed toward the single corridor leading to the cliffs.

The wild Ramp was ebbing, a crazed burst he couldn't sustain. Anton reached into the silence, drawing forth an edge of speed, and closed on the praetorian.

Anton lashed forward with the Blue Dragon, and struck a second and a third time – the short vampire deflecting each blow at the last moment. He slashed across the vampire's chest with a reverse cut, the blow didn't land.

The short praetorian leaped high into the air, flipping upside down, running steps along the ceiling before dropping back amongst his comrades.

Anton whirled around, his focus on Li's killer, his back to the shadows leading to the cliff edge. His rage was subsiding, becoming cold fury, his senses reached out through the chamber.

Kain laughed madly, swinging a sword wildly. Jay cut off his laugh as well as his head, which bounced and rolled along the flagstones.

Francis, Peter, and Chiara fought the other three vampires, the one disarmed by Li, was now wielding Luther's katana.

With the short praetorian joining his comrades, it would be five against four. Anton strode forward, a dreadful certainty filled his soul – he would have vengeance tonight or die trying.

* * *

Chloe embraced Marcus, whispering into his ear, "For love and duty."

She stepped back, they looked down along the corridor into the Gossamer chamber. She'd shutdown the Gossamer system, it had fulfilled her purpose perfectly. Li Wu was dead, and the situation was descending into chaos, the Mirovar force team falling upon the Red Empire vampires like vengeful angels. Kain had allowed himself to be drawn into the fight, suffering the intoxication of blood drunkenness, he'd believed himself to be invincible.

The Mirovar force team had closed off the loose end of Ramin Kain for her.

"Buy me five more minutes, it's all I need to advance our cause."

Marcus nodded grimly.

Chloe leaned up, kissed him for the last time and promised softly, "Your courage will not be forgotten."

He nodded again, and said with quiet sincerity, "I've always loved you."

She stared into his face for a long moment and said, "I know."

He turned away, walking down the corridor toward the chamber, rolling his shoulders, and limbering up his battle-axe and a nine-foot-long whip-like black chain.

She expected him to do his best, if it was enough to survive, then Anton Slayne was not the weapon to defeat Cornelius Crane, and she would begin again. If Marcus didn't survive and Anton Slayne did, especially if Marcus died by Anton's hand, then the game was very much alive.

It was time for Anton to walk the true path of vengeance, a pathway soaked in blood, suffering, and wrath.

She stepped out to the edge of the cliff face. Dark clouds obscured the sky, the rainfall had reduced to a fine drizzle. Sheer rock walls rose a hundred feet above her and fell another hundred feet below her to the ocean. She leaped twenty feet upward, fingers like steel stabbing into the rock face. She moved upward, scaling the rock wall with ease, in moments she reached the upper cliff and stood tall on the precipice.

Her manor house rose before her, the ground lights illuminating the purpose written in the hard intensity of her face. The lights of Whitby glimmered in the distance, she turned toward the town, making her way to the rendezvous point.

Chloe had barely four hundred yards to travel, the way lay shrouded with stands of ancient trees growing back from the cliffs. In the distance a clearing waited for her. One known from her childhood so many years in the past. She advanced toward it, it matched the coordinates provided by the Raven. She needed to meet Juliette Mirovar and Joan Lewis. She had business to complete with the loremasters of the Order of Thoth.

It was the next essential step in her plan.

* * *

"Behind you!" Peter shouted.

Anton whirled around, ducking instinctively, a thick black chain slashing through the air above his head, sparking and scoring an inch-deep groove on the stone wall.

The chain clattered to the flagstones, before skittering away behind Marcus Drake. He stood a dozen feet in front of Anton, the length of chain dangling from his right hand and a massive double-bladed battle-axe in his left. A corridor stretched behind him, wreathed in ever-deepening shadows until it merged with the pitch-black night beyond the cliff.

They stared at each other for a brief moment, Anton's mind immediately shifting gears to meet the new threat.

"Where's my father?" Anton demanded, circling to the left, fury flowing like a river of ice through his soul. He hoped to pull Drake deeper into the light.

Drake's eyes tightened, as he counter-moved to the right. "As if I would tell you?"

Anton stepped backward, perhaps he could draw Drake forward. "You will tell me before this is done."

Drake grinned, but his eyes were glacial. "You are a child, full of idle boasts. Kill me and the secret of your father's location will die with me."

He's trying to make me hesitate.

"You've killed him anyway," Anton spat, watching Drake carefully. He'd never fought anyone using a chain before. It would be like a whip, the tip moving lightning fast would rip through anything in its way. It was too late to attempt to use a gun against Drake, by the time he drew his weapon and it fired, Drake would be upon him with the battle-axe or the broadsword sheathed at his hip.

"No," Drake offered slowly, shaking his head. "He is very much alive."

Drake's words rang true, and Anton's heart sank. "A vampire?"

"And imprisoned in silver," Drake declared, taking a step forward, putting Anton within range of the chain. "Unlike the Order, we keep our promises."

Drake's right hand blurred, the chain speared forward toward Anton's chest.

Anton blurred to his right, the tip of the chain brushing past his left shoulder, before slithering back behind Drake.

"Your parents lied to you for your whole life. You join the Order, and they lie to you again and again. You know nothing."

Anton bit back a reflex denial, he had to admit Drake was speaking the truth, but it didn't matter – not this time – Drake was trying to bait him, to fill him with doubts and weaken his ability to fight.

Anton stared hard at Drake and promised, "I will free my father."

Drake arched an eyebrow, moving back toward the shadows. "You will let a vampire loose on the world?"

Anton followed him, grim-faced, and promised darkly, "I will free him."

Drake laughed, a grim, barking sound. The black chain lashed forward out of the gloom.

Anton blurred left, away from the nearest wall, straight into the path of a thrown battle-axe. The leading edge of the axe was a thick crescent shape of dark iron between the two blades, it slammed into his chest, catching the flat of the Blue Dragon's blade in a diagonal across his body.

The meteoric-iron of the katana saved Anton's life, distributing the force of the blow across a much larger area as the axe lifted him off the floor and threw him backward twenty feet.

A white sheet of agony flashed through him. He rolled as he landed, coming back to his feet, his katana on guard, his chest heaving as he attempted to get air back into his lungs. A pair of shallow cuts beneath his nipples from the tips of the axe's blades began bleeding into his shirt.

Drake, his broadsword drawn, the black chain whistling through the air like a demonic serpent was upon him a moment later.

The fight hadn't started well.

* * *

For love and duty.

The words echoed in Marcus' mind. He knew that Chloe didn't love him, it was enough that he loved her. He would kill the boy. It would prove he wasn't what she believed he could be – a genuine threat to Crane.

With Anton Slayne out of the way, there would be time to find another way to breach Allemande's curse, and he would be where he belonged – at her side again.

By sheer luck, the boy had survived his thrown battle-axe and was still on his feet. He'd evaded Marcus' follow-on attack with an astonishing burst of speed.

They stood a dozen feet apart, the boy's face paled, his blue eyes stared with a wild intensity at Marcus, a thin line of foam appearing on his lips.

What the hell is happening to him?

Whatever it was, best to kill the boy quickly, he flourished his sword and prepared his next strike with the chain, striding forward to bring the boy within range.

* * *

Anton's Ramp went wild, dark lightning coruscating through his body.

Anton's right hand reversed on the Blue Dragon's handle, grasping it like an oversized dagger for an overhead strike. He blurred forward, suddenly appearing in front of Drake. He hammered the Blue Dragon down in a stabbing motion, piercing Drake's armored breastplate between his heart and his left shoulder. The meteoric iron of the blade tore through the ceramic nano-fibers of the armor, skewering flesh and bone before disappearing up to the hilt, half the blade appearing outside Drake's back, sending a red ribbon of his blood splashing into the shadows behind him.

Drake staggered back under the impact of the blow. His eyes widened, he snarled, his right fist wrapped with chain links pummeled Anton's chest, sending him spinning backward a dozen feet without the Blue Dragon.

The chain followed; a lethal black whip whistling through the air.

Anton landed, twisting blindly back toward Drake. The tip of the chain slammed into the side of his face, entering next to his left eye. It continued forward, obliterating his nightglasses and gouging a furrow an inch deep through his left eye and the top of his nose.

A red mist composed of his own blood and fragments of bone bloomed in front of him. His heart burst with a torrent of rage, pain, and grief. The wild ramp overtook him again, he instinctively drew upon his training in hooded darkness and blurred forward, reaching across his body for the Blue Dragon with his left hand.

Drake's broadsword had been in his left hand, his counterstrike would come from Anton's right. Anton's right hand flashed up in a block, his forearm connecting with Drake's wrist, he was within Drake's guard, his broadsword had over-reached past Anton's right shoulder.

The Blue Dragon's handle smacked into his left hand; his grip tightened around it. There was heavy resistance to moving the blade, it remained embedded in Drake's chest, and surrounded by armor front and back.

Drake cried out, "No!"

Anton screamed in inarticulate agony, his muscles rippling; he drew the Blue Dragon out in a massive draw cut, the blade shearing through Drake's heart, spine, right lung and chest wall.

Anton stepped backward.

Drake slumped to the floor in front of him, blood splashing across the flagstones in a torrent.

The Blue Dragon crashed to the floor. Anton's left hand rose to his ruined eye. His heart thudded in his chest, he sobbed once, a vision of his mother's head falling to the floor assaulting him like a lash from beyond the grave.

He sucked in a great breath, whirled around, searching for Li with his good right eye. She still lay where she'd fallen, the battle between the Mirovar force team and the praetorians raging near her body.

"Li!" he cried, scooping up the Blue Dragon, he rushed toward her body and the fighters swirling around her.

* * *

Li woke up, her eyes were already open, but she couldn't move them.

She couldn't move anything.

Oh my God, I'm paralyzed.

The battle stormed around her, she'd crumpled forward unconscious and lay with her face to one side. She'd been stabbed. The entry wound between her left shoulder and neck had stung, then everything had gone black.

Why am I still alive? I should have bled out by now.

Her father's voice whispered in her mind, *'There are secret strikes that don't cause any real damage but appear deadly.*

But what had knocked her unconscious? The vampire had tapped her next to the spine, it must have been a pressure point technique. That was good, the paralysis would most likely wear off in a while.

Most likely … but what on Earth was his motive?

A praetorian blurred into view. Anton and Jay overwhelmed his defenses in a flurry of strikes, and he slumped to the floor, his heart's blood spreading in a pool beneath him.

The battle was turning, the two forces had been evenly balanced, but as one team gained ascendancy, numbers would become telling, and suddenly it would be over.

There was a gurgle behind her, and a low grunt, weapons clattered to the stone floor.

Francis called out, "Non, Anton! Let him go, come back and bring Li's body, we don't leave anyone behind."

Footfalls rapidly retreated into the distance; two final pairs approached on the flagstones.

Anton knelt down next to her and rolled her over onto her back. His face was a mess, covered with blood, his left eye socket ripped open – a red ruin. Tears had carved furrows amongst the blood and grime covering the rest of his face.

He pushed his hands underneath her shoulders and hips, holding her close with tender gentleness. He rocked backward, smoothly lifting her as he stood up.

Peter's voice, his tone grim, came from somewhere behind him, "C'mon Anton, follow me, we have to catch up with the others."

Anton whirled around, running after Peter.

Li was able to scan the chamber as Anton turned, she counted six bodies, Kain, Luther, Drake, and three praetorians. The short vampire who had stabbed her and seemed to be the strange praetorian's leader had vanished.

She appeared to owe him her life.

Anton held her close, jogging steadily up the spiral staircase to the manor house. His chest was tight as a drum, his heart thudding near her ear. His breathing would catch on every breath. He couldn't breathe properly, he'd been badly hurt, more broken ribs and perhaps a cracked sternum to add to the smashed eye socket.

But it wasn't the physical damage that tore at her heart, it was his words whispered over and over, "Not Li too, not Li, not now, not her too…"

Li's heart rate had dropped to the single digits per minute, and she was breathing too slowly to be noticeable.

What on earth did that vampire do to me?

I hope they work out I'm not dead?

A vision of her grave overtook her. Clods of dirt falling onto her limp body, lumps of clay catching in her open mouth, darkness obliterating everything. She screamed once in utter silence before regaining control of her emotions.

Surely it wouldn't come to that?

C'mon Anton, see me, I'm alive.

I'm alive!

Chapter Twenty Seven

"Never give up on your friends. Never give up your faith in them. It's when everything is worse than you could ever imagine it could be, that you'll need your friends the most." – Juliette Mirovar

* * *

Armitage Manor, The Cliffs, Yorkshire, August 22nd, 20:52

Black clouds bloomed over a night sky, backlit by a brilliant sea of stars. The edge of each cloud illuminated with a ghostly, silvery light that was millions of years old.

Chloe moved stealthily beneath the trees, her steps silent on the soft grasses and wet leaves. She caressed rough bark on the trunk of the nearest tree, the air was rich with the scent of the ocean and the recently passed storm.

The clearing was in sight, there were two Order warriors on guard, facing out into the darkness and wearing what appeared to be sunglasses. The same technology the pair of Order operatives who had infiltrated the dungeon that morning had been wearing. They stood in wary watchful postures, well equipped with light intensifier technology overlaid with data supplied by their loremasters.

Kain had indeed been a treasure trove of information.

Chloe positioned herself next to a tree, she was about forty yards back from the clearing. The two guards stood clear of the rest, a young, blond woman, and a tall man with a touch of gray in his hair. They looked like a pair, not lovers, but trained to fight with each other, together they would not be a simple kill.

Beyond them were three others, Juliette and Yvette Mirovar, and Joan Lewis, the loremaster for the United Kingdom force team. The loremasters were not much of a threat, it was Yvette that presented a risk, but she was favoring her left arm. Chloe arched an eyebrow for a moment. The young Mirovar must have taken a wound earlier in the day and was not at full strength.

That would make all the difference.

It pained her that Yvette was here. It was possible she was the Raven; it would be a setback to lose the Raven at this point in the game. It was a risk that was now unavoidable, everyone in the clearing would have to die.

Chloe stepped away from the tree, there was no time to waste, she drew the Red Dragon and blurred toward the rendezvous site.

* * *

Juliette leaned back against the trunk of a large tree.

With the help of her Order nightglasses, the world was a twilight-lit realm instead of pitch-black night. From where she sat, she could see the lights of the manor house in the distance. She'd picked her seat in the hope of seeing Francis, and the rest of the team come toward the rendezvous site.

Joan Lewis, the local loremaster sat next to her. She'd been working feverishly on her laptop for the last eight minutes in a vain attempt to break the jamming of the tactical comms link.

To Juliette's left was the cliff edge, where Yvette stood looking out into the night. Mary Turner and David Wilkinson guarded the approaches to the clearing. They stood watch, armed with H&K MP5 submachine guns and their katanas.

She was worried, this was the first time the team had been in combat without her tactical oversight, and the long running battles had exhausted their strength. With the loss of communications there was no way of knowing what was happening, and to make matters worse, the identity of the Red Empire spy was still unknown.

But ... all the pieces of the puzzle suddenly snapped into place. The spy had confronted Walker about guarding the wounded once he announced the split to the rendezvous point. Juliette had asked them if they were okay. They were frightened of something, and they'd wanted to be here – to protect the wounded.

But that would mean—

A figure clad in black, gray, and tan combat fatigues, and wielding a dragon-blade katana flew through the air toward the middle of the clearing.

Juliette gasped out. "Armitage!"

The threat was overwhelming and instinctive, Juliette ramped on reflex.

Turner and Wilkinson opened up with their H&Ks: flames stabbing from the throats of their submachine guns, bullets slashing through the clearing, rounds striking bark from the trees, and zipping off into the night,

Yvette's sword hissed free of its scabbard.

Juliette reached for her crutches, she had to get to her feet.

Joan leaped to her feet, stretching out her hand to grasp Juliette's arm. She shrieked a single word, "Run!"

* * *

The deadly streams of 9mm rounds reeked of silver.

Chloe landed in a fighting crouch between the two Order warriors. They both stopped firing to avoid hitting each other. It was the wrong move, they should have kept firing to guarantee a hit regardless of the risk to each other, but a fighting pair became instinctive about not hitting each other in a melee.

It was an exploitable weakness, allowing Chloe to draw them into a fight on her terms. However, whoever she attacked first, the other would advance on her undefended back. A skilled and experienced pair of Order warriors was not to be trifled with.

There was no time for uncertainty, she drew upon her capability for a supreme Ramp. Time slowed precipitously, her heart paused between beats, energy exploded from the base of her spine, flooding through bone, sinew, and nerve.

Her mind raced.

The male warrior was coming toward her, his blade arcing through a diagonal slash that would cut her from shoulder to hip – if it landed.

Chloe moved to her right, the Red Dragon snapping up to her left to meet his descending sword. The two blades connected, his katana deflecting away to her left in a shower of sparks as her sword consumed its edge. She kept moving, rotating her wrists flat, running the Red Dragon horizontally across his abdomen as she passed him on the right.

She whirled to face the clearing.

The man was faltering, falling forward, bright blood splashing to the left and right.

The girl rushed upon Chloe, her gaze intense, ferocious, her mouth a grim slash, her sword angled for Chloe's heart.

Chloe's supreme Ramp was peaking, she waited until the final moment to bring her katana into play. The tip of the Red Dragon's blade met the tip of the girl's sword, pushing the opposing blade aside by a matter of inches. Chloe leaned away to her left, her sword traveling along the length of the girl's blade.

The girl realized the danger and began moving aside – too late.

Chloe's katana ripped through her chest, as the girl ran upon the Red Dragon, its bloody tip appearing a foot outside her back.

Chloe ripped the sword out through the girl's side, opening her up like a gutted fish. She blurred to the left, the Red Dragon flicking up into guard, the supreme ramp fading.

Yvette's first strike slammed against her sword, and then Yvette was past her.

Chloe circled back into the middle of the clearing, Yvette pacing her at a dozen feet.

The two women faced each other, Chloe with the Red Dragon, dripping with fresh gore, Yvette with her katana poised in guard position over her left shoulder, her red hair storm-swept and wet on her forehead.

Their gazes met with deadly intent.

* * *

Yvette stared at Chloe Armitage.

To her left, Joan helped Juliette to her feet.

Her left shoulder hadn't healed from the gunshot wound, even with system zero epigenetics she'd only experienced the equivalent of four days of healing in the last nine hours, and it wasn't enough to restore her to full strength.

Still, she was no novice, and she would rather die than leave her adoptive mother and Joan Lewis to Armitage's tender mercies.

Her heart thudded in her chest, her body instinctively recognizing the predator standing opposite her. Armitage had cut through Wilkinson and Turner like they'd been standing still. Her speed was amazing – if she could continue at that pace, Yvette knew she wouldn't last much longer than the others had.

Lasting long enough was the key to her strategy. She had to believe the rest of the Mirovar force team were on their way. If she could survive long enough, Francis, Jay, Peter, Chiara, Li and Anton would arrive, and together they would end Armitage forever.

She had to buy time, she had to play a defensive game – the sort of game she excelled at.

A breeze blew in off the ocean, riffing Armitage's hair beneath her cap, she sighed with disappointment. "With your wounds, there is no honor in killing you, but take your life I must."

"Why?" Yvette asked dryly, wondering how much time Armitage would burn talking.

Armitage glanced at the loremasters, then looked at Yvette and shrugged her shoulders. "You're in my way – I'm sure you won't tolerate what I need to do."

"Which is what?"

Armitage smiled. "I admire your bravery, and of course, you hope to slow me down long enough for help to arrive – but you will not succeed."

Yvette scowled. "Just bring it!"

"With pleasure."

Yvette drew upon every ounce of training she'd received at the hands of Francis Mirovar, and Jay Creeley, her primary training partner. She'd mastered an array of defensive techniques that had proved impervious to everyone except a berserk Anton Slayne. She reached deep into silence, her mind dropping into a fathomless quiet, golden light bloomed from within her deepest being and stormed along her limbs.

Armitage flew toward her, the famous Red Dragon arcing down for a head strike – a sudden death move designed to end the fight before it began.

Her katana, a faithful blade gifted to her by Jay Creeley, arced forward. She blurred hard to the left, her sword catching the Red Dragon in a deflection to her right.

The shock of the blow reverberated along her arms; her left shoulder threatened to tear apart. She barely avoided the near irresistible force of Armitage's strike; blurring further to the left, she swapped positions with the vampire general.

Armitage had done her best to kill her and failed, all she had to do was keep defending at the same level, and she would hold Armitage here until help arrived.

Armitage inclined her head respectfully and promised, "I will not forget you."

"You won't get the chance," Yvette promised in turn, happy to steal every second she could.

Armitage blurred toward her, the Red Dragon arcing down in a perfect diagonal slash.

Yvette's blade rose to meet it.

It was a feint, Armitage pulled the blade back, her left foot lashing out to catch Yvette in the solar plexus.

Yvette twisted aside, turning Armitage's kick into a glancing blow. She whirled away, her sword lashing instinctively toward Armitage, whose own blade swept back against her own with a clang.

Armitage, it seemed – was impossible to touch with an edged weapon.

They stood opposite each other again.

The storm clouds were breaking up, bright stars appearing overhead. A cool sea breeze caressed Yvette's face.

Joan Lewis pulled on Juliette's arm, it was time to flee, but her mother resisted. It was no more possible for Juliette to abandon her daughter to Armitage than it was for Yvette to abandon her mother.

Their destinies were bound together. The skills of Yvette's masterful defenses versus Chloe Armitage's terrifying capabilities would determine their fate tonight.

Armitage frowned, the first show of concern. Yvette took it as a small victory of sorts, perhaps Armitage would make a mistake Yvette could capitalize on. Time was on Yvette's side, if she could drag this out long enough, she would survive, and her friends would destroy the vampire facing her.

Armitage's eyes narrowed, her face stilling with intense concentration. She launched herself forward, the Red Dragon arcing down toward Yvette.

Thousands of hours of training and combat experience kicked into high gear. Yvette's movements flowed like a perfectly formed symphony, her silence complete, her mind a still point of certainty. Her blade rose to meet Armitage's descending sword, her body moving toward the left to avoid the inevitable deflection.

The Red Dragon smashed through her katana, cutting straight into her right shoulder a couple of inches away from her neck. Tiny droplets of superheated steel struck the side of her face. The glow of the blooming cloud of metal illuminating Armitage's face before her, her eyes gleaming with a silvery light.

Armitage's strike continued deep into her chest, her right arm disappearing from her awareness. Cold steel ripped through flesh, blood, and bone with relentless force, a wave of shock and horror slammed through her.

Her sword fell from nerveless fingers.

The inevitable draw cut came an instant later, followed by merciful oblivion.

* * *

Juliette cried out in grief.

Yvette crashed to the ground, Armitage stepping away from her, the Red Dragon flicking through the air to rid itself of Yvette's blood.

Juliette stood in front of the same tree she'd been sitting at, Joan at her side.

Joan pulled a 9mm automatic from her hip and fired at Armitage. She blurred left and right, the bullets flying harmlessly past her. The pistol clicked on empty, Joan threw it away and blurred to her right.

Armitage blurred toward Juliette.

Juliette attempted to move aside, but her left leg wouldn't carry the forces of a ramp, and she barely moved half a foot.

The Red Dragon's impact pushed her up against the tree. The cold meteoric-iron blade running through her chest, thudding into the trunk behind her with a wooden crack that echoed away from the cliff.

Juliette's world faded, it was a heart strike – she was dying, her blood running freely past the blade to soak her shirt.

Joan appeared to her right, Wilkinson's katana in her hands, swinging in hard toward Armitage.

Armitage dragged back on the Red Dragon, but it was stuck fast in the tree. Her left foot kicked out, connecting with Joan's blade which swung wide.

Armitage dragged on the blade again with more force, this time it came free, just in time to impale Joan Lewis as she attempted to strike a second time.

Juliette staggered forward a step, dragged in a ragged breath, stilled her mind and ramped. Her right hand blurred forward, the silver dagger given to her by Francis, appearing in the middle of Armitage's right forearm.

The pointed tip, red with Armitage's blood jutted three inches out the other side. Her face chalk white with horror, she staggered back a step and launched herself with a mighty leap backward over the cliff edge.

Juliette, her strength spent, slumped to her knees and toppled forward. Joan rocked backward and forward and then fell next to her.

Twin pools of blood began spreading slowly from their bodies, soaking into the grass.

* * *

The silver dagger pierced Chloe's right forearm.

A dreadful numbing cold raced up her arm. Her fist had frozen on the handle of the Red Dragon, if the knife had been in her opposite arm, she wouldn't have hesitated to cut it off with her sword.

She flew backward through the air. She had a single chance to rid herself of the thrall of silver or be lost forever to a catatonic paralysis until the dagger was removed.

Her left hand brushed clumsily at her right arm, her left arm felt like a wet noodle, barely under her control.

Had she struck the dagger clear, she couldn't feel enough to tell. Her body became rigid, she descended past the cliff edge, falling toward the rocks and ocean below.

Rocks and ocean ... rocks and ocean ... rocks and ocean.

* * *

The Raven followed Francis and Jay into the clearing, the rest of the Mirovar force team were behind them.

Francis and Jay rushed toward Juliette and Yvette; their voices filled with desperate hope. Hope, the Raven knew would evaporate like snowflakes on hot stones as reality sank in.

Everyone was dead, Juliette was slumped with Joan Lewis next to a tree, a few feet away Yvette lay in disarray, while the other Order team fighters lay in pools of their own blood and entrails.

The Raven watched, dissociated from events, numb, their mind in perfect denial of what their eyes could plainly see.

Then their world shifted violently, their breathing became ragged, their chest heaving helplessly, their heart thudding in their chest. A wave of nausea overwhelmed them, and they fell to their knees, vomiting the thin contents of their stomach onto the wet grass.

It wasn't the brutality of death; they'd seen worse. It wasn't the loss of a beloved mother and sister, although the thin, cruel talons of grief were already clawing at their soul.

It was the dark, inescapable guilt rising like a tidal wave over everything else.

The Raven staggered to their feet; their eyes wide, unable to look away from the horror before them.

Jay cried out, holding Yvette's body in his arms while rocking back and forth, his voice lost to strangled sobs.

"Mon Dieu, her silver dagger, it's gone," Francis wailed, flailing around for the lost dagger as if its recovery would restore Juliette to life.

Their other teammate stood still, their face stricken with helpless horror, their hands on their head in disbelief.

Francis fell forward over Juliette, his arms cradling her blood-soaked torso. He prayed for release with thin, desperate words.

The Raven looked back down the path, Anton was running toward the clearing, Li's body in his arms.

It was too much, the loss, the catastrophe; the guilt was beyond what they could bear. They turned toward the cliff edge, blurring forward to the enveloping darkness beyond it.

They hit the edge stepping off into space. A strong arm snaked around their waist, and a hard body tackled them sideways to the ground.

Anton rolled them over onto their back, away from the cliff edge, his face was pale, angry but controlled. He shouted at them, "Do you think we can afford to lose you too?" he slammed his own chest and grimaced through the pain. "Do you think your hurting worse than everyone else here!" he leaned in close, his one good eye holding a mixture of intense wildness and adamantine purpose. "We don't stop here. We move forward. We fight for each other, and we damn well fight back."

Anton rocked back on his heels, stood up and snapped his hand out. "Get up. You're coming with me. I can't do this without you."

The Raven stared at Anton for a second, then took his hand and stood up. Inwardly, they lay lost, drowning in a dark sea, but Anton's hand was strong, his bearing filled with purpose, his command a lifeline to a safe harbor.

The Raven, tears streaming down their face, accepted Anton's leadership.

They were no longer an agent of the Red Empire, that time was past. They would follow Anton to whatever end, and perhaps, one day they would find honor again.

If it was still possible to find honor.

* * *

"What's this?" Anton asked, staring at something on the ground a foot back from the edge of the cliff.

He picked it up, it was a silver dagger, still slick with blood. He studied it for a long moment, piecing together a likely sequence of events. A grim smile touching the corners of his mouth; apparently, someone had stuck Armitage with a silvered blade.

Peter said behind him, "That's Juliette's, I think Francis gave it to her earlier." He strode to the cliff edge and peered over into the darkness.

Anton joined him. The ocean was rolling in, wave after wave crashing against great black rocks. If Armitage had taken a hit of silver before falling over the edge, she might have died upon the rocks below.

The violence of the waves scoured the rocks clear every ten or twenty seconds. The sea would have taken her body almost immediately.

"Without her body," Anton declared. "We must assume she is alive until proven otherwise."

Peter raised an eyebrow. "It's the only safe assumption."

The two men stepped away from the cliff edge, Anton tucking the dagger into his belt, he would give it back to Francis later.

Once they'd reached some measure of safety.

"We all take a body – no one gets left behind," Anton commanded. "Francis with Juliette, Jay with Yvette, Chiara, and Peter can manage the other three, and I will carry Li. Quickly now, down to the docks before anything else happens."

Francis was too distraught to argue Anton's assumption of command. Jay nodded his assent, his face streaked with tears.

Less than a minute later, the remnants of the Mirovar force team left the blood-drenched clearing and strode single file down the hill toward the Whitby docks.

* * *

The fishing trawler was driving north, half a mile off the Scottish coastline.

Anton stood with Peter on the deck, leaning on the rails, facing out toward the ocean. He shook his head, a rueful smile kept appearing on his face despite the circumstances.

Li was alive, she'd woken up, and started moving. It had freaked everyone out when it had happened. Anton's first thought had been that she was coming back as a vampire.

Then she'd hugged him and then slapped him for not realizing that she was alive. He was happy, things were back to normal between them.

Francis had asked Chiara to retrieve the implants from Juliette's and Joan's forearms. The implants were at the forefront of Order technology and could not be lost.

Most of the team were asleep, Peter and Anton had taken the first watch. The Order helpers, a pair of old salts in their sixties who knew this coastline and waters better than they knew their own wives manned the trawler.

Li was sleeping, her wound was surprisingly light, somehow the blade had missed every vital organ in her body. Clearly, the short vampire had his own agenda. Whatever it was, Anton was thankful there appeared to be at least one vampire who was working against Armitage and Crane.

He blinked and looked up at the stars overhead. It would be easy to be overwhelmed by the challenges ahead. The UK team had been utterly destroyed, the Mirovar force team had just been smashed, and the loss of two loremasters was a third of the Order's total complement.

There would be no way to mask their operations or travel from the Panopticon.

Now there was a target, Anton thought, if only they could find it, they could blind the Vampire Dominion.

Peter clasped his shoulder and said, "We'll have to get you an eye patch."

Anton stared out at the sea with his one good eye, his left hand lifting reflexively to the bandages covering the left side of his face. "It will have to be black."

Peter nodded. "Fitting…"

The two young men stared out at the rolling waves. The storm had exhausted its fury, a wreath of stars graced the heavens, providing a faint ghostly light beneath a shroud of infinite darkness.

Marcus Drake was dead, proof that Anton could take down his enemies. Now there was only Armitage and Crane to destroy, and he would have justice for his mother and father.

Juliette had been lost and Yvette with her. The Mirovar force team was badly wounded, its leaders dead or maimed with grief. There was work to be done, they would have to rebuild, and refocus on a new mission.

It was time to step up and make a real difference to what was happening in the world.

Armitage was gone, but he felt she was still alive, still out there, still an agent of her master's will. Without her cold body as definitive proof, it would be foolish to assume she was dead, but it was Crane who was the architect behind her actions. It was Crane who had ordered the murder of his parents. It was Crane who had to be destroyed. With Kain's secret collusion with the vampires exposed, it was time to take the battle to the Vampire Dominion.

Anton said quietly, "We must cut off the head of the snake."

"Amen to that," Peter responded.

The ocean's endless darkness drank in their quiet words, a mute answer to the crystal purity of their shared purpose.

Anton stared out into the night and considered his visions. He had thought to discuss them with Juliette, she'd asked him to do exactly that after the vision of Peter's death, but now she was dead that conversation was never going to happen.

It probably didn't matter, there were too many real world things to do. They didn't seem to be causing any harm and might even be helpful, hadn't the vision today indicated the importance of saving Peter?

Anton decided to remain silent on the topic of visions. There was no need to tell Li or anyone else, after all, there were friends to keep safe and vampires to kill.

And that was enough for any man to deal with.

* * *

Chloe was the sole occupant of the cabin of her Spike 512 supersonic business jet. It was half-past ten at night, the flight was more than fifty thousand feet above sea level over the mid-Atlantic.

The pilot and co-pilot, her surviving retainers, had stayed at the airport during the day. As humans, and mistakenly deemed innocents, they'd been left alone by the UK force team when they'd investigated the hangars that morning.

Her mind turned to recent events.

Juliette Mirovar had nearly claimed her life with her silver dagger.

Chloe had leaped far enough out from the cliff to miss the rocks – just barely. She'd been underwater for nearly thirty minutes and swept out into the North Sea. The silver-induced catalepsy had reduced her metabolism to a level that had ironically saved her from drowning.

With the dagger removed, she'd revived in time and swam back to shore. Coming out on a beach a couple of miles north of Whitby. She'd run back through the night at speed, making for her private airport outside Goathland.

Now onboard her flight, showered, and wearing an elegant silk dressing gown, she relaxed in her favorite chair with a glass of chilled Krug champagne. She studied the high-def screen in front of her, it displayed recorded feeds from the Gossamer chamber at her manor house.

Li had died as planned, and Anton had killed Marcus in a frenzy of violence.

He had a talent, just like his grandfather. A capacity for an enhanced burst of speed, much like her supreme ramp. He was becoming the weapon she needed to defeat Crane, although he did seem to be quite berserk when he went off on a rampage.

She'd watched the footage of the death of Marcus three times, from different angles. Anton had moved so fast; he'd penetrated inside Marcus' defense before he could move. It was quite stunning, and then using the Blue Dragon like it was a dagger – she pursed her lips, *What was in control when that was happening?*

Chloe tilted her head slightly, *Talents – there's always one or two quirks in there.*

She took another sip of champagne; it really was excellent and the perfect ending to a difficult two days. She could visualize Crane and Anton in combat, it would be a bloody mess, but there was no certainty that Crane would win. She looked absently at the bubbles rising in her glass and decided that Anton was indeed the 'one,' to kill Crane for her. He'd proven it tonight when he'd killed Marcus.

Marcus – she would miss him, but omelets, broken eggs and all that.

Anton would one day free her, an act that would usher in an entirely new world.

She took a deep breath and sighed, *Mechanics.*

The Raven was still in place, an essential link into the Mirovar force team. Their information on the rendezvous point proved they were still working to her advantage.

But still, there was a question over them, would they remain loyal? She determined to test the Raven soon, to ensure they were still committed to their mission. Upon reflection, it had become clear the Raven had not gone to the rendezvous site and must be either Peter Lamb or Chiara Romano.

Her thoughts turned to her destination, and Cornelius Crane.

Crane was a terror in combat, faster and stronger than any other vampire, except herself – if she used her supreme Ramp, she was faster, stronger, harder, but Crane knew nothing of her power, and she couldn't use it due to Allemande's curse.

The source of Crane's powers was a mystery, he'd hinted it was due to his great age, being nearly a thousand years old, but Chloe suspected it was something else. Crane was a man who kept his own secrets.

She finished watching the recordings and wiped the data, the images preserved forever in her eidetic memory. There was one last thing to do to complete the evidence for the story she would tell Crane. She set her screen to a sole camera feed at the entrance gate to her manor house. The camera swiveled around to face the manor.

She ran a command on her smartphone. Less than a second later, the manor house silently disappeared in a fountain of fire, dust, flying masonry and billowing clouds of smoke.

Chloe sipped her champagne. She would tell Crane a tale about many splendid things: Red Empire assassins targeting her, battling with the UK Order force team, brave Marcus fighting them all to the death, and finally, the bombing of her ancestral home.

She lifted her champagne flute and watched bubbles stream to the surface. She would detail how the encounters of the UK Shadowstone squadron with the Mirovar force team had produced Order losses, including Ramin Kain, his head of staff, Samuel Luther, the warrior Yvette Mirovar and the loremasters Juliette Mirovar and Joan Lewis.

While Crane's forces had paid a high price, the events of today had eliminated the Order in the United Kingdom, diminished their force of loremasters and seriously weakened the Mirovar force team, a result Crane could easily deem a victory for the Vampire Dominion.

The smoke cleared from the screen, the light intensifiers on the camera feed revealed a great gouge in the ground, like a giant's hand had reached down and scooped the manor house, the dungeons underneath, and half the cliff away and deposited it into the North Sea.

Chloe drank the last of her glass of Krug, savoring the exquisite and refined flavors. She put down the glass and declared softly to the empty cabin, "The past must die so the future may live."

It seemed apropos.

Chloe spent the rest of her flight reviewing her plans. The Order would hold a conclave that she must disrupt to cement her position with Crane. There were new allies to recruit to her cause, members of an ancient predator species whose powers would be extremely useful in the coming war.

For war would come, and chaos would be its avid handmaiden.

She would have her liberty, and she would bring a new order to the world, one that reflected the truth of how the world really worked.

She would make deception obsolete.

It was her destiny.

* * *

Standard operating procedure for the Red Empire when building a camera sensor network was to build in a secret pathway through it.

After breaking contact with the Order force team, Tamsah al Ramil had left the manor house using the pathway he'd built himself. He expected

Armitage would scan the camera feeds, and his exit from the manor house would remain hidden. His deception would leave her with the belief he'd remained in the doomed manor house.

He'd seen the explosion on the horizon far to the south, she would think he was now dead, his body consumed in the destruction of her original home.

He felt betrayed, he and his fist team had been sold to the vampires for no discernible gain. It was against the precepts of the Way of the Faithful. It was wrong in so many ways, and there must be an accounting for the Red Ghost's actions.

If necessary, Tamsah vowed that he would be the agent of a terrifying and remorseless retribution, the Way could not be denied – there would be justice, or there would be death – there were no other options.

He passed through a stand of trees; dark shadows illumined in silvery starlight. He was tracking a fishing trawler north along the coast, the ship visible a mile offshore. He moved through the darkness like a shadow, easily keeping pace with his quarry. He would have to find shelter soon, for the sun would rise in a couple of hours, but he would pick up the trail again come nightfall.

There was a girl onboard the trawler, a young woman of extraordinary skills. She interested him, there was something about her that resonated within himself. She was a key of sorts, a key to his own strange fate. There were powers swirling around her and her friends, and he planned to find out who those powers were, and if appropriate, he would thwart them.

She'd spoken truth to him, and he'd felt deeply ashamed, and it seemed a lifetime had passed since that last happened.

He'd done nothing wrong. He'd acted with honor at all times, and yet, he was now a vampire. The only answer was that a power beyond his understanding was moving through his life. There must be a greater purpose behind what was happening. The only thing he had left was his faith in the Way, and it would be his sole guiding light.

It would have to be enough.

Tamsah al Ramil, the Sand Crocodile, initiate of the second level of the test of the Olgoi Khorkhoi and Red Empire fist team leader vowed to bring justice to the world.

He smiled slightly, he now had two guides: faith and justice. Since honor remained denied to him, they would fill him up.

Tamsah would be their willing and terrible servant, for none could stand before the might of faith and justice together.

He stared out at the trawler. He must protect the truth speaker; her fate was his fate. There was something there, something beyond definition or knowledge, a calling beyond oaths or allegiance.

As the Way proposed, in the end, there was only 'the truth,' and those who were shameless before the truth would be honored above all others. Her words had cut him more deeply than any sword could have done. She'd awakened a fire within him that once lit, could not be extinguished. There were those like the Red Ghost who had lost the 'Way,' and would need to be corrected, but the truth speaker was someone else, she was something else.

If need be, Tamsah would protect her with his life.

The End

The story will continue with the next instalment of The Metaframe War.

The Day Guard

IT'S A HOT WAR.

Cornelius Crane, King of the Vampire Dominion has his eyes fixed on the final destruction of the Mirovar force team and Anton Slayne.

The Day Guard is ready. Crane's new super-soldiers can fight the Ramp masters of the Order of Thoth and the Red Empire during daylight.

The Order of Thoth has called a secret conclave to decide who will lead. The faceless men who run the Order will stop at nothing to ensure Francis Mirovar does not become the next Head of the Order

Rogue vampire general, Chloe Armitage, seeks a new alliance with an ancient foe. A terrible power Anton Slayne has never seen before.

Will the Day Guard tip the balance of power in favor of Cornelius Crane? Will the faceless men of the Order secure their grip on power? Will Chloe Armitage advance her enigmatic cause?

Will Anton Slayne and his friends prevail, or will the last true hope of humanity versus the vampires be extinguished forever?

www.ingramcontent.com/pod-product-compliance
Lightning Source LLC
Chambersburg PA
CBHW020241030726
47499CB00001B/15